THE MANTIS AND THE MIRRORED SKY

RAGE OF LIONS BOOK SIX
MATT BARRON

BLADE OF TRUTH PUBLISHING COMPANY

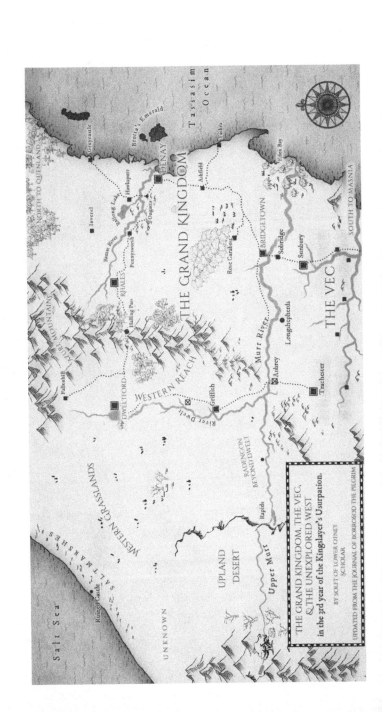

THE GRAND KINGDOM, THE VEC, & THE UNEXPLORED WEST, in the 3rd year of the Kingslayer's Usurpation.

BY SOLFIT OF LOWER OJNEY SCHOLAR

UPDATED FROM THE JOURNAL OF BORROSGOO THE PILGRIM

PROLOGUE

"We have been seen," Dahyoor muttered.

The fey rider watched the green-blue witchlight wings of a will-o'-the-wisp dancing in the shadows under the woodland branches. Looking up through the densely layered canopy of the deep forest, he could barely tell it was daytime. So little light penetrated the old growth that the ground itself was in perpetual twilight. This was the kind of thicket-dense land that no common mortal—no *kreff*—would ever dare to enter, a land of primeval memories. Of course, Dahyoor was fey, not *kreff*, so he and his companion should have had nothing to fear from places even as ancient as this in the land. However, Dahyoor was fey from the mountains and the grasslands, born to the saddle and the bow. The sages of his people kept memories the world had forgotten, and their knowledge stretched back unto the convulsions of the earth when the mountain was cast into the sea. Yet even those atavists admitted that they did not know everything that had ever been.

There is nothing new under the sun, so it was said, but the creation was so old. Could things primeval become so forgotten that when they were rediscovered, they would seem new to even the eldest and wisest who lived now?

Awkward from being forced to share his saddle, Dahyoor drew his bow from its embroidered case and nocked an arrow. He sighted the will-o'-the-wisp, tracking it as it flitted and leapt like a leaf in an updraft. Then, he loosed. The shaft flew true,

and the iron point passed straight through the glowing creature's body, falling away into the gloom, but the tiny dancing
light remained undisturbed, continuing its crazed flight. No
arrow would deter the blithe threat. Dahyoor felt it mocking
him.

"We have been seen," he muttered again.

"We pass unseen," Uyrlaan replied from behind him. In
fact, Uyrlaan's injuries made his words so slurred that he could
barely pronounce them, but Dahyoor understood him all the
same. Any Wind Rising fey would know the words—it was
the ethos by which their people had lived for a thousand years,
but even that timeless truth was changing into something new
now as well. The war that had come upon the lands to the
west of the mountains had shattered so many other accepted
realities that Dahyoor supposed he should not be surprised by
anything anymore. Even here, in these pockets of forest that
remembered all the secrets of the world, something else new had
happened—something that his people never imagined could be.
The elders and the sages had to be told. And so, with the dying
Uyrlaan riding behind him in the saddle they shared, Dahyoor
aimed for the pass in the mountains, desperate to win clear
of the forest and the long southern water and return to his
people. His pursuers were doing their best to keep him pressed
southward to trap him.

With his bow still in hand, the fey rider turned his mount
around trees and through dense undergrowth by his knees. He
was making little better than walking pace amidst the scree,
and it made him want to curse. The will-o'-the-wisp had no
difficulty keeping up with him, even with its crazed motion.
If they had been on the open plain, or even just in the lifeless
foothills and the fringes of the forest, his pony could swiftly
outdistance the damnable dancing light. It would take him no
time at all. But here, there was nothing for Dahyoor to do except
allow the bright little spy to follow him. Wisps were the eyes
of the forest, and what they saw, the Verdant fey would know.

There was no chance he and Uyrlaan would pass unseen now. Bow still in hand, he heard from behind the sound of a horn echoing through the forest.

Even now, they were closing in.

Rounding the base of another vast hardwood tree twenty paces across in the trunk at least, Dahyoor came into a relatively open dell, though still shadowed from the sky. On a ridge no more than thirty paces away, he caught sight of a Verdant rider. Tall, with pointed ears and fair hair, the lithe figure showed that he was of the same original heritage as the two fleeing horsemen, but after that the similarities ceased. Where Dahyoor and Uyrlaan were tanned from their life under the sun, the Verdant fey were pale, with skin the color of milk. The proud forest hunter wore a tunic woven of green leaves that had been treated by some arcana to be as supple and strong as leather. Where the Mountain fey were consummate archers on foot or in the saddle, the Verdant rider carried a kit of very different weapons.

In a sheath tied around his mount's neck, the rider had a sword called a falx, which the fey of the forest forged to mimic the curve of the Rampart—the bright ribbon of light that stretched across the northern sky at night. The falx blade was not a saber, though, for its edge was on the inside of the curve, akin to a scythe or sickle, and the savage weapon made brutal slashes when it struck; that much the two riders could testify to from experience. Uyrlaan was dying from the savagery of a falx's cut. Hanging from one of his hands was the Verdant hunter's other weapon, looking like nothing so much as a green length of vine. A sling—grown as much as fashioned, just like the rider's armor—it could whip a stone or metal bullet as fast as an arrow's flight, and the masters of the art were every bit as deadly as any archer. It was a deceptive weapon, seemingly simple but powerful, nonetheless. Deadly and effective, it was easy to make but supremely difficult to master.

Most different of all from Dahyoor and Uyrlaan was the Verdant fey's mount, no mere horse or pony. The hunting rider sat bareback upon a mighty stag—Monarch of the Forest—with branching horns almost as broad across as the length of its body. Dahyoor could scarcely comprehend that the powerful beast was able to make its way through the deep green without tangling its antlers on every second branch. Nevertheless, the proud creature truly belonged in this primeval wilderness, and it moved through the dense growth as naturally as a fish swam in water or a bird flew through the air; and on its back, the Verdant fey rider moved with it.

Dahyoor turned aside and spurred his pony to a gallop, risking a fall or crash with every stride. Even for his sure-footed mountain beast, this kind of rush through the undergrowth was all but suicidally dangerous. Branches batted at mount and rider. Thorns clawed at Dahyoor's corselet and tore the skin of his arms. Behind him, Uyrlaan whimpered and bounced about in agony, barely holding on. The Verdant rider had dropped out of sight, but the horn blew again. The pony whinnied in terror as a sudden boulder appeared through the undergrowth. It twisted away just in time, and Dahyoor moved naturally with it, but his companion almost fell from the saddle. By the time he had settled Uyrlaan back behind him, Dahyoor had completely lost control of their ride. The pony was picking its own course now, and infected with its riders' fear, it would likely run itself to death. Recognizing that fact, a cold pragmatism settled into Dahyoor's heart. The Verdant fey were looking for a horse and rider carrying a wounded companion. Maybe they did not know who, or how many, were wounded. There was perhaps a chance for them in that. The pair were seeking to escape because they had a dire message that must reach their people. But two on a horse in this forest were too slow to escape, and it did not take two to bring a message.

Now barely clinging to his saddle himself, Dahyoor fitted his bow back into its case with his few remaining arrows and unfastened the container. Tucking it under his arm, he half twisted in the saddle to pass the reins back to the nearly insensible Uyrlaan. The wounded fey took the leather more from habit than choice.

"Ride to the horizon, *keshmiryaa*," Dahyoor whispered to his childhood friend. Then he leaned out, snatched at a long, hanging branch, and flipped from the saddle into the tall brush, landing amongst the boughs with the litheness of his people before his feet even touched the ground. He scrambled through the tree limbs like a cat, his light form disturbing the leaves no more than a breeze. Finding a hiding spot he hoped would conceal him, he managed to watch as his forsaken friend and horse bounced away. He expected to lose sight of them in a short time, but as it happened, their headlong flight was terminated all too quickly. A single stone whipped through the brush from somewhere Dahyoor could not see, and the supreme shot took Uyrlaan in the head, almost certainly slaying him outright. The Verdant hunter and his elk-sized stag then burst into view, and even as the stag was leaping through the air, the rider's falx bit into the pony's neck, killing it and driving rider and mount to the ground. A second Verdant fey, this one mounted on a smaller but still powerfully built hind, joined the first hunter as he wiped blood from his blade on the leaves of a nearby bush.

"Fully passed," the doe-rider said to his compatriot as he hopped down to investigate Uyrlaan's corpse. The stag rider scanned the forest through slitted eyes.

"There were two; one was wounded," he said.

"He might have fallen. They were battered with stones as they fled, and your blade has cut true many times in recent days."

"We will search and make sure. Call the others."

The rider of the hind put a horn to his lips and gave it a long blast that echoed through the twilit green. Dahyoor pressed himself back into the deepest shadows and found a cleft in a trunk where he could be further obscured. Drawing his legs up close and moving the branches as little as he could, he sought to make himself as near to invisible as his skill at stealth and his people's ancient craft could make him.

"We pass unseen," he whispered to himself under his breath, so earnestly that it was almost a prayer. Then he *did* pray. "Maker of all things, who sweetens the gall that poisons the world and rescues the light out of shadows, if ever you have allowed even one of my people to hide, hide me now. Let me pass unseen, unseen by all but you."

More Verdant fey arrived, some riding but as many again on foot, and they began to search Dahyoor's path and the surrounds. Not daring to even turn his head to look, the hidden horseman-without-a-horse strained his ears to listen to their footsteps and judge how far they were from him. His muscles ached with tension as he kept himself poised to spring forth if discovered. He knew it was a fruitless hope to expect to win free of these hunters if they found him again, but he would never simply accept defeat. Above him he heard a scratching noise, no louder than the rustle of leaves itself. Risking a glance upward, he saw a little climbing creature, about the size of a hare, making its way cautiously down the tree trunk toward him. Knowing nothing of the possums, stoats, or whatever kind of forest dweller this might be, Dahyoor watched the creature with trepidation, holding his breath. It gripped the rough bark with black claws as long as a finger joint. They seemed dagger sharp, and the fey man wondered if the creature would claw at his face with them, aiming for an eye. Or would it suddenly screech in alarm. At any moment the watchful little beast could ruin Dahyoor's concealment, and he wanted nothing more than to swat the thing with his saddle axe, except his axe was still with his dead pony.

The little forest creature's nose twitched for a moment, as if it was considering which particular betrayal it wanted to visit on the fugitive. Then it turned around and, flicking its tail upward, sprayed him with a squirt of heavy-smelling musk. Then the creature scampered up the trunk and disappeared amongst the leaves. The spray had managed to miss Dahyoor's eyes, and he was thankful for that, but the aroma was so pungent that he teared up anyway while some droplets ran down his cheek. It made him want to cough and spit, and inwardly he cursed. This stench would be detectable so far away. He despised the little creature for a moment, but then he realized that this was a natural smell, a forest smell. He cautiously reached one hand up and wiped at the noxious fluid and began to spread it on other parts of himself.

I pass unseen and perhaps un-smelled, he thought.

As if to confirm his hope, two Verdant fey rode nearby, their deer mounts snuffling the air as they moved past. Both animals snorted and shied slightly from the revolting stink, and when their riders sniffed the air with them, they seemed to dismiss it without even questioning. They calmed their mounts and moved on, searching for the escaping mountain fey who still hid in the bole of a tree behind them.

Dahyoor remained in his refuge until the dark of forest shadow became the black of night. As the sun barely penetrated the canopy, so the branches and leaves overhead now shut out moon, stars, and Rampart. Nevertheless, the fey man knew he could wait no longer. He slipped to the earth and, listening and watchful, trusted his instincts to find east in the darkness. He had no horse and no axe, but he still had his bow and his message—the message that must reach the elders. The Serpent Witch who had enslaved his people with blood magick still lived.

And their kin had betrayed them.

CHAPTER 1

Crickets chirruped and frogs croaked in the reeds and rushes as the river boats landed on the lake's southwest bank just before sundown, exactly as planned. Twilight was the perfect time for an ambush—a time of shadows—and on the waters of the Western Reach there was a war going on in the shadows. Prentice watched the sun touch the horizon just as his boat ran aground, and he threw himself over the side to wade ashore. Around him, his two handpicked cohorts, each one of a hundred White Lion veterans—mostly sword-and-shield armed Fangs and Roar—were leaping from their own lighters and quickly making for dry ground. This small force had left Dweltford sparse hours before, their rivercraft pushing hard to cross the water before any warning could be brought ahead of them. From their landing spot, Prentice could look back northeast straight across the open water and just make out the tower tops of Dweltford Castle as the sandstone walls lit a flaming orange in the last rays of the sun.

"Shall we light 'em now, Captain?" asked Gennet, newly promoted sergeant and Prentice's second-in-command on this mission. The captain nodded, and Gennet passed the whispered word for the Roarsmen—the Lions' matchlock gunners—to light their weapon fuses, ready for combat. Hot coals hidden in clay pots were breathed back into full flame, and long-matches were dipped inside and ignited. The fuel-soaked strings fizzed and sparked to smoldering life, giving off their tell-tale curlicues of smoke. Soon, the distinctive smell of those fumes would drift to the enemy's nostrils, but by then it would be too late, assuming everything continued as planned.

"I still can scarce believe they're so close to the town," Brother Whilte, the White Lions' chaplain, marveled quietly as he joined Prentice, his wooden leg sinking into the mud of the lakeside and almost toppling him where he stood. He managed to keep his balance by leaning on his staff, what the Lions had taken to calling his "prophet's rod"—a spear with a symbolically broken blade. It had been made to commemorate the broken pike with which the chaplain had rebuked the magick of the Serpent Witch and had been fashioned from Prentice's own winged partisan spear. When Prentice had presented it, Whilte had laughed and declared it the perfect symbol of his chaplaincy—"a broken weapon for a broken warrior, remade in God's service."

"The Ragmother insists this is an old skip's-nest," Prentice told Whilte, using the smuggler term for a hideout. A river smuggler was a "tariff-skip," someone who dodged or "skipped" the taxes on river cargo. A skip's-nest was where they stored contraband and pilfered goods until they could get them into Dweltford or down the river. In that light, the secret little boat haven they were seeking, hidden amidst the reeds and trees of a copse-like fen on the bank of the lake, was almost perfect for its purpose.

"I mean, surely it is a great risk for them," Whilte persisted.

"Perhaps. But consider that this has been here for years by all accounts, and if the Ragmother had not told us, we would never have known."

Brother Whilte nodded, accepting the logic of that observation. Prentice did not begrudge the chaplain his musings. He had put this raid together as soon as he learned of the hideout, with the possibility that it concealed not only river criminals but also Redlanders of some stripe. After years of bloodthirsty war, no one took the threat of the invaders from the west lightly. Nonetheless, the captain did not want to talk. He wanted to hunt, and he had one especial prey in mind—the Serpent Witch. She had eluded him all winter, and now there was a hint, an echo of a rumor, and he would not waste the chance. Prentice had almost come to accept that the Redlander priestess must have fled the Reach. It was the most sensible thing she could have done. To draw this close to the capital would be reckless, but it was exactly the kind of arrogant recklessness she had favored, using cunning and stealth. To aid her, the word was that she and other Redlanders had begun proselytising, making converts amongst ordinary Reacherfolk. The river smugglers were her preferred initiates. Like her, they favored stealth.

From landward only a league or two away across the tops of the paperbark trees and bloodwoods, a single mournful trumpet blast was heard. That was the signal. Prentice's own stealthy allies were now in place and would be moving into the fen, driving the smuggler cultists toward his men.

"Go," Prentice commanded, and the cohorts fanned out, a light or lantern with every ten-man squad, called a line, even though there would be no battle lines in tonight's action. Prentice shouted further orders to the silhouetted figures around him. "Take prisoner any who yield. We want to interrogate all that we can. But remember, we also want their boats. A skip without his boat is just a thug waiting for the bailiffs to take him, and tonight, we are the bailiffs. That is how we will take them."

And the Witch, if you find her, he thought but did not say. *Her, we want most of all.*

The entire company began to bound clumsily through the reeds, lantern lights ranging into the shadows under the trees, matchlock wicks already looking like lit smoking pipes in the dark. A year ago, this area had been bone dry, but since the breaking of the drought, the winter had given almost more rain than the land could bear. All up and down the Dwelt there was flooding, and the lake was now at the highest level in living memory. Even so, they were reliably informed that there was only one channel in the swampy ground that was deep enough for riverboats. It was so well concealed that even with specific instructions on how to find it, it had taken Prentice's sharp-eyed fey scouts almost two full days to discover its exact location. Of course, their task had been complicated by the need to do their work quietly so the smugglers would not know they had been given away, but that was why he had sent the fey in the first place. No one in the Western Reach excelled them in stealth—not mere smugglers and not even sorcerously empowered Redlanders.

Over the splashing and the clank of armor, Prentice strained his ears to hear sounds of his prey. He leaped and stumbled through the sedge and shallow water to the hideout's boats, up above the waterline. The nest itself was somewhere further in amongst the trees. Like so many wild-grown woodlands, the deceptively small area was a maze on the inside. The native trees—paperbark and bloodwood—had wood either too weak or too difficult to work for lumbermen to take up residence, so the pocket wilderness thrived amidst farms and meadows.

A handful of figures rushed out of the shadows toward charging militiamen, and the first clashes began. Shouts demanded that smugglers yield, and there was a flash to Prentice's left as at least one matchlock was discharged. Steel clashed once or twice, but these sounds were short lived. Typically clad rivermen were wrestled into lamplights, and militia demanded to know how many more there were and where they were hiding. The formerly peaceful evening was sudden chaos. The White Lions had only brought a fraction of their total company, but it was still many times the number of smugglers they expected to find, and that was before the fey riders were counted. The few actual fights around Prentice were swiftly one sided.

The dark shape of a grounded riverboat arose out of the grasses in front of him, and Prentice vaulted the gunwale, stepping up to the upraised prow to try for a better look at the progress of their ambush. He was scanning the crazed lamplight when he felt the craft shudder under him, and he turned to see a heavy-limbed man climbing over the stern. Broad shouldered, with a thickly muscled neck, the escaping smuggler looked like a typical dockworker, a man who spent his whole life hefting heavy cargo and dragging boats like this one in and out of the water. Prentice could just make out the curve and spike of a billhook in the man's right hand.

"Oh, bugger you!" the smuggler cursed as his shadowed eyes met Prentice's, and the man set himself to fight.

Since the summer, Prentice had taken to habitually not wearing his leg armor for speed on foot, especially not in actions like this one where the ground under him was un-certain. Nevertheless, he still had his leather and plate brig-andine on his chest, as well as his helmet, gauntlets, and spaulders protecting much of the rest of him. It was a lighter suit of armor than a full knight's harness, or even a frontline White Lion's for that matter, but it was still heavy enough to make the smuggler's tool-like weapon a minor threat. Add to that, the captain was also carrying a new Fang's round shield and was wielding the jagged steel baton that was his swordbreaker. After being peppered by arrows in ambushes by fey horse archers, Prentice had sent an order to the workshops in the north for a larger kind of shield for his Fangs, and tonight was their inaugural battle. Their old bucklers were the size of a helmet, or a dinner plate, and the traditional companion to a sidesword, fast and ideal for dueling. The new round shields were large enough to protect a man-at-arms from neck to waist, almost but not quite as large as the typical Redlander spearman's own wood and leather shields. These new shields were steel, thinner and ironically both stronger and lighter than their enemy's counterpart. Best of all, they were broad enough to be held overhead and protect most of the body from falling arrows. The militia had already nicknamed them "umbrellas."

"Do not be a fool," Prentice told the smuggler who seemed to be trying to stare him down in the flickering gloom. "Yield in the name of the archduchess."

Suddenly another matchlock fired nearby, and both men were half lit by the flash. The smuggler must have thought it a good distraction, and he took the opportunity to charge at Prentice, leading with his billhook but apparently thinking also to barge his opponent off the boat completely. Unfortunately for the riverman, Prentice was not distracted. He checked the short blade's thrust with his shield and shifted his weight so that he deflected the charging body to one side. The boat under them moved suddenly with the change of balance, and it was the smuggler who was tipped over the side into the muddy grass. Prentice had meant to follow his shield with a strike from the swordbreaker, but he found himself falling in the same direction as the toppled smuggler, so he chose to make the fall his attack, landing knees first on the tumbling man's back. They both crashed into the sludge, and Prentice did his best to roll with the motion. Even so, he ended up on his side, scrambling in the dark and wet to get to his feet. He need not have worried, as in the shadow of the tipped boat, the smuggler groaned in anguished pain.

"Me hand!" he wailed. "You mongrel, you cut me hand off."

From out of the shadows, Brother Whilte hobbled around the side of the tipped boat, a lit lantern in his free hand. The sucking mud wrenched at his wooden leg and prophet's rod with every step. Soon enough his light fell on the smuggler who was writhing on the ground, gripping his right hand to his chest. The flow of crimson down the man's tunic was obvious. Prentice wondered what had happened a moment before he realized that when the man had fallen, he landed hand first on his own blade. The sharp billhook had gone straight through his palm and sheared away most of the fingers with it.

"Me hand," the man moaned pitifully again as he looked at it in the light.

"Well, it's not cut off, but you've lost those fingers, that's for sure," Whilte said in the gentle, matter-of-fact way that healers often discussed injuries. "Keep still and I'll stop the bleeding."

"That's most o' me hand! He's ruined me. That's me livel-hood. He's made a beggar out o' me!"

Livelihood, Prentice said to himself, reflexively correcting the man in his own thoughts. Looking at the wound, he was sure the smuggler was right in every other respect. He would never make his way as a docker or riverman with only one good hand. *That went easier than expected.*

"You did that to yourself," Whilte chided the man like a schoolmaster with a belligerent child. "You heard him call on you to yield."

Prentice turned away from the two on the ground, confident the situation no longer needed his attention, and looked about the dark under the trees. More lanterns were being lit, and by their light he could see the few prisoners being taken and tied together into coffles to escort back to Dweltford for trial. Prentice did not envy the captives their fates. Magistrates were not known to be kind to tariff skips.

This cannot be all of them, he thought, looking back toward the middle of the fen. He had been warned of more than a single cargo boat crew's worth.

"Captain! Captain Ash!"

CHAPTER 2

A way from the high-water mark where the smugglers hid their boats, the fen became even more unreliable. The few Claws in the company went ahead of the little squads with their long pikes, using their weapons like sounding poles to test the depth at every step. Even so, men weighed down with armor slipped and slid regularly, even up to their waists, or wrenched sideway as the mud underfoot gave way or sucked at a boot. With so many lights, Prentice had hoped that seeing the way would not be too difficult, but as men began to push further into the trees, the shafts of lanterns danced crazily, splitting endlessly around harsh shadows. The mass of silhouettes soon resembled a life-sized shadow play of a battlefield, a discordant visual madness that might as likely hide an enemy as easily as full darkness.

Prentice advanced slowly in the direction he was called, eyes alert, head swiveling back and forth for danger in every inky spot around him. As his tension built with the continued hunt, he wished he could take his helmet off to give his ears a better chance to hear the tiny, telltale signs of an attack coming, but he dared not. He also could not risk obscuring his vision further by lowering the protective visor. As much as his sallet reduced his hearing, the protection it gave against an unexpected strike was too valuable to relinquish. He strained to listen for danger, just as his eyes never stopped searching. It shocked him as he realized how quickly he found himself effectively alone. Brother

Whilte had remained behind to treat the wounded man, and other Lions were no more than ten paces away, but the trees, the shallows, and the shadows between meant that no ally could reach him swiftly if he was bushwhacked. It was unnerving to be so vulnerable amidst so many comrades.

Then he was called for again.

"Over here," he shouted back.

"We found somethin', Captain," a militiaman declared, splashing up with a comrade who carried a lantern. They both slapped out mud-spattered salutes. "Over by some thicket."

"Show me!" Prentice commanded, hoping it was the skip's nest proper. He followed the men to a spot between a pair of trees and was disappointed to find only a post, as thick as a man's arm, sunk into a small lump of earth above the waterline. On top of the post was a green shape of some kind, too flat to be a plant. As he rounded to its front, Prentice realized it was like a mask, carved in wood and overlaid with beaten copper. It was the metal that was green, patinaed in verdigris from the moist air. It could have been there for decades from the state of the corrosion, but the post it stood upon was freshly cut and pale, even in the shadows. The mask had an insect-like appearance, antennae extending from the top and mandibles in the bottom. Eye slits were made up of tiny holes, mimicking the facets of a bug's eyes. The artifact was held in place by a fresh iron nail, unrusted, driven straight through the forehead and pinning it to the wood.

What is this? Prentice wondered. His hand reached out almost of its own volition to touch the artifact, but he caught himself, pulling it back and then waving the lantern closer. As the light shone full upon the copper, it was as if the empty eyes were staring straight at him. He had a sudden, rushing feeling of vertigo, as if he might fall into the tiny holes in the metal, and he recoiled.

"What was that?" one of the men next to him whispered, telling him that they must have felt the strange pull as well.

"I do not know."

There was a drumbeat some further distance away and another call for the captain.

"West," Prentice said, looking upward through the branches and figuring the direction of the new call. "Stay here and keep watch on that...thing. Keep the light off it, and no one is to look at it. In fact, if one of you has a cloak or if someone else turns up with one, cover it. Wait for Brother Whilte."

Since his confrontation with the Serpent Witch at Prentice's side last summer, Chaplain Whilte had become the militia's first line of defense against any forms of sorcery that were discovered. The other religious man Prentice most trusted, Sacrist Fostermae, was yet tending to the folk of Halling Pass, brutalized survivors of another of the Serpent Witch's plots.

Prentice moved into the shadows and again he felt suddenly alone. It reminded him of the story Archduchess Amelia told of a little wood in the far west on the shore of the salt sea where a tiny hermit woman had practiced prophecy from ages past until Daven Marcus had her executed.

Whatever mystic power has taken refuge in this swamp, it is not a kindly prophetess, he thought. *And I will not abide it so close to my liege lady's home.* He began to think the safest thing for them to do would be to bring oil and torches and burn the whole cursed fen to the water. Other Lions sloshed out of the shadows toward him, and he gave the evening's password.

"Were you the ones that called?" he asked.

Both men nodded, their faces pale, and then one of them bent at the waist and vomited up the contents of his stomach.

"Is your man alright?" Prentice asked, eyes narrowed. He did not want to find out he had militiamen with him who were drunk. The night was chaotic enough as it was.

"Just a little fearsome, Captain," the standing man, a line first, reassured his commander. "It's a...well, it's a foul thing we found, is all."

"You looked at it?"

"A little. Made me guts water, I swear, just lookin'. Urlbe here, he took a longer look, and it's spooked him. I run after him 'cause you told us no fewer than twos for safety."

Should follow my own orders, Prentice told himself.

The man Urlbe lifted himself up, wiping the bile from his lips and saluting.

"I ain't craven, Captain, I swear," the man insisted. Prentice put his hand up to stop the explanation.

"A mask?" he asked. The two Lions' eyes went wide with surprise, as if their leader's insight was as magickal as the artifact from which they had just fled. They nodded. "Show me."

The line first pointed the way, and while he lost his sense of direction once, he soon led Prentice to a second post, the twin of the first, with copper mask and iron nail. The dread power of this visage was enhanced by the presence of a rotting body slumped at the foot of the post. The maggoty flesh was chained in place, arms behind its back, and a moldy rag was stuffed into its mouth. Another three militiamen were standing around the post, looking as disturbed as Urlbe and his line first, along with a young drummer, barely eight years old, who had his face pressed against one of the men's buff coats.

"Seems like they left him here to starve," one of them said as Prentice crouched down to examine the corpse. It was a reasonable assumption. There was no sign of any injury, other than the putrefaction in most of the flesh, and no blood on the rotting clothes.

"Smell alone's enough to make a man want to run, I'd reckon," added another militiaman, loyally excusing Urlbe's lapse to the captain of the militia. Prentice recognized the instinct and even approved, but his mind was more focused on these bizarre artifacts. He had come expecting a clutch of converts, not an unholy site dedicated to the Redlander's demon gods, assuming that was their purpose.

"Find something to cover that thing with," he commanded them, pointing to the mask as he stood from examining the corpse. "And then get your lad away and report this to the chaplain. This is not something for young eyes. Brother Whilte is some distance back that way..."

Prentice trailed off, hearing drums again and recognizing the beat as yet another summons.

Not a third mask? he wondered. *Are there any actual cultists in this muck?*

As he looked in that direction and then up to get his bearings again, a new thought occurred to him. He pointed to a nearby tree.

"Give me a boost," he said, and when two men cupped their hands for his foot, he stepped up and grabbed a branch. His armored weight must have been burden enough for his two men, strong as they were, but it was almost more than he himself could haul as he strove to climb the bloodwood's narrow trunk to where the branches actually started. He finally hooked his arms around one and dragged himself upward while it creaked ominously. At last, he was able to twist his leg around the trunk and find the remnant shoulder of a broken branch, and he pushed his foot onto that. That managed to get him a fair distance above the ground, but nothing like enough to clear the canopy.

"What can you see, Captain?" one of the men asked.

Prentice felt his limbs, cold-stiffened from hours sitting in armor in a boat on the water, protesting and burning just from holding his armored weight off the ground.

He looked heavenward for a moment, orienting himself by the Rampart, and then down to the directions of the first mask and of the new signal, then back to the lakeside, hoping to see some glow of the lights as the prisoners were loaded onto the riverboats. An instinct gripped his thoughts and he slid to the ground, half shinnying, half falling. He crashed to the dirt with a grunt, then turned even as he was rising and led his men in a new direction.

"The call came from more over that way, Captain," the line first said after him, pointing. Prentice did not bother to correct him or to explain but led them an angled course between the first mask and from where the third call was coming.

"Just follow me," he ordered.

One of the Claws in the group was a pikeman, and Prentice pointed ahead of himself a step for the man to test the way. As swiftly as caution allowed, with the pike shaft dipping into the mud and water every few paces, they made their way to what he was becoming sure was a midpoint between at least three and probably four masks enshrined at cardinal points around the fen.

"Order your lad to beat rally," he said. "And be ready."

CHAPTER 3

"It's like a millpond," Gennet whispered as he emerged from under trees to find Prentice standing in the shadows at the edge of a broad opening in the middle of the fen. The sun was long set now, but the moon had not risen. As it was, the night sky overhead shone the Rampart's soft glow down into the clearing, and the open surface of the water reflected that light, along with the orange flickers of a gathering cluster of Lions' torches and lanterns—flames and heavenly silver dancing over unknown black depths. It *was* still like a millpond, but that was not what Prentice was reminded of when he looked at it. In his mind, he heard the roar of a lion and the hissing squall of five other animal heads on the body of a vast serpent. He watched, waiting to see if another vision like the first one he had had when the invasion began years ago would come upon him. He could feel his men beside him becoming restless.

"And that looks like an encampment of sorts, or a stack of stores over that way," Gennet continued, pointing across the water slightly to his left at a large patch of deep shadows. "I thought I caught a glint as of a hidden...there it is again. Did you see that? A shuttered lamp, I'd say."

"I know," was all Prentice said. He had already seen the hidden camp, suitable for twenty or even twice that number. Carefully maintained fires there burned low to keep down the smoke that might be smelled out upon the lake, and bedrolls were laid between mounds of purloined river cargo, bales and barrels in neat stacks. Everything looked to be set upon waxed canvas, pulled up around the sides to prevent the water seeping from the mud, and then covered with even more canvas to protect from the weather. Except for its secrecy, the whole arrangement could have been a legitimate trading post. Other than the sliver-thin flash of the shuttered lantern, the only signs of movement looked to be other Lions, loudly and openly approaching, mostly from the direction of Lake Dweltford.

"I reckon that over there is the boat channel," Sergeant Gennet muttered, pointing to a stretch of open water unimpeded by sedge grasses that looked to meander eastward. "They've got their own little port harbor here."

A shadow shifted in Prentice's sight, and he smiled.

I knew I saw you there, he thought. No vision from the heavenlies had come upon him, but he had observed an important detail.

"Is there something we're waiting for, Captain?" Gennet said, and Prentice could hear the urgency rising in the sergeant's voice. He obviously did not understand why their leader was standing motionless while any remaining smugglers or cultists might be fleeing their camp before the noose closed around them.

"Sergeant, do you see that little piece of dry ground?" Prentice asked. "There, a hummock just off to the right of the middle?"

"Uh, maybe, Captain." Gennet's tone made it clear he could only barely make out the spot to which Prentice was referring.

"It looks to have a single tree on it," Prentice added.

"I guess I can make it out, just. Skinny, like a post almost, with just one branching, like opening arms at 'bout the height of a man's head."

"That's what I see," Prentice confirmed. "I think we have someone waiting for us on that hummock, Sergeant."

Waiting for me, he thought and hoped it was the Serpent Witch.

"I don't know, Captain. I can't see nothin'."

"Have you found any masks tonight?" Prentice knew he was being needlessly enigmatic, but he felt the icy eagerness inside himself, the longing to come to grips with his foe. It had been his weakness when the drought broke in the river-bend village that let the enemy sorceress escape, and the devoted part of him that loved his liege was determined to correct that failure.

"Someone brought word from Brother Whilte, something about magicky masks in shrines, Captain. But I ain't seen any myself," Gennet said. "Are we safe?"

"I do not know, Sergeant. What I do know is that little island is in the middle of the two other visages I have seen tonight, and they were both looking this way," Prentice explained. He could feel his skin crawl even as he said it. Whatever power those graven insectoid eyes possessed, it was focused upon this point. "They were both looking through the woods to that tree. I would wager that if we crossed the water and went about thirty paces straight north, we would find a third mask, looking back this way. In fact, there could be many others, all lurking and looking at the island."

"What for?"

"I do not know, but when the chaplain arrives, I mean to find out."

As he watched, Prentice searched his memory for what he had learned at the Academy about the kinds of sorceries that could supposedly be conjured from the earth by means of secret lines marked with standing stones. Or else mystical paths, shaped like magickal runes or other symbols, which occultists would walk in their rituals to raise up the powers of the spirit realm. But what dominion were the cultists trying to invoke with their posts all looking to a center point?

The militia numbers around Prentice continued to grow, and he could hear them shift, arms swinging weapons impatiently at the air. Their eagerness was an almost palpable thing, like hunting hounds when they have scented the prey. They were waiting for his order, straining forward for the command to run to the hunt.

There were no more sounds of conflict now. Whoever of this smuggler cabal meant to flee, they had done so already. Any who remained were waiting in ambush.

Cocky, Prentice thought, and he shook his head with a wry smile.

"We gonna go soon?" muttered someone from behind Prentice's right shoulder.

"We go when the captain says so, you bull-at-a-gate," Gennet rebuked in the shadows.

Prentice was about to explain that he wanted Whilte with them to protect against what he was sure would be Redlander sorcery, but a sudden clamor arose from around the supplies in the encampment and new lights speared across the still water from that side. Another group of Lions had stumbled into the middle of the skips' nest from the northwest. Immediately, there was a fresh crash of steel, and powder flashes burst under the trees. The new sources of light silhouetted the figure Prentice was sure he had seen waiting on the island. It did not look female, but there was no time to second guess that.

"No more waiting," he shouted, fearful that the new melee would spook his target. "Now, we hunt!"

CHAPTER 4

It was no charge; how could it be? Prentice and his men lumbered slowly through the sedge, lifting their legs high just to clear the sucking water and muck. They shouted and splashed, and more than one almost fell face first, but soon enough two lines worth were on the firmer, if slippery, shore of the little hummock island with its one tree. Prentice was the first, but Gennet was only a pace behind, halberd in hand, using the butt to keep his balance. The rest fanned out as the captain's attention was swiftly drawn to a low voice from the shadows under the single spindly tree.

"Well come, Ashen Man."

Ashen Man? Prentice thought. *It has been some time since they called me that.*

Ashen Man was the title the Redlander champion, the Horned Man, had used to address him at the Battle of the Brook. As far as the captain knew, it had arisen from some legend of the invaders, and while others had thought it a badge of honor to be valued, Prentice had happily forgotten it until he confronted the Serpent Witch. Even as the memory of facing the Horned Man in the bloody waters of the little stream ran through his thoughts, Prentice realized something more, something he could not have expected. The voice that had spoken was *not* that of the Serpent Witch, nor of any woman. Yet, more astonishingly, it was not a Redlander voice at all, but the clear, well-spoken accent of an educated man of the Grand Kingdom.

"You have me at a disadvantage," he told the shadow, pointing with his sword-breaker. "Step into the light that we may exchange proper introductions."

A bullseye's shutters were pulled back by a militiaman nearby with a loud clack that seemed to echo over the water despite the growing clamor from the smuggler camp on the other shore. The focused shaft of oil flame's light pierced the ink like an arrow, and there, at the tree's foot, was a man of noble bearing, with dark eyes, a hawk nose, and prominent cheek bones. His high brow was topped with close-cropped, brown hair and a simple circlet of gold.

"Brother Elder Inxyphos," the man said, bowing formally, as if being presented to a noble at court.

"'Brother Elder'?" Prentice repeated, as if he had not heard properly. The title was a rank of holy orders. Was the man declaring himself as a Church knight? As if to answer Prentice's unspoken question, Inxyphos swept his heavy cloak back over his shoulders to reveal a silvered mail byrnie, long-sleeved and hanging to his knees. Over that he wore a tabard of pure white silk, with three overlapping, embroidered crosses upon the breast—one gold, one black, and one flaming orange. Prentice felt his breath catch at the sight of it. Knights of the Church only bore two crosses upon their tabards and standards, a gold representing the glory of heaven, and a black, signifying power upon the earth—"like Christ's rod of iron," as the initiates were taught. Different religious orders had other colors in their fields but always the two crosses. Except one.

"Inquisition," Prentice breathed, scarcely able to comprehend that a lone man-at-arms sworn to the Church's most secretive sect would be standing here, openly, in the midst of a cultists' lair. The third cross, the flaming one, represented the fires of Hell and the sovereign justice of God that sent mortals there. God or the Inquisition, Prentice doubted the Almighty actually much liked the Church's usurpation of his rights as judge of men's souls. The merciless preachers of mercy, the fey called them.

"Have a care, Reachermen," Prentice told his men loudly, "The brother elder here is an old friend of Bluebird's."

There was a low growl from the militiamen. Bluebird was the assassin who used magickal artifice to facilitate his missions. He had almost been successful in killing the archduchess and installing her rebel Earl Sebastian in her place, not to mention using his magick to help the Serpent Witch take Prentice and Brother Whilte captive. Everyone present knew the tales, and while few had the exact details, every loyal man wanted a piece of the professional killer-minstrel while being wary of his powers.

"Ah yes, Cerulean sends his compliments," Inxyphos said politely.

"How is his knee?"

"It heals," the Inquisition man-at-arms said with a dismissive gesture of his hand that caused several of the Lions to flinch or even step back. He raised a mocking eyebrow and smiled with self-satisfaction. "He often bids his comrades to make a point of taking a kneecap from each of the bitch's ladies-in-waiting when they punish her—the ones in the lace masks. One of them is your wife, is she not? Cerulean says he doesn't know which of them specifically did the damage, so both will have to be made to pay. The order normally frowns on petty vendettas, but he is like to be indulged in this one request after what he suffered."

"After what *he* suffered?" Gennet demanded indignantly, lowering his halberd to point straight at the Church militant. Prentice dropped his swordbreaker across the sergeant's path to keep him from charging. Something was very wrong, and it was not only Inxyphos's presence nor his easy calm.

He must know how vulnerable he is.

Prentice was used to the arrogance of Kingdom knights and nobles and their disdain for low-born soldiers. To a noble man-at-arms of the Grand Kingdom, a militiaman was little more than a rogue with pretensions, and rogues were mere blade fodder, good for blooding an edge but nothing else. Church knights were typically wiser than that and often better trained at strategy and tactics. Even if his sense of superiority were overwhelming, surely this man Inxyphos did not think he could face down twenty or more of them at once?

Across the water, the melee in the smuggler camp was continuing. Prentice could see it over Inxyphos's shoulder. As he watched out of the corner of his eye, he thought he could make out sounds of whinnying horses, and he was certain it was not his fey allies' mounts he heard. More Inquisition men-at-arms, and mounted?

In a swamp? Almost all the horseman's advantages would be negated, and that was not counting the fact that the White Lions were specialists in fighting men-at-arms ahorse. There had to be something else. Prentice lifted his eyes to the tree over Inxyphos's head. The religious knight saw him look and smiled, the flickering torchlight giving his expression a ghoulish cast.

"Yes," said Inxyphos. "There's one up there as well."

"What do they do?"

Inxyphos refused to answer, shaking his head.

"Someone, get some powder by that tree and set the thing alight," Prentice commanded. He pointed at Inxyphos. "If he tries to stop you, put him down."

"I will not try to stop you, but I wouldn't try it, if I were you," the Inquisition militant told them, his eyes looking across the line, apparently searching out the Lion bold enough to enact their captain's order to break this eerie standoff. "Powerful things those mantis works, products of a fiendish craft."

"We have faced mantis men before," Prentice declared, and several of his men chuckled or made confident noises of disdain. "Faced and beaten. We are not afraid."

"My how you bark. What a bold, loyal mutt you are."

"The captain *took* the golden horns," Gennet snapped angrily. "He weren't the one fool enough to *wear* 'em. The gull was one of yours."

The sergeant was talking about an offensive song that cunningly insulted both Prentice and his liege lady, Amelia, which had come to the Reach via the lips of Bluebird. The tavern ditty portrayed Prentice as a mongrel dog. If this agent of the Inquisition recognized the reference, he did not show it. He kept looking at Prentice.

"You have no idea how they hate you," he said, and for a moment there was an almost respectful undertone to his mocking voice. "They sell their souls in pacts of blood to devils, but *you*? You haunt their nightmares, Ashen Man—whatever nightmares come to a folk who burn their own children alive."

The Redlanders?

Prentice's thoughts were racing, and though he tried to remain focused on the immediate situation, watching for the inevitable ambush for which Inxyphos was certainly posing as bait, he could not help hearing the broader implications of the man's words. The captain knew that Bluebird had made contact with the Serpent Witch and helped her with her plans, to a point, but he had always assumed that their cooperation had been a pact of convenience. And the Serpent Witch had always seemed somehow separate from her own people, as if acting on her own. When they were freed from her eldritch control, the fey explained that she had planned to make herself queen over the Western Reach, a depraved mirror of the land's rightful ruling lady. Yet Inxyphos's words made it sound as if the contact and exchanges between the Inquisition and the invader cult was even deeper than Prentice's worst fears. An Inquisition that played its own hand in the politics of the land was evil enough, but for them to sit down at the table and play partners with the Redlanders? That would be heresy in anyone's eyes. For all their brutality, the Inquisition was supposed to be the Grand Kingdom's first and last line against heresy. What then if they had fallen to heresy? Who could defend the Church and the throne now?

Who watches the watchmen?

Prentice resolved at that moment, regardless of how Inxyphos's plan played out, that the man must be taken alive and questioned. It would probably mean torture, if they were to get anything useful from him, but that was a moral boundary Prentice was ready to violate or uphold on the morrow. For now, Inxyphos must not be allowed to escape. Prentice set himself for a charge straight at his target, but before he could shout the order, there was a shift in the air to utter stillness. It was as if there had been a storm around them that they had not noticed, and it suddenly, instantly went calm.

"Bleed or shed blood, that is their nonsensical credo," Inxyphos said with a disturbing sense of satisfaction, lifting his eyes. "Yours was part of their price for the pact, so we will give it to them. As a mercy, let me comfort you with this thought: we will not leave the Broken Kings their other trophies for long. The Western Reach will be cleansed of their filth and returned to the bosom of the Denay throne, only not by your hand and not in the name of your fool bitch."

Prentice looked up at the top of the tree, watchful for some power of the tarnished copper mask there, but then he realized that Inxyphos was looking higher, to the sky itself. He looked into the starlit vault and his mind rebelled.

CHAPTER 5

"God in heaven, preserve us," someone shouted.

Prentice had no words to name what was happening. All he knew for a fact was that there was a wrongness to it as the sky above him shifted and changed. His first thought was of the monstrous Night of the Red Sky, when a massive blood sacrifice had stained the whole world crimson; but though it felt similar, this was not that—not least because there was no sovereign blood being spilled. Also, rather than projecting crimson into the sky, this magick, which was clearly centered upon this little island and the mask hidden in its one sapling, seemed to be drawing a part of the sky downward, so that the open space amongst the trees suddenly felt as if it had a roof over it just above the tallest branches.

At first, it seemed as if this drawn-down patch of sky was a reflection of the ground beneath it, a polished mirror, mimicking and distorting the likeness of the pond. But as he watched, Prentice realized that the image above was not a reflection because the island on which they were standing was not there. He was looking up into a picture of dark water, which he could tell by the reflections of moonlight and 'part-light on the surface of the other fluid. The stillness in the air intensified, so that even the sounds of the battle in the smuggler camp were dimmed. Had the fighting stopped?

"It's going to flood us," one of his men shouted in panic, and Prentice understood that fear. He was wondering himself why the water did not fall down upon them like a deluge. Or why they did not fall into that upside down lake beneath-above them. His thoughts and perceptions made war upon each other, refusing to concede that the laws of the universe had been so corrupted. He could not fault his militiamen for a moment of panic.

Then a buzzing began to arise, as of the sound of a fly's wings but writ large, so that the very air thrummed with it, vibrating upon their skin and causing the muscles in Prentice's jaw to ache with tension. A light like the almost rainbow glow of iridescent insect wings spread across the mirrored water above them, and as it lit that surface, he saw a spoon or a bowl—something made of wood but almond shaped and full of small things.

"Rest in hell, Prentice Ash," Inxyphos shouted over the drone. "Comes your doom."

The thrumming grew and the pain in Prentice's head increased. Just as it reached its crescendo, he realized what he was looking at—it was a boat, seen from far above, and the little objects in it were armed men. Redlanders.

"'Ware the sky!" he shouted, hardly hearing his own voice over the noise of monstrous insect wings. Then the black water above and the water around them were somehow connected. The iridescence flooded the intervening space until it was obliterated, the multi-hued glow reflected back from each mirrored surface, penetrating the waters and making them one. Men howled and Prentice felt his own flesh try to revolt. Then it stopped, and the boat he had seen as if from a bird's eyes far above was sitting calm in the pond water beside them, crowded to the gunwales with Redlander warriors, including at least three or four wolfen figures already leaping over the side in their eagerness for bloodshed.

"Form on me!" Prentice bellowed and was pleased that the familiar command broke many of his men out of their confusion. When faced with the unknown, mortals naturally defaulted to the familiar, and the Lions drilled until their battle order was as familiar to them as breathing. They fell into a pair of rough lines even as the first beast-man thrashed his way up onto the hummock. The captain had a momentary thought that he hoped Brother Whilte was not far away. It occurred to a quiet inner part of his mind that if Solomon had been here, he could have had the young drummer beat out rally-on-the-standard to summon his entire force to this point. But it was too late to worry about such things. With shield and breaker in front of himself, he set his stance to fend off the dagger-like claws of the wolfen warrior.

Bodies went flying as the ambush's first wave crashed on Prentice's small group. Lions were at their strongest in forma-tion, but with so few and the uneven ground of the island, they were only a skirmish line, and that was too evenly matched in numbers with even the first wave of this crew. While none of the Fangs and Claws around him was the untried recruits they might have been, man-for-man they were still barely equal to Redlanders in full fury.

"Keep them in the water," Prentice shouted. If they could keep the invaders from getting onto solid ground, it would be at least some advantage. Unfortunately, they were too few to prevent the Redlanders from sweeping around them to their flanks. There were a few lit torches on the newly arrived boat, as well as the lantern light reeling across the water more insanely now than ever. Nevertheless, the darkness favored the bestial warriors, black fur almost invisible against dark water or tat-tooed faces screaming like demons in the flickering shadows. For their part, the Lions held their ground, pulling together tightly to fight in their most useful fashion, with their three pikemen at the back, wielding long pole-weapons choked-grip in the close space. They thrust over the heads of their comrades, who formed a defensive front line with swords and "umbrellas." A wolfen man leaped at Prentice out of the shallows, only to be caught by a pike point in the mouth, tearing open its jowl in a spray. The creature snarled with more frustration than pain as it fell back into the water and righted itself for another spring. Swords beat on leather-bound shields and enemy spears scraped over hard steel armor forged in Fallenhill. It was an affray, a brawl. There was some positioning but not the neat, strategic battle Prentice had wanted when he first envisaged the White Lions on the battlefields of the Horned Man's invasion. Nonetheless, these were the two forces in their purest forms, their purpose-built warfare in microcosm—Redlanders hunting for him and the militia he had built to stop them.

What kind of hate drives men and women to this? he wondered. *To slay their children and lust for the blood of men they can hardly know?*

The shadows and shallows raged in the night. Prentice's breaker rose and fell again and again, shield always forward, covering now his head, now his body. He reminded himself to do nothing fancy. This was no duel or demonstration. Formation was more important than technique here. His intent to capture Inxyphos was all but evaporated now. He doubted the man was still even on the island. Over the shouts and clamor, he heard a thrum and worried for a moment that a second boat was coming through the mirrored sky, then realized it was bowstrings at a distance. The wounded beast-man surged out of the water another time, and even as Prentice clubbed its head with his steel baton, another White Lion was thrusting his backsword's point into its underside, twisting in its belly. Again, the beast-man fell into the water, and this time he did not rise.

A quick glance around him told Prentice that many of his men had fallen, but if anything, he had more in the ranks beside him now than when the fight had started. They were being reinforced. Other search parties must have found them. He set himself to be ready if more Redlanders emerged out of the dark water to assault his part of the line, and then, as suddenly as the boat had appeared, the fight was done. Beside him, men went to one knee or bent over their weapons, gasping for breath.

"Sergeant?" Prentice called, feeling a little winded himself. "Sergeant Gennet? Are you living?"

"Over here, Captain," the sergeant responded, and Prentice found him holding a man with a bleeding face from falling into the water.

"Good man. Take a moment and then we will get as many lights here as we can." The noise of the other melee caught Prentice's attention and he looked up. "After we deal with *that*."

He crossed the little island in a dozen paces and tried to see a good spot to risk a crossing in the dark water on the other side. Just before he stepped off to take the risk, he called a last set of orders to his second-in-command.

"Cut that damnable post down and cover its mask. And look out for that Inquisition man. If you find him, take him prisoner."

"If we find him, Captain," Gennet answered, "but with any luck the bastard's a pincushion already."

I hope not, Prentice thought, but he knew it was a slender hope.

CHAPTER 6

P rentice was thigh deep and halfway across the water when the fight he was wading toward seemed to crumble suddenly. There was a momentary run of surprised shouts and the sounds of mounts moving heavily through the brush. As he watched, it looked like the Church knights were breaking out of the fight and fleeing.

Doubtless taking their man Inxyphos with them, he thought. *What is the bet they already have a ready path planned for their escape?*

He was sure they would not be hindered by tree branches or unseen swamp water in the darkness. There was an occasional thrum of bowshot, but nowhere near as many as Prentice would have liked to hear. He hoped at least some of those few arrows had taken down a fleeing knight or his mount, but that was all he could do as he finally found a patch of denser mud underfoot and made quick progress to the other bank. There, in the remains of the melee, he found militiamen surrounding a small knot of smugglers who had clearly been fighting beside the Inquisition men-at-arms and had now been left to fend for themselves. Lions were being fended off with gaff-hooked poles, and some were calling on trapped cultists to surrender, but to no avail.

"No more!" commanded Brother Whilte's voice, and Prentice followed it to find the chaplain standing to one side, his prophet's rod raised high like a herald issuing a decree. He was wet and filthy down one side, from his matted hair to his wooden leg. "Leave off this foolishness and live."

"Have a fall, Brother?" Prentice asked as he drew near.

"Headfirst into a fen when my peg caught between two logs," Whilte said happily. Then he looked Prentice up and down, noticing the captain was in all respects just as filthy. "What's your excuse?"

Prentice smiled but kept his attention on this last crew of holdouts. There were as many bodies lying about as were left standing, many with multiple arrow shafts sticking out of their torsos. The Inquisition and Redlanders might have planned a fiendish ambush, but fey archers were the masters of surprise attack, practitioners without equal. Their attention had been focused here, which likely explained why few shots had been loosed at the fleeing Inquisition on horseback. Once they cleared the fight, the Church militants would have been obscured by the trees and hanging mosses. Prentice had asked his archer allies not to be too ruthless if they were forced to attack. Apparently, half the enemy slain was the Mountain fey equivalent of merciful.

"They're quite determined, Captain," Whilte commented as three of the militia made a feinting surge and the smugglers only clustered tighter, poles out like a hedge of spears. Prentice knew what this kind of last-ditch effort felt like—weapon gripped tight like the final lifeline of a drowning man.

"Yield and you will be treated fairly," he commanded in loud tone.

"Bollocks to that!" a smuggler in the middle of his friends shouted back.

"You have my word."

"And who are you? Why should we trust your word?"

"I am Prentice Ash, Captain of the White Lions," Prentice answered, and he stepped closer to a nearby lantern just forward of the rest of the militia.

"He's the one they want," another smuggler muttered, audible in the growing quiet now that the battles were all but over and the sorcerous sky had faded to mundane night.

"Bulldust! You ain't him!" the defiant first man said when he could see Prentice clearly. "The lion's longdog carries that magick curved sword. It's where he gets his powers from. You're just a filthy bailiff with a borrowed shield."

Prentice blinked in surprise. As it happened, he normally would be carrying the curved sword that he had won in his famous duel with Baron Carron Ironworth, Knight Marshal and king's champion—famous or infamous, depending on one's politics. However, he had never heard it called magickal before and neither had he realized that it had become so synonymous with his identity. Far from being magick, the blade was almost too heavy for him, and it almost perpetually aggravated the lingering shoulder injury he had taken winning the duel against Ironworth. In fact, that was the main reason he did not have it with him on this night. Having heard him complain of the pain it caused him one too many times, his wife had conspired to take the blade away and hide it somewhere "until your arm has a chance to heal proper," so she said. It was a situation that would have annoyed Prentice if he had not been so delighted by his wife's defiant devotion. When a wild rose was beautiful enough, he did not mind the occasional thorn, and Righteous was his wild rose.

"I *am* the captain," he said flatly, pushing thoughts of his wife to the back of his mind. "And you know Lions do not hunt for mere tariff-skips. We want the supplicants amongst you. It is only the ones with the mark who are facing the noose for sure."

A "supplicant" was the first and lowest rung on the Blood Sect ladder of faith, and its adherents accepted a tell-tale tattoo somewhere on their body as the sign of their commitment. Prentice had learned that fact during the campaign to the south some years ago. What he hoped was that one or two of these would-be cultists were less devout than the rest and might accept a chance to surrender if they believed they would live. Every religion, true or false, had its pragmatists. He watched as two or three of the resisting smugglers cast doubting glances at each other.

Not all are converts, he thought with satisfaction.

One man started to lower his barge pole when another voice from the back of the group cursed them.

"Useless cowards! Bleed or shed blood! It is the only path to power."

Prentice thought he could see someone behind the rest, pushing backward. Thinking the figure was trying to retreat in the shadows and realizing the group's resolve was weakening, he barked a sudden order to attack. His men rushed forward and all but one of the smugglers threw their poles down in panic. The last one resisted a moment, but heavily outnumbered, he was taken swiftly with only a shallow cut to his scalp.

None of that was Prentice's concern, though, as he charged around the final conflict at the retreating figure at the rear. He saw the shadowy form duck behind some wool bales and followed, expecting to have to run down the fleeing man. Instead, he came upon him almost immediately as the fellow had stopped and was holding a wooden mask in his hand, one without metal that Prentice could see but otherwise a copy to those on the poles around the fen.

"Put it down," he commanded, but the wild-eyed man ignored him. He lifted the mask toward his face but reversed it, with its mandibular mouth at the top. The wood on the graven fangs seemed wet, some kind of fluid running slowly from them as if the mask had just been dipped in oil, and Prentice watched fascinated and disgusted as the cultist put the edge to his lips, sucking on the liquid.

"Last chance!" the captain shouted, raising his 'breaker and stepping forward.

"For you," the cultist declared, his voice cracking in near madness. "The stag and the serpent have failed, but the mantis has opened the mirrored sky. They will come in a multitude to consume your land. It is prophesied. River and grass, on wings of sail, we will sweep you away."

He triumphantly pushed the mask to his face, and Prentice deliberately paused to watch but only for a moment. Even that little hesitation was a risk, of course, but he had never seen beast-men transform so close at hand before and never through the power of an icon.

"Lions, to me!" he shouted as he watched the wood of the effigy bite into the cultist's face. He wanted to learn as much as he could of how the sorcery worked, but he had no intention of facing a mantis-man alone if the simple object did have the power to truly transform this cultist into one.

The convert screamed in agony, and for a moment Prentice thought the thing had killed him. Militiamen rushed to join him, gasping with horror. Even at this late stage, the night had new terrors to reveal to them. Prentice watched as the carved shape of mandibles on the front of the mask were swelling, growing from image to fully solid parts of the man's jaw. The wood's grain began to smooth itself over his skin, turning it insect green, and his clothing ripped apart as his flesh was torn through with jagged, chitinous protrusions. The cultist's limbs cracked and twisted to fit the proportions of a man-shaped insect. It perversely reminded Prentice of a torture victim being drawn on a rack, their limbs disjointed by the tension of the ropes, and he wondered what kind of devotion to spiritual powers could persuade a man to do this to himself voluntarily.

"Be ready," Prentice commanded his men as they cursed or prayed under their breaths. "We will take him alive if we can. Someone call for cables."

Swallowing his revulsion, Prentice led by example and dove at the cultist, throwing down his baton, smacking the half-made beast-man in the head with his shield and tackling the transforming body to the ground. Even though he was smaller than Prentice, wrestling with the man proved physically as well as mentally formidable as the flesh under his skin writhed like the coils of a serpent trapped in a bag even as it hardened. Prentice could barely keep any grip on the man. One or two of his militiamen rushed to try and help, but the fray was now so unruly that the rest could not easily involve themselves. Doubtless, some were also a little intimidated. Grappling this sorcerous fiend in the gloom as his transforming mouth began to chirrup and clack with enormous mandibles was unnerving to say the least. Prentice smelt as much as felt a drip of the ichor mantis-men produced in their mouths, and he shifted his weight quickly to get away from the cultist's head. Mantis-men were not known to be as venomous as Blood Sects' serpent priestesses, but their spittle was not pleasant either. A gobbet of it burst out and fumed on one of the wool bales where it landed.

As he moved in the grapple, trying to push one of the other militiamen clear of the fluid at the same time, Prentice felt the body under him sit up with inhuman strength. The transformation was complete, and he now stared into an impossible head with bulging eyes and a triangular shape. Prentice was about to go for its throat to control that head and its new fangs and call again for ropes when he heard once more the twang of a bowstring—once and then once again almost instantly.

"No!" he cried out as two arrows buried themselves into the mantis-man's face, one through an eye and the other in the odd opening that was all that remained of the transformed nose. The cultist fell dead, and Prentice punched the suddenly still body in sheer frustration. He looked furiously up at the lightless edges of the swamp clearing, but there was nothing to see in the night. From out of the darkness a fey-accented voice called.

"*Brakkis effar.*"

CHAPTER 7

"*Brakkis effar?*"

"It means beast-man," Brother Whilte explained to Sergeant Gennet. "Or at least it is their term for them."

"And they hate 'em, do they?"

"As fire does hate water."

The sergeant looked to Prentice, who nodded wordlessly. What else was there to say? Whilte's description was poetic, but it was no exaggeration. The fey had suffered at least as much as the rest of the Western Reach at the hands of the Redlanders, arguably more so, and the *brakkis effar* were at the center of that suffering. If they seemed heartless as ambushers in general, the horse archers were indefatigably vengeful toward the invaders and their bestial champions most especially. Prentice shook his head. He should have known the fey would not have wanted a beast-man left alive to be taken captive.

"Speak o' the devil," Gennet muttered as a pony emerged from the dark of night carrying a fey rider on its back—a lithely muscular figure with long, pointed ears and a high-boned face. His fair hair was shaved on the sides of his head and his skin was nut-brown, as from a life spent in the sun.

Whilte tutted at Gennet's minor blasphemy but made no more objection than that. He would know the man meant no harm by it. As a military chaplain in a war with devilish forces, the brother was far more concerned with the truths of his faith than with the niceties of its form. Prentice appreciated the distinction more than he cared to admit. There had been a time, when he and Whilte had both been students at the Church Academy in Ashford, that the pair of them would have enforced every point of holy writ as devout zealots and debated every uncertain piece of punctuation on the page. Now, both captain and chaplain had witnessed the ruinous powers firsthand and tasted the corruption that lurked behind strict walls of tradition and injunction within the Mother Church—corruption that empowered men like Inxyphos. There was a time and place for debate and searching the scriptures, and the battlefield was not it. When the drums beat and the trumpet sounded, the man or woman who did not know their faith well enough yet would soon find out which were the key questions and which could be left for the quieter hours.

"Our search is done," said the fey rider, neither dismounting nor even saluting. "You have them all prisoner and those marked by the Untrue are slain."

Prentice frowned and lowered his head a moment, pausing to make sure his temper was in hand before he spoke. He rubbed the back of his head where the scalp itched under hair matted from sweating in his helmet.

"What of the riders who fled to the south at the end there, Benjamin?" he asked at last.

"What of them?" the fey asked.

Prentice shook his head wearily. "Did you capture any of them?"

"They were your men, were they not?"

Prentice looked up coldly, eyes narrowed. "What in perdition made you think that?" he demanded.

"You set us to track boatmen in a swamp. They do not use horses on the long waters, west or south," Benjamin the fey replied indifferently. "Redlanders do not ride, and we do not ride in steel."

He slapped at the stiff corslet of embroidered, waxed linen on his chest to emphasize the truth of his statement. "Who else would there have been but your slow riders?"

"Church knights," Whilte explained, but Benjamin cocked his head as if the words made no sense.

"Friends of the bluebird," Prentice told the fey man, and Benjamin's demeanor shifted. He hissed and scowled, seizing up his reins.

"We will hunt them now," he declared, looking over his shoulder and obviously planning to leave.

"Hold one moment," Prentice commanded, suppressing a sigh. The fey skill in the land and with bow and horse made them deadly enemies and invaluable allies, but they were their own people, and even as friends, they were proving insular and hostile.

Like herding cats, Prentice thought, a Veckander expression he had learned from Farringdon, former prince of that southern country.

"I do not doubt the fey folk of the mountains could run those slow fiends down in short order," he said, hoping some flattery might help him get his meaning across. "But until this night we had no idea the Inquisition had any instruments still on this side of the mountains. They are not like your people, Benjamin, but they have passed unseen by ours, nonetheless. Tonight's crew might be their whole cadre, or they might be only a few of many. We need to find them all and know that all have been found."

"We will find them all," Benjamin declared with confidence. "The word will be spoken in every mountain valley. There will be nowhere for them to hide!"

Now Prentice did sigh, and despite himself he cast a distempered glance at Whilte and Gennet. He knew they understood his frustration.

"Hunting them out is only half the task, Benjamin," he said flatly, nervous of offending the prickly man but past being diffident. "The Lioness Mother needs to know what they know and what they want. I want you to track them for me, trail them as none but the fey can, then return to me with the report. I will decide when and how they are to be taken."

Benjamin sat back in his saddle and stared at the three White Lions disdainfully. If he was not such a deadly warrior, the diminutive rider could have been mistaken for a pouty teenager.

"Mark me, I speak with the voice of an elder," Prentice persisted, hoping he was using his strangely-won authority correctly. For his service to the fey people, he had been given a place of respect and authority within their culture, but he still had almost no idea of its power or limits.

"We will do as you command," Benjamin said, to Prentice's unmitigated relief, "but they will not be permitted to escape. We carry blood debt in our saddles for Bluebird's evils."

With that, he wheeled his mount about and rode into the darkness. It was an almost disdainful gesture, but Prentice suspected he mostly wanted to be gone before the non-fey could lay any more limitations upon him and his people. The sound of his pony's hoofs faded almost immediately, and he was gone into the night like a ghost. Fey stealth always seemed to border on the mystical, so guileful were they.

"'Benjamin,' Captain?" Gennet asked after a moment, eyebrows raised in confusion and surprise.

"'Tis hardly a fey name, is it?" Whilte agreed with a smile.

"He will not tell us his real name," Prentice explained, staring into the shadows of the fen. "By their traditions, I am the only Reacherman supposed to have even heard any of their names."

"Coz they made you an elder?" asked Gennet.

Prentice nodded. "That is the main of it," he said. "To them I am *kreff enkreffra,* which means 'the blind one we allow to see us.' The rest of the Reacherfolk are still just *kreff*."

"Blind?" asked Gennet.

"Aye, and that is their word for us," Whilte confirmed. "They think of us as strange, hairless moles. We live above the ground but are just as sightless, to a fey's way of thinking."

"But we *can* see 'em," Gennet protested.

"Only when they let us," Prentice said. The sergeant furrowed his brows for a moment, then shrugged and nodded, acknowledging the truth of his captain's words. All three men had a hard-won respect for fey cunning, both as allies and enemies.

"Benjamin took a Kingdom folk name so he can speak with us more conveniently. He is the one they have elected to be the connector between us," Prentice explained further. "Like a herald but with none of the glory. I get the feeling he considers it something like a punishment."

"They don't salute or tug the 'lock or nothin', that's for sure."

"Doubtless our ways are as alien to them as theirs are to us," said Whilte. He scratched at his nose and looked into the small fire in front of him. The other two followed his example, staring into the low, ruddy flames for a moment until Gennet spat into the fire and shook his head.

"Well, I guess I'll leave all that thinking to you, Captain, if you don't mind," he said. "I trust your thoughts have cargo space enough to carry all that. Me? I got enough to do drilling the ranks and keeping the layabouts from shirking. I'll get back to that, if it's alright? It'll sure be dawn soon, I'd say."

He turned to Prentice, and when he had received his commander's nod, he saluted and went off to other duties.

"A good man, that one," Brother Whilte said when he was gone.

"Joined free as well. Not former a convict," said Prentice, only half listening. His thoughts were still on Inxyphos's words and the power of the Redlander boat to sail through the sky.

No, not sail, he thought, but he could not think what other word to use to describe it.

"You have a knack for drawing such folk around you, if you don't mind me saying, Captain."

That drew Prentice out of his thoughts for a moment, and his mind was suddenly flooded with names and memories of the men and women he had led and stood beside since the day he had first seen the invaders come out of the west. So many of them were dead now, and it weighed on him in the quiet watches—good folk like Gant and Felix and Baron Ironworth. Then there were the folk who were far from good, like the convict Treff, who for all his faults had still died to preserve the Reach, fighting until his last breath. Quite suddenly and unexpectedly, Prentice realized the uncanny similarity between Treff's name and the fey name for all Reacherfolk. Treff the *kreff*.

In spite of himself, he laughed.

"You think I am joking?" Whilte asked him, not understanding the source of the captain's humor. "Or do you suspect I count myself amongst those good folk? I do not."

Prentice blinked at the chaplain's harsh humility.

"You should," he said before he thought to stop himself. "Your service to the Lions and to me personally has become invaluable. Many of us still draw breath because of your efforts."

That assertion was a simple fact to Prentice's mind. Although not the best healer he had ever known, Brother Whilte had nonetheless saved many a wounded man's life just in the short year he had been chaplain. They both turned back to the fire and Prentice realized that the dawn light was slowly rising, just as Gennet had said.

"I was jealous of you, you know," Whilte told him quietly. "At the Academy."

Prentice's brows knotted as he listened to the chaplain's new revelation. The normally eloquent clergyman spoke in a low, hesitant tone, as if he feared to even broach the subject, which was likely the case.

"I hated you for my brother's suicide, of course," Whilte went on, "but when I look into my memories, I realize that I was filled with resentment long before that."

"Truly?" was all Prentice could think to say.

"Oh truly, Prentice." The chaplain almost never used Prentice's name anymore, and the captain read it as a clear gesture of sincerity. "You were so skilled at everything. Every lesson, every teaching. Whenever the instructors turned us to a new study, I would look and there you were, at the head of the class."

"Not every class," Prentice countered. "I never mastered the longsword nor horse riding either."

"You were better with the knight's blade than you think," Whilte responded. "You thrashed my brother, as you'll recall, and he was older and bigger than you. And you've grown so much more skilled with long blades since then as well. Baron Ironworth was no little foe to defeat."

Prentice felt his eyes go wide, surprised to hear such effusive compliments from a man who had once been his sworn enemy.

"And my horsemanship?" he asked, his voice now as quiet as the brother's.

Whilte's lip upturned sardonically. "Well, you're not old yet. There's still time for you to learn."

The two men chuckled and looked back to the fire.

"I was envious of you, too," Prentice said, "if we are making confessions."

"I imagine most lower-born folk are when they look to the advantages of those of rank."

"No," Prentice disagreed, shaking his head. "It was not your station or your wealth but your way with people. You made friends and allies so readily. Whatever else you *were*, Brother, you are a charismatic man, and I envied *that* in you. I may have been at the head of almost every class, but I was there alone, I assure you."

"But now, alone no longer," Whilte said, turning the conversation back to his point. "With many good folk around you."

"True enough, but when I look at it, I have to confess to you it is not by my hand. If men are drawn to me then it is by the hand of God or fate, I swear."

"Fate is what men call the hand of God, when they refuse to see Him at work," Whilte said piously, reminding Prentice that for all their warrior's brotherhood, he was a clergyman as well. "Nevertheless, I was a proud and jealous fool in my youth, and it cost you your dreams. For that the Almighty laid me low, took away my dreams and my leg for good measure. Now I will limp the rest of my life like Jacob the Patriarch. You say that you were an envious youth as well, but I see in you a life redeemed to an awesome purpose. God has formed of you a weapon to defend against unspeakable evil. You and the archduchess are making something beautiful here in the Western Reach, something that might found a new age for men and fey. And we are drawn to you, to help you in that purpose, however much or little we understand it."

Drawn to me? Forced, more like. Over half of the Lions are transported convicts, Prentice thought. *I am making them fight for the Reach in exchange for their freedom.*

"Thank you, Brother," he said, choosing not to share his thoughts.

His name was called from the direction of the water and a runner arrived to tell him the boats had returned from taking the prisoners to Dweltford. He would be able to return to town on one of those while the others were being loaded with the liberated contraband. Whilte would remain with the wounded to make sure they were sound enough to be moved. That was a task for full daylight.

As he walked to the lakeside, Prentice turned the chaplain's words over in his mind. He did not know how much he agreed with them, although he certainly liked the life he had now better than the one he had expected to have when he was a young man training to be a Church knight. With a wife he adored, a child on the way, and a place of command in the Reach's military structure, it was, in its way, a beautiful life. Or at least it had the beauty of purpose, though that made it bittersweet as well, turning him back once more to memories of lost comrades.

Perhaps God has made of me a blade to defend the Reach, he thought. *And a blade* can *be beautiful, but a blade's purpose is forever bloody.*

CHAPTER 8

"At least we are pennant bright," Archduchess Amelia whispered absentmindedly as she adjusted herself yet again in the carved, high-backed chair on the dais at one end of the Counting Hall. Seated upon an appropriately less splendid bench to Amelia's right, Lady Dalflitch gave her a quizzical look. Amelia nodded down at her fine gown and then at her lady-in-waiting's equally lavish attire. "Pennant bright," she repeated, "but without gold or silver in our purses.

"If we are pennants, Your Grace, then we fly over a field of charcoal and sable," Dalflitch whispered back, her eyes surveying the crowded trade hall. Amelia allowed herself a small smile at the lady's apt extension of her metaphor. In this gathering of ranking merchants and senior guildsmen, black coats and fur lined robes were ubiquitous. Virtually all present were clad in such dark colors. By comparison, Amelia and her lady-in-waiting were like vivid flowers growing in the ashes of a burned-out fire. The archduchess wore a gown of fern-green silk under a quilted linen overdress in Reach blue, embroidered with fiery orange thread. Her lady-in-waiting was vibrant in yellow under crimson. Both wore pearled coif headpieces, with their hair gathered by gilded netting. Their four military escorts had blue brigandines and polished steel plate on their limbs. The archduchess's Lace Fangs, her usual lady bodyguards, were not present this day. Lady Righteous was in the last third of her pregnancy, and Lady Spindle had not yet returned from a journey she had taken with her newlywed husband, Selectman Caius Welburne.

"If it is a field of ash, My Lady, then it is a rich field for the miner's guild," Amelia joked. Although the crowd was dressed in dour colors, everyone present sported gems and jewelery in a wide array, from medallions on heavy gold chains to rings and signets of sizes ranging from petite to as large as a walnut. And then there were the ever-present livery pins, worn on the breast and declaring the wearer's guild membership. In such august company, gold pins were most common, but even the few that were not were journeymen's pins cast of solid silver.

"A rich field, Your Grace, but sadly it is you they have come to mine this day," Dalflitch said, and Amelia nodded.

They were both fully aware of the reasons the hall was as full as it was, but ever the consummate courtier, Dalflitch was making witty conversation. The truth was that, with a few exceptions, the room contained folk to whom the archduchess—and through her the entire Western Reach—was deeply indebted. It was early spring, and the winter past had seen the end of a long and bitter drought. The archduchess's lands had survived the heat and dry but only through the expenditure of her every reserve of wealth. She had spent her last coppers to feed her people, and while future taxes would raise more wealth to replace the loss, in the meantime she had more invoices to honor, the payroll of her White Lions militia not being the least of those. The time had come for the Reach to take loans to pay those who could not wait to be paid. That was why this meeting had been called, so that the bankers could loan her the coin at high interest, and she could hand it straight to her creditors. On a table beside her, Lady Dalflitch had three heavy, leather-bound ledgers listing all the province's accounts.

And so I sit here, poor and pretty, to beg for alms to pay my debts.

Amelia rolled her eyes at her own self-pitying thoughts. It was no great strangeness for a noble to take loans. More than half the peers of the Grand Kingdom likely owed heavily to one or more lending houses. Nobles were wont to live more exorbitantly than their finances should allow. It was a point of pride that the high-born did not "care" about money—a point of pride but a lie as well. Even so, debt was nothing new. Amelia's own first marriage had been built upon an exchange of finance, her dowry paying her betrothed's loans. Amelia turned all these thoughts over in her mind as she awaited the arrival of the new set of consolidating creditors—bankers of the realm and foreign lands who were lending for the prestige of having nobility indebted to them.

And for extortionate interest, Amelia thought.

While they sat waiting for the bankers' arrival, the continuous low mutter of other business rolled through the hall like a swarm of insects that couldn't escape.

"Do you think they are making us wait deliberately?" she asked Dalflitch.

"Presumptuous of them if they are," the raven-haired beauty replied, her eyes continuing to regard the hall with transcendent disdain. The perfect noblewoman in so many ways, Dalflitch could make a king feel small and insignificant with a single glance or calculated expression.

"We cannot fault them for wanting to make a grand entrance, My Lady."

"Can we not, Your Grace? You and I both have paid court to the Throne in Denay itself, not to mention being witness to the peacock nonsense of Daven Marcus in full flight. Do they think to impress us with some contracts and coffers of coins?

"Unless you have been lowborn, My Lady," Amelia chided good-naturedly, "you cannot imagine how valuable the chance to draw near to nobility is to a yeoman. Even more so patricians, who are separated from the peerage by a thin but nearly impenetrable veil of birth. You and I have rank over these bankers who make us wait, but they have more money than I, and they will relish this chance to make me pay for the superiority that I enjoy over them at every other time."

"Money is beneath you, Your Grace," Dalflitch sniffed, pretending to examine the hem of one of her sleeves. Amelia nearly laughed out loud, only holding back the undignified act by sheer force of will. Lady Dalflitch was embodying all the classic attitudes and mores of Grand Kingdom nobility, but the archduchess knew it was all a mask, as much as the actual lace masks her other ladies-in-waiting wore in public. Dalflitch was too shrewd and calculating a mind to give credence to appearances. Finery and courtesy were mere weapons to the former countess, which she wielded in political and financial circles with the same level of cunning strategy that Prentice Ash showed upon a battlefield. Together, captain and courtier were a pair of advisors the equal of any in all the world, and Amelia was thankful every day for their loyalty to her.

Conversation in the hall suddenly stilled as a heavy thumping noise beat upon the double doors at the opposite end from Amelia's dais. They were opened a small way, and a bailiff stepped through. Amelia could barely see him over the intervening crowd, but he looked to have his hair wetted and slicked back.

"Pray make way for these men what has business wiff 'er Grace, Archduchess Amelia of the Western Reach," the bailiff bellowed, his common speech at odds with the elevated role he was trying to fulfill.

"Oh, for mercy's sake," Dalflitch muttered in disbelief, and she lowered her head to her hand, covering her eyes as if her temples ached. "Next, they'll be wanting to ride in on chargers to a trumpet's fanfare. Watch out, they'll be preceded by heralds and ambassadors yet."

"Shh," Amelia whispered. Her lady was not wrong about the coming financiers' presumptuous behavior, but the time for witticisms had passed. The next few moments demanded deft handling. Yeoman and patricians might envy the peerage, but

Amelia knew that no merchant respected a proud beggar. She had influence and prestige but no money, and the loan contracts were not inked and sealed just yet. It was within the power of offended lenders to make their expensive service more expensive still. She would have to negotiate the next hours with some care.

The double doors were thrown wide and five men in a line of three, followed by a pair, began to walk into the Hall like a religious procession. Ahead of them the crowd parted, some nodding their heads and at least one lower guildsman tugging his forelock. The archduchess wondered what that craftsman owed to which banker that he felt obliged to offer such excessive respects, but only momentarily. The main of her attention was fixed upon the lenders' men themselves. The front three were exactly the kind of men she had expected, although she only knew the one in the middle by name, a rotund fellow named Master Porcel, a selectman of Dweltford's own Conclave and respected throughout the town. He led the others down the growing aisle belly first, his heavy, fur-lined robe swishing on the floorboards with every step. Porcel had a florid, pudgy face that made him always look half drunk. He was the Reach's lone representative of a lending house called the Pin Makers. The emblem of his office was a belt made of large, interlinked gold rings that barely held his belly. In the center of each ring was an archaic version of the Pin Maker's Guild symbol. Centuries ago, the guild had been a small one, concerned only with the fine metalwork of making pins and needles, scarcely more than tinkers' trade. Then they had also taken hold of the weaving of gilt thread, braiding, and lace, as well as other fine services that used small and focused craft skills. Gilt thread was woven from silver and gold, and in short order, the guild's new crafts made it wealthy, catering as it did to only the most affluent clientele. From there, it was only a short step to offering loans from their treasury to others and becoming the bankers this selectman was now representing. The two men to either side of Master Porcel were similar in size and as richly robed, but neither had Porcel's glorious paraphernalia. Both wore only banker's versions of the typical guild pins that most every other man in the room, and not a few women, possessed.

The two financiers in the second line were of a different cast, it seemed to Amelia's eye. One was short, almost small enough to still be a child, though his face was mature, and some greying wisps of hair escaped from under his embroidered felt skullcap. Despite his lesser stature, he still seemed fit, and what Amelia could see of his hands and wrists made her think he was likely quite strong. The last man stood out so much from the others, and indeed from the rest of the hall, that he was more like the ducal party than anyone else. Tall, with a shaved head—a rare fashion in the Reach—his facial hair was an equally exotic goatee rather than the full beard or shaved chin favored by men of the west. Instead of the traditional black robe of a merchant, he wore a high-collared, quilted doublet in bright yellow silk of a foreign cut that buttoned close to his throat and fell to mid-thigh. The material had a repeating pattern of large black and yellow dots dyed upon it, and as he drew close enough for Amelia to see, she realized the dots encompassed a picture of a long-legged bird in inverse silhouette.

The Golden Heron, she thought, recognizing the symbol. This man was Jerrod Froster, Reach factor of the richest lending house in the known world. She smiled. The Reach had had successful dealings with the Heron in the past. Given his employers' vast fame and wealth, it struck her as curious that Froster had chosen to follow behind others. He would surely have had the right to take the lead if he wanted it.

Master Porcel reached the cleared space in front of the dais and stopped still. He risked impertinence by looking up into the archduchess's face, and as he appeared reassured that her eyes were fixed upon him, he lifted his right hand high in the air. Amelia blinked as he held it there for a long breath, and then, with an exaggerated sweep, he threw it to the floor, executing the most grandiose bow she had ever seen. She wondered for a moment if he might be about to throw himself off balance.

"Your Grace, I am named Porcel, Selectman of the Dweltford Guild Conclave, and I present myself to you as factor of the grand and loyal Pin Makers of Denay, Rhales, the Grand Kingdom, and beyond," he declared at full volume, his voice treacly rich. It echoed over the crowd and through the open narrow windows that lined one wall. Amelia thought she heard the flutter of birds taking flight outside, startled by his proud rhetoric.

You've been practicing some while for this moment, haven't you? she thought, looking at Porcel, although she schooled her face to courtly reserve. She was the archduchess, sovereign within her realm, and dignity was her duty.

"On my right..." Porcel went on, but Lady Dalfitch interrupted him.

"There is no need to make a feast of the introductions, Master," the lady said with cold, clipped speech. "Her grace is well aware who you all are."

"Good Lady, I must object," Porcel said with a scowl. "Introductions are seemly."

"Then you should not have come so late. Her grace has been made to wait for you, not to mention the entire of her land's mercantile class." Dalfitch cast an eye over the whole room, encompassing the "mercantile class" of the Reach, and then she looked back to Porcel. "If you meant to use some of your precious time with your liege lady to make speeches, you should have been more prompt."

There was a small muttering around the room, more an expression of emotions than actual words being exchanged, but Amelia understood. Few present, if any, would ever have been to a noble's court. These folk would know only stories of the kinds of clever banter and calculated conversations that were common in such esteemed society. For her part, Dalfitch was only fulfilling an important role on her mistress's behalf. The archduchess could not be seen to lose her temper or to be angry over petty points like lateness, so it fell to her lady-in-waiting to be annoyed on her behalf. Amelia saw the room's populace watching closely and wondered how many were merely happy to look and how many were inwardly cheering on their man Porcel. Finally, a chance for a patrician to speak straight with the proud muckity-mucks from the castle, with their bright clothes and empty purses. Amelia realized that she had become distracted and was not listening as Porcel was speaking, his right hand now flourishing with the end of every sentence. As she paid attention once more, she realized he was giving a long-winded explanation of each merchant's absence, using the excuse-making as a backhanded way to have his introductions after all. He turned to look back at the man Froster next.

"And Master Jerrod here..." he began, but Amelia had had enough. With the gentlest touch of her fingertips to Dalflitch's arm, she gave a signal, and the lady-in-waiting cleared her throat loudly.

"Master Porcel, if her grace had wished a sermon, she would have invited you to join her in church," she said with a sweet tone that was nonetheless as hard edged as a fighting knife. "Rest assured that your arrival, gentlemen, is welcome, however late you come, and introductions are unnecessary. The archduchess is prepared to move on to matters of commerce. This is, after all, a house of commerce."

"It ain't a playhouse neither," an anonymous voice called from the crowd. "Some of us can't waste half a day waiting to get paid."

"Who said that?" Porcel demanded, looking back at the crowd. No one volunteered themselves, but the master was not prepared to let it go. "Watch your tongues, all of you. There is an order to this hall, and you all know it. The select of the Conclave will not endure unruliness. We can order the room cleared and you can await your betters' business in the street."

Amelia sighed, not loudly, but just so that Dalflitch could hear her. Dignity and reserve were one thing, but her patience was truly ended. Her lady-in-waiting reached out and touched the arm of the corporal commanding their escort. The junior officer hammered the butt of his halberd down on the dais boards and it echoed as loudly as the bailiff's cudgel had on the door.

"Silence for Her Grace," the man bellowed with parade ground voice, rougher by far than Porcel's rhetorical speech but all the more commanding for the fact. The Pin Makers' man turned to look, an anxious expression upon his face.

Good, Amelia thought. *My turn.*

CHAPTER 9

"Good gentlemen, I do thank your masters for sending you to us today," she began, smiling benevolently. "They are much respected, and I do not doubt every man and woman present knows how valuable they are to the Western Reach. Without your masters and their indispensable service, surely all our endeavors would suffer."

Amelia paused a moment to let the five men present recognize the implications of her words. They were present, as far as she was concerned, only as representatives of their respective lending houses. For more than that, she had no interest. She looked aside to the table next to Dalflitch with its massive ledgers.

"As you can see, my lady factor has come prepared with a full accounting of the amounts I seek to commission from your houses. What say you that we get down to business, have our haggles, and see the silvers to the right purses."

"Ah, well..." Porcel said, speaking hesitantly for the first time since he had entered the Counting Hall.

"Master, I cannot help but notice that you have no coffers or secure chests with you," Dalflitch observed suddenly, and Amelia could hear the subtle note of tension in her voice. The archduchess had not noted this fact before this and now wondered what it boded. Dalflitch went on. "Are they perhaps beyond the hall doors, secured by armed men of your hire?"

"No," Porcel replied, frowning as if the word tasted unpleasant in his mouth.

"No?" Dalflitch repeated, eyebrow raised. She paused a moment, and when the banker was not more forthcoming, she cocked her head. "The funds are elsewhere in Dweltford then? Somewhere secure?"

Porcel looked to his companions and all the men shared apprehensive frowns, all except for Froster, who stepped forward between them, responding to their nervous demeanors with a stern nod. Once he was in the front, he bowed to Amelia in an odd, double-handed manner and then stood straight once more, placing his hands into the sleeves of his doublet.

"Your Grace, we have brought no money because there is none," he said with a heavy Vec accent.

"What do you mean by that?" she asked.

"We will not be making any loans today."

The insect buzz of conversation flared instantly through the hall, and now it had an angry undertone that gave Amelia a momentary chill. She felt her fingers gripping her chair arms as she stared.

"You are Jerrod Froster of the Golden Heron, are you not?" she asked him, hearing the unwanted brittleness in her own voice. He nodded. "Are you here to tell me that the Heron will not loan to the Reach?"

"I am saying, Your Grace, that none of the finance houses will."

Amelia gasped and the buzzing arose afresh until someone called out, "Why not?"

Obviously unnerved by the rising tension, Master Porcel stepped up beside Froster and swept his rhetorical hand around once more.

"See the matter from our position," he shouted, and his rich tone started to show signs of cracking.

"What position is that?" demanded one of the crowd, a man near the front with the hammer-and-nails guild pin of a carpenter on his heavy grey doublet.

"There is war," Porcel declared, as if revealing a secret the crowd could not have known. "War, and famine, and disasters. You cannot expect us to take excessive risks. Our houses have duties to their members."

Amelia listened to his words and did her best to contain her rising anger. Had these men truly come here just to tell her no? All five? Was this why they were late? Her eyes fixed on Froster, the odd one out and the clear leader, despite Porcel's attempts to be their principal.

"Jerrod Froster," she said loudly, and the angry hornets stilled to a quiet hush. Every ear was listening now. What before had been a curiosity was now become a matter of their livelihoods. If their duchess secured no loans, many would not be paid. "Is this some form of negotiation tactic, common elsewhere but unknown in the Reach? In days past, the Golden Heron has been happy, even eager, to loan to us."

"As you say, Your Grace, 'in days past,'" Froster responded. "These are not, I fear, those days."

"What days are they then, banker?" Dalflitch interjected, her tone now all steel and no charm. The velvet glove had been removed from the iron fist.

"Uncertain, hazardous," Froster answered readily. "Whether on this side of the great Azure Mountains or the other, troubles beset all our houses. My masters in Sunbury have instructed that we will undertake no new loans at this time. I promise you I am being neither petulant nor insolent. I am acting under directions from my superiors, directions which I cannot refuse."

"And the Heron speaks for you all?"

The other bankers looked at each other timidly and Porcel held up his hands, apologetic.

"It is the war," he said.

"I do not remember any of *you* standing beside us against the rebel," Amelia declared, her voice rising despite her attempts at self-control. Dignity was a fading concern now, and it was taking most of her will not to stand and denounce these men with pointed finger, like a penny prophet accusing sinners in the street.

"Your Grace...?"

"When the outcast earl and his rebel knights rose to overthrow the Reach, I do not remember you standing by my side to defend our people. There has been war, but the Reach has peace now, rebels cast down and Redlanders expelled from our lands. All this has been at the hands of my militia and bought by their blood. You have your place in the Reach because of their sacrifices, and you speak to me of the 'hazards' of war?"

Amelia knew she was exaggerating, that the war with the Redlanders was far from truly ended, but the last winter had been more secure than any period they had known since the Horned Man first marched out of the western grasses. All of that was because of the White Lions who now awaited their pay. She glared at the lenders' men, and while Froster seemed unconcerned, the others at least had the decency to cringe from her displeasure.

"You leant me fifty guilders to cover wool shipping to Griffith only last week," the carpenter said, pointing to the banker on Porcel's right. There were more angry rumbles.

"Is this true?" Dalfltich demanded, but it was Froster who answered. He turned for the first time, rudely presenting his back fully to the archduchess.

"It is not to the Reach as a whole that our doors must close," he declared to the crowd, and though she could not see his face, it sounded to Amelia as if he must be smiling as he said it. "It is the military adventures and conflicts between thrones which we must refuse."

"Since when?" Amelia muttered, trying to think how this inconceivable turn of events had come to pass. Surely not every great lender was against her. Who could arrange such an un-precedented level of cooperation?

"What about Daven Marcus?" she all but shouted, following a sudden intuition.

Jerrod Froster looked at her over his shoulder, blinking with what seemed like mild surprise but unwilling to yield his place as the current center of attention.

"Pardon, Your Grace?" he asked, and now he, too, looked to be losing some of his aplomb.

"Do you lend to the Usurper, Daven Marcus?" Amelia asked, only just managing not to sneer at the name.

Now it was Froster's turn to look to his fellows for support.

"Answer her, Heron's man!" Dalflitch commanded, and the banker's politeness and discomfort hardened suddenly into pure disdain, a man of wealth and influence now indignant at being pinned to the spot.

"Yes, the Heron still does business in the Grand Kingdom proper, and our factors are yet in Denay and Rhales."

"Traitors," muttered more than one guildsman, and the entire room was gripped with simmering fury now, from high-est-born to least.

Froster addressed the Hall once more.

"Questions and usurpations make the matters of peers too complex to risk," he said, and now he sounded like he was reciting a speech. "But we are still loyal—loyal to our customers of every other rank. We will even loan to cover losses the Reach cannot pay. We do not mean you to starve."

"That's their plan," Dalflitch hissed, and Amelia could see it, too. Not only were they in all likelihood still doing business with Daven Marcus and his allies, it also looked like they were doing his bidding, shutting her out. Worse, by offering funds to cover her debts, they were trying to buy her own citizens out from under her.

"We are not perfidious, Your Grace, I swear," Porcel pleaded, all sense of pride evaporating in the face of the crowd's growing displeasure. "We are merely men under instructions. Good Reachermen need not fear for their livelihood. We only must stand apart from the questions of thrones."

"My own guild sponsor has had three of his family in Denay taken before king's courts and others are in the hands of the Inquisition," protested another of the financiers, his voice a high-pitched squeak. He also turned to the crowd to plead with them. "We cannot risk being ascribed as rebels or heretics. What would you do?"

The collective anger seemed to abate a moment as no doubt all present considered the fearsome question. Most guild merchants had contacts across the mountains and likely relatives as well. Merchants were a traveling class. The wealthier the merchant the further their business reached and the greater number of authorities they had to not offend.

Their bluebird missed his mark, so they will strike any who might stand behind me, however distantly, Amelia thought, and the misery of that notion twisted her lips finally into a snarl-like frown. *But they will reward the ones who turn on me, just enough to keep them indebted.*

Perhaps the Heron was a loyal ally of Daven Marcus, as the Inquisition seemed to be, or maybe they were just being opportunistic. Amelia bowed her head and listened to the once more hushed room. Her entire domain felt balanced on a knife's edge yet again.

"All our houses have had visits from the quiet arm of the Church in Denay, Your Grace," Froster confirmed, and without looking Amelia could hear the confidence returning to his voice.

"Even the princes of the Vec are stirred against you, *Lioness,*" he went on, emphasizing her sobriquet with a layer of oily contempt. "You have been bold, and yes, snatched victory from the jaws of sure defeat more than once, but eventually even your luck must run out."

"Get out!" Amelia commanded, not looking up.

"This is the Conclave," Porcel said, his tone aghast. "There are traditions. Not even you may order us from here..."

"Get out!" she shouted again, looking up and standing all in one motion. "Get out and do not return until you are ready to beg my forgiveness."

"It is you who should beg forgiveness," Froster retorted. "You speak of hazards and dangers, but it is you who have made these good folk face war and chaos without the protection of the rightful throne in Denay—you and your stiff-necked pride. They should throw you out until *you* are ready to beg forgiveness."

The muttering hornet buzz rose to a sudden crescendo like an unexpected cloudburst, and the hall surged forward. Amelia fixed herself to stand stiff and unyielding in the face of a rebellious crowd, but she was not their target. Misjudging the power of his own rhetoric, Froster cried out in alarm as he was seized bodily by a half dozen hands and hoisted into the air. The other lenders' men were similarly scooped up. Struggling vainly on the shoulders of the crowd, they were carried towards the doors, chants of "Out! Out!" echoing from the rafters. Soon the dais end of the Counting Hall was empty, and Amelia slowly sank to her seat, relieved even as she absorbed the terrible portent of the day's events. As she looked around her, she noticed that all four White Lions were standing in fighting stances, their halberds lowered toward the diminishing crowd. She realized that they had set themselves immediately the room began to surge, ready to defend her with their lives.

"Thank you, good Lions," she said sincerely.

"You are the Lioness, like he said, Your Grace," the corporal responded. "The pride will not abandon you, though it cost us our lives."

It was an impertinent thing for a man of his rank to say, and Amelia was delighted to hear it. It made her smile.

Lady Dalflitch gave her a querying glance to see that she was alright. When Amelia nodded, the lady-in-waiting's regal manner reestablished itself as if it were a player's mask which she could put on just by lifting it to her face. "We will wait a moment for the crowd to clear some more," she told the militiamen. "Then you will escort her grace and myself out the rear entrance and back to the castle."

The corporal nodded and saluted.

CHAPTER 10

"A deaf what?" Lady Righteous asked as she played her card, her pregnant belly momentarily butting awkwardly up against the table.

"A defenestration," Dalflitch repeated as she drew her own card from her hand and played it with precise delicacy.

"What's that?"

"It is when someone is thrown from a building," Dalflitch explained, and Righteous looked up from her cards with wide eyes.

"They got a word for that?" she asked.

"Indeed, 'they' do."

"Strictly speaking, My Lady, a defenestration is when one is thrown through a window," Amelia said from her stone bench under the solar's own windows. This was one of her favorite places to think, staring out over the lake water as the sun set. After the day's disaster with bankers and the Conclave, which Dalflitch was recounting to Righteous while the two ladies played cards, Amelia had needed a long moment to think. The implications were not small.

"The particular opening through which one is thrown is not the point, if you'll permit me, Your Grace," Dalflitch countered her mistress's objection. "The fact that your people rose up in your defense and ejected the pompous fools is."

"Yes," Amelia agreed pensively, "and it will cost my people dearly in coming days, I do not doubt."

"Ships and castles," Righteous announced proudly, laying her completed hand upon the table.

"What? How?" Dalflitch demanded, looking from her own hand to the cards in her opponent's completed contract. Presently she accepted her defeat with an impatient tsk and swept the table to gather the deck. "I think you are swindling me, mother-to-be. You told me you could not play cards."

"That was when I thought you played some sort of high-born game, far above what I knew," Righteous explained as she accepted the deck from Dalflitch and began to shuffle and deal adroitly. "When you said to wager for silver, you put me aback. I ain't never played for more than coppers in my entire life." She started to deal out a fresh hand. "Then it turned out you were just playing some fancy version of cobble flip, using the chicanes from horseshoes. Well, that was easy. I been playin' them games since I was a lass. Three Streets' master, Krepps a'Krepps, he never let us go home after a lesson without a hand or five of some kind of shuffle and deal."

"You know I understood less than half of what you just said?" Dalflitch asked rhetorically as she took up her fresh hand. "Just as long as this Krepps a'Krepps didn't teach you to sharp."

Righteous cocked an eyebrow—the one not covered by her half-mask of black lace—at the implication that she might cheat at cards, that she might "sharp." Sharpers were accursed in every tavern, inn, and bawdy house in the Grand Kingdom as the lowest criminal dogs, despised even by brigands and cutpurses.

"You best be thankful I'm a proper lady now," the Lace Fang said with a gentle edge to her voice, "or else you wouldn't beat my dagger to the door, makin' accusations like that!"

Amelia smiled again. When they had first met, both women had had an almost instant dislike for each other, coming as they did from opposite ends of the social order. However, they had grown in respect for one another over the years, and since last summer when they had survived a particularly violent encounter in the back of a smugglers' tavern together, they had become fast friends. It was as if they were natural opposites of their husbands, just as their husbands were in so many ways the opposites of each other, and so they all now fit together as if made to do so from birth.

"I accuse you of nothing," said Dalflitch primly, but as she gathered her cards, Amelia saw the beauty give her counterpart a sly wink.

"Good, 'cause my back's too sore to clean up the blood after," Righteous said, taking up her own hand from the table. "And I can't well ask her grace to do it."

"Well, of course not," Dalflitch agreed. "Most improper."

Amelia shook her head, grinning at the distraction of their banter, knowing that Righteous could well make good on her threat, even as fully pregnant as she was. She looked back out the window and saw that the sun was now fully below the horizon and she needed to send for candles. There would be no need to set a fire in the hearth since the evenings were already mild. Before she could summon a steward, however, the solar door opened and the Marquis Consort Farringdon, former Prince of Aubrey and Amelia's husband, entered the room, carrying a long, cloth-wrapped bundle under one arm. He looked around and went immediately to her when he saw where she sat. She had just enough time to rise as he laid the bundle upon the seat beside her and then allowed him to take her into his arms. They had been married for not even two seasons and already she was astonished at how much she found his presence a comfort in her life.

"I heard there was trouble at the Counting Hall," he said, nuzzling his head against hers so that his soft brown curls tickled her cheek. He pushed back and looked into her eyes. "Are you alright?"

"I am quite hale and unharmed, my husband," she said, enjoying the emotion of using the term. She sometimes wondered if the pleasure would wear off, as if it were a mere novelty that would fade with familiarity. She hoped not. Putting her fingers on his forehead, she traced down the crook of his nose, the bone badly healed from where it had been broken when his homeland was conquered by the invaders. It made him quite unhandsome, and yet somehow, she found him only more attractive for it. Her touch upon his face was an intimacy they shared, and it seemed to comfort them both.

"How went your own day?" she asked. He looked at her closely for a moment, obviously searching for any signs of hurt that she might be concealing, then accepted her simple explanation without further question.

"My day, my love, was as the sweetness of spring sunshine, almost as deeply as are you to my eyes."

Amelia raised a finger in front of his face.

"This is not a time for poetry and sweet speech, Marquis Consort. We are not alone."

She cast a telling glance to the table where Dalflitch and Righteous were continuing their game of cards with silent, assiduous attention, as if there was nothing else in the room, certainly not two ranking nobles experiencing an intimate moment.

"Of course, Your Grace," Farringdon said, stepping fully back and bowing. It was an agreement between them that, when not alone, he would always remember, and honor, their respective ranks. He had relinquished his princedom to her as his wedding pledge, and as such, while he would be her husband and she his wife in matters of family, in matters of state and public duty he would always stand and walk one step behind. He looked to the bundle he had left beside her, and Amelia followed his gaze.

"Is it...?" she asked, and he nodded, a boyish smile splitting his lips.

"Master Sent gave it to me when he presented the cannons and the rest of the triggers for the lancers' arms," he told her. "I wrapped it in the cloth myself. It is impressive."

Amelia understood her husband's enthusiasm for the new weapons he and Yentow Sent had been working on through the winter, but in light of the day's events, all she could think of was the even greater debts she now owed to the weaponsmiths of Fallenhill. The master smith's creations were not cheap.

"And is he coming?" she asked.

"Master Sent? No, he's staying in the town...oh, you mean...?" Her husband nodded and his smile took on a guilty cast. "Steward Turley is bringing him now, I believe. Shall I send for candles?"

"Please do," Amelia told him, but as he headed to the door, she called an extra question after him. "Does the captain know why he is being summoned?"

"I shouldn't think so, Your Grace," he replied before he ducked out. "Not unless someone told him."

They better not have, Amelia thought.

What she intended to do this evening was not at all what she wanted. She had planned for something quite different, but once again, circumstances were forcing her hand. While her mind had been fixed on the bankers' meeting for the afternoon, she had also received a report of the previous night's action on the edge of Dweltford Lake, and the description of enemy men-at-arms ahorse troubled her. She needed more horsemen of her own to replace the exiled knights and nobles who had been banished with Earl Sebastian. She also needed someone to command them, to replace the earl's role as knight captain. That meant she had an awkward conversation coming with Prentice Ash.

"Does he know? Has anyone told him, Ladies?" she asked the pair at the table. Neither player answered her until Righteous looked up, surprised to realize that the question was not rhetorical.

"Well, I ain't told him," she said defensively. "He's a fearsome canny man, my husband, but he can't read minds."

"Even if it seems sometimes that he can," Dalflitch added. Amelia nodded, not sure if Prentice finding out ahead of time would make matters more or less difficult.

"'Course, Lady Dalflitch's husband? I wouldn't vouch for him to keep a secret," Righteous went on. "His tongue can wag ever long sometimes."

"I will vouch for my husband," Dalflitch said with the dignity of a Church elder, refusing to rise to Righteous's bait.

"Really, my beauty? What am I being accused of in this case?" asked Turley, having heard the last of his wife's comment just as he entered the room, holding the door open ahead of two kitchen maids and a junior steward, all carrying two lit silver candelabras apiece. Each servant bobbed or bowed as they diverted to different quarters of the room with the new lights. Behind them came Marquis Farringdon, and following him was Captain Ash.

"It seems Steward Turley had already anticipated our needs, Your Grace," the marquis said, "and diverted his escort via the kitchens to fetch light. Ever the diligent man, a retainer worthy of praise."

"You are too kind, My Lord," Turley said with a self-satisfied grin.

"Indeed, he is," Dalflitch interjected, turning her formal tone upon her husband. She clearly disapproved of him being so familiar with someone of the marquis's rank. "Especially considering you are given to speaking out of turn at every opportunity. Lady Righteous, I might have to withdraw my vouchsafe for his behavior. I wonder if he could ever hold his tongue long enough."

"You wound me, love," Turley told his wife, his hand pressed dramatically to his chest, roguish smile dancing.

"Hush, Steward," she responded, less sternly but somehow more seriously. "All joking aside, remember we are in our liege's presence."

As if he had only just noticed Amelia in the room, Dalflitch's husband turned to the archduchess and bowed with almost perfect formality, his face instantly honest and serious. She smiled and nodded, accepting his gesture of apology. The truth was that she indulged him far beyond what any normal household servant would be permitted, and while his jovial nature regularly transgressed minor boundaries of decorum, he never failed to protect her interests or uphold her dignity.

It was not Turley that concerned Amelia in the main, though, and her eyes followed his best friend as Captain Ash made his way directly across the room to present himself to his liege lady, pausing only once on the way to smile at his pregnant wife as he passed. Prentice stood in front of Amelia and knelt on one knee, bowing his head.

"Welcome, Prentice," the archduchess said and drew in a breath to steel herself. In the usual scheme of things, what she had to discuss with her militia captain would be a positive thing, something for which she should have no misgivings, but so much of her relationship with this man was not within the usual scheme of things.

"Your Grace," he began, rising from his knee, but she held up her hand and nodded in the direction of the servants who were finishing up the placing of the candles. The next hour's business was not something for listening ears.

CHAPTER 11

"The Inquisition? The Inquisition and Redlanders in collusion?"

The archduchess roamed about the room, absorbing the implications as Prentice unfolded the full tale of the previous night's action. She had bid him begin as soon as the servants left and the door was closed behind them, but before he had even half finished his account, Amelia found herself on her feet, pacing back and forth.

"We knew they had been before, Your Grace," Lady Dalflitch said, clearly referring to the cooperation between the Serpent Witch and the assassin Bluebird in the drought.

"Aye, My Lady, but to this degree?" Amelia retorted. Prentice's account made them sound almost like allies, and this man, Inxyphos? In her mind's eye he was another Bluebird, civil and even charming but murderously vile. Even now, she sometimes awoke in the night, terrified that the shadows of her room hid the minstrel assassin, putting the castle to sleep with his eldritch music before he plunged a dagger into her heart. During those nights, Farringdon would sense her fear in the bed next to her and wake to hold her until she fell once more into restless sleep.

Amelia looked up and noticed Prentice watching her attentively. Their eyes met and she could read the seriousness of his thoughts there. She wondered if he had been able to snatch even a few hours of sleep since the night before. His mind would have been turning over each new piece of information continually, trying to weave the many threads into a coherent tapestry. After years of war, the archduchess had come to see sleep as a luxury that true leaders were often denied.

How has a force of the Inquisition come so far, so secretly, into my lands? she wondered. It was bad enough to have been invaded from the west, but the Azure Mountains were supposed to be a barrier to her enemies in the east. Surely, they were not as mystically stealthy as the fey from the mountains. Almost instantly, Amelia knew the answer to her questions.

"The refugees," she said quietly, and as soon as she did, Prentice nodded his head, following her thoughts even before she spoke them. It reminded her of Lady Righteous's insistence that her husband could not read minds. Sometimes Amelia was not so sure.

"That seems the most likely way," Prentice said. "Posing as newcome folk would not have been that difficult, even bringing mounts and arms, as long as they were careful. There are a myriad former men-at-arms and lesser peers amongst the refugees, many with their horses and armors. And the newcome folk are a horde for them to hide amidst." Prentice seemed to stop his last sentence short, as if a new thought had occurred to him, but before Amelia could ask him about it, Lady Dalflitch spoke.

"As many as a hundred thousand, is my best count," said the lady-in-waiting. As seneschal, she was charged with keeping all the province's accounts, including the populace and visitors. "Obviously that number is conjecture; I most certainly have not conducted a true census, but we have all seen the shanty town growing outside Dweltford's walls. It is easily five or more times the size of the encampment when Daven Marcus was there a few years ago. There are similar newcome settlements all up and down the Reach, and word from Griffith is that theirs is as large, if not larger, than ours."

"Conjecture?" Turley asked quietly of no one in particular.

"It means a guess," Farringdon whispered, not too quietly, and the steward tugged his forelock in thanks.

Amelia shook her head. Even without the Inquisition hiding among them, the refugees were another major problem for her. They were folk caught between, displaced from their old lives by the Usurper's civil war and now in a new land without a set place for them. They had already been a large number during the days of the drought, and if anything, the flow of humanity over the mountains had only increased since the rains returned. She knew they were not criminal people, only desperate, but if desperation was allowed to fester, it would turn to criminality soon enough.

A hundred thousand? That was almost the full population of the capital Denay. It was the same as if God had reached down from heaven and snatched up the whole city and deposited it into her land. That reminded her of the most fantastic part of Prentice's story of the previous night.

"And boats that fly?" she said. He seemed not to hear her at first, and by the time he did, she waved away his objection before he could even raise it. "No, not fly. Move through the sky you say but...not...fly?"

"As between two mirrored surfaces of water," Prentice told her. Amelia shook her head. What could that mean?

"I saw it and I do not understand it," he said. "Not fully."

"Well, understand it or not, it is just another in a long line of magickal threats that our enemies have presented us with. We will need to find a solution to this one as we have all the others."

Amelia paused and pinched the bridge of her nose, feeling momentarily overwhelmed by the seemingly endless array of tribulations besetting her lands.

I need a rest and space to think, she thought, then shook her head. *Too bad. The Reach has needs, and it falls to me to supply them. To live in the castle is to take up these responsibilities. We stood against the drought, the rebellion, and the condemnation of the Church—well, the part that is in Daven Marcus's grasp, at least.*

Her eyes fell upon the table and the ladies' game of cards. Prentice often spoke in card-game metaphors. Perhaps she could make use of that thinking, too. She went back to the stone bench under the window where she had been sitting and from one end took up a small stack of documents and folios. She left the cloth bundle behind on the other end for now, a complicated matter in its own right, and returned to the center of the room.

"Ladies, I must ask you to yield the table," she said to the two playing cards, and they instantly swept and folded their game away. Amelia put her documents down.

"The Reach has too many problems, and at present they are dancing about like drunkards around a maypole. I would have them put into better order so that I may address them and send these rowdy carousers to their beds." She looked round the room at everyone present and then put her hand on the stack of parchments in front of her. "So, that is the game and this is the deck. Let's turn our cards over and see more clearly exactly what kind of hand we've been dealt."

"A tortured metaphor, my love," said Farringdon, good-naturedly.

"Perhaps, but apt all the same," Lady Dalflitch added. Already her expression had shifted to its shrewd cast—the calculating look she almost never showed to others because it revealed too much of the sharp mind behind the beautiful face.

"All of you help me," Amelia told them. "Set your minds to this. What is the first card?"

The archduchess's inner circle looked back and forth between each other. It seemed for a moment that none knew who should begin, but then Prentice stepped to the table.

"We have the mountain passes secured and the land is recovering from the drought, swiftly in fact. It could be as little as a few years and the Reach will be prosperous again," he said. "The western grasses across the Dwelt are patrolled for us by the fey, who can ride more leagues a day than any other mortals.

Nothing will escape their notice, and they will be able to slow anything short of a horde of Redlanders."

He trailed off again, and Amelia was sure there must be something teasing at his mind. She decided to trust him to bring it to her attention if and when it was relevant.

"That still leaves the southern border—Aubrey and the bridge across the Murr," said Farringdon. "I know it is my homeland and I have a personal interest, but you have asserted your claim over Aubrey, the town *and* the province, Your Grace. If you do not act to fully absorb it into your rulership soon, other forces will make your claim moot. Reports were that my uncle, Prince Garrodmin, was already moving to invade before the winter came."

"That is significant," Amelia agreed. "And, my husband, your love for your homeland and your people is not an unworthy consideration, not in my eyes." His fidelity to his own folk was one of the things she most loved in him. She reached into the stack of parchments and drew two out, putting them in a smaller stack by themselves upon the table.

"Aubrey," she named that "card," then pulled another folio out and put it next to the pair. "And the rest of our borders."

Each little stack was made up of summary documents of what her seneschal and the Conclave reported to her of their subjects—lists of trades or events in various villages; problems of crafts and guilds, as well as strange happenings and reports of possible enemy actions; and of course, taxation reports.

"For both of these cards, the correct play is the White Lions," Amelia continued, pulling forth a third document, a much thicker folio, and laying it in a triangle with the other two. "But that only gives our hand another penalty card."

She pulled out the largest single folio in her whole "deck."

"Our debts and the bankers who will not lend to help us pay them," said Dalflitch. The folio was the lady seneschal's own summary report of the larger codices that had sat beside her in the Counting Hall. "The Lions are going too long without payment."

"The bankers will not lend?" Prentice asked. Apparently, he had not yet heard of the day's fiscal events.

"The Inquisition's put the screws to 'em for Daven Marcus," Righteous explained to her husband. "The Conclave gave 'em a chucking out once the merchants discovered their credit's no good no more."

Prentice raised his eyebrows in further surprise. Amelia nodded at him.

"The lending houses only refused the Reach itself, not the local merchants," she explained. "It was a strike at me, not all the folk."

"But in a display of unexpected patriotism, the Conclave *did* rise up and eject the five agents," Dalfitch added.

"On their shoulders and into the street," Righteous finished off, clearly taken with that aspect of events. It was somewhat satisfying to Amelia as well, as she remembered it happening, especially given the difficulties the financiers had visited upon her.

"That is unhelpful news, Your Grace," Prentice said, "Perhaps even moreso than you realize. Because I was going to say that you need to expend yet more on the Lions to increase their numbers."

"More men-at-arms?" Dalflitch asked, and it was clear she was not happy. Already the White Lions were the largest single expenditure of the Reach's treasury.

"We are stretched thin," Prentice told them. "Even if we had not lost almost all the Reach's nobles-at-arms to Sebastian's exile, we would not have forces enough for all our needs. As it is, I am going to have to detach a few cohorts now to capture these Inquisition men, as well as others for hunting out any other converts to the Redlander cult."

He cast a glance at Lady Dalflitch and Amelia saw them share an unspoken resolution. It was the lady senschal's sources that had revealed the cult's hideout across the lake in the first place.

"All of that must happen, and then we must marshal whatever forces you choose to deploy to the taking of Aubrey," the captain concluded.

"You don't trust them fey to hunt the Inquisition lads by themselves?" Turley asked. "Your story made it sound like they might've let the knight fellas make a run for it on purpose. Could they be in cahoots?"

That idea had not occurred to Amelia, but before it troubled her any further, Prentice was already shaking his head.

"The fey hate the Inquisition like they hate the Redlanders," he said confidently. "They might leave these Church knights for a chance at the Serpent Witch, but they would circle back and finish the task, I assure you. That is not our problem."

"Then what is?" the steward asked his old friend.

"We do not know how far we can trust them, beyond their hate." Prentice turned to look at Amelia, an earnest expression on his face. "I do not think they plot treachery, Your Grace, but we cannot afford to forget they are a skilled military who have for the first time stepped into the open after a thousand years of hiding behind a veil of myth and legend. Even if they mean us only good, they are more uncomfortable than they have ever been. We are allies that represent a threat to their ways almost as dire as their enemies."

"Even just having allies is a threat to them," Farringdon concurred.

Amelia waited a moment, absorbing Prentice's words. She reached into her stack and drew out the single sheet that held the written summary of the raid across the lake. It was the only part of the whole "deck" that contained any clear discussion of the fey, their actions or their motives. The smallness of the one sheet next to all the other stacks was a perfect representation of the problem—they simply knew too little about these allies to rely on them too heavily at this time.

"Well, Prentice, you brought me this force. You know them best. What is your advice?"

"Knights ahorse, Your Grace," Prentice said, and it sounded to her like he had to force the words out through gritted teeth. She cocked an eyebrow.

"My lancers are a part of that solution, Prentice," Farringdon said, and he leaned over, waiting a moment for Amelia to nod her permission, then pulled another "card" from the deck to place into their "hand." From the document's red string binding, she recognized it as Farringdon's account of training a new kind of heavy horse, equipping them mainly with captured arms and horses from the exiled rebels, refurbished and retrained to suit new owners. He put his card onto the table. Inside, it also explained the progress of Farringdon's other new major contribution to the White Lions—new cannons. Amelia shuddered inwardly just at the thought of such weapons. She had once come under their terrible fire and lived, never wanting to go near such things again. The tremulous emotion reminded her of the feelings her nightmares gave her when she awoke in the night.

"The lancers will go a long way to cover the gap, My Lord," Prentice said, "but even if they could replace the knights ahorse right now, we would still need more foot."

The certainty in his tone gave his words a finality that seemed to close off conversation for a moment. There was a long, pensive quiet.

CHAPTER 12

"Is a levy not the obvious solution?" Dalflitch asked, addressing her words to the whole room. "We have a vast population that must be settled and a shortfall of men-at-arms afoot. Why not use the one to solve the other?"

"A levy, sweetheart?" Turley asked his wife, moving close enough to put a gentle hand on her shoulder as she still sat at the table. If she heard the unhappy tone in his voice, she did not show it.

"Why not?" she said, her attention on the archduchess. "It's what any other noble in your position would do, Your Grace. And better, for you have this horde of displaced folk to draw upon. You can fill your ranks without taking a single farmer out of the fields or guildsman away from his craft."

"And how would her grace draw this levy, love?" Turley persisted, his voice soft. From his expression, Amelia could see he was more hurt than angered by her words. "Would her grace send press gangs out to gather the numbers? Run through the shanties, snatching up every hale body they can get their hands on? Maybe take them out of any chains they're in. She could give the word to the magistrates to go a bit harder in their judgements, get a few more onto prison sentences. Would you offer a bounty, perhaps? Grease some palms for extra men, the ones no one would miss."

"We're trying to *save* money husband," Dalflitch said, and half turned toward him. As she did so, it obviously dawned upon her what it was that she was suggesting. Her expression fell and she gripped Turley's hand, pressing it to her lips, aghast. "Oh, husband, I am so sorry. I wasn't thinking. No of course, we cannot do that, Your Grace."

"There will never be rogues 'foot in the Reach again," Amelia said flatly, not angry with Dalflitch's suggestion but wanting everyone to recognize that her resolve on this matter was not to be questioned. Half the room had been convicts in her service at one time and the thought now sickened her. She wondered how it had ever not. Looking, she saw that Righteous was scowling at the suggestion under her lace mask, though she uncharacteristically kept her tongue. Amelia looked to Prentice, who met her gaze with icy resolve. She was certain he would rather die than put any man on a chain to fight.

"It would be different if we could pay them," Farringdon said. "A recruitment would raise us a fresh host out of the new-come folk in short order. Especially offering a roof and meals to boot."

"Which only returns us to today's disaster in the Conclave," Amelia told her husband with a wan smile, resting her finger on the debt "card" on the table.

"Not if we play another card, Your Grace," Prentice said, his expression shrewd. "A card that has the potential to tie our hand together into a winner."

"Is there such a trump in this deck, Prentice?" she asked, looking down at the table.

"Not yet, Your Grace, but we could fashion a new one. Creating an archduchy has opened some new pathways. Perhaps it is time to walk a few of them."

He paused, clearly waiting to see if she would realize his new idea for herself, but she was not following yet. She nodded to indicate he should go on.

"An archduchess is sovereign in her own realm," he explained. "A princess in all but name, with all the rights thereof, including warranting many things, such as town charters."

He stopped right there and let his words hang. Amelia was chewing them over in her mind when their implication struck her. Under Grand Kingdom law, a town was a very specific kind of settlement, distinguished not only by size but also by having its own guild conclave, with the right to levy taxes in the liege noble's name, all secured by an official charter. Every town had to have a charter, and they could only be issued by a throne, either from Denay or Rhales. Or now from Dweltford.

"The Reach is vast," Farringdon said, his enthusiasm unmistakable in his tone. "It's nearly a third the area of the Vec, and the newcome refugees add a princedom's worth of folk to the populace just by themselves. Yet there are only three major towns." He looked to Prentice. "Not counting Fallenhill, if you'll forgive me, Captain."

Prentice blinked at the marquis, clearly nonplussed. He nodded readily but did not show any understanding as to why Farringdon might have singled him out. Amelia understood and realized that her husband was moving toward the other issue she had left to one side so far this evening. It was clever thinking on his part. This idea of town charters had the potential to open the question naturally, assuming she handled it with care.

"It's an excellent idea," Dalflitch said, smiling as enthusiastically as Farringdon. "Kings and princes have sold warrants for town charters to wealthy nobles for centuries. It's practically a tradition. They've even been known to go to war just so they could sack a town and force the ruling noble to seek a new warrant and build a replacement."

"But who would pay me for these warrants?" Amelia asked, ignoring the horror of wrecking a town just to raise more money. "The Reach is down a few nobles at present, perhaps you had all noticed."

"Sometimes guilds can buy a warrant on their own or put up a petty lord while covering the cost for him," Dalflitch explained, warming to the notion further. "Imagine how many selectmen of the Conclave would jump at the chance to form conclaves of their own? To become Alderman Masters, first amongst equals in their own communities?"

"How would they pay?" Amelia objected. "The bankers have closed off their loans."

"You know yourself, Your Grace, that most merchants keep something squirreled away to stave off poverty," Dalflitch said happily. "Guildmasters too, I'd venture. I doubt there's a select-man who wouldn't be able to scrape together the coin. Or they can form pacts amongst themselves."

"You can bet guilders to gobbets that more than one or two newcome folk managed to stash some coin in their luggage when they crossed the mountains, Your Grace," Turley offered. "If you're to let merchants form compacts, then why not some of the refugee folk?"

"And even those who don't have merchants, newcome or yeomen even, there will be many who'll sell all they can to buy into a compact," Farringdon added. The enthusiasm was spreading, and Amelia was almost feeling forced into agreeing just because of the infectious approval.

"Sell their own sons and daughters even, for the chance to be kings o' their own little hills," Righteous said, and that brought the good mood's rise to a halt, smiles fading almost instantly. The lace-masked lady looked around her, confused about the sudden change of atmosphere. "What? You surely don't think it's only back-alley doxies and wretched folk as have one too many bubs and sell 'em off to a workhouse?"

Amelia scowled but forced her expression into a gentler frown.

"No one doubts the truth of your words, My Lady," she said quietly. She looked back to Prentice, who had let his suggestion flow without guiding its path in the conversation. "But you do raise a good point, Righteous. New towns would require rulers. Guild conclaves would be appointed to civil affairs, but I would need new nobles as well to maintain my peace and execute my judgements."

"To replace the disloyal ones exiled for rebellion," Prentice said. "The earldom of Griffith stands empty, and you cannot fill that, but you can create knighthoods, baronetcies, and baronies, Your Grace. You could split the town off from the rest of the pale and make two baronies of Griffith. Then there is Fallenhill, another empty barony. Sell warrants to charter four or five new towns with their own barons or even viscounts, plus one or two baronets. If each raises a banner for his own sworn knights, you could replace the main of the Reach's nobility within the year."

The sweep of the captain's idea was almost breathtaking, although no matter how seductive it was, she felt he was exaggerating about the speed at which it could be done. Amelia smiled and looked at her husband. He returned her expression and then looked over at the parcel he had brought her, sitting on the bench. She nodded to him, and he headed that way.

"And whom should I choose to fill these peerages?" she asked, turning back to Prentice.

"Surely Marquis Farringdon's lancers have more than one former noble driven off his rightful lands by Daven Marcus' forces. Close to half are like that, from what the marquis has told me."

Prentice's tone of voice made it sound as if he thought his answer was obvious. Amelia caught Dalflitch's eye and gave her a subtle nod. The lady seneschal took her meaning.

"You would replace our old nobility with a new nobility of the same stripe, Prentice?" she asked. "Bring us back to our old problems and awaiting a repeat of the same crisis?"

"Not at all, My Lady," the captain responded sharply, then addressed Amelia again. "These will be titles and ranks which you create, Your Grace, not dispensed by you in the name of another throne. You may set the oaths you require, phrased however you wish. Have them swear to you first, every bannerman a vassal of yours before even his own banner lord."

"And you think former nobles will accept such a condition?" The question of to whom a peer owed their first loyalty had always been the key threat to Amelia's power in the Reach. Prentice's plan would codify a solution to that problem. Every knight of the Western Reach would owe *her* their allegiance, obeying no power before her and loyal only to any other throne above hers, if she chose to be. It would be perfect if it worked. Prentice had a typically ruthless opinion on that subject.

"If they refuse the oath, they can refuse the peerage," he said flatly.

"What if there are not enough to allow them to refuse?" Dalflitch persisted. "There might not be enough newcome former peers. By my count, you plan five or six barons, twice that number of baronets, and knights as many as they can raise. That is quite the number of instant peers."

"Then appoint proven others," Prentice answered. "Every would-be Reacher noble will have to prove themselves anyway. There are no claims of birth left. Let only those knights who have shown their loyalty without doubt be raised, and others too, if they be worthy."

"You think there would be many such men or women?" Dalflitch asked. Amelia watched the interchange between captain and lady closely, happy that Dalflitch was carrying this part of the discussion for her. She wanted to observe Prentice as he discussed this situation. It was close to the matter she had been dreading, and she had already asked almost everyone present what they thought he would think. This was her last chance to get her own impression before unpleasant truths made pure honesty impossible.

"I can name a half dozen such men in the Lions right at this moment, My Lady," Prentice said, the edge in his voice sharpening yet further. "Even in this very room."

"Is that so?"

"Master Turley, your husband for one, My Lady," Prentice said, pointing to the Chief Steward, who jumped in surprise.

"Who, me?" he asked reflexively, then clamped his mouth shut, apparently uncharacteristically aware that this was not the right time for one of his usual cheeky witticisms.

"He gave his arm saving her grace and yourself," Prentice continued. "He runs her household with the precision of a master architect, and he is married to you. Do you not think his service worthy of a knighthood? You were once a countess. Would you not like your ladyship to be anchored to a peerage once more?"

Dalflitch blinked a little, surprised, it seemed, by Prentice's sudden intensity and the direct question concerning her own status. She looked askance at the table a moment with her face turned away from Prentice, who still stood back a little. Amelia thought it was to gather her thoughts, and she realized just how much the formerly ambitious countess had given up by marrying a commoner like Turley.

Of course, I will knight him, My Lady, she thought. *And for just service, not merely to return you to a peerage.*

The archduchess looked over her shoulder and was pleased that her husband was there. The bundle was in his arms, and he smiled at her confidently. There was only one more misgiving Amelia wanted settled before she would ask for its contents.

"It will take some time to choose this new nobility for myself, not to mention drafting the warrants and charters," she said, allowing her eyes to roam over her closest confidants. She felt a sudden sadness that Spindle was not with them. She would have liked her to share in this moment as well. Nevertheless, Spindle was with her new husband and happy, and they would meet again soon enough. Amelia finally let her eyes rest again on her militia captain. "That would leave the post of knight captain vacant for a good while. Too long, in fact, given the threats we still face."

"You could appoint a new knight captain before midnight, Your Grace, if you wished," Prentice said readily, the hard edge in his voice now unmistakable. "You could have done so a month ago."

Well, here it is, Amelia said. She was not one to shirk a duty, no matter how unpleasant. She had faced down the pride of kings and princes, and ordered men executed in front of her. The Archduchess of the Western Reach was not made of spun sugar. And this duty was something she had known she would have to do for the whole of winter at least. Leaving it and hoping for a more ideal moment had only made it so much more difficult.

"Whom would you recommend for the post, Captain Ash?"

There was a long pause, and it felt as if everyone in the room might be holding their breath. The very air was still as a painting. Prentice looked her straight in the eye, and she suddenly shivered. That was the face that men about to die saw when they tried to stand between him and his goal, and she knew it—an expression not of hate but of cold fury, as of a deluge surging inexorably down a river channel.

"I would recommend your husband, of course, Your Grace. Marquis Consort Farringdon should be your knight captain."

CHAPTER 13

Prentice knew he was staring at Archduchess Amelia in a manner that even the most lenient of nobles would consider impertinent. She had more than once told him to treat her as a friend in private, to leave many of the niceties of rank aside between them, but this was not quite private enough for that. Even if it were, he knew his attitude was not acceptable, but he was struggling to restrain himself even this much. He felt betrayed.

Do you really think I would put my own name forward, Your Grace? he thought, wishing he could ask her the question directly. *After all these years, do you imagine I would embarrass you with such crass ambition?*

If knighthoods were to be awarded to the commoners who had rendered service, Prentice had no doubt his name would be on the list of possibles. The archduchess was a faithful liege and loyal friend, and he had as much to credit his service as any other. It was no boast to think so, and he knew he did not have to put his own name forward. In fact, it occurred to him that he was actually more vehement in his hope for several others than himself. If Amelia were to knight Turley, then perhaps Markas the standard bearer or Sergeant Franken who was training recruits up at Fallenhill could receive such an honor. If they were chosen, Prentice might even be content to go without himself, almost. He managed to pull his eyes away from the archduchess for a moment to look at his wife, who was watching him with an expression he did not recognize. For her sake, for the sake of their children unborn, he would have to seek a knighthood. Providing for their future was his other duty, as strong as his loyalty to his liege.

Gennet as well, in a year or two, he thought, adding his current sergeant to the list of those he would recommend if she ever asked him again. Given how he had reacted this time, which he was sure she would have noticed, he would not be surprised if her grace never raised the question a second time.

"I am pleased to hear you say this, Captain," Amelia told him, and she smiled.

Prentice felt some of his ire recede as the archduchess turned to her husband.

"Marquis Consort Farringdon of the Western Reach," she said, addressing him formally, "will you accept the rank of Knight Captain of the Reach, leader of the knights martial of my house?"

"With honor," Farringdon replied and bowed his head.

"I...," the archduchess began and then paused. When she spoke next, there was a sense of amusement to her words. "I was about to apologize that our circumstances do not allow us to give your accession the pomp it is due, but the truth is that it is now practically the tradition that knight captains of the Reach are appointed swiftly and without ceremony."

Prentice thought about her words and realized it was true. Liam, Gullden, and even Sebastian had all had been appointed brevet without the typical military honors. The demands of war had given the archduchess no other choice.

"The promotion is the honor, Your Grace," Farringdon said politely. "What ceremony is needed can be taken as if done."

He bowed again, and when he lifted his head, he smiled. While Prentice could not see Amelia's face as she was turned away, it was obvious that the newlywed husband and wife were exchanging some sort of unspoken notions. When she nodded and looked back to the room, Prentice felt relief. He did not resent the need for these moments between them, but he was eager to return to hunting down the Inquisition's force that was currently riding away into the southwest. For now, he had little fear of the Church militants going into hiding. The fey hunters were much too skilled for that. But given their revealed relationship with the Redlanders, they were his best chance to ultimately track the Serpent Witch. He did not want to leave this task waiting.

Yet before that, there was something else teasing at his mind like an itch, and it was connected to what the mantis cultist had said last night just before the fey killed him. It was something he needed to discuss with the archduchess. He stared down at the Reach's "hand of cards" on the table and used it to track his immediate duties and guide his planning while the liege and her husband concluded their interactions. The marquis's next words caused him to snap his head up in shock.

"Your Grace, I thank you for this honor, but I feel constrained to raise an important concern," Farringdon said. "You are *Archduchess* of the Reach now. Prentice Ash cannot remain captain of your militia."

Prentice was astonished. He stared at the marquis as the nobleman began to unwrap the cloth bundle in his hands. There was no anger in him, just disbelief.

"Of course, you are right," the archduchess agreed, and Prentice could only shake his head. Sebastian had tried to have him removed from the militia command out of loyalty to the old order, the old nobility. Prentice had never feared that happening, and even if Amelia had done as Sebastian demanded, he would not have objected. He understood the political pressures that weighed upon her. Even so... this? This he had not foreseen, could not have foreseen. He counted Farringdon as a friend. He had never imagined that the former prince would show such treachery. Was it envy? Fear of a challenger to his new authority? If the young man worried about Prentice's relationship with his new wife, then perhaps that made a kind of sense, but everyone in this room knew there was nothing of romance between himself and his liege. It was a crass rumor that no loyal Reacherman would tolerate being spread.

"Step forward, Prentice Ash," the archduchess told him, and unthinkingly he looked to his wife. She was still watching him with that strange expression, her hand on her belly. His heart constricted in his chest, but he forced his legs to move, and he walked to stand in front of his liege, ready for her to strip away his rank. He had not realized until just this moment how much he loved the role. He knew it was what he was made for, grim though its duties so often were. He set himself at attention and bowed three paces in front of the archduchess. As he lifted his head, Farringdon laid the cloth from the bundle on the floor in the space between them, but Prentice hardly saw him. His eyes were fixed on Amelia's, and there was an uncertainty in them. He was reminded of a night many years ago on a riverman's barge, poling up the Dwelt away from the riverbend village, when she had asked him to forgive her for not releasing him from convict servitude. He had been cold to her then, and he wanted to be cold again. She could do almost anything she wanted to him—he was her bondsman—but he would not let her ask him to comfort her if her conscience could not bear her actions.

"An archduchess *is* sovereign as you said Prentice, a princess in her own realm," she told him, though he hardly heard the words. Why would he want to? "Princes are not served by knight captains but by knight commanders, as Lord Ironworth was knight commander to Prince Mercad. However, a knight commander cannot be a mere knight. It is not fitting. Kneel Captain."

Prentice did as he was bid, confused, his mind recognizing that something unexpected was happening. There was no ritual form for dismissing someone as lowly as a militia leader. Kneeling on the cloth, he watched as Farringdon presented his wife with a scabbarded sword held in two hands; apparently it had been wrapped in the bundle with the cloth. He offered it to her, hilt first, and she drew it forth from the sheath to hold it up in front of them. Prentice recognized it immediately by its long curve. It was his champion blade, the one he had won from Baron Ironworth and which his wife had hidden from him—more than hidden, it seemed, and it made him wonder how long this ritual had been planned. He watched as Archduchess Amelia lowered the sword and turned it blade-down in front of her, its point resting on the cloth as well.

"Master Yentow Sent has brought this back to us today, so it seems this is the propitious moment," she said.

Studying the weapon more closely, Prentice could tell that it must indeed have received Yentow Sent's attentions in its time away from him. The blade's profile had changed, its point now being re-ground, and long fullers had been grooved in its sides. It would surely be lighter now. Its grip, too, had been changed. The former leather-wrapped wood had been replaced by what at first looked like a carved piece of bone, with silver cord wrapped around it in a spiral. It was the spiral that revealed its true nature, though, as Prentice realized with a shock that it was the horn of the unicorn slain last year and polished now to an ivory gleam. The master smith had also fitted a new silver pommel, graven like a lion's head. The lion had a small silver ring in its mouth and from that ring hung a tassel of snow-white hair—a brilliant tuft of unicorn mane. It could be nothing else. Prentice shuddered at the sight of the magnificent weapon. He knew he had blood upon his hands, and as the scripture said, God delighted not in the death of any man, but somehow the death of the unicorn, whom he had killed as a mercy, weighed especially upon his soul. It was as if he had killed beauty or purity itself, as if a man could slay a sunrise. Yet, as sad as the reminder of the glorious beast dead at his hands was, Prentice still marveled. He had not even imagined the horn and mane might be worked like this.

The archduchess lifted his sword over his head, and for the first time Prentice fully understood what was about to happen. She brought the flat of the blade down on one shoulder and then on the other, and as she did so, she made a pronouncement Prentice never imagined he would ever hear.

"Prentice, called Ash. Ashen Man. Hero of the Brook."

He thought he saw her lip twitch in the direction of a smile at that title. He knew Amelia would delight in finally, officially, taking the honor of the Brook back from Liam's memory.

"Vanquisher of the honorable Baron Ironworth. Captain and founder of the White Lions. First to be seen by the fey and permitted to see them in return. My loyal friend. I have my life by your hand. My lands have their freedom by your toil, your wisdom and your blood shed on our behalf. All here, all the Reach, know your honor, your devotion and your worthiness. For all this, I now create you Lord Prentice Ash, Baron of Fallenhill and the Northern Azures, and I appoint you Knight Commander of the Western Reach, my sovereign advisor in all military matters and first commander in the field. May your word be law over all the men-at-arms in the Western Reach."

Prentice looked up at his liege, and though she was smiling, he thought he saw some uncertainty still. She gestured for him to take the sword, and when he placed his hand upon the pommel, she put hers upon his.

"There are pledges that a noble gives to accede, oaths to his liege," Amelia said. "But I have had your pledge since the night before the Brook, and it is an oath of steel that has never failed me. Please, accept this honor."

Again, the uncertainty. What could she fear in this moment? That he would refuse? Behind him he heard a chair scrape on the flagstones and a moment later Lady Dalflitch was standing beside him, holding a document from the table that he had not seen before.

"Here is the writ of your ennoblement, Prentice," she said. "It awaits only your seal and signature."

"I do not have a seal," he said, feeling foolish. Even as he said it, Dalflitch, Farringdon, and Amelia all shook their heads.

"Not so," said the lady-in-waiting, and she held out a gold ring with a carved, semi-precious stone boss—a blue-green opal by the look. "This is your signet and your heraldry."

She nodded at the floor beneath him, and he looked down to see that the cloth was in fact a standard banner, like the White Lions, but instead of a lion, the rampant beast was a gryphon, its wings flaring behind it. Unlike the typical heraldic animals of its kind, instead of eagle's talons for its forelegs, all four of its lower limbs were like a lion's.

"I suggested a unicorn," the archduchess said to him as he stared at the embroidery, "but Righteous insisted it was not a victory you wished to commemorate that way."

Prentice nodded and looked back over his shoulder to smile at his wife. She was right. No one knew him as she did.

And now I have an inheritance for our children, Wild Rose, he thought. *A name, a title and an inheritance.*

"Will you accept, Prentice? Does this please you?"

The archduchess seemed almost to be pleading with him. He gave her a smile as well, different from the one for his wife, and stood, taking up his sword. As he expected, it was significantly lighter than it had been. It should be much less trouble for him to wield now.

"I accept with honor, Your Grace," he told her. "As you say, I have been your sworn man too long to turn away at this point."

With that, Dalflitch led him back to the table and laid the writ down. Turley had already brought a candle closer and there was sealing wax ready. Prentice looked around himself at everyone's faces, all smiling happily. They had all known this was coming, he realized now, probably since Righteous had snagged his sword and sent it away to Fallenhill to be refitted for him. Perhaps longer.

"Spindle did the banner," Righteous said to him, reaching out and taking his hand, "before she went off with Welburne. She insisted."

That was before the winter solstice, so this had been a long time coming indeed.

He was given a quill and he dipped it into a silver inkpot, then signed the bottom of his writ. Then the archduchess stepped up beside him and signed her own name. Hot wax was dripped upon the page and Prentice pressed his new seal into it, then she did the same, using the very signet ring he had once borne in her name.

"Done," she said to him, and he realized just how true that simple statement was. Since the day he had been born, it had been the quest laid upon his life to rise as a man-at-arms in order to attain a hereditary title, all for the sake of his family's ambitions. The path had been almost infinitely harsher than they had imagined, and in its twists and turns, they had cursed him and disowned him, but now that he was here, their ambition for him fulfilled, they would own no part of it. All the family he wished to share his glory with was with him in this room, save perhaps for Solomon, his drummer and ward.

"It's a pity," Turley said quietly, stepping up next to him and offering him a silver cup of what looked like brandy. "When you suggested me for a knight, I thought there might be a chance that I'd get to have you bowin' down to me first afore I had to give you the noble treatment. Might've been nice."

Prentice smirked at his friend and took the cup.

"You ever try to give me 'the noble treatment,' and I will hand you another thumping."

"Another?" Turley repeated in mock offence. "I don't readily recall you ever giving me a thumping."

"That is because it was such a good one, I knocked the memory from your head," Prentice told him. Turley blinked as if he was struggling to remember something.

"I suppose it's possible," he said at last. Then he offered Prentice his hand with a smile. "Baron Ash."

"Master Turley... for now?" Prentice smiled as well and then looked to the archduchess.

She nodded, returning his expression.

They toasted Prentice then, and Righteous, as Lord and Lady Ash of Fallenhill. It was a sweet moment, a welcome pause amidst the bleak duties that still confronted them.

CHAPTER 14

"Did you truly think I might refuse, Your Grace?" Prentice asked. The candles in the solar had burned halfway and everyone still present was sat around the table, drinking and finishing their plans. The newly raised Baroness Righteous had retired to her bed in a bower attached to the ducal chambers, complaining of back pain, and Turley had gone to the kitchens to see that the staff were finishing the day and leaving everything ready for the morning.

"Bellam tells me that someone's mucking about with the stores," the chief steward said at the door as he left. "If they're pilfering for themselves or sellin' to someone in the market, I'll have their guts for garters."

"Pilfering is theft, and that is a matter of law, husband," Dalflitch had told him. "If someone is stealing from the archduchess, then the bailiffs should be informed, and they will be put in irons for trial."

"Ah, I *says* pilfering, but only as a figure...you know...of speech like," Turley replied. "It ain't like anyone's actually stealing. You'll see."

Then he was gone.

"That was odd," said Farringdon innocently.

"He will not favor courts as a punishment," Prentice explained. "It is a rare ex-convict that willingly trusts another man to the bailiffs, honest or dishonest. He will root out the thieves, if there are thieves, and give them a thrashing they will not forget, but you will not hear of it."

"Does that include you?" Dalflitch asked, but Prentice chose not to answer her question. More brandy was poured and so they reached the moment when Prentice felt he could ask Amelia his question.

"Are you surprised that I might expect you to refuse, Baron?" Amelia asked him in return. "We have only just discussed an ex-convict's distaste for the authorities of the land. If any in all the Reach have cause to hate the nobility from highest to lowest, it is surely you, and that is true even against the likes of myself, Lady Dalflitch here, and your own goodwife. I feared you would consider it a hypocrisy. How many times in my service alone have you suffered more to be rewarded with less?"

Prentice accepted her explanation with a nod and took another sip.

"And this goodwife of mine, she knew about all this and kept it a secret?" he asked.

"Quite so, My Lord," said Farringdon, smiling broadly. The marquis was taking every opportunity to use Prentice's new term of respect, clearly enjoying his friend's increased status.

"Goodwife, perhaps; bloody vixen, without doubt," Prentice muttered, and the other three chuckled. He looked at the documents on the table, with three candlesticks, the brandy bottle, and their cups placed in the few bare spots of wood between parchments.

"When we march in the morning, I will take only four or five cohorts and few, if any, wagons. Just enough to supply us. We will be making swift time."

"Must you go first thing?" the archduchess asked. "I can give you leave to remain here with your wife until she delivers, Prentice."

He smiled but shook his head.

"I would like nothing more, Your Grace, but the longer we let them ride the greater the chance they escape us. We cannot afford to let that happen."

"The fey are trackers without peer," said Farringdon.

"Yes, but you know what they did last night. I wanted any cultists as prisoners, and they knew that, but it made not the least difference to them. If I am not with them when they catch the Inquisition knights, or at least nearby, I do not believe we will get a chance to capture one of them either."

He gave the marquis and the archduchess an optimistic smile.

"If the Lord favors us, then we will run them down swiftly and be back before my child is born."

"Let us drink to that," said the archduchess, and she raised her cup. They all joined her in the toast. "And when you return, we can speak about a plan to liberate Aubrey from any Vec pretenders and bring it into the fold."

Prentice saw Farringdon nod in thanks to his wife, but the new nobleman did not agree.

"It would be a mistake to wait, Your Grace," he said.

"How's that?" It was clear that his comment surprised her.

"The militia is costing the Reach dearly, is it not?" he began and looked to Lady Dalflitch.

"Dearly," she agreed emphatically.

"So, you gain nothing, Your Grace, to have them stand around, waiting the return of my little company."

"You want me to send them off without a leader?" Amelia's brows were furrowed.

"Knight Captain Farringdon will command them."

Farringdon now sat up and put his drink down in the manner of a drunk who suddenly decides he must have had too much already.

"Prentice, the plan is for me to command the lancers in the manner that other knight captains have commanded the knights ahorse previously. You truly are knight commander; there is no plan to usurp you."

The knight commander shook his head again.

"Sebastian was an intractable fool, Your Grace," he explained, "but he was not wholly mistaken when he claimed that divided command is not the correct way for an army to be led."

"But you just said you wanted to divide the Lions," Dalflitch objected. "Some with you, some with the marquis."

"This is not the same," Prentice answered, and the lady seneschal cocked her head slightly, signaling that she was ready to hear his explanation of the difference. Prentice could see that the other two at the table were similarly attentive. He was mostly accustomed to such respect from the archduchess herself, but he felt a strange flush of pride, nonetheless. Finally, after years of having to fight against tradition and hidebound institutions to justify his place in his liege's inner circle, he now had a position that was unquestioned.

Do not let it go to your head, he warned himself. *A man who is not questioned is a man who must see all his own mistakes for himself.*

He leaned forward in his seat and took hold of two of the small document stacks and laid them side by side.

"Until now we have had foot and horse, each unto themselves, because knights would not deign to march and rogues do not ride," he placed one hand on each symbolically, indicating that the stack on the right were to be the horses, the left hand the footmen. "Each has had their own leaders, and from between the two, you, Your Grace, picked an overall commander."

He symbolically drew a finger from the top of each stack, tracing a line along the table to a point in between the two. Then just before the two fingers touched, he joined his hands together as of two men shaking in agreement, a partnership.

"When it was Sir Gant and myself, it worked well because we respected each other and always thought to put strategic needs first. But with other knights captain?"

He pulled his hands apart and formed fists. Then he butted the knuckles together and his symbolism was obvious.

"You clashed," said Amelia, nodding.

"Said mildly, Your Grace," Prentice agreed. "Even when they respected my judgement, which I believe Viscount Gullden did, their loyalty to the pride of the old order made it almost impossible for them to cooperate regardless."

"And when you were unproven with men like Sebastian, that pride and loyalty hardened so much that you were never given a chance to prove yourself," said Farringdon, and Prentice nodded.

"You are a baron now, Prentice," Amelia told him. "That objection is put paid to."

"Assuming he is accepted," Dalflitch said quickly over a sip of brandy. "If some resented a former convict raised to the rank of militia captain, they will likely be incensed to see him as their peer."

She finished her sip, and then her eyes widened in horror as she recognized the bluntness of her own words.

"Oh, forgive me, Prenti...I mean, My Lord," she said, nodding her head in a seated bow. "I spoke honestly but meant no offence."

Prentice smiled at her warmly. He had great respect for Dalflitch. Her intellect was peerless to his way of thinking, especially in political matters, and he had affection for her built almost exclusively on the fact that she was his best friend's beloved wife. For either reason alone, he would happily extend her a great latitude, especially when it came to social graces, which he wasn't sure he even cared about.

"We will all be having such lapses in coming days, My Lady, of that I am sure," he said calmly. "When they happen, comfort yourself with the knowledge that you enjoy your husband's favor with me always, and he has done worse many times."

Dalflitch nodded demurely, and her smile was so alluring that Prentice was glad he had a wife to love already. He would have hated to have to fight off jealousy over this woman's beauty and her love for rough-and-ready Turley.

"Well, if this is the problem and raising you to knight commander is not the whole solution, what is?" asked Amelia.

Prentice took hold of the side-by-side parchments and moved them so that they formed a column, one following the other. Then he took two more and formed a second column beside it. Then he started at the top, pointing again at the right-hand column and tracing down the table as he spoke.

"Two separate banners—the knight commander, his footmen, his horsemen." He moved his finger to the top of the left column and started downward a second time. "The knight captain, his footmen, his horsemen."

"Two separate armies?" the archduchess asked.

"In most respects, yes."

"But dividing forces leads to weakness," she objected. "All the sources agree on this."

"In battles, Your Grace, that is true," Prentice said. "But in a broader war such as we face, we have only needed your full force upon the field once or twice. The rest of the time we skirmish, as we did against the fey while we rescued the trapped riverboats last summer. With two full banner armies you could post one to watch the west across the river, the other in the south and mountains."

As Prentice was talking, Farringdon took up two of the empty cups and put one at the end of each column.

"What are they?" asked Amelia.

"My cannon and the baron's war wagons," the marquis explained, and he looked to Prentice, who gave him an accepting shrug. Frankly, Prentice was less concerned that the war engines be equally shared. Whichever banner was set to watch the west would not need cannon, and even wagons would slow them too much for a frontier guard force. That banner would have to be able to move swiftly. When he marched west in the morning,

Prentice intended to take no more than one or two wagons with him, and neither of them would be the slow, heavy, battle type.

"Do we not already have two banners? One horse, one foot," asked Dalflitch.

Prentice suppressed a sigh as he thought of the times he had been abandoned by proud knights on the battlefield when his plans for coordinated actions had been thwarted by men-at-arms ahorse resenting his lowly birth. Simply making him a baron was a poor solution, as she had observed. If every man fighting together, horse or foot, acknowledged one leader and had loyalty to his fellows in the other half of the banner, that division would become unthinkable. Devoted men would not have to die for the pride of fools, at least not so much.

"We have two types of fighters for her grace, separated by too many facets," Prentice told Dalflitch. "Birth, tradition, tactics, weapons. All the advantages of having both types are neutered by keeping them separate. Combining them and teaching each one, from the lowliest recruit to the knights commanding, to see the combination as natural will hone those advantages to an edge that will cut through armies, I swear. Then the only advantage we will lack will be numbers, and for that requirement, we combine the armies on the field as we would with any allies. The two banners come together to fight side-by-side when needed, knight captain yielding overall tactical leadership to the knight commander for the battle."

"It is very similar to the practice of the emperors of Masnia," Farringdon observed, and Prentice gave him a much more emphatic nod this time. This idea was based on what Prentice knew of the Masnian system, which he had learned of when he was at Ashfield. The empire had stood unchallenged by foreign enemies for centuries in the far south, protected by its banner armies.

"No wonder you wish for many more recruits, Prentice," the archduchess said, shaking her head. Her expression was not negative but showed awe at the enormity of the task. "You say you wish to divide into two banners now but not evenly. Why not?"

"We do not know how large a force the Inquisition has lurking among us, but it cannot be too large or else it would already have been noticed. Five hundred should be enough to force them to surrender when we catch them or else win a reasonably bloodless victory. Aubrey and the southern frontier have the possibility of being a true campaign, Your Grace. Warfare against a Vec prince. Better you have the main of the forces with you there, including the wagons we have and Marquis Farringdon's new cannon. The battles there are more like to be set pieces, for which these are the ideal weapons. Once I bring our prisoners back, I can take my five cohorts up to Fallenhill, along with whatever recruits we have, and begin building the second banner around that core of experience."

"So soon? How will you make your numbers?" asked the archduchess. Her eyes were ranging over the table. Her "hand of cards" was now a scattered mess, but the problems were not gone. As she watched, Lady Dalflitch took up her report of the treasury.

"Your Grace, I know you owe almost every merchant from here to the Azures and up and down the Dwelt," she said, holding the folio in one hand like a preacher's tract. "But if today's defenestration proves anything, it's that your people are loyal to you and that loyalty has not yet found its limit. It might be an ugly thing to do, but a not untypical thing, for you to exploit some of that fealty."

"Exploit, My Lady?" It was clear that the archduchess did not like the implications of that word.

"Let them carry your debts for a season or two, even extend them," Dalflitch said. "I promise they will let you ask. They may even compete to extend you more credit to show their fealty. It will not be the easy coin that the banker's loans would have been, but they can give you the other resources needed to raise a second company of Lions—metal, cloth, leather, wood, and food. We could even let them offer goods against the future cost of the town charters. Give us what we need now and pay less for the warrant when it's offered."

Archduchess Amelia nodded as she listened, her expression serious and thoughtful. As much as she would hate to misuse people's loyalty, Prentice imagined she would have fewer qualms about playing upon their greed.

"Do you really think this sense of devotion is so deep? We live in a time when even ancient fealties have become fickle."

"I think, Your Grace, that if we play this part of your hand cautiously, we can possibly set the Conclave into a frenzy, competing with each other to show who has the greater commitment to the Reach. They will gee each other on, boasting just for the prestige. We could even auction the charters, let them drive the price up for us..."

"I think that is enough for now, My Lady," Amelia interrupted. "This is starting to sound too much like a forfeits council for my taste."

The lady seneschal bowed her head and fell silent. Prentice waited a moment to allow his liege her thoughts. After a while, he asked the archduchess the question that had been troubling him since the previous night.

"Your Grace, do you remember what Duggan said to you?" he asked, and he could see her surprise. It seemed as if the room were suddenly darker, but Prentice realized that the candles had been burning down and that his concentration on other matters had kept him from noticing before now.

"When...?" the archduchess began but stopped. Prentice could see that she knew what he meant. "His final words?"

Prentice nodded.

"I know he spat curses upon you as he died, Your Grace. But just before that, when he was on his knees, I have been told he made some kind of prognostication—a 'hanged man's prophecy,' as it were."

"I don't...," Amelia paused and looked away into the corners of the room, doubtless recalling that ugly night. Prentice knew that while she never flinched, the archduchess had taken no pleasure from Duggan's execution on the Great Hall flagstones. He also knew that that night was the first time she had ever received a vision—at least that was what she had told him.

"I remember he said there was more than we knew about, more Redlanders," she said softly. "Daven Marcus mocked him for that, but given all we have learned about the Redlanders and the fey, Duggan was closer to truth than any of us guessed that night."

"I wonder if he was even more prescient than that," Prentice said thoughtfully.

The air in the room was still, and Farringdon's chair creaked loudly as he leaned over to take his wife's hand, like a man worried his unmoored boat was about to float away on an ebbing tide.

"You wonder about what the Widow told him," Amelia said, appearing to follow Prentice's train of thought. "What he heard from the prophetess?"

"Prophetess? Is this the Widow of the Wood?" Dalflitch asked, but no one bothered to answer the question.

"When Gant and I captured Folper trying to flee, he told us that Duggan had been nearly mad with fears of what he had seen in the little woman's visions," Prentice explained. "They were vivid to him, so Folper claimed, as real as the world under a noon sun. And central to those visions was an army as vast as a horde of locusts, covering the whole land."

"Locusts?" Farrindon breathed. Knowing looks were shared around the table, and Prentice could see they were making the connection that had troubled him most of the night.

"The cultist who transformed," Amelia said. "You say that he spoke as if from prophecy. Did he say there was a multitude coming, a multitude of mantises?"

Prentice nodded solemnly.

"He did, Your Grace. Two prophecies from different sources. If you saw them in a vision, could you pick a mantis from a locust?"

"God save us," Amelia breathed. "Duggan saw these Redlanders?"

"Or their spiritual types."

Prentice knew from his own experience that often in visions animals stood for kinds of people or even whole clans or nations. If Duggan had been given a prophecy of locusts, it could well have been the mantises of the Redlander invaders. Worse than that...

"We do not know how many of their boats can travel through the sky at once, Your Grace. Imagine a fleet, such as the one you saw on the salt sea in the west, suddenly appearing on the lake outside the castle. There are no defenses on the waterside. They would sweep over us before we even knew we were invaded."

A somber mood fell upon the table as each one present contemplated the grim possibility. Lady Dalflitch audibly sucked in a calming breath and released it slowly. As with the archduchess, she had actually been present to see the Redlander fleet. She did not have to *imagine* the horror. She had already lived it.

The room's stillness took on an unnerving edge. It seemed so long ago that Duggan had rebelled, though in truth it was barely a few years. So much had happened in the intervening time. To think now that he might have something to tell them this long after his death was also unpleasant.

"The stag and the serpent have failed," Prentice said.

"And those were the cultist's exact words?" Farringdon whispered.

"The Horned Man?" Amelia mused, making the obvious connection between the crazed convert's pronouncement and recent history.

"And the Serpent Witch," Prentice agreed, nodding slowly. He laid his hand on the tabletop in front of him and thoughtfully rapped his fingers a moment, letting them find a marching rhythm of their own accord.

"What does it mean?" Farringdon asked.

"Five heads, five kings, five kinds of beasts," Prentice said. This was the core of his understanding of the Redlanders, what he had learned in his visions of the giant, multi-headed serpent from scholar Solft's researches and from fighting the Redlanders time and again. "They have factions as the Grand Kingdom does, noble houses or religious orders, after a kind."

"Sacrilegious orders, more like," Dalflitch added, and while it was a poor jest, no one commented. They had all experienced the cruelty of Redlander religion one way or another. She was entitled to any lame witticism she liked.

"The Broken Kings, that was what Bluebird called them," Amelia added.

Prentice nodded. So had Inxyphos. It was another fragment of information to thread into what they knew, another card in their opponent's hand. Yet still, he felt there was too much happening about which he knew nothing, and too many of the archduchess's enemies knew more than he did. The Inquisition clearly knew vastly much more and had probably been playing at this game much longer than anyone suspected, but like the Usurper in Denay, they were playing the game for their own victory. They had allied themselves with Daven Marcus, but somehow that felt like a marriage of convenience to Prentice. As Farringdon knew the Redlanders from bitter experience, so Prentice knew the Inquisition. They were too patient, too self-controlled to bind themselves fully to the brash fool now calling himself king.

"So where does this leave us, Knight Commander?" the archduchess asked.

"It leaves us with a new set of questions, Your Grace, the most significant of which is this: have we seen the force that drove Duggan mad, or is it yet to come? As violent as the storm has been up 'til now, are there stronger winds yet in our future?"

"We need answers to those questions," she said.

"And until we have them, we need to build the largest force we can to protect your lands and your people, Your Grace," Prentice told her, and he was pleased to see all three people at the table nod in agreement.

"You must go, Knight Commander," Amelia told him, the resolve in her voice unmistakable. "Capture us as many of these Inquisition men-at-arms as you can. They may be invincible to interrogation, knowing the devotion to secrecy that the Inquisition has shown us. They are not called the 'quiet arm' of the Church for nothing. Nevertheless, we must try."

She turned to Lady Dalflitch.

"In the meantime, we will progress with the new town warrants and let word slip that they will soon be available. Let those with wealth know there is a reason to turn it to our needs. I will have to suffer the discomfort of extending my debts against their loyalty, however manipulative it may feel. Also, have criers sent, especially among the newcome folk, that land is promised to all who do their seven years honest service in the Lions. By the time Baron Ash returns from the west, we must have as many recruits available to send to Fallenhill as we can."

Everyone nodded, and the archduchess sighed like a weary mother with fractious children who refuse to settle. She turned her head to the dark window that looked out over the lake, and Prentice saw her shiver momentarily. He suspected she was imagining the Redlander fleet suddenly appearing at this moment and the slaughter that would inevitably result.

"Franken is already training some recruits in Fallenhill," Prentice said. "Do not wait for me to return. Send as many as wish to join straight north as soon as possible to join the training. Better we not delay."

He paused as another idea occurred to him.

"I will send Righteous up that way as well, if you will permit, Your Grace."

"You wish to keep her safe?"

"No," Prentice said and then corrected himself. "Yes, I do, but that is not my reason. I want her in Fallenhill to assist Franken. She will deliver soon, but even if it takes her weeks to recover from the birth, she is still the best trainer with sword and shield that I have free. Just having her eye to watch for him will help."

The archduchess nodded and put her hands on the arms of her chair.

"Well, gentles," she said, "it seems we have many fresh duties and dangers awaiting us with the dawn. Let us get what sleep we can and be ready. The Western Reach is depending upon us."

She stood, and they rose with her. Prentice was looking forward to a few hours resting beside Righteous, but at the solar door, Dalflitch touched his elbow.

"Might I speak a moment more with you, My Lord?" she said politely. "I have a quiet matter I think you should hear before you march in the morning."

CHAPTER 15

L eading the way through the late-night peace of the kitchens, Dalflitch brought Prentice to a locked door in a disregarded corner, half hidden behind a stack of oil barrels and empty potato baskets.

"Do you know where this leads, Baron?" she asked as she put her hand on the latch.

Prentice shook his head, although he did remember waking up one morning with a savage headache from sleeping on flour sacks not ten paces from where they were.

"Until last year, there was a vegetable garden out this way. Why they ever thought they needed to lock a door to the carrots and spinach is beyond me," Dalflitch explained. "Come the drought, it all died away. Now it's just dirt."

Reaching into the winged sleeve of her dress, she drew forth a simple iron key, holding it up in the sparse light.

"Apart from this one," she said, "every other key to this door is locked away in the duchy's treasury. I am the only one who can turn this lock."

"What need do you have for a vegetable patch?" Prentice asked, but then he realized what must be hidden behind the door. There was one particular secret the lady seneschal absolutely needed to keep locked away.

"You see, don't you?" Dalflitch said, watching his face. She turned the lock and opened the door. Taking up a candle in a clay holder, she led the way into the night. The old vegetable garden was now just a flat piece of earth, a tiny dirt courtyard in the midst of high castle walls. The Rampart glowed in the sky above, and the cool of the spring evening had a mildness that foreshadowed the coming heat of summer. Prentice looked up a moment but managed to resist conjuring the memory of the reflective night sky. With their one candle, it was not possible to see into the lurking corners of the yard, even as small as it was, but Prentice knew there would be no other way in or out of this space that did not involve scaling a sheer stone surface.

"Over here."

Picking her way gently over the barely seen, uneven ground, the former countess led her new superior to another door. Unlike the one from the kitchen, this one led nowhere except to a single cell-like room built into the base of a curtain wall's tower. It had formerly been used to hold the gardener's tools. Now that there was no garden, there was no need for the tools, and Lady Dalflitch had found it perfect for an entirely new use. As the pair approached, a sparse yellow warmth glowed in the gap under the door. Despite the late hour, no one would be sleeping on the other side. Years of habit would not be broken, even at this final stage.

Dalflitch knocked on the door.

"Evening, mother," she called. "I've brought you a visitor."

She pushed the door and the light of a small iron brazier spilled out, revealing the Ragmother, ancient smuggler crone, seated on a simple cot mattress and knitting something with her gnarled, arthritic fingers.

"D'you bring me some more gin?" she said, smacking her gums around a set of wooden teeth. "I'm just 'bout out."

"Next time, mother," Dalflitch said. Her words were respectful, but her tone was cold. She turned to Prentice, making a formal introduction as if this were any other appointment between equals. "This is Knight Commander Prentice Ash, now Baron Ash of Fallenhill."

"I remember," the Ragmother said, all pretense of a doddering old woman falling away to reveal a heart as cold as a venomous snake's. "You the one that done for my Fulford, my golden boy."

"My wife did, actually," Prentice corrected, just as coldly. The Ragmother sniffed at the distinction.

"Baron and baroness now, is it?" the Ragmother asked. "Is that the reward the Lioness give you both for doing in my grandson and heir?"

In spite of the woman's ancient frailty, she seemed so consumed with hate, like a predatory animal, that she could launch herself at them at any moment. Prentice clearly was not intimidated, but that was not from lack of respect for the woman. The frail and failing body contained a will that would frighten a devil. He fixed her with his gaze and set his jaw hard.

"Her grace would hardly lower herself to notice a rodent as small and insignificant as your grandson," he said. "What was between my wife and him was between them, and at his instigation. If he did not want to die, he should not have dangled my safety in front of her. A fool who dips his hand in blood and then offers it to the lion's mouth gets what he deserves."

Knight commander and old smuggler boss regarded one another for such a long moment that it was almost as if Dalflitch wasn't even there. Then the Ragmother shrugged, her expression softening from hatred to surly resignation.

"Well, that's as may be, but Fulford was family," she said, her eyes going back to her woolwork. "And family's family."

"Of course," Prentice agreed, his own expression softening somewhat. "Righteous did not kill him just for the pleasure. He was threatening *her* family."

The Ragmother huffed but said no more. Dalflitch breathed a quiet sigh of relief that nonetheless sounded loud in the tight confines.

"Many things are changing," she said. "I am so used to the ways of courtly life where deadly conflicts were never settled by ladies, demure and desirable as we were. That was what you seduced a young fool for. It was his task to live and die for your honor."

"Not in the Reach, dearie," the Ragmother said, not looking up from her needles.

"Quite so." Dalflitch turned to Prentice. "My Lord, it can scarcely have escaped your notice that the Lace Fangs are not at present able to protect the archduchess as they once did. Spindle is away and your wife is indisposed."

"She would not thank you for saying that," Prentice said with a wry half-smile, "once you explained what it meant."

"Oh, I know. Why do you think I'm having this conversation with you?" Dalflitch said, returning his smile, and Prentice glimpsed the bewitching presence with which she must have seduced many a "young fool." Poor Turley. The old womanizer had never stood a chance.

Prentice looked down on the Ragmother, then back to Dalflitch, cocking an eyebrow. What did all this have to do with the old smuggler?

"The Ragmother here," Dalflitch explained, and then she put a hand on the crone's shoulder, "and stop me, mother, if I get anything wrong. It's your story I am telling, after all. The Ragmother came up amongst the riverfolk, running her own crews in a world that produced the likes of that monster you speak about sometimes—Malden. Think about the kind of will it takes to fashion a river boss out of a young woman."

Prentice nodded. He could well imagine.

"We've been chatting over the winter, she and I, and she tells me she wasn't the only one who tried what she did over the years—just the only one who survived."

"They didn't have the eye to see the snags and banks under the water," the Ragmother agreed off-handedly, using a riverfolk metaphor. "They couldn't tell a bluff catch from true."

"And you did not think to help them?" Dalflitch asked rhetorically. The Ragmother answered the question anyway.

"Why should I teach them how to beat me? They weren't my crew."

Typical underworld logic, Prentice thought, still wondering where this was all leading.

"But things change, do they not?" Dalflitch continued. The Ragmother sniffed, as if disinterested in the question, but the lady-in-waiting to the Lioness of the Reach ploughed on with her line of reasoning. "The Ragmother tells me that there's a significant number of young women amongst the riverfolk, grown up in the ways of smuggling and tariff skipping, accustomed to a hard life and perhaps ready to seek something more for themselves, as you and I have done in our different ways."

In the quiet of the next moment, the Ragmother finally looked up.

"The river crews is family," the old woman explained. "A handful o' families any rate. Men on the boats mostly, hauling the cargo. Womenfolk on the riverside, raising the babes and watchin' the business. But when the times get tough..."

"As they were in the drought," Dalflitch interjected.

"In times like them," the deposed riverboss continued, "the menfolk on the river go farther afield to greener pastures or go to ground, and the women folk fend for 'emselves too often. It's alright for a season."

"But with more than a year of drought..." Dalflitch added once more, and this time Prentice finished her thought.

"The womenfolk are fed up with the whole practice?"

"That's right. Prentice, My Lord, *two* Lace Fangs have been invaluable to her grace. Imagine what twenty could do? Twenty women, trained to fight by Righteous, and Spindle when she returns. Taught from my experience to behave as courtly ladies. Wearing their masks so that even their true identities might be obscured. Raised on the river to know all the skips' tricks. Imagine?"

Prentice was almost shocked by what he was hearing. Not that it was unthinkable, but that it was so audacious. He turned the notions over in his mind.

"You're wondering what she gets out of it, Baron?" Dalflitch asked, studying his expression.

It was certainly one of the first questions he was considering.

"I thought you did not help others on the river," he said to the Ragmother.

"Me, dearie? Once maybe, but I got no more heirs. I still got a niece though. She's about sixteen and her husband shot through to the Vec last summer. Ain't been heard from since, near as I know. 'Course I been out o' the way since my grandson died." She paused and shrugged, her bony shoulders poking up against her shawl. "What I do know is she needs a better future than that lout or the one she's shacked up with now. No more heirs, but mayhaps an heiress?"

"And what do you think *she* will get out of it?" Prentice asked, fairly certain he knew what the answer would be, but wanting to hear it from the old woman's mouth.

"A place in the world that's shaded from the sun and warm against the wind," the Ragmother said, using another riverfolker adage. "I can give you twenty strong lasses, sharp-eyed and canny, and still fair enough to make into ladies, leastwise once you get one o' them pretty lace masks on 'em."

"And what is to stop one of these damsels of yours putting a dagger in my wife when her back is turned? An old woman with nothing else to live for might send a girl on a suicide mission to avenge her lost grandson."

"I figure she can put the steel back to 'em easily enough," the Ragmother answered with a chuckle. "It's what I would do. I mean, they didn't call her *Cutter* 'cause she was good at slicin' bread, did they?"

Prentice marveled at the breadth of the old woman's knowledge. Few, if any, people called Righteous by her old name anymore. He looked from the Ragmother to Dalflitch.

"It is a fair plan," he said flatly. "But I do not like the risk to my wife nor to the archduchess."

Dalflitch looked at the Ragmother. "Tell him the rest of it!" she commanded, and her tone was much sharper.

The old woman looked down at her knitting again, as if to ignore the command, but Dalflitch slapped her shoulder. The little woman looked up to glare hatefully at her, and then burst into a cackle. "Fickle fate," she laughed, spitting around her dentures, "if Fulford had married the like o' you instead o' takin' up with whores, *I'd* be the archduchess o' the Reach, with all the power by now!"

"As if I would've shared it with you, old woman," Dalflitch retorted, but that only brought another delighted, phlegmy chuckle. She looked at Prentice with a conspiratorial expression.

"You do well in that skip's nest, didya, bold captain man?" she asked. "I didn't steer you wrong none, did I?"

"We took the nest," Prentice answered, noncommittal.

"And how many d'you figure's like that up and down the flow, hhmmm? How many crews have how many nests stashed away in little streams and hidden docksides?" She paused and then leaned in, as if she was telling a tale to frighten children around a night's fire. "And how many of them crews do you ken have already fallen to the animal head's lying preachers? Blood Sects they call 'emselves, and hoo, don't they love blood!"

These were questions that Prentice expected to ask the Inquisition men once he captured them, however many he managed to take. Finding how far the Redlander's had burrowed into the riverfolk and tariff skip communities would be another matter, in many ways a worse challenge than hunting out the fey had been. His men could spend whole years searching up and down the Dwelt while the skips relocated themselves, one step ahead of the ever more exhausted Lions. If he were the Redlanders, it was what he would do—keep the Reach chasing rumors while he built his invasion somewhere else and then dropped the hammer upon them when they were at their limits.

"You're offering to sell out the whole river?" he asked the Ragmother, trying to sound skeptical but hoping that that was exactly what she *was* offering. A sense of where to hunt on the Dwelt for other mantis masks would be an invaluable relief.

"I'm a poor old widow in prison," the Ragmother said, her tone and expression seeming like anything but. "What have I to sell, dearies, 'specially to such high worthies as you are?"

"What then?"

"Young'uns like Fulford, they think it's all steel in the 'part-light and actin' brassy. I tried to teach him, but that's all water downriver now." She shook her head and a moment's sadness touched her eyes. "Still, I have some crew out there yet, loyal and not gulls. The animal-heads are eatin' up all the skip crews and slittin' the throats o' the resisters. By end o' summer, won't be a free skip on the river. They'll all be sold and blooded to the sects. Unless...the Lioness gives 'em safe haven."

"Your gang is too small to survive, so join a bigger gang?" Prentice summed up and the Ragmother smiled, nodding happily. Even with all she was offering, Prentice was tempted to tell her she could take her secrets to the grave. There was too great a risk. Dalflitch took him by the elbow and stepped back to whisper.

"Nothing happens in the shadows of the Reach that the smuggler crews aren't aware of," she told him. "If I grab them now, I can make spies of some, and send them back into the crews to watch for me. Noone'll get as close as that nest over the lake again."

The possibility of Dalflitch's plan was clear. She wanted to build a cadre of spies for the archduchess, a shadow complement to the White Lions. And from her comments about training Lace Fangs, she imagined her espionagers working not only amongst the lowborn of the docks and riversides. She was planning a network that would be able to infiltrate great houses, noble institutions, and even the royal courts if they could.

But could it be done?

Prentice chewed the inside of his cheek, recognizing that there would never be a way to make this happen that did not make them vulnerable to treachery. How vulnerable?

"We would send the girls to Fallenhill with Righteous to start with," he said. "Once she has birthed, she will want to start training them with knives."

"My girlies know more 'bout a gaff or billhook than you might think," the Ragmother offered.

"Not like my wife does, they do not," Prentice told her. "And fight training will be a good test to see if they have the mettle and to give Baroness Righteous a chance to sniff them out. If she suspects anything, if one of your 'girlies' even looks at her askance or mutters an unkind word, I swear to you, old crone, I will burn your precious riverside to the waterline. There will be nothing for the Redlander cults but blacker ashes than Fallenhill."

The Ragmother chuckled again.

"See," she said, clapping her hands and pointing them at Prentice, clasped together. "That's why we want to join *your* crew."

CHAPTER 16

Prentice carried a wooden tray into the chamber he shared
with Righteous, where his wife was still in bed. Shards
of early morning light were piercing through the gap between
the one window and its curtain. This room, usually for guests,
had been allowed to them by the archduchess, since Righteous would not be going into the kind of seclusion typical of
high-ranking mothers-to-be. Once the tray was on the side-
board, Prentice took up a bowl and spoon, and moved over to
the bed. His sleeping wife stirred as he looked down on her.
He wanted this one moment on their first morning as nobles,
a memory to share, but his mind was not really here with her.
Every moment that passed was another the prey were getting
further ahead of him, so that even the four fitful hours of rest
he had snatched in bed beside his darling wife had seemed an
almost wasteful extravagance. Nonetheless, he was forcing himself to take the time to break fast with her. Her eyes opened fully,
and she smiled. He sat beside her on the edge of the bed.

"Direct from the kitchens," Prentice told her as he handed
her the bowl of fresh curds and preserved fruits in their juices.

"You're not turning steward on me, are you husband?" she
frowned as she levered herself awkwardly up in the bed and took
the bowl. "Her grace plans to make Turley a knight, but she did
raise you over him, you know that, right? I didn't see you raised
this high just to have you actin' all lowly."

Prentice smiled at her sour-tempered joke.

"You will have all manner of servants and retainers to watch over you and do your bidding in coming days," he said, pushing his concerns to the back of his mind by sheer force of will. "While that's happening, I will be marching west in the sun-scorched grasses."

"You are a baron, now," Righteous persisted through spoonsful of her breakfast. "You're supposed to have servants of your own to set to servin'. We can order a few of her grace's stewards about until we get our own. She won't mind."

"Husbands, love your wives as Christ loved the Church, giving up his life for her," Prentice recited, still smiling.

"What's that then?"

"That, wild rose, is holy scripture, and I will obey it because I value the finest blessing God in heaven ever bestowed on any man."

Prentice laid his hand gently on his wife's belly, and for a moment he thought he might have felt a kick through the fine cloth. His smile broadened and Righteous stared up at him with eyes that seemed like lenses to some sapphire lantern. Then her smile soured as she clearly tasted bile. Their child's motions were upsetting her stomach.

"Oh, hells bells, stop it," she said. "It's fancy talkin' like that that got me in this bally way." She let out a small, painful-sounding belch and scowled at the taste it left in her mouth.

"When're you leavin'?" she asked before risking another spoonful.

"Within the hour," Prentice said, frowning.

"I figured. Well go get 'em, and come back in time for the birth."

"I will do my best, but before I go, I have something for *you* as well." He quickly outlined the plans for her to go to Fallenhill to take up a role in the training once more.

"You want me to make a whole gaggle of new Spindles?" she asked. "And to help Franken train the new Fangs? You do remember that I'm carryin' a baby, husband?"

"Would you trust the task to anyone else?"

Righteous's brows narrowed, and she frowned again.

"Not bloody likely," she declared.

"There you go," Prentice said and stood up. "I will send Solomon with you. You will need the help, I expect, both with the pregnancy and the training."

"How's he gonna help with my birthin'?"

"He can be a runner for you, as he has all winter. Besides, I know you want to start training him for the Lions in full. Fallenhill is where he should be." An orphan adopted by the White Lions to be a drummer, not even Solomon knew for sure how old he was, but in the recent winter, he had suddenly shot up like a climbing vine and had the first fuzz on his upper lip. He was starting to look less like a boy and more like the man he would become.

"He won't like it," Righteous said, and Prentice knew she was right.

"He is a Lion," he told her. "He will do as he is ordered. If he grouses, tell him I will be returning soon anyway."

"See, that's how you should be orderin' servants about," Righteous said.

Prentice shook his head and smiled. He leaned down to kiss her goodbye, being careful not to promise that he would return soon. He certainly would if it was possible, but she was so close to her time, he knew he could be swift as a hawk and still be late.

"I will miss you, Baroness," he told her at the door, mostly for the pleasure of using her new title.

"I'll probably be fond to think of you too, Baron," she answered back, giving him a wink.

Marching across the 'bridge and down Castle Road, Prentice was already working through his mental list of all the duties he had to fulfil before his contingent marched when he was intercepted by the richly dressed figure of Master Solft, renegade scholar and former head of the now burned-out Paper House. The archduchess had all but promised to fund the scattered scholars again, if they returned, but so far very few had. With Solft was Brother Whilte, leaning upon his prophet's rod and smiling in the sunshine.

"Good morrow on this fine spring morning, Captain," Solft said, then ducked his head in an apologetic bow, his pudding-bowl haircut flopping up and down over his eyes. "Forgive me, My Lord, Baron."

"You have heard then?" Prentice asked them.

"Master Turley sent word to camp last night," Whilte said. "The whole company is quite taken with the news."

"Of course, he did."

Prentice rolled his eyes at the thought of Turley going ahead and stealing his thunder. It was exactly the chief steward's kind of prank, but as he thought about it, he realized that his mischievous friend had done him a favor. It would save him the trouble of having to announce himself as acceded to the nobility. He had no idea how he might do such a thing without seeming condescending or self-important. He and all his men marched together, tasted the same dust in the air, and slept on the same ground. Prentice didn't think he could command them if they thought he counted himself superior.

"What service may a new baron be to you gentlemen this morning?" he asked as he started off again toward Within Walls.

"Master Solft has learned of our mission into the west and has asked to accompany us, and I have said that I would seek your grant for him," Whilte explained.

Prentice looked at the scholar, prepared to reflexively refuse the request. They would be moving swiftly, and it would not be an easy march for a man not accustomed to hard travel. Before he could speak, though, he realized that Master Solft was not quite as he remembered. Formerly, he had been a man of stodge, a soft body containing an astute mind, which though it lacked much strength or courage, was nonetheless fearless in pursuit of historical truths. The fact that he was still in Dweltford after Bluebird had tried to have him and all his fellows murdered spoke to his character being unchanged, but his person was a different matter. His face was more jowly than it had once been, and his clothes looked like a much poorer fit. Before, he had always had an element of wealth and indulgence about him, but now there was a marked shabbiness. Then Prentice realized the stout man had lost weight, and not a little. He was likely only three-fourths the heaviness he had been when he first met him years before.

"You have been trying to live amongst the fey, have you not Master?" Prentice asked, remembering now what he had last heard of the man.

"I have, My Lord," Solft confirmed. "I've been learning some of their native tongue and trying to get them to tell me some of their history. They say their sages have tales of the past remembered that date back even to the fall of the mountain. Perhaps they know something of these Broken Kings driven west."

Piecing together the lost history of multiple kings from the beginning of the Grand Kingdom was Solft's life mission. It had earned him an excommunication from Mother Church for heresy, but he would not relent. Prentice and Amelia both facilitated the man's research because there appeared to be some kind of connection between the Redlanders and this lost history. Since Bluebird's failed attempt at assassination, it was clear that the Inquisition was also somehow involved. It was little wonder that Solft wanted to travel with the Lions if they were hunting invaders and Inquisition both.

"Why, then, did you not ride with the fey when they left?" Prentice asked. Solft gave him a pained expression and looked away, ashamed.

"I cannot keep up with them," he said simply. His tone was almost mournful as his eyes fixed on the cobbles. "I've learned a good deal of their speech. I promise I will be useful to you, but I could practice from here to doomsday and never be their equal in the saddle."

"Few of us could," Prentice responded honestly.

"When the master learned that I would be going, he asked to accompany my wagon. He has a mule, it seems," Whilte said. "If you are amenable, one more such beast would make little enough difference to *my* speed."

Prentice had to accept the reasonableness of that assertion. Whilte's was one of the few wagons he was planning to have with them. The one-legged chaplain could never keep up any other way, and Prentice would not do without the devout man's power to neutralize enemy sorcery.

"Very well, Master Solft, you may come with us. We will not abandon you, but be warned, once we encounter the enemy there is no knowing what the precise state of affairs will be. You might find yourself in great danger."

Solft tugged his forelock, a gesture Prentice found hard not to be angered by.

"I've been in quite a few 'great dangers' in recent years, My Lord," he said. "Yet here I am, still. Until the Almighty decides it is my time, I will seek the truth wherever I must."

From the other side of his body, he hefted a leather satchel, full to overflowing with scrolls of parchment, books, and other papers. There were also three writing quills thrust into a pocket on one side.

"Here, and in my saddlebags, I have everything the Reach knows about the far west," he said. "I realize it's a pittance, but perhaps I will be able to find useful facts for you so that you might be forewarned."

Prentice wondered what the minor trove of documents might contain. Since his first day in the Reach, the River Dwelt had been a hard boundary in the mind of every Reacherman. Ignorance of the grasslands beyond the water was virtually a pillar of Reach culture.

"You see, Master, as I said, the knight commander is a reasonable man," Whilte told Solft with a broad smile, clapping the shorter man upon the shoulder. "And do not be too hard on yourself that you aren't equal to the fey in the saddle—you are hardly the only one."

Prentice did not need to check to know that Whilte would be looking at him—he could hear the taunt in the chaplain's voice.

"Which reminds me, Commander," he went on, "when Turley's man delivered the news of your accession, he also brought you a gift from the archduchess and Marquis Consort Farringdon."

Another gift? Prentice had no idea what that would be, and he turned to Whilte to see if the man was making fun still, another kind of teasing.

"What gift?"

"A mount," the chaplain explained cheerily, the look in his eyes making it clear that he knew exactly how Prentice would receive this news.

"I already have a mount," Prentice told him, "A previous gift from her grace."

"Oh, I believe she knows. Since a long overland journey will require a change of horses to keep the animals from exhaustion, she has sent this second one."

"Every adult fey keeps two mounts at least," Solft said, happy as any scholar to share titbits of his learning. "It's a mark of maturity when they receive their second. Most of Benjamin's archers have four. It is a secret of their swiftness overland, so they say."

Prentice doubted merely having a change of mounts was enough to explain the fey journey speed. It also seemed like not much of a secret. Grand Kingdom knights all travelled with multiple mounts, especially since heavy destriers trained for battle were built with more strength and less endurance. Better to ride a lighter mount to the battle and then switch to the fresher warhorse for the fight itself. The archduchess's gift was practical, and Prentice did not resent it, but he was immediately thinking to have the creature stabled before they marched, along with his other horse, since he had no interest in learning to ride while he was aiming for the Inquisition.

"Her grace's gift arrived with instructions," Whilte added cheerily. "You are to be told that barons, knight commanders, and obedient retainers all ride. As such, you are without excuse on three accounts. You are to make a diligent study of horsemanship, learning the saddle at every opportunity, beginning with this particular journey. She avows your skill at learning and your love of new ideas, so she commands you turn such abilities to this task."

Prentice scowled. So much for stabling the horses while he marched. He had resisted this for many years now, but no longer, it seemed. No wonder Whilte was teasing him about it. Being lowborn, he had had no childhood experience with riding, and it had been the one knightly skill he had never mastered at Ashfield. Whilte's mockery was well-deserved. Even with his missing leg, the chaplain was probably still a better horseman than Prentice. The fey had seen the captain on one of their horses once and declared him *palpolon*, which in their language meant something inert tied to a saddle, specifically something that was badly tied and about to fall off.

"You are enjoying this, Chaplain," he said to Whilte who did not bother trying to hide a smirk.

"When a man rises to a certain greatness, the Almighty sometimes grants him a thorn in his flesh so that his pride might not grow too boundless," the chaplain said. He bent down, holding onto his staff, and slapped his own wooden leg. "Some are thornier than others. You do not begrudge me a trifle of mirth at this, do you?"

Prentice sighed. There were worse things than being forced to endure a few aches and pains and the amusement of those close to him.

"Very well, Brother, in that case, before we march today I would like you to go to the apothecaries and purchase me as much lanolin as they can spare."

"Wool wax? Why is that?" Whilte was surprised.

"Because I have saddle sores in my future, good chaplain, and while my respect for your healing gifts is absolute, I will not ask for them in this case."

Whilte laughed out loud at that, and even Solft smirked, though he did his best to hide it. Prentice shook his head. This was exactly why he would need the lanolin. He liked to think he was not a proud man, but he would need to be a much humbler man indeed before he asked Whilte to lay hands upon his backside, saddle sores or no.

CHAPTER 17

"You *will* remain standard bearer of the Lion company, Markas," Prentice told his faithful militiaman, sighing and looking him in the eye. Markas's face showed a soul in agony, as if his dearest mother had just disowned him.

"But why can I not march with you?" Markas almost pleaded. "I've been your man since that day on the walls. Don't you trust me?"

"Trust you? Good Lord, man, there are few in all the Lions I trust more!"

Prentice felt himself struggling to keep his temper. He had walked out of Dweltford's gates and through the burgeoning refugee township beyond. For the entire time he was watching those around him—the haunted and exhausted looks of folk clinging to whatever fragments of life war had left them. They were not starving, but they were not thriving either. That made them vulnerable, not only to the hazards of their own forced poverty but to the seductions of cruel and brutal liars like the Redlander Blood Sects. The same proselytizers that were converting the smuggler crews would find rich pickings here, there was no doubt. Lady Dalflitch's planned spy network would have to start recruiting newcome folk just to keep ahead of the cult. Enlisting the hale men into the Lions would help that process as well, he expected, especially by offering those who served rewards of land. That should spread some hope.

A lot will have families already, he had thought, watching children play, their youthfulness less dispirited than their parents' hearts. *Those families will follow the recruits north when they go to train.*

The Lions' new recruitment drive was about to deliver Fallenhill an influx of new citizens. He would have to send warning to Sergeant Franken and the village headman Grice to prepare for that. All these serious matters had been turning over in Prentice's thoughts as he walked alone past the refugees and the fields beyond, towards the Lion's encampment. Whilte and Solft had both left him at Within Walls to buy the wool wax he had asked for, as well as any extra ink they could scare up for Solft. The scholar was planning a "chronicle" of the campaign, apparently.

Prentice was still a hundred or more paces from the militia camp when the shouting began. Lions in their buffcoats rushed from their tents, cheering and grinning like drunkards. He tried to ask what was going on, but it was fruitless as they seized him up and carried him on their shoulders into camp like a conquering hero. The entire company cadre of drummers was there, including Solomon, and they beat rally-on-the-standard as a dozen rambunctious men carried their commander to the Lions' banner in the center of camp. On its own pole beside the rampant lion of the Western Reach was the blue and silver gryphon banner—*his* banner. They deposited him in front of Sergeant Gennet in full panoply, brilliantly polished helmet in the crook of his left arm like a knight in his liege's presence.

"Welcome, My Lord, Knight Commander Baron Ash," Gennet said loudly in what sounded like a well-rehearsed fashion. He lifted his right hand to halfway between his chest and head. "Do I salute or tug the forelock now?"

"You try tugging the forelock to me, Sergeant, and you will lose one of the fingers you do it with!" Prentice replied, his voice parade-ground loud. "Highest to lowest, White Lions salute each other. Whatever you may have heard, that does not change."

Gennet snapped to attention and his gauntleted fist thumped hard into his brigandine-protected chest. Prentice returned the salute with as much enthusiasm, smiling in spite of himself. It took at least ten minutes of the candle to finally get the cheering to die down. Once he had brought the camp back to some semblance of order, Prentice had intended to write commands to Fallenhill and begin the process of giving leadership of the Lion banner over to Marquis Farringdon. That had been his great mistake. Knowing that the force their knight commander was taking to hunt the Inquisition would form the basis of the second banner when they returned, the banner Prentice would continue to personally command, suddenly he was inundated with a stream of requests from men who rarely asked him anything other than where to march and whom to use their weapons on when they got there. Markas was not the first, and as Prentice let his eyes range over the camp that was supposed to be preparing itself to accept the new marquis knight captain, he saw far too many other little groups of men lurking nearby, looking busy, but unmistakably waiting for their own chance to make a "polite" request of him to take them with him.

"Listen now, Markas," Prentice told his standard bearer. "You have served faithfully every day and every night, and I promise you I know your value. After Franken, you are my best man, and that is why I want you with the Lion banner. Marquis Farringdon is a good man, and a skilled warrior, but he has no command experience—well, little enough, at any rate. He needs someone who understands the Lions—how they march; what problems will come up every day; and what matters he must fix now and what he can leave until the morning. That is why I need *him* to have *you*. The marquis I trust because of his heart. *You* I trust because you are a proven man."

Markas's expression shifted, his eyes almost staring as he listened to his commander. Prentice could see it in the man's face—he was realizing this was not a dismissal. It was a promotion, and he was glad Markas seemed to be recognizing that.

"From now on, you are the Lion Banner's Sergeant of the Colors. On the battlefield, the honor of our original standard is trusted to you, as it always has been, but now you will have to step up to greater authority."

"I would rather carry *your* standard," Markas said. It was the most insubordinate he had ever been since Prentice had spared his life in Fallenhill. He still proudly wore the symbolic noose around his neck, reminder of that day.

"You are a Lion, Markas," Prentice told him quietly. "Archduchess Amelia has made me a baron, and that means I have the right to present men to her for knighting, to swear to my banner. I have marked you for that, I promise. And when the second company is ready, and Marquis Farringdon settled to command the first, I will call you back Markas. You will carry the gryphon—you have earned the right."

Markas swallowed. Prentice met his eyes and could hardly remember the desperate convict who had tried to push him off a wall years before. That man was long gone. He saluted and Prentice returned it.

"Marquis Farringdon will be here soon," Prentice said, relieved to finally be wrapping up the conversation. "When he arrives, I want you to have picked out some fresh corporals. Take them from line firsts or even trusted militiamen and promote them rather than existing ranks if you can. I will not pick the eyes out of our command structure, but I will be taking more experienced officers than you will find comfortable. Inquisition knights are dire foes."

Markas turned to leave, but as he went, Prentice called after him.

"And not a breath about what we have discussed here sergeant. Keep it quiet until I announce it, understand?"

When he was gone, Prentice was thinking to quickly get to his tent and begin writing his orders. Before he could take three steps, however, Solomon was in front of him, saluting. This was the conversation the new baron had been dreading the most, but as it turned out, he need not have worried. Solomon had already been informed where he would be going.

"Baroness Righteous sent me her summons in the night, Capt...I mean Knight Commander," the lad said cheerily, his scarred cheek twisting oddly with the expression. The damaged flesh was healed, but the inflamed color of the scar had not yet settled.

"The baroness already told you, but not her husband," Prentice repeated, shaking his head. Solomon grinned, clearly aware that he was in on a joke. Righteous and Turley both—the pair would certainly have conspired to "help" without bothering to let Prentice know. It also showed that his wife could easily anticipate his intentions toward her. She had to have warned Solomon even before Prentice had raised the notion with her that morning in bed. "You understand why?"

"She wants me to keep training, to step up to a pike or halberd."

"She will make a Fang out of you, if she can," Prentice assured him, but even that felt like it would fall short of his wife's ambitions for their young ward.

By the time she is finished with you, you will be a killer, my lad, he thought. *If you are not ready to take my place in ten years, she will not let you forget it.*

Their coming babe was Prentice and Righteous's first child, perhaps their only one, but Solomon was family all the same, and the former street-fighting lady was determined to teach him the family trade. All winter he had been at Righteous's side day and night, fetching and carrying for her as her pregnancy grew. When she had no chores for him, she drilled him in knife work and wrestling as stringently as any military trainer. Solomon running about the castle, drenched in sweat from a training session, had become a familiar sight to the arch-duchess's household. Now, with Lady Dalflitch's plan to create a corps of Lace Fangs, Righteous would have an additional duty for Solomon—that of senior student to assist in martial instruction. He would be her training demonstration dummy, teaching a gaggle of young women how to fight.

"Just make sure the baroness does not get you married off too young," Prentice told him and nearly laughed out loud at the stricken look on the young lad's face. Solomon had fought a bloody duel and stood on more battlefields than most grown men twice his age, but the thought of talking to girls clearly filled the young man with dread. As it should.

"What...what does that mean, Captain?" Solomon asked, so nervous he forgot Prentice's changed rank.

"Ask your new mistress, lad. The baroness will be glad to explain it to you."

Prentice dismissed him and smiled to himself. He could create a little trouble for his wife as well. He did feel a bit sorry that he'd used Solomon to do it, but the youth would get over that soon enough. He would have liked to come up with something similar for his chief steward friend, but the time for playful thoughts was over. He still wanted to get his pursuit force across the river before nightfall.

CHAPTER 18

The first few days into the western grasses, aiming away from the Dwelt as much southward as west, went as smoothly as Prentice hoped, although on the morning of the second day after they left the river behind, he had emerged from his tent to a surprise. His first horse from the archduchess was a buckskin with a black mane that he had never bothered to name, and the newer was a white-socked, reddish bay color. The socks were prized, Prentice knew, but he had never learned a consistent reason why. Some said it showed a more spirited creature. Others claimed that it pointed to deeper endurance. Whatever the truth was, he had named the newer horse Boots, at Whilte's encouragement.

"He'll like you better if you give him a name and talk to him often," the chaplain had said of the gelding. Prentice had always felt foolish talking to a horse—or any animal for that matter—but better horsemen than he took it for granted.

So, as Boots was a gift for his accession to baron, he had named the horse for the first thing he had bought himself when the duchess had raised him out of convictry—a new pair of boots. On that second morning, Prentice awoke, stiff and sore, to find Boots saddled and ready, a White Lion standing at his bridle.

"I noticed you lacked a groom or squire, my Lord Knight Commander," he said and there was a clipped precision to his speech that caught Prentice's ear. Looking him up and down, the knight commander saw a typical militiaman in many ways, but there were also signs of something more. His dark beard was rough, but it was growing out from a more well-groomed state. His expression was deferential, but his eyes were bright when they looked at Prentice's face. This was not a man accustomed to looking down when faced with a member of the peerage. There were a number of other minor indicators that added up to one clear impression in Prentice's mind—a former noble, and by his accent, not a Reacherman. Newcome then?

"I thought until you picked one, it might be useful for someone to look to those duties," the militiaman continued. Prentice had made a point of choosing his officers for the march, and those were militiamen he knew and trusted by name, but there were still easily a hundred men with him he did not know personally.

"What is your name?" he asked.

"Lyrach," the man answered after a moment's hesitation.

Not used to not giving your name without mentioning your title and birth, Militiaman Lyrach? Prentice thought.

"And where are you from?"

"Northeast, near Quenland," Lyrach answered more easily this time, and Prentice realized that he could not confirm that by the man's accent.

"You are what, twenty years old?" he asked next.

"About that, My Lord Knight Commander." Lyrach's easy manner appeared to be becoming even more comfortable as the conversation went on. Prentice walked past the young man and down Boots' side, examining the clearly professional job Lyrach had done in readying the knight commander's horse.

"I checked his shoes as well," the young man reported. "All still fitted tight and no stones or damage. I can see to your other mount, too, if you need."

Prentice nodded and let his gaze casually shift to scan the west. There was nothing there to see but endless, waist-high grass, green from its winter growth, a veridian carpet all the way to the horizon.

"So, when did your knight sponsor die?"

That question shattered Lyrach's ease like a hammer through stained glass. The ex-noble startled like a shying colt.

"How...how do you know about my sponsor?"

Prentice turned his gaze back upon him.

"You are of an age to have won your spurs, but you are not fighting in the east," Prentice explained. "You said you are from Quenland, so perhaps you were under a traditionalist faction, and there are no battlefield promotions there since there are no acknowledged kings or princes to bestow them. But you would still have a chance to ride as a squire. Better than humping foot after foot on the march in our militia. So, I am left to think it is more likely you were never sworn, not even to ride for your spurs. That would only have happened if you had no knight sponsor to vouchsafe your training and birth. Did you kill him?"

Lyrach flashed Prentice a murderously cold glance and then looked away.

"Collinwall, Sir Collinwall of Ramat Farms, that was my sponsor's name, and no I did not kill him," he said quietly, the tension in his voice revealing how hard he was working to keep his temper. "He died of an infection from a lance thrust in a tourney."

"How long ago?" Prentice asked. He had never heard of Collinwall, but that was not surprising.

"Several summers," Lyrach responded. "Or what would have passed for summers, if your drought hadn't lasted as long as they say."

Your drought? Prentice thought. *Not* our *drought, or* the *drought?*

That meant Lyrach had come across the mountains in the winter. He was a true newcome recruit. Prentice had not thought there would be any in this smaller force. He had wanted only the most reliable men. How had someone as fresh as this Lyrach come to be amongst their number, and whose idea had it been?

"I rode to King Chrostmer's call at Aubrey, hoping to win them there," Lyrach said, continuing the story of his unwon spurs. "But you know how that all washed out. Since that time, I've ridden with some other knights, but no one with a fiefdom to swear to or money enough to pay for my losses. My horse went down in a fracas south of Rhales, and I spent a season as a footman for some less reputable elements of the war."

"Did you serve the Usurper?"

"No, but not for want of trying," Lyrach admitted honestly. "I wanted my spurs, and the only faction offering them was the one with a king on a throne, kingslayer or not."

That admission, while brutally honest, also cut to the heart of Prentice's misgivings about this man. He was alert and clearly confident in a military setting. Likely, he was a good fighter, perhaps even the equal of any others with them on the march, but this Lyrach was still a knight in his heart. That was why he was taking this chance to presume upon his commander's needs like this. Newly recruited, he already had one eye on promotion, and for a knight, that came through the favor of the higher ranks.

"Ambitious, are you, former Squire Lyrach?" Prentice asked, but he did not need an answer. He could see the truth of it already.

"If God has put talent in a man's hand and strength in his limbs, then surely ambition is the best use of that potential," Lyrach said, and a flicker of a sly smile revealed that he did not really mind being found out. Perhaps he still expected Prentice to approve of his cunning and politicking for advantage. He was about to be disappointed.

"Well, Lyrach, in the archduchess' militia, the only ambition we allow is to serve loyally and fight hard..."

"Oh, I can do...!" Lyrach started to declare, but Prentice held up a hand for silence and he stopped.

"Listen now and hear me, Lyrach. It is possible for any man to rise in the White Lions—any man—but there are no favors and no shortcuts. Battle is the only fire that shows the temper of our blades, and there are many here with more fires behind them than you."

Lyrach bristled and Prentice wondered if the man would finally lose his temper, but he did not.

"If God *has* granted you talent and ambition, then he will grant you opportunity to fulfill them. Wait for the right moment and you will win through."

"And what if that moment doesn't come?" Lyrach asked, and his youthful frustration was unmistakable.

"Then you will live, or die, as a White Lion, just like all the men-at-arms you see around you. You are dismissed."

Prentice saluted and Lyrach returned it, unenthusiastically, then handed over Boots's reins, turning to leave. Prentice watched him go, annoyed not at the young man or his presumption but that Lyrach had hit upon something true. He really did require a groom. He had too many duties as it was to look after his horses as they needed. It had not even occurred to him to check their shoes and feet, for instance.

Perhaps I am just looking a gift horse in the mouth, he told himself, not smiling at the easy pun. *But I cannot just take you on face value, Lyrach. Unknown things are deadly in the Reach.*

On the one hand, appointing Lyrach as a groom would make perfect sense. A former squire would have a wealth of military knowledge and combat skill to offer. In fact, given that he was supposed to be binding some men to knighthoods, a position as a squire was also in keeping with Prentice's new status. But there were no squires in the White Lions. Even the horsemen that Farringdon was recruiting and training were not like that. Each man rode as one of the company.

Then there was Lyrach's obvious experience and confidence. Even if every word of his story was a lie, he was likely skilled at any number of military arts. Unless he was an abject coward, anything less than a rank of line first, or even a corporal, would be a waste of that learning. Of course, that only raised the most important question: a squire from the east was a part of the peerage, even if only its lowest level, and there was no way to tell what part of the nobility Lyrach hailed from. Perhaps he was the ill-fated victim of the social order, slipped out of his place by no fault of his own, just as he claimed. Or he could be a second cousin to Daven Marcus himself, hoping for a chance to win the kingslayer Usurper's favor by wreaking havoc in the enemy's army, maybe even assassinating the Reach's new knight commander. Lyrach could be hoping to get near to Prentice and put a dagger to his throat in the night, then ride back east on Boots before anyone knew. Or he could have the same plan but in the fallen Earl Sebastian's service. Worst of all, Lyrach could have learned his knightly skills at Ashfield, or wherever else the Inquisition trained its militants. He could be here on behalf of Inxyphos.

The canny thing to do would be to send him back today, Prentice thought, but as he stepped up into the stirrup and levered his sore legs over Boots's saddle, he realized he still had a need for a proper groom. And having chosen this force for its fighting experience, men-at-arms afoot every one of them, it was probable that Lyrach was the only one, besides perhaps Brother Whilte, with any art for the task.

Prentice sighed heavily. As if he did not have enough to occupy his thoughts, he had to find Master Solft now. The scholar had something important to discuss with him as well, apparently.

"Welcome to rank and privilege, Baron Ash," he muttered under his breath and touched his heels to Boots's flanks.

CHAPTER 19

P rentice found Solft waiting beside Whilte's wagon, sitting on an upturned barrel at a small wooden table with parchments and two folios spread out upon it. The knight commander dismounted from Boots and joined the scholar.

"Baron," Solft said, tugging his forelock and standing. Prentice forced himself not to frown.

You are a peer now, he told himself. *Get used to it.*

"You have something for me, Master?" he asked, looking over the various documents.

"I do, My Lord, but this is only half of it," Solft replied. "A fey scout arrived just after dawn to say that Benjamin is coming to us and we should wait here."

"Why can the scout not guide us to Benjamin?"

"I don't know, My Lord. But he did say that Benjamin was bringing word of the Serpent Witch. She is hiding with the others of her kind in the west."

Prentice felt himself scowl at this frustrating good news. Solid word of the Witch was a prize, and one worth waiting for, but he still wanted to hunt for the Inquisition, and waiting made that feel like letting them escape. He comforted himself with the certainty that whatever reason Benjamin had to make him wait, it was not to help the "quiet" militants.

"We don't *have* to do what they want, Baron," Solft said tremulously, as if he feared Prentice's wrath for himself.

Prentice raised his head and looked east. Already they had come far enough west that the Azure Mountains were out of sight beneath the horizon. The sun rose over a straight flat line. He turned about completely and looked west, then southwest. In every direction was nothing but grassland, seemingly uninterrupted save by the occasional scrub trees. Somewhere in that direction was Benjamin's *keshiyaa*, his brotherhood of closest warriors, like a noble's sworn bannermen. From what little Prentice had learned of the fey culture, a *keshiyaa* could be as few as ten or as many as hundreds in the case of a great war leader. Benjamin commanded close to a hundred, and that made Prentice shake his head as he looked to the southwest horizon. A hundred riders, each with more than one change of mount, so ultimately a herd of three or four hundred beasts, and not one sign of their passing—no trampled grass, no worn trails, nothing. By rights they should be crushing a road through the land under their hoofs. But the fey were not merely skilled. Their tie to the earth was mystical; there could be no other name for it, even more so when he considered that Benjamin's was not the only *keshiyaa* in the west, nor by all accounts the largest. Exactly how many fey riders rode between the Azure Mountains and the western grasses was anyone's guess. Prentice doubted even the fey themselves had an absolute count.

"If we do not wait, there is no chance we will find them by ourselves," Prentice told Solft wearily, trying to still the frustration within himself with resignation, but it was a poor tool for the task. He did not like being told to wait, and not merely because he wanted to move swiftly after his enemy. Benjamin's word amounted virtually to an order, and that was not the nature of their alliance. Supposedly, Prentice had some authority in fey society, but individual fey like Benjamin did things whichever way they chose and only explained if they felt so inclined, which seemed to be almost never—none of which was Solft's fault, however. The scholar was still watching him nervously. Prentice shook his head and sighed.

"So, we must wait," he said. "What else did you wish to show me?"

Solft looked so relieved he seemed like a criminal receiving a reprieve.

"I have managed to find a map for you, Baron," he said, turning back to the table with a smile. He sat down and opened a bound codex to a place he had marked with a feather. The book's pages were barely a handspan wide, but on one there was a clearly illuminated rendering of the Western Reach, with the two main rivers and the Azure Mountains on the right-hand length of the page. The left side contained only a stylized tuft of grass and the words "bereft of cultivation." Prentice took up the small book and turned it over to look at its cover. It was undyed leather without inscription, so he opened it to its inner plate.

"Borrosod the Pilgrim?" he said, reading the author's inscription out loud. It was an obscure but unknown name. "This is eighty years old, at least, surely."

Solft frowned apologetically. "It is the most recent I have to hand, though I would dare say it is likely the most recent in all existence, unless her grace has a survey commissioned by the late duke that was never copied."

Prentice sighed again and looked at the map once more. It dated from a time before the Reach had even been a contested land, let alone a unified duchy. Aubrey was there on the page, and Dweltford, though the provincial capital was marked as a Broken Barony, which was the town's old status. Fallenhill was marked without a name, and Griffith was present only as "Veckander trading post." The map did show the Murr rising from mountains in the far southwest at the bottom left of the page, but other than that, the area was blank, even emptier than the rest of the western side, except, he noted, for an illumination of a dragonfly in the corner of the page just below the lake. It had a matching partner in the opposite corner. So much of Grand Kingdom cartography was elegant but impractical.

"This cannot much inform our march," he said sourly. Not having to depend on his fey guides would have given him some comfort. He looked up at Solft. "Which is no failing of yours, Master. Please forgive me if I seem churlish. Thank you for your effort."

Solft shook his head and smiled politely, his drooping jowls making his face seem almost like a sad hound's.

"I appreciate your frustration, My Lord" he said. "Nevertheless, I have made you a larger copy for easier consultation."

He lifted a broad sheet of vellum from under other documents. It had the basic outline of the map copied upon it, with Solft's usual fine skill at reproduction, though without the folio's embellishments and with the names of settlements updated. As with its tiny progenitor, the large sheet was essentially half blank.

"It seems we will have to fill in the details as we go," Prentice observed wryly.

"I have taken the liberty of one update already, My Lord," Solft said, and he waved his hand over the lower left part of the page where the Murr River traced back to its source, which appeared to be a forest in some hills. The words "Radengon Beyond Dwelt" had been written in, giving the region its current name. "I realize it is not *much* help."

Prentice nodded and looked the map over. The phrase Broken Barony caught his eye. He had known it for years. Griffith, Dweltford, and Fallenhill were the three Broken Baronies that had been reformed after Kolber's defeat to make the singular Western Reach Dukedom.

The Broken Kings? he thought, remembering what Inxyphos had called the Redlanders and what the archduchess had told him of Bluebird's words to her. Why was everything on the west of the mountains "broken"? He picked up the codex by Borrosod and flicked through it. It was a journal of the scholar's expedition to the wilds beyond the mountains. Prentice almost laughed out loud when he saw an engraving of a knight fighting with a manticore, its bat-like wings flapping in a brilliant sunset. On the opposing page was the writer's surely fictitious account of the combat. The unnamed knight was victorious but died of the creature's poison. Prentice was reminded of the different *brakkis effar* and their venomous natures. If only Borrosod the Pilgrim had warned the Grand Kingdom of what was really on the other side of the Azures.

He was about to put the little book away as next to useless when he caught sight of a line on one page. It read, "...so far are these lands from civilization that they need not have border earls set to their defense; with the river on one side and the mountains the other, they are defended by impenetrable natural boundaries. If ever a prison were to have such walls, it would be inescapable."

"Bastard," Prentice swore, casting the book upon the table. He knew it was irrational, but suddenly all his controlled fury and past hurts gripped his thoughts, and he almost shook from the overwhelming emotions. It was likely that Borrosod was not the only one, perhaps not even the first, to imagine transportation across the mountains as punishment for convicts, but here it was in writing—the authorship of so much of his torment. And not just his, but Turley's, Righteous's, Bellam's and too many others. If the author had been right there next to him, Prentice was sure he could have throttled the life from the man. He would not have even wasted the time to draw his sword. Without a word to Solft he walked to Boots and mounted up, geeing his horse to a canter and riding straight away from the Lion's camp. He was not about to lose his temper in front of his men.

As it happened, his saddle sores helped bring him back to reality fast enough. Although the lanolin was aiding with the discomfort, every time he rode, his backside and thighs burned from the unfamiliar movement. He knew that eventually his flesh would toughen against the pain and injury, but in the meantime, it made him smile at his other troubles. It was hard to maintain righteous anger at ancient slights when such mundane and embarrassing discomfort could govern his thoughts alongside it. He had lived and worked for years with the sores and irritations of iron fetters around his ankles; a few weeks with sore buttocks was little enough burden. He had completed two circuits of the entire company, practicing cantering and walking alternately, grimacing at the saddle sores most of the way, when a sentry gave cry that there were riders coming in from the south. Prentice awkwardly turned Boots about in a wide circle and was halfway to the southern side of the camp when Solft came bouncing out to join him, riding on the back of a mule.

"Oh, Holy Lord God," Prentice prayed softly. "Please let me look better than that when I ride."

CHAPTER 20

"If you'll permit me, My Lord, I will join you in this conference," Solft said as he drew alongside, his lower mount meaning that his head was barely equal height with Prentice's waist. "I would keep an account of all the interactions between our two peoples, if I may. I can also translate a little, I think."

"Then count yourself welcome," Prentice told him. "Though I would not have ridden fast. You could have come on foot." The scholar had his writing bag with him, obviously hastily slung over his mule and threatening to fall with every bounce.

Solft shook his head.

"With respect, Baron Ash, that would be a great error," he said. "A mule has little value in fey eyes, but even that is better than walking. A man who approaches the fire or approaches the camp without a saddle is less than a man in their society."

Solft's words made sense to Prentice when he thought about it, but he was still surprised by them—not simply because they were something he did not know, but because of his memories of his first meeting with the fey last year in the mountains above Fallenhill. It had given him a picture of just how desperate the fey were at the time that their elders had thought to meet with him, even though he came to them on foot, and how much they had humbled themselves by their own standards to accept him at their fire.

"Let us ride to meet with Benjamin then," he said.

By the time Prentice and Solft had ridden around the camp, three fey ponies were waiting about a hundred paces farther south, riders sitting comfortably in their saddles. There was something odd about the one in the middle, which was Benjamin. He was between the other riders, as if they were an honor guard.

Just don't wince, Prentice told himself as he walked Boots closer. As he neared the three, he realized that Benjamin looked strange because there was a fourth fey man seated in his saddle behind him. Remembering Solft's recent comments about fey warriors and being mounted, Prentice wondered what it meant that this one was only a passenger on someone else's horse.

"Welcome to our camp, Benjamin, men of the mountains," Prentice called loudly when he was only a dozen or so paces away. One of the two escorts said something in the fey tongue and the other replied, but Benjamin only stared at the knight commander and his companion. Prentice thought he made out the word *palpolon* but did not know whether they meant him or Solft.

Probably both, he decided.

"Could you translate any of that Master?" he asked Solft.

"I would prefer not to, My Lord," came the reply.

"Fair enough." Prentice smirked and did not try to hide it from the fey. Let them wonder if he understood their disdain better than they realized. "Are we obliged to set a fire to meet around, Master?"

"I don't...think...so," said Solft.

The two parties sat their mounts for a long moment, the breeze that stirred the grass the only movement between them. The fey escorts were exchanging more soft words, their eyes fixed on Prentice, when suddenly Benjamin raised his double-bitted saddle axe and spoke a single word.

"He's commanding them to 'riding silence,'" Solft explained. "It's what they call it when they move with stealth."

You are not used to kreff being able to understand, are you, Benjamin? Prentice thought. *Your people will have to decide soon just how far you are willing to open up to us to get what you need.*

It was likely that there were internal conflicts amongst the fey at the changes to their society, just as Archduchess Amelia's changes to the Reach had disturbed the nobility's pride and ultimately led Sebastian to rebellion. The thought that the fey might similarly split amongst themselves was not a pleasant one. Allies were little use if they were at war with their own factions.

"You sent us word that the Serpent Witch is found," he said eventually, deciding that it must be his obligation to start the conversation. "This is welcome news."

"It is," Benjamin agreed and then said something to the fey man behind him. The passenger slid down out of the saddle and shuffled forward a short distance, then dropped heavily to a crouching position. As if exhausted, he ultimately sank to sit cross-legged, head hanging low to one side, almost resting on his knee. He wore the buckskin leggings typical of a fey rider, but on his torso he had only a simple shift of cloth rather than the usual color-threaded corselet. The shaved sides of his head had started to grow out, and his hand resting on the ground at his side looked claw-like, it was so skeletal.

You have known the 'mercies' of the Redlanders, Prentice thought, remembering the haggard and haunted looks he had seen on the fey who had been forced to ride for the Serpent Witch.

While Prentice watched the broken fey man closely, Benjamin dismounted and took his saddle from his horse. Recognizing the gesture from his meeting with the elders in the northern Azures, Prentice also dismounted and moved to a point opposite Benjamin's saddle, with the exhausted fey seated upon the ground between them.

"Careful, Baron, if I may," Solft counseled with a quiet voice. "I don't know what is right here."

Prentice understood Solft's worry, but he felt comfortable that this was acceptable conduct. He sat down and rested as comfortably as he could, cross-legged on the grass, doing his best not to reveal how gingerly he was doing it. Prentice felt a little foolish with the long grass fronds almost hiding him from sight and wondered if they should have tamped some down first to create a meeting space of some sort. Benjamin sat his saddle calmly, however, with the same sense of distant superiority he always showed. The two leaders watched each other for a long moment with the forlorn rider between them.

How much longer does this go on? Prentice wondered, starting to suspect that Benjamin might want him to begin their interaction. When knights met, they recounted each other's deeds of honor, nobles raised their house colors and heraldry, and 'skips and street gangs stood and dared each other to bare steel. Showing respect was universal, and Prentice was willing to give the fey whatever due their ways demanded. However, with nothing but instinct and Solft's nervousness to guide him, it was not an experience he wanted to go on longer than it must.

"Since the first rain of winter fell, we have not forsaken our debt of blood to the Serpent," Benjamin began finally. Prentice shivered despite the warm sun overhead, and the image of the witch slithering away from him in the mud that night filled his mind. If he had not been so wounded, he would have caught her then. Just one true cut with his blade and she would have been no more instead of a figure of undelivered justice sitting always in his thoughts, like a toad upon a rock. Vengeance is mine, said God Almighty in his scripture, but to let that fiend go unpunished was not something Prentice's conscience could bear. It was not a petty revenge he sought. Let God judge her as he saw fit. It was that, while she lived, she remained a potential threat to every free person, fey or mortal, who dwelt in the Western Reach. Her magicks had scorched the land to a near desert once already. There was no reason to think she could not do the same again, or something worse, if she was given the time to try.

"We *kreff* are pleased to hear of your people's diligence in the hunt for justice," Prentice said to Benjamin, and he had a sudden insight concerning the broken fey sitting between them. What had happened to this rider during his hunt for the Serpent Witch?

Benjamin nodded ever so slightly, accepting the compliment for his people.

"Did your hunters find the Redlander homeland when they were searching for the Witch?" Prentice urged hopefully but was disappointed when Benjamin shook his head.

"How could we? It is far beyond the salty sea. We do not sail," he declared, his expression one of true disbelief. "The ones you call Redlanders sail, even through the sky, for the land will not tolerate their defiled steps."

Did that mean that their transporting sorcery only worked on waters? Prentice wanted to ask Benjamin for more on that, but he had a more pressing matter first.

"I was told you found where the Witch hides and where the Redlanders come from," Prentice said, wondering why Solft had told him this if it wasn't true. Had someone lied or was it only a misunderstanding?

"We found where their boats come from when they move through the sky."

Prentice looked from Benjamin to the broken fey, blinking his eyes.

"Are they not the same place?"

The notion that Redlander magick to move boats might not be based in their homeland had never occurred to Prentice, though as soon as it did, he realized that he might have guessed. The invader's fleet, the one the archduchess had seen upon the western coast, had had to come from somewhere, and their homeland was the most likely source. But if their magick was in their homeland, why bother sending the fleet across the salty sea in the first place? Why not send it straight through the sky? The thought gave Prentice a sudden flare of hope. The Redlanders had to sail from their land to somewhere nearer to the Reach, and from there they moved through the sky. That meant the source of their movement might be reached and destroyed without having to face the whole of whatever evil their homeland could produce. It also raised another question: just how many strongholds and sorcerous places of power did they possess across the world? Was their entire existence one of secret havens and hidden dominions? If so, it was little wonder they found common cause with the river smugglers.

"The long southern water," Benjamin said enigmatically.

Prentice furrowed his brows, but the fey leader was not forthcoming with an explanation.

"It is what they call the Murr, My Lord," Solft said from behind, but that drew a reproachful hiss from Benjamin.

"The long southern water," Benjamin said again. "Its beginning is far—farther than *kreff* have ever traveled—but it is not too far for us."

"What does...?" Prentice began but quickly realized what Benjamin was saying. "The Murr? The headwaters of the Murr River? Is it from there that they send their boats?"

The fey nodded solemnly.

"Far west, far south, there is a higher land. Beyond that are mountains, and behind those the sun sets each night. In those mountains there is a lake, so deep that its water springs pure from the heart of all land. It gives life, such as is not remembered except by the sages. No curse of summer can drain the life of this lake, and it feeds the long southern water. So full is this cup of life from the earth that all the southern water lives from its overflow."

Benjamin made a gesture like raising a cup and pouring out its contents in a long, slow trickle. Between them, the broken fey looked up fully, and for the first time Prentice saw clearly his withered features as full sunlight fell upon them. He was a scarecrow creature, his leathern skin pulled tight like a rictus against his skull. His cheekbones seemed to want to cut through to the surface, and in their sockets, his eyes glittered like dark gems—bright but empty. Had the talk of an endless source of life caught the attention of this living cadaver because he hoped to be restored? Or because however the hunt had cost him so much vitality, it had begun when he reached this fabled headwater lake?

"Your people hunted the Serpent Witch to this water?" Prentice asked. "Did they see the mantis men there as well?"

Benjamin looked to his broken comrade, but the man had let his head sink once again. The fey leader turned back to Prentice and shrugged.

"The Untrue bind themselves to animals, mingling their blood with different beasts, but though they are separate to each other, they are always united to their foes."

Prentice frowned at that, annoyed at the deliberate obfuscation. He began to shake his head when behind him he heard Solft speak softly again. This time Benjamin did not object.

"Where one kind is, we can expect to find others."

That is what we are supposed to think, Prentice thought, watching the fey leader and trying to read his inscrutable features. *But my money says you do not know or care, do you, Benjamin?*

"Can we reach this place?" he asked.

Benjamin grunted at the one between them and the cross-legged fey looked up again.

"We rode the way there," he said, his words slurring and his accent thick. "But I returned…"

The fey man's speech continued in his own tongue. Prentice did not expect to understand the words, but behind him he heard Solft draw in a shocked breath.

"Master?" Prentice called over his shoulder for a translation.

"He says his name is…was Dahyoor, and he returned alone, on foot," Solft said, and the disbelief in his tone was easy to hear.

Prentice nodded, thinking he understood the implications. A man returning alone was a survivor from a defeated force, and there would always be a question over why. Was he alive because he was cunning or because he was a coward? Double that by having him return to his rider people without his mount. No wonder he hung his head in shame, but to have his name denied to him as well? Prentice wondered how long ago this fey man had been forced onto his feet and what had driven him to continue back to his people despite such a level of shame. Most men of honor he knew would have chosen to kill themselves rather than suffer the equivalent humiliation in Grand Kingdom society.

"You also can travel the waters in the natural way," Benjamin explained. "If you ride to the southern water and take your boats, you may follow it to the rise, drag them up to the height, and ride them much of the way to the mountains. To the forests at the foothills, at least. If you go now, you would be there before the end of summer."

Benjamin sat back, arms folded. Prentice thought about that suggestion, calling up Solft's nearly empty map of the west in his mind. He could choose to send his men straight south to the Murr and look to find enough boats amongst the Radengoners to carry his five cohorts upriver. Or he could march back to the Dwelt, secure boats from the duchy and ride them south and then west. Both were possibilities.

"What about the riders in steel I set you to track?" Prentice asked. "The Inquisition men-at-arms?"

"Leave them to us," Benjamin said. "We will make anteaters of them." A typical fey threat. Anteaters had a myriad of protective spines on their backs. Benjamin was promising to fill them full of arrows so that their bodies looked "spined."

Dead or captured was the ultimate aim of Prentice's mission against the Inquisition militants, but Benjamin's suggestion was unacceptable to him. He needed prisoners.

"We will go with you to where these riders in steel are," he told the fey leader. "We will act together and take some of them prisoner so that the Lioness Mother may learn their secrets. Then we will turn south to the southern water and make the journey westward to this lake. That way we combine our strengths in both tasks and will not come up short."

That last comment was a matter of simple strategy, just as the archduchess had observed back in Dweltford. To divide one's forces was to risk weakening them. Even as he said all this, though, Prentice realized this plan was committing him to miss the birth of his child. He hoped his wife would forgive him.

Benjamin scowled.

"This is not necessary," he declared in a tone that made it clear he intended not to cooperate. "At the lake water they are no more than *imzuss*. We do not need you to finish the riders merciless. Go to the southern water now. It will be better."

"'*Imzuss*', Master Solft?" Prentice asked for a translation.

"A coven, I think, Baron," came the uncertain reply. "Or something similar. A small group that shares a secret. Not of warriors, I think."

So, there was a small enough number at this lake that his lesser contingent of Lions could defeat it by themselves. Benjamin could send them ahead safely. That was convenient. Prentice rubbed his bearded chin and studied Benjamin's face.

Why? he wondered, trying to guess what might be motivating this intransigence. Simple efficiency? A lust for vengeance? Maybe Benjamin did not trust his Reach allies. He might fear that Prentice or Archduchess Amelia would pardon the Inquisition men-at-arms since they were both mortals and of the same faith, ostensibly. Those explanations made sense, but Prentice could not forget that these enemies were on the loose in the western grasses because the fey had let them ride away on the night of the ambush. It seemed incredible, but he could not completely ignore the possibility that there was a link between the fey and the Inquisition that he did not know about. They seemed like dire enemies, but Prentice just could not shake some of his doubts.

"No," he said at last. "We will take the merciless preachers of mercy together and then we will go to this lake together."

Benjamin shook his head.

"We will not..." he began to say, but Prentice cut him off.

"I speak as an elder," he said, and Benjamin flinched. The fey leader looked over his shoulder at his two escort riders before looking back, visibly displeased. Then he nodded slowly.

"It will be as you say," he said.

We will see, Prentice thought, not at all convinced that this was the conclusion of the matter.

CHAPTER 21

Hoofbeats hammered the soil, and the vibration arose through the bones in Amelia's feet and legs so that she felt it all over her body. It took courage to stand and watch as a rank of twenty riders in heavy steel harness hammered across the open field so close to her, even knowing she was not their target. Skilled in the saddle, each rider was leaning forward in their stirrups, their mounts galloping to the charge. Despite their breakneck speed, the squadron kept order almost perfectly, as if the entire twenty were all tied to one length of taut rope. As Amelia watched, the advancing rank seemed to slip slightly to the side of their line of charge and, as one, the armored figures leveled simple-seeming weapons in their right hands, aiming forward while they drifted left. When they were still seventy paces back from where the archduchess stood, the twenty fired as one, and flame spat from twenty barrels. A cloud of smoke trailed them as the riders came on.

Almost as soon as that first volley fired, the line began to veer to its right and they all leveled their left-handed guns. These, too, fired and a second cloud of smoke trailed behind. They were now barely fifteen or twenty paces away, and the rank split suddenly down its middle, ten men on each side veering off to ride away in columns. The nearest ten circled around Amelia and Farringdon beside her. As she watched, she could see the riders returning their two handguns to leather sheaths on the front of their saddles. By the time the split rank had swept to its starting point and begun to reform, their firearms were stowed, and each rider was detaching a long, spear-like lance from another holster, this one on the back of the saddle. Barely even slowing as they readied this new weapon, the rank came on once again, and they executed a lance charge that, while perhaps not the equal of a company of the best Grand Kingdom knights, would nonetheless put no men-at-arms to shame. The rank charged straight past Amelia before splitting as before and veering to either side of the field.

"So, Your Grace, what do you think?" asked Farringdon.

Amelia put her hand to her chest, the bones within seeming to remember the vibrations of the charge. She looked at her husband and then over his shoulder at the lancers who were reining in their mounts to return at a walk. When her consort had first come to her with the notion of mounted hand-gunners, the idea had seemed ludicrous. A compromise between Kingdom knights and fey horse archers—that had been his description—and it had only been her desire not to disrespect him that had kept her from scoffing outright. All winter he had recruited and trained these horsemen, ignoring questions of birth and privilege, intent only on producing a new type of man-at-arms—Farringdon's lancers.

"Well, My Lord," Amelia said, making a point of showing her husband the same level of respect that he gave her, "it certainly looks to work exactly as you promised, assuming the shots do not all go wild."

"A charging horse-gunner *is* much less accurate than a Roarsman of course, but accuracy is not the point," Farringdon answered readily. "The two volleys will strike from close, and we both know what happens when hot iron begins to fly, what it does to an enemy's nerve, even if the shots never actually land a wound."

Amelia could not argue with that.

"And you plan for them to come on in such small waves?" she asked.

Farringdon shook his head. "Only for now. It's taken all winter just to get a hundred horsemen up to this standard. And we have few enough of these."

The marquis hefted a firearm in his hand, of the same kind the lancers had wielded in pairs. It was much shorter than a White Lions Roarsman's matchlock. More distinctive still was the trigger mechanism. While the Roar's guns had a serpentine lever and a long, slow-burning wick that set fire to the black powder in the open pan, this device concealed the entire triggering process inside a turning wheel with a little handle on the side. Farringdon had explained that the powder within was fired by means of a spark scratched by spring-loaded metal when the trigger was pulled. It sounded almost fearsomely complex to Amelia. The enclosed nature of the mechanism meant a horseman could use the handgun without fear of the powder in the pan spilling or being knocked free by the horse's gait. Unfortunately, it also made the entire trigger complicated to load and thus too slow for repeated firing in a battle situation. That was why each rider had only two, one for each hand, and then went to their lances for the rest of the fight. The complexity of the trigger mechanisms also made the weapons extremely expensive.

"Master Sent has not fully solved the riddle of their construction?" Amelia asked.

As the archduchy's chief armorer, Master Yentow Sent and his workshops produced virtually all the province's weapons. It was he who had introduced Prentice to serpentine firearms, and the man had a fascination for any form of the new weapon. Master Sent was also a rabid perfectionist, who insisted that every constructed piece that left his workshops was of the highest quality. That meant that what he produced was almost always flawless but was also slow in arriving when ordered. After a whole winter, Farringdon's new company still only had the weapons that had been imported from the far south. As winter had broken, the master came to Dweltford to bring the products of his most recent labors and was now marching with the Lion Banner company as they campaigned down the Dwelt toward the Reach's southern border.

"The master smith says that the ten or so new triggers he brought with him are...," Farringdon began to explain, then paused as he remembered Yentow Sent's exact words, "a 'serviceable facsimile' of the wheel-lock triggers we bought from Gwetlan. He is not yet satisfied that his versions will surpass those, and so he has not yet commenced full production. He seems quite frustrated."

Amelia cocked an eyebrow quizzically. Seeing it, Farringdon shrugged.

"Master Sent used a number of Masnian words. I do not know the language, but from the context I assume they were curses."

The archduchess nodded with a smile.

"So, we have these two hundred only?"

"Give or take. Enough to equip one cohort of riders. And we have the canons."

Amelia flinched inwardly even at the mention of the mightiest gunpowder engines of war. She had seen the wheel-mounted long tubes of black iron which Master Sent had brought with him from Fallenhill. They seemed almost laughably small compared to the enormous ancient monsters which were the royal house's Bronze Dragons, but she was reliably assured that each could fling an iron ball larger than a man's fist a thousand or more paces with force enough to smash walls to dust and men to meat. Every time she thought of them, an involuntary thrill of fear at the memory of having to stand under the horror of cannon fire rushed through her. She refused to yield to it, but it seemed to always be there, refusing to be forgotten.

"Has he focused too much time on his engines of destruction?" Amelia asked, knowing that in spite of her wishes, her lurking fear was souring her opinion of the weapons and that her husband could surely hear it in her voice. "Are we short of lancers for the sake of his iron brutes?"

"*My* iron brutes, Your Grace," Farringdon responded. "Master Sent is taking his instructions from me and fulfilling them to the letter."

Amelia smiled at her husband. He was such a just man, refusing to let another suffer her displeasure on his behalf. It was another of the traits that kept building her love for him—another solid stone in the castle of their marriage. That thought made her smile. It was such a warlike metaphor for a young wife to use, yet it was so apt. She stepped up to Farringdon and took his hand, placing her other upon his polished breastplate.

"They seem very fine horsemen, my love," she said reassuringly. "And doubtless the cannons are most powerful. I suppose I am anxious that there are so many new things in our Reach. Earl Sebastian and High Sacrist Quellion, they both accused me of making wreckage of the old order, like a wild colt kicking its stable apart, but in truth I have never sought much change to traditional ways, not in my heart. I sometimes think that if I had never met Prentice, I might also never have learned to care about the plight of the convicts who built so much of the Reach. I want to seek a better future for all the west, you know this, but I fear we might discard worthy traditions with unworthy if we make too many changes too swiftly. Surely not everything that came before was evil."

Farringdon nodded.

"Prentice agrees with me about the cannons," he said. "He is persuaded the lancers will be a force to reckon with on the battlefield as well."

Amelia sighed and lifted her hand to his cheek, holding his gaze.

"Husband, I trust you, truly I do," she told him earnestly. "You do not have to invoke Prentice's name and opinion to win my approval."

Farringdon kissed her hand.

"You trust his word more than mine on matters of war," he said, and it stung Amelia to hear it. Once she had wanted nothing more in life than to be a nobleman's excellent wife. Now she had grown to be so much more, but that ambition had not died within her. It pained her to think her husband felt the need to compete with any other man for her favor. Farringdon must have seen something of her emotions in her eyes because he shook his head.

"Fear not, my love. You *should,* at least for now."

He looked over her head at his lancers, waiting patiently in their saddles some distance away.

"My ideas are yet fresh and green, like the spring around us. Prentice's strategies are proven, standing strong on many fields. One day, I mean to be to you as he is, but for now, his word carries a great deal more weight."

Amelia looked back to the lancers as well and remembered some of the things she had read in war treatises. She was suddenly of a mind to engage her own knowledge in order to test her theory against her husband's skill and ideas.

"It looks like it will be a sure enough tactic against infantry," she said. "Against knights, will it not become more difficult to execute?"

"How so?" Farringdon asked her, blinking in surprise. She was sure he had not expected her ask a question quite so professionally minded. It made her smile.

"If a company of knights sees your lancers charging at them, they will not wait politely to receive the attack, surely?" Amelia explained her thinking. She was drawing upon the famous tract of Lord Rossman and his musings on the nature of different kinds of men-at-arms. "Will there not be a good chance they will countercharge? That will cut down the time your men have to fire. Your lancers might be lucky to get even one shot off before they are engaged in melee, and you say the whole point of your new horsemen is that they should not get into melee with knights in full harness."

Farringdon stared at her agape for a long moment.

"Have I sprouted a second head, husband, that you drill your eyes into me so?" she teased, and he suddenly smiled back. Then he settled himself to seriousness once more and addressed her questions.

"That is a solid objection, Your Grace," he acknowledged, and his eyes narrowed as he thought. A moment later they brightened with a fresh idea. "They're already training to ride in waves. When we face infantry, it can be all guns first and then lances, as I have planned. If we find ourselves against knights, we can alternate the waves—first with gun and then the second wave with lance to exploit the openings immediately."

"And if the guns make no openings?"

"Then the lance line splits and wheels away without engaging, and the next gun wave takes their shot."

"Knights ahorse will follow them."

"They can try," Farringdon declared confidently, and Amelia had to accept his confidence was probably justified. The whole point of his new type of cavalry was to create a compromise between a knight's power and a fey archer's mobility. In a short charge, knights' destriers should be able to match Farringdon's coursers for pace, but even over a middling distance, the heavy warhorses would quickly fall back. Amelia knew that was why Kingdom knights used footmen in the first place, to tie the enemy down as best as possible and line them up for a few crushing charges by the heaviest of horsemen. Prentice had explained that to her years ago, and his Lions had proved the truth of it on more than one battlefield.

"How many horses still shy from the fire and smoke?" she asked.

"None of those ones, as you saw. We've pretty fairly weeded out the high-strung mounts already. We'll foal from this stock and a decade from now have the basis of a whole new breed of warhorse—less powerful but unafraid of powder and shot."

"Your Grace! Your Grace!" a young lad in a ragged blue tabard over his bare chest shouted as he raced up, arms pumping. He stopped, breathless, and saluted Lions' fashion, then tugged his forelock. Even after years, militiamen still became confused as to how they were to show respect when it came to the archduchess. She could hardly fault this child, who was probably a drummer as Solomon had once been.

"I got a message for you, Your Grace."

Amelia stepped back from standing so close to her husband and then nodded in his direction.

"The knight captain is your commander, boy," she said. "You should ask his permission first."

Without hesitation the lad turned to Farringdon and repeated the salute and forelock before announcing he had a message for the archduchess. Farringdon gave him permission to deliver it.

"Please, Your Grace, but Sergeant Markas says to ask you, polite as I can, rally on the banner. There's a visitor for you—a truly important lady, so he says."

Rally on the banner? Amelia wondered. It was likely the easiest way for a drummer to understand the message. Then she realized that he had said the visitor was a lady.

"Who is this lady?" she asked him.

"A pretty noblewoman, all of a mystery," the boy said, his voice tinged with awe.

"A mystery?"

"They said she's a needly woman, though I don't know what that rightly means. She's in fine clothes, though, just like you, Your Grace. And she's masked in lace."

Masked in lace? Amelia started as she realized who it must be.

"Spindle," she said happily. Although she knew her other Lace Fang was somewhere in the south, she had not expected to encounter her on this march, at least not so soon.

"Take me to her," she ordered the lad, and the boy turned upon his heel, walking away like a marching Lion, obviously proud to be escorting the highest ranking noble in his world.

CHAPTER 22

"Your Grace, it is a pleasure to be with you again," said Lady Spindle as she curtseyed. She was wearing a forest green overdress that was embroidered with what looked like genuine gold thread, no doubt a product of the woman's own skill. Her lace half-mask covered the cruel scarring upon her face and scalp and helped to create the image the young messenger had described—beautiful and mysterious.

"And to see you, dear Spindle," Amelia said. "A pleasure and a marvel, that you are returned so soon from the south. Have you cut your sojourn short? I trust it was not unpleasant."

Spindle had travelled south with her new husband, an infamously charmless merchant named Caius Welburne. An odd-seeming match for the archduchess's former convict lady, Master Welburne was more a cold fish of a man than actually cruel or violent, but nonetheless, Amelia had feared for her lady in this new relationship.

"Our journeyings have been quite pleasant, Your Grace," Spindle said with a smile that seemed genuine. "Caius has sent me north while he attends to an urgent matter. I think I should tell you about it away from other ears, if you'll permit."

"Of course, My Lady," Amelia replied.

Spindle then turned to two men-at-arms standing a short distance behind her. They had simple conical helms and wore coats of mail under tabards of a similar green to Spindle's dress. They carried maces hanging from their belts.

"I will be safe here for now," she told them. "Go back to the others and see that our tents are set for the evening. We will be staying with the Lions from now on."

"We're supposed to escort you at all times," one of the two objected.

"My husband hired you to keep me safe," Spindle corrected. "I am safer now than I have been since we left Redfern. The Lions will defend me as well as you could, and if one of them meant me harm, there would be nothing you could do to stop it."

The two guards looked sour at her dismissive treatment, but they accepted her instructions and left. Spindle turned back to Amelia and smiled demurely.

"At your pleasure, Your Grace."

Amelia led the short distance to her and Farringdon's tent, set not far from the Lion banner in the middle of the company encampment. Since leaving Dweltford, the Lion Banner Company had camped four times as patrols were sent out to scour the banks of the nearby Dwelt River for smuggler's hideouts. They were using a list of known boltholes and skips' nests provided by the infamous Ragmother. So far, the list had proved astonishingly accurate, and Amelia sometimes wondered whether the old smuggler would have conquered the whole river if she had had a sufficiently large crew of cutthroats, ruling it from the shadows. The archduchess was comforted by the notion that the woman's exceptional knowledge was now helping to purge the river of the infiltrating Redlander religion.

"We are doing the Inquisition's true job for them," she had remarked bitterly to Farringdon more than once.

Once they were inside the archduchess's tent, Amelia offered Spindle her own chair while she took her husband's. This new tent was larger than the one she had travelled in for so many years in previous campaigns.

Still nothing like Daven Marcus's monstrosity though, she thought as she settled herself and offered some watered wine.

"How fares your new marriage, Your Grace?" Spindle asked, noting the larger bed in the other half of the tent with a politely raised eyebrow.

"It blesses my days," Amelia answered. "And yours?"

"Much the same." Spindle sipped from her silver cup. "If I may say, Your Grace, it very much seems to suit you. You look quite well."

"Suits me? What about you?" Amelia blurted out, unable to keep her wonder contained any longer. Where was the Spindle she had known only a few months before—the harsh, scarred knife-fighter who had risen beside the deadly Lady Righteous and now seemed to have been replaced by a true patrician lady, a courtier in poise and manners? "Marriage has left you transformed."

Spindle nodded politely and raised her cup again, but before she could take another sip, she suddenly chuckled and the old Spindle was returned.

"Oh, sorry, Your Grace, but I just couldn't hold it any longer," she said. "You should see your face."

Amelia could well imagine the look of astonishment she must have been wearing. It would only match how she felt.

"A few months back, before midwinter," Spindle began to tell her, "me and my Caius were in a town called Shepparton. It's in the Vec, south, a long way off. Anyhows, when we were there, we met this woman called Forever Countess. True as I sit here, her name was Forever Countess. And she really was like a countess, if Dalflitch is anything to go by. They could have made a pair, I swear."

Spindle took another drink, her previous reserved sip replaced with a hefty slug.

"Anyhows, turned out this woman, she's a teacher of manners, of all things. She ain't nothin' noble, leastwise that's what she says, but she teaches all the noble the bearin' a lady's s'posed to have, like it's an apprenticeship. Takes in girls and makes 'em proper. Did you know they had such things?"

Amelia had heard of instructors for ladies. Although they were uncommon in the Grand Kingdom, they were not unknown. In a sense, the noble mistress who had accepted her into service, Baroness Jayne Switch, had been a trainer of ladies. Of course, the baroness would never have done so for something as crass as mere payment. Until the end of her days, the baroness would consider Amelia to be indebted to her, but only to owe favors. She would never stoop to ask for money, even though she starved.

"Lady Dalflitch is such a teacher, you realize that?" the archduchess said, but Spindle shook her head.

"No, see that's not the same. Dalflitch is teachin' me and Righteous cause we're part of the same household, your chamber ladies. This Forever Countess, she does it for pay. I tell you, just like a guildsman and apprentices. Apprenticed ladies."

Spindle shook her head in wonder.

"And I take it she taught something to you?" Amelia asked, making the obvious connection.

"Did she what! My Caius hired her for me as a tutor, just 'cause I asked. No question, nothin'. Just a 'certainly, my wife,' and the next morning the Forever Countess is at our lodging door."

That's the second time you have called him 'your Caius,' My Lady, Amelia thought. *It seems I need not fear for the happiness of* your *marriage.*

"She taught you some more of lady-like behavior, I take it?" Amelia asked. The lady-in-waiting sat upright in her chair, and in an instant the new Spindle was back in place, as if it was a second mask, as easy as her lace one to take on or off.

"Does it not seem as if I have acq..." Spindle paused and was clearly trying to remember the word she wanted. She scowled and slapped her hand on her thigh.

"Acquired?" Amelia offered and Spindle nodded.

"That's the one, Your Grace. Forever Countess always says, don't reach too far for it if it don't feel natural. Doesn't have to be fancy, just not coarse. A lady speaks well or does not speak. Let 'em guess what you mean or think if you have to be silent a while. You are elegance and they must be in awe."

Amelia nodded at the courtly wisdom. "Lady Dalfitch would agree, I'm sure."

"Oh, yea. I can't wait to show her what I've learned."

The two women smiled at each other and then burst into girlish laughter, enjoying the ridiculous side of the manners that governed so much of their lives and the lives of all in the peerage. Amelia swiftly calmed them down though. Freeing as the moment was, it wasn't seemly to be giggling in the middle of an armed camp on campaign. War was still a serious business.

"All this is wonderful, Spindle, but what is it that has caused your husband to send you north early?"

Spindle's expression grew deadly serious.

"I bring a warning, Your Grace. There is conspiring in the Vec against you and against the Reach."

Amelia nodded.

"We have heard," she said.

Spindle's lips twisted in an annoyed frown.

"Well, what was the point of rushing...?" she began to say, then her new lady's persona resettled over her emotions like a second mask once more.

"No, it is good you heard as early as you did, Your Grace," she said, holding her hands up as if her feelings were a runaway animal that she was trying to calm. "I am pleased to learn that your need was served."

The words were so at odds with the old Spindle that Amelia almost broke into laughter once more. Only her appreciation for her friend and lady's efforts helped her to keep her own poise.

"I value your loyalty, My Lady," she said, her tone mimicking Spindle's formality. "And it is good you came so quickly, for what you have heard may be different or more than I know. Tell me the tale, if you please."

Spindle seemed to almost grow in her chair, she was so puffed with pleasure, and she folded her hands in her lap with concentrated composure. Amelia could see how much it delighted Spindle to converse like this, the way she must imagine two ladies of rank speaking together privately.

"When we traveled south," Spindle began, "Caius was mostly concerned with seeing to his holdings. He owns a..."

She paused, apparently contemplating the correct word.

"He owns a large number of holdings," she said, choosing simplicity over pretension as her new instructor had taught. Amelia smiled encouragingly.

"At first, I thought it was to be all trading, with me along to occupy his nights, if that ain...*is not* too coarse to say. Except it wasn't. I mean, we've had our husband-and-wife time, and you've never met a kindlier man. I swear, Your Grace, I think he's had years of love saved up and didn't even know it until he had me there to share it with. It's like a cask that's been so long in a cellar and no one's really sure how long anymore, but when you tap it..."

She raised her fingers to her lips and kissed them. Her expression turned wistful for a moment before she appeared to remember the serious purpose for the conversation.

"Sorry, Your Grace," she said. "You know how it is sometimes, I'm sure, when you're fresh married."

"I do," Amelia agreed, trying in her thoughts to reconcile the kind of warm affection she shared with Farringdon with what she knew of Caius Welburne. She smiled and forced herself not to show any disbelief or even wonder. She did not want to undermine her friend's joy.

"Well, anyhows, as Caius was doing business and looking to his accounts, he had to speak to other merchants, and not a few conclaves. He's a respected man in so many quarters, I never've guessed. In some of these places he started to hear stories and questions."

"Questions, My Lady," Amelia prompted, starting to feel a growing impatience and doing her best to keep it leashed.

"How's the Reach doing? Is it as bad as they say with the mad woman in charge? They meant you when they said that. I'm sorry, Your Grace."

Spindle's joy of a moment before, recalling her new marriage, was swept away and her eyes narrowed angrily, brows knotted.

"Merchants sure gossip. Caius says they all can talk, but the smart ones listen to guess which way the winds of business are blowing. To me it just sounds like wretched fishwife gossip, and they should keep it to themselves. Things they said about you, they were lucky I promised Righteous not to stick anyone while I was down there."

That was news to Amelia, and she wondered why the matter would even have occurred to Righteous in the first place. Were wives more likely to get into knife fights in the Vec? But Spindle was moving on, getting to the crux of the story.

"It all came out one night at a dinner we were invited to by a minor nobleman. Real fancy affair. If I hadn't had you and Dalflitch's examples, Your Grace, and Forever Countess' lessons, oh, the fool I would likely have made of myself. Still, everything is going well, and Caius is talking to some men he calls fin...finan..."

She drew in a breath and chose a different word.

"They were men of lending houses. Coin merchants. Well dressed, with lots of gold and tiny, sneery mouths. They were drinking and laughing, while Caius was leading them round to talk of loans. Then one of them let drop that it was good Caius had left the Reach cause no more coin was going up here from the Vec, not a copper. When asked what that meant, they said that the really big house, the Golden Heron, they had made some deal with someone in the Grand Kingdom to shut the Reach out of all trade, if it could be done. Where the Heron goes, the others follow, so Caius says, so all these sot's banks were going to close loans. Silver is the blood of business, that's what Caius says, and they can choke off that blood for you and the rest of us, Your Grace. Like throttling a little animal. These banker men, they laughed, said a woman fool enough to take up with heretics has invited trouble. And they said it was your fault the Redlanders had come. Can you believe that? All you've done, all Captain Prentice has done, and they blame you for everything. Ooh, my Caius was furious that night."

Amelia nodded. She could well imagine how angry she herself would have been in the presence of such men, even though it was exactly what she would have expected. It was only a slight variation of what Sebastian and the other exiles would be saying in the Grand Kingdom proper. In fact, it was exactly what Daven Marcus had said publicly more than once, by all accounts. Amelia was pleased to hear that Caius Welburne felt offended by such talk though.

"So, having learned of this, your husband sent you straight back home to tell me while he remained behind to continue with his business?" she asked. "That is most loyal."

Spindle shook her head and her eyes glittered with a fresh eagerness.

"Oh no, Your Grace, that's just the beginning. See, after that night, the first thing Caius did was to talk to other folk he knows in all sorts of places. You won't believe how jinxed all that went, like someone's right put the mockers on anyone coming out of the Reach. Eventually, someone told him there were agents, quiet men like, secretive. They sounded like stand-over lads to me, like a gang runs to collect protection, but one of Caius' friends insist they were Churcher types. I didn't even know the Church went into the Vec, the way sacrists go on all the time about heresy and splitting from the ordained throne and all that. But Caius says it's like an open-air secret that there's Church folk still in the Vec. Some of them's good ones, too, like Fostermae. These other ones, they're like some kind of smuggler types in the back rooms, running things quietly."

As she continued her story, Spindle's newly learned forms of speech were slipping more and more. Her eagerness to give the details to Amelia was obvious. For herself, Amelia was listening intently to the substance, not the form, focused on not missing any fresh detail that might be a key to unpicking the knots being tied around her lands. It was bad enough that the Inquisition had militants riding free in the Reach, able to cause who knew what harm, but to have their agents whispering against her in far lands was effrontery.

"Then, my Caius, with friends so far afield they come from places I hadn't even heard of, learned that there is a different word in Masnia. Seemed some of these agent types went that far south but got themselves caught up in something shocking. No one was clear what, but it was scandalous. Men were hanged and a whole flock of sacrists was expelled from the country. So, Caius figured he might go a bit farther afield and see what was what down there. He bid me wait for word from him, which only took like four days. They've got so many rivers in the Vec, boats are going all the time. It's like the High Road on a holy day, Your Grace, but with boats on rivers. One fellow I met claims he can walk from one side of the river to the other without his feet getting wet most days. They can travel so far, so fast."

"Fascinating," Amelia said, not meaning it in the least. She was much more interested in what Caius Welburne had learned in Masnia. "What was your husband's word?"

"Lifeblood, Your Grace," Spindle answered with a beaming smile. "Lifeblood."

"I don't understand." Amelia shook her head.

"Masnian merchants, they can't get past the Veckanders. Vec conclaves don't let any direct trade through from Masnia to the Grand Kingdom if they can help it. They tariff everything. And every prince gets his cut as well. It's like the whole land's a tollgate and the Masnians are furious about it. Caius has made touch with a handful of rich Masnians—real rich, by all accounts—and they want you to promise to make Aubrey open to them. There's a western path out of their land that comes close to Aubrey through some rough country with almost no patrols or Veckander bailiffs to tariff them on the way through. And they're ready to pay for the privilege."

"Pay?" Amelia asked, finding herself rising out of her chair in excitement.

"Gold, Your Grace. Seems they don't have silver like we do, not so much, but they have gold coins, and when they make big trades and compacts, then they use lots of gold. The Masnians want to cover your debts. Caius is putting it together now, an armed caravan to bring all sorts of goods, along with two strongboxes filled to the brim with Masnian gold coins."

Amelia wanted to laugh and cry at the same time. This news was such a relief. She jumped from her seat and embraced Spindle.

"Bless you, My Lady," she said as she held her friend close. "God bless you and your husband."

"Don't bless us just yet, Your Grace," Spindle said, returning the hug, but not without some hesitancy. "That caravan's coming the wild way to test the path. Until the gold's here, Caius says not to take anything for granted. The deal's not done until the coin changes hands, as he says."

"We are already heading south to assert my claim over Aubrey, Spindle," Amelia said as she released her lady and stepped back. "We will take the town into the Reach officially and secure the northern end of their journey. That caravan *will* bring us its cargo if we can do anything about it."

The archduchess looked about her tent and realized that she wanted to go back to her husband and see if there was any way they could gee their campaign southward from this walking pace to a proper trot, or even a gallop. She suddenly wanted to be in Aubrey as soon as possible.

CHAPTER 23

*D*ear Lord, don't let me chuck again, Righteous prayed inwardly. *Not here like this.*

The new baroness's morning sickness had not diminished, though her due day was nearer and nearer, despite what the midwives had told her to expect. Even on the mornings when her stomach was less upset, she felt queasy with worry for her babe until it kicked or moved again, which settled her fears but only added to her nausea in more typical ways.

"T'ain't fair," she muttered, thinking her words would be swallowed by the creak of the open carriage's wheels over the rough dirt track that had pretensions of being a road. As it was, her only fellow passenger was too attentive to miss even a single comment.

"Sorry, Baroness Righteous?" Solomon said, leaning forward. "I didn't hear what you said."

Righteous waved him away. She was content to make misery comments to herself, but she did not actually want to discuss her condition, especially not with a lad with only one foot on the last ladder to manhood. Maybe with her grace, Lady Dalflitch, or even Spindle, if she was back in the Reach. Otherwise, Righteous preferred to enjoy her discomfort on her own. For at least the first day of their journey to Fallenhill, that had been no problem. As expected, Solomon had been quiet, even a little sullen, disappointed as any other youth might have been to be given what they saw as a demotion in rank or responsibility.

In fact, in a quiet moment that night, Righteous had thought to give the lad some comfort, shine up his brass a little, and she reassured him that this would only be a temporary matter.

"I need you to help train these lasses, but you aren't just some flesh-and-blood pell," she had told him—a pell being a training post for swordsmen to practice against when an actual partner wasn't available. Often it had a single length of wood poking out in front to represent an enemy's sword arm. "You ain't just a dummy to thump on. Once these hopeful ladies-in-waiting are trained up and tested for loyalty, you'll be into a recruit cohort in Fallenhill yourself to become a militiaman in full. And while we're teaching these lasses, don't doubt I'll be giving you my canniest pointers. You're a dabber hand already than I think you realize."

For his part, Solomon had seen through her motives almost instantly, apologizing for his mood, even though she had said nothing about his dourness.

"I am a White Lion, My Lady," he'd said, as earnest as a sacrist preaching hellfire. "I go where my captain commands, no grousing and no hesitations! That is our way."

Righteous had accepted his words as she would a pledge of loyalty, but watching him later in the evening, tending to his chores, she found herself marveling somewhat.

You really have spent years marching at my Prentice's side, ain't you lad? she thought. *So straight up and spit-polished. We got to find you a proper lady to be betrothed to soon, or some twit doxy will scoop you up and ruin you.*

That, she would not have.

The carriage kept rocking and the rising morning sun warmed the day, making Righteous thirsty. Even the pleasant aroma of spring blooms that carpeted the fields beside the road in bright golds and whites, reds, purples and blues threatened to turn her stomach. She longed for a drink but refused to take more than a sip from the skin she kept with her in the carriage because these days anything she drank went straight

through her. The baby inside her left little space for her blad-
der to fill, and she refused to stop the company's march every
half a candle-mark to relieve herself—not because she feared
inconveniencing the militiamen. They were well enough
trained to do whatever they were commanded without question, just like Solomon had said *he* would. Besides, she was a
baroness now, and if she could not force a stop to take a pee
now and then, what good was her title?

"Must be nice, bein' able to ride in a carriage in the pleasant mornin' sun," called a voice from behind Righteous, reminding her why she would not call a halt for a latrine break.

At the vehicle's rear marched eighteen young women,
red-faced and sweating under bundles that contained all
their worldly goods—the would-be Lace Fangs. More in a
crowd than anything that resembled an actual column, the
soon-to-be trainees had hitched their skirts and huffed their
way between the carriage and the column's rearguard. The
Lions had initially made the occasional catcall to the young
women in front until their corporal enforced discipline with
threats of punishment. Now the men marched in silence, but
the women had no such junior officer to bring them to heel.
When they found the breath to make a comment, they felt
free to indulge themselves.

"You can't expect proper ladies to walk like us com-
mon-as-river-mucks, Daisy," another woman sounded off, her
voice shrill with the effort of making sure she would be heard.
"She's right better than us, no matter what is said 'bout her!"

Righteous was hard fixed on ignoring every word they
said, which was not as difficult as it might have been since
feeling ill took up most of her attention. Nonetheless, hot sun
and nausea made for a poor temper, and the yeoman sport of
anonymous cheek was starting to wear on her nerves.

"You can't blame 'er girls," the original voice said.
"Wouldn't you like a chance to ride like a duchess, drink in
hand and pleasant male company to boot?"

Drink in hand? If only, Righteous thought, but it was the "male company" that drew the other women's attention.

"I think it's male, Daisy, but I wouldn't call it pleasant," said one.

"Oh ay," another chimed in. "We had a suckling pig in my da's house last season, and it had a finer face than that one, even after we roasted it."

Righteous looked to Solomon, who was riding facing the rear and thus was fully visible to the mocking maidens. His face was red with embarrassment, and he put one hand to his scarred cheek, trying to hide it but only drawing more attention to the damaged skin.

"I don't know, I heard she likes 'em pig-faced like that," offered Daisy, clearly warming to her role as ringleader. "They say that husband o' hers is a right mass o' mangled old flesh."

That's true enough, Righteous thought, feeling her teeth begin to grind. *Though it's none o' your wretched business.*

It was offensive enough that they would tease loyal Solomon, but as far as the baroness was concerned, comments about her husband were tantamount to fighting words.

"Oh, he's not *all* scars," one of the women countered, her tone full of a mocking smile. "I seen him once down on the dockside. He's got a clean face and strong, with them deep grey eyes that are like cold, clean water. Gives you chills right down inside, like the first time your swain holds you tight, if you know what I mean. I'd sure step out with him once or twice at least, 'specially now they say he's a baron into the bargain."

"As if you'd be so lucky," Righteous shouted, spinning in her seat before she realized she was doing it. She scanned the women's faces, hoping to see which one had thought to make a claim on her husband's affections, eyes narrow like a hungry predator's. "If he noticed any o' you lot at all, it'd be to scrape you off like a clod o' dirt from the side o' his boot, and as pretty to him as all that, too!"

In her fury, there was nothing she wanted more than to skin one of her stickers and jump down from the carriage, challenging each woman in turn to make a comment to her face in the sight of bared steel. It was what Cutter Sal would have done once if some floosy had made comment about her man on the street. But Cutter Sal was gone, and in her place was Baroness Righteous, lady-in-waiting to the dignified and glorious Archduchess Amelia. Baronesses did not mix it up with mouthy maids, even maids on the path to ladyhood themselves. On top of which, Righteous's back ached, and even if she wanted to get down and make a knife fight of the issue, she had that sack of flour tied to the front of her belly—precious—but weighing her down all the same. Realizing how foolish she looked glaring at them, she flipped herself around in her seat, wanting to seem disdainfully superior and knowing she probably looked most like just another pouty lass.

"You told *them* off," Solomon whispered appreciatively, but Righteous shook her head.

"No, my colt-y lad," she told him. "All I done is show them where I'm weak, where they can poke me to get a rise. You watch, there'll be snidey remarks 'bout Captain Prentice every chance they get from now on. And 'bout your face, too, sorry to say."

"Knight Commander," Solomon corrected her, his scarred cheek twitching in an impudent grin. Righteous scowled, then felt her expression turn to a cunning smile as well.

"Don't you go forgettin' your place either, my colt!" she rebuked him quietly. "I won't take cheek from you any more than I'll take it from them riverside scolds, you hear me?"

Solomon returned her smile, but then his hand went to his cheek again and the still-vivid scar. It clenched Righteous's heart that her moment with this boy she loved like a nephew or even a son was stained by his fear of being ugly, or the thought that when she said "cheek" it had had some double meaning. He turned away to look at the fields and she let him. They rode on in silence but for the creak of the wheels, the buzzing of insects, and the tromp of marching feet.

Some while later, the company arrived at Fallenhill, marching around the village in its dale and up into the old town, now the training camp of the White Lions' recruits. Inside the gates, the corporal handed off to Sergeant Franken, commander of the training company. After a polite welcome for the new lady of the barony, Franken started ordering the newly arrived men-at-arms to their billets, giving them time to take water and food to refresh themselves before settling into whatever duties they would have while they were in the garrison.

Around the open parade ground and on the walls, the seemingly small numbers of recruits paused to watch the new arrivals, fascinated as all trainees were by the presence of fully uniformed fighters of the company. Here were the warriors the recruits aspired to become. A line first or corporal somewhere bellowed for his charges to return to their work, and around the marshalling yard and barracks huts similar orders echoed, bringing the entire armed camp back to its prime purpose. Remembering the days when Fallenhill had been a ruin and she had been cowering here with over two thousand other recruits, cold and hungry, the brightly sunny and orderly encampment seemed almost empty to Righteous's eyes, with only a few hundred trainees, though it would fill to the same numbers in the next few weeks. Adding a second banner to the Western Reach's military structure would double the number of the archduchy's men under arms before the end of summer. Another of her husband's military miracles, and it filled Righteous with pride.

Behind the carriage, with no officer overseeing them, the riverfolk women milled about a moment, taking in their surroundings with more hesitation and less satisfaction on their faces than Righteous felt. One of them noticed men drawing water from a well across the parade ground and a pair of them headed off in that direction. They had not gone a dozen paces when Righteous's voice sounded sharply after them.

"Where do you think you lot are off to, missies?" she demanded, standing in the carriage.

"We're thirsty is all," responded one of the two, and Righteous recognized her by her voice.

"You the one...," she began, but the effort of shouting had brought bile to her mouth. She coughed, then hawked and spat over the carriage side in an act as unladylike as any she could imagine. In her thoughts she heard the archduchess's voice chastising her.

You are a member of my chamber, Lady Righteous. You cannot be casting spittle about like an ostler with a mouth full of chew!

"Sorry, Your Grace," Righteous whispered, as if the archduchess were standing right there with her. There had been a time when the archduchess had struggled to get Righteous to even wear a dress. Not so anymore. The archduchess's honor was always a priority in her mind now. This situation, however, called for something different. "Forgive me, Your Grace, I'm going to have to be a bit rough for a moment."

Righteous looked the waiting women over with a cold glare, daring any one of them to laugh or even smirk at her "joyous" debilitation. Pointing to the carriage driver's goad, she told Solomon to hand her the thin, flexible pole. It was almost as long as she was tall.

"Right, startin' again," she shouted, rapping the goad on the carriage's side. "You the one called Daisy?"

"Ay," answered the woman with a round face and thick brown hair tied back in a braid that more resembled a rough boat cable than a lady's hairstyle.

We'll soon fix that, Righteous thought. *Once I'm done, just wait 'til Dalflitch gets her hands on you.*

"Well, Daisy, it seems to me that if you lot all had enough breath left to make all that conversing while you walked, it must mean that it wasn't too taxin' for you. Bein' as I'm a high-and-mighty baroness, a lacy little lady-thing, I 'course found it almost overwhelmin' just ridin' in the back o' this here wagon. But you and your riverfolker sisters there are all made o' sterner stuff, no doubt. So, I figure you don't need a drink, not just yet."

The women looked at each other in disgusted surprise, and Righteous was pleased to see more than one give Daisy an accusing glance. If the girl wanted to be a ringleader, she could take responsibility for where she led them.

"Solomon, get down," Righteous commanded, and the lad jumped readily to the ground. He might have expected to be required to help Righteous from the carriage, like a steward, and he stood clearly ready for the duty, but she had other ideas.

"You remember how to run the walls, Solomon?"

"Sure, I do...," Solomon began, but then he looked straight at Righteous's face, and she was glad he recognized the seriousness of her expression. Suddenly he snapped to attention and struck his fist to his chest. "Yes, My Lady, I do."

"Explain it to them."

Solomon looked around the walls, pointing as he described the circuit. "Up the west steps, along the ramparts all the way north, behind the workshops, then all the way down the east wall and down to the ground at the gatehouse step there."

"You feel like stretching your legs, colt?" Righteous asked him.

"I'd say I do."

She nodded, but before sending the youth off on Fallenhill's classic training run, she turned to face the women once more.

"Drop your bundles there, and when I send Solomon off, you'll go with him. Keep up and follow him every step, girlies, because when he comes back and is standing right here in front of me, I will begin counting off like this."

She rapped the goad on the carriage again, maintaining a count like the slow beat of a village dance.

"Whoever is not back standing here next to him by the time I reach a count of ten will be going back around the whole circuit another time before she's released to get herself a drink. Oh, and the last two, whoever they are, will be doing everyone's washing for the next week, hear me?"

"Why a count of ten?" asked Daisy with a surly look.

"And how fast is he?" demanded another.

"He's right quick on them long legs, my missies," Righteous said with a sneer. "I don't call him colt for nothin', don't you mind. And as for a count o' ten? Well, I'm such a lace-headed lady that I never learned how to count higher than that. Why would I? What do I count but stitches in needlework or number o' children I given my husband?"

The women all scowled at her, but Righteous enjoyed her moment of mockery, knowing that her common vernacular put paid to any claim of high birth. That would teach them to despise her. If they were proud of the hardship they had endured in their riverside life, then let them learn how proud she was of her own hardships.

"This is your first lesson in ladyhood," she declared.

"What, how to run behind an ugly fancy boy?" Daisy demanded.

"No, how to keep your mouth shut or pay the piper for the dance you called." She turned to Solomon and nodded. "Off you go, lad."

Solomon saluted again, then spun on his heel and dashed away like a runner in a foot race.

"Oh, bloody hell," one of the women called as they started off after him. "Never mind a colt, he's swift like one o' them fey ponies!"

"Shouldn't 'a called him pig face, should you?" Righteous called after them.

She watched the little parade of women as they lifted their skirts to rush up the first set of stairs. Solomon was already loping along the rampart, deftly avoiding squads of trainees that were certain to slow the women coming after him. Righteous sighed and sat again, resting her back for a moment and enjoying her petty victory. She wondered how her husband, or the archduchess, would have responded to this situation. Neither favored revenge for its own sake, but Righteous suspected that Prentice would have chosen some kind of punishment, such as a run, and for exactly the same reason she had—because discipline was core. The former pit fighter and street rowdy knew she was nothing like the self-possessed archduchess, much less than her iron-willed husband. But she saw the value of the self-control they practiced and had induced some measure into her own wild character. Cutter Sal had been a frenzied fool of a young woman who had gotten herself branded, raped, and nearly killed. Baroness Righteous had to rise above such wildness, at least somewhat, both for the dignity of her liege and the needs of her new lands. Wild nobles made for poor rulers, like the kingslayer Usurper.

But woe betide any twit that thinks my high rank means I was highborn, with nothin' but lace and fluff between my ears, she thought. The first lesson she wanted these hopefuls to learn was that she was nobody's fool, least of all theirs.

CHAPTER 24

"An ugly little saltpan, Commander," Gennet whispered as he crouched beside Prentice in the long grass on a low rise looking down into a broad, shallow dale where the Inquisition riders had made a camp for themselves. The middle of the dale was a depression filled with murky water, almost certainly undrinkable. At the water's edges the dark mud was bleached pale, a sign that there was a good deal of salt leaching from the earth into the tiny sump-water. Some dead trees were dotted around the edges of the water, as well as in it, indicating that it was not very deep at all. With only the worthless water and the sweeping green grass of the open plain, there was little about the location to recommend it for a campsite.

Despite this, the Inquisition force had constructed a strongly defended bivouac, with several of the trees cut down to form improvised barricades on three sides. Only the waterside of their camp, which butted right up against the murky shore, had any opening. It looked like they must ride in and out through the shallows.

"I wouldn't camp here," Gennet said quietly, expressing the obvious sentiment of everyone in this little scouting party. Besides Prentice and the sergeant, they had Benjamin and another fey archer, as well as two Fangs. Claws, with their halberds and pikes, would have had too much difficulty staying hidden. One of the two men Prentice had ordered along was Lyrach, the ex-squire. The knight commander did not want to reward the man's obvious politicking, but he also did not want to have him out of sight for too long—not until he was sure where the man's loyalties lay.

"I think we can safely say this spot has other advantages to recommend it, Sergeant," Prentice said.

"You think this water has masks or other powers, Commander?" Lyrach asked, but Gennet ordered him to mind his tongue. Prentice did not interfere, but he was glad Lyrach had recognized the true danger of the situation. He looked at Benjamin.

"Have you seen them use any mask magicks?" he asked.

"No," was the fey leader's typical reticent response.

"They might have used them without you noticing," Lyrach said, not taking Gennet's rebuke at all to heart.

"We have watched," Benjamin responded.

"But if they saw you, they might've known to hide their actions."

"We pass unseen."

"It's all very well to say that, but if they are truly cunning, how would you know?" Lyrach persisted.

"We pass unseen," Benajamin repeated, and there was a brittleness to his voice.

"Lyrach, shut your mouth now or you'll be digging the whole company's latrines for the rest of the march, d'you hear me!" Gennet whispered savagely.

Prentice ignored the interaction. Gennet knew how to keep order and needed no help. The knight commander kept his attention on the trees in the water, picking out the best guesses for masks to be placed. He thought he could see an opposing pair of dead trunks that made likely candidates, though at this distance any mantis mask nailed to them was invisible to him. There was another tree just in front of the Inquisition camp that could have served as a third cardinal point to mount a mask, but the camp's tree-trunk fence obscured most of it from his vision.

He drew his comrades' attention to the one possible mask tree farthest to the east, the one most visible from their vantage.

"What do you see around its base?" he asked.

"Something like roots or bundles of sticks," Gennet said.

"Bones," said Benjamin confidently. Prentice nodded. That had been his thought as well. Sergeant Gennet looked from his leader to the fey and then back.

"That's a big pile, if it's bones," he said.

"About what you would expect if a number of people had been chained to the trunk and left to starve?" Prentice suggested. They all nodded grimly in agreement, remembering the bodies of the sacrificed in the swamp by Lake Dweltford. Bleed or shed blood—it was clear now that sacrifice was how the Redlanders sanctified their sites to whatever demon gods they worshipped.

"Can these be truly Church knights?" Lyrach asked, forgetting his place once again. "Wouldn't Inquisition men-at-arms take such vile shrines apart? Is that not their duty?"

"You got a lot to learn, mate," said the other Fang present, a corporal, and this time Gennet did not bother to command silence. Even with their combined experiences, men often forgot themselves when confronted with the invaders' horrors.

Prentice kept watching the camp for what must have been nearly half an hour, making plans and testing them in his mind against what he could see. At one point, four of the knights in armor mounted up and rode out of the rough stockade. He wondered for a minute if they had been spotted, but the four rode in an outward-spiraling circuit around the water. Their horses' hoofs kicked up the salty dust in filthy, grey puffs.

"A patrol," Prentice said to himself, then he looked to Benjamin. "How often do these happen?"

"Three times a day," said the fey leader.

"And do they circle as far out as this?"

"Sometimes."

"Then we better be gone before they get here," Prentice commanded, and he pointed behind himself north to where the rest of the Lions were camped a few leagues away. If the patrol spotted them before they managed to get back to their main body, there was a good chance that would be the end of them. Three leagues was enough distance for the riders on patrol to return, rouse the whole Inquisition camp, and bring it down upon them before Prentice and his companions could even get close enough to call for help.

"We pass unseen," Benjamin said, as if repeating the refrain of a hymn, but then he looked at the Lions. "But you will leave marks of your passage, if they are diligent to look for them."

"Nothing we can do about that now," Prentice said sourly, and he led the small cadre as they half crawled, half duck-walked their way north, doing their best to keep their heads below the level of the grass. It was only after they had gone several hundred paces and allowed another sweep of hummocks and undulations in the land to give them some cover that Prentice permitted his men to half stand and walk bent over.

"Benjamin, can your riders circle around to the south of their camp before dawn tomorrow?" Prentice asked after looking to the sky a moment. It was not long before dusk. For an answer, Benjamin only sniffed derisively.

"Alright, then this is what we will do," Prentice explained as they continued northward. He was reasonably confident the patrol would not find them now, at least not before they reached the strength and safety of the others.

"Tonight, the fey will ride around to the south of that water and wait, hidden. The rest of us will sneak up directly in the dark and set ourselves behind that rise we were on. At dawn, or just before, we will form up and make a noisy assault, marching to their camp. While we do that, Benjamin—as soon as you hear the drums, in fact—I want your riders to come up and encircle the water. You will stop any who tries to escape. At the same time, look for masks and destroy them. We do not want another nasty surprise dropping upon us out of the sky."

"We can do this," Benjamin replied, nodding once.

"When it comes to the camp itself, leave that to the Lions," Prentice said, taking the time to meet Benjamin's gaze. "Mark me, Benjamin, the ones in the camp are ours. I want prisoners this time. Any that flee, make anteaters of them as much as you want. Those that remain, even if they are *brakkis effar*, are my prisoners. I speak as an elder on this."

Benjamin's face twitched slightly and the other fey man with them said something in their own tongue, but Benjamin did not reply. Prentice wished he could have Solft translate, but he knew there was no way he would remember any of the unfamiliar words to repeat them later.

"Seems simple enough, Knight Commander," said Lyrach readily, and his eager expression turned to a resentful frown when Sergeant Gennet cuffed him across the back of the head.

"Get yourself a shovel when we get back," Gennet commanded. "If you're going to be as thick as two short planks, then we'll have to make sure you get the kinds of simple duties you can't foul up."

Lyrach looked past the sergeant at Prentice, as if he hoped for a reprieve, but when it did not come he hung his head resignedly and marched the rest of the way back in silence. Later, when Gennet rolled his eyes behind Lyrach's back, Prentice gave his sergeant an approving nod. Lyrach was starting to seem too eager, too impatient even, to be a spy of any kind. However, that just made him needful of other attentions, and Prentice was happy to leave that duty to Sergeant Gennet.

"Tell the men quietly no huzzahs," the knight commander told the second-in-command as they returned to the Lions, "but ready them for battle in the morning."

CHAPTER 25

The Lion Banner Company approached the Aubrey bridge across the Murr River under the shoulder of the last ridge of the mountains. Even as she rode in the bright sunlight, Archduchess Amelia felt a momentary chill when she looked up to the ridge and saw the burned-out remains of the watchtower where she had lodged two years earlier. The memory of that time had dimmed in light of more recent events, but seeing the ruined pile so close brought back many of the emotions of those terrifying nights and the days that followed.

"Have we sent scouts to the tower?" Amelia asked her husband, riding beside her. "It looks as if it remains a ruin, but it might be being used as a lookout."

"Good thinking, my love," Farringdon said and wheeled his horse about to find riders to send to the task. Amelia kept herself upright in the saddle, projecting the dignity of a ruling peer, sovereign in her own lands. The green meadows around her, flush with the verdant grass of winter and the vibrant flowers of spring, seemed too joyous for her memories, as if the sacrifices of her men-at-arms were somehow dishonored by this new life.

Most likely it is the sudden clash of the bright present with my gloomy recollections, she thought, though a sudden mix of aromas on the breeze threatened to turn her stomach for a moment. Spring was not normally such a riot of smells, and she shook her head to throw off the melancholy of her thoughts. The dead would not be honored by living in endless grief.

Farringdon returned at a canter. "I've detached a handful of lancers to investigate, Your Grace," he said.

It made Amelia smile at the way he maintained his commitment to guard her dignity. It seemed almost every other day he found ways to honor his oath to her that he would never try to overmaster her place as the preeminent ruler of the Reach. He was her husband, and in private he might exert some authority, although she had yet to see him do it. In public, she was Archduchess, supreme over even her own spouse.

"I doubt the Redlanders would set one of the knight commander's magick mask shrines up there so far from the river and the water," Farringdon said, "but you are right, of course, that we must be sure."

In fact, Amelia had been thinking that some bandits or sentinels from a Veckander force might have taken up residence in the ruined tower. The notion of another clutch of Redlander converts secreted away had not occurred to her.

"I suppose we will have to get into the habit of looking under every rock and behind every bush," she mused sadly, her hope for happiness further driven back by unpleasant thoughts. Even with the Ragmother's advice, being watchful was surely the wisest course. She looked to her right where the River Dwelt was flowing broad and strong to its consummation with the Murr. The river's edge was a tangle of high reeds.

"I trust we have scouts poking through the riverside as well," she asked, and Farringdon smiled back.

"That, at least, I have managed to think of for myself."

"Of course, Knight Captain," Amelia said and sighed. The thought that any dark corner of her land might conceal a monster galled her deeply. Her people should not have to live in fear, although of course she knew this was the way of the world to some degree. In a sense, such was the purpose of things like fey tales—they taught children to be wary in a world where, if not witches and grumpkins, there were at least wild animals and untrustworthy folk that could endanger them beyond the edges of civilization. Except, of course, that now the dark shadows contained not only the usual dangers of outlaws and beasts but also actual witches and fey from legends. For centuries, the Grand Kingdom and its neighbors had been spreading the influences of civilization, following the scripture's injunction to "go forth into the world and subdue it," and now it seemed that all their progress was folly, built on arrogant self-deception. The world was far from subdued and perhaps never would be. Worse, the institutions entrusted to lead the way, like the throne and the Inquisition, were actively fighting that civilizing mission. At least that was how it seemed to Amelia.

For another hour the company marched in the sunlight, the jingle of their harness and tromp of their feet mingling with the calls of birds and humming of insects. As Amelia let her thoughts brood, she worked them to the present and then brought them back to their mission here in the south, planning what next moves they would have to make once they arrived at Aubrey.

All of which are flights of fancy until I know what we will actually be facing, she thought.

When the bridge across the Murr came into view, Amelia was surprised at how normal it seemed. She realized that she did not really know what she had expected to see, but her last memory of it was from the night of the Red Sky and the days immediately after. It would not have seemed shocking if the ancient bridge had been completely gone. Shortly after arriving, she and Farringdon had ridden with an escort up to the little hilltop where King Chrostmer had mounted his accursed Bronze Dragons and shot fire and stone down upon the Redlander's boat bridge.

And my loyal men, she recalled bitterly.

From the hilltop, the ground in every direction seemed to have forgotten the battle, although when she looked closely at the earth beneath Silvermane's hooves, she could see the ruts that the cannon's wheels had dug into the ground. Farringdon pointed to a shape on the bank of the Murr a short distance upriver from the bridge.

"That would be one of their boats, I think," he said. "We'll have to look to that. And there's another one, or half of one."

He pointed to one of the bridge's stone footings. Amelia felt a mild sense of satisfaction that there was at least some memory of her enemy's suffering also in this place. Now that she was here, however, the past was not her primary concern. Sitting up in the saddle, she strained to look across the river to the region on the opposite bank called Cattlefields, the little Crossroads village, and Aubrey itself. The town's walls still stood, lichen growing on cut stone, and the ground in front of them was as green with grass as the rest of the fields and meadows. Amidst that grass was a little cluster of huts which reminded Amelia of the refugee shantytowns outside the Reach's major settlements. It made her wonder if there were refugees from the war crossing the Murr as well as the Azures. She would have thought the Vec princes would deny them, but perhaps that was part of Aubrey missing its ruler.

"That is my uncle's army, I would say," Farringdon said and pointed toward a camp of tents off to their left, just north of Crossroads. There were colorful pennants flying from poles, and sunlight glinted off polished steel as men marched about.

"Will Prince Garrodmin oppose us, do you think?" Amelia asked.

"He contests our marriage, which means he contests your claim, Your Grace," Farringdon said. "The letters I've received have made it clear he thinks Aubrey is his."

Amelia looked over the far encampment and then back towards the town.

"Why isn't he inside the walls then?" she asked. "Surely that is the stronger position. Why not billet his men there? If that is all he has, it is not more than we have. Aubrey's walls could swallow the whole of our force and not even notice."

"Word is that Aubrey's haunted," said the lancer sergeant leading their escort. He noticed that both nobles were looking at him and he pointed in the town's direction, waving at the walls. "That's what the hovels are, My Lady, Captain. The few of the Aubrey folk still alive won't go back in there to live, so they have made what they can outside. Tis a grim life."

Amelia was so shocked by the rider's words that it did not even occur to her to correct his misused term of respect.

Is that truly all that remains? she wondered. What she had thought was a refuge addition to the outside of Aubrey was actually the remnant of its total population. She knew the stories of the brutality and starvation the occupation had inflicted, but this news made it suddenly and freshly real to her.

"Your uncle thinks to seize the land but does not seem to think of the people, leaving them in poverty?" Amelia declared through gritted teeth as she looked from the wattle and daub huts to the bright tents.

"My uncle is not a strong man," Farringdon said quietly in response. "Sorry to say."

"Strong enough to try to take what does not belong to him, though."

Her husband bowed his head. Amelia knew he was only showing dutiful respect for his family, but Farringdon's explanations for his uncle's behavior were beginning to annoy her. Even as they watched, a rider could be seen leaving the Vec camp, aiming straight to the bridge, striking his mount's flanks with his reigns and driving it to a full gallop.

"A messenger, do you think?" asked Farringdon. "A call to parley? They have likely seen us by now."

The rest of the Lion Banner was already marching near the bank of the river under the shadow of their hill. Any Veckander lookouts on the southern side of the river had to have seen them by now.

"He's surely going hell for leather," the lancer sergeant observed. The rider did not spare his horse as he reached the bridge, and even from a distance, the mount's iron-shod hooves could be heard clattering on the boards as it made the crossing. Man and mount drummed over the river at full pelt. Then the rider turned his horse back northeast, away from Amelia's army and toward the heart of the Grand Kingdom.

"If he is a messenger, his message is not for us," Amelia said. She watched the lone man recede into the eastern distance, the long-grassed meadows and overgrown croplands swallowing him up. When he was out of her sight, she looked past the land to the manor house, with its garden courtyard where then Prince Daven Marcus had slain his father and seized his throne. She shuddered once again and could feel her thoughts turn darker still. The Redlander invasion had been a horror, a blight upon the lands for years before, but it was that act of treason on that night that had set fire to the whole world.

"How tired are our men-at-arms, Knight Captain?" Amelia asked, her tone turning imperious to reflect the simmering anger in her soul at so much death, so much destruction and slaughter, and the petty noblemen who dispensed it for their own selfish ends and promptly forgot. Perhaps they thought new seasons would spring afresh upon society and new growth would cover their sins, as spring grass covered the scenes of their crimes. Well, no more. She would not allow it.

Farringdon looked to the sun.

"It is past noon, Your Grace," he said. "We could array for battle this afternoon if you command, but I would prefer to wait for morning, if you'll permit."

"Will that not simply give your uncle more time to prepare?"

"It will, but it will also give us the same time," Farringdon explained. "And I am confident that both our mettle and our preparations will be the superior."

Amelia felt some satisfaction at his confidence. Her growing fury was crying out for justice, for retribution, and as the land's liege and highest judge, she intended to deliver it. She was, however, able to hold her feelings enough in control to realize that they did not have to rush.

"Very well, go to, Knight Captain. We will cross the bridge on the morrow and drive your uncle and his men out of my lands."

Farringdon bowed in the saddle and turned to his lancer sergeant.

"Send word to set camp near to the foot of this hill to control our end of the bridge. Wherever that rider went, we must make sure he is the last. Also, tell the waggoneers and ostlers to bring the cannons up here."

Amelia shot her husband a disturbed glance, the mention of cannons on this hilltop offending her sense of justice with the memory of the last time such weapons had been here, as well as the way they had been used.

"You think that right?" she asked indignantly, and Farringdon looked at her, brows knotted.

"If they are as accurate as Master Sent believes, from here we could control the approach to the bridge from the other side, as well as much of the far bank both east and west," he said, giving the military justification. "This is by far the best vantage for them, Your Grace."

"King Chrostmer thought exactly the same for his Bronze Dragons," Amelia said, suddenly overwhelmed by a sense of disgust with her husband. It was unjust, she knew, but somehow she could not control it, not fully. She wheeled Silvermane about, looking to leave before her tongue got loose and said something she might regret. Nonetheless, she threw a cold rebuke at him before she rode away.

"However accurate these new war engines of yours are, Knight Captain, see to it that they are better aimed than the dead king's were. I will sacrifice no more White Lions to such engines of war."

"Where are you going, love?" Farringdon asked her. He had surely sensed her shift in mood, and it concerned him enough to be more familiar with her in public. It was not a lapse as such, more an attempt to see to her needs. Even so, for some reason, it only increased her distemper.

"I am going, husband, to find some place that is not so well suited to machines of murder. If you can think of such a place, then look for me there."

She put her heels to Silvermane's flanks and left her husband to his preparations for battle. Tomorrow, the order would be given for further combat on these fields that had already seen so much, and more folk would suffer and die. If she were forced to stay amidst the preparations for the bloodshed, she knew she would end the day by screaming in tears and rage. And such would not be seemly for an archduchess, not even the Lioness of the Reach.

CHAPTER 26

Dawn crested the grassed horizon and Prentice gave his men the nod. Drummers stood as they had been instructed, and his five cohorts rose from their hiding spots. They had been waiting, lying in the tall prairie fauna, since just after midnight. In shifts they had snatched hours of sleep while the rest kept watch. Through the tense hours they had kept alert, fearful they would be discovered, but no other patrols left the Inquisition camp. Behind their branch-and-trunk fence, the enemy had spent the night around their fires, horses whickering occasionally. Only once did someone emerge—two men in armor—who walked around the fence with a lit torch, apparently checking for signs of wild animals.

Now the day was on them, and the ambush began.

Fangs and Claws were set in tight squares, eighty men each, while the Roar—a hundred gunners in total—were divided into two concentrated corps on the flanks. Prentice wanted to maximize their fire. If the enemy knights made another ride for freedom, his gunners might only get a single volley away, and this would give them a better chance to make that one shot count. As a coherent front, the whole company marched straight down into the shallow dell toward the fenced enclosure. Prentice had already explained to Gennet and the cohort corporals that he planned to march around the east side of the little fort and then to wheel right and capture the one entry point.

"If any ride out, let them have iron shot," he told them, "But concentrate on capturing those that remain behind."

They had managed to cross half the distance to the camp before the first trumpet sounded within, and they were close enough that Prentice could see men inside, moving about rapidly. The sounds from the horses made him think they were mounting up.

Good, he thought. *Sally, you mongrels. You can learn the Lions' way of war firsthand.*

Even though the wooden fence was a rough defense that was almost too humble to even be named a fort, it was still an advantage to any who would hide within it. Prentice would much rather face knights on an open field where the White Lions were at their strongest.

There was another blast of the trumpet and Prentice wondered if some were coming out already. He tried to think whether it would be better for him to slow their march and let the riders emerge or to continue the swift pace to prevent escape. Their marching line was already to the east of the camp, and he could see most of the mudflat with its salt-poisoned trees. It was nothing like as dense as the swamp on the edge of Dweltford Lake had been, and on the far side he could make out the fey riders gathering, some splashing through the shallows. That was good; any evacuees would be intercepted. Benjamin would likely not take prisoners but having them stopped would be good enough. Prisoners to interrogate would be invaluable, but destroying the Inquisition presence in the Reach was the ultimate goal, and Prentice would accept that. He just hoped the fey would find any masks before it became an issue. He had no idea how easily these heretical Church men might be able to call upon their bloodthirsty allies.

So, we go fast and hard, he thought and kept his post in the middle of the line beside the Gryphon standard. His horse, Boots, was tied to a tent peg back with Master Solft, Brother Whilte, and the rest of their sparse luggage. Learning to ride was one thing, but mounted combat was not a skill Prentice ever expected to acquire. Leaving the chaplain behind had been a difficult choice, but one Prentice felt was best. As a renegade member of the clergy, the Inquisition horsemen might target him as a high-value prize.

The line came close to level with the fort's other side and Prentice gave word for the company to wheel, the right end forming an anchor point while the rest of the line turned a quarter circle. It was a simple enough maneuver, and one every Lion had drilled hundreds of times, but as the left end came around, they started marching into the shallow water, and that end began to break up as the militiamen's feet were sucked at by mud or tangled in hidden branches or other hazards. Thus delayed, by the time the maneuver was complete Prentice could see the entry in the southern fence—a simple gap, three or four paces wide. Sitting in the middle were two knights ahorse, clad in steel harness with their triple-cross tabards and helmets in place. Behind them, through the small gaps in the fence, Prentice could make out the rest of the enemy force, or most of them, at least, all mounted and ready to ride out. One of the two in the gateway lifted the visor of his helmet.

"Inxyphos," Prentice said under his breath, recognizing the enemy leader.

"Good Lord, Ashen Man?" Inxyphos said in a tone that made it sound like he had just come across an unexpected guest at a friend's banquet. "Well, aren't you just the faithful and dogged little retainer?"

"Did you imagine we would not come for you—you and your men, Inxyphos?" Prentice shouted back. He was happy to parley a little while the fey continued their search and he judged the distance from his force to the gateway. There was no way they would get to the opening before the knights could enact whatever defense they had planned, but he could simply order an assault to force the issue. If he did that, though, it would disrupt the company's formation, as maneuvering through the shallows had demonstrated. That could even be what Inxyphos was hoping for. Lions in close order were the superior of even the best Kingdom knights, but there was nothing a horseman loved better as a target than a group of men afoot with a broken formation. Such were significantly easier meat to chew.

"In truth, *Captain*, I imagined you dead," Inxyphos said sardonically, an arch tone emphasizing his pronunciation of Prentice's rank. "That's what we were promised. Still, I suppose you have a fair list of slain behind you who all promised the same thing. Perhaps I should not be so surprised. You ever exceed the boasters."

"Knight Commander now," Prentice said, not exactly sure why he bothered to correct Inxyphos. "And Baron as well. Baron Ash."

His revelation seemed to truly surprise the Inquisition leader, and Inxyphos cocked his head to one side, as much as his armor allowed.

"How could that...?" he began, and then he seemed to realize. "Oh, of course. The lion bitch is making full use of her purloined authority, I see. Well, don't put too much store in it, loyal hound. It will not save you from the noose when the time comes. No headsman's sword for you. That is reserved for true nobility, I'm afraid."

"It is also for those who are defeated and captured first," Prentice retorted. "As you have mentioned already, there are more who thought to do that than have actually achieved it. Best not to get ahead of yourself."

In the ranks around him, several of the men chuckled at his comment and Prentice saw Inxyphos scowl. That made him smile, but as he did so, he felt strong tension in his jaw, and it surprised him. He had not realized he felt so taut. So far, everything was going as he had hoped. Then he realized that the tension was not from his emotions but was in the atmosphere around him. He could hear his men shifting uncomfortably, water splashing around their ankles. The air was starting to hum, and in the bright morning sun he could see it causing fine ripples on the surface of the brackish water.

Around the other side of the boggy ground, he saw the fey riders coming about the water's edge in a column, trailing their second and third horses. Prentice watched and wondered what they were doing. They were supposed to be hunting out those masks.

And now it was too late.

The insect-wing drone echoed around the dell, rising until it made Prentice's ears ache. He felt a sudden fury with Benjamin and the rest of the fey. In their obsession with revenge, they had not even bothered to try to find the masks. They wanted the kill, and now he and they would have to face Inxyphos's knights, as well as whatever force was coming through the sky.

"Take warning! 'Ware the sky! The sky!" Sergeant Gennet shouted, also recognizing what was coming, and men watched as the dell acquired a mirrored roof. Prentice had already briefed his men that this was a possibility, and every corporal and line first gave his charges the order to be ready for whatever was coming.

How many boats this time? Prentice thought. In broad daylight and with his men in formation, the knight commander favored his force's chances against even two or three Redlander boat crews. Any more than that, added to the Inquisition knights who were sure to sally forth now and attack, could prove a challenge, at least until the fey started raining down arrows across the water.

And straight at us, Prentice thought, even more annoyed by Benjamin's insubordinate behavior. With the enemy between them, any arrows of the fey that went wide or long would be landing amongst Prentice's men. Surely even such magnificent archers were about to wound at least some of their allies.

The knight sitting next to Inxyphos drew his leader's attention, pointing at the fey riders approaching.

"Well, well, *Baron* Ashen Man," the Inquisition militant said, "you really have come to play, haven't you? Sad to say though, I simply cannot stay for a game. I have a previous assignation, and my masters would be most unhappy if I missed it."

The droning grew, and as water appeared in the sky over their heads, the daylight began to glitter with iridescence. Prentice watched it play over himself and the water, over the entire dell, and he was suddenly struck with the memory of the dragonfly drawn in the corner of Solft's little codex. The shifting colors were much like the glitter of dragonfly wings. He stared up into the warping sky, desperate to see if there was such a creature there, imagining something enormous and terrifying. He was sure it must be, and that meant that whatever other fancies the author Borossod had invented for his book, the ancient writer must either have seen or learned of the lake Benjamin had spoken of. What other secrets did the little tome contain?

Inxyphos suddenly yelled a command and spurred his mount. A trained warhorse, built for explosive power, it was into a gallop almost immediately. The man next to Inxyphos did the same, followed by all the others behind in column. Prentice steeled himself for the charge, sword drawn and ready for the coming melee. Inxyphos did not lead his column to attack the Lions, however. Neither did they wheel toward the fey or try to make a dash for escape. Instead, they charged straight at the water, as if following a road under the surface directly into the space where the iridescence was deepest, the air there alive with a coruscation of gold and green, purple and red.

"Fire," Prentice bellowed, suddenly realizing the Inquisition knights' true intent. The Roar on the ends of the line fired, and at least two knights fell, while others had shot ringing on their armor. Prentice looked through the colored air at the fey, expecting to see a swarm of arrows flying like angry hunting birds at the retreating enemy, but not a single fey he could see had their bow to hand. Rather, Benjamin stood in the stirrups and raised his saddle axe over his head, wheeling it about, and the column of fey charged into the water toward the knights.

"Damned fool!" Prentice swore. What possessed Benjamin to think he could fight the knights hand-to-hand? He looked to Inxyphos's force as it was reaching the middle of the water. Through the droplets sprayed from the charging destriers and the deep, impossible colors of the air, Prentice had already lost sight of the front of their column. Soon they would be gone to the dragonfly lake at the far end of the Murr. All Prentice could hope for now was that they had left some clues behind in their camp, anything that might shed more light on the Inquisition's plans and agents in the Reach. Perhaps one or both knights who'd been felled by shot were still alive.

"Damn, they're going in after them," he heard Lyrach shout from his place elsewhere in the line, the former squire's voice now unmistakable to Prentice's ear. For the first time, the knight commander felt no urge to rebuke the ambitious young man for speaking out of turn. Lyrach was right. As they all stood, ankle-deep in foul water, their allies splashed through the magickal light, fading into it as if into a deep fog, and suddenly the droning stopped. The air was the clear, bright sunshine of a summer morning now flashing in the reflections on the agitated water. Everything was quiet. It was all over. Inxyphos and his knights had escaped again, and Benjamin had taken his *keshiyaa* with them.

"What do we do now, Commander?" Gennet asked, his voice conveying what they all must feel—disappointment mixed with utter bewilderment.

"Fall out, Sergeant," Prentice told him. He looked to the now-empty fortification. "Go see if either of those two that fell is still alive, and the rest of us will see if the bastards left us any food or drinking water."

Sergeant Gennet gave the orders and the Lions moved to obey. Prentice stood and watched for a long moment, trying to absorb what had just happened. At last, he moved to join the rest of his men.

"Damn them," he cursed under his breath. What else was there to say?

CHAPTER 27

A t dawn, the Lion Banner Company was already arrayed by cohorts, just to the west of the Aubrey bridge. Archduchess Amelia was ready with them, sitting her saddle on Silvermane's back. Summer was fully upon the land now, so that almost as soon as the sun crested the horizon, the air was warming quickly.

It is like to be a hot day, Amelia thought, watching daylight stretch over the land. *Best if this business is settled early.*

Farringdon assured her that the day would bring a victory. Scouts, sent up and down the river in the night to see what they could across the water, had returned with news that the bridge itself was guarded only by a few sentries making a desultory effort to watch their end of the crossing.

"I would have had at least a cohort's worth there, my love," he had told her once he heard that news in the hours before dawn. "The bridge is a perfect choke point to bottle us up."

"Why so few then?" Amelia asked in response.

"I think, my love, that they do not rate us a great chance of winning."

"I thought we outnumbered them," she said. She had seen glimpses of the enemy camp in the meadows across the river from multiple points during the previous day, and everyone she spoke to had estimated about the same number of Veckander troops—approximately a thousand—which was less than half the Lions' number.

"And our weapons are far the superior," Farringdon added. "My only thought is that they underestimate our mettle because..."

His voice trailed away, and Amelia realized why he did not finish his sentence. He did not wish to offend her.

"Because we are led by a woman?" she asked rhetorically, cocking an eyebrow at her husband. He grimaced apologetically, but she was not angry at him. "How many will make this mistake before they learn? Liam, Duggan, Sebastian, even Daven Marcus—all of them underestimated me, and here I am yet."

"Lioness of the Reach," Farringdon said and bowed to her. "Perhaps we could publish a chronicle of your victories, spread your fame abroad in the world?"

Amelia had wondered if he were teasing her, but he seemed at least mostly serious. She shook her head at the notion.

"Even if they read of it, they would not believe it."

"Then it must be a lesson we teach them all until there are none left who do not know it," Farringdon had declared and then kissed her hand.

Until there are none left who do not know it, Amelia thought as she waited for the army to march. From where she was, she could not quite see all the way across Cattlefields to the Veckander camp, but there were no sounds of an enemy army rapidly marshaling anywhere in the south. If they were watching, they should have seen the Lions in array and be readying themselves to fight.

The order was given, and the drumbeat began for the march. Amelia sat up higher in her saddle, back straight. Amidst her troops, she had made sure to dress in Reach colors, wearing her blue overdress with the two embroidered silver lions opposed rampant upon the skirt—one male, one female. When she rode with the Lions, no one should mistake her place in the pride. Not that she would ride in the vanguard. That dangerous duty was given to the most experienced cohort, a hundred militiamen that Farringdon was already calling the "prime." Instead, the archduchess was in the middle of the column with the lancers, sitting Silvermane beside the sergeant who had commanded her escort the day before.

"What is your name?" she asked him as they began to walk to the bridge.

"Nunel, My Lady," he told her.

"I am Your Grace," she corrected him. He nodded with an unconcerned smile that reminded her somewhat of Turley and his insouciance.

"Yes, I am sorry, Your Grace," he said. "The knight captain mentioned it last night, but I forgot."

Amelia accepted the apology with a nod of her own. It did not sound insincere precisely, just not attached to any emotion. She suspected he meant no offense, but he also did not especially fear offending her.

"Where are you from, Sergeant Nunel? I cannot place your accent."

"Boorne, Your Grace, about a hundred or so leagues south southeast of here."

"You are a Veckander?" Amelia looked at him in surprise. She knew, of course, that there were likely to be southerners amongst her militia. The Reach was a land of settlers from foreign places. Perhaps only the fey could claim to be truly local. Nevertheless, now on the very cusp of battle with a Vec prince, it unnerved her a little to be confronted with the reality.

"I hope this will not be too difficult for you, Sergeant, to fight against your own people," she said, knowing that this was precisely the worst time to sound out his loyalty and yet not quite able to stop herself.

"I shouldn't think so," Nunel responded calmly. "It didn't trouble me any when I rode against them for Vec captains, and I've done that in three separate little wars."

An experienced man-at-arms, Amelia thought, recognizing immediately why her husband must have appointed Nunel to the rank of sergeant. But that experience also spoke to an aspect of warfare that Amelia could not abide.

"You are a mercenary then?" she asked.

"I was."

"I do not like mercenaries."

"Neither do I much," Nunel said flatly. Amelia looked at him, astonished, and when she caught his eye, he shrugged. "War's too bloody a business and men's lives too precious to throw them away on mere coin."

Amelia blinked and shook her head.

"Then why? Why become one?" she asked. He shrugged again. It was an odd gesture in his plate cuirass, with the whole metal on his chest and back, not to mention the spaulders on his shoulders, lifting a finger span and dropping back into place.

"I like to ride, and I like to fight," he said, giving the most mundane answer Amelia could imagine. "It seemed like this was the trade for me. But if I may, Your Grace, that's not the question you want to ask me, is it? You want to know if you can trust me?"

"You are quite impertinent, Sergeant Nunel, to ask a direct question of your liege like that."

Nunel did not respond to her admonition. There were finally sounds of the Vec army beginning to form up, and the sergeant looked ahead to where the bridge was coming near. Soon, the vanguard would be crossing, and though they were at last coming out of their camp, the enemy army still had not engaged the Lions' crossing.

"There's a lass in the camp followers," the sergeant said, calmly. "Fair thing, ready to marry. She does washing for the lancers and doesn't charge me like she does the others. She seems to think a sergeant's rank and pay is a high enough esteem for her to aim for. I've promised her that when we get back to Dweltford, I'll ask her father's blessing and make it all right and true in a church."

"Why are you telling me this, Sergeant?" Amelia asked.

"You promise good pay, Your Grace, and you make serious effort to keep your word. I mean to use my silver from this campaign to buy us a little plot of land in one of those new towns I hear you have planned. I want you to know, I'm here for the Reach, because it's here that my future is."

Amelia smiled and was about to thank the man for his honest answers when Farringdon rode up on a charger, the sun flashing off the brow ridges of his polished salet helmet.

"Your Grace," he said, bowing in the saddle. Amelia was momentarily fascinated at just how adept these men were at moving in their heavy protection. She had never really considered it before. She remembered how even the ancient Prince Mercad, frail and only days from his death, had moved so seemingly freely in his well-made harness. Perhaps she should have something of armor made for herself. It need only be parade armor, not the heavy harness of a full suit of plates. Would it project a martial presence, or would she just look even more like a little girl playing at war?

"What is it, Knight Captain?" she asked him.

"Something has...developed, to the east, on this side of the river," Farringdon said. "I would ask that you accompany me to the hilltop where it will be easier to show you than to explain."

"Very well," Amelia said, turning Silvermane aside from the march to the bridge. Already, the prime cohort was beginning to cross, their boots tromping loudly off the ancient wood.

"Did you want us to wait, Captain?" Nunel asked.

Farringdon paused to think and then nodded his head.

"Yes, wait on this bank until we know which side is more determined. Sergeant Sedgemark knows his orders for the Lions afoot, and they outnumber the Veckander force by themselves. They should be able to hold our bridgehead for a while. If he asks for any orders, just remind him to keep his men back under the range of our cannons."

"No more than thirty paces ahead of the bridge, Captain," Nunel said, showing he remembered the orders. The lancer sergeant called his men to a halt and move aside for the rest of the infantry to cross the bridge, following the first cohort. Amelia reined her mount about and rode with her husband the short distance to the hilltop.

Chapter 28

"At least now we know where that rider was going," Farringdon said as he drew Amelia's attention east toward the tumble-down manor farm. There, in an overgrown grainfield, was a company of men-at-arms ahorse, arrayed in two squares. "I make them to be about five hundred or so."

"And we can guess who sent them," Amelia said, noting the two enormous banner poles lifted above each formation. On the left was a white- and yellow-striped field with the black and gold cross upon it. The righthand ranks were under a banner of royal red, with the Denay king's eagle. Church knights and Daven Marcus's men. For a moment Amelia wondered if the Usurper himself was with them but doubted that. Every word from the Grand Kingdom was that the false king was fighting in the north, somewhere near Quenland.

"Will they attack us here now?" she asked.

"They will regret it if they do," said Yentow Sent with his usual self-confidence. The master smith was supervising the cannons, dressed in a long leather coat that hung to his knees and had a brass buckle at one shoulder. It was designed to protect him from sparks and embers, and with a single pull of the buckle it could be removed almost instantly if it caught fire.

"I have already ordered the good master here to reposition these three cannons to cover the east," Farringdon said, and Sent bowed his head as if he had just been paid a compliment.

Amelia looked around her at the hilltop and did her best not to think of King Chrostmer's night under the red sky. Three of Farringdon's new cannons were aimed over the river toward his uncle's army, but three more had been redeployed to face eastward, looking out over a little ridge, like a lesser hilltop halfway down the eastern slope.

"They are almost within range now," Yentow Sent declared. "If they attack, we will have little trouble striking them, as long as these aim true."

He waved his hands at the Lions who were working as gun crews, four to each weapon. They were wearing layered woolen buffcoats that must have been hot on such a warm day, as well as open-faced helmets. The woolen clothes were to protect from fire as well, apparently. The crews were hauling barrels of black powder about and stacking iron balls beside their weapons, readying for the coming fight. Amelia was reminded of the diligent Bronze Dragon gunners, but as she watched, she also remembered that her forces had already defeated the king's cannons once and wondered if these were vulnerable as well.

"I thought cavalry could sweep upon cannon too swiftly for them to fight alone?" she said.

Yentow Sent gave her a dismissive glance, but Farringdon acknowledged her question with a ready smile.

"That's true, Your Grace," he said, "which is why we have also ordered up some of the wagons."

He pointed north and west a short distance, and Amelia saw four of the company's battlewagons being hauled by bullocks across the rough ground north of the hill. There was a half cohort of mixed men-at-arms helping them move.

"We'll put them down there on the secondary ridge," Farringdon explained, pointing down the slope in front of the east-facing cannons. "They will form a bastion, like a castle wall, from behind which the cannons will fire, protected and effective."

Amelia looked at the three cannons mounted on their large cartwheels. The black iron tubes looked ribbed, like the sides of a half-starved animal, with bones showing through the skin. Farringdon had explained to her that the ribs were additional iron bands, forged to wrap around the barrels to reinforce them. Iron could not be melted and cast, as the barrels of the Bronze Dragons had been, so additional rings were needed for strength. To Amelia's mind they made these newer cannons seem at once more complicated and less sophisticated. Nonetheless, her retainers seemed to lack no confidence in them.

"Envoys riding," someone called, and she looked eastward again to see the two banners flying as they were carried by standard bearers in a crowd of six or seven knights. Polishing armor steel was universal to prevent corrosion and the weakness it brought with it, but even by the standards of bright steel that most men-at-arms wore, this group shone in the morning sun, their armor adorned in many places with silver and gold. For the second time this morning, Amelia was reminded of Prince Mercad and his entourage at the Battle of the Brook. Then she remembered another morning when Mercad's seemingly glorious heir, Prince Daven Marcus, had arrived in Dweltford, coming as a savior but all too eager to damn himself by his actions.

Let us see you again at the end of this day, gentles, Amelia thought coldly. *Your silver and gold will wear blood and dirt, do not doubt.*

"Is there an easy way from here to that ridge?" she asked. "And fetch me a speaking trumpet."

Farringdon guided his wife down to the lower height, still halfway up a difficult slope for a horse to climb. The only easy way to the hilltop proper was on the north side, and to get there the enemy force would have to ride under the fire of Roar on wagons on the lower ridge and the cannons on the top. To make their task even more difficult, Farringdon ordered one of the wagons to block the path on the north side as well. By the time the envoy riders arrived, Amelia and her knight captain were sitting their horses on the ridge, looking down on the enemy, while behind them a three-wagon wall was fully crewed with Roar gunners and Claws to defend them. The archduchess felt very calm and ready to hear the enemy's talk of terms. Whatever was offered, she did not expect to like it.

"Rebel Amelia of the Western Reach," a man-at-arms in a brigandine of dyed stripes, the same as the field of the Church banner, bellowed up the slope. Amelia wondered what order it belonged to but realized that she did not really care. "By entering here, the lands of the Grand Kingdom, and bringing your rabble with you, you have once more rebelled against the throne of Denay. By bringing your heretic servitor with you, you have again sinned against God and Mother Church."

"You are a rebel who has rebelled again, my love," Farringdon whispered without looking at her. "How very scandalous."

Amelia smirked a little, but otherwise held herself calm. She put the speaking trumpet to her lips. There was little chance she would be heard and understood across the distance without it. She could not bawl like a man-at-arms.

"This man is no heretic servitor," she said. "He is my knight captain and husband." She thought about introducing Farringdon as Marquis Consort, but the churchman did not wait for her to say more.

"This depraved false marriage you speak of has already been denounced by the ecclesiarchs in synod," he shouted. "It is Church law that no Veckander prince or noble can be married in righteousness while the Vec is yet in heretical rebellion. Your depravity is null in God's eyes."

The Vec is in heretical rebellion, Amelia thought, *but your Inquisition doesn't hesitate to recruit them to your assistance all the same.* She resisted the urge to look south to Prince Garrodmin's army across the river.

"The fathers of the Church are to be commended for their continued diligent attention to my marital affairs," she said into the trumpet. "Nevertheless, is it seemly for old celibate men to inquire so deeply into a young lady's chamber?"

Several of the Lions behind her chuckled, but what surprised Amelia was that she could also hear laughter from the enemy group, a single voice echoing loudly, as if heard from inside a locked room. As she searched the visors of the envoys, a knight in the finest plate, with a bright golden eagle embossed on the chest, lifted his helmet's face covering. From within, Amelia could see a mocking smile, cruel dark eyes, and a perfectly manicured moustache and beard. She knew the face immediately.

"Baron Robant," she called, recognizing Daven Marcus's most loyal knight. "Is the Usurper with you, or have you slipped your master's leash?"

"I am here on my master's business," Robant shouted to her. "And it's Duke Robant now."

"I would congratulate you," Amelia responded, "but to rise in a kingslayer's service is surely to descend in righteousness."

The church knight scowled, apparently disgusted by her mockery, but Robant only shook his head happily.

"A man's rise, or fall, are matters for God," he declared. "I only serve my king's throne to the fullness of my abilities. There is no more for me than that."

Amelia scoffed openly. She doubted Robant even believed in God, and if he did, it was only as his master did, as a justification for his own abuses of power. The fact that the political church supported such men while they called her depraved made her sick to her stomach.

"Why are you here?" Farringdon demanded.

Robant looked at him with derisive curiosity. "To ask *you* that question, of course, and to prevent you coming a step further eastward," he said.

"You should have brought more men then," Farringdon retorted.

"There are two armies for you to face today, fool false prince," the church knight shouted, sneering. "You are caught in the jaws of the wolf, and you will be torn apart by its fangs."

"Lions do not fear wolves," Farringdon called back breezily, and Amelia loved the confidence he projected. He had come so far since he had last been here. "And these lions have a new roar to give. You would do well not to wait to hear it."

He looked over his shoulder to the three cannons above the ridge, but Amelia was struck by something else. Although the messenger sent by the Vec prince to summon Robant's force here was evidence enough, it was clear from Robant's words that cooperation between the Vec and the Usurper, with the help of the Inquisition, was a known fact. No one was hiding it, and the hypocrisy of that burned her blood. Now she almost longed for them to attack so she could see their evil punished as it deserved. If God was generous, perhaps foul Robant could meet his end at the hands of a cannonball, preferably through his golden-eagled chest plate.

"I must offer you a correction, as well, sir," Farringdon was saying. "You call me a false prince, but this is not true. I have gone to my knee and repented my ancestor's rebellion. I am Marquis Consort Farringdon now, and Aubrey, my once-rebel province, is returned to the throne via the throne of Archduchess Amelia. When the kingslayer Usurper is removed to make way for a true king, I will go to my knee once again, in Denay."

"You always were clever with the laws, bitch," Robant shouted at Amelia, his expression seeming to show grudging respect but hard for her to know for sure at this distance. "But the prince across the river disagrees with your man's assessment."

"We shall persuade him presently, if he insists on pressing the issue," Amelia spoke into the trumpet, while the men deploying on the wagons behind her muttered angrily at the bald-faced insult of calling their liege lady a "bitch."

"If you have no other matters for me than these worthless denunciations, I will bid you goodbye. There is another, more significant party awaiting me in the south. I will leave you here with my men to attend you."

"You can run away in a moment, girl," Robant said coldly. Then he nodded to the Church knight. "The brother elder here has something to tell you first."

Amelia watched as the Church knight, now revealed to be a brother elder, a somewhat senior officer in whatever knightly order he belonged to, stand in his stirrups and produce a sheet of parchment like a herald.

"Amelia, wayward wife, whore, renegade, heretic and witch, hear now the words of the Mother Church, speaking with the authority of God himself and carrying the full danger of his wrath and judgement," he began.

Well, they certainly aren't holding back, she thought.

"God has seen your many fell acts and depravities and judged them. More than this, he has seen your devilish engines of war with which you oppose his chosen men and their righteous authority. As such, your engines of war are accursed, and if you do not forsake them, the fire of His wrath shall fall upon you."

What do you know of the fire of His wrath? Amelia thought. She had seen the angel of God fall upon the enemies of the Lord in more dreams and visions than she ever wanted to recall. Expressions like "fire of God's wrath" sounded hollow in this white-washed sepulchre's mouth.

"If you fear fiery wrath, I invite you to press your attack," she shouted into the trumpet, feeling her anger drive her voice to a shriller tone. "Otherwise, cease from wasting my time with your prattle."

The envoy party turned and left, and it was clear it had only ever been their intention to read this parchment of denunciation. They intended to attack no matter what her response. That suited Amelia quite fine. Let them suffer *her* wrath for a change.

"Did you wish to go south now, my love?" Farringdon asked.

"I will wait and watch awhile, if you don't mind, husband," Amelia said.

"Of course. I suggest we move back some though, for best safety."

Amelia nodded and let him lead the way back up to the cannon park on the hilltop.

CHAPTER 29

Once Duke Robant and the envoys had returned to their company of knights, there was a fanfare of trumpets and the Grand Kingdom force began to advance in their twin formations, walking at first to arrange themselves into lines for the charge. As Amelia watched them, another trumpet blast sounded from the south, answering the first.

"The Veckanders are moving to attack," a sharp-eyed look-out beside the south-facing guns shouted.

"Excellent," Farrindon called back. "Load up and be ready to test your range."

The gun crews saluted like any other Lions and began preparing their opening salvos. Amelia watched in dread fascination as sacks of the deadly black powder, filled from larger kegs, were thrust into the cannon barrels, followed by the heavy iron cannonballs. She felt a sudden thrill of discomfort, being so close to so much danger.

"They attack both at once, just as promised," Farringdon observed.

"Like the jaws of a wolf," Amelia muttered, momentarily tasting the bitterness of her feelings in the back of her throat. She had forgotten how unnerving an open battlefield could be. The last time she had stood beside her Lions in combat, she had had Castle Dweltford at her back, and she had not realized until this moment how comforting its presence had been. She shook her head and swallowed the bile in her mouth.

"Master Sent, do you not wish to observe the cannons firing?" Farringdon asked, and the weaponsmith shook his head. He was already standing by the east-facing guns, a linstock in his hand, the pole's slow-match already smoking away, ready to light the cannons.

"The combat in the south will last longer than this one," the Masnian declared with confidence. "I will watch here until these ones are driven away and then watch the rest of the southern fight."

Farringdon conceded that assessment with a nod and gave his permission for the guns to fire as soon as the enemy came within range.

Amelia watched eastward as one of the two knight formations rode ahead, the one under Daven Marcus's banner geeing their horses to a trot. Men and destriers wrapped in heavy plate were still several hundred paces away and would take their time to build their speed, saving their energy to gallop the last fifty. The archduchess looked down past the three wagons forming the little bastion on the lower ridge and wondered at how the knights thought to charge up that slope. She knew that at the Battle of the Brook the Redlanders had exhausted Prince Mercad's knights by forcing them to charge uphill, and while that had been a much longer slope, it had also been nowhere near as steep.

Will they never learn? she wondered.

"How close will you fire, Master Sent?" Farringdon asked professionally, as if discussing target practice.

"I have sighted for the purple flowers," Sent replied, and looking into the field, Amelia could see the little crop of wildflowers that he meant. "When they cross that, we will light our first."

The enemy eagle banner flew in the wind as the men-at-arms drew near to Yentow Sent's ranging marker blooms. It seemed almost perverse to Amelia that something so beautiful and innocent could be used so bloodily.

Like the unicorn? she asked herself, and she felt a fresh disdain for the war around her and the eager hate with which she had wished for these knights to make their charge, just so she could bloody them for their masters' arrogance. She suddenly wanted to pray for humility. As a noble with a mighty force—a conquering army—pride was too easy a temptation. *Let me never forget the price of our pride is paid in the lives of too many innocents.*

Yentow Sent put the linstock match to the nearest cannon touchhole and the thunderous fire and smoke belched forth. Almost immediately following, the second and third cannons fired as well. For a long moment Amelia could see nothing beyond—the smoke was too thick—but a lookout standing some way to one side called out a hit and the men on the wagons cheered as well. Soon the air was clear enough for her to see and she watched the knights closing gaps in their line as they spurred to the final length of the charge. The hoofbeats hammered the ground as the Roarsmen on the wagons began to fire their weapons.

"Have we disrupted them that much?" she asked her husband.

"I'm sorry, Your Grace?" Farringdon replied, only half listening. He was watching as the cannon crews were already beginning to reload their weapons.

"Knights are not normally so disordered," she told him, and he looked to the charge. Every knightly charge Amelia had observed had been almost architecturally precise, even over rougher ground, so well trained were the masters of Grand Kingdom warfare. Yet this line was already wavering as it reached the foot of the hill. Behind them they had left two pairs of horses and riders, one blasted to crimson ruin by the cannonball, the other fallen from his horse and wrestling weakly to disentangle himself from his stirrup while his mount wandered confused. It would not normally have been enough damage to unnerve a charge.

"Are these *not* knights?" she wondered out loud, but Farringdon did not reply.

At the foot of the hill, the charge tried to keep its pace as it climbed, but it quickly broke apart so that only three mounted men even reached the wagons, easily fended away by Claws with their pikes and halberds. A Roar-shot killed one of the three, and the other two turned to withdraw. So did the rest of the force, and the Lions threw jeers at their retreating forms.

"Have they no stomach for the fight?" Farringdon wondered out loud. As if to answer him, the trumpets sounded again, and the second Kingdom formation began to walk forward. The knight captain smiled at his weaponsmith. "Ready yourself, Master Sent. Here come your next customers."

The gunners chuckled, but suddenly the whole affair seemed pointlessly murderous to Amelia. Her men had the upper hand and would not struggle in this fight. Knights would die empty deaths to uphold Daven Marcus's evil ambitions. When they were defeated, she resolved to bring Baron Robant—*Duke* Robant, she corrected herself—to trial for his part in the Usurper's crimes.

Whose dukedom did he give you, Robant? And did you have to kill them yourself to receive it? she thought. It was one of the questions she promised herself to ask at his trial. Turning away from the newly gathering charge in disgust, she noticed that her husband was frowning at the southern-facing cannon crews.

"Why are you not firing?" he demanded, and Amelia realized that she had not heard those guns fire at all.

"The Lions have moved forward, Captain," the lookout answered him. "They're right in our range."

"What? I told Nunel to keep Sedgemark on a leash," Farringdon said furiously, and he slapped his hand on his pommel. "Can they not follow orders?"

Amelia was surprised at the intensity of her husband's reaction. Was his new-found strength as a knight captain making him into the kind of tyrannical noble she was afraid she might become? One short-tempered moment was hardly proof of anything, but in her tense mind she could not quite dismiss the possibility.

"If they don't pull back, we'll be unable to use the cannon on the southern battle at all," Farringdon said, and he turned his mount to ride down the north slope pathway.

"Where are you going, husband?" Amelia asked as she followed.

"To tell Nunel to fulfill my orders."

"Is it so important to you that these death machines rain hell upon those men? Please tell me you are not falling in love with their lethal might."

Farringdon stopped his horse just downslope of the hilltop and turned to her, a look of shocked disbelief on his face. She brought her mount close to his.

"Do you think I am Daven Marcus that you ask that question?" Farringdon asked, and the pain in his expression was unmistakable.

"Are you?" she asked him back, tension giving freer voice to her fears than they deserved.

"My love, our cannon can engage our enemy, break them, or even drive them away without any risk to our own forces at the same time. This is what makes the Bronze Dragons such horrors, and why the kings have kept them for themselves. I do not love their power except that it can make our men safer. The men engaged across the river right now could be holding back while we hammer Prince Garrodmin's force from here."

Amelia felt almost shamed by his answer, and she smiled at him. There was no time to apologize, though, as Master Sent demanded their attention.

"The time for the next firing is near, Marquis," he shouted from back on the hilltop. "Are you going to miss it?"

"I will return soon, Master," Farringdon promised loudly. "Continue firing as you will."

Looking back, Amelia saw the Masnian nod with a satisfied expression and put the linstock to the touchhole once more. Her husband turned back to her and smiled. Then everything behind him was instantly engulfed in a cloud of dust, flame, and smoke as the thunderous fist of God's wrath fell upon the hilltop.

CHAPTER 30

"You were right Commander," said Sergeant Gennet. "They had themselves a nice little stock of food and water. The water's stale and their victuals for fifty won't stretch far across our near five hundred, but it's still a bit of restock, I'd say."

Prentice accepted the report with a salute and bade the sergeant to see all the rest of their supplies and equipment moved into the fenced enclosure to turn it into a temporary depot while they camped outside. He had already set teams to find and destroy any mantis masks in the trees nearby under Brother Whilte's supervision, so this location should be safe enough for one night while he decided what they should do next. Other than a single lean-to and a hand full of old tree trunks carved out for use as water troughs for horses, the entire fenced area was open to the air and empty. The Inquisition force had been bedding down straight on the ground. It was in keeping with the kind of humility Church knights were supposed to exemplify, but it surprised Prentice all the same.

"I have the codex and the map, My Lord," Master Solft said as he approached the lean-to where Prentice was standing beside a large, upturned barrel that had been used by his enemy as a table of sorts.

"Spread the map out here, if you will," the knight commander instructed, pointing to the barrel. As Solft unfolded his draft chart, the corners drooped over the sides. Prentice took the copy of pilgrim Borrosod's travelog from under Solft's arm and opened it, turning first to the page with the map's original. There in the bottom corner was the dragonfly illumination, just as he remembered. Solft looked up from placing the map.

"Have you found something significant, My Lord?" he asked.

"Just the dragonflies," Prentice answered. Solft's brow crinkled at the enigmatic response. There were little flakes of peeled skin on his nose and cheeks. After days in the sun, his pale flesh stubbornly refused to brown. It burned to a painful-looking redness, then cracked and peeled, revealing fresh pink skin beneath that would pale over a few days and then burn once more. It hardly even produced freckles either. Prentice pitied the man some and had offered him free use of the lanolin.

Solft's expression changed as he seemed to recognize Prentice's subject.

"I overheard some of the Lions talking of hornets," he said, nodding solemnly. "They heard such a swarm during the attack, but say they saw nary a one. Is that part of the Redlander magick?"

"A sound, as of insect wings beating the air," Prentice agreed. "Deep and thrumming though, as if the insects were enormous."

"A disturbing notion," Solft said, the horror unmistakable in his eyes.

"My Lord Knight Commander," Brother Whilte called out, thumping purposefully into the enclosure, carrying something made of bone in his hands. It occurred to Prentice that the chaplain, a former Church knight himself, was the only one who said his new rank with any sense of familiarity. In everyone else's mouth it still carried a tone of uncertainty, as if he had been raised so high above his men that they no longer knew him. As he recognized this, he also realized that he'd been sensing it since the day they left Dweltford, and it had been contributing to his unease as they hunted the Inquisition militants.

"How fares your task, Brother?" Prentice asked, finding himself with a new reason to appreciate this man he once hated with murderous venom. Of course, a former knight would not be intimidated by the rank of a knight commander.

"We have fulfilled your instructions," Whilte said, tugging his forelock. "Every mask we could find is destroyed, and I have prayed that the Lord will release the magick from within the pieces. It is all I know to do. I will say they seemed much older than the ones near Dweltford. The wood on the back was bleached and cracked, and the corrosion was like thick-grown moss. They were almost ready to fall apart, so destroying them was not hard."

"Pity the damned Inquisition did not take it upon themselves to do it for us already," Prentice cursed. "It is their remit, after all. What is that thing?"

As Whilte lifted the object, Prentice could see it was a skull, a human skull, and from its sides projected two antlers. His immediate thought was of the Horned Man, that this might have been the remains of another such *brakkis effar*, but as Whilte turned it over, it was obvious from the underside that the horns were attached by metal nails.

"A totem?" Prentice asked.

"I believe so," Whilte answered. "It was beneath the tree with the middle mantis mask, set up as if in a shrine at the base of the trunk. There were other bones there, as of sacrifices chained to the tree."

Prentice looked south and wondered what it might have been like to have died of thirst, chained in place, with undrinkable brackish swamp water all about. The torment would have been unspeakable.

"Master Solft, if you would be of service, could you fetch Sergeant Gennet for me?" he said as he looked at the map on the barrel for a moment. Solft rushed away.

"I will see this artifact destroyed, Knight Commander," Whilte told him. "I only let it be to show you first. I thought you would want to see it."

Prentice understood the chaplain's thinking. Whilte was one of very few men in the Lions who had actually stood the field against the mighty Horned Man, and he would have no desire to see another such enemy champion. Except perhaps for the monstrous bull *brakkis effar*, the Horned Man had been the mightiest of the enemy they had ever encountered.

"Wait one moment if you will, Brother," Prentice said, continuing to study Solft's map, putting details together in his mind. Outside the enclosure he could hear men grunting and swearing as they cut wood for fires and prepared to camp. Their few horses were whickering, and he heard someone whispering to calm one of them. To make for best speed, they had hitched teams of two pairs to each of their supply wagons rather than the usual slower bullocks. The sound made Prentice think of the speed of the fey as they ranged. Their *keshiyaa* drove a herd of rugged ponies with them as remounts, eating horsemeat cured under their saddles and drinking mare's milk. And they slept as they rode. He shook his head, marveling at the fleet-footed efficiency of his allies' forces. Then he paused in his thoughts. Were they still his allies?

"You wanted me, Commander?" Gennet asked as he returned with Whilte. Prentice nodded without looking up from the map.

"How far is that distance?" Prentice asked the scholar, using two fingers on the same hand to mark a space on the parchment. Solft peered closely, brows knotted. The others leaned in as well.

"Dweltford to the crossroads?" Solft said, brushing away his bowl-cut hair behind his ears as he leaned forward. "I do not have the exact leagues my Lord, but you know yourself it is three days regular travel. Traveling light, a messenger can do it in just under two."

Prentice nodded.

"And this distance?" he asked again, marking now from Dweltford to Fallenhill.

"Well, that's different. The river makes travel swifter, especially if coming with the flow from the north. It can be done in three easy days north to south. South to north *can* be that quick, but not easily and not by many."

"And the fey?"

"Oh, the fey could do it in less than two, if they rode hard," Solft said with a dismissive tone, as if comparing a fey rider to a regular Reacherman was like comparing a waddling duckling to a diving hawk.

"Have you ever known our friends from the mountains to *not* ride hard?" Prentice asked rhetorically, and Gennet gave a sneering chuckle, obviously thinking Prentice to be joking when he called the fey "friends." Prentice looked at him sternly and he shrugged and nodded, acknowledging the truth of the base observation. The knight commander put his two fingers back down to the page, marking the distance from Fallenhill to Dweltford.

"So that is about two days," he said. He moved his fingers so that the distance between them stayed fixed, but the start on Fallenhill now began on Dweltford Lake, and the other rested on a point in the blank part of the map, southwest of Dweltford. "Benjamin came to us roughly here with his lone survivor and word of a lake there."

With his free hand he pointed to the bottom left corner of the map that was hanging over the edge of the barrel.

"That one fey man had returned from a search that began almost as soon as the rains returned with winter, no?"

Solft nodded, but his eyes were studying the empty portion of the map just like the knight commander's in the way of a learned man who realizes he might be about to acquire some new and important information. A sincere scholar never ceased to be a student in his heart. The master was undoubtedly one of the most learned men in the Western Reach, if not the world, but he never failed to recognize he had more yet to learn.

"So, almost half a year," Prentice said, outlining his thinking. "Let us subtract a month for searching at the other end of the journey, locating the exact tributary of the Murr that began at this magickal lake. Another month scouting the region to locate this coven we're told is there—a generous amount, but it will serve our purposes. That leaves us one month there and three months back on foot, roughly speaking."

A distance being twice as long on foot as horseback was a more typical assessment, but these were fey riders they were discussing, so Prentice chose three to one.

"If you say so, My Lord, but I don't see..." Solft agreed, but Brother Whilte stilled him with a hand upon his shoulder. Prentice fixed his fingers' distance, and counting by twos for two days' travel by fey ahorse, he began walking his fingers westward across the map.

"Two, four, six, eight, ten, twelve."

Already his leading finger had reached the end of the Murr in the unknown eastern mountains marked on the edge of the page. He kept going, and soon his hand was "walking" off the barrel and into the air beside it, and still he kept counting.

"Good Lord," Solft breathed as he now recognized the lesson, and Whilte and Gennet both nodded in agreement.

"Twenty-six, twenty-eight, thirty." Prentice finished his count and held his hand out in the air.

CHAPTER 31

"This map is wrong," Solft breathed, recognizing the significance of this one insight. "Very wrong. Radengon Beyond Dwelt could be only one of a half dozen provinces between here and there. There could be whole countries yet of which we know nothing."

"Or a wilderness vaster than the grasslands that are 'bereft,'" Prentice added. With his finger he now traced a circle further up the map's left side. "The salt sea must begin about here, but in the south, Benjamin's scouts never encountered it, or perhaps skirted its coast. Yet we know the Redlanders can link their boats from that water to this far-flung lake."

"We do?"

Prentice nodded but kept his eyes on the chart that was transforming to a better map in his mind.

"Recall the archduchess saw their fleet sailing south on the salt sea," he said, "only mere weeks before the conquest of Aubrey began. They must have moved from one to the other either by their sorcery or by another river that flows from the lake or nearby."

"Unless they have built themselves a canal or dragged their boats over the land by some means," Whilte offered in the way of a thoughtful person simply exploring an idea without placing limits on their contemplations.

Prentice was forced to concede the point, but it did not comfort him. In some ways, the notion that the Redlanders might have such long-term commitment to their conquest that they would build canals hundreds of leagues long or simply drag boats such a distance overland was almost as frightening as the notion that they did it all by occult power. The sheer force of will such feats would require boggled the mind.

"Dragging would not bring their boats to the Murr swiftly enough," Prentice asserted, "not unless the salt sea draws right up to the shores of this damnable lake, and Benjamin made no mention of that."

Solft coughed lightly.

"Would the fey have been forthcoming on that, My Lord?" he asked, and his pained expression made it clear he thought they should probably doubt Benjamin's every word up until now. Prentice was not so sure. The fey had defied his wishes and followed their own plans, but he was not entirely convinced it was an act of pure treachery. After all, Benjamin's proposed plan originally had been for the Lions to reach this lake, just later than either Inxyphos's men or Benjamin's own *keshiyaa*. Whatever their intent, it had not seemed to be open rebellion, not to Prentice's eyes. He told the three men around him as much.

"If you say so, Commander," Gennet said, though he did not sound persuaded.

"Well, Knight Commander, your reasoning seems sound, but what is the upshot?" Whilte asked. Prentice looked from one to the other.

"This is what I think, Brother," he said, and he took the skull out of Whilte's hands, grabbing it by one horn and placing it upon the map.

"Let us assume no other lies, for now," he began, realizing that strictly speaking Benjamin had never lied about his intent, only concealed it. It was possible that even now, on that far mystical lakeshore, the fey were engaged in battle with Inxyphos's men. Pity they could not have done it back in the swamp near Dweltford.

Prentice shook his head to cast that pointless regret out.

"The Redlanders come from somewhere over the salt sea, which washes up on our lands around here."

He waved at the approximate section of the map.

"It seems most likely that they must come at least some distance across that sea before their boats can be lifted through the sky, because they sailed their whole fleet here before it appeared on the Murr weeks later. The Horned Man and his force were in the Reach a full two seasons before that fleet, spreading terror ahead of their arrival."

"Warning us to be ready, ultimately," Gennet said dismissively. "If it weren't for him and his cutthroats, the West would've been meat for that invading fleet. Aubrey surely was."

"They were scouting out our strength," Whilte said, but Prentice shook his head and pointed at the skull on top of the map.

"They were based here," he told them. "That was why elements of his force were encountered south of Dweltford first. And their purpose was likely to create other secret sites for them to transfer into the Reach directly."

"Like the one on the lakeside," said Solft.

"Then why did the others go to Aubrey, and why did the Horned Man do so much to draw Prince Mercad to battle so far away in the north?" Whilte objected. "They had so many coming to the assault. Why not wait and join the rest, attack in full force?"

"Bleed or shed blood," Prentice answered. "That's their credo. We know they take mystical power from bloodshed, and the Horned Man's force had just conquered Fallenhill, swiftly and easily. Perhaps he felt powerful enough to make the assault himself."

"The glory of victory kept for himself," Whilte acknowledged.

"One thing the Redlanders do not seem to be is restrained," Solft observed.

"Yea, but how powerful did they have to feel to think they could take the whole Western Reach with that small force?" Sergeant Gennet asked, mostly rhetorically, but Prentice had an answer for that question, too.

"Do not think them too foolish, Sergeant," he said. "Overeager perhaps, but I think the truth is the Horned Man had no idea the size of the enemy he was confronting."

"Well, he was the biggest bugger I've ever heard of," Gennet retorted.

"I was speaking about the Grand Kingdom, Sergeant, about nations," Prentice said, shaking his head but smiling. "Master Solft here has found some vague old references to what might be the origins of the Redlanders, but they all date from a thousand years ago."

Gennet whistled at that revelation, but Whilte only nodded. He already knew much of this. It was only news to the sergeant.

"After a millennium, all we have is fragments of legends and lost tales," Prentice continued. "I think the Redlanders know as much about us as we do about them, or near enough. Maybe they remember us better to hate us, but they only know what we were, not who we are. I think the Horned Man had no idea that the Western Reach was only a border. I doubt he knew about the Vec or Masnia either."

"If any people could cling to their hate while all other details were lost to time, surely it would be the Redlanders and their religion," Whilte said.

"The Inquisition has done a fair job of clinging to old memories and old hate," Prentice said grimly. He still could not fathom the multi-layered dishonesty it would take to serve God and Church and still make pacts, even temporary ones, with the invaders. He wondered just how long the Inquisition had known about this fell waterhole in the middle of nowhere and its usefulness to the Redlanders. Did it date all the way back to the Broken Kings, or had the Inquisition and Blood Sects renewed contact over the centuries?

"Whelp, Commander, knowin' all this, what are your orders?" Gennet asked, and Prentice started out of his thoughts. He grabbed the lower left corner of the map and lifted it, pointing his finger at where, on the codex page, the dragonfly picture was drawn.

"Benjamin, Inxyphos, and the Serpent Witch are all here, and I have business with all three." Prentice paused. That was true, but what he planned was not motivated by personal need. He had service to his liege to perform. "More than that, somehow the Redlanders can use some kind of dragonfly magick at this lake. I mean to find a way to put an end to *that* for once and all. If the Redlanders want to attack the Reach, let them march over the grasslands like the rest of us."

"We are not supplied for the kind of march you are imagining, Knight Commander," Gennet said.

Prentice sighed and bowed his head, scratching at his scalp that was itchy with sweat in the afternoon heat. He looked up and pointed to the map one last time.

"We will bear straight south, aiming for the Murr," he said. "Then we will find a river town, a trading post, something, and send word back down the river and up the Dwelt to the archduchess, calling for more supplies and boats."

"And we'll wait for them there?"

"No, we will try to source boats from the Radengoners ourselves, and if they have none, we will start to march west anyway. Time is too short for any kind of waiting."

"Assuming we don't run out of food," Solft said glumly.

CHAPTER 32

Amelia was nearly thrown from the saddle by the force that buffeted her, her ears ringing as a cloud suddenly engulfed her. At the same moment, Silvermane reared. Amelia barely held herself in the saddle. Then a second thunderous blast sounded, and the air suddenly filled with the smells of flame, smoke, and dirt. Silvermane panicked and bolted. The mare had been a little agitated already by the sound of the cannon fire, but these overwhelming blasts, accompanied with the sudden changes to the air around her, had broken her nerve. Amelia herself had no clear notion of what was happening, and as a third, somewhat lesser blast echoed a short distance away, she was borne down the hill's northside path.

Although there was barely any way to see through the suddenly smoke-clouded air, in a sense Silvermane's panic served the archduchess well because it carried her away from danger and forced her to deal with a mundane trouble first. Something horrific had happened and Amelia's mind could not apprehend it through the haze of terror, but years of equestrian experience made dealing with her mount's panic an easy priority upon which to focus. Using the one-rein technique she had first been taught as a teenager, she forced Silvermane to cease her flight, just as the battlewagon guarding the path loomed out of the smoke. Unnerved militiamen crouching on the back of the wagon startled when they saw the archduchess and her horse suddenly appear, crying out and forcing Amelia to ready herself to stop another bolting.

"What's happened, Your Grace?" the line first asked, his voice awash with terror.

The leader in Amelia could see he needed reassurance, to be calmed, but she needed that for herself. She wanted to project strength, as she had less than half an hour before with Robant and the Inquisition knight. Yet what could she say? God's judgement had fallen upon the cannons, just as the Church's proclamation had declared.

Robant's trumpeters sounded another fanfare, and as she looked east through the slowly clearing gloom, she faintly heard a fresh sound of onrushing hooves. They were renewing their attack, coming to complete the destruction.

"Amelia? Amelia!?" a furious voice called from the hilltop, and a dire-looking figure in blackened metal stalked through the smoke and dust. For a moment it seemed to Amelia's terrified mind that this must be some demon sent by the Devil to drag her down to damnation for her arrogance—an ironclad fiend, whose hell-forged metal had first conquered her cannons and now hunted for her very soul. It stalked toward panicked horse and rider, bellowing her name, eyes within its helm dark and full of rage.

"Amelia? Oh, thank God you live," Farringdon's voice declared from within the demon's form, and suddenly it was transformed in her eyes into her husband. His steel armor was dented and blackened by earth and flame, and there was blood trickling down his neck from inside his helmet. He approached awkwardly, clearly favoring one leg, and tried to take her mount's bridle, but she turned Silvermane aside before he could, continuing to walk the mare in a tight hourglass back and forth on the path.

"Amelia, dear wife, stop!" Farringdon shouted, and in the chaotic insanity of the moment, the commonplace danger of a panicked horse was a refuge for the archduchess's mind again.

"I dare not, husband," she said. "She's spooked. She has to be let to move. If I try to hold her too still now, she'll only bolt once more."

Farringdon stopped trying to control the horse's movement at that point and nodded.

"Of course, my...Your Grace," he said, bowing, and as he raised his head he cried out in pain. Amelia's fears of judgement and hell flared a little once more, but the knight captain pulled his helmet strap and removed the protection. Even as he lowered it, she could see a heavy dent in the back. His gauntleted fingers rubbed the damage thoughtfully.

"That was a piece of the cannon, I would guess," he said with a professional air, and for a moment he was almost her academically minded husband once again—another element of the mundane to help calm her inwardly. Then he looked up and she could see why his eyes had looked so dark under the helmet. His left eye was utterly bloodshot, so that virtually no white could be seen, and more blood trickled from his left ear. That must have been the side of his helmet that had been struck by the flying shrapnel.

"Unspeakably lucky hit," he was saying, a notion that Amelia could barely fathom. "Glanced right off the curve of the steel. A finger's width further across and it might well have torn my head off. Killed me at least, that's for sure. Ooh, God in heaven, that hurts."

He gingerly rubbed the back of his skull. It sounded as if his speech had a slight slur to it and Amelia feared he was about to slip into unconsciousness as the pain made him stumble for a moment. From the lower hill there came the sound of hoofbeats, and she looked over her shoulder, fearing to see their enemy assaulting the slope.

"We must flee, husband," she said. "The day is lost."

Farringdon shook his head slowly, doubtless because of the pain, but it only made him seem more lost to the reality around them, as if he was drunk. From the other side of the defending wagon three riders appeared, lancers in Reach colors, and she saw it was Sergeant Nunel and an escort.

"My Lord, Knight Captain," Nunel shouted as he rounded the wagon and noticed Farringdon standing there.

"Marquis Farringdon is wounded," Amelia told the lancer. "We must withdraw immediately, for we are caught in the jaws of the wolf."

Nunel gave her no more than a single glance, barely even bothering to acknowledge her existence. He looked back to Farringdon.

"Knight Captain?"

"Do you think to ignore me, Sergeant?" Amelia demanded, her voice cracking. Silvermane's agitated movement made it hard for her to keep looking in the man's direction, which only served to make her fury feel less impactful. She would not be undermined by a Veckander mercenary. Later, she would realize just how much the explosion had scattered her calm, as completely as it had upheaved the earth of the hilltop, but at this moment she only knew she was afraid, insulted, and desperate to get her people to safety, away from the consequences of God's curse for her arrogance.

"I am commanding you to order a withdrawal, or our force will be destroyed," she insisted, feeling her voice grow shrill and hating how weak it sounded to her. "My husband is wounded, and we must..."

"No," said Farringdon suddenly, countermanding her. Without looking to anyone in particular—in fact, still seeming to be unsure of himself or his surroundings—he began to brief his officer.

"The Kingdom force is attacking," he said, and as if to confirm his word, there came war cries and the clash of steel from the direction of the bastion on the lower ridge. Matchlocks fired, their crackling shots sounding so much less frightening in the memory of the explosions just passed. "A cannon burst has destroyed our battery whole cloth. Ripped Fortitude right out from under me."

Fortitude was the name of Farringdon's horse. Amelia looked back up the hill, and with the smoke clearing, she thought she could see the poor creature's body lying upon the ground like a child's discarded toy.

"Shall we look for survivors?" asked Nunel.

"No!" Farringdon shouted and the passion in his voice shocked Amelia. As uneven as her own emotions felt, *he* seemed so much more disturbed to her. She wanted nothing so much as to see him to somewhere safe. Before she could give another order to retreat, he continued apprising the sergeant.

"There's like to be fires up there and still some remnant powder," he explained. "If it catches, there'll be more blasts and we'll lose more of us. It's not safe. The only reason the archduchess and I are still alive is that we were just below the crest of the top. The blast went out over our heads, in the main, hers more than mine. If we had been but paces higher, we should have been blown from the summit like leaves in a storm."

Amelia blinked, astonished at how rational that explanation sounded. How had he determined it so swiftly?

"These are your orders," Farringdon continued. "Firstly, give the archduchess an escort and go via the camp. Take word that everything is to be left and all are to flee to the bridge immediately."

"Husband?" Amelia burst out, terrified that he seemed to be sending her into danger, but he did not answer her.

"Sedgemark has our beachhead, and our safest strength is there. The escort is to ride the archduchess straight to the Lions afoot and give word for him to finish the job against the Vec force. The rest of the lancers are to round the south of the hill and attack the Kingdom knights on their flank. We will cover the bastion's retreat."

"Husband?" Amelia demanded with a near scream, desperate for his attention and furious that she did not have it. "You cannot throw your life away for glory! We must withdraw. It is not cowardice! Captain Ash—"

"Enough, wife!" Farringdon bellowed, and Amelia shuddered for a moment. Her nerve was frayed, and her indignance was at its peak. How dare the man who had sworn to honor her rank and dignity treat her so disdainfully? Her husband was not finished, however.

"We are in a fight for our lives," he said. "The bastion is still safe for now, but if those men try to flee, Robant's knights will slaughter them. Then they will ride on to our camp and take everyone there captive as well. To the south, Sedgemark is engaged, but he is winning. That is where our strength and safety is. Knight Commander Baron Ash would know this and understand the sense of my instructions."

Farringdon, correcting her misuse of Prentice's rank, caught Amelia's attention, strangely revealing the scattered nature of her thoughts just as the practicality needed to calm Silvermane had helped before. She had been so afraid that Farringdon was lost to her, his mind clouded by his injuries, and yet he was forcing his pained head to find a solution to their problem.

"The lancers are trained for this fight, Your Grace," he said. "If God is kind, Robant will keep his men ahorse and wear them out before he thinks to fight on foot. That will create a space for the Lions to withdraw and cross the bridge, but first we must see the Lioness to safety. Now cease arguing and let your knight captain do his duty."

Amelia was stunned, and for the first time since the cannons had exploded, she felt a moment of relative calm. Even Silvermane was a little less fractious beneath her. Neither she nor her horse resisted as one of the lancers took the reins from her hands and led off down the hill. In a daze, she rode as she had on the day her barge had been attacked by the Redlanders on the riverbank. Then, as now, knights were fighting to keep her alive, and this time there was no Prentice Ash to come to her defense. Looking over her shoulder where the sounds of combat from the bastion were rising, she realized that she no longer needed Prentice, for he had replaced himself with an entire corps, competent and faithful, led by her devoted husband.

"Don't let him die, please, Lord," she prayed as her escort made for the bridge, diverting first to take warning to the camp.

CHAPTER 33

Days marching straight south brought the Gryphon Banner Company into the gentle rolling grasslands of Radengon-Beyond-Dwelt. Many small streams trickled through the land, making it easy for the company to refresh their waterskins and barrels, and occasional farmsteads began to appear. The first were tiny, little more than a hut and an animal pen, and Prentice made sure his men marched a wide berth around those. Such farms would be too small to have any useful surplus to sell and the company's presence was more likely to terrify the farmers than anything else. Two more days and the land began to grow more populous, the farmsteads larger. One or two were almost enough to deserve the title of village.

"They've got livestock," Sergeant Gennet said as he walked at Prentice's stirrup. The company was passing a group of huts ringed by a low stone wall. On the far side of the little clutch of structures was a field that looked to be tilled and growing new wheat, or some similar grain, and the orderliness of the planting made it stand out against the natural grasses.

"Even these probably do not have enough to trade with us, Sergeant, and my order still stands. Anyone who takes so much as a hen's egg he does not pay for will be hanged as a plunderer. Make sure everyone understands that."

"They do, Commander," Gennet replied, and Prentice knew the admonition had been unnecessary. It was his own fear that he was responding to—the fear that anyone, anywhere, might see his force as abusive conquerors like the knights of the Grand Kingdom who pillaged so freely that hundreds of thousands fled across the Azure Mountains to escape them.

"Call a halt, Sergeant. I will take Brother Whilte and we will see if we can get some directions from the locals. I imagine they can spare us that much, at least."

While the drumbeat commanded the company to rest, Prentice fetched Whilte.

"You don't want me to bless the hearth again, do you?" the chaplain asked, referencing a cunning ploy Prentice had used the religious man for when they had been hunting for the fey. As effective as the trick had been, Whilte had never been comfortable with the deception.

"Nothing like that, Brother," Prentice reassured him. "A sacrist's presence might help comfort them, though. Make us seem like something more than rapacious men-at-arms."

"You know I'm not a proper sacrist?"

"Close enough," Prentice said, pointing to Whilte's shaved tonsure.

Whilte dismounted his wagon and walked beside Prentice's horse as they made their way around the ring wall at a polite distance until they found the entry, a closed gate that had three men standing at it, holding hay forks and shovels for weapons. It was a gesture at defense that seemed at once both forlorn and courageous.

"We ain't got naught to spare and no reason to let you take what we do have," one of the three farmers shouted as Prentice and Whilte approached. While they were still a good ten paces distant, Prentice dismounted with a groan and squatted to flex his sore legs. The saddle sores were beginning to heal, but riding was still a far from casual experience for him.

"We will be taking nothing. You and your families are safe," Prentice shouted back, as he stood up. "Save some guidance, if you are willing to share it."

"Guidance to where?" the farmer demanded, his expression showing he was not in the least persuaded by Prentice's reassurances.

"The Murr River, and the nearest town or settlement."

"The Murr's that way," the farmer said pointing southward. "A day and a half's walk. You keep going and you'll reach it afore sundown tomorrow."

"They want us gone," Whilte said quietly, more reflecting on the obvious than revealing anything.

"And we will give them what they want," Prentice muttered back. "But first..."

He lifted his head to shout again.

"The nearest settlement?"

The three farmers exchanged looks, as if wondering if they should answer the question. Perhaps they thought they would be betraying whichever place they directed the Lions towards. Prentice understood the kinds of problems bandits could cause on truly wild frontiers like this. With the mantis masks having been only a handful of days to the north, there was a good chance these folk had experienced raids by Redlanders as well. He wondered how much destruction the invaders had wrought when they switched their fleet to coming up the Murr.

"Nearest settlement's a trading post on the north bank, downriver a day or so," the farmer said at last. "You plannin' on robbing them?"

Prentice shook his head. "We will trade with them, if they will allow. No more than that, and no robbery. We come in the name of Archduchess Amelia of the Western Reach."

"Never heard of her," said the farmer, and Prentice laughed.

"That is surely a lie," Whilte said quietly. Prentice thought he was right, but it did not really matter. This conversation was almost over.

"When we get to this trading post, will they have enough livestock to spare some for us? Some extra grain perhaps?" he asked.

"Couldn't say," came the answer. "Like as not you'll find their gates shut to you. Word's spreading fast that you lot're ranging about. Ain't many folks as like your kind 'round these parts."

Prentice smirked. That was a bold thing for a farmer to say to a man with five hundred men-at-arms at his back. He nodded to the farmer and mounted up.

"Good day and thanks," he said calmly. "We will be gone within the hour. If ever you come to the Reach, speak the name Prentice Ash to the archduchess' factor and you will be assured a fair price on any produce you think to sell."

The farmer snorted dismissively, and his two fellows looked at each other in disbelief, as if Prentice had just declared himself to be a dragon who baked pastries for a trade.

"Only get to the trading post two or three times a year," said the lead farmer. "Can't see as how we'd ever go as far afield as Dweltford."

Prentice nodded, acknowledging the man's point. "Nevertheless," he said. "If you do, remember my name. I will see you are received."

"You know they'll never see Dweltford," Whilte said as he and Prentice returned to the company."

"It is unlikely," the knight commander conceded. "But you heard him. Word is already going out ahead of our coming. The archduchess wants to build a relationship with the Radengonner folk. When we behave honorably and give them our names honestly, that news will start to spread, and we prepare ground for her aims."

Whilte thrust out his lower lip and nodded thoughtfully, acknowledging the wisdom of Prentice's words.

"In the meantime, do we head south and then east?" he asked.

Prentice was reluctant to turn back east. His target was westward, and even a day's journey felt like too great a step backwards. The trading post was their best option, however, so he knew he had no choice.

"South and then east, Brother," he said reluctantly. "If you could pray to Almighty God that they have some large river boats we can buy from them, I would appreciate you putting in the good word for us."

"I can do that," Whilte said happily, "but I encourage you to ask him for yourself."

"I already am, Brother. I already am."

CHAPTER 34

"No! No! No! Quick on your feet, like a cat with its tail on fire," Righteous told the young women with their skirts hiked up as they practiced the basic Three Streets Vipers' footwork.

The pregnant baroness cursed under her breath and did her best to cover a wince as the pain in her back flared once more. She leaned more heavily for a moment on the sheathed Claws' sword she had taken to using as a walking stick, teeth clenched. When the sharp bite in her muscles receded, she put one hand to the spot and watched over the little, red-faced class, drilling in a quiet place between the north wall and the hut that had been commandeered for their quarters. The spot was virtually ideal—flat and open to allow combat drills but out of sight of most of the rest of Fallenhill. The last thing Righteous wanted was her gaggle of ripe maidens being made to jump and run with bare legs under the watchful eyes of hundreds of militiamen, easily distracted by the novelty of women in camp. Temptations were numerous enough without making a show of them.

Almost without thinking, Righteous cast a surreptitious glance to her right, to a seemingly meaningless spot on the fortress's rear rampart. It was just there that she had watched her not-yet-husband face a knight in full armor with nothing but a practice sword, such as the ones her new students would soon be learning with.

My heart in my throat the whole damn time! she remembered. That was the day she realized she was falling in love, when she watched her proud lion throw himself at steel like he had no fear. He could easily have fallen to his death or ended up spitted on a longsword like a hog. *But he hadn't.*

She smiled, then shook her head and walked into the midst of the huffing women and Solomon, who was daily becoming more and more useful as her training dummy, since he was able to demonstrate the moves she felt simply too pregnant to execute. By the time these women had finished their training, he would likely be ready to "walk the twine spiral," the ritual test that every Three Streets' Vipers student went through to prove themselves worthy to enter fully into the school's membership. Righteous had gone through it at thirteen, about the same age as Solomon was now.

Hell's bells, by that time, he'll likely be ready to give Spindle a run for her money, she thought. *In the meantime, I better make sure they all get the basics right, at least. Master Elmantin would skin my hide if I taught slow Vipers. If he's still alive.*

"Swift or dead, little Sally. Make your choice." Her old instructor's voice still echoed in her memories as she walked amongst her own students, looking them over with the same stern expression Elmantin the Flenser had used on his pupils.

Walk? More like waddle, she thought and then scowled at them.

"And still I got more grace than you heifers," she muttered as if they had been privy to her thoughts and would understand the comment.

"We're tired," one of the girls said quietly, but not so quietly as to not be heard.

"Oh, tired, are you?" Righteous whirled on one of the maids, the dark-haired, round-faced creature with fair skin and freckles. She might be a riverfolker, but she would never have the typical tanned complexion that most of her people had. The sun would only ever dust her button nose with ever more freckles.

Her hair was thick and darkly colored, tied back in a simple plait, but other than that, her appearance had nothing to recommend it. She was no Dalflitch.

Then again, neither am I, Righteous thought. She sized the heavily breathing trainee up the way she remembered her own master doing years before, the way she had with those first squads of Lions' Fangs that she had trained not far from this very spot.

"What do you think you're going to do when an assassin comes in the night to slaughter our liege lady and you along with her?" Righteous demanded. "Will you just bend over at the waist and whine at him. 'Oh, I'm tired. Poor little thing that I am.' Such a fine Lace Fang you'll make!"

"All your lace is in that mask!" the freckle faced woman retorted, and Righteous was simultaneously shocked and pleased. That took some brass, but it was the wrong kind of brass. Fearlessness was good, but only if it could be harnessed. Time to show them how that worked.

"Daisy, isn't it?" she asked as if she did not already know. She had made a point to learn all their names by now, but Daisy had been the first. The young woman straightened herself upright and put both fists on her hips defiantly, though Righteous thought she saw a spark of uncertainty behind her eyes, like a young'un who had taken things too far without thinking and now feared a clip across the ear.

"That's right."

"You're the mouthy one from the march." Righteous stared Daisy in the eye and smiled as the woman met her gaze unflinchingly.

Ooh, I'm gonna rub the brass off you, little girl, she thought. The pain in her back flared another time, and she almost snarled as it seemed to swirl all the way through her abdomen as well. Now was not the time for her little one to start kicking, damn it.

"You don't like learning to move like a proper fighter?" she asked, though the pain made her clench her teeth.

"I don't like bein' made to prance and gambol for your pleasure while you play lady-o'-the-castle. I come to learn to be a lioness, not your dancing girl! I coulda done that at a tavern back in Dweltford and been paid better for it and all! You play noble, but it's just a mask, like that silly piece of frippery on your face."

"Solomon's doing everything I make you do, too," Righteous said mildly, but knowing her fury coiling within herself. She felt her lips lift in an icy smile, like the one her husband sometimes got, and she gave Solomon a casual glance. Accustomed as he was to marching, running, and drilling, the young drummer looked as fresh as the late spring morning around them, his steps still light and swift.

I could say he looks fresh as a daisy, Righteous thought as she returned her cool gaze to the challenger in front of her. *Except he's far fresher than you, Daisy girl.*

"You don't hear him complaining, do you?" she asked.

"Then give him the damn mask," another girl jeered from behind Righteous's left shoulder. "He can cover his pig-ugly face."

"Then you could show us how *you* do it!" Daisy added.

There was an obligatory round of snickers, and out of the corner of her eye Righteous could see Solomon blush and turn the scarred side of his face away, covering it with his hand. Righteous scoured the giggling girls with her brittle gaze, making it clear that they wanted no part of what was happening here and that she did not need their opinion of her training assistant. She was pleased that more than one dipped her eyes reflexively, and one almost lifted her hand to tug her forelock.

Don't let 'em shame you, lad, Righteous thought. *Five years from now and you'll be the dashing and dangerous young man-at-arms that'll set them all hearts aflutter. You just got to get past this coltish phase.*

She flinched as the pain gave her another quick lash, like a stroke from a whip across her lower back and around her side to her belly. Even with that annoying distraction, Righteous found she was enjoying herself. This challenge to her authority was like dozens of other back-street confrontations she had had in her lifetime, and while she was supposed to be above such things as a baroness, she found this was too much fun. She may have become Baroness Righteous of Fallenhill, but deep inside she still remembered what it was to be Sally, to be Cutter Sal and Cutter. She would happily *cut* any man who tried to remind her of her past, but that did not mean she had forgotten it herself.

Sorry, my love, she thought to her husband. *I want to be a proper lady for you, I do, but this is a bill-hook haggle, and I mean to make this jump-up pay her due.*

Even as she thought it, she felt a flush of deeper joy, because as much as she wanted to be a fine noblewoman for Prentice, he loved her even as Cutter Sal and Cutter, raped and broken like shards of glass. She knew that when she told him about this day, he would tut and shake his head like a disappointed school master, but he would smile at her all the same. Then he would laugh and take her to bed, kiss and hold her all night like she was his whole heart, which she was.

But first, let's deal with you, my wild little filly from the riverside.

Not taking her gaze from Daisy's face, she carefully untied her lace mask from about her head. She spun it in the air, to catch the ties one handed, then held it out.

"Solomon, take this will you, please," she said, still not looking away from her rebellious student. "And see you do not put it near your face. It's a thing for ladies, not Lions."

Solomon took it from her, and it looked like he quickly hid it behind his back. With one hand on her walking-stick sword, she used her now freed other hand to point to the brand under her eye, exposed by the removal of her mask.

"You ken this?" she asked, letting all pretense of speaking like a fine lady fall away. "I got this for gutter gullin' a fool with a dirk on the Denay dockside. Surely you girls have wondered what's 'neath the lace, ain't you? Didn't you hear no rumors?"

Hiding another wince behind her sneer, Righteous settled her weight across both feet and lifted the sword in her hand, holding the hilt out to Daisy.

"You want me to show you somethin' more than—what was it?—prancin' and gambolin'? Alright then. Feel the weight."

Daisy hesitated, then reached out to the sword's hilt.

"Go on," Righteous insisted.

The young woman let her fingers wrap around the handle, then just as Righteous felt Daisy take some of the weight, she wrenched the scabbard back, so that the blade was bared, glinting in the sunlight. Every woman present drew her breath in—a soft sound, but collected all together, clearly audible. This was the first time any of them had held a genuine weapon during Righteous's drills.

"Now you have a sword, young Daisy girl, and all I got me is a stick." Righteous flourished the scabbard like a singlestick. "You got the plum hand in this game, the trump card, but you better have learned how to play it."

Daisy's expression became puzzled, but her eyes went wide as Righteous stepped adroitly to her right and slapped the scabbard down to strike the side of the girl's knee. She yelped and jumped back.

"That's better girlie, but still too slow."

"Warn me next time!" Daisy said sullenly, flexing her leg to relieve the pain.

"Warn ye? Warn ye? What d'ye think this is, Daisy girl? An honor duel? If it was, I'd have me a sharp steel to match yours, no mistake. You have the sword. If you think it's hard goin' to face just a stick, then you need to ask Solomon there what it's like to go bared steel to bared steel. He's got that face, and he *won* his duel. And you, scared of a little stick."

Several of the young women looked to Solomon again, and this time Righteous was sure there was less laughter in their expressions. That pleased her, but she wasn't done teaching the day's proper lesson. She looked to Daisy once more.

"You better ready that cutter o' yours my lass, cause my stick is ever so twitchy today."

Righteous moved again and was pleased to see Daisy at least make an effort to protect herself with the blade in her hand. The baroness streetfighter knew she was being unfair. Almost everyone was unnerved the first time they drew live steel, doubly so if they did not actually want to hurt or kill anyone. Daisy had been mouthing off, not actually issuing a challenge. But body-guarding was a serious matter, and it was time that lesson was pressed home. Righteous had had this lesson taught to her in a hot, low-roofed room at the back of a warehouse the first time she ran her mouth at Master Elmantin. She knew her Prentice had learned the same lesson even younger than she had. And Solomon...well Solomon was probably the only young buck Righteous had ever met that was canny enough to know this lesson without having to be taught.

Now it was Daisy's turn.

Feinting in one direction, Righteous sidestepped easily, despite the pain in her back and abdomen that was refusing to recede, and whipped the scabbard in a circle to clap Daisy on the shoulder. Before the girl could recoil, the tip of the improvised singlestick dropped to her wrist and knocked the sword expertly from her grasp. It fell to the dirt and Daisy rubbed at her arm and hand.

"Pick it up!" Righteous ordered firmly but without raising her voice. Daisy shook her head warily. "No? How 'bout you?"

The baroness whirled upon the loudmouth who had called Solomon "pig faced." That girl also shook her head.

"No?"

In spite of the pain, Righteous found she was smiling, a kind of wild, gritted-teeth joy governing her thoughts. She danced back towards Daisy, flicking the girl with the scabbard a fourth time before spinning in place and surging toward the loudmouth, clouting her on the forehead. Now the entire class was withdrawing, keeping back from her as they would from a feral animal. It felt wonderful. Righteous stood grimacing at them, the fallen sword only a pace in front of her.

"You think this is going to be pretty dresses and maybe flashin' a bit of brass now and then? You think I'm teaching you to put an unwanted sweetheart on his arse when he's got an overeager gaff in his cod? Is that what you think? The Lioness has real enemies, my fillies. They come in the night with swords and maces and sometimes even magicks, and she ain't got no time for lacey fripperies if they ain't draped around hard steel. So, someone better pick that sword up!"

Still the young maiden trainees held back, their eyes wide with uncertainty and no small amount of fear.

"Right, well let's put it this way," Righteous declared, raising her voice as she upped the ante. "If none of you tries for that sword and right soon, then none of you eats tonight or at breaking fast tomorrow. And we'll come back here tomorrow morning and do this again until one of you gets her courage up, or I send you all back to squat in the river muck again."

One of the young women made a half-hearted start out of the ring that now surrounded the furious, red-faced instructress with her "stick," but Righteous moved one step toward her and the girl flinched back. The baroness's legs were aching, and her back was burning, but she faced them all down, delighted at a bared-steel moment for once. The pain and the weight in her belly made her sweat, and she could feel it running down her face, but she did not care. This was too much fun. She was surprised when Solomon stepped out of the ring toward her.

"You still get to eat, lad," she said, her voice rasping. "This ain't your game."

"Ain't so, My Lady," he answered her. "If the cubs go hungry, then the cubs *all* go hungry. Lions eat together, march together, and fight together."

He stopped, standing astride the sword.

"I won't let 'em eat if you take it for 'em," the baroness warned him.

"I figured," Solomon said, and he smiled her smile back at her—the smile of tempered courage that only the blooded can share. "But I can get in the way while someone else takes it."

"I won't spare ye!" Righteous hissed, and she meant it, though she bore him no ill-will for his intervention.

"I know."

Just to test him, Righteous slapped his upper arm just as she had Daisy's. He barely flinched.

"Someone grab that bloody sword," he shouted, his voice cracking high as he did so. Then he rushed at Righteous, arms held forward, clearly to protect his head. It was akin to the maneuver he had used to win his duel last year—a strong charge. Righteous was so distracted with how proud of him she was that she almost didn't react in time. As it happened, she only managed one barely effective thrust with the stick, and though it twisted him about some, it was not strong enough to fully deflect his oncoming mass. With his youth, it was easy to forget that he was as tall as she was and likely just as heavy. One day he would certainly be a tall, well-built man indeed. However, it was not Solomon's weight that caused Righteous her main problem. It was her own. Her swollen, painful belly threw her balance far out of line, and when Solomon adjusted his direction to keep coming at her despite her deflection, she was wrongfooted, slipping to one knee. She spun her scabbard, trying to bat him away, but he took the two swift strokes on his back with no more than a grunt and then wrapped his arms around hers, pinning her from further strikes.

"Don't you try wrestlin' me, you cheeky devil," Righteous panted, but before she could fight back against his clinch, she felt a wetness on her legs and wondered if they had somehow ended up on top of the dropped sword. Had she cut herself on the bared edge? Then her first strong contraction hit her, and she realized what the pain she had been ignoring all morning was. She released a long moan from her chest and gasped. She had been cut, beaten, and raped in her life, and none of that was like this. It wasn't worse, necessarily, just more undeniable. Her sight blurred as her eyes filled with tears. She felt rather than saw Solomon release her, but no sooner had he stepped back than suddenly a half dozen other pairs of hands were upon her, lifting her to her feet and guiding her toward the women's hut.

"Prentice?" she gasped through gritted teeth as she half stumbled through the doorway, tears streaming down her face. "Where's my Prentice?"

CHAPTER 35

"Aha, you are servants of the lovely duchess of Dweltford," said the swarthy trader Master Jannomoch after Prentice had explained who he and his men were. Big-bellied, even by the standards of wealthy merchants, Jannomoch had that strong-limbed size that spoke of a man who still worked with his hands. His stature reminded Prentice of the dead smuggler-merchant Vardian Malden, but where Malden had the lumpen face and twisted knuckles of a retired pit-fighter, not to mention a snake's cold manner about him, Jannomoch was soft-skinned, gregarious and welcoming. His bright smile opened his dark lips readily, revealing a full set of white teeth, except for one that was grey and likely soon to need pulling. Prentice knew the man's heritage suggested he was from a land in the northeast on the other side of the Grand Kingdom, but he did not know the region's name or else had forgotten it.

"I had the good fortune to meet her grace, did you know?" Jannomoch asked. Prentice shook his head. "Yes. Last year in Griffith. I was there as a guest of the conclave, and she addressed them. Her need was great, and I desired to assist her, but I had already committed my treasury for that pilgrimage."

"Pilgrimage?" Brother Whilte asked, confused by the use of the word. There was nowhere in the Griffith region, or the Pale, where the devout made pilgrimage, at least as far as Prentice knew.

Master Jannomoch laughed, a rich, melodious sound that seemed to echo up from his belly. "It is what I call my annual trip into the Reach," he said. "The folk on the farms hereabouts give me their orders and I go to the bigger market in Griffith to get them the prices I can, as well as to sell produce and some stock. The grasses in Radongen make for a particularly flavourful breed of lamb, and the wool is thick, too."

Prentice shared a look with Whilte. By Grand Kingdom standards, the market in Griffith was barely worthy of note. It was not even as large as Within Walls. To hear it called a bigger market and a place of pilgrimage was quite ironic.

I suppose such matters are relative, Prentice thought.

"Well, I was not privy to any of that meeting," he told the merchant, "But I do know that her grace is intent upon opening more trade with your region and the folk of Raden-gon-Beyond-Dwelt."

Prentice looked around him, as if marveling at a new and exotic town or land. In truth Jannomoch's trading post was a fenced compound that surrounded a single jetty on the north bank of the Murr. From what he could see, the place supported perhaps as many as fifty people, a handful of huts, and two barn-like warehouses. There were other fenced enclosures just outside the compound for livestock, but only one of these held animals and was only half full at that.

"For now, Master Jannomoch, we are intent on traveling up the Murr to its headwaters."

"You seek to punish the invaders?" Jannomoch asked, eyes suddenly narrowing in suspicion.

Prentice nodded, watchful of the sudden change in the merchant's mood.

"What do you want from us?" Jannomoch continued.

"Boats and supplies," Prentice told him, "whatever you can spare. We will rent the watercraft if we can, or if you do not trust us to return them, we will buy."

"There are not many barges in Radengon that will suit your needs, and most are well spoken for this season. What of supplies? How much do you want?"

"Whatever you can spare," Whilte said. Jannomoch nodded to the chaplain but turned his shrewd gaze back on Prentice.

"And what if we can spare nothing? We did not have your drought, but heaven was not generous to us last season either."

"What you cannot spare, we will not take," Prentice told him flatly and stared him straight in the eye as he did so. Jannomoch met his gaze for a long moment.

"We cannot spare," the merchant said slowly, as if testing uncertain ground, like wading into a swamp and watching to see if there was an unexpected depth waiting to suck folk down.

"Then we will enjoy your field for a camp this night, with your permission, and march in the morning," Prentice said. "I will ask if there is a riverman's boat that can run messages for me up the Dwelt to Dweltford. I would tell my liege of our progress and send a letter to my wife."

Jannomoch held Prentice's gaze a moment longer, and then his convivial smile broke out again, like the sun coming from behind a cloud.

"This is excellent, and yes, the cost of a messenger to take a boat will not be too great."

"Will you accept a promissory note?" Prentice asked, since he had no more than a handful of coins with him. He had always planned to ask for credit but was glad now that it was only for a messenger boat to take letters instead of boats and provisions for five hundred militiamen. He held out his hand for the merchant to see his new signet ring. "I will affix my seal to the claim."

Jannomoch looked it over, assessing it as he might any other trade good. He nodded.

"For this I will take the word of the Lioness' men. I have seen into her eyes and trust her. She is just and faithful to God and to her people."

"Then I will have the letters written for you when we leave in the morning," Prentice said, ready now to return to his men and reexamine their supply situation. Perhaps some of the farms west would be willing to give up a few of these "desirable" sheep.

He and Whilte had gone no more than a step when Jannomoch followed them, coming up beside them once more. "Tell me, Knight Baron, are you intent on boats? You mean to send for them with your letter, no?"

Prentice smiled and looked to Whilte a moment. The chaplain wore an amused expression. They both had some idea of what was coming. Having apologized that he cannot help them except for the barest service of a messenger, Jannomoch was about to offer them something that had "just" occurred to him—something that would be a difficult favor for him to provide. It would be some great effort to arrange and all the more expensive for that, but he would be willing to try for them. And his profit margin would be many times greater than just providing them the food or boats would have been.

"A few years ago, I might have been able to fetch you some boats from the docks in Aubrey," the merchant said thoughtfully, as if their need for transport had become an intricate puzzle he felt morally obliged to aid with. "Of course, that is in ruin now. But we do still run down to Bridgetown, and they have boats aplenty. If you could wait a fortnight, I might be able to buy barges for you from a skilled wright I know there. Best builder on all the waters. Vec princes ride in his boats. They have them carried over the land to their inner rivers since no water of the Murr connects to the Vec rivers, not since Mannerisk filled in the canal, may God curse him for a paranoid fool."

All Prentice knew of a man named Mannerisk was a Vec figure of some importance who had died when Prentice was still a boy.

"That is a very generous offer, Master Jannomoch," he said, trying not to smirk at the merchant's obvious scheming. "However, two weeks is too long to wait."

"Ah, it would probably not have been possible anyway," Jannomoch said with exaggerated disappointment. He hung his head and sighed enormously, like the huff of a laboring bullock. "And in truth I would have felt bad taking your money for so poor a tool."

What did that mean?

Prentice looked at Whilte and it was clear that neither of them had understood Jannomoch's import. The merchant smiled and shrugged apologetically.

"You cannot take boats more than a week upriver, perhaps less," he explained.

"Why not?"

"The land, it rises sudden and steep. The river comes down from the heights over rapids. There is no way to take a boat to the upper water save to haul it up a ridge. A hard journey indeed."

"If it is so difficult, how do folk on this upper land come down here?" Whilte asks.

"There are no folk on the upper land," Jannomoch said, and his smile dimmed, a look in his eyes of fear or awe. "It is an empty place, full of ghosts and death. Nothing lives there."

"Except the Redlanders?" Prentice offered. Jannomoch obviously did not know the term, but he quickly seemed to puzzle it out.

"The painted raiders? The men with animal faces and skin like pelts of beasts?" the merchant asked, shaking his head. "No, even they do not live there. Wherever they live, it is beyond that plain. Fitting do you not think? Only men who have forsaken their mortality for the power of beasts and demons could dwell in a land beyond a dead land."

Fitting indeed, Prentice thought, instinctively thinking of Jannomoch's words as legend or fey tale but reminding himself that they were living in an age of legends and frightening stories become real. Perhaps nothing could be utterly unbelievable in such a world. The merchant became very serious for a moment.

"I have respect for Lady Amelia, truly I do," he said, squeezing his hands together earnestly in front of his chest. The pink skin of his palms contrasted with the darkness of the flesh on the back. "And I do not doubt your bravery, not even of the least boy who marches with you, but now you go to your death, don't you?"

"We are not inexperienced in fighting the painted men and their bestial champions," Whilte said, his tone suggesting he was trying to be encouraging.

"It will not matter," Jannomoch said, shaking his head pityingly. "Do not mistake me, My Lords. I do not despise your effort, and your might is becoming remarked, even here so far from your lands. Yet it will not be enough. If I thought you might succeed, then I would buy you boats and all the food you could need myself. I would indebt myself to every man and woman of Radengon-Beyond-Dwelt to aid you."

He started to walk away, head still down, like a mourner leaving a graveside. He turned back for one last comment.

"I will send your messages. I will not even ask for payment. But make sure you write your most important words, especially to your wife. They will be the last she receives from you."

Prentice nodded, and he and Whilte left the trading post compound through the landward gate. They turned left and headed to where the company was setting its camp for the night.

"Well, that was quite the dire prognostication," Whilte said with what sounded like forced cheer. "Let us hope it is not a true prophecy."

Prentice only kept his eyes on the ground, barely listening to his companion's words. His mind was on the problems they now faced. As he turned it over, he realized that it had been hopeful optimism to imagine this frontier land would be able to provide enough to resupply him and his men. If the haunted upland Jannomoch had described was truly a week upriver, he could send a letter by fast boat to Dweltford and they might send him some food in that time, especially if they rushed, and if the town's storehouses had enough easily to hand. Dalflitch would pull whatever favors she could to stock a barge or two for his needs, but it would be another burden on the Reach. At least he was only taking five hundred souls with him.

Of course, the Redlanders are hiding on the other side of a haunted land, he thought, hardly noticing as Whilte left him to his rumination. He remembered the picture in Borrosod's codex, the knight fighting a manticore. What else might be in this upland plain, waiting to put them in their graves?

Reaching his own tent, same size as all the others, Prentice sat on his simple wood-frame cot and pulled out his scribing board, a little table designed to hang by a cord around a writer's neck, with a compartment that held a few sheets of parchment and a quill. A little notch fitted his glass ink bottle. Prentice did not bother with the hanging cord, only sitting the board flat on his lap as he composed first his letter to the archduchess, addressing it to both her and Lady Dalflitch as factor and seneschal. When he was done, he took a long moment to consider what he wanted to write to his wife. He wondered if he should make it a goodbye of sorts, as Jannomoch had urged. He tried to imagine Righteous listening as someone read the text to her. For a moment he pictured it being Solomon, even though Solomon was still only a novice at reading. Prentice imagined himself dead, and this text as the last connection drummer and baroness had to him. He had friends and allies in his life now, more and closer than he once had ever imagined he might, but these two, woman and boy, were the two he loved most in the whole world—them and his babe, whom he prayed was now brought safely into life.

"I will not say goodbye," he muttered to himself and began to pen the missive. Come ghosts, come manticores—let this land send him whatever it would. He would fight them all and win his way back to his beloved. Benjamin's scout had managed it, which meant it could be done. Come what may, he would find this dragonfly lake and return, ghosts and Redlanders be damned.

CHAPTER 36

"Next time I see him I'm gonna skin his scraggly hide and wear it for a bonnet, I swear!" Righteous gasped through gritted teeth, the last words choking off in another red-faced groan of agony. "He did this to me!"

"Sure'n I'll bet ye were more'n willin' when it happened," muttered the midwife in a tone of good-natured rebuke. The elder woman from the village at the foot of Fallenhill's valley held up Righteous's skirt, watching her body's progress.

"O'course I was willing," Righteous huffed, getting her breath back as the contraction receded. "That's 'cause no one tells you that sweet nights in your marriage bed lead to hours like this!"

The midwife chuckled and stood from where she was sitting at the end of the bed. The bent-backed old woman shuffled over to a small table where she had laid out a handful of tools Righteous could not see and did not understand. Didn't she just need some catgut to tie off the cord and a sharp knife to cut it? What else was wanted?

"You know, I think we keep this part a mystery, especially to the menfolk, for good reason," the midwife said as she returned. "After all, what do they want to know about us huffin' and pantin' and screamin'. And I am well certain that if they knew exactly what it looked like for us to go through this, they'd never touch us for fear o' puttin' us through it all. Most husbands care about us at least that much."

"Not all the ones who put us through this are loving husbands though, not by a long shot," Righteous retorted, scowling at the memory of her worst night, always ready to raise itself in her thoughts if she let it. The midwife nodded soberly.

"Ye've been on the receivin' end o' that, too, in yer time, I can see," she agreed.

Righteous let out an involuntary whimper that made her disgusted with herself for its display of weakness, but exhausted as she was, she had no strength left to care. It broke her heart to think that there were scars on her body that revealed that she had once been raped and beaten. Worse, it clenched that broken heart in a crushing grip to think that her beloved husband could see those marks every time he looked on her naked. Every time they were one with each other, was he confronted with those scars? Was her escape from the memories only purchased by forcing him to face them for her? Righteous knew how that would feel. Sometimes at night, when Prentice was asleep beside her and there was moonlight to see by, she would trace some of the scars in his flesh, trying to imagine what horrific tools had inflicted those injuries and what it had taken to heal them to this level. She often ardently wished she could fly like an angel across the mountains and backward through the years to rescue him from the pit where the Inquisition had tortured him.

The deep, warning whispers of the next contraction drew her thoughts from the past and into the present.

"Well, never mind all that," the midwife was saying. "Soon enough ye'll have a fresh babe in yer arms, and its sweet face will start ye to forgettin' all about the pain. Before ye know it, yer thoughts'll be turnin' to getting' yer man back from the wars so ye can both start on makin' the next one."

"Some chance!" Righteous cursed, listening to her body and its warnings of a building contraction. As much as she did not want it, she found she was wishing it would come on quicker rather than tormenting her with waiting. "But you think I'll deliver? It's coming alive?"

"Why would ye worry 'bout...oh. Well don't ye waste thoughts on that sort o' thinkin'. Ye just fix on lovin' the little'un when it gets here." The midwife looked Righteous over. "Seems to me that we might be reachin' the last bit, so if ye think ye're needin' a drink o' somethin' to get through the pushin', now's the time we get one o' the girlies to fetch it."

"Damnation no!" Righteous declared, glaring angrily at the older woman. "I didn't pack 'em off earlier just to have 'em come in and gawk at me like this!"

"Why be like that? Girls need to see this part so that when their time comes, they know what to 'spect."

"Well, let 'em watch some other goodwife's struggles. I know what they must be saying about me behind my back. I don't need to feed 'em more gossip fodder."

"What are ye on about? What do ye think they're sayin'?"

Righteous wanted to vent her spleen, to pour out a stream of invective for all the contempt and insults she had been imagining her students had been making as they mocked her privately for her being lower born than even they were and now playing queen-of-the-castle over them.

"Unkind things," was all she could find the will to tell the midwife, however.

"Fie on that," the old woman said matter-of-factly, looking Righteous dead in the eye for a moment. "They worship the ground ye walk on, don't ye doubt it!"

"What are you talki...aargh?" Righteous's words were cut short as the muscles in her belly clenched again, driving the air from her lungs. The midwife took her hand and patted it as she endured the contraction, and slowly, with time, the pain receded. Even before she recovered her breath, she looked, gasping, for the midwife to explain her impossible assertion.

"Ye haven't heard what they actually do say 'bout ye. How ye're a back-alley shanker, deadly as any man they ever known of. There was some bloke named Fulford, I hear?"

Righteous nodded, recognizing the name of the ambitious young smuggler boss she had killed the previous summer.

"Right, well seems he was known for takin' liberties with dock maids in Dweltford. And ye put an end to him, s'that right? Well, that makes ye some kind o' avengin' angel in their eyes, and no mistake. A man deservin' o' the noose, by the stories I hear."

Now Righteous shook her head, and for the first time since she had collapsed in the training yard, she almost forgot the pain she was going through. Fulford had certainly been a conniving, murderous dockland boss, and it came as no surprise to her that he might have been in the habit of forcing himself upon young women in his community. Of course, she also imagined that he must have kept that reasonably secret. She could not believe that his granny, the Ragmother, would have thought too highly of such behavior.

"But they're always giving me such grief," she protested weakly to the watching elder woman.

"O'course they do!" the midwife responded as if what she was saying was obvious. "Ye're the swordmaid bodyguard o' the Lioness o' the Reach. They know ye're nastier than a rabid dog and sharper than one o' them spears the militia fellas out there carry. They want ye to think they're tough like ye are!"

"So why don't they just do what I say and show me?"

"Cause they's girls, ain't they?"

Again, Righteous shook her head, and this time she truly did not understand the midwife's point at all. The woman rolled her eyes.

"Ye grew up with boys mainly, didn't ye?" she asked. Righteous nodded. "It shows. Ye're thick-headed 'bout some things, just like a boy would be. Girls don't brawl; ye know that much at least, I hope? Girls whisper and catpad around each other's backs, which I suppose is what ye kenned must o' been happenin', so ye're not quite young-boy thick-headed, but ye're close still. Boys do their fightin' straight all through their childhood, roughhousin' and wrestlin'. By the time they're the age o' yer stepson out there, they know what fightin' words are, what they sound like, and how to say 'em. And they're ready to learn how to speak close to 'em without goin' out o' bounds, to be respectful and challengin' all in one bag o' words. But girls? They just whisper and snipe over their sewin' or milkin' until one of 'em cries. They don't know how to thread the needle 'tween grovellin' and fightin' words the way strong good men are with each other, and ain't no one want to teach 'em how until you come."

Righteous was stunned at how obvious it was now that the midwife had spelled it out. The riverfolk maids she was training knew that she wanted them to be tough and fearless, but they had no notion how to show it to her, and she had the wrong idea of what it would look like. Righteous had assumed that they had her street fighting experience, the knowledge gained from years runnin'-the-cobbles that she took for granted. If they had spoken to her in some back alley the way they did here, they would have learned quick smart what it meant to challenge Cutter Sal.

"I'm used to training men," she muttered half to herself, and that one observation settled everything into place in her mind. "They kept making me prove myself, prove I was worthy to teach them, so I never imagined any one of them would want to prove himself to me."

The midwife nodded.

"And that's menfolk, who, for all their ox-brained skulls, at least know 'bout provin' themselves in a fight. What's young'un fillies know 'bout that?"

"I've not been much of a teacher," Righteous said and shook her head. The motion reminded her that her body was still in the midst of a significant occasion, and she swallowed, waiting for the next bout.

"Ye're not so bad as all that," the midwife said comfortingly, patting her hand again. "And ye're teachin' 'em to be swordmaids and ladies all at once. Can't be no easy feat."

Again, Righteous shook her head and it set off a bout of nausea that made her think she might throw up, but that faded into the aching pain of another building contraction soon enough.

"I'm not teaching ladyship all that much," she huffed, feeling the coming agony-filled wave. "I'm still learning all that myself. I don't even remember to speak right half the time. It's Dalflitch'll teach 'em all that just like she's teaching me."

"Well, ye do about as much like a lady as I ever seen. Now wait there a space while I go fetch one o' them girlies to help us in this next part."

"What? Why?"

"Because we're comin' to the dawn, my deary, and when the real bright light hits ye, ye're goin' to want to hold onto someone for dear life. It can't be me, cause I'll be busy at the other end, so best to get you Daisy to grip onto while you get through."

"Her...ooooh," Righteous tried to object, but the pain had its own ideas.

"Yes, her, milady," the midwife insisted, using the correct term of respect for the first time since she had arrived from the village. "Girl's got more midwifery in her than any o' the others by a long league. She's the one that told me to be ready, that ye'd be deliverin' sometime in these past few days."

"She knew?" Righteous could barely believe her ears, but contraction pain had reached a peak that no surprise could distract her from. She groaned in agony.

"She did indeed, milady. Now after this one's passed, I'll go fetch her and the pair of us'll have you off this bed and bent over, better to deliver."

"Like a cow?"

"Like womenfolk 'ave been doin' this since Eve left the garden, yer Ladyship. No matter how high an' mighty ye get, this'll bring ye back to earth with the rest of us mere mortals."

The contraction slowly faded to its lower level of pain, which was now much higher than it had been between earlier phases. Righteous hoped it would all be done soon, but she was still afraid. To go through all this and deliver stillborn could truly break her, she thought. She was sure she would never look her husband in the eye again if that happened, and that thought brought fresh tears to her eyes that she was too tired to care about. They streamed down her cheeks.

Yet only an hour later, Daisy and the midwife were fussing over the unfathomably precious, *living* product of Righteous's labor.

"There we go, Baroness, nice and warm. Still a little mucky, but newborns is filthy creatures, don't you doubt."

Righteous lay on her back, glad for the chance to rest after the previous hour of pushing and birthing her first crying, wriggling, living daughter. She wrapped her arms around the little bundle on her chest and wept with relief. Her child had arrived.

"You hold 'er for just a little while," the midwife was saying. "We might have to take 'er back while you deliver the afterbirth but maybe not. That can go easy or hard, no way to tell yet, but ye're lookin' hale enough. Once that's out, we'll get yer littlun on the teat. Get 'er and yer body acquainted with their new way 'tween 'em. She'll be there a lot for some years yet."

Righteous was too happy with her newborn daughter to really listen, more delighted than she had ever imagined she would be by the sounds of an infant, even when it had been crying at first. The midwife insisted the little thing was only cold, and now that she had been wrapped in a woolen blanket, the baby was settling calmly.

"She's beautiful," Daisy said, leaning in to look at the smeared pink face amidst the folds.

"Aye, she is," Righteous agreed. Despite their history to this point, the baroness had found Daisy to be every bit the helpful presence the midwife had assured her she would be. She looked up and smiled at Daisy. "I hear you knew I was near my time?"

"Seemed like to me," the young woman answered, shrugging shyly. She was almost a different person altogether at this moment to Righteous. The aggressive belligerence was gone, replaced with a simple happiness. She wiped some of the sweat from Righteous's brow.

"Thank you," the new mother told the girl.

"Do you know what you're to name her?"

"We have some thoughts, but nothing picked for sure yet," Righteous said, then frowned in renewed discomfort. "Ooh, something's moving again."

"The afterbirth, my dear," said the midwife.

"Almost all over," Daisy added, and after a nod from the elder woman, she reached out to take baby back for a moment. Righteous was reluctant already to hand her off but too tired to resist. She could feel herself delivering the last of her newborn's direct connection to her body.

"It stings a bit like a cut," she said, thinking that otherwise it was not as painful as it had been.

"That's 'cause ye've torn a little," said the midwife.

"It's not much," Daisy said comfortingly. "Most mam's tear some their first time."

"Not just their first times," the midwife muttered.

"Torn?" Righteous asked, suddenly alarmed. She lifted her head to look directly at the midwife still between her legs. "What's torn?"

The midwife rolled her eyes. "Oh, what do ye think tore? Daft girl."

"Don't be afraid, it's all for the good..." Daisy started to say, but Righteous cut her off with another groan. The pain in her abdomen started up swiftly once more.

"What are ye...?" the midwife asked rhetorically and crawled up the bed slightly to put her hands on Righteous's belly. The woman's soft-skinned, wrinkled fingers pushed with surprising strength into the baroness's flesh. Righteous could not feel the stinging sensation anymore. This was like the contractions. She felt her breath catch in her throat as a sudden fear gripped her. Sometimes the afterbirth did not deliver right. She had heard of that. A babe could come but would tear itself free of a mother so harshly that she bled to death right there on the birthing bed. Only a moment ago she was just getting to know her daughter, and now this? She had fought so hard to come this far, and she'd won the fight. It wasn't right to have her fall after the victory like this. Fresh tears stung her eyes.

"Oh no, Lord God," she wailed and prayed all at once. "Don't take me away so soon. Let me stay, please. Even just a little while?"

"What are ye going on about?" the midwife demanded. The elderly woman pushed herself back onto her knees on the bed and looked down sternly on Righteous.

"I know what it means when afterbirth don't come out right," Righteous spat back, feeling angry at the woman's apparent disdain.

"Daft cow, the afterbirth's been out o' ye awhile now."

"What? Then why am I still...oowwa?"

"Does that answer yer question?"

The midwife pushed herself back to be standing once more, as she had been earlier.

"No," Righteous wailed. "What's happenin'? Tell me, please, what's happenin'?"

"What's happenin' your ladyship is that we ain't done with this evening's business."

Righteous had not even noticed that the labor had been ongoing so long that now it had become night. Even as the midwife said it, the baroness spared not a thought for the dark outside the shuttered window.

"What's still to happen?"

"Ye've got to finish yer work and bring yer other child into the world," the midwife said, and Righteous could not make any sense of the words.

"You're having twins," Daisy explained with a beaming smile as she held Righteous's swaddled little girl close to her breast.

Oh my good Lord, thank you so much, Righteous thought joyfully, and when the pain spiked again swiftly, she gritted her teeth and smiled her fighting smile. She had suffered and now knew what this pain was as well. This did not frighten her anymore. She was going to beat this down, just like she had beaten Malden and Fulford and all the twits that took her for a little girl, easy prey. And when she was done and Prentice came home, she was going to present her husband with their *two* children. The contraction throttled her exhausted torso and Righteous almost laughed like a madwoman. She could hardly remember ever being so happy.

CHAPTER 37

Amelia sat in a tent, staring at the canvass side, barely hearing the sounds without. It was dark now, long after sundown. Someone had brought a small oil lamp sometime earlier, but she had not spoken or even turned to acknowledge them. Everything was wrong, and she had no idea how to come back from this place to where she belonged. Everything was wrong. She was sitting on a wooden camp chair that did not belong to her, and the tent was not hers either. These were on the periphery of her thoughts though, hardly more acknowledged than the servant with the lamp had been.

I am not dead, she thought, as she had now for hours. It was the impossible notion to which her thoughts returned continually. In her nostrils she could still smell the smoke and fire, the hot iron, and the blood. Later, there had been shouts and cries, pain and fear from so many of her sworn men-at-arms, but her thoughts were trapped, chained to the hilltop where everyone else had died.

I am not dead.

Someone new came into the tent, steel harness clanking as they moved. A figure in armor stood next to her and then crouched down—more a shadow in the edge of her vision than an actual person. For a long stretch she only focused on the tent's blank wall until the person beside her removed their gauntlets and took her hand in theirs. Amelia turned to look and saw it was a man, and as she noticed that, his features became sensible to her mind. It was her Farringdon. Yet even as she recognized him, she saw the blood from his ear still upon his neck and the one dark eye, and she recoiled in horror. It was him but he was monstrous in her sight. Even as she tried to pull away, he gripped her hands tighter, almost painfully.

"Amelia," he whispered to her vehemently, pulling her to him against her terror. "Amelia, my love. I'm so sorry."

He embraced her, and the press of his armor hard against her cheek reminded her of how safe she usually felt in his arms. Suddenly, she flung herself into the hug, straining her arms to pull him closer, as if she could press herself through his breastplate and into him, merging them into one being. She let herself forget everything she could to cling to the memory of shelter. When she had been rescued from Bluebird, he had held her like this, shielding her from danger with his own body.

"How badly are we defeated, husband?" she whispered in his ear at last, as her thoughts returned her to herself a little. Farringdon pushed back from her to look her in the eyes. His left one was so dark with blood that it was almost black in the weak lamplight. Even ignoring her fear of it, she stared. How could he see through that much blood?

"Who told you we are defeated?" he asked her.

"Is it not obvious?" she asked forlornly.

He smiled at her gently. "Today is no resounding victory, Your Grace," he said, switching to her title. "But we are far from defeated."

Amelia could not understand his meaning. She looked around the shadowy tent, firelights glowing on the other sides of the canvass.

"Am I not a prisoner?" she asked, more confused than trying to make a point.

"No, Your Grace," Farringdon told her, cocking an eyebrow in surprise. "This is my uncle's tent."

Amelia blinked again, and as her questioning mind began to assert itself more fully, she felt the cloud of horror and memory begin to fade. There was a sun burning off the battle fog, it seemed.

"Where are we, My Lord?"

"Cattlefields, Your Grace."

"Across the river?"

Vaguely, Amelia remembered the rush from their camp to the bridge, lancer escort about her, shouting for all the stewards and other camp followers to flee with them to safety. Spindle had been there at one point, surrounded by her mailed body-guards. Amelia remembered being relieved for her lady-in-waiting's safety.

Then she had dismounted and pressed herself against Sil-vermane's flanks, while on the northside of the river the lancers fought against Robant's knights and just mere paces south of her, the Lions afoot battled tooth and nail against the Vec. In the confusion, she had become isolated in her mind, as if alone amidst a crowd, and the smell of fire and smoke followed her from the hill, obscuring all thought. She had been destined to die under God's hand of judgement and yet she was still alive. She was not dead.

"Tell me what happened."

"We defeated my uncle's force—soundly, as it happens," Farringdon said, and he pushed himself upright again, groaning wearily at the effort, his armor pieces grinding against them-selves quietly. "We took nearly half of them prisoner and cap-tured their camp. All their supplies are ours now."

"Your uncle?" Amelia asked, expecting to hear he had es-caped, that he would be somewhere nearby, rallying his men for further battles. Her husband shook his head grimly.

"He refused to yield," Farringdon said, and his voice was a mix of pity and fury. "Time and again he led his horse contin-gent in a charge against the line. It was Liam all over again, so some of the veterans who were there tell me. Sedgemark held his nerve like a man several years his senior, and the Lions stood fast with him. Markas gave an excellent recommendation when he put his name forward for sergeant. I should never have ordered him to hold back. He told me he saw Uncle Garro go down under Roar fire sometime around noon. The Vec foot troops kept their discipline for another hour, fighting longspear to pike but lacking Fangs to make unexpected gaps under the opposing polemen. It took time, but we ultimately broke them. The Roar he had left also hammered their one flank. It was brutal, by all accounts, but never a truly close contest."

Amelia looked down, working hard to keep her mind from drifting away again as she listened to Farringdon's report. She focused on his voice, trying not to let her thoughts offer up images to match pictures to his words. As it was, what she had seen was still too chaotic to put into a coherent series of facts. She remembered meeting with Prentice barely two or three leagues away across the Murr after the Night of the Red Sky when he had seemed more like a grim ogre in armor than the man she had known. Was this how he had been feeling that morning? How had he brought his mind back to himself? Her thoughts suddenly attached themselves to a surprising piece of Farringdon's report.

"The Roar he had *left*?" she repeated and looked at her husband. What had happened to the matchlocks? Had they been judged as the cannons had?

"Clever beggar is Sergeant Sedgemark, no mistake. He could see he had the whole field under his heel," Farringdon said, smiling appreciatively as a man who cannot help being impressed by something he has seen or heard. "So, he detached half his Roar contingent and sent them to watch the bridge for us. Dashed cunning. We needed it at the end."

Feeling her neck starting to hurt from looking up at him so close, Amelia stood slowly, somewhat unsteadily. Farringdon held out his hand to help, but she realized it was just that her limbs were stiff from sitting so long. She declined his aid with a gentle wave of her hand.

"Why did you need the Roar on the bridge, Knight Captain?" she asked, feeling more of herself returning with each passing moment. Despite her fear that it would never end, the chaos in her mind was receding under the ordering influence of his report, as if the spoken version of events was suppressing the unruly experiences. She would have nightmares tonight, she was sure, and likely for nights to come. But for now, she felt the Lioness coming back to life in her heart.

"The lancers..." Farringdon was saying, answering her question. He shook his head sadly. "They were effective...*we*...were effective. But there were too few. Nunel and I led them around the south of the hill, and we hit the Kingdom knights upon their left rear flank. I think Robant expected our militiamen to break after the explosion, but the Lions on the bastion were solid. They knew a rout would be their death, so they held, and while the knights were engaged with them, we struck. Robant was forced into retreat."

"That sounds like a victory, My Lord," Amelia said.

Farringdon shook his head.

"It was but one exchange of blows in a duel that lasted most of the day. Daven Marcus' man Robant may be many things, few of them righteous, but the man is a fiendish warrior and an excellent tactician. He kept maneuvering over the old estate's fields with a cunning I would never have credited. I was right that our chargers could outrun his destriers in retreat, but his numbers were so much greater, five to one, and he set more than one ambush. In the end it cost us nearly a quarter of our number, dead or wounded."

The anguish at his rider's sacrifices was unmistakable in Farringdon's voice. Amelia felt his pain, and her fears that remained stubborn within her were quelled by her concern for him and the loyal men who had suffered with him.

"Why did you not retreat?"

"Firstly, we had to ensure that the bastion detachment and the remaining servants from the camp had a chance to withdraw in safety. Robant had his men rallied so swiftly, if we had left the field, he'd have made a slaughter of our people on foot. After that, we kept up the game of tag because the outcome on the south bank was not resolved. We had to keep the wolf's jaws open as long as we could. In the end, I heard the drums beating rally from the bridge and saw the Roarsmen ready to cover our withdrawal, and we made for safety as swiftly as we could. Robant tried to run us to ground, but his mounts were done. Armored horses carrying armored men cannot run all day. A few thought to canter onto the bridge, make a melee of it, but the Roar dissuaded them."

Amelia absorbed her husband's words and realized he was right. The day was hardly a defeat. It might even be called a victory, depending on who wrote the ultimate chronical. Then she remembered the Church knight's pronouncement, his cursing words echoing up the hill.

"How many from the cannoneers have survived?" she asked as in her mind's eye she saw again Master Sent touch the linstock to the gun, the fizzing spark, and then the instant cloud of flame and thunder. Farringdon's expression told her what she had feared.

"Only you and I, my love," he said softly. "I think because we had started down, the ridge of the hill's peak protected us from the worst of the blast."

We were protected? Amelia thought, looking at her husband's injured face and remembering her own near death, almost being thrown from her horse.

"Master Sent's cannon exploded," Farringdon continued. "The flames from that detonated the powder stores of the other guns. There was no chance of escape."

"Can anyone escape God's judgement?" Amelia said, and guilt suddenly washed over her like a wave. So many dead just to punish her hubris.

"Judgement? No, Your Grace, you must not think like that," Farringdon said earnestly, taking her hand. "This was horrible, but we need not invoke God's wrath to understand it. One of the gun's likely had a flaw in its manufacture. Once this campaign is done, I'm sure we will be able to discern the cause so that the next ones will be better. The tragedy of Master Sent's death will only be compounded by the loss of his skills, of course, but..."

Amelia recoiled from her husband, snatching back her fingers from his grip as if his hand was painfully hot. Suddenly all the horror and fear that had been settling stirred back to life in her mind, like a wild animal awakening to the scent of prey.

"Are you a *fool*?" she demanded, not sure if she was more shocked or angry. Both emotions were surely mixed in her in equal measure. "You wish to make more of those damned devices?"

Farringdon was clearly shocked by her sudden change in mood.

"We don't give up all swords just because one breaks," he protested.

"These monstrosities are not swords, and I want nothing more to do with them!"

"My love, please, consider..."

Amelia refused to let him finish.

"You will not speak to me again of cannons, unless it is to tell me of how you plan to destroy the ones of our enemies. Do you understand me, *Marquis Consort*?" She emphasized his inferior rank as a way to control him, to make him stop speaking and obey her. Her inner turmoil demanded nothing less. He seemed to understand that was her intent as he watched her a moment, his shadowed face showing no emotion. For some reason that annoyed her even further, though she knew there was no reason it should. He bowed to her formally, as any courtier would to their liege.

"As you command," he said, and his voice sounded controlled but brittle. "With your permission, I will withdraw and see to the camp. I still have many duties."

"Yes, you do," Amelia told him imperiously. Some small part of her knew that what she was about to say next was a mistake, a cruel thing that would only make matters worse between them, but somehow she could not stop herself. The emotions inside would not be denied. "Do not think, Knight Captain, that the way you mishandled me and defied me on the battlefield has been forgotten either. At some time that will have to be addressed."

Farringdon nodded and turned to leave the tent. At the flap, he regarded her over his shoulder.

"You know Prentice has done the same thing more than once," he said. "And to your benefit."

"Knight Commander Baron Ash has earned the privilege," she retorted, recognizing that she was undermining all the effort she had made to comfort her husband that he did not have to compete with Prentice for her respect. "If you can do the same, then you will enjoy the same privilege."

He left, and Amelia hated to see him go. Why was she battering at the man who loved her best in all the world? She was angry, but it was at herself. The judgement was pronounced against her, not Farringdon, and not her people. They were only faithful and loyal, and wounded for it or slain outright. Grief started to push tears into her eyes, but she wiped at them with her sleeve, harsh in her self-disgust, so that she was almost battering her own face to wipe away the salty water. When she finally stopped, she let her hands and head drop. Looking down, she could see dirt and stains on her dress, but her eyes were drawn to the wet smears of blood on the cuffs of her sleeve. She touched her face, and her fingers came away with a wet, rust-red grit. There had been dried blood on her face and the tears had loosened it.

When was I injured? she wondered, far more puzzled than afraid. In fact, in her current mood, it pleased her that she might have been wounded in the battle. It was not fitting that so many should suffer for her while she passed through unscathed.

Lady Spindle leaned through the tent flap, a wooden bowl full of steaming water in her hands and a cloth over her shoulder.

"I thought you might want to wash some of the muck away, Your Grace, afore you came outside," she said politely.

"Yes," Amelia agreed with a soft tone, feeling the blanket of unnatural calm beginning to settle back upon her. She shook her head vehemently and realized that a part of her scalp was very sore and likely the source of the blood. It would be so comforting to withdraw into that broken-minded stillness, but she forced herself not to. Her responsibility was to the Reach and to Aubrey. Men had suffered and died for her today. Angry with him or not, she would not leave the duty of leading her army solely to Farringdon. She let Spindle begin to bathe her face and stood waiting, impatient to leave this captured tent.

CHAPTER 38

"It seems we move faster than others," said Brother Whilte. Six days' march west brought the Gryphon Banner Company to the rise in the land Jannomoch had told them of a day earlier than the merchant had claimed. Prentice might have been pleased that they had made such good time, since it likely indicated that morale was still high; however, his mind was already moving on to the next set of problems. As they had approached, it had looked like they were advancing on a low range of hills with strangely jagged tops. A day ago, however, the panorama had resolved to show that it was an escarpment—a long, flat ridge rising to an upland plateau—and the jagged tops were mountain peaks somewhere much more distant beyond that upland. The scarp was not quite a cliff, but it might as well have been. Facing west, Prentice looked to his right and left to see the ground sweep upward a hundred or so feet in an increasingly steep curve that would straddle the boundary between a walkable slope and a proper rock climb.

"So, we have to get up there, do we?" Whilte asked rhetorically as he looked up as well. He looked right and left. "Perhaps there's an easier way up somewhere not too far."

"Perhaps," Prentice said without enthusiasm. He turned to face the Murr water no more than twenty paces to their left. "But first we must deal with that!"

The river was flowing down the scarp, cascading over enormous boulders, spraying and pooling all the way down the slope, so that the falls covered several hundred paces across the face of the gradient. Jannomoch had not been exaggerating when he said there was no possibility for a cargo barge to traverse that in either direction. Looking at it, Prentice doubted a well-made barrel would survive being rolled down it, and whatever it contained would be battered to paste inside if it did. The rapids, however, were not his main concern.

At the foot of the scarp, the falling water pooled to form a lake, two hundred paces across, with willows and paperbarks growing on the banks. The water looked deep and dark, and about fifty paces from the north bank was a sandstone plinth, poking up from the surface, with an obelisk ten feet tall on top. Square sided and carved, the pillar had something affixed to its peak. From the bank it was hard to discern what that object was, but Prentice was sure none of his fellows doubted what it might be—another mantis mask. A thorough search of the lakeside had discovered no masks in any of the trees on this side of the river, and Prentice had spent close on half an hour studying the rapids to see if there might be a point where a mask could have been safely placed there.

There could be a hundred nooks or crannies to hide one in, he had concluded grimly, and he would likely lose one or more men to injury if he tried to have the rapids searched. So, his mind returned to the obelisk.

"What do you think of it?" he asked Whilte as he led them back to the water's edge.

"It's no mere post stuck in the ground, that's for certain," the chaplain answered. "Perhaps it is significantly different in other ways—ways we cannot even see."

That much made sense. Whilte knew his first duty was to deal with the Redlander artifacts and sorcery, and his hard-set expression showed that he was as troubled by the lack of cardinal point masks as Prentice was.

"Perhaps Solft has something," the knight commander mused, and they ducked under the branches to get close to the water. There, crouched amidst the reeds and the water bugs, Master Solft had a scribing board on hand, sketching the entire scene in charcoal, making multiple drawings of the obelisk especially.

"What say you, Master?" Prentice asked as he crouched down next to the scholar and looked at his diagrams.

"I think that the carving is writing of some sort?" Solft said, nodding at the stone. "There are none on the base that I can see, though I have no idea if that means anything or nothing."

"Sorcery?" Prentice asked, giving Whilte a glance. With the awkwardness of his wooden leg, the chaplain was choosing to stay standing, since rising again once he had lowered himself into the muddy reeds would be an awkward chore.

"I have no way to tell, My Lord," Solft said happily, not exactly apologizing. Rapt in scholarly curiosity, his usual timidity was diminished as a result. He was never so confident and fearless as he was when he was researching.

"What I *can* tell you," the scholar went on, "is that if it is magick writing, it is not the same as the blood-scribed sigils the Redlanders use. Or at least if it is, it is of a graphological structure quite distinct from the usual."

"Which means?" Whilte asked.

"Which means if it is Redlander writing, it was made in a way we have never seen before," Prentice explained.

"From the little I can make out, Baron, I would say it most likely isn't Redlander at all. It could be the same magick but not by the same hand. It would be akin to words that are the same but in different languages with a different alphabet." Solft was quite pleased with his analogy, it seemed, making approving noises as he went back to his sketching.

"Is that even possible?" Brother Whilte was an educated man, but this kind of academic thinking was clearly at the limit of his mind's talents.

"Of course, it is," Solft said, still sketching and looking across the water. "We have a myriad of leftover words from past kingdoms and countries, some over a thousand years old. They had their own alphabets for their languages, but we use their words and spell them in our own fashion."

Whilte nodded, stroking his beard, but it was clear he did not find the concept as self-explanatory as Solft seemed to think it was.

"Stonework is something new for the Redlanders," Prentice said. The invaders had never shown an interest in producing anything so permanent before now.

"Indeed," Solft agreed.

"Or something old," Prentice continued, and that made Solft stop and look at him. The scholar nodded.

"Something which prefigures them? An interesting notion indeed. Of course, that raises the further question: is this even theirs, or is it something that they have borrowed from a past folk, as we have borrowed ancient words?"

Prentice understood Solft's fascination, but history was only his concern in so much as it impacted on his current purpose, and that purpose was to end Redlander power. He stood and began to loosen the buckles on his brigandine.

"Do you have a plan I should know about, My Lord Knight Commander? Or perhaps something about which Sergeant Gennet should be informed?" Whilte asked, watching as Prentice shrugged his body armor off and dropped it into the grass.

"Whatever else this is, we cannot leave that mask there," he said, nodding to the obelisk. "You know that."

"And so your plan is to swim out there yourself? Surely we have some riverfolk among the militiamen who would make a better job of it. Do you even know how?"

"To swim? We all had to learn at the Academy," Prentice said, feeling a little puzzled that Whilte might not remember. He drew off his doublet and then bent down to remove his boots.

"I remember at least half of us treated it as a waste of time," Whilte objected, then he rolled his eyes. "But of course, diligent young Prentice took the lessons to heart and mastered the skill like a Denay coast sailor."

"Don't be daft," Prentice retorted with a smile. "Those sailors can swim in the spray of a storm surf. Waves like that would sweep me away into the depths."

"Oh aye. And what do you think *these* depths might be hiding from you? Are you sure there are no sharp-teethed fish in there to make your swim a hazard?"

"We will soon find out," Prentice told him, and as he finally was stripped down to his trews, he took his dirk in its sheath from his belt, thrust it into his waistband and dove into the water. It was cool and fresh, and he enjoyed the feeling as he swam out towards the plinth. The depth was surprising, but he could see the fronds of river grasses growing up into the light from the shadowy bottom. No sign of Whilte's predatory fish.

He reached the squared stone plinth, which was slightly broader across than the obelisk it supported, so that there was a narrow ledge all around the bottom just above the waterline. That ledge was green and slippery with wet lichen. He used it to support some of his weight as he swam around the plinth, examining all four sides. There were no steps or other elements to make it easy to climb up out of the water, but that was not surprising. If he had to judge, whoever had placed it expected to come and go by boat. Looking up, he could see that the carving on the sides did indeed seem like writing, though in keeping with Solft's ruminations it was not in any alphabet Prentice recognized, not even the Redlander blood runes, which he had seen enough times to feel he could identify them by sight. He raised his hand above the water and used his other to pull himself up on the ledge, moving the flat of his palm toward the obelisk's face.

"Take care Knight Commander," Whilte shouted from the shore, and Prentice nearly barked a laugh.

What do you think I am doing? he thought. His hand hovered near the carvings and nothing happened. Thinking he should be able to climb onto the plinth without touching the obelisk itself, he lifted himself from the water. It was even more awkward than he anticipated, and he felt himself brush against the stone side before he got his balance.

Well, still drawing breath, he thought. *That is a good sign.*

He tried to study the carved writings, but looking up and down the plinth was difficult given how little space he had to lean back. Even making his way around the whole ledge was a risky proposition, and his bare feet nearly slipped more than once. He was about to give his investigation up as a waste of time when a dark-winged waterbird, a coot with a bright red beak, flapped over the water and landed on top of the obelisk above him. It warbled as it shook its wet feathers, and he chuckled. That noise so close seemed enough to surprise the avian and it took flight again almost immediately. Prentice waved at it as it flew off.

"Thank you, master bird," he said happily. The Redlander death magick slew everything with its power, all the way down to mice and even insects. If the bird could land, then likely he was safe. With a short prayer entrusting his life to God in heaven, he put first one hand on the plinth carvings and then the other.

CHAPTER 39

"Well, that worked as well," he said to himself gladly. Smiling as he felt around the stone surface, looking for places to grab, he realized that he was genuinely enjoying himself and wondered at the sensation. He gripped hard on the carvings, half wrapping one arm around the corner of the obelisk for better leverage, and then put his toe into another spot where the stone was cracked and lifted his weight off the plinth.

Searching for the next handhold, he realized that the pleasure he was feeling came from the demanding simplicity of the task in front of him. The carvings were barely a single finger joint deep, so they were just enough to grip with the tips of his fingers. Same with the few cracks he could find. That meant he had to keep much of his body under tension just to maintain his grasp. It was a physical exertion but not beyond his strength. Best of all, it involved danger to no one but himself. No men faced death or injury at his command in this task. In fact, it was a service he could perform for his men, making the effort to remove the Redlander artifact from the top. In short order he was two thirds of the way up, and as the sides sloped gently inwards, he could make out the edge of the artifact, projecting slightly over the lip.

The sound of voices from the bank drew his attention and he adjusted his position slightly so that he could look back over his shoulder. Amongst the reeds on the bank, a number of militiamen had gathered to watch his efforts. It seemed that they were loudly discussing his progress, some apparently calling other militiamen from further afield.

"Marvelous," he muttered, turning back to the sandstone. He was glad to do this for his men, but an audience had not been a part of his plan.

One slip and I will never live it down, he thought. In truth, as he neared the obelisk's full ten-foot height, he was starting to realize how great his risk actually was. If he fell and made it clear of the pillar, he would be safe hitting the water, but if he slid down, he risked striking the ledge, and that could do him serious injury.

Bit late now, he thought and pushed himself the last distance until his head crested the top. Sure enough, there was a mantis mask, but like the obelisk itself, this Redlander artifact was different to the others he had seen. For a start, it was made of solid iron, finger-width thick in places. It had almost certainly been in place for many years, perhaps even decades or centuries, as the surface was pitted and flaking with rust. In shape, though, it did not seem much different than the wood-and-copper masks, although he thought he could make out some kind of markings in the corroded metal.

Prentice felt his grip slipping and he moved himself around the top, pushing up a little higher, his feet positioned on pieces of the carvings on two sides. With his toes, he gripped the narrow bits of stone as tightly as he could. Carefully, using only one hand at a time, he drew out the sewn cord that held his trousers up under his doublet when he was wearing it. The soaked material of his trews meant that they clung to his legs, and he had little concern of them falling down without their tie. He made a loop out of the wet cord and hooked it around the top of the obelisk so he could use it like a safety line of sorts, making his position less exhausting and allowing him to exert more strength. He was determined to pull the mask down and expected it to be nailed in place like the others.

He swore out loud when the iron piece moved almost readily, nearly causing him to fall before it stopped and clung stubbornly to the stone. Once he reset his balance, he ducked low to
look underneath, searching for how it was anchored. The mask
was held in place by an iron chain, fixed to a ring in the stone.
As he looked, he noticed that there had once been two such
rings and two chains. One was still connected, but the other had
corroded away or somehow been damaged.

*Perhaps I am not the first one to come here to do away with
you,* Prentice thought. From the look of the connection, some
attempt had been made to chip away the stone around the two
rings, and the second one was now loose in its place. If someone
had tried to remove the mask before, they had stopped close to
completing the task. With one hand, Prentice tried to wrench at
the mask and chain, but it did not budge. The task clearly called
for a chisel and hammer, as well as a more convenient perch
from which to use them. Lacking those, he considered trying
his dagger to scratch some of the stone away, but that was just a
recipe for a ruined blade.

"Leverage, that is what I need," he muttered and considered
his options. A plan formed in his mind, and he looked over to
the waterside where the number watching him had grown significant indeed. He shook his head, knowing how his audience
would react to the foolishness he plotted. Ignoring what could
not be avoided, he took his sheathed dagger from his trousers
and put it on the stone under the mask. Then he pulled the
iron artifact forward so that it hung on the edge of the obelisk,
the chain pulled to its full extension. Once that was in place, he
transferred his weight from the pants' cord to the mask, hanging
from the iron piece and the one chain.

*You watch, this'll be where the mongrel thing does its sorcery,
so it will,* Prentice heard Turley's voice in his mind, deriding the
folly of his plan. *Fool daft notion, this is.*

Prentice shook his head and nearly laughed. He knew he
was taking a risk, but it was a calculated one. Masks could be

touched; they had determined that already. Whatever awakened their magicks, it should not simply be touch. Besides, he had rescued Turley from the consequences of enough "daft notions" in their time as friends that he was due one of his own. The only problem with that thought, of course, was that Turley was not here to pull Prentice out if things went wrong, except as a voice in his mind.

"Sorry, old friend," he muttered, smiling to himself. "This is just something I have to do."

As he said it, he wondered why he would even think such a thing. What was so important about him doing this now, by himself? He was taking several risks he need not take. Where was his usual watchful caution? Poised on the top of this ancient marker of Redlander power, the exertion beginning to make his limbs shake, Prentice found himself experiencing something more primeval than his usual approach to the world. His characteristic will was still within him, as was his analytical mind, but they seemed all fixed and focused, unwilling to yield to this iron mask, resenting even its very existence. It was like a duel, a battle to the death, and in his heart he found he was exalting in it. The sun was bright and warm, the water cool and fresh. It was the perfect day for a battle, and this was one he wanted to fight.

Quickly tying the dagger to himself with the pants' cord, he moved himself into position, square on to the mask as it hung over the edge. Both hands on the mantis, he drew his knees up to his chest and began to pull backwards with all his might. For a long moment there was nothing, not the least bit of movement, but he refused to give up. Groaning as the muscles in his limbs began to burn, he kept the pressure on. His fingers on the edge of the mask began to sting, and he expected he was cutting them on the metal.

The groan in his chest grew to an enraged shout, and voices on the bank started to cheer him on. Pausing for a long, agonized breath, he heard a second groaning sound and realized that the

iron was moving, the links of the chain pulling apart almost un-
bearably slowly. Refusing to be denied, he pushed out further,
every ounce of strength devoted to the task. His knuckles were
agonized white, and he caught a flash of crimson forcing itself
up between them. There was a loud crack, a moment as if he
were suspended in space, leaned back so far that he was almost
horizontal, and then the mask tore free and he was falling, the
heavy iron still in his hands.

He struck the water back-first, the cool engulfing his hot,
straining flesh. The weight of the mask in his hands added to the
slapping impact, and he found himself sinking into the depths
faster than he imagined he could have. As the water rose around
him, the sunlit sky blurred, and the shadowy depth darkened
the bottom of his vision. He tried to kick, keeping hold of the
mask. If he let go, it would sink irretrievably, and there was no
way to be sure the magick would not still work underwater,
making this entire adventure pointless. Moving the thing about
in his grip to give himself one free hand to swim with, he caught
sight of it moving across the light from the surface so that the
bent rays shone through the compound holes of the eyes.

And he saw another place...

CHAPTER 40

I t was an obelisk, another one, a copy of the one from which he had just fallen. He knew it was not the same one because this one was enormous, like a castle's tower, and at its top there was a dragonfly—a statue of one, at least—not in copper or iron but gold. Its wings were a fine gilded latticework, fitted with faceted glass or crystal, mimicking the intricacies of the true insect's wing with a level of craftsmanship Prentice had never imagined was possible. Certainly, no Kingdom goldsmith could have achieved it, and he doubted the Redlanders had such talent. Above the obelisk, Prentice could see towering mountains, basalt cliffs rising sheer from thin strips of swarded slopes. He was in the lake at the end of the Murr, deep in a ravine somewhere in the west, and at the far end of that lake was the dragonfly perched upon its obelisk. The sun was high over the shoulder of one mount, but its light felt distant, and the shadows of the cliff shut out much of its warmth.

Staring up at the vast carved stone he could see that it must have been cut from the land itself, even though the obelisk was the color of the sandstone native to the Azures, not the basalt of the mountains on either side. What power could have moved a monolith that size from somewhere else in the world to this cleft amidst a titanic landscape? It was criss-crossed by lengths of iron chains up its sides, with gigantically carven runes like the one he had just broken at the falls. Hanging from the chains at points up and down the stone edifice were bodies in varying states of decay. Some were skeletal, long rotted away, while others were almost fresh, the stains of their blood running rusty down the engraved rock. Each one wore a mantis mask, and Prentice did not have to look closely with this strange mystic vision to see that the objects were nailed to the skulls they covered. In a flash, he was sure Master Solft was right, that these obelisks were not of Redlander construction but were borrowed from another magick—looted and corrupted, twisted by blood sacrifice to their new masters' purposes. As grotesque as the sight was, the insight gave him a flicker of hope that Redlander power might be broken, taken from them in irreplaceable ways. If the obelisks could be cleansed, or better yet destroyed, the Redlander's power to enter the Reach through its waters would go with them.

Bleed or shed blood, he thought as he looked at the brutalized victims.

Then he remembered his fingers had bled upon the mask and now, somehow, the sorcery had taken his sight far away to the headwaters of the Murr—not through the sky as the Redlander boats travelled, though. He knew somehow that he was not actually in this far lake. It was as if the lake's surface was now his eyes, and the notion seemed suddenly confirmed as he thought to look elsewhere around the valley. He could see in all directions, even across the water itself, and he knew the lake was vast—leagues in length—with steep-sided shores covered in deep green grasses.

Can my body drown while my sight is here? he wondered. He had a sensation, as of his body suspended in the cool waters at the foot of the falls, sinking, but ever so slowly. How long could he hold his breath?

His sight moved, as if swiftly drawn across the lake to the other end of the valley where there were some kind of huts—a settlement—clustered on one side of the water. The shelters seemed built of pale wood, stacked upon one another like grapes on the vine, and as if truly upon a vine, they climbed the mountain cliff on that side of the valley a hundred feet or more. He tried to imagine how many might live in such a community and realized that if they had spaces cut into the cliff behind, he would have no way to know. This could be a town the size of Dweltford, or even larger still.

The village touched the ground and grew right out to the shore in the valley's only flat space on that side of the lake at the opposite end from the great dragonfly. Although made of wood, the little huts almost appeared to have grown in place, as the poles, beams and boards seemed to twist around one another, like trees that had grown up beside and into each other to become one living thing. Perhaps they were indeed grown that way, though by what art, Prentice could not begin to guess. Beyond the village, he could see the entrance of the valley itself, where a surprisingly wide river flowed over a weir of some sort—doubtless the Murr at its headwater. It left the valley and flowed almost immediately beneath the boughs of a forest so dense that it was dark as night within, despite the high sun above.

Prentice did not watch the forest for long, as his sight moved once more, drawn to a broad stone platform in the water in front of the village, connected to the shore by a narrow, raised path. It reminded him of the archduchess's description of the causeway that connected the shore to a lone castle in the salt sea. Had both been made by the same people? And if so, was this their village?

There *were* people in the village and on the platform, and of several distinct kinds, in fact. In the open spaces between the huts, and all along the shore, folk were on their knees, facing the dais platform in the water. They were dressed in clothes that resembled bark and leaves to Prentice's mind. What else would folk who could make their homes "grow" wear? Men and women both were present, and Prentice thought they might be fey by their general builds and distinctive ears. If they were, he could also see in an instant that they were not riders of Benjamin's *keshiyaa*. Mountain fey were tanned from the sun, and these folk were pale, with skin the color of fresh snow. As so many of them knelt, he did not think they were at prayer, for they all had their eyes fixed upon the dais, and in their expressions was the haunted despair that fey riders in the Reach had when they had been bound by blood to the Serpent Witch.

Mingled amongst them were Redlanders, standing over them with painted skin that made them stand out beside the pale fey. A moment later, Prentice realized that most were not Redlanders, not as he knew them, but were, in fact, milky skinned fey people. They were tattooed, as Blood Sect warriors typically were, but they were definitely fey under their markings. They had risen in the cult, it seemed, something no convert in the Grand Kingdom was known to have achieved, at least not yet. Until this moment Prentice had always assumed the Redlanders reserved the inner part of their religion to their own kind, and that they counted themselves some kind of chosen people, perhaps descended from whomever the Broken Kings had originally been.

Upon the stone dais were other types of folk, and these Prentice did not have to wonder about. Most obvious were *brakkis effar*. He saw one wolf, pacing back and forth like a watchdog, gazing down on the oppressed fey upon the shore. Another was a mantis man, so transformed that even his hands were no more than serrated, chitinous blades. His mandibles were moving such that Prentice thought he must be speaking, but this vision brought no sound with it. The rest of the *brakkis effar*, at least ten of them, were serpent women, all fully transformed and naked, seeming so strange. As women, their faces were human shaped, allowing for the fangs in their mouths and the slits in their eyes. Their bodies also had some lingering semblance of a female shape under their scaled skins, but as serpents do not suckle their young, so they had no breasts or other femininity about them. Indeed, calling them naked seemed ludicrous to Prentice's thoughts, for while they wore no clothes, they were so animalistic that it hardly mattered. One of their number was subordinate to her sisters, it seemed, as she crouched upon the stones, wearing a metal collar around her throat with a chain leash, the other end of which was anchored to the flagstones. It was hard to tell, so indistinct was one serpent woman from another, but Prentice was convinced the one enchained was the Serpent Witch, who had thought to make herself queen over the Reach.

Was she being humbled for her hubris or for her failure?

There were two other kinds of folk upon the stone platform, and their presence turned Prentice's analytical curiosity to horrified fury. The first was a fey, mountain fey, and most likely one of Benjamin's band. He was stripped to the waist and tied to an X-shaped cross. Red stripes and dark bruises crisscrossed his flesh, and as Prentice watched, two of the serpent women sliced at his skin, drawing forth fresh trickles of blood. They used the same kind of copper and bone knives he had once witnessed the Serpent Witch use in her ritual to bind the unicorn. To what purpose this crimson rite was being put, he could not say, but watching closely as it was practiced were two men in the armor and tabards of the Inquisition knights. Indeed, to say they were "watching" was to understate their intense examination of the process. They were studying, and worse yet, they were learning. One of the serpents stepped aside and offered her bone blade to one of the knights. As if moving into light from a shadow, the man's identity suddenly became clear, and Prentice knew Inxyphos.

Disgust overwhelmed the knight commander, such that if he still had connection with his body he would have spat upon the ground. Instead, Prentice was helpless to do anything as he watched Inxyphos take the knife and look to the point on the fey rider's body where the serpent priestess indicated. The man stepped forward and dispassionately surveyed the prisoner's torso, perhaps enjoying his suffering, perhaps simply memorizing the previous placement of cuts that led to this point in the rite. Prentice remembered the coldly aloof way in which his interrogation had been conducted, the Inquisitor assessing the best points of his flesh to cut or burn with a professional dispassion. Was Inxyphos trained as an Inquisitor as well as a knight?

Then the bone blade was thrust up under the ribs and surely into the heart. It was a killing blow, and Prentice watched the light fade from the fey rider's eyes as his lifeblood spilled upon the stones. A priestess all but pushed Inxyphos out of the way while she presented a bowl under the wound to capture the falling crimson. The other priestesses began to writhe, and Prentice imagined they were making some kind of sound, their mouths opened as in song. Inxyphos stepped back and looked to his compatriot with a bemused frown. Prentice wondered if they were troubled by the prospect of recreating this ritual themselves by having to contort their bodies as the *brakkis effar* now were. If not for the slaughter, Prentice might have found the prospect amusing.

The priestess's gestures became focused upon the water, seemingly looking straight at Prentice but not seeing him. Rather, they began to reach out across the lake to the obelisk. They spoke or sang or shouted words Prentice could not make out from their lipless mouths, but from their attentive expressions, it seemed Inxyphos and his man were doing their best to learn and memorize them. Watching from the same distance, unable to control his point of view, Prentice saw the dragonfly on top of the vast edifice begin to move, its wings starting to beat as an insect's would. The air thrummed, and the surface of the water vibrated with power. He half wondered if the artificial creature would actually take to the air and flit over the lake the way a true dragonfly might. It did not. Instead, its multi-faceted wings set the valley ablaze with coruscating refractions and the air came alive. The priestesses now looked to the sky, and the whole valley was roofed in the warping mirror, slowly resolving to show another water—how far away Prentice could only guess.

As the sister cultists summoned the sky down, the above-below water showed waves and a coastline. Puzzled as he had been the first time he witnessed this power, Prentice realized that this transition was beginning from a greater height. Whereas before he had looked down upon the water as if from one of the village huts that climbed the cliff beside the lake, now he had the perspective of a bird, and one that flew high indeed. He was reminded of the scripture and how the deceiver had taken the Christ to a mountaintop to tempt him with the kingdoms of the world. With that insight, he recognized what he could see in that far water and upon its edge—people, encamped in array on the shore, thousands and thousands again. And in the water, buffeted by thin white lines that Prentice now realized must be waves rolling into the beach, were boats—more than he could count. This was the swarm of locusts Duggan had feared, and it seemed ready.

Anguish gripped Prentice's thoughts. He was late. The Redlander fleet would come through the sky to this lake. They would be so many that the highland mere would be crowded like cattle herded in for market day, but that would not matter. If there was even one mask shrine in the Reach, these witches would send their raiders through before he could even warn his people. The prophesied dread future had arrived and there was nothing he could do but watch.

He was too late.

Suddenly he remembered the day he had first faced the Redlanders in battle, the invincible-seeming army of the Horned Man waiting upon their hill, patiently keeping time. The Reach, the Grand Kingdom, its princes and knights and beaten-down convicts had not been ready. They had come late to the realization of the enemy's power. Yet for all their pride and cruel sins, God had not abandoned them, had not forsaken those who sought Him and his protection before their own glory.

For God resists the proud but gives grace to the humble.

The words of scripture sounded in Prentice's thoughts, though he had no memory of where he must have read them. He remembered the lion angel, falling with thunder and fire amongst the *brakkis effar* and scattering them like autumn leaves rising from a bonfire.

Was there anything humbler than a man drowning in a murky lake far from his home, his wife, and the children he would never see? Give me grace, mighty God, Prentice thought, and he opened his mouth that was far from his mind and his sight. Through the murky water that flooded into his throat and lungs, he cried out with all the leonine fury he had ever known. He would drown for certain now, but the words had to be spoken, shouted into the crushing chill depth—the plea of rejection that was the core of Brother Whilte's power over Red-lander magick, the one-word prayer addressed to the Righteous Maker of all things.

"Dear God, no!"

The sound made no sense to Prentice's ears. Even if the water had not garbled the words, his own breath-starved blood, hammering in his ears, overpowered the suppressed cry. If he was to do magick, the sorcerous formula would doubtless have been spoiled. No power could be invoked by such humble sounds.

But God gives grace to the humble.

The serpent ritual ceased. There was no noise, no opposing symbols or flashes of lightning or thunder from heaven. The magicks simply stopped and the mirrored sky vanished. The dragonfly became still, and the light became as normal day-light, overshadowed by mountain peaks. The priestesses began to keen and wail, terrified confusion in their eyes, and Prentice realized suddenly that he could hear them. He wondered if that meant his spirit had been surrendered to the water, if he had become one of the drowned dead, consigned to the bottom to be disgorged by the seas at the judgement. In a far-off sense, he knew he could taste mud and weed in his mouth, and he felt a distant burning sensation that made him think his lungs must be failing him. He felt oddly calm but hoped Gennet would continue the quest to the lake without him. The invasion had been stopped, but the obelisk remained. How soon would it be before the Redlander cultists would try again?

"Ashen Man!"

Prentice heard a voice scream, and he looked back to the dais to see the Serpent Witch, the first but least of her kind, still crouched at her sisters' feet. She was pointing into the water, staring straight at him, as if he were physically present. A hideous chorus of hisses arose from the priestesses, and they dipped their hands into the bowl of shed blood, drawing power from it in whatever fashion their fell beliefs permitted, and they began to throw curses upon the water. Prentice felt a growing pressure and thought for sure his drowning body was finished, water within him and all around. The bloodthirsty fury that these reptile women cast upon him almost made him laugh. It was too late for their hatred to do anything, and as much as he died with some regrets, he would die glad to have thwarted them even once.

The dais was descending into chaos as the priestesses drove themselves to greater frenzies, venting further and further hatred upon the water of the lake where their enemy now watched them without fear. They spat their venom, but it only splashed like raindrops. Behind them, Inxyphos and his man were withdrawing some distance down the causeway, still watching with the same dispassion. Nothing, it seemed, could assault the Inquisition's sense of superiority. The wolf howled, its baying cry echoing off the cliffs. Suddenly, with a strangely human sense of impatience, the mantis man leapt from the stone platform into the shallows and waded to the shore. Without even breaking his inhuman stride as he emerged from the water, he thrust his chitin-bladed hand through the chest of one of the convert fey, killing the tattooed woman instantly. Hefting her up on the serrations of his arm, he threw her over his head and into the water, clicking in his own bestial tongue. As the body struck the lake, Prentice felt a heavy push, as if he had been physically shoved, but after that, nothing.

The mantis stared at the water a moment and then turned its head, apparently looking to the dais for confirmation that his killing had made a difference. As far as Prentice could tell it had not, and the cacophony of invocations and curses continued. The mantis looked around it, apparently searching for another victim, and the other fey, kneeling and tattooed, stood and pushed back in terror. Prentice doubted they would be able to outrun the insectoid beast-man when he struck. Instead, the mantis paused, and its head swiveled back to the dais again. The motion seemed almost thoughtful, and Prentice wondered what might have occurred to the barely human mind inside the bug. Turning and springing as only an insect could, the mantis man was suddenly upon the causeway, striding in an ungainly fashion back to the wailing priestesses. As he reached the serpent closest to the edge, he thrust his serrated, bladed forearm through her back and lifted her, screaming, into the air. As it did so, the mantis spoke yet more, and the clacking of his words was a staccato rhythm in Prentice's mind. The impaled *brakkis effar* writhed in agony, and the mantis threw her at the water. As she struck, Prentice felt suddenly thrown backwards, out of the lake and into his own body.

In an instant, his consciousness was overwhelmed by the myriad sensations of dying flesh that fights for life. His limbs began to thrash, and the inside of his chest burned. His back had touched the bottom, and the lakebed around him was being stirred to a cloud of murk. Seeing barely the dimmest hope of sunlight above, he twisted his feet under him and kicked against the mud. Rising through the water, he felt heavy, heavier even than his weary, breath-starved muscles should have felt. He realized that he still had the iron mask in one hand. To live, he would have been better served to discard it, but he refused. He was alive yet, and he had a duty to fulfil, even though it killed him.

He kicked and rose almost not at all. Again, he kicked and knew he was making no progress. Already, the light above was darkening, though he did not know if it was because he was sinking again or if death was finally claiming him. He strained upward—his one free hand desperate to touch the surface that was high above him. It was too far. Then something grabbed his reaching hand, and he was being dragged upward. For a minute, he felt as if his legs were entangled, as if the weeds on the bottom would not release him. His exhausted mind's last thought was to wonder if the Redlanders were using magick to drag him back to drown, and then he felt his loose trousers slip free as he was pulled up to the surface. Too tired even to draw in the gasping breaths his lungs demanded, he let himself be carried through the water, nearly insensible. At last, he was dragged naked onto the bank and up beyond the reeds. Folk who knew what to do with a nearly drowned man turned him on his side and let him cough forth the mucky water in his lungs. Someone took the iron mask from his fingers.

"The eyes," he muttered. "Do not look..." He was too weak to finish the warning, and more water spilled from his lips.

At last, he heard Whilte's voice praying for his recovery and felt a weary sense of peace gradually enter his body. He was going to live. It made him smile.

"Proud of ourselves, are we?" Whilte asked, like a stern parent with a foolish child.

Prentice blinked the water out of his eyes and looked blurrily up at the chaplain. He shook his head, which ached.

"No, not proud," he said. "Not proud but pleased."

Then he let his head lie back and the brother returned to his prayer.

CHAPTER 41

After Spindle helped Amelia wash her face and treated her scalp injury with vinegar, the lady-in-waiting fetched some cheese and wine, which refreshed the archduchess's spirits much more than she imagined it could. When the simple meal was done, however, she felt suddenly weary again. Spindle had two camp stewards bring in bundles of fresh-cut meadow grasses, which they used to make a peasant bed, although covered with cloth of finer linen than ever likely graced any beds of actual peasants. Spindle apologized for the rudeness of the setting, but Amelia waved her away with a fatigued smile.

"I've slept nights in filthy straw, don't forget," she said as she lay down, "This will be no burden."

Soon enough, Amelia fell into a much less troubled sleep than she had expected, not waking until the dawn drumbeat echoed over the camp. Rising to find herself alone, she left the tent and was astonished by the sight that greeted her. In spite of her husband's reassurances, she had fully expected to awaken in the midst of the chaos of a routed army. She had imagined the wounded laying about wherever they could find space, while the healthier competed to escape the field, with the few retainers still loyal struggling futilely to keep order. Instead, she walked in the early morning light surrounded on all sides by discipline, peace, and calm. Indeed, except for the fact that they were camping in the classically colorful tents of a mercenary force, awakening this morning felt not really any different than it had on any other morning of the march.

Just outside the tent were four men—two Lions with buffcoats and halberds, and two of Spindle's bodyguard. Amelia looked to the militiamen and asked after her lady-in-waiting.

"The lady arose just afore you, Your Grace," the Lion said, touching his knuckle to the brim of his open-faced salet helm, mimicking tugging the forelock. "She's at the fire just around that other tent, if you seek her. Our orders're to escort you anywhere you are today, though we get swapped over at mid-morning and again later today."

Amelia nodded and looked quizzically at the mailed bodyguards standing equally attentively on the other side of the tent flap.

"They's the Lady Spindle's men, and we're not to interfere 'less they make any threat to yourself, Your Grace," said the sentry when he noticed her interest. The hired men heard the comment and one turned to repeat the gesture of respect the Lion sentry had just given.

"We are hired to protect the safety of the Lady Spindle Welburne," the man said, not using Amelia's honorific, but otherwise speaking respectfully. "She has two others of our detail with her now as escort. When there is fear of assassination, it is considered wisest that some remain near to the Lady's quarters so that none may hide themselves in her absence."

"You speak as if from much experience," Amelia observed.

"Our company are the finest bodyguards in the Vec," the sentry responded, and it was clear from his tone that he considered his words not a boast but a statement of fact.

Amelia looked from one pair of men to the other, wondering how the two groups might interpret their overlapping duties. From their expressions, though, it seemed as if they must have come to some form of accommodation, as she saw none of the rivalry and disdain that so often infected proud men-at-arms in competing loyalties. She smiled at all four.

"Thank you for your loyal service," she said. The Lions saluted, fists thumping their chests. The hired men knuckled their brows. Following the sentry's directions, and with them accompanying her, Amelia found Spindle at a campfire amidst a number of other camp women, preparing to break their fast—a warmed small beer porridge that the lady-in-waiting served in a clay tankard with a silver spoon.

"Silver?" Amelia asked, surprised.

"From your uncle-in-law's canteen, Your Grace," Spindle explained. "A fair helping got purloined before the quartermaster merchants got to it, but we still have some for you to use."

Amelia shook her head, disappointed not by the loss of the booty but by the lack of discipline it represented. "Prentice would never have allowed such a breakdown of order."

Spindle seemed troubled by those words, but Amelia was more surprised to hear one of the sentries behind her cough tellingly. She looked to see the other scowling at his partner.

"You have something to say?" she asked. The man sheepishly began to shake his head but clearly did have an objection of some kind.

"It's just..." he looked to his comrade, who shook his head in a warning gesture.

"Speak," Amelia commanded, lowering her mug of grains and ale.

"I know it's out o' turn, Your Grace, but I just felt that you should know it weren't us," the sentry explained. "The lootin', that is."

"I did not suspect you two," she responded. That had been assumed as a matter of course. Men who stood loyal duty should not be the first accused of a crime.

"With all respect, Your Grace," said the cougher's partner, "he means it wasn't the Lions, nor them hired fellows. The Veckander prince's force was more than half mercenary, and when they broke, they made sure to try to fetch off with whatever they could carry. I guess they figured they weren't going to be paid any other way. I think we captured more'n half o' them cause of that."

"The paymaster's come late this season," the coughing sentry added, "but we all know you're good for it, Your Grace. Vec bankers be damned. We would never embarrass you by turning to pillage, and neither would Knight Captain Farringdon nor the baron, I swear."

The baron? Amelia wondered, knowing whom the man meant, but surprised to hear Prentice spoken of in that manner. Spindle must have understood her lady's thoughts, as she nodded when their eyes met.

"It seems Prentice's men have accepted his accession much more readily than he did," Spindle said with an amused flicker of a smile on her lips. Amelia nodded and looked back to the sentries.

"Thank you once again," she said, "And forgive me for slandering your loyal service. You deserve better."

The two men stood proudly, almost boyish for a moment as they enjoyed her simple compliment. She marveled at their devotion and realized in that moment that it was a devotion built for her on hard work and suffering. She also noticed that Farringdon had not been excluded from the man's protestation of fealty. It made her think of her harsh words to her husband the night before, but she thrust those thoughts aside. She might regret the way she had spoken, but she hadn't changed her mind about the substance. The cannons disgusted her, had cost good and loyal men like these their lives, and until Farringdon released his love for the monsters he was in the wrong with her.

Taking a short time standing in the pleasant sunshine while finishing her breakfast, Amelia suggested that she should inspect their new camp. She and Spindle, escorted by two Lions and two hired guards, began to walk through the tents, receiving salutes and surveying the state of her forces. One pavilion near the western edge had been set aside for the badly wounded, and fifty or so men lay on grass beds, groaning softly while they were attended to by a chirurgeon and a healer.

"Some few won't make it," she was told by a line first attending, but he seemed happy to make that report. "Most'll live, and more than a few will return to service. We done much better than them lot."

The junior officer cocked his head towards the open portion of Cattlefields between the camp and the town of Aubrey where corrals of prisoners had been formed, dejected men sitting in small crowds upon the ground. Two full cohorts of Lions were standing guard on the edges and walking patrols through lanes between the groups.

"What is to be done with them?" Spindle asked.

"Knight Captain has a scribe going through, getting name's and swearings," the line first explained. "Mercenaries pick their own officers, so they say, and more than a few didn't make it out of yesterday's fracas or else lit out when they broke. Once they pick someone who can speak for them, the scribe'll take their pledges and we can pack them off to whatever border we like."

The "pledge" was an official signature of surrender coupled with a promise not to return to make war on the Western Reach for one year and one day. It was possible, of course, that a pledge could be ignored, but if a man who had given it was captured once more within that time, he would be subject to summary execution. Amelia knew that, from one perspective, such rules of war were nonsense. How could men so determined to slay one another care about such niceties? But the longer this war went on, the more she realized that without them the suffering of all peoples involved would only be many times worse. Indeed, the greatest horrors always occurred at the hands of those who thought the rules of war did not apply to them—the Redlanders for example, and knights like Duke Robant and the Usurper. Like the weapons and armor of a warrior, rules of chivalry were not flawed unto themselves. It was when they were used only in one direction to serve only one part of society that they failed.

Amelia stared westward over the seated prisoners to the shanties outside the walls of Aubrey.

"We should look to our beset folk as well, My Lady," she told Spindle. "Best we do that from horseback, wouldn't you say?"

Spindle accepted her words as a command, and they went in search of their horses and an escort that could ride with them.

CHAPTER 42

"Ghosts and death," Prentice muttered, standing in the stirrups as he surveyed the upland plain at the top of the scarp. The pain in his chest reminded him that his lungs had nowhere near fully recovered from his almost drowning the day before, and despite the difficulty, he had determined to let Boots make the uphill journey. His lack of riding skill notwithstanding, it had not taken too much effort to pick out a reasonable trail up the slope, leading a small cadre of companions to investigate the next challenge of their mission westward. Now that Boots was standing on the ridge itself, it seemed as if this single geographical feature was like a line drawn north to south upon the landscape by the hand of God. To the east of that line, the land was grassed and green, thriving even in the early summer after a wet winter and spring. Next there was the upward slope, and as it climbed, the grass thinned, and the few trees petered out completely a third of the way up.

Then came the ridgetop, and into the west there was only crushed rock and dust—flat, open, and windswept. Almost everything Prentice could see was the same dun color—a pale, dusty earth. Barely even dotted with shriveled pieces of some kind of weeds, more dead-seeming than alive, the only true greenery to be found was the slender strip at the banks of the river. On this upland plain, the Murr River itself was different as well. Before it cascaded over the falls to the grasses of Radengon, it was dark and deep—not poisonous or unrefreshing it seemed, since it supported vivid green reeds on its banks, but inky, like frozen mountain water, black as under ice. From east to west, there was the green of grass, the line of the scarp, and then bleakness.

"Lord ha'mercy, that's bloody desolate," Lyrach swore, standing at Boots's bridle. Given his limited riding experience, Prentice had thought a groom to help his mount up the slope was a sensible notion.

Nothing, Prentice thought, understanding Lyrach's sentiment and astonished at how apt Jannomoch's description of the terrain had turned out to be. *There really is nothing but the river.*

Soon enough, the rest of his companions on this scouting mission had drawn up the last of the slope and each had their moment of shock.

"Is this what we expected, Knight Commander?" Sergeant Gennet asked after he whistled in astonishment.

"I do not know what we expected, Sergeant," Prentice told him honestly. "Some of those boulders should be heavy enough to tie to and run cables from. Once we get that done, hauling men, supplies and animals up should be easy enough, at least."

The knight commander looked back east and down at the contingent camp by the river and the falls lake. Last evening, as Prentice was resting from his drowned vision, a small flotilla of rivercraft had arrived, sent from Dweltford by Lady Dalflitch with orders to move at best speed. A barge with grain and other foodstuffs had been most welcome, but more important by far had been the two lighters with a twenty-animal mule team divided between them, along with the ostlers to manage them. Not only would Prentice's cohorts be well supplied for the upland phase of the journey but they would not be forced to carry their own food the whole way. If the distance proved to be even further than anticipated, the mules could become extra meals on the hoof, albeit unappetizing.

"Did you want me to get to that right away?" Gennet asked.

"Just a moment," Prentice told him, and he swung out of the saddle. Once on the ground he crouched down and, removing his gloves, took up a handful of the chalky earth, letting the grains fall through his fingers. He stood back up and clapped the dust from his hands. "Before we move on to the next stage, I want you all to know what I learned yesterday."

Aside from Lyrach and Gennet, Prentice had Brother Whilte, Master Solft and two senior corporals with him—an older man named Porth who was of the Claws and an ex-convict with multiple judicial brands on his cheeks named Guillam, a Roarsman. Corporal Guillam's scars made it hard to guess his age from his face, but he had a manner about him that spoke of maturity and experience. As they all listened attentively, Prentice outlined the key points of his vision while he had been underwater. There had once been a time when he would never have spoken so openly of such things, cautious that folk would think him mad or heretical. Now though, visions and sorceries had been proved more truth than legend too many times to worry about it. Moreover, every militiaman with him knew they were hunting down Inquisition men-at-arms, as well as Redlanders, so questions of heresy were pretty much moot. Prentice wondered sometimes if any of his troops were experiencing troubled consciences for so openly opposing a part of Mother Church. If they were, nothing had so far been said.

"So, those are mountains off that way," Gennet said, looking to the jagged line of the horizon in the west. "And in those mountains, somewhere at the end of this river, is a lake valley behind a forest valley."

"And in that valley are more fey, living up the side of a cliff," said Lyrach.

"Different fey," Porth said, making it clear he had listened and absorbed the details of Prentice's story well.

"Not to mention some kind of cabal of Redlander witches," Whilte added, his attention no doubt drawn naturally to his key responsibility.

"The fey call such a group an *imzuss*," said Solft, and Whilte accepted the correction without comment.

Prentice nodded, affirming their understanding, but giving them no guidance. The main purpose of conversations like this was to let other minds see things he had not, if they could, which they would not do if he told them what he thought first.

"The power in this lake, this dragonfly...?" Solft wondered out loud, letting the sentence hang in the air a moment. "And you say it was bound by chains and sacrifices?"

"That is what I saw. The obelisk, at any rate," Prentice confirmed.

"Sounds like a hell of an adventure, Commander," said Guillam with a veteran's casual impertinence. Gennet scowled at the junior officer, but Prentice only shook his head with a wry smile.

"You and Master Solft wondered if the carved pillars were or were not Redlander make yesterday, Knight Commander," said Whilte. "I think this settles that question."

Prentice nodded, and the others joined him, though most wore expressions that showed they did not necessarily understand why. Lyrach was honest in his lack of understanding at least.

"How do you know?" the ex-knight asked.

"Because of the haphazard way they wield the power," Prentice explained. "They did not even know I was there at first, and then when they did, they could not eject me. I was there by the power of one of their own masks, coupled to whatever dwells in the stones, and it took the blood of one of their own to banish me."

"Power or not Commander, they got the sky to open for them again, and you say you saw a fleet? Like the one that took Aubrey two years ago? Bigger even?"

"That was how it seemed from my strange vantage," Prentice confirmed, and most present shook their heads somberly. Of all of them, only Lyrach had not been at the Battle of Red

Sky, either to face that fleet's raiders or at least to witness the combat, as in the case of Master Solft and Brother Whilte.

"They were well swift taking Fallenhill, and Aubrey, too," Gennet said grimly. "A fleet in Dweltford Lake and we'll lose the archduchess, no doubt."

"The Lady Dalflitch's letter says her grace is currently in Aubrey with the rest of the Lions," Prentice explained.

"So at least she can try to take Dweltford back if they've already seized it," Lyrach said, and several others scowled at him. Seeing the resounding disapproval, he became defensive. "What? Weren't you thinking it too?"

"Maybe we were, lad," said Porth, "but you might've seen we were all too canny to speak it out. Should've given you the tip-off."

Lyrach looked ready to make yet another argument, but Prentice tutted once and shook his head, stilling the young man's ire.

"Let us not forget, the baron knight commander's prayer sealed the sky once again," Brother Whilte counseled.

"The two happened at the same time," Prentice responded, "I would not say the one was the result of the other, necessarily."

The last thing he wanted was his men-at-arms imagining him as some kind of holy prophet, wielding the power of God as he led them into battle. Hubris and disaster were the only things he could see at the end of that path. It was enough that he had a chaplain like Whilte with them, a man actually devoted to serving the Lord, willing both to pay the cost of that service and to call it no cost at all. Knowing the icy fury that abided in the depth of his soul, Prentice had no illusions he could be such a man. Faith was one thing; peace was another, and both were worthy. Holiness was a third thing altogether, and while Prentice was willing to choose the first and pursue the second, he could not see how the third could be his, not with all the blood upon his hands.

"However it came to pass, I think we can take faith that God has closed their power over the sky, at least for a time," Whilte continued, obviously seeking to encourage their belief. Prentice appreciated that.

"What if it isn't long enough?" asked Guillam sourly.

"You think the Almighty wants to torment us?" Whilte asked with raised eyebrows. "He has given us a hope through this vision, and when we get there we will find what? That he plans to kick our legs out from under us?"

"He done it to you once already, ain't he?" Guillam countered, looking down at Whilte's wooden leg. Despite the sharpness of his words, the man did not seem angry, only grousing almost as if from habit. The chaplain for his part did not seem offended. He bent down and slapped his knee where it met the prosthetic.

"This? My pride and sin did this," he said calmly. "If God in heaven had kicked my legs out from under me as I deserved, I'd have neither left, nor my hands nor tongue, I'd wager, Corporal. I thank him every day that this was all it took to open my eyes."

"Pretty sentiment," Guillam muttered, but it was clear he could tell he was wearing out his grace for speaking his mind. He lowered his head and looked away.

"Theology and faith aside, we are going to make the best speed we can for this lake," Prentice told them. "Whether or not we can stop the cabal before the full fleet is moved through the sky, we have to make it so that no other boats can ever travel so."

"How?" asked Gennet, and Prentice met his eyes. The sergeant waited for an explanation, but then the answer to his question occurred to him. "You think we'll have enough powder for something like that?"

"We will have to make sure we do," Prentice told him, then looked to the others. It was important to him that they understood that this was his ultimate aim. The magickal dragonfly had to be destroyed. He was sure that if it were, the Redlanders could never replace it. Detonate the ancient artifact and any mask shrines the mantis or their supplicants set up in the Reach would be useless. Hunting out the cult would then be a task that could almost be handed over to bailiffs.

"Won't the Redlander fleet crews just come at us overland then from that salt sea they say is to the northwest?" asked Lyrach.

"Let 'em," said Porth. "We all know what it's like havin' to face fey in them grasslands. An overland march through that'll take a lot o' the stiffness out o' their leather plates."

"If them pointy heads is still on our side," Guillam groused once more. "I thought they swapped banners on us, didn't they?"

"Actually, I think the baron's vision gives us some hope on that matter, as well," Solft interjected, and the martially minded men all looked upon the soft-skinned scholar. He shrugged but did not withdraw his comment. "Consider what was seen—another tribe of fey different than the mountain folk but under the Redlander thumb all the same. And if anything, perhaps even more abused in their subservience. More than that, the only rider Baron Prentice saw was a victim tied in place."

"This gives you hope, Master? Why?" Whilte asked.

"At least hope that Benjamin has not tried to betray us. I think..." he paused and looked at the desolate landscape across the entire west. "I think these other fey are accursed and Benjamin rode to free them."

Guillam scoffed outright, and Porth and Lyrach shook their heads as if the scholar was making a bad joke.

"Why would you think that?" Whilte persisted, but Prentice thought he understood the rationale.

"The Redlander's ancestors and the fey crossed the Azures together centuries ago," he said, and Solft began to nod eagerly. "They were driven out by the crusaders. The master here has discovered reference to a civil war at the founding of the Grand Kingdom, with seven lesser kings fighting over the new throne in Denay. One king was slain and five others driven out. That is why the Inquisition calls the Redlanders the Broken Kings."

"You what?" asked Guillam. Porth and Gennet held their tongues, but both seemed as unbelieving of this claim as the scar-faced corporal. "The Redlanders is Kingdom folk?"

"Once perhaps, although plainly no longer," Whilte confirmed. Lyrach whistled once again and shook his head in wonder.

"Where they been then that makes 'em like they is now?"

"Over the salty sea, obviously," Lyrach said, but Prentice knew the young man might as well have been saying off beyond the Rampart in the stars for all he had reason to think they were connected.

"There is a tale," Prentice continued, "that when the Broken Kings, the fey, and their followers fled westward and found the sea, they fell out, and their alliance broke down. The fleeing kings made boats and crossed the sea, while the fey left them there and went somewhere else. The Broken Kings cursed them for traitors so that whenever the fey make alliances their land is punished under them."

"You do see it, don't you, Baron?" Solft said, still nodding and smiling.

"See what?" demanded Lyrach.

"Most of us who learned this tale have assumed the fey allowed the Broken Kings to sail away and become future Redlanders while they themselves returned to the Azures to hide away, allies to no one. But what if there were others who went somewhere else, say to the south, or south and then west around the coast of the salt sea? What if being close to that coast let them maintain some contact with the Redlanders-to-be, a contact that let them fall under their sway as the mountain fey did when the Serpent Witch came to them?"

"But where're they gonna have settled?" demanded Guillam.

"Here," said Solft, smiling his approval at Prentice's insight. It was clear he was persuaded by the story.

"Why would anyone try to settle here?" Guillam said disdainfully. The question seemed obvious given the wasteland all about them. Lyrach similarly showed confusion, but Gennet began to shake his head, and when his gaze met Porth's eyes, Prentice could see by their look that they had figured it out for themselves.

"Oh, hell's bells," Porth muttered. "The drought."

"What?" demanded Guillam.

"The curse brought drought to the Reach in just one year after the Serpent Witch bound the fey to cooperate with her. What do you think the Reach would have looked like if that drought had lasted fifty years? Or a hundred?" Prentice asked.

The whole group looked around once more in horrified appreciation of what it implied.

"They cursed their own land?" Lyrach muttered aghast.

"What the hell for?"

"Benjamin's people say they did not remember the curse when the Witch arrived," Solft explained. "Not even their most elder history keepers. It seems likely the Redlanders have long forgotten it as well. The elders only knew to mistrust the beast-folk, not why or the possible consequences. Perhaps these other fey do not remember either."

"How do we remember it then?" asked Gennet.

"From the words of an ancient prophet," Prentice told them in a tone he hoped made it clear he did not intend to explain that any further. The tale of the Widow of the Wood was not something he felt free to share openly, belonging as it did to the archduchess rather than himself.

"But Knight Commander, you said there was a dark forest near where these other fey are, this lake," Lyrach objected, and Prentice could not fault the man this time. It was exactly the kind of interrogation every new thought needed.

"They can open the sky to move a boat or horsemen," Solft answered readily enough. "Why not to bring rain to a parched land, or at least on one forest valley?"

"So, the Redlanders bound the fey up here in this plain a long time ago, and it's made this desert out of everything," Lyrach walked through the reasoning slowly. "Why did they do it? Just to control the fey? What do they want?"

"The dragonfly," Prentice told him, "At least now. Who knows why originally, if it was hundreds of years ago. Perhaps they used them for slaves or took their forests for the wood."

Surely there were endless possible reasons the Redlanders and fey might have come back together in this southern realm.

"Well, it's a mongrel dog's leavings for *them*, if it's true," Gennet said at last. "What does it mean for us though, Commander?"

"It means that we have a long trek over a wasteland ahead of us, a wasteland that might or might not have fey riders ranging over it, waiting to give us the horse archer treatment."

"At least it won't be like the grasslands," Gennet said. Prentice appreciated his assertion but did not think they could rely on it.

"I would like to think that even Benjamin and *his* people could not stay hidden in land like this, Sergeant, but I would not bet our lives on it," he said. Fey stealth never seemed to rely upon the ground under them. "What I am hoping is that whatever lies between here and there, we can make the trek at speed and arrive at this lake to find a new fey people ready to be liberated as the mountain riders were, as well as the main of Benjamin's riders not slain to demon gods. Then we break the Redlander power, purge that valley, and come back to a Western Reach with safe waters and breathing room to finish training the rest of the White Lions to defend it."

The whole group nodded one last time, and Prentice was glad they all now had a broad appreciation of the challenge still ahead of them. He was also pleased that none of them pointed out that his plan made no mention of the Serpent Witch or Inxyphos and the Inquisition company of militants. It surprised Prentice how little the Serpent Witch even mattered to him now. She had been a haunting presence all through the winter, and now that he had seen her chained at the feet of her own kind, he hardly even cared.

It does not matter whether I care, he told himself. Stopping the one serpent had expanded to stopping her entire cabal, her *imzuss*, whether she ruled it or was its slave.

As for Inxyphos, the truth was that the knight commander had no idea how he wanted to handle the Inquisition men-at-arms, but he certainly hoped the fey in this far lake valley would assist him against them. Perhaps they would be able to reveal details of the Inquisition's mission to the Redlanders, as well as why it was that the curse that harried the fey with the Broken Kings had no effect upon the Church men or the Reach.

Prentice dismissed his men and looked westward to the jagged horizon before he mounted Boots once more. He shook his head in wonder. No matter how much he and the Reach learned about the invaders out of the far west, there were always yet more questions and more mysteries. From the first day he had seen the Redlanders emerge from under the trees by the riverside, the Grand Kingdom had been guessing, bumbling about in the dark, searching for a candle or lantern that they were not even sure was there. Now, as they found a wick or two to light, they only discovered that the cave of ignorance they were in stretched in every direction, the darkness still ruling beyond the boundary of their trifling glow.

"They've pinned us on this side, well and truly at this point, Your Grace," Sergeant Sedgemark said with a matter-of-fact tone as he explained the situation at the Murr River bridge. A search for escort riders had led Amelia and Spindle to the southern bank where a handful of wounded lancers were using their handguns to support the cohorts guarding the Lions' end of the crossing, all under the young Sedgemark's command.

"'Tis better you not get too close, if you'll pardon my saying, Your Grace," the red-haired sergeant advised. "They've not many bows over there, but there are a few rangers or the like in their number. It would not do for an overoptimistic archer to land his best arrow ever at the sight of your ladies' dresses."

Amelia recognized the wisdom of the advice and gladly remained back several dozen paces from the bridge. This put her in the section of the road that had seen the main of the fighting the day before, and while the bodies had been gathered and were now burning in an oily smoked pyre some distance away, the ground was still churned and the air smelled foul. A stack of broken weapons and equipment had been piled up on the other side of the road and was now being picked over by two women in threadbare shawls and patched skirts.

"Is the bridge safe otherwise?" she asked.

"As much as we can make it," said Sedgemark. "The knight captain ordered up the wagons we managed to cross yesterday, making a barricade for us to defend. The knights over there tried to ride the bridge last afternoon, just as the sun went down. We flung them back handily. Later in the evening they came again, dismounted, but that was easier, in a sense. Even in the dark, the bridge is a narrow target. Aim straight and a Roarsman's bound to hit something."

"Will they keep attacking?"

The sergeant shook his head.

"Not if they have any sense," he said. "That's why the knight captain's got lancers riding up and down the bank, keeping an eye out. If they're canny at all, the Kingdom men'll try to get a team over by boat for a night attack, disrupt us from this side and then come at the bridge in force. We've been eyes and ears out all night, watching for every shadow. Hope we took some gin or something when we captured the camp. Lot of tense blokes gonna need something to help 'em sleep tonight."

Amelia scowled at that notion, and when he noted her disapproval, Sedgemark ducked his head apologetically.

"Not like drunkards, I mean, Your Grace. Just to take some of the tension out of the guy lines, as it were."

It's hardly a shock to hear, Amelia told herself, surprised at the intensity of her disapproval. She had even taken some brandy herself with her meal the night before. It would be rank hypocrisy to demean in others what she allowed for herself.

"If you're seeking, the knight captain is just on the riverside, not far," Sedgemark said, interrupting Amelia's thoughts. He pointed to the bank not two or three hundred paces west of the bridge where a small cluster of men were laboring almost out of sight amidst the long reeds.

"Thank you, Sergeant," the archduchess said, forcing herself to smile, and led the way for Spindle and their guards through the meadow grass parallel to the river but a safe distance back from it. It was a short walk to the spot indicated, and even as they drew close, the sound of men grunting and groaning with exertion floated through the tall fronds.

"Get the other rope tied under that bit," someone commanded. "If it's safe?"

"Should be. It's part of the carriage axel," Amelia heard her husband answer. She was surprised at how pleased she was to hear his voice and felt a sudden urgency to speak with him. After the harshness of their parting the night before, she found she was quite eager to reconcile. She picked her way carefully toward the group. Two men suddenly burst from the reeds directly in front of her, hauling red-faced on a boat cable. They stopped abruptly upon seeing her and released their rope to bow their heads and tug the forelock. From deeper in the grasses there came a splashing and men cursing.

"What are you twits about?" shouted a voice. "Warn a fellow, will you?"

"Tush, you jackanapes!" one of the two haulers shouted back over his shoulder. "'Tis the Lioness!"

"You what?" demanded the voice, and a third man emerged, clearly ready to require an explanation of the neglectful workers. All three men were heavily thewed, suggesting lives of hard work, but the third man revealed himself to be likely a blacksmith, because apart from the thick muscles of his arms and barreled chest, the skin of his wrists was peppered with the many little burn scars a man acquired by working hot iron, flames, and sparks every day.

"Oh! Beggin' your pardon, Your Grace. Never thought to see you here by the waterside." He tugged the forelock in an exaggerated gesture of respect, apparently fearful his gruff manner might draw Amelia's displeasure. The archduchess only smiled.

"Is that you, my love?" she heard Farringdon ask, and he followed the impatient smith out of the grasses, approaching her and bowing formally when he was but a few paces away. She felt a sudden desire to embrace him, and even though she knew such a thing would not be seemly in this company, she was nonetheless disappointed that he did not attempt to violate protocol that way, just this once.

After the way you beat him down last night? she thought. *Not likely.*

"Come to see what we're about, Your Grace?" Farringdon asked, and he smiled warmly. Amelia knew it as his problem-solving smile, the expression he had when he was wrestling with something unknown that fascinated him, such as repairing a wagon hitch or rediverting a stream to bring water to fields where it was needed. It made her think that if he bore her any ill-will for the previous night, he was not letting it overwhelm their relationship. That was a happy notion.

"Indeed, Marquis? Have you found treasure on the riverbank?" Amelia asked, feeling almost playful suddenly.

"Not exactly, but Hilderman the smith here did find something of importance," Farringdon explained. "And given the moment of quiet, I thought to help getting it seen to immediately. The distraction of simple tasks and all that."

The scarred smith bowed his head, accepting the marquis's words as a compliment. Nearby, one of the two laborers was less appreciative and scoffed quietly under his breath.

"Simple, my left buttock," he muttered, but the smith wheeled upon him.

"All you had to do was haul! Simple enough even mutton-headed bullocks like you two should'a been able, but no, couldn't even do that right!"

The indignant man seemed ready to make more of an argument, but a quick glance at the archduchess's armed guards put paid to that temptation. Behind Amelia, Spindle tutted imperiously, and the archduchess could imagine the lady-in-waiting shaking her head in superior disappointment, her lace mask making her seem an even more frightening presence.

"Perhaps I could show you, Your Grace," Farringdon offered, and he held out his hand to Amelia. Accepting it, she stepped down to the reed level from the bank. The ground beneath her squelched somewhat, but her body was light enough not to press down to the wet mud itself. That prompted another smile. With so many aspects of recent days weighing her down, the notion of something proving her to be lighter, even if purely physical, was oddly pleasing. Silly as the thought was, she cherished it as she did the bright morning sunshine.

"There it is," Farringdon said, pulling aside the cattails and fronds of long fennel, the distinctive aroma rising from the river herb as he did so. There, in a crushed area that led right down to the waterline, was an indistinct piece of black metal with the cable tied to two hooks upon it. Amelia had no idea what she was looking at.

"You are to be commended on your eyes, good smith," she said, slightly bemused. "It is a wonder that you saw such a thing so well hidden at the water's edge."

"Oh, well, I saw it land, Your Grace," the smith explained, though the words only added to Amelia's mystification.

"Land?" she repeated.

"Oh aye. I was watching from the camp across there yesterday morning."

He pointed a thick, callused finger in the direction of the White Lions' previous bivouac beyond the north shore. Even from this distance some of the abandoned tent-tops could be seen.

"This bit flew through the air like a drunken bird, I swear. Whee, all the way from the hilltop, over the river and plonk, down here in the water, trailing smoke the whole way."

The man used his finger to trace loop-the-loops in the air, showing the path of the chunk of metal he claimed to have seen, and Amelia realized what she was looking at. She whirled on her husband.

"A piece of damned cannon?" she shouted in fury. Pushing off him as if he were a tree or similar object, she thrust herself out of the reeds and back towards the bank proper.

"I commanded you!" she raged, feet slipping in the trodden reeds.

"My love?" Farringdon pleaded, following her and offering a hand to help her balance. She shoved it away disdainfully, causing her to almost slip as her foot caught on the hem of her dress. She hardly cared for the cloth. It was already dirty, and when a fresh piece of clothing was ready, she would take it off and never wear it again. Her proud blue and silver Lioness overdress just felt like another symbol of her hubris now.

"I commanded you to have nothing to do with these things ever again!" Amelia said, facing her husband once she was standing on solid ground once more. "Now, only a day later I find you playing with one by the riverside like a truant child!"

"With respect, that is not what you commanded," Farringdon objected, and Amelia was shocked that he would openly contradict her. All around, in the corners of her vision, she could see the others present looking away, embarrassed or fearful to be here in the midst of a marital argument between the Reach's two highest peers.

"Your exact words were that I should never speak to you of them, except as to how they are to be destroyed," he said tersely, and it seemed to Amelia that he clenched his jaw as he did so. "Even if we are to never learn again of their manufacture or whatever flaw it was that caused the explosion, surely the best way to learn to destroy a thing is to study one that has already been destroyed?"

"Study them?" Amelia demanded, and she realized her emotions were slipping away very quickly. While she had come a long way back from the shattered mindlessness of the immediate aftermath of the battle, it seemed her inner walls were not restored enough to hold her feelings completely in check just yet. She did her best to grip the reins, as she had with the unnerved Silvermane, but her emotions were proving to be a wilder beast than she expected, even spooked as she was by the preceding day.

"They do not need to be studied! They need to be banished to the perdition from which they sprang! They are works of evil to be loathed by every righteous soul. You heard the words of the Church in synod pronounced yesterday. These monstrosities are accursed!"

"So is our marriage," Farringdon said quietly, "if we are to believe the words of that pronouncement."

Without thinking, Amelia slapped him across the cheek, striking just below his bloodshot eye. He flinched heavily, and in her inner thoughts she realized that the blow had probably hurt his existing wounds. Her blood was up, however, and she found herself unwilling to show him any pity.

"I made you my knight captain to defend our lands, not to speak poison or waste lives!" she told him, her fury carrying her past any hope of reconciliation now. "Go to your duty, Marquis Consort, lest I come to fully regret my choices."

Farringdon saluted her and bowed his head. Then he stepped to one side and up onto the bank beside her, facing away in the direction of the bridge. He seemed about ready to walk off, then paused.

"I promised the smith here the right of salvage over the iron and steel once we were done," the knight captain said without turning to face his wife-liege-lady. "Would you have me retract that pledge, Your Grace?"

"Let the man do whatever he will with it," she said, also not turning to look at Farringdon. "Have him melt it down to make nails if he wishes. I am told that one does not use good iron to make a nail, after all."

Farringdon nodded once more and then marched away. Everyone else stood around, waiting silently for any kind of signal as to what was acceptable to do now that the awkward moment was waning. Recognizing their discomfort as her own inner turmoil receded, Amelia waved at the workmen down amongst the reeds.

"Go to your salvage, yeomen," she said, and the men tugged their forelocks.

Amelia turned away, but not wanting to follow the path her husband had just taken toward the bridge and the road, she led them off across the field, straight south from the river. The waist-high grass waved in the pleasant summer breeze, and a pair of young goats cropped at the greenery a little way ahead. The two animals capered away as the ladies and their escorts approached, and Amelia noticed a small redbrush bush a short distance farther on. She turned to their escorts.

"If you will, I would speak privately with my lady a space, by that bush," she told them. "If you could keep watch from here, I would be grateful."

The escorts were happy to let the ladies go on to the bush, and the women sat beside one another in the shade on the grass. Amelia drew in the pleasant lemony scent with a deep breath and then let it out. She bit her lower lip.

"Spindle, I just gave my husband a dressing down in front of God and man," she said cautiously, as if admitting what had just happened might somehow make the whole event worse. "And he told me he thinks our marriage is accursed."

"You know that isn't what he said, Your Grace," Spindle said quietly, and Amelia's first instinct was to turn on her own lady-in-waiting but recognized, in fact, that Spindle was correct. Farringdon had not said their marriage was cursed. He only pointed out that if his cannons were cursed, then by the same reasoning, so were they. It was a reasonably logical piece of thought, but she still could not believe he had been so cruel as to say it to her like that.

"It's like he loves those things more than me," Amelia said, and even as Spindle gave her a raised eyebrow and doubtful frown, she knew the comment for pure self-pity. She shook her head and laughed at herself, though somewhat bitterly. Spindle chuckled as well, then looked away at the pleasant scene. As long as they did not look too far in any direction, and ignored the suffering folk of Aubrey, the armed camps, and prisoners on the edges of Cattlefields, they were in effect in the midst of a summer idyll—meadow and late morning sunshine.

"I'm struggling, Lady Spindle," Amelia said with another lemon-scented sigh. "My nerve is taut, and my heart runs around without my guidance. Why can I not single-rein my spooked emotions as I do with Silvermane?"

"Well, Your Grace, it's not as if you haven't been through a true upheaval. And every time something bad happens and a sour-tongued sacrist has been there to add his 'this is a curse from God' to the feelings, it's only natural it keeps you from getting your feet back under you."

"But I'm supposed to be the Lioness," Amelia protested. "I'm supposed to be steel-hearted and true. Not some harridan who keeps berating the man she loves every time he sneezes in a direction she doesn't approve."

Spindle cocked her head with a smile, politely acknowledging the truth of that interpretation of the archduchess's recent interaction with her spouse. The lady had a knowing smile as she delicately spread the creases in her own skirt.

"It's not that uncommon, Your Grace, given the way you're in," she said, still courteously looking away at other matters, such as a loose thread on the hem of her own overdress. "You should hear the stories Righteous tells, and surely she is as steel hard as any of us."

"What stories?"

"Well, she nearly cut Prentice's—sorry, Baron Prentice's—throat during a fight last year," Spindle explained.

"She did?" Amelia asked, astonished. Baroness Righteous was a ferocious creature when enraged, but even for her, cutting her husband's throat seemed at least one pace beyond normal.

"Right on the steps outside your chamber, so she said," Spindle assured her mistress. "Had her sweet ripper right to his windpipe and all. Said she actually thought about it even, except, of course, he made no move to fight her back. There was no way Righteous could hurt him when he showed her that much trust, even being *how* she was at the time."

"He trusts her that much?" Amelia wondered. She was about to tell herself that she wished Farringdon had the same trust in her, when two thoughts struck her at exactly the same time. The first was that, in fact, Farringdon did trust her as much as could be expected given their history—more even. It would just be another attempt at self-pity to think anything else. The other thought was to remember something Spindle had said a moment before.

"What do you mean, the 'way' that I am in?"

"Well, in the early days, like Righteous was last year," Spindle said, her tone making it clear she thought her meaning was obvious. "This was back the last time she and Baron Prentice saw each other before the fey and Bluebird got him. She was terrified that was to be the last time they spoke, too. Of course, that's part of the topsy turvy heart of many a new mam in the first days. Eventually, the body wakes up to its growing blessing and the glow comes on a girl so everyone forgets how the first few months can make a shrew out of her, specially if she gets some ugly upsets, like having a hilltop go all thunderclap and fire around her."

Amelia blinked and then stared, unable to form thoughts for a moment. It was as if Spindle had been speaking in a foreign language that Amelia thought she knew but suddenly could not understand.

"Are you saying you think I'm pregnant?" she asked at last.

"Are you not, Your Grace? I conjured you as two to three months in. Should be your body'll settle to the fact soon and start to show proper. You'll be needing new underdresses, and believe me, I've got some ideas where to get the soft linen for them for you."

Amelia looked down at the grass but with unfocused eyes as inwardly she was calculating when she had last had her time. Counting in her head, she could not believe she had not noticed the weeks passing. The winter had been hectic for a wet season, as so much work had been needed to ensure the province recovered from the drought. Of course, she and Farringdon had taken moments together as husband and wife, as any newly married couple would, but beyond growing in intimacy with her spouse, Amelia had not really considered the implications. She nodded, realizing that Spindle was almost certainly correct.

"I have a child," she whispered and looked up into her smiling lady's eyes.

"Not here yet, but soon enough, God willing."

The two embraced comfortingly.

"See, once he hears that, I'd wager the marquis consort isn't going to remember much of a few harsh words said in a difficult moment," Spindle said as she sat back from their hug. There were happy tears in her eyes, and as she saw them, Amelia realized she had them in her own eyes as well.

CHAPTER 44

I t took almost two full days to lift all the supplies, the mule team, and the entire Gryphon Banner Company up the scarp and onto the higher plain. In truth, Prentice had to admit the whole endeavor was completed as swiftly as could be expected, and not a single man of the company was injured and almost nothing lost. Even so, every day's delay worked at his mind. Come dawn of the third day, he was pleased finally to begin the forced march toward the distant mountains.

Lacking riders to act as scouts, he detached a number of ten-man "lines" to form teams and roam ahead and north of their column, having them move off on foot but without armor or packs. Each team had a couple of Roar with them to give them some capacity to fend off wild animals or small groups of enemies, but every scout had orders to stay within running distance of the main company and to retreat before becoming engaged in anything like true combat. The first day all teams reported back exactly the same thing—nothing had been seen but desert and the river.

When they camped that night, some of the Lions tried their hands at fishing in the waters of the upper Murr, but they all reported the same thing. They not only caught no fish but saw no sign of any either—no spoor or eggs in the usual places, no freshwater crustaceans, and no frogs or other amphibians amongst the shallows. It took a while for them to notice, but they even found there were no midges or insects of any kind.

Aside from the green grass of the edge, there was nothing living, not even in the water of the Murr River.

"At least it's drinkable," Brother Whilte said when he and Prentice discussed it that night. "But who could imagine something so bereft?"

"Not just of cultivation," Prentice agreed, remembering the map from Borrosod the Pilgrim's codex, which Solft was still bringing with them. "Bereft of almost all life."

What has the power to curse so thoroughly? he wondered, knowing that he might not be glad to learn the answer.

"I've had more than a few men come to me, looking for prayer and counsel," Whilte told him. "This emptiness is wearing upon their souls. It might get worse, too, spread to more of them. I'd like to hold a dawn service before we march if you'll permit."

"You know how little time we can spare," Prentice objected reflexively.

"I do, but if we don't make allowance now, spirits will..." Whilte began to explain, but Prentice held up his hand to stop him.

"I know. I know," he said, nodding and sighing. "You have good reason to ask. Let those who wish to attend do so but make it a small service and completed at dawn."

"A small service, indeed," Whilte said, shaking his head. "The men's spirits may need a little more, you know?"

"Ten years on the chain and no one cared a moment what a convict's spirit needed, no matter how far we marched or how hard we were worked," Prentice retorted bitterly. Whilte seemed ready to make more argument, but Prentice cut him off. "Of course, no one expected convicts to maintain high morale to face a foe at the end of those marches, except once, and we both know how that ended up."

Whilte tugged his forelock and thanked the knight commander, adding one more comment before he left for his own bed for the night.

"There's not a shirker among them, Prentice, not a one. They just don't know what to make of this strange land that you and Solft say is cursed."

Prentice accepted that with a silent nod, but he didn't know exactly what to make of it either. The next morning, Whilte was true to his word, and his dawn prayer service, which included a breaking of camp bread downed with boiled river water, was concluded as the streaks of dawn lit the open flats.

At midmorning, Prentice was approached by Solft, who bounced along on his personal mule, looking up at the knight commander, higher in his saddle and riding his changeover horse, whom he had decided to name Dusty, since its buckskin color reminded him of the parched landscape of the uplands.

"I say, Baron, do you see that mound out there in the distance?"

Solft pointed to an odd-looking lump in the terrain, perhaps a couple of hundred paces north of where the column was following the path of the river. It was the closest thing to a geographical feature the plains had produced in that direction since the march began. It might have been only a dune of sorts or an outcrop of rock.

"I have seen it, Master," Prentice answered.

"I was thinking to investigate it."

"Do you imagine there is much there to investigate?" the knight commander asked with a slightly mocking tone. Solft appeared to take the question in the good-natured spirit it was intended.

"Probably not, My Lord, but as there is so little else to investigate, I might as well direct my curiosity some way."

"I cannot argue with that rationale," Prentice said. "In fact, I will escort you, Master, to ensure your safety."

"Do you think there will be danger?" Solft asked, not sounding much afraid.

"Probably not, Master, but as there is so little else to exercise my martial skill upon, I might as well direct my abilities to something."

"Oh, very clever," Solft said with a smile and clapped his heels to his mule's flanks. Prentice looked over his shoulder where Lyrach was marching diligently a little behind his commander, leading the unmounted Boots. Prentice felt his training at Ashfield returning to life in a fashion he had not expected, but he still found Lyrach's service as a groom useful. He no longer much suspected the ex-squire of plotting treachery, but it annoyed him that the ambitious man had effectively managed to circumvent the natural order of the Lions, nonetheless. It had already occurred to Prentice that the best use of Lyrach might be to pack him off to serve as one of Farringdon's lancers.

Of course, that would leave me needing a groom again, he thought. Perhaps the best thing would be to make the knight commander's groom a permanent position and assign it to one of the lancers as a matter of honor. If Solomon could be taught the skills, Prentice would gladly give the lad the role, but he suspected it would be a different waste of talent. Solomon had the makings of an excellent foot officer.

"Tell Sergeant Gennet where I am going, Lyrach," Prentice commanded. "Solft and I will rejoin the march before midday or else send word back with one of the scouting parties."

Lyrach saluted, and leading Boots in a wide circle, started walking back to pass the message to Gennet at the head of the main cohort. Prentice turned Dusty out of the line and headed north after Master Solft's receding mule. It was not a long ride before he caught up, and soon after that the two men reached the mound in the parched earth. Approaching it, they found a long trough in the dirt, a kind of shallow line, worn in the ground leading straight to it. Looking back over his shoulder, Prentice could easily make out the green line of the river, going back and forth across the land to the south. The shallow trough headed directly towards that, and Prentice stopped Dusty to look down at it while Solft went on ahead to circle around the mound itself.

"I think it's stonework under the wind-blown grit," the scholar said, studying the low hump that barely rose to the height of his mule's shoulder above the plain. Prentice was still studying the trough leading up to the mound. In any part of the Reach or Grand Kingdom, or indeed anywhere in any civilized lands, a small geographical feature like this would be utterly unremarkable. It was obvious that this was an irrigation ditch. The farmlands of the world were crisscrossed with them like a weaver's discarded yarn ball.

Bereft of cultivation? Prentice wondered. *Perhaps a group of settlers from Radengon tried their hand at it?* Someone had had to give Jannomoch the tale of a land of ghosts and death, but what would prompt a group of farmsteaders to abandon the lush grass of the lowlands and climb up here to attempt the monumental effort of converting dust to soil?

"Baron Prentice, come see this," Solft called eagerly, and Prentice looked to see the man had ridden up the mound and was now dismounting to look more closely at something upon the summit. Prentice geed Dusty to a walk and was shocked as he closed the last few paces to see that it was no mound at all, and no natural feature. It was a pit with stonewalled sides that rose like a battlement above the height of the plain itself. Around that wall the wind had pushed banks of sand, so that the wall was surrounded by an earthen bulwark, a sloped ring over a pace wide. Solft's mule was now stopped on that bulwark while its master was looking down into the pit in the middle.

"It's an entry into the earth," the scholar said, happily surprised by his discovery. The pit was a spiral of sorts, with walls of rough-cut stone the same color as the dust and earth. It twisted, screw-like, into the ground, forming a downward pathway broad enough for people to walk single file. Solft was already eagerly making his way around the spiral toward the bottom which seemed to be full of sand. Prentice was still wondering at the construction's purpose when Solft reached the lowest level. He traced the point where the stone wall met the earth and then crossed the bottom to the other side, measuring by his steps.

"It's silted up by the wind, I'd say," Solft declared, his eager voice echoing up the sides of the pit. "It almost certainly goes someway farther down. The question is, to what purpose?"

Prentice stood in his stirrups and scanned the plain to the north. The shallow trough he could see stretching south toward the river stopped at this pit, but as he looked farther to the north, he thought he could make out other, similar marks in the ground. The air over the land shimmered in the sunlight, making it harder to tell for sure, but he also seemed to see a similar mound perhaps another four or five hundred paces north.

"Could it have been a well, perhaps?" Solft was musing as he began the curving walk back to the surface. "I should very much like to dig it out to discover what the wind and sand have hidden."

He reached the surface and took his mule's reins, then stood looking up at Prentice still in the saddle.

"I say, My Lord, did you hear me?" he asked, an unusually forward question for the normally respectful scholar. Prentice blinked as he realized he had truly not been listening to Solft's words. He traced back through his recent memory of the speech he had been half-ignoring, looking for the question.

"No, Master, we do not have time to dig this out," he said, recognizing at least that implicit request.

"No, I didn't think so," Solft said with a sorrowful nod. "Well, perhaps when our campaign is done, I might come back with some workmen."

"It is not a well," Prentice said flatly, still more absorbed in his own thoughts than his companion's. He looked over his shoulder again at the upper Murr, not far enough distant to justify a well here. "This is part of a qanat."

"A what...oh, that is unusual," Solft mused, recognizing the obscure word. A qanat was a kind of underground aqueduct, a tunneled way to bring water from a distant source across land where the sun might punish an open-air flow. It was the kind of construction the Reach might have used to combat the drought, bringing water from aquifers in the Azures down to the farms and towns where the surface rivers and streams had dried up. The only problem was that even a single qanat would take miners years, if not decades, to build. As far as Prentice knew there were none still in use in the Grand Kingdom. He only knew the word himself from his studies, producing it from the vaults of memory where the long-ago lessons of Ashfield were still stored, along with his all but forgotten meager skills in horsemanship.

"This is not farmersteaders," Prentice muttered as he surveyed the ground about. "This is the work of a nation, a civilization."

In his mind's eye he could imagine the other fey, the ones who had settled here after severing from the Broken Kings. They must have occupied much of this plain, with farms and towns, perhaps even their own kings or queens. Then, sometime after they had forgotten the curse on their former allies, they came under the sway of the Redlanders once more.

"You think they fought against the drought?" Solft said, sifting Prentice's words in his own thoughts. "It must have been upon them for many years to make the effort seem worthwhile."

Prentice nodded. He could imagine a drought parching their land. The Murr must have kept running, perhaps because of the magick in the lake at its headwaters, or perhaps the fey built the dragonfly obelisk to make it flow. If they did, the art was now as lost to them as cannon-making was in the Grand Kingdom, Prentice was sure of that. Otherwise, the Redlanders would have had these southern fey making them new obelisks, not using blood sacrifices to enslave the existing ones.

"I think we will find more like this the farther we march west, Master Solft," Prentice said. The thought made Jannomoch's words about ghosts take on new meaning. They were marching almost literally through the graveyard of a dead civilization.

"They must have been so numerous," Solft said, and he shook his head as he turned around and mounted awkwardly onto his mule.

"Equal to the Grand Kingdom today, I would guess," Prentice said grimly. In his mind's eye he was watching ordinary fey farmers and craftsmen going about their daily business, banding together to dig these trenches and wells, connecting them by qanat tunnels to the river—their hope of life. And slowly the curse overwhelmed them.

"We know nothing of them," Solft marveled. "They settled here, rose and thrived, then declined and perished, and not a word of them reached our ears."

"You know whom we have to thank for that," Prentice told him.

The two men rode back toward the river, catching up with the marching column, which had stopped to drink at midday.

CHAPTER 45

That evening, Prentice was still contemplating the dead fey civilization as he walked by the riverside. It was a surprisingly solitary space, even though his entire camp was only a handful of paces away on the dirt. That was because of the feeling the upland Murr engendered in all the Reachermen. The Western Reach was a land bounded by life-giving rivers, and whether or not they had been riverfolk before they swore to the Lions, all Reacherfolk knew the power and value of a strong river to commerce, to society, to life itself. This lifeless flow by which they were forced to live was an abomination that all of them felt, even if no one spoke it aloud. Every evening as they camped, the militiamen assigned to refill the waterskins and barrels came and did so, taking the cool water away to be boiled and then did not return to the river. None came to bathe or swim, to refresh themselves as men on the march beside any other waterway might at the end of a day. Even the sedge was bitter and inedible. A couple of the hardier types had tried to chew some, almost out of pure bravado, demonstrating their manliness, but after they had developed violent stomach aches, Prentice had ordered the practice stopped. It was a redundant command. The Gryphon Banner Company wanted nothing to do with the upland Murr beyond its water.

"Fresh, yet unrefreshing," Prentice muttered as he looked at the surface that mirrored in ripples the glow of the Rampart over the sky. It, too, reminded him of the swampy pond where the lion angel had first visited him on a night when he had raged against God and men. The terrifying sublime being had arrived amidst the reeds that night and begun Prentice's lessons in what true rage against injustice was like. Bowing his head, he gave a gentle prayer of thanks—not so much for the visitation or the revelation it brought but for the fact that in his woundedness, God had not simply swept him away as a great and raging wall of floodwater might have done. He had tasted the divine fury at the evils visited upon creation, and in comparison, his own sufferings were one small ripple in the tempest-tossed ocean.

"What rage did *you* feel?" he asked the dead fey in his imagination. "Did you curse God? Did you fight to your last breaths, fists clenched, demanding that somehow your efforts might yield survival? That you might preserve the land you built against a forgotten curse that gripped your nation?"

Pity arose in Prentice's heart like mist rising in a chilled land. He could imagine the anger of the fey and wondered where they might have directed it. The fury of his own conviction and exile had made him angry at God, even though he could easily see that the Church which endorsed convict servitude had long forgotten too many of God's truths. *The merciless preachers of mercy*, the mountain fey called them. God's name was invoked, but His actual presence was too often not invited.

Walking through the low grasses, Prentice wondered if these fey had turned their rage upon the Redlanders at all. At first, the idea seemed foolish, since of course the two groups were yet bound together, but the more he thought about it, the more Prentice realized that it almost certainly had happened. After all, however many of the remaining fey there were at the end of the Murr, they were clearly slaves of the Redlander cabal. He had seen that for himself.

"So why has it taken them so long to come looking for us?"

The iron mask he had plucked from the obelisk at the base of the rapids was ancient and pockmarked with rust. Solft had it now, studying its craft, having first stopped up the eyeholes with

river clay to block the magick. It seemed a ham-fisted solution but appeared to work, nonetheless. Brother Whilte
was keeping regular watch upon the artifact, and thus far
no danger had been perceived. The item's age was the main
clue for Prentice though. Its condition suggested it had been
placed a hundred or more years ago. Yet, if the Redlanders
had conquered this upland fey nation that long in the past,
how had it taken so much time for them to come east? He
could hardly imagine the Blood Sects being patient in their
lust for conquest. However much they remembered of the
true history of the Broken Kings—and Prentice suspected
that Solft was correct in saying it was not much—they did
remember that they hated the folk of the Grand Kingdom.
And the Redlanders were not a people slow to punish that
which they hated. Of course, it was possible that the Redlanders had only seized control of the fey lands recently, but the
desert around them spoke of a curse that had lain upon the
land for generations, and the mask Solft was studying was
ancient. Whatever the exact history, Prentice had to admit
that his imagination was not up to the task of guessing it all.

He chuckled and thought about the instructors at Ashfield who had taught him history and law, secular and religious, and what they would have said of a student who
imagined his reasoning alone was enough to reach the truth
without any reference to evidence or study. Corruption may
have blinded Mother Church, but that did not mean there
were no wise men or women in its corpus.

"Thank you, even for the wisdom of those who now hate
me," he muttered, trying to be humble. He was about to
leave the riverside to go back to camp when he noticed a light
moving in the water's reflection some distance ahead of him.
He looked into the sky, thinking to see a shooting star or
something similar, but there was nothing there. The heavens
were as steady as they ever were. Looking back to the water,
he wondered if this was a firefly and suddenly hoped it was.

Even a single living thing might be a cause for optimism, he thought.

Prentice stood still a moment, watching the light grow slowly to the brightness of a candle flame. It danced about like a firefly, but was not yellow like that insect, nor as a candle or rushlight. It was not the same kind of brightness either. Rather, it was a single, bluish, luminous fire that flickered and bounced over the surface of the water, weaving through the grasses.

A firefly? A will-o'-the-wisp?

Prentice shook his head slightly, not turning away from the approaching glow. It drew closer, and when it finally lifted itself to flit at his face, he could see that unlike a firefly, which pulsed a glow from its thorax, this creature was most like unto a butterfly but with wings seemingly of blue and green fire. Most scholars considered the will-o'-the-wisp to be a simple glow, the light from a firefly thorax detached from its body by an unknown natural process. They dismissed the legends of witchlights and pixies living under mushrooms as the fancies of ill-bred serfs.

Yet here it was—a fully glowing creature, insect-like unto itself. A part of Prentice wanted to be curious, to reach out and touch the thing, perhaps even catch it, and yet he was frozen in place, and he felt the space around him fill as if the shadows by the lifeless river contained unseen folk—beings possessed of dark emotions. He wondered if the restless ghosts of the dead fey civilization had arisen to vent their frustrations upon him, upon his force and their intrusion. The air around him became a vapor of loathing and bitterness, every breath chilling his heart, which was beating in his chest like the clenching and unclenching of a fist, so that his blood hammered in his ears. And still the bright little glow danced around him, blithe in the riverside darkness.

Fear, the witchlight whispered into his soul. *Flee in fear. Flee to the water and be safe. Hide in the depths.*

There were no words, not truly, but the sentiment was unmistakable. As if the thing was a perversion of a true conscience, the will-o'-the-wisp was trying to persuade him that the only right course was to throw himself into the water to escape terror by hiding in the depths. He stared at the dark surface, his jaw clenched against the dread, not moving for fear that he would follow the monstrous advice and throw himself in to drown. The wisp flittered back to the surface, as if beckoning him into the water. A part of Prentice's own thoughts began to wonder if this was someone reaching out to contact him, to draw him to a new vision like the one he'd had with the mask. He had barely survived that experience. Days later his chest still felt uncomfortable when he drew deep breaths. For a long time, he stared at the water, feeling a tug upon himself like a hook and cable, embedded in his soul and dragging him below the surface.

"What if there is another vision there?" he wondered out loud, his voice sounding distant even to his own ears. The wisp danced anew, as if it heard him speak.

Another vision. Another. Another.

Prentice felt his weight shift forward suddenly, as if to follow the little fire-creature's insistence. He stopped himself, but it was difficult—an exertion of will. Even so, his eyes were still drawn to the water, and the wisp still tried to entice him. He had no idea how long he had been standing there. It could be after midnight or even near to dawn.

"How long?" he muttered, and the wisp answered again.

Forever. Rest and peace. Forever.

A cold battle-smile, the joy of fearlessness in the face of fear, came over Prentice's face, and looking at the surface of the water he saw the reflected lights of the sky, the stars, and moon, and Rampart. Seeing them, the dark of the water was transformed, because he remembered something else he had also seen more than once—the dark between the stars reflected in the angel lion's eyes. In comparison, the dark at the bottom of the water was shallow, washed out, and strangely pale.

He barked a sudden, furious laugh.

"Your masters hear what you hear, don't they?" he asked the flickering light as it suddenly projected annoyance. It did not like him laughing. "Do they see what you see? Can they see me?"

Prentice stared at the light, not in fascination anymore, but to see beyond it to whoever had sent it.

"Wisp," he said, and now his voice felt increasingly under his control, stronger and clearer. "Well are you named, for you are a whisperer, a weak and fearful thing."

It did not appear to like being called "weak" or "fearful" either, though exactly how Prentice knew that he would never be able to explain to someone else. As he had thought at the first, it was simply as if the creature spoke the way a conscience spoke. Only it was a liar, he was sure of that much now.

"You wish to see me drown? That was the other day," he told it. "You missed your chance. Whisper to me as often as you like, your words cannot control me. I have heard the lion roar in the night and in the day. I have seen it do battle with the serpent that has your masters in its grip. I have spoken with its voice and broken the chains of the serpent's priestesses."

Feeling control of his limbs fully returning to him, Prentice took a forceful step toward the will-o'-the-wisp, but not to enter water, only to show he was not afraid.

"Tell them I am coming," he said, and the years of his education melded suddenly in his thinking with the years of his conviction and the years of war. Moreover, they linked together with the supposed prophecy which the Redlanders had of him.

"I am coming on the back of a red horse, with my sword held high," he told them through their little representative light. "I lead beasts of war into your land, and we come with the dust of your ancestors upon us, crying out for vengeance. The land long accursed bids us find you. Run, hide, weep, and wail—bleed or shed blood—it will not matter. Whisper what fears you will; when you hear the hot-iron roar of the lion, then you will *know* fear."

"Knight Commander, is that you?" called a voice, and Prentice turned to see one of the camp sentries—a Claw holding a long pike and carrying a reed torch—coming toward him. "I thought I heard someone talking."

"No, that was me, militiaman," Prentice answered. "I was just…" He looked around and realized that the will-o'-the-wisp had vanished. It did not surprise him.

I was just declaring myself one of the four horsemen of the Apocalypse to a mystical insect, sentry, he thought and shook his head with a chuckle. *All perfectly normal.*

"How goes your night?" he asked the man on duty. The Claw shrugged his shoulder.

"Quiet enough, Commander. Gives me the willies sometimes, the empty flatness, like. But in the end, empty means quiet, and quiet's better than under attack."

"Not a bad way to look at it, I would say," Prentice agreed. He cocked his head. "Have you seen nothing odd then?"

"Odd how?"

"Lights on the water?"

The sentry looked past Prentice to the surface of the river and scanned it up and down, as if he had only just realized the water was even there.

"Not that I've noticed. You thinking things like fireflies?"

"Things like that," Prentice agreed. The sentry frowned and shook his head.

"Nope, Commander. Does it matter? Fireflies ain't dangerous, are they?" the man asked.

"Usually not," Prentice answered and then paused. He wasn't sure yet just how much he wanted to share about his latest numinous experience. He thought about what to tell the sentry. "Of course, the only river grass around is poison, so whatever can live on *it* probably is not much good for us either."

The Claw nodded slowly, likely willing to accept his commander's word, even if he did not fully follow the reasoning. Prentice saluted the man and turned away.

"Did you see fireflies, Knight Commander?" the sentry asked.

"I thought I might have," Prentice answered. "Pass the word to the other sentries. If they do, just keep clear."

"Aye, Commander."

Prentice left the riverside in search of his bed, ready to rest for the next day's journey. He resolved to explain to Gennet and Whilte in the morning what had happened, as well as to Master Solft. It would be a curiosity that the scholar could add to his chronicle if nothing else. As it happened, when dawn arose and the drumbeat sounded to wake the company, two sentries from the last watch were found to be missing. One was lost completely, but the other was eventually located, face down on the bank of the river. His drowned face was blackened from the blood settling downslope toward his head. Prentice cursed the two men's deaths, and after Whilte said prayers and the one that had been found was interred in the dusty soil, he mounted Boots and set a demanding pace for the day's march.

CHAPTER 46

"They've sent a hundred or more up the Dwelt, burning the villages and whatnot," said the militiaman, sitting and dripping river water in such a heavy puddle that the ground at his feet was turning to mud. He shivered despite the summer evening's warmth.

"Redlanders?" Amelia asked, horrified that her force, or Prentice's, must have missed a mask shrine somewhere.

Unless this is a new one, she thought, which only unnerved her further. They still had no fresh word from Lady Dalflitch and her newborn spy network. It was impossible to know what the riverfolk cultists might be doing in the Reach while the Lion Banner Company was trapped across the Murr. Amelia was little comforted, even though the swimming scout shook his head.

"Knights under the dog, Robant," the scout said, and he spat as water dripped from his hair, down his face, and into his mouth. "He's given 'em orders to rape and pillage, so I was told. They ain't gotten as far up as Griffith, but there's no river-banker hut in the lower east o' the Dwelt that ain't burned to the waterline."

"Damn them," was all Amelia could think to say. Rampaging against peasants was a typical Grand Kingdom tactic. It promoted chaos, disrupted the economic base upon which a land's power was built, and forced the liege to divert troops which might otherwise be used to attack or form a defense force.

For all that it was typical strategy, it still offended Amelia to her core.

"T'ain't all, Your Grace," the scout added, his expression earnest. "They've taken a spot near the mouth where it's narrowest before the flow reaches the Murr. They've thieved some boats and are fetching up chains and cables."

"What for?" asked Lady Spindle, but Amelia was not so slow to understand.

"They intend to blockade us," she said. "Keep us trapped here with no means of escape."

"And the whole o' the Reach trade bottled up, too," added the scout, "So's the word from some farmwives whose fellas are bein' held for buildin' labor, at any rate. The dog Robant's makin' no secret of it, seems like. He means to intercept every rivercraft up or down, so there's no trade of any sort."

So much for word from Lady Dalflitch, Amelia thought, *at least until the second White Lion company is brought to bear. Another two to four thousand militia marching down the Dwelt will likely clear any blockade quick smart. Until then, we must look to taking back the bridge. Oh, for just one of those messenger birds.*

She nodded and dismissed the scout, thanking him for his service. She bade the corporal who escorted him to see the man well fed and given a place by a fire to warm himself. Once they were gone, Amelia turned back into her defeated in-law's command tent, with Spindle dutifully following. Since capturing the Vec army's encampment almost whole, her own force had little fear from starving since Prince Garrodmin had been well stocked. He seemed to have imagined he would be maintaining his position in the field for some time.

Little wonder, given the state of Aubrey, Amelia thought bitterly. Three days ago, she had bitten down on the strap and visited the ruins and the sparse village outside it. Scarecrow-thin folk subsisting on tree roots and wild greens had watched sullenly as the new archduchess and her escort arrived amongst them. Amelia had brought a purse of silver with the intention of giving alms and encouraging the wretched folk to buy from her own quartermaster merchants, but even that seemed a mockery to the filthy, wearied people too weak and too dejected to even be afraid.

"See they receive whatever food they want," she had told Nunel, the leader of her escort that day. Knowing now that Duke Robant planned to make it difficult or even impossible for her force to be revictualed from the Reach or evacuated by boat, Amelia wondered if her generosity might have been misplaced. She wondered how many of the Lions camped around her now remembered first-hand the bitter near starvation of the Fallenhill siege.

The town of Aubrey itself had been a different heartbreak, with a distinct flavor all its own. Amelia thought she had known what to expect as she rode through the broken-down gates. She'd anticipated the emptiness of the streets, the weeds poking through every crack in the cobbles, the vines and the collapsing roofs. Nonetheless, the brutalized town still had dismays to reveal to her. Bones lay in clusters about altars built in the streets, as if the bodies of the sacrificed were simply slung to the side while more victims were fetched. Skulls were cast into corners like children's balls. Some houses were nailed shut, their occupants doubtless long since starved away or else gutted completely by fire, broken walls surrounding ashen pits, like enormous, tumbledown chimneys. Even within the first few streets from the gate, Amelia had been astonished that some random fire had not burned the whole town to the ground.

Ghosts they had been warned about, yet worse were the living horrors. Carrion birds still roosted in vast flocks, turning tiled roofs into hateful colonies. There had been vermin hidden in every crack in the roads and rubble. More than once their escort force had disturbed swarms of flies that filled the air with menacing buzzing, dense clouds that shadowed the sunlight.

Prentice had led a tiny force into Aubrey the day the Red-lander's occupation here had been broken, and in his account of that action he had emphasized the presence of their sorceries in the form of dark writings on portals and roadways. The arcane lines were said to kill all living things outright, forming barriers more absolute than the sturdiest wall. As such, every member of the escort had been instructed to keep their eyes out for any writing of any kind. While an occasional word was spotted in an obscure corner, whole lines were long gone, worn away by the elements.

Then they had come upon the closest thing to real ghosts—not spectres as were found in fey tales but something every bit as dark and forlorn. It happened as they were riding out of High Street where it emptied onto a large market square fronting upon the abandoned prince's palace. Shaped like a roundhouse keep, with crenelations on its battlements, the palace was no true defensive work, despite the martial aspect of its construction. Its walls were plastered and whitewashed and accented with fired tiles of brilliant blue glaze. Unlike the keeps in the Reach, it stood back from its town's walls and only mimicked a defensive structure. In fact, apart from the over-grown gardens at its foot, the palace had seemed the least damaged part of the entire town. Its pleasant height overshadowed the low block building beside it—Aubrey's infamous Ditch Prison. The market square itself had been transformed by years of weather into almost a meadow, weeds and grasses growing up through the cobbles and sprouting on the destroyed remnants of merchants' booths and tables.

As they had ridden into that odd field-in-the-midst-of-a-town, two figures had emerged from somewhere to the escort riders' right side. As thin as the survivors outside the walls, but more raggedy even, almost naked in their few clothing scraps, the pair had sprung from hiding like wild animals, hooting and screaming as they rushed at the lancers. Nunel had feared an assassination attempt and immediately ordered his men to guard the archduchess, but it was not necessary. The two were not assassins, but rather were hungry predators, or at least saw themselves as such. They threw themselves at the nearest horses as if they were wolves falling upon a flock of sheep. One began to bite uselessly at a horse's flank until the rider cuffed the assailant, causing them to fall back to the ground. The other attacker was intercepted by another rider who did not fancy letting a crazed woman—or man, it was hard to tell—bite his mount. Catching the attacker just beneath one arm, he was astonished as the assailant suddenly crawled insect-like up his limb and bit at his face. He shouted furiously and beat the attacker off with his gauntleted hand. That one also fell to the grass and cobbles, moaning and snarling from the impact before regaining their feet.

"They've gone feral," Nunel had said as the pair now began to stalk back and forth at a distance, like hunting wolves.

"Damned beast-men," the lancer with the bitten face cursed, but his fellows scoffed at that.

"If they'd been true beast-men, they'd have taken you straight out of your saddle, no mistake," another lancer said, clearly speaking from experience. "They're mad mayhaps, but they ain't no proper beast-folk."

The bitten man sneered, and Amelia could understand his confusion. As the pair of mad assailants continued to snarl and hiss, she could see that their teeth, what few they had left, had been filed to sharp points, mimicking animal fangs. Angry at the way their behavior was beginning to annoy his mount, one of the lancers turned at them, and it was enough to break the pair's commitment to their "hunt." They fled suddenly through the long grass and into whatever back streets they considered their lair.

"I guess they were better than ghosts," Nunel had said with a shrug.

"No, not ghosts, just bloody cannibals," the bitten man answered.

"No, not much better," Amelia had said, shaking her head sadly. She had no way of knowing if those two were rare or part of a pack of such folk, mimicking beasts as thoroughly as the Redlanders ever did, even without the sorcerous power to change their skins. If Aubrey were ever to be renewed, such folk would have to be caught, although what the proper way to deal with them would be the archduchess could not begin to imagine. It reminded her of the broken-minded Baroness Stopher who had been found chained just before the Battle of the Brook. Wherever they went, the Redlanders left bloodshed and madness in their wake.

From the market square, the archduchess and her escort had ridden to the dockland, hoping to find boats to allow her forces to cross back over the Murr, or even to send messages up the Dwelt. Although by that stage she and her husband had not spoken again since their confrontation on the riverbank, Amelia had heard that he was looking for boats for that purpose himself. She decided that taking the time to investigate Aubrey's abandoned dockland might yield fruit in that quest, but she had been deeply mistaken.

Aubrey's dockside occupied the southern frontage of the town, although the stone walls curved almost entirely around that side as well. With piers built of fired clay bricks, it had once been a vibrant, bustling harbor, the end point of at least half of all trade journeys that left Dweltford far in the north. Amelia had never seen it in those days. The docks themselves fronted onto an artificial waterway that had been expanded from a small tributary of the Murr, which curved around the town's west side. A hundred or more rivercraft had been based there in its heyday. Amelia could see that with her own eyes, for the entire harbor was now a mass of wreckage, with boats of every kind sunk but visible just under the water or poking through the sunlight-dappled surface. What had once been a hub of trade was now a sunken graveyard for Aubrey's main industry to match the sepulchral nature of the rest of the town.

Did the Redlanders do this in revenge for their defeat after the Red Sky? the archduchess had wondered as she looked over the debris-choked water. Whatever boats there might have been to find, there were none in ruined Aubrey.

And now, even if we could find boats, Robant means to make it impossible for us to retreat or even send messages. Amelia shook her head.

"Perhaps the knight captain has found some boats. It would be a sweet hope, but if he has, he hasn't sent any word," Amelia responded. Spindle politely nodded her head, neither agreeing nor disagreeing. Amelia couldn't blame her. Since their confrontation on the bank of the Murr, the archduchess had hardly spoken a word about her husband. Indeed, she had only seen him at a distance two or three times. It was becoming clear that he must be avoiding her, and while it seemed petty to Amelia, she was not about to go running after him like a lovesick girl. Besides, if his wounded pride became a genuine impediment, she would simply summon him as liege of the Western Reach. An archduchess was sovereign, after all.

"He never mentioned boats, Your Grace," Spindle said gently, and her words snapped Amelia out of her thoughts.

"Never mentioned? When was it that you spoke with him?" she asked, wondering if Farringdon had deliberately consulted her lady-in-waiting as some kind of mean-spirited tactic.

"Two days ago, Your Grace."

"You didn't think to mention that fact to me?"

"I assumed you would have heard from the marquis directly, Your Grace," Spindle told her.

Amelia suddenly found it difficult to read Spindle's expression, realizing for the first time ever that the lace mask she wore had the power to maintain mystery against enemies and allies both. "So, what did you discuss if not boats two days ago?" Amelia could feel annoyance growing within her, along with a sense of hurt. Playing courtly games of favorites and disapproving snubs was not uncommon among peers' marriages across the Grand Kingdom. To hear Dalflitch tell it, pettiness was a lifestyle unto itself amongst the nobility. But until this moment, Amelia had not realized how greatly she had seen herself and Farringdon as removed from such heartless traditions.

"The marquis asked me about my husband and what I knew of the path he was trying to come by," Spindle explained. "He said he planned to scout it out himself and to leave a small company of lancers waiting for Caius to arrive, seeing as how the coin he was bringing was so needed."

"The coin?" Amelia wondered out loud. In the chaos since the battle, she had virtually forgotten about the secondary reason they had to be here in Aubrey—to secure the new trade route and the loan from Masnia. It seemed that Knight Captain Marquis Consort Farringdon had not.

CHAPTER 47

"You're looking well, My Lady," Sergeant Franken said, tugging his forelock to Righteous as she sat under a waxed-leather sunshade, nursing her daughter discreetly under a linen shawl. The baroness/new mother gave the White Lion officer a withering glance. She could hear the mockery in his tone as he said, "My Lady."

"Been practising saying that awhile, have you?" she said archly.

"For weeks," Franken answered with a smile. "Every night afore I go to bed. Can't make it not sound like a joke, no matter what I do."

"I'll wager."

Franken was one of the original convict Lions, a broad-shouldered brute of a man who'd once made his living as a traveling prize fighter, beating challengers unconscious for the cheering crowd on market days. Ironically, he had never killed anyone prior to becoming a part of Prentice Ash's militia. He had been convicted and transported across the mountains for thieving, having been tempted by a particularly disdainful merchant's gold and silver dinner service. He and Righteous had long respected each other, which naturally meant they took every opportunity to mock and insult one another.

"Still, you look like you're settlin' to motherhood," Franken followed up. "Sure'n you'll make a proper lady one day, if old age don't take you first."

"Did I give you the impression I called you here to play jester?" Righteous asked him.

"No, Baroness, not at all, My Lady. So sorry, so sorry," Franken said, mimicking a panicked courtier, or at least the way he probably thought a panicked courtier behaved. He tugged his forelock several more times.

"Oh stop, before you sour my milk," she told him and paused to adjust the weight of her babe. She looked across at the twin boy, asleep in the wide crib that he shared with his sister. The little wooden piece of furniture was also protected by the sunshade. It was anyone's guess each feeding which of the two squallers would demand to go first. This morning the boy had had his fill and fallen back to sleep, leaving his mother to nurse his sister.

The boy? Righteous thought. *Going to have to give them names sometime soon. Can't keep saying the girl or the boy.* She was reluctant to pick a name for either since she had not yet had time to ask Prentice, and she did not want to become attached to a name he would not agree to. Of course, a part of her felt that if he wanted a say in the naming, he could just hurry up and get back sooner.

"So, what was it you *did* want me for, Lady Righteous?" Franken asked, his expression more serious.

"I need some of your lads for my fillies to train with."

"Train with?" Franken lifted his eyebrow in mock suspicion. "Is that what they call it nowa...?"

"Just you stop your mouth right there, Sergeant," Righteous almost shouted, only just managing not to disturb her daughter. "Don't you impugn me or my ladies-in-training, you hear!"

"'Imp-ewe-n'," Franken repeated, sounding out the word. "What's that mean?"

"It means insulting their honor, without saying the exact words," Righteous explained, having learned the term herself from Lady Dalflitch, who could impugn the characters of an entire noble household with one twitch of her lower lip.

"I would never do that," Franken said, and though his smile had not faded, she could tell he was more serious now. He was mostly an upright fellow, and like so many of the serving convicts, devotedly loyal to Righteous's husband.

"I thought the duelist was seeing to training with 'em?" the sergeant went on, referring to Solomon. Righteous had been pleased to learn that while her girls might laugh at Solomon for his adolescent awkwardness and scarred face, the Lions themselves had nothing but the utmost respect for the lad, for his courage especially. They called him "the duelist" because they all knew the story of his victory over the snooty knight's page, Kirkin—an honor duel fought for blood.

"He's got them all chasin' after 'im now, don't he?"

"Morning run of the battlements," Righteous nodded. From where she was seated, she could not see much of the battlements, but running the circuit had become a daily drill for all her recruits. Solomon still led the whole way, but some girls at least were beginning to make him work for it. "But there's an upper limit to how much I can make him do in a day. And while each girl takes her turn, I got the others all standing by doing sod all but watching."

"Oh, well we can't have anyone doing 'sod all,' My Lady," Franken said with a chuckle, mocking the juxtaposition between Righteous's turn of phrase and her new status in life.

"No, we can't. Idle hands are the devil's playground." Righteous had no idea where such a stern saying had come into her mind from, but it felt like the sort of thing a baroness would say, especially a baroness with near-on twenty ripe young women in her charge.

"If you're fearing them playing up, then maybe puttin' 'em together with some recruit fellows might not be the wisest notion," Franken mused.

"Is that right?" Righteous began, but paused as her daughter detached from suckling, asleep like her brother at last. The new mother brought the little bundle out from under her shawl and leaned over to lay her next to her twin. Then she gave Franken a knowing expression and pointed for him to look away while she rearranged her bodice, which he did willingly.

"Are you telling me that in all of Fallenhill you don't have twenty trustworthy recruits who could be relied on to keep their minds out of their britches?" she demanded after her clothing was back in place and she was able to stand up. Her pregnancy belly was still loose under her clothes, but with the weight of her twins gone from her body, the pleasure of being able to stretch her back and legs properly was surprisingly enjoyable. "Can't you keep discipline, Sergeant Franken of the White Lions? What kind of training camp are you running here?"

Franken whirled back, eyes narrowed. He towered over her, but as she met his gaze, his angry expression dissolved into a laugh, recognizing that after all his needling she had managed to prick his pride with such ease.

"Despite you running them bare-legged fillies all over my fine and disciplined training company, Baroness, I have made it clear that I'll sure'n geld the first twit that thinks to go near them. Ain't none o' my lads got his mind in britches, believe it."

Righteous shook her head, as if she was disappointed with him.

"I think you might have a few candidates for the knacker's knife, in that case," she said. "One or two's been lingerin' at odd times, hopin' to *accidentally* run into someone. Already I got one girl who's mutterin' about goin' off to marry some fellow, and another's just lit out without word. Last we heard she had some recruit she figured to elope with."

Franken stared at Righteous's face for a long moment, and she realized he was not sure if she was still joking. She nodded solemnly and the sergeant scowled in fury.

"Who?" he demanded. If he had a sworn recruit about to go on the lam, the sergeant would not stand for it. Righteous knew that much.

"*I* don't know their names!" Righteous spat back. "It's not me they're sniffing about for."

"No, that's for surely not," Franken said, his eyes unfocused as he was clearly running through his mind to see if he could guess any likely perpetrators. Then she came back into his vision and his eyes went wide, aghast as he realized what he had just said. "Oh Righteous, I never meant it like that! You know that's not what I meant. You're the baroness and Captain Prentice is your man. There's not a colt in all the Reach would be fool enough to angle for you behind his back. It's just that."

Righteous smiled at him and never even cared that he used her name familiarly instead of her title. She patted him on the forearm.

"I ken exactly what you meant, you big oaf. The one who cried off has asked to marry a carder down in the village. Nothing to do with your charges. The other girl? She's with whoever's missing from your night count."

They smiled at each other, and Righteous was glad there were such loyal men around her, ready to defend her honor and her marriage.

"This is what I get for playing the fool," Franken said, shaking his head, and he tugged his forelock sincerely for the first time that morning. Righteous bowed her head, bestowing her grace upon him, exactly as Dalflitch had taught her and as she had seen Archduchess Amelia do many times. Franken still looked thoughtful, clearly trying to think who might be missing or about to go that way. Flick, the girl who had run off, had been gone two days already, so if her beau had not been noticed missing, perhaps he hadn't been a recruit after all.

"I'll go now and scare you up some useful men, ones you can trust for training. Are your girls that advanced already?"

Righteous shook her head.

"Not even close," she said. "But the fastest way to get them ready is to put them up against partners. Best if you can spare some Fang recruits. They need the close fighting experience, daggers and short blades."

"I'll see to it," Franken said, turning to leave as Solomon loped up to them from the training run, two long-legged girls only a handful of paces behind him. "Still got 'em chasin' you I see, lad. Must be your charm and wit, 'less o' course you've got another secret you've not shared with us?"

The sergeant gave Solomon a knowing look, which the young man only smiled at, waving away the implication. The two girls behind him, however, scowled and blushed over and above the color from their exertions.

Good, thought Righteous. *'Bout time you gossipy lot got to learn what it feels like.*

The baroness was looking forward to putting her students through some serious training, wooden blades to wooden blades, with would-be Fangs. Time was getting tight, and Righteous expected word from the archduchess any day, summoning the first new Lace Fangs back to Dweltford to begin their proper lady-in-waiting training and incorporating into her grace's chamber.

CHAPTER 48

Each evening at the end of the march over the next few days, will-o'-the-wisps were sighted by sentries on the riverside. Each time, the men on duty alerted others and kept their distance, watchful and avoiding contact. Nevertheless, on the morning of the fourth day another sentry was found dead in the water. When his corpse was drawn out, he had a cracked skull and several cuts on the unarmored parts of his body.

"Weren't no fireflies did this," Sergeant Gennet remarked, and Prentice had to agree.

"Could it be a wild animal?" asked Solft. The cuts had a similar nature to claw marks, gathered in three- and four-stripe clusters on the man's skin, but Prentice was not convinced.

"I would say he was likely already dead when these cuts were made," he told his men. "His heart had already stopped; you can see that by how little blood is scattered around on the grass. And look where it *has* stained the grass—under the body, straight down from where it dripped from each wound."

"So, they cut him to make it look like an animal," Whilte said, nodding grimly.

"It would seem that way."

"You've quite the huntsman's talents, Baron," Solft complimented him, but Prentice ignored the praise, making eye contact with Whilte, who only tipped his head to one side quizzically. Prentice was certain there would be fifty or more men in this company alone who would have just as easily seen what he had seen. Better than that, a true forester would likely have known without even having to think through the clues.

"Double the sentries on the river tonight, Commander?" Gennet asked.

Prentice chewed the inside of his cheek, thinking over his options. It seemed clear that the river was still how the enemy was moving, even though they had discovered no new masks. However, the possibility existed that this new attack had not been made from the river but from the plains, and the false claw-marks were to confuse the issue. Perhaps the attackers thought to persuade them there was some kind of monster lurking in the river. That would make him move his nightly camps farther back from the water and thus make them more vulnerable to a full desert raid. There was only one way to find out for certain.

"Keep the number of sentries on the river the same," he commanded, "but put a line of blind sentries in between the river and the camp."

"*Blind* sentries, Baron?" Solft demanded, plainly unfamiliar with the nickname for watchers with no lanterns or other sources of light. They were not truly blind, of course, and Gennet leaned closer to the scholar to explain that quietly.

"Put another blind line on the desert side as well," Prentice continued. "We need to be sure exactly what our fey-assisted enemy is doing before we do anything else."

"I thought you said the fey had not betrayed us?"

"In my vision I saw that one of Benjamin's people had been used as a sacrifice," Prentice told them. "From that, I assume Benjamin did not betray us to the Redlanders or the Inquisition."

Prentice paused at that. He had reiterated this point to himself a number of times since he had been dragged from the water with the iron mask in hand. Inwardly, though, he still realized that it was possible that Benjamin's betrayal *was*, in fact, so vile, and that he was secretly so depraved that he would

willingly surrender his own people to Redlander blood sacrifice. Of course, it was possible. In the vision itself, Prentice
had seen the mantis man sacrifice a serpent woman just for
additional power to expel him from the lake. Even so, that did
not ring true to Prentice. He knew the hatred the mountain
fey had for the Redlanders, and Benjamin's personal hatred
had never seemed feigned.

"What was that, Sergeant?" Prentice asked as he realized Gennet had asked a question while he was lost in his
thoughts.

"Just saying, Commander, if they didn't betray us for
either of the other factions in this three-faction fight we're
marching toward, then who did they betray us for?"

"I still say that perhaps they don't see it as a betrayal,"
Solft protested. Ever since Benjamin had led his riders into
the iridescent air, Solft had been insistent that their motives
were not clear. When he had learned that Prentice had seen
one of them being tortured and slaughtered in his vision, the
scholar had eagerly taken that as evidence that their fey allies
were not traitors. He had been so pleased by the notion that it
had taken him some time to realize his vindication would be
at the cost of a fey-man's tormented death. And all that was
only if Benjamin was not some secret convert to the blood
sects, giving up his own closest followers for power.

"Betrayal or not, we cannot say why Benjamin did what
he did. Not yet," Prentice asserted, and while Solft's smile
showed he felt vindicated, Gennet's scowl was likely a better reflection of the average militiaman's attitude. Hateful
treachery or not, the fey had betrayed their commitment as
allies, and that would have to be settled. But that was for later.

"What we *can* say, Sergeant, is that there are not three
factions at the end of this river but four," the knight commander continued. "The Redlanders; Inxyphos's Inquisition militants; Benjamin's riders—however many are left and
to whomever they swear—and this other type of fey."

"*Lake*...fey? Forest fey?" Whilte offered and Prentice shrugged. Either was as good a name as the other.

"What I can tell you about these is that they are not the same as the mountain fey of the Reach, but they are in a similar position. I saw their faces in my vision. I looked into their eyes. Many are as haunted, as beaten down, as Benjamin's people were under the Serpent Witch. I cannot say whether they began as willing partners or even converts to the vile faith, but I promise you they have many who are victims of it now."

"Seems like with these Redlanders, their lower orders are just first in line for the knife once the enemies run out," Whilte said.

"Way of the world, isn't it?" Gennet commented, but when even Prentice showed disapproval, he shook his head at his own cynicism. "No, maybe not quite the whole world."

"Whatever way it is, pass the word tonight," Prentice said flatly. "No one sleeps on sentry duty. No crafty kips, snuck off under a tree. Make sure they know the wrath of God falls on every twit who tries it."

"The wrath of God, Knight Commander?" Whilte asked with a raised eyebrow.

"Forgive me, Brother." Prentice bowed his head, accepting the mild theological chastisement. "The wrath of the Knight Commander."

"That's fearsome enough, I should think."

Everyone chuckled and Prentice dismissed them to bury the dead sentry, then to make ready for the day's march. That evening the watchmen were set as Prentice had ordered. It was around midnight that the cry for help went up, and men already tense rushed toward the riverside.

CHAPTER 49

"This way! I swear I saw something moving downriver," shouted one voice as lantern lights danced over the thin green sward of the riverside. As soon as the alarm was raised, the number of militiamen near the water swelled, frustrated searchers ready to catch whatever enemy had been raiding in the night. Prentice joined them but made no effort to take control. The truth was he wanted the search to be noisy and a little chaotic. He was certain the enemy's plan involved building a sense of fear and tension amongst his men-at-arms. If they saw disciplined fighters behaving in an orderly fashion, they would likely change their tactics, and Prentice did not want them to change anything, not until he had a better sense of their overall strategy. So, he let the search be a fraction too wild and disorderly.

For himself, while he kept his eyes open for any actual raiders, Prentice did not expect to catch sight of them. The mountain fey were masters of stealth, and he expected their lakeside forest cousins to be no different. No, his primary purpose was to speak with three specific people. The first was whoever raised the alarm. It took a little while in the dark and general disarray, but at last he located the attacked watchman, seated in the wet grass and being attended to by Brother Whilte and a Fang holding a lantern to light the pair. The injured sentry tried to rise when he saw the knight commander arrive, but the healing chaplain pushed him back down, so he saluted while sitting.

"How are you?" Prentice asked him.

"Gonna have a bally headache the rest of the night, I reckon," the watchman said, leaning his head forward to show the back of his scalp. In the poor light, there was nothing Prentice could see by way of an injury. Certainly, there was no blood. "Good thing I was wearing me helmet, that's all I can say. It was one hell of a hit, beggin' *your* pardon chaplain."

Whilte only turned the man's head back around so that he could continue his ministrations.

"Did you see who hit you?" Prentice asked.

"Nothing, sorry to say, Commander," the sentry replied. "It was all quiet and safe-seeming. No lights on the water and no sounds, except from the camp. Then whack! Didn't knock me off my feet, but damned near... sorry, chaplain."

"I'll say it did," added the other sentry who was holding the lantern. In his other hand he had the sitting man's helmet. There was a fresh ding in the steel at the back. "I was twenty paces off and I heard it ring off his helm like a bell. Right clang it was."

"And did you see anyone?"

"Sorry, but no, Commander. I swear I was looking out, and soon as I heard that hit, I was on the run. Your man Dellep there wasn't even fully back straightened up when I reached him."

"No one thinks you were shirking, Fangsman, do not fear," Prentice reassured his man. With a clap of encouragement on the sentry Dellep's shoulder, Prentice left the trio in search of his second conversation with the nearest blind sentries to the attack. When placed that evening by Sergeant Gennet, these watchmen had been given strict orders not to respond to any alarms. Only a direct command, prefaced with a specific word known to Prentice, Gennet, and the two corporals could direct them from their posts. As he found the nearest sentry, Prentice was surprised to see that it was, in fact, one of the corporals—the sour man Guillam.

"How's our lad, Knight Commander?" the corporal asked from the shadows. Prentice could only barely make out the man's shape as he stood, leaning on the haft of a halberd, borrowed it seemed since he was a Roarsman, typically. There was a hawking sound that made Prentice think Guillam must have just spat out some chew or something similar.

"He will live, Corporal," Prentice said. "He took some kind of thump to the back of his helmet. Left a good, broad dent."

"So, not an arrow then?" Guillam mused and Prentice agreed. His thoughts were already trending that way as well. "Didn't think it would be when I heard it hit. Figured it for like a cudgel strike, good bell-clapper of a hit. 'Cept I can't see as how they did it. I was lookin' that way, soon as I heard it. I would've seen a shadow, somethin'."

"Are you sure?" Prentice asked.

Guillam sucked at his teeth. "I been crouched down most of the night. It puts more of the distance up against the night sky. The dark of the sky ain't like the dark on the ground. I could see that man silhouetted against the stars on and off again all night. If someone had footpadded him with a club across the noggin, I'd 've made out their outline, least a little wise. There ain't no way they got in that close, clopped him one, and got away, all without being seen, not unless they was pressed flat to the ground the whole way."

Prentice nodded, acknowledging the possibility of that kind of ambush, but he was almost certain it had not happened that way.

"Our man will live, and you have done your duty this night, Corporal," he said. He could almost hear the sneer in Guillam's response.

"Just remember that in the morning, Knight Commander, when I'm a little slower on the march for not having had a night's sleep."

"You're no crawler, are you?" Prentice asked, impressed with the man's brass. "How is it you have made the rank of corporal?"

"Because I do what I'm ordered, when I'm ordered, and I know how to keep my mouth shut in the meantime."

"You do?" Prentice asked, smiling in the darkness. "All evidence to the contrary, of course."

"You think? Did you even know my name afore I become a corporal?"

Prentice thought about it and realized he had not. Before he could ask the significance of that fact, Guillam explained voluntarily.

"I came across the Azures with the whole horde that Daven Marcus brung with him," he said. "Two and half thousand of us—hungry, footsore. Then I was up in Fallenhill. I stood right next to Sacrist Fostermae on the steps the day you almost hanged Markas, did you know that?"

"No," was all Prentice said in response. His recollections of that day were vivid, but he could not pick Guillam's face from amongst the crowd in his memory.

"I was there, and I saluted, just like the rest of them fools. Faster even, I might confess. I'd never seen a boss-man like you. Not a noble or a patrician. Not even some filthy homespun hetman put over the rest of his village but still covered in dung smears. Everyone takes advantage except you. We were all tired, hungry, cold and scared. And so were you, holding the whole cursed lot of us together like trying to grip water in your fist."

Guillam paused and sighed. Prentice remembered well those days and nights in the ruins. Compared to that time, camping on balmy nights in the middle of this empty plain was virtually bucolic.

"I ain't a kindly man by nature," the corporal continued finally. "But then again, neither are you, Commander, if we're bein' honest. And that's what makes us both good leaders, I'd reckon. I been keeping my head down every day since I made that first salute, bitin' my griping tongue and doin' whatever you ordered 'cause I knew whatever the hell it was you was goin' to be right there beside us, marchin' into the teeth of it.

"Then some weeks back, you let Gennet name me a picked man to come on this little adventure, and even more, you started bringin' me into your leader talks. I'm content to keep my barker shut to my betters, but you invited open talk. Ordered us to it, in point of fact. So, my reckoning is, if you ask for honest talk, you get my honest thoughts, gripes and all. You order me to shut up again, I promise you, Commander, you won't hear another word from me except 'yes, no, and who do I kill, My Lord.'"

Prentice chuckled in the dark, shaking his head. In any other time or place in the Grand Kingdom, this bitter, plain-spoken yeoman would have been doomed. Even with his boasted talent for keeping his mouth shut, he would inevitably have offended against a sumptuary law or the dignity of someone higher up the social order, and that would have been the end of him. In the Lions, he had become a loyal, inspired, and competent junior officer.

"I will make you a compact, Guillam," he told the corporal. "You curb your tongue in the open, show a little more deference when non-Lions are amongst us, and I will never punish you for any honesty when we speak within the pride."

There was a long moment's pause, and then Prentice thought he could make out Guillam's silhouette nodding in the darkness.

"So, in front of the scholar man, or the ostlers, you want 'yes, Knight Commander,' 'no, Knight Commander,' but when it's only militiamen...?"

"Corporals and above," Prentice confirmed, wanting to make sure he was explicit. He was starting to think Guillam was a man who followed orders quite explicitly.

"Then you want straight talk?"

"That's right."

"Well, if that's the word, since it's just us two here, you know, Knight Commander, that these fey-not-fey-new-fey-whoever-they-are, they're tryin' to put the willies up us. They want us good and spooked."

"I had come to that conclusion myself," Prentice agreed.

"It's a sure bet that they don't think they can scare us off just like this though," Guillam continued. He paused, but Prentice only waited quietly "You understand why that's important, don't you, Knight Commander?"

"If they want us afraid, it is because they plan to use that fear against us," Prentice said.

"Rightly so. Just so you know. I trust you have a plan for that."

"Some ideas in mind, Corporal, yes," Prentice responded, enjoying the moment's direct speech.

"Good, 'cause if this little adventure does turn awry, then we are far too far out of our place to just go runnin' back to the Reach. If they force us into a retreat, I'll offer you a sheep for a shaved silver ain't one of us makin' it back alive."

Prentice accepted Guillam's assessment and left him to his sentry duty. The corporal's grasp of the overall strategic situation was excellent and matched Prentice's own. This far west, with nothing but a dead river and dust for days behind them, there truly was no hope of successful retreat if the enemy did manage to meet them decisively. He looked westward in the night, even though he knew he would see nothing of the horizon. Nevertheless, with every day the distant mountains grew more visible. Soon they would be in the foothills and searching for some way through to the forest valley and the lake valley beyond it.

CHAPTER 50

T he third conversation Prentice wanted to have was with the blind sentries on the desert side of the company camp. As he expected, none of the watchmen there had seen or heard anything, either before or after the alarm was raised. After speaking with four, he left them and returned to the river, finding a lantern and slowly searching outward in a spiral from the spot where the sentry had been attacked. Half an hour after the sun crested the horizon and the drummers hammered out the dawn beat, Sergeant Gennet, Lyrach, and the two corporals found the knight commander standing alone on the riverbank, staring at the water.

"Commander, is there uh...are we marching today?" Porth asked. "Only it's just that you haven't given us the order."

"Just enjoying a moment's breath, Corporal, in the cool of the morning," Prentice said. In truth, having spent the whole night searching and only finding what he was looking for just after dawn, he had spent the rest of the time considering the implications. He was also enjoying the moist air by the waterside before the sun rose higher and the day heated up. He turned to face his men, holding up his treasure from the night's dredging through the riverside grasses.

"Do you know what this is?" he asked, holding up a rounded object half the width of his palm.

"A rock?" Lyrach answered, staring at the object with a confused expression. Prentice shook his head and tossed it to Gennet, who caught it and whistled immediately in surprise.

"That's heavy!" he said and rubbed at the dust with his hand. "Sure'n that's no rock. What is it? Lead?"

"I would say so," Prentice told them. Gennet tossed the rounded piece of lead to Porth, who made a show of weighing it in his hand, then passed it off to Guillam.

"It's an odd, smooth lump," Lyrach observed as he watched it in Guillam's hand and then took his own turn to study it. "Almost like a ball."

"That is because it is not a lump," Prentice explained. "It is a slingstone."

Gennet whistled again and Porth tutted, but Guillam was unconvinced. "A sling? What village lads use to hunt out rodents and small birds? You couldn't throw something this weight with a little length of twine."

Prentice shook his head.

"I know you're a wretched former convict, Guillam, but did your father never take you once off to church? Do you not know the story of Goliath the giant and David the shepherd?"

Porth smirked and Lyrach tutted, but Guillam cast a querying look at the ex-squire.

"Is this 'in the pride,' Commander?" the corporal asked. Prentice nodded. "Right well, in that case, Bible stories or not, are you sayin' we're to be fightin' giants now? Or giant-killers?"

Prentice was going to answer, but Lyrach spoke first. The knight commander was pleasantly surprised that what he said was exactly right, though.

"Would it be so much of a surprise to face giants?" he demanded. "After everything else we have seen these last years?"

Guillam sucked his teeth again and scratched at one of the scars on his face where the bristles refused to grow.

"What sort of range does a sling that can throw one of them get?" asked Sergeant Gennet, turning his subordinates' thoughts onto professional matters.

"From what I remember reading," Prentice reported, "equal to all but the most powerful bows."

"Oh, surely not," Lyrach protested.

"What, too much of a surprise?" Guillam needled him.

"This is what struck Dellep in the back o' the head, isn't it?" Porth reasoned. "You done well to find it, Knight Commander. And he was daft lucky he had his salet on."

"And that he was facing away," Prentice added. At least half the Lions wore steel helmets that were open-faced, without visors. A lead sling bullet at full force could easily have smashed Dellep's face in or killed him if it struck his forehead or temple. Just like Goliath.

"Should we make it the rule for sentries to keep their helmets on?" Gennet asked.

"I think we should make it the rule for everyone to keep his helmet on whenever he is standing up," Prentice replied. "Night and day. The days have been ours up until now, but I think we can expect them to start twisting the noose tighter soon enough."

"That's a grim image, if I might say, Commander," offered the more elderly Porth. He stroked his drooping moustache with his thumb and forefinger, grooming it away from his lips. "D'you really think we have our necks in a noose?"

"The Redlanders think they have us in one," Prentice told them. They all looked at him thoughtfully, their full attention focused on what he said. A sudden memory of all the times he had had to fight to be heard, fight to be believed came to him—all the meetings of the high-born where it was offensive for him to even have his own thoughts—and now here he was, the outright, ultimate authority. And no one would question his orders. The pressure to be right—to make no mistakes, give no foolish commands—suddenly felt astonishingly real, like the weight of the iron fetters that never let a convict forget he was on the absolute bottom of a very heavy and pitiless social structure.

"Since they came out of the west, the Redlanders have shown a fondness for certain tactics," Prentice explained to his subordinates. He had spent the night thinking, and it was time to test his thoughts against theirs once more. "They like to spread terror and harry their foes. To drive them to rash action."

"They're certainly tryin' that on," Guillam said.

"But we're not afraid, Knight Commander," Lyrach objected. "Morale is still high."

"Morale? Pfft!" Guillam muttered and spat upon the ground, as if he felt the word was too high minded and needed to be shown an appropriate amount of contempt, to be put in its place, as it were.

"Expect the attacks to increase," Prentice said, thankful Lyrach did not take too deep an offense at being so dismissed. The young man really was learning his place, it seemed. "In fact, from now on I want the mule team and the ostlers in the middle of camp every night as well. And no one is to be off alone, not even for a call of nature. Bring the sentries in closer, too."

"That'll make everyone safer," Gennet said.

"And make us look like we're all ready to wet our britches," Guillam added.

"Which is all to the good."

"How's that, Commander?"

"The other thing the Redlanders like in war is to choose the field they want to fight upon," Prentice explained. "They tease and torment their enemies while the whole time leading to the spot they have already prepared for the battle. The Brook was like that. They led old Prince Mercad's knights a merry dance until they were champing at the bit. Then the Horned Man waited with his people and let the prince march his force straight into the ambush."

"That was the day the angel saved the Reach, so they say," Lyrach said. From the look on his face, it seemed to Prentice that the young man was hoping to hear the tale.

"The knight commander and his chosen rats did more than their share that day as well," said Porth.

"We were not yet called the rats at that point," Prentice told them, self-effacingly. "And the circumstance was the only one doing any choosing."

He shook his head. They were getting off track.

"A similar thing happened at the Murr with the Red Sky. King Chrostmer had them bottled up at the bridge, safe as town walls. So, the Redlanders built their own bridge of boats and called down the crimson sky to freeze the Murr in its place. Then they crossed where they wanted and struck the Lions full force. We held them, but it was a mongrel of a night battle—a bath of fire, mud, and blood. I am sure most of us remember what it was like, and if not, then find a veteran and ask them."

Guillam and Gennet nodded solemnly. Corporal Porth had not been present at that time, as far as Prentice knew, but he was veteran enough of other campaigns. Lyrach looked to each of the senior men, and it was obvious he wanted what they had—the comradeship of battle. The younger man had stood upon battlefields, so he had combat experience, but not the brotherhood. Now he longed for nothing more than to endure a trial like the Brook or Red Sky, to stand beside the men he had joined and to be called their brother. It was a better ambition than the mere promotion he had angled for when he first arrived in Prentice's new company, and the knight commander just hoped it did not get the young man killed. The history of war was filled with the anonymous corpses of would-be heroes who died seeking glory and brotherhood.

"They're harrying us to a battlefield they have already chosen," Prentice continued, reasonably confident he was correct. "They will step up the attacks to two or three times a night, and they will mostly come from the riverside. When they get us where they want, we will find ourselves hit with a full force, a proper sledgehammer, and likely from multiple points at once to either try to destroy us whole cloth or break us and run us all the way back to Radengon."

"If they let us get that far," Guillam muttered, and Prentice nodded.

"Quite so. With all this ahead of us, here is my plan. I am going to take a page out of Prince Mercad's book, using his failed strategy to our advantage, and march half days from now on."

"I thought we were in a hurry, Commander?" Gennet asked with a raised eyebrow. From their faces, all of the men present were surprised by Prentice's new order.

"We were...we are...," Prentice said. "We must reach that lake before the Redlanders recover the power to transfer that fleet of theirs through the sky to Dweltford. I am sure they are rushing to restore that power to themselves as best they can."

"So how can we delay?" asked Lyrach.

"Because they are taking the time to drive us into an ambush." Prentice let that statement hang in the air a moment. Lyrach looked back and forth at the junior officers who were all heads down in thought.

"It's a big fleet they've got, as big as Red Sky, the commander says," Gennet observed, sharing glances with Porth and Guillam.

"Full o' painted men and beast-men," Guillam continued, nodding.

"Not to mention how many o' these slingstone chuckers they got to throw at us," Porth added. Prentice was glad the experienced fighters comprehended the situation.

"I don't understand," Lyrach said, and it almost came out like a whine. Prentice felt a stir of pity. Lyrach was so desperate to be involved, to find a status to replace the knighthood that was denied him. Ironically, it might be the thing that held him back from finding it. Proven men did not whine and did not respect those who did.

"If they can open the sky to their big fleet already, then they ain't got no reason to play tactics and strategy with us," Guillam explained to Lyrach, and Prentice was surprised by how little contempt there was in Guillam's tone this time. "If they could, they would just open their magick mirror water and send a vast fleet through to thump us down, like a hammer on a nail stuck up out of a floorboard."

"Or else just skip right past us to Dweltford and leave just a few fellas waitin' in their magick forest or lake or whatever to grind us away on whatever tricksy defenses they like to set for 'emselves," Porth added.

"So, the fact that they are harrying us means they don't have the strength to smash us or ignore us yet?" Lyrach asked, and Prentice confirmed that with a nod. "But they do have the strength to maybe draw us into a fair fight?"

"Especially if they can pick the ground and set an ambush for us," Prentice finished for the young man. "And I mean to spring their ambush upon them, break them as they try to break us. To that end, we will march half days, so that if we come upon this ambush at the end of a day's march, we will still have the strength to fight. We fight them, we beat them, and then we have a clear run straight through to the headwaters of the Murr."

"That easy?" said Lyrach. Everyone else chuckled.

"Who said anything 'bout easy?" said Guillam, and Lyrach shrugged, smiling a little shamefacedly.

"Scouts out ahead still?" Gennet asked.

"Yes," Prentice told him, "I want as much advance notice as we can risk."

"And what about this ambush site? What exactly are we looking for?"

"I will be able to tell you *exactly* once we find it, Sergeant."

"Oh, good." Gennet chuckled again, shaking his head with rueful humor. Prentice dismissed them to their duties, telling them to be ready for a call to march after the high sun of the afternoon. He hoped that the extra time to rest would do the company some good, give them the opportunity to repair any worn or damaged equipment, especially boots, or just to take their ease off their feet.

"Just one more question, if I may, My Lord Knight Commander?" Lyrach said as the rest started to move away.

"What is it?"

"It's just that you haven't made mention of the Inquisition men-at-arms. I know they're a small force, but they are full knights and Church-sworn. I was always taught that a Church knight was the purest of warriors, the equal of any five."

"Then we should be fine, Lyrach," Prentice said flippantly. "We have them ten to one, our five hundred to their fifty."

"But Church-sworn? What if we're wrong and they have the right of it? What if God is on their side?"

Prentice looked Lyrach straight in the eye. The question was a simple one to Prentice's way of thinking. Men who made pacts or even peace with a bloodlust cult like the Redlanders could not possibly have God's approval. War was a brutal business, and too often confused in its motives and meanings. Two factions might easily boast that God was on their side, seeking his blessings for their "righteous cause." Sacrists and Church elders might declare themselves for either or both, claiming that scripture or prophecy supported their chosen faction. It was an age-old problem, and the confusion wracking the Grand Kingdom was, in one way, just that problem writ large, with a great crowd of factions instead of just two or three. But for all that, there had always been certain things for which God had never shown any patience and little mercy, and human sacrifice to demonic entities was one of those things.

"Just by sitting down to make even temporary peace with the Redlanders, Inxyphos shows that he cannot have approval from God in heaven," Prentice told Lyrach. "Inquisition or not, Church-sworn or not, God is not with them! If you doubt me, go to Brother Whilte, and he will explain."

Lyrach nodded, but hesitantly. "I want to believe you, Knight Commander, I swear I do, it's just…"

"Look to your duties, militiaman Lyrach," Gennet commanded, his voice taking on its unyielding sergeant's tone. "Do your best at whatever comes into your hands to do and leave such lofty questions for your betters. Don't forget what a privilege it is just to have the knight commander admit you into his conferences, understand?"

Lyrach nodded and turned to salute Prentice. In all likelihood, his misgivings were not going to be settled so easily, and Prentice doubted he was the only one struggling with the notion of whose side God was on in this war, which was increasingly as theological as it was political. When Lyrach turned away, Guillam wrapped an unexpectedly comradely arm around his shoulder.

"If you're frettin' 'bout it, then look at it this way," he said in the ex-squire's ear. "If the commander's got the wrong of it and the Church is full against us and God with them, you ain't got much to worry 'bout."

"How do you see it that way?" asked Lyrach, his brows raised in complete surprise.

"Well, look where you is. It's a dry desert in all directions or a drownin' river full of deadly nixie magicks. You're marchin' every day beside convicts, murderers, thieves, and rapists—sinners, one and all. The way I reckon it, you're already three-quarters to hell as it is. If they damn you on top of all that, well, t'ain't that far to fall, wouldn't you say?"

Lyrach looked aghast at Guillam's casual disregard for the disposition of their souls. Prentice tutted loudly and the corporal looked back over his shoulder.

"Too far, Knight Commander?" he asked with a sardonic smile.

"Just go to, Corporal Guillam. Another word and the militiamen under you are going to find themselves with an abundance of extra duties, and be assured they will know they have you to thank for it."

Guillam shook his head, but his smile did not dim. If anything, it grew a little broader.

"It's like I said, Knight Commander," he joked as he pulled a piece of chewing tobacco from a pouch on his belt and thrust it into his mouth. "You may be of gentle rank now, but you ain't a kindly fellow. Nope, you're just 'bout as cold in heart as the depths o' that river."

Gennet cast Prentice a glance, as if to ask whether Guillam's comment needed a disciplinary response, but Prentice waved him off with a short shake of the head and a wry smile. It was not as if Corporal Guillam was wrong.

CHAPTER 51

Four empty days after the scout had swum the Murr to bring news of Duke Robant's developing river blockade, Amelia was again in her looted tent reading the quartermaster merchants' assessments of the captured plunder. She also had the written and signed list of the first group of prisoners who had sworn peace with the Reach and were being marched eastward to the border with the next Vec princedom, a province reportedly smaller even than Aubrey named Longshepherds. The archduchess had no expectation that she would recognize any of the names among the surrendered men-at-arms, but she felt an obligation to read the list, nonetheless. It also wasn't as if she had much else to do.

Not since the return march from the Brook and being shut out of Dweltford by the rebel Duggan had Amelia felt at quite such a loose end. She was not in immediate danger, and despite Farringdon's continued absence, the Lions maintained their discipline and held the bridge against Robant's force without difficulty. She stroked her belly where it seemed a new life was growing but left signs only noticeable to the sharpest eyes. For herself, Amelia felt nothing there yet, and while the notion of a child filled her with the kinds of emotions she would have expected, the reality had not truly dawned upon her, she did not think.

I'm sure you will soon be the better part of my whole world, she said inwardly to her unborn. *For now, though, you are not even a pleasant distraction.*

In a sense, even the desperation Amelia had felt during the previous accursedly long summer had been preferable to her mind than this kind of paralyzed redundancy. More than once, she had contemplated trying to parley over the bridge with Daven Marcus's lapdog duke, just to relieve the boredom. Only the memory of the last time she had spoken to Robant and the curse pronounced upon her kept her from trying a new negotiation. Of course, that memory led her mind back to the destruction of the cannons and the ongoing feud with her husband that it had prompted. And so, once around again, she longed for something to fully occupy her mind.

"I could perhaps begin drawing up plans for the rehabilitation of Aubrey," she muttered to herself, looking through her limited collection of parchment and quill laid upon the bed, seeking a blank sheet. Then she remembered how some of the expectant first mothers had occupied their time when she had been a lady-in-waiting in Baroness Switch's chamber. "Or a list of possible names for my coming child?"

Before she could find any such writing tools to distract herself with, Lady Spindle stepped into the tent and executed a perfect curtsey, demonstrating her rapidly developing courtly skills.

"Your pardon, Your Grace, but I have excellent news," the Lace Fang announced. The lady's half-mask seemed to have acquired new layers of lace, revealing to Amelia what Spindle must have been doing to keep herself occupied during this period of her liege's inactivity.

Perhaps I should turn my hand back to a lady's chamber duties, Amelia thought. She could not remember the last time she had had needle and thread in hand. Odds were, if she tried it, she would only end up setting her fingertips to bleeding all over whatever cloth she might work upon.

"Excellent news is welcome, My Lady," she said earnestly. "Though in truth, at this stage, I doubt I would be unhappy even with dire news."

"Well, Your Grace, that is a..." Spindle paused, clearly reaching for a word. "A claim that we shall not have to put to the test. Marquis Consort Farringdon has returned with my husband, Master Caius Welburne. He is now in camp and receiving food and succor."

Amelia jumped up, eyes glittering as she smiled broadly. She clasped Spindle's hands in hers.

"Spindle, this is wonderful! Excellent news, indeed. But what are you doing here? Come, let's see to your husband's wellbeing."

And to perhaps reconciling with my own husband, the archduchess thought, but did not add.

Lady Spindle led the way from Amelia's tent to another nearby, almost as fine in brightly striped yellow, green, and red. It had apparently belonged to one of the Vec mercenary captains, a man who had also not survived Prince Garrodmin's battle with the White Lions. Inside, they found the merchant Caius Welburne lying on a peasant bed of fresh-cut reeds, his haggard features looking as pale and cadaverous as ever. It was also the first time Amelia had ever seen him unshaven or even unkempt.

The merchant did his best to rise in his rush bed when his archduchess entered the tent, clutching at his black robe that was serving as a blanket, but immediately, Spindle knelt beside him and put her hand upon his shoulder, pushing him back down gently. Amelia was so used to the prickly Welburne who stood apart from all others—his fellow conclave members and even his own business partners—that she half expected him to scold his younger wife for her impertinence. Instead, he merely nodded at Spindle and laid back.

"I ask you to forgive my husband the usual courtesies, if it please you, Your Grace," Spindle said.

"Are you not whole, good merchant?" Amelia asked as she nodded, acknowledging Spindle's request to break with formality. It was not as if she would ever deny her loyal lady anything so simple. Spindle had long since earned such indulgence.

"I am no closer to death's door than I have ever been, despite my ordeal," Welburne croaked in reply. "Forgive me that I do not rise, but the newly appointed sentinel over my welfare refuses me permission."

He looked askance at his wife, whose eyes narrowed in return.

"I'll not be widowed young because of the pettiness of some Veckander mercenaries and their purse-holder. You need rest."

Spindle looked around and saw a pewter cup and ewer on a tray upon the ground. Taking them up, she poured her husband watered wine and then put the cup to his lips.

"You were hounded on your journey?" Amelia asked after Welburne had taken a sip.

"Indeed so, Your Grace, though between my hired guards and the Marquis Farringdon's lancers, once they found us, we were in little enough danger."

"The lancers provided goodly escort then?" Amelia asked, surprising herself by deliberately not mentioning her husband by name.

"Indeed so. Excellently, in point of fact," Welburne said, the words sounding like they hurt his throat to speak. Perhaps he had taken a chill upon the journey. If he and his escort had been hunted through the wilderness, there had likely been nights of cold camps with no fires to warm them. Even in summer, that might well have proved hard on the older merchant's constitution.

"Truly, Your Grace, the Marquis' knowledge of the herders' paths through the hills kept us out of sight of the company sent to run us down before we even reached the southern border of Aubrey. If you would accept my thanks and mention it also to him, I would be doubly grateful."

The merchant nodded his head, the closest he could do to a bow while lying down.

"I will do that," Amelia said, and while she meant it, she could not keep from scowling. Odds were that Welburne had spoken a significant amount more to Farringdon than she had in recent days.

Welburne laid his head back and closed his eyes.

"I think I shall rest now, Your Grace," he said and there was something of his more typical emotionless reserve in the tone of his voice. "With your permission, of course. A nap and the satisfaction that the Heron wasted its money on mercenaries that did not stop us will prove all the cure I need, I would think."

"The Heron?" Amelia asked, her scowl becoming a more perplexed frown.

"The Golden Heron Bank, Your Grace," Welburne explained, not opening his eyes.

"The men hunting you were not servants of Garrodmin or some other prince?" Amelia realized she had assumed that her foes here in the Vec were only the princes who might oppose her claim to Aubrey upon political grounds. The idea that the Golden Heron might be prompting direct actions against her, just as the finance house had closed off all loans to her, was something she had not considered. No wonder Garrodmin had a large mercenary force and such a wealth of supplies. He had been being backed by the richest bank in the known world.

"Mercenaries under the Heron's own banner," Welburne said, and his croaking voice had started to slur. Amelia looked to the cup still in Spindle's hand and realized that the wine must have had something else mixed in, some physic to assist her husband to rest. "But their factor in Launcensbeem was fool enough to let slip what was happening. My contacts warned us to watch out for the Heron's paid men."

Amelia shook her head in wonder, marveling that her ongoing conflict with a kingslayer and usurper in Denay could have a bank in the Vec hiring soldiers to hound her representative in Masnia. Would this war not end until every land and every great house—royal, religious, or mercantile—was dragged into the crucible?

"Well, whoever was paying these men who hunted you, Master Welburne, thanks to your efforts, the gold you bring will be able to pay my Lions."

"Pay? Gold?" Welburne repeated, and his voice was taking on a dreamy quality, an uncharacteristic smile lighting his lips. "I bring no gold."

"What?" Amelia whispered, her hand to her mouth. Had the Heron succeeded despite Welburne's escape? Had yet another plan been brought to naught? She looked to Spindle, but the lady-in-waiting only shrugged.

"I've not heard, Your Grace," she said. "I assumed he had the gold with him."

As if hearing his wife say the word gold triggered some part of Caius Welburne's somnolent mind, he suddenly reached up and clutched her sleeve. His face developed a look of almost childlike cunning, like a player on a stage acting a goblin or similar trickster creature.

"Fools figured us to bring the gold by the west path," he muttered, the slur of his speech moderated by the awakened sense of sly satisfaction. "But why? We had to make the journey to prove the route, but why would we take strongboxes full of gold into the wilds? So they can be robbed away? Pah! No one comes to wealth being that doltish! *I* came the west way with a Masnian to prove the path. The gold is coming through the bridge, hidden in two different caravans."

Caius waggled his finger at Spindle, like a parent speaking to a young child.

"The north of the bridge is in the hands of Duke Robant," Amelia said, increasingly horrified by what she was hearing. "We control the south. Why send the gold to the bridge? Is he mad?"

"Mad? Mad? I'm furious, and canny. Know who you can trust and keep a small house in the bridge on the town...no, the town on the bridge."

The town on the...? Amelia wondered and she realized what the merchant's drugged consciousness was unfolding in its confused fashion. There were two great bridges across the Murr River between the Vec and the Grand Kingdom—the lesser bridge that she and Duke Robant now faced each other across, and the greater bridge farther east, which controlled the main of the trade between the two otherwise enemy nations. The bridge that was an earldom unto itself. Caius had sent the gold separately through Bridgetown.

Amelia did not know whether to laugh or weep. The cunning of keeping a heavy load of gold away from the Heron's mercenaries pleased her, but by sending the coin through the Bridgetown trade routes, Caius Welburne had delayed it reaching Amelia's hands. Not only that, but he risked it being stolen by whomever he entrusted it to, not to mention other agents of the Golden Heron, if they discovered it. As she thought about it, there was also the Earl of Bridgetown to consider, or any other lordling who might have turned brigand in the civil war. Merchant caravans were typical targets of men-at-arms who thought to support themselves with banditry.

Except, of course, that from Bridgetown the gold could be loaded on riverboats and shipped up the Dwelt, Amelia thought, and her heart sank to the bottom like a stone. Any gold loaded on boats traveling up the Dwelt would be seized by Duke Robant's blockade.

"Your Grace?" asked a militiaman who had just poked his helmeted head through the tent flap. "Message for you."

"What is it, militiaman?" Spindle asked, rising to perform her primary duty as a lady-in-waiting, forming a barrier between the liege and any unwanted intrusions.

"With My Lord's compliments," the man said, clearly repeating a phrase he had been instructed to use. "The knight captain, Marquis Farringdon, requests her grace's presence at the bridge. The enemy's doing somethin' odd."

"Odd?" Spindle asked, investing the one word with such imperious weight that for a moment she could have been Dalflitch.

"That's what I was bid to say, and no more. Will her grace come, or am I to send her regrets?"

Spindle looked to Amelia for her decision, but the archduchess was still trying to wrap her head around the shifting fortunes concerning her loan from Masnia, which might be secure, or given that something "odd" was happening at the bridge, might already be in enemy hands. She nodded to her lady-in-waiting, and Spindle turned to the militiaman.

"Tell his lordship that his wife, her grace, will attend the bridge shortly."

"What now?" was all Amelia could think to say once the messenger was gone. Then she looked down at the now sleeping Welburne. She smiled wanly at Spindle. "It is excellent news to see your husband returned to you."

CHAPTER 52

B arely ten days since the White Lions had crossed the Aubrey Bridge and already their side of the river had been transformed. The wagons that had been used to fortify the southern end had been reinforced at the sides by bulwarks made of large wicker baskets filled with earth and slowly being covered with mud to form adobe walls, so that even if one of the wagons was pushed over or smashed apart somehow, any assault would still be forced into a channel toward the road, preventing them fanning out or otherwise escaping the Roar's gunfire.

Beyond that, on the riverbank to either side of the bridge, further earthwork bastions were being built up, and behind their ramparts a whole cohort of Roarsmen kept watch, fifty on each side. From their firesteps, the matchlock gunners could target the southern half of the bridge with ease. Of course, the bridge's thigh-high stone parapet provided some protection from their iron shot, as did the pillars of the footings, which rose almost to shoulder height every ten paces. Even so, any knights attempting to assault the southern bank would not only be receiving fire from the wagons on that end but also all along their flanks as well.

Amelia was received on the road well back from all these fortifications by a line first Claw who had been set to watch for her coming. A waiting militiaman took Silvermane's rein and held him while Amelia dismounted, and then he took charge of Spindle's mount as well.

"I am here to see the Knight Captain," Amelia told the line first, who tugged his forelock while standing at attention.

"Your Grace, my name is Quilks. I have been bid to greet you and ask that you await here in safety," the militiaman said formally, with a precise accent that made Amelia think he must have been an educated man before he joined the Lions.

Like Prentice, she thought—courteous enough to be able to tell her what to do while making it sound like a polite request. Regardless, Amelia was not of a mind to wait.

"Thank you for your welcome, Quilks, but you will take me directly to..." she paused a moment, wanting to say, "to my husband," but reluctant, as if the conflict between them made it hard for her to remind others she and Farringdon were, in fact, married. "...to the Knight Captain."

"Directly?" Quilks asked, swallowing a little in poorly concealed panic. Clearly, whatever briefing he had received, it did not involve the archduchess having her own ideas.

"Her Grace should not have to repeat herself, Line First Quilks," Spindle chided dutifully. "Lead now and fulfil her instructions."

The man tugged his forelock once again and turned on his heel. Amelia heard him draw in a deep breath, like a man about to dive from a height into uncertain water, and then he led off toward the bridge. Weaving between armed and armored men going about the various duties of an active defense, in short order Quilks stopped just behind the line of wagons and looked around the corner.

"If I could ask you to wait here, Your Grace," he said, almost pleading. "It isn't safe past this point. The knight captain's just down there. I'll fetch him up for you, if he allows, 'course."

Spindle nodded on Amelia's behalf and the archduchess stood amidst her men-at-arms. When they heard Quilks's words, several standing duty on the wagons knuckled the brims of their helmets. Amelia accepted the obeisance with a smile, but almost as if she couldn't help herself, she leaned out around the corner of the wagon to see where the line first had gone. Some way ahead, she saw Quilks standing with three other men beside the bridge's stone footings on this bank. In the ground amongst their feet there were arrows sticking out of the mud, explaining Quilks concern for her safety. If the armored men felt any concern for their own wellbeing, they gave no sign.

As she watched, Amelia realized that she recognized each of the men, even though they mostly had their backs to her and were all wearing their salets. Besides Quilks, there was the redheaded Sedgemark, his hair poking out from under the ridge of his helmet. Next to him was a former convict Amelia had met only once, the standard bearer named Markas. He was recognizable by the woven white noose around his neck, which always looked to the archduchess like a neckerchief for a corpse, even though she understood its grim symbolism. Last of the men was her husband, Marquis Knight Captain Farringdon, whose identity was obvious to her, not only by the many little marks that a wife will note of her spouse, but by the hurriedly repaired dent in the back of his helmet. The steel had been hammered back into shape, but time had not been taken to polish away the imperfections of the restoration.

Farringdon and his companions were pointing to a spot under the bridge about halfway along where there were boats, apparently caught upon one of the bridge's pillars. From the bastion to her left, a Roar fired his matchlock and the bullet bit into a high wooden side of one of the boats. Farringdon said something to Markas and the standard bearer waved at the bastion.

"Hold fire," he bellowed, arms above his head. "They've come ready for that."

Wondering at the claim, Amelia looked beyond to the boat that had been shot at and realized that it did, in fact, have a strange appearance, its darkly tarred lower boards topped by a newly built wall of paler planks. Rising awkwardly above the little craft's gunwales, these overlapping protections, freshly nailed into place, clearly unbalanced the boats in the flow of the Murr, and that was what had caused them to be caught on the bridge. Looking closely as she dared, Amelia imagined the boats had been built to ferry knights safely across the river under the fire of her Roarsmen. Based on the one shot she had witnessed, she thought the boats might well have done the job if they had been sounder for basic water navigation.

Quilks spoke to Farringdon, and he looked back over his shoulder to see Amelia looking at him. The knight captain nodded and called his men back from the lower bank to the relative safety of the wagon line. When he was beside her, he removed his helmet, tucking it into the crook of his arm and bowing formally. Seemingly instructed not to stay close, the other Lions moved aside, as if they could give their lieges privacy simply by taking a pace or two away.

"Your Grace," Farringdon said, greeting her as formally as Quilks had, but with the added detail that he looked her directly in the eye as his rank and place as her husband allowed. Meeting his gaze, she was pleased to see that his injured eye was at least halfway healed, so that he was coming back to his usual self. Almost as soon as she thought that, however, she realized that he had dark circles under his eyes and the bones of his face were more pronounced. He looked haggard, as if he might have lost ten or more pounds in weight. Nevertheless, he held himself with composure. Amelia wanted to ask if he was well, to say she was glad he was healing from his injury, to tell him she thought she was pregnant, and to chastise him for keeping away from her—all of those things all at once.

"You asked for me?" she said, falling back on formality in the face of her own confusion.

"I did, Your Grace," Farringdon said and then gestured towards some simple wooden steps up to the wagons. Preceding her, he climbed to the wooden "battlement" and offered her his hand to help her ascend. Roar and Claw on duty stepped aside to make space for them both, and Farringdon pointed down the length of the bridge. Looking, Amelia could see a kind of temporary wall built at about the halfway point.

"We are not the only ones to fortify our claim, I see," she said, trying to sound unconcerned. In truth she was puzzled and a little worried. Didn't the presence of such constructions only make it easier for Robant's forces to cross the bridge if they wanted? They could march half the distance in safety now.

"Are we not concerned, Knight Captain?" she asked Farringdon. "Or have we surrendered that part of our bridge already?"

"We have surrendered nothing, Your Grace," Farringdon replied, and Amelia felt a small, inward shiver. She had never heard him use so cold a tone with her before. "These are not much more than pavises, temporary and easily within the power of our axes to clear. They were brought up in the night and only as far as they could be before our Roar-shot would punch through them. Another step and they would stop providing cover. I would already have ordered them cleared, but as you can see, a banner is raised for parley."

Looking beyond the improvised wall, Amelia could see Robant's banner raised on its pole, a white pennant flying with it. The archduchess rolled her eyes and sneered.

Well, this is what you wanted, sovereign lady, she told herself. *What happens now?*

"Shall we raise our own banner?" Farringdon asked. Amelia nodded. The signal was given to Markas back on the ground, and he lifted the White Lions standard and marched it up onto the wagons, two of the Claws jumping down to make space on the now crowded planks. Amelia watched the other side, expecting to be made to wait as a runner would be sent to Duke Robant saying she was here and ready to talk. It was the kind of petty gesture for which he was known.

"Those boats were built to survive our gunners?" she mused as they waited for a response.

"So it would seem, Your Grace," Farringdon said.

"Why send only two? Especially if they were calling for parley?"

"As I sent word, Your Grace, something odd is happening."

Amelia looked at her husband directly, though he did not turn from looking straight across the bridge. She felt a sudden desperation for him to treat her like his wife. For the first time ever, she regretted his capacity to keep formal etiquette between them. They hadn't spoken in a week, and instead of smiling at her, kissing her, even just holding her hand, he was as upright and cold as an iron fencepost. She was reaching for something more to say to connect to the gentle man she knew was in him when there was movement beyond the opposite defenses. A trumpet blast announced the arrival of Duke Robant. Two additional protections were raised above the height of the temporary wall, painted pavises of stiff, wax-boiled leather. At this distance, the arrow protections might deflect a Roarsman's bullet, but even if not, they concealed most of the armored body of the Duke as he stood behind them.

"Is that you, rebel witch Amelia?" Robant shouted through a speaking trumpet.

Markas offered Amelia a leather cone of her own with which to converse, and she accepted it. Putting it to her lips, she answered.

"If we are dispensing with titles, Robant, then perhaps we might dispense with insults as well?" she offered. "Having to continuously refer to you as the Usurper's lapdog footpad will only make conversation tedious, wouldn't you agree?"

If Robant was offended by her response, Amelia could not tell by his tone of voice, and his helmeted expression was too difficult to read at a distance.

"If you wish, then let us make this brief. For myself, I would not waste breath with this conferring at all. I would command you crushed for your offences and your misguided servitors with you."

I thought you were going to be brief, Amelia thought. If there was one thing Robant and his master Daven Marcus had in common, it was their love for the sound of their own voices.

"Nevertheless, the Patriarchs of merciful Mother Church have insisted I offer you a chance to recant, in the face of the recent demonstration of God's wrath falling upon you."

Knowing the duke referred to the terrible destruction of their cannons, Amelia tried to resist looking at her husband, but the pressure of the conflict between them was more than she could overcome. Farringdon, for his part, was still fixed upon the duke, saying nothing and showing no emotion. Amelia hardly knew how to respond. In her heart she was still uncertain, and she knew it was a self-doubt that had not truly abated since that day. She could not believe that elders who fostered the Inquisition and prospered by its evils would have the approval of the Almighty, yet exactly as pronounced, hellish wrath had fallen on the war engines within moments of the reading of the prophecy. What else was she to think?

"No answer, harlot?" Robant's shouted query shook Amelia from her thoughts and she realized that she had been chewing her lower lip in the tension.

"Very well. King Daven Marcus, Unchallenged Sovereign of the Grand Kingdom, has issued his judgement," the duke went on. There was a round of scoffs and chuckles amongst the White Lions. While "unchallenged sovereign" was a known title for Denay kings, it was a rather ridiculous epithet to apply to the most contested man in recorded history to ever sit that throne. "For your rebellion and heresy, the Western Reach is formally withdrawn from your hands. The duchy is hereby awarded to his loyal retainer Robant, to be held in trust for the throne, with all the rights and responsibilities thereto."

Amelia barked a laugh and the men around her began to jeer.

"Try to take it!" Amelia shouted into the trumpet. When at last her men had quieted from their mockery, Duke Robant continued his pronouncement with the same calm voice.

"I have already begun to do so. This bridge has been sealed to you and all other illegitimate Veckander pretenders. I have likewise closed off the River Dwelt until such time as the province is returned to its true sovereign. If any resist, they will be made to yield."

"Not with a few hundred second-rate knights they won't," Markas muttered behind Amelia's shoulder. She was encouraged by his confidence, since he was one of Prentice's most trusted men.

"I am bid by his majesty's pronouncement to inform you that you are formally exiled, heretic rebel Amelia. Should you set foot in the Reach or the Grand Kingdom proper again, you will be subject to summary execution. Hanging, drawing, and quartering is preferred, but the king permits any execution of his judgement to loyal folk. You will die however the first to seize you chooses.

"Of those who serve you, they will go into exile with you, unless they show their loyalty by seizing you now themselves and executing the rightful king's judgement. By that act alone may they find the king's forgiveness and return to the Grand Kingdom."

Amelia looked around her, and those Lions who risked cheekily meeting her gaze at all smiled loyally or shook their heads. Not one of them was prompted to rebel against their liege. This was the pride of the White Lions, the loyal militia Prentice had built for her. Even though she had trusted their fealty, Amelia was a little ashamed that a small part of her was relieved. There had been other moments like this, such as with the rebel Earl Sebastian, where someone had tried to prompt her men-at-arms to rise up against her. Each time her Lions proved faithful. One day she hoped to trust them utterly without question.

"Very well," Robant shouted after more silence, and Amelia thought she heard some sense of eagerness in his voice, as if he had wanted this to happen. There was a creaking sound, followed by a wooden clack as a post with a leading bar was raised behind the barricade where Robant was standing. It took no guessing to realize that it was an improvised gallows. There was a rope that seemed to be draped along the crossbar, running through a number of pulleys.

Not the usual arrangement, Amelia thought.

The section of the rope that was draped off the end of the bar came into view as a prisoner was marched up whatever was serving as the platform behind the wooden wall. The man had a noose already in place around his neck, and his hands were tied behind his back.

"Who are you?" Robant demanded of the man theatrically. The prisoner muttered something, but the duke cut him off swiftly. "No. No! Loudly, so everyone can hear."

"My name is Onsman," the man shouted, his voice cracking with fear so that he was hard to understand at such distance. "I'm a steward of Her Grace, the Archduchess Amelia."

"There is no such person in all the Grand Kingdom," Robant declared, "but an exiled witch in the Vec makes such silly claims. If you are hers, why are you not there with her?"

The man began to mutter once more, but it looked like the duke cuffed him across the head and so he started shouting again.

"I was in the camp when it was attacked. I fell behind and was captured by your men."

"Ah, so God has delivered you into the hands of true justice."

Amelia felt her fingers twisting against each other as she gripped her own hands in fury. To hear Robant boast that he was doing God's work was so disgusting that she wondered why heaven did not open and strike the bridge as it had her cannons upon the hilltop. Perhaps God really was on the Usurper's side. The notion chilled her to her pregnant belly.

"For the sake of your soul, do you recant your commitment to the exiled witch and pledge yourself to the rightful king, Daven Marcus?"

The poor steward lifted his head and directed a fearful sneer at his tormentor. It was as brave an act as any man-at-arms who stood the field. Faced with the choice between loyalty and death, the man was steeling himself for the coming horror.

"I am a loyal Reacherman!" he shouted. "I am her grace's man..."

He might have said more if he had been given the chance, but by some unseen signal, the rope was pulled, the little pully wheels squealed, and the captured steward was hauled bodily into the air. His face turned rapidly red, then to bruise-purple, and his struggles for breath could just be heard at the distance.

"If you will not recant following the witch, then you will suffer her path into Hell as the Patriarchs in synod and the throne have determined," Robant said. His tone was as unconcerned as it had been up until this point, as if hanging men for heresy was the most natural business of a summer's day. "You will be hanged, then drawn behind horses and quartered. We will send one section of you back to your heretic mistress to help her contemplate her inevitable fate."

Already the condemned man was dancing the gallows' jig, his legs pumping in the vain hope that some movement, any movement at all, might relieve the pain in his throat. Amelia felt tears as she watched, her heart rending, knowing that not only was this man suffering for his loyalty to her, but possibly also in the belief that he was going to Hell for it as well.

"Oh, dear God, someone help him," she moaned involuntarily.

There was the snap of a trigger spring, followed by the tell-tale pause and then the flash and roar of a matchlock. The dangling man's chest had a wound suddenly tear through his tunic, and the horrifying dance ended.

CHAPTER 53

"I said help him!" Amelia all but shouted at the Roars-man who had made the shot, but before she could say any more, Farringdon interposed himself between her and the militiaman.

"We did," he said. "We gave Onsman what help we could."

"I meant that he should be rescued," Amelia said with rising fury. "And you know it. Why did you defy me?"

"I did not think to defy you," Farringdon replied quietly. "I have ever sought to fulfil your commands."

Amelia blinked as she stared at him, irate disbelief making it almost impossible for her to form a clear thought. How could he say such a thing? Time and again it seemed he defied her, then hid from her to prevent the matter being resolved. In her inner self there was a quiet part that recognized her temper was out of her control and that this was not how she normally behaved. Later, she would wonder if it was the changes to her moods that her growing child was producing within her, but for now, she had no option but to ride the emotions forward, regardless of the damage they did. She opened her mouth to speak, but in the delay as she tried to order her thoughts, Robant's voice echoed out once again.

"Not able to stomach the consequences of your rebellion, lying wench?" he shouted as the dead Osman was lowered be-hind the barricade. "Hide from the lessons of Mother Church however you wish, but each one you kill is spared the righteous suffering that will purge their guilt. You only send them to Hell the swifter."

Another body was hoisted up, the new prisoner choking, unnamed. Amelia groaned in anguish at the sight and wondered how many more prisoners Robant had to torture to death in front of her. She turned back upon her husband, who seemed to regard her almost as disdainfully as the hateful duke slaying her loyal servants.

"You said your axes could easily sweep those pavises away," she snarled at him, enraged at the distance he had put between them. Where was the loving man she thought she had married? "No righteous man who could do such a thing would stand by and watch this monstrousness."

"You mean, Knight Commander Baron Prentice would not stand by and watch," Farringdon replied. "And with respect, Your Grace, you are mistaken."

"You dare? He would not..." Amelia gasped. Her fingers clenched into fists, and she looked around her. Most men present were turning their faces away, or watching the brutal execution, waiting for the signal to give the next victim a mercy shot. Then Markas, the standard bearer, met her gaze.

"I mean no disrespect, Your Grace, but Knight Commander Ash would not."

Again, in the deep, quiet part of her mind, Amelia remembered the story of the day Markas had first come to wear the abominable lanyard around his neck, how Prentice and his fellow rats in the walls of Fallenhill had had to watch as Liam had a prisoner similarly tortured and executed outside the town's walls. The thought that Markas and Farringdon might be right only made her want to rescue whatever prisoners Robant held all the more. Nobles of the Grand Kingdom did not hesitate to kill mere yeomen to make a point.

"You boast that you obey me," she hissed. "Then obey me in this!"

"Your men will die," Farringdon said. At no point had he lost his temper in the face of her rage, and that only drove her anger onward.

"My men are already dying!" she shouted. "I had to drive Earl Sebastian to his duty last year. Is this the tradition amongst my knight captains?"

A twitch in Farringdon's cheek, as of a frown or sneer restrained, revealed that her latest rejoinder at least had landed. It brought her no satisfaction, and her anger began to crumble to fear as the marquis turned to the standard bearer and they shared a grim nod.

"I'd like to come, if I may, Knight Captain," Markas said quietly.

"I will not deny you," the knight captain replied. "First, go tell Sedgemark I am leading an assault and to send up the men set for the task. Give my order to the Roars to pepper the sides ahead of us. Then return here. We should have an opening ready in that time."

Markas jumped from the wagon, and as he left, Amelia wanted to reach out to her husband. He really was about to assault Robant's defense on her order, and though he said he was confident, she could not bear the thought that he would go without their reconciling. As she turned back to him, she saw the hanged prisoner being lowered so that they could be tied behind a horse and drawn to wherever they would be quartered. Her own loss would not matter if this murder went on. Hardly knowing what to say or think, Amelia was offered the hand of another militiaman to step across from the wagon she was standing in—the middle one—to the one on the left of the makeshift defense. The plan was apparently to move the middle wagon aside to allow the assault. No sooner was she moved than men began to heave upon that middle wagon, shifting it out of the way. Amelia wondered why her *husband* had not thought to escort her across the tiny distance, but when she looked to him, the urge to berate him growing up in her thoughts once again, she found him leaning over the side of their wagon, handing someone a hunting horn.

Where had he found *that* on this battlefield?

"You know what to look for?" he was asking whoever he was handing the horn to. Amelia could not make out the mumbled reply. "Good. As soon as you see it, if you do."

Amelia drew close just as Farringdon turned around. He looked her in the eyes and his expression was sober, stern even. Nonetheless, he bowed, and before she could say anything more, jumped down where a militiaman was waiting to hand him a Fang's round shield, as well as a swordbelt with a Fang's backsword and a sheathed lancer's handgun. He handed over his own longsword and asked the man if the firearm was loaded. When he received a positive reply, he settled the belt over his breastplate to sit at the faulds and waited. Soon enough he was joined by Markas and two lines of mixed Claws and Fangs. At least five of the Fangs had their swords sheathed, shields on their backs, and were carrying woodsmen's axes with heavy steel heads for splitting boards and logs. With these serious-faced men came Sergeant Sedgemark, as well.

"Your cohorts are ready?" Farringdon asked the sergeant. Sedgemark nodded. "Good. Do not follow us until the signal. If they make a greater resistance than we expect, we'll want to be able to come back quick smart. Have some men on the wagon to close it behind us. If all goes well, we will call you up and the bridge will soon be ours from end to end."

"And the other matter?" the sergeant asked.

"In the hands of a man you trust most. I will justify him."

"I'll do it myself."

What other matter? Amelia wondered. She wanted to ask, but a sudden gust of wind caused the Lion banner to snap near her head and she wondered when Markas had handed it off. By the time she turned back, Farringdon was leading the small squadron of men crouching onto the bridge, and Sedgemark was bellowing an order for the Roar on the riverbanks to begin firing. On the wagons still in place, other gunners fired as well, and shot bit into the pavises over the heads of Farringdon's men. There was no man hanging from the gallows, and it seemed that Robant himself had withdrawn from his half-hidden position. Perhaps this would be easier than everyone feared.

With a shout, Farringdon's force charged the last ten paces to the barricade and threw themselves upon it. The axemen hacked at the planks while other Fangs held shields to protect them, and Claws pushed their polearms against the thinner pavises above, knocking one of them back. The Roar beside Amelia ceased fire, lest they shoot their own comrades. On the riverbanks, firing continued. From further behind the barricade, still mostly obscured, a handful of archers suddenly loosed a volley in a high arc to fall on the assault. Two struck shields, but the rest fell ineffectually.

"Have they no one on the barricades?" Amelia wondered out loud. She was watching, astonished, as Farringdon's small force rapidly demolished the defensive construction, and she realized that apart from the thin volley of arrows, they were meeting no resistance. Why were there no men-at-arms fighting to hold the defensive point? Robant was no coward, for all his evil. It seemed impossible he had simply run away.

Another volley of arrows fell, and Amelia estimated they could have no more than ten archers in their defense. Through the growing gap in the barricade, she thought perhaps she could make out some of them on the bridge. Even as she watched, though, the men with bows appeared to be withdrawing quickly. Then Farringdon's squad was beating their way through the gap. It was slow going, and several of them seemed to fall over each other.

"They've laid caltrops," one of the Lions on the opposite wagon shouted. His view was obviously better than Amelia's. Caltrops were spikes laid on the ground, usually to impede horses, but in a narrow space, placed densely enough, they would slow attackers on foot. They would also slow defenders, though.

Suddenly, from the ground at the left side of Amelia's wagon, the sound of the hunting horn howled out over the water. The long, deep rumble sounded in her chest, and she leaned over the edge to see a militiaman with the instrument to his lips. When he was done, he pointed along the side of the bridge. Looking to where he was indicating, Amelia saw two men leaning out over the parapet, risking being shot by her gunners. They snapped back into cover away from a volley of shot, but as they did, the archduchess noticed something odd amongst the puffs of dust or flying splinters where missed shots struck. It was a tiny fizzing spark. Before she could fully make it out, Amelia felt herself bodily hefted from the wagon and dragged down to the ground. Trying to comprehend what was happening, she heard boots hammering on the bridge planks. Her vision was confused as all around her Lions were leaping from the wagons and the assault force was retreating at full speed. She caught sight of Farringdon for a moment, seeing him with his arm under another fellow's shoulder, urging him along. The man seemed wounded.

Then Amelia felt a pause that let her get her feet under her and she looked to see that Sedgemark had been carrying her with his arm around her waist. She wanted to demand an explanation, but he had put her down only to get a better grip. Almost immediately whisked back into motion, she yelped once before hearing a cry of "Get to ground" echoing over the bridge. Sedgemark all but threw her down in a depression in the earth near to one of the Roar bulwarks. Then he dropped almost completely on top of her, and she realized he was shielding her with his own body.

"Sorry, Your Grace," he said with an expression of embarrassed amusement, clearly ashamed by his actions. "Knight captain's orders."

"Why?" she asked, but before he could answer, there was a heavy whumping sound, and the ground underneath her shook. It was not as horrid as the day on the hilltop, but she realized what must have happened. There was a sound of water splashing all around and the same sudden smell of smoke.

Duke Robant had blown up the bridge with black powder. That had been what the two jammed boats had been for, and he had waited until her soldiers were on the bridge to do it. Looking into Sedgemark's face, she could see by his expression that he had been expecting this, and he smiled at her, reaching up to tug his forelock.

"Knight Captain Farringdon suspected something like this might happen," he said, "Soon as he saw the boats."

Amelia had no idea what to think. She was about to thank the sergeant when a dark shape descended suddenly from the sky and a heavy piece of bridge planking fell straight upon Sedgemark's back, crushing the sergeant's brigandine against her ribs and driving the breath from her lungs.

CHAPTER 54

"You asked me what the ambush site would look like," Prentice said, shaking his head with a wry smile. "Well, redoubtable men of the Reach, *that* is what it looks like."

For three days the Gryphon Banner Company had continued its half-marches, harried each night from near midnight until an hour or two before dawn. Not many militiamen had died, but several had been injured, slung lead bullets breaking bones or knocking men senseless, even through their helmets. The slinger fey were every bit as deadly in ambush as the horse archers of the Azures. One of the mules had been badly lamed and the ostlers put it down, redistributing its load and roasting the unappetizing meat.

Now, with less than an hour before sundown on the third day, the company faced a sudden rise to a ridge at the foothills of the far western mountains that had no name. The rise was not as high as the escarpment that was so many days march behind them, but it was steeper, almost a true cliff, and far beyond their ability to surmount before the sun set. As they approached, Prentice had gathered all his officers and made sure they all appreciated the challenge they were facing. They looked up at the ridge from an oddly bowl-shaped depression, filled with softer drifts of the desert sand than the hard-packed dust they had been marching in so far. To their left, as they studied the ground, the Murr fell not in rapids but in an unusually regular-seeming cascade, switching back and forth down the bluff like a set of steps. The entire location was a perfect place for a group of slingers, or javelineers, or indeed any missile troops to hammer down upon an enemy from the looming clifftop.

"Scouts report that the ridge slopes down to this level 'bout a half dozen leagues north. They say it's all trees up there, but they're dead, just dry trunks and spindly branches," Corporal Guillam told them. A few bleached trunks were visible from where they were standing, clinging tenaciously to the ridgeline.

"They had a lock system here once," Prentice declared, studying the water flow, "to bring boats up and down that rise."

"Oh, of course, My Lord," Solft said, looking at the cascade with fresh eyes. "It's broken down now, but as you say it, it becomes obvious."

The military men mostly shrugged at the scholar's sense of wonder. However obvious it seemed to Master Solft, they did not really care. Prentice pointed at the sandy bowl around them and then northward, perpendicular to the flow of the river, where a broad, channel-like depression, also sand-silted, ran away from them.

"That was a canal," he explained. "They would have brought boats down here and then either sailed north or east. This was the interchange."

"Like the meeting of the Dwelt and the Murr, Knight Commander?" Lyrach asked, recognizing the similarity.

Prentice nodded.

Like the Dwelt and the Murr, he thought. *But with one exception—this was a canal, a waterway dug by mortal hands.* As the days passed in this dead land, he was starting to guess at the parameters of the magick that had blighted it, and perhaps its limitations. The curse brought drought, but the Murr still flowed because of whatever ancient power there was in the headwater lake. Nevertheless, almost nothing lived or grew in its waters until it reached Radengon. Its natural vigor was enough to preserve it against eldritch drought, but only just.

All other waterways failed—wells, irrigations, even canals and purpose-built qanats. Nothing could quench the thirsty land.

"They'll be pummeling us from up there, I suppose," Porth muttered, surveying the ridgeline. Fifty or so feet high at this point, the summit was about the height of a good castle tower, enough to add to a slinger's range without diminishing their aim too greatly. Ideal.

"We can expect their foot to come at us from the east," Prentice told them, looking back the way they had just marched. "They have been harrying us nightly from the river, making it a double barrier for us so none of us will think to swim for it and so we will not put our backs to it in a battle. We will be pinned between slingstones from a ridge we cannot hope to assault and spearmen coming from behind us out of the dark. We will have no choice but to retreat north."

"Why north?" asked Solft.

"Drive us into the desert, Master," Gennet readily explained, which Prentice backed up with a nod. "We'll be out on that empty plain, disorganized, wounded, most likely, and quickly gettin' thirsty."

"They will not have to harry us anymore, in that case," Prentice finished off. "They would be able to hunt us openly and easily. They might even take their time doing it. After all, their main purpose in this is to get their fleet through to Lake Dweltford. We are an impediment, not a target."

"Alright, so that's the rabid mongrel we're facin' down," Guillam said, sucking black saliva from his mouthful of chew. "What're we gonna do 'bout it, Commander?"

"First, we are going to set up our tents," Prentice told them. "Then, we will have some work to do."

As Prentice predicted, the combined fey and Redlander ambush came from both the east and the west, from on the ridge and along the river. Scouts had never yet found a mantis mask on the upland Murr, but perhaps it did not matter. The will-o'-the-wisps and the secret harriers had always appeared on the river seemingly at will. So, while the slingstones began to fall from the bluff, striking the few sentries in sight amidst the tents and the campfires, from out of the dark east, chariots bearing beast-men rolled ahead of a body of painted spearmen, charging in the open skirmish order Redlanders used when raiding. Wolfen and mantis men leapt from the chariots to smash aside the few sentries who had not fallen to stones. Wheels rode roughshod over some tents, while other shelters were torn open by talons and spearpoints, seeking vulnerable, resting bodies to slay. The whooping frenzy reigned in the night as the Redlanders gave full vent to their bloodlust. Fires were spread, coals kicked around to spark whatever fuel they could, so that the shadows in the darkness only raged ever more chaotically.

So utterly intent upon destruction were they that it was almost a quarter of an hour before the raiders realized that not one of them had made a genuine kill. The sentries they had first assaulted turned out to all be made of sticks and reed bundles, holding up empty suits of armor. All the tents were empty, too. Even the mule team and its handlers were nowhere to be found. As the berserker madness began to cool slightly, the Redlanders looked about in confusion. Where was their foe?

Then, from the north a drumbeat began to thump, rolling down the ancient, parched canal and echoing off the bluff.

CHAPTER 55

"That is our signal," Prentice whispered.

The word was passed, and around him eighty Roar lying flat upon the ground to be out of sight began to light their long-matches from hot coals hidden in clay pots, blowing the embers to life.

Eighty gunners, fully four-fifths of the Gryphon's total Roar, along with four lines of Fangs, forty swordsman, had force-marched north in the darkness after sundown with Prentice at their head and Brother Whilte keeping uncomfortable pace with them on the back of one of the mule team. Since the company had ascended the scarp, leaving his wagon behind, he had kept up on his one good leg better than any would have predicted. This march needed as much swiftness as possible, however. In the north, the Roar detachment found the location the scouts had described where the ridge slipped downward and then mounted it to turn back south and return on the heights. Guessing that moonrise was somehow a part of the fey power to move through the Murr, since they never struck before then, Prentice had wanted to get his separate force back to the height above their "camp" before the slingers ever appeared, which meant his detachment had driven themselves hard in the few hours between the summer sundown and the imminent midnight. A night march before moonrise over uneven ground near a growing cliffside was no easy task, however, and so Prentice's force had arrived just as the fey slingers were emerging from the dead trees to attack from the ridge, with barely enough time to throw themselves to the ground, hoping to pass unseen.

Down in the dried-out canal, the rest of the company under Gennet's command had formed up north of the faked encampment with instructions to let the Redlanders in as close as they would come. Once it seemed likely that the raiders would have noticed where the ambush was waiting, that was the moment to march to the fight. Expecting the enemy to squeeze his company between two sides to drive them north, Prentice's plan was for the Gryphon Banner to do exactly the same thing back. Gennet's force, the majority of the melee troops, would push the Redlanders against the river, while on the ridge Prentice would use the Roar to drive off the slingers and then fire down on the Redlander flank.

So, it was as the drumbeat down below began, booted feet tromped in the sand and every Roarsman signaled quietly that he was ready to shoot, that Prentice gave the order for his unit to stand and advance. Light from the fires in the camp leapt up to the ridgeline, and the slingers were visible enough to target, standing in a long, thin formation. There were at least a hundred, perhaps twice that number, and while they were focused on hammering stones on the ground beneath them, it would surely be only moments before the closest ones noticed the line advancing upon their flank. If they had been watchful, they would likely have known an hour or more ago that Prentice's force had been coming, but they were not. Why would they be watchful? This was *their* ambush site, after all. They had ruled the night since the Lions had first come to this highland plain, this empty land that had been a fey possession for nearly a thousand years. This was where the persistent, irritating men of the ancient enemy were to be broken and driven into the desert to die.

Prentice had ordered his Roarsmen to fire in two corps of forty in off-set volleys so that as one half of the gunners fired, the others were reloading, allowing for a nearly continuous shooting. The first forty raised their matchlocks to their shoulders and forty iron "hornets" launched themselves through fire, smoke, and thunder to rip into the fey flank. Screams of pain and shouts of alarm sounded southward along the ridge.

Down in the dry canal, the first elements of the Redlander force, painted men rapidly whipping themselves back into a frenzy, launched at the massed Lions marching in formation out of the dark. Only once before had painted men faced White Lions in the dark, and the likelihood was that few, if any, of these had been at that battle as well. As the skirmishers attacked, expecting to find unnerved yeomen levies, they were instantly repelled by the forest of sharp steel that was the Claw's formation of pike and halberd. A handful thought to drive past the pikes with their shields to get their own spears into range, but no sooner did they beat past the first line than the next rank and the third, polearms wielded over and between comrades in tight order, hacked and bit into the invaders. Those mad, courageous raiders who let their bloodlust rule them all fell first.

On the ridgeline, the fey slingers fell into disorder of their own as they tried to comprehend what kind of assault they were under. Prentice watched as best he could as a third volley lit the night under the dead trees. Every flash of shot played havoc with his night vision, not to mention the cloud of smoke that was growing to further dim the darkness. Even so, he peered into the dire shadow play, looking for whichever fey was trying to rally their force to redeploy for the officers or champions who commanded. They were the danger he most feared. The horse archers had been a single form, highest to lowest all fighting the same, but they had only been bound to the Serpent Witch for a year or so. These fey had years, centuries probably, of subjugation to the cult. How many had converted in that time? How many were secretly *brakkis effar*, happy to use their traditional weapons but able to transform and bring real Blood Sect sorcery to bear? How many of these fey were mantis or serpents? That was why Prentice had brought twenty Fangs with him, in case magick changed the parameters of the combat. The fourth volley echoed in the night and the knight commander kept close watch.

After the initial ineffectual attacks, the Redlanders' champions barked new orders from inhuman throats and the raiders drew back. They were not retreating. All Gennet's men had been warned not to expect an easy fight. The outwitted ambushers were reorganizing themselves, bringing spearmen together into the tight shield wall, leather and wood defenses overlapping while the spears poked out in a hedge that was like the Lions'. As the enemy built a column to assault the Lions' matching corps, their *brakkis effar* remounted the chariots and the drivers whipped the horses, sending them out into the dark to sweep around the Lions' flank. There was no space for them to fit between the Lions and the bluff, so they could only flank on the desert side, which was all to the good as far as Gennet was concerned. He could keep his men-at-arms up against that near-cliff because his knight commander above was tying up the slingers. His troops were safe on their right flank, which meant he could put all of his Roar on his left flank. As the sweeping chariots reemerged from the darkness, their wheels bit into the soft sand of the canal and slowed suddenly. Horses whinnied at the sudden increase in their labor, the drivers whipping their flanks even more brutally. Beast-men snarled in frustration at being denied the extra speed that their chariot charge usually gave them in an assault. And then the slowed vehicles felt the rage of the remaining forty Lions' Roar. Horses died, drivers and *brakkis effar* were wounded, and more than one chariot tipped over in the silted ground.

Some slingstones were beginning to come back against the iron shot on the ridgetop, but too few to be significant. Every Roarsman had been ordered to wear his full panoply, buffcoats and helms especially, despite the heat and exertion of the forced march. Added to that, the Fangs with them held their shields aloft, giving additional, if haphazard, protection to near comrades. Prentice himself had opted to carry a round shield and to use his champion sword one handed. It was a challenging but not unknown way to wield a longsword, and the work Yentow Sent had done to reduce the weapon's weight made it an almost negligible problem. Prentice told himself he would thank the crochety smith again when he returned from this campaign, assuming he did. He held his shield aloft, ignoring his tired muscles. A sore shoulder was better than a broken arm. His spaulders and rerebraces could likely deflect the lead missile, but if the slinger managed to hit on a joint—an elbow or wrist—that could easily be a break.

Moving east along his force's firing line, Prentice reached the ridge and spared a glance down into the canal. As they had at the Battle of the Brook, the Redlanders had formed their tight column and were drumming their own marching rhythm on their shields. The chariots, what he could see of them, were bogged or still being peppered by shot. One beast-man, a mantis, had managed to leap into the main body of the Lions, doubtless hoping to cleave away the furious gunners, but once in amongst them, his slaughter was opposed by the Fangs awaiting him. The densely packed, painted spearmen looked ready to hold their own, though. Prentice performed a quick head count and estimated there were around another two hundred, roughly equal in number to Gennet's force. That was expected. Once he had control of the ridge, Prentice would order his gunners to fire down into the massed Redlanders and make them suffer the same kind of flanking shots the fey had planned for his Lions.

A hunting horn echoed like the wail of a mournful ghost, and at the other flank of his Roarsmen, Prentice saw a new contingent of mighty fey warriors burst from within the dead forest, blades flashing in the crazed firelight. The battle's turning point had arrived.

CHAPTER 56

The horn's wail was still echoing through the night as Prentice started to run back from the edge of the bluff toward the forest where the fey counterattack had just emerged. The rush of battle let him push his weary legs to a sprint, and he had just enough time to hope that Brother Whilte was close to hand. As the only one in the entire company capable of directly opposing Blood Sect magicks, it had been an open question where he would best be deployed. Since he had no clear idea what the limits of the fey were, Prentice had chosen to bring Whilte up onto the ridge. Now the knight commander needed his chaplain ready to help oppose whatever the fey were bringing to bear.

As he rushed behind his gunners, shield still awkwardly over his head, Prentice tried to understand what he was seeing coming out of the forest to assault his men. In the crazed shadows, his first thought was that the fey had somehow made the trees walk like mortals and attack the Lions because what he thought he saw was long clusters of branches sweeping his Fangs aside. His mind deciphered the confusion, however, and he realized what he thought were branches were in fact horns—impossibly broad antlers, as of mighty deer. Prentice skidded to a halt, his shield lowering to his shoulder involuntarily as one fearful thought crashed into his mind.

Another Horned Man?

It had been years since his near suicidal hand-to-hand fight with the Horned Man at the Battle of the Brook. That mighty *brakkis effar*, the first he had ever faced and still one of the strongest, had almost crushed the life from his body. Did he have the strength to face another like that? Almost as soon as he had the thought, Prentice knew the answer was irrelevant. There was no choice but to face the coming monster.

Starting to run once again, Prentice blinked in pain as shafts of pure light shone through the darkness from his right. Through the now starker outlines of trees and terrain, he saw Brother Whilte holding his broken-spear rod aloft, commanding whatever power God placed in his prayers. The greater radiance revealed to Prentice that it was no horned man ahead of him, but a genuine deer as large as a warhorse, with branching antlers almost as wide across as the animal was long. These horns were not chased in metal as the Horned Man's had been, but they were thicker at the base and branched many times more. As the stag surged forward, it lowered its head, and its antlers were every bit the hedge of deadly points that a formation of Claw militiamen were. Prentice saw two Fangs try to resist the sweeping charge. One was able to protect himself from the points with his shield but was knocked aside by the beast's mighty strength. The other was caught in the tine-like points, pierced in numerous places, and then screamed as he was hefted bodily into the air. As he writhed, a flash of steel clove into his buffcoat. The stag had a rider upon its back, a pallid but proud fey who wore armor dyed green, wielding a curved sword. Its edge must have been inhumanly sharp, because where it struck the hapless Fang, his buffcoat separated and a line of blood showed, perhaps not fatal but long and brutal. As the crimson dripped down its horns, the stag tossed the wounded man aside with a shake of its neck and then lifted its head to bellow into the night.

As the echoes rang out, Prentice realized that what he had thought was a hunting horn a moment ago was actually the mighty creature's sovereign cry, announcing its dominion, just as a lion's roar or a wolf's howl. The sound was answered by several other deer and riders who were following on behind this Monarch of the Forest and his master. None of the others was the equal of the lead beast in size or power, but it did not matter. Their antlers were still as potentially deadly. At least half the Fangs who had marched to protect the Roar had been slain now, or at least badly wounded, and the deer riders were searching the night for more victims. Some nearby gunners realized the danger they were in and turned from firing after the scattering slingers to target the newly arrived sylvan cavalry. Prentice felt a rush of pride at their discipline and nerve, as not a single one broke from his fellows. That was followed by a singular flash of sadness as he realized it would not save them.

Then, like a sudden deluge, all other emotions were sluiced away in an icy torrent of battle fury, a rage from within him that had never and would not ever yield to any enemy. Prentice would never willingly save his own life at the expense of any one of his militiamen. He lowered his sword and pointed it at the mighty stag and rider just as the fey commander looked in his direction. They were too distant, and it was too dark for their eyes to truly meet, but nonetheless, the two seemed held in each other's glare for a moment. The stag bellowed again, stamping one foot on the dusty earth and also looking at Prentice, as if rider and mount shared the same sense of enemies and danger. Last summer, the lion angel of Prentice's visions had loaned him its voice to speak one word of unfathomable power against the evil of the Serpent Witch and her Reachermen *brakkis effar*. For a moment, he wished he could have that power flow through him once more to rebuke this enemy who disdained his men's lives.

Then he smiled his predator's smile. Lions roared to announce themselves, but they could hunt silently in the night just as well. And now, he was not only a lion but a gryphon lion. Prentice hated honor duels and pointless gestures of heroism. Wars were won by discipline and determination, not by glory-seeking. Yet in this moment, as knight commander and gryphon, bearer of the unicorn-hilted champion sword and facing the enemy's commander across a distance of barely twenty paces, Prentice knew this was between champions. This was not only battle; it was spiritual, symbolic warfare. A man-at-arms might need only skill, stout armor, and a sharp sword, but the more the enemy embraced powers ancient and eldritch, the further the combat moved beyond those practicalities. A gryphon—lion and eagle in equal measure—was made of two creatures that hunted without fear, not because they were invincible, but because fear was pointless.

Let me soar on wings like an eagle, Prentice prayed, and he launched himself forward. The stag leaped into a gallop, more agile than the best chargers. Shield forward, Prentice rushed upon the lowered forest of antler spikes, smiling, furious. The stag swept its horns to pierce and entangle him and lift him from his feet as it had the other Fangs. Prentice had different ideas and protected himself with his round shield. However, where the previous Fang had tried to deflect the horns, vainly matching his mass and strength against the stag's vast might, Prentice angled his shield downward, jumping upward and forwards at the same time. Since the drought, he had never bothered to wear his armor leg pieces, choosing fleetness of foot over pure protection. Now, while that choice increased the risk of his legs being injured, it also made it easier for him to gain speed and height. The shield caught the antlers, and as he tucked his legs behind it, Prentice was lifted bodily into the air, flying over the stag's head, safely above the deadly points. He found himself momentarily face-to-face with the enemy commander, the fey's eyes wide with enraged disbelief.

Even shocked as he was, the rider managed to swing his unusual sword with impressive speed. Prentice had no time to protect himself from the blow, only hoping that his shield would catch some of the rising cut. It did, but he was astonished as the inwardly curved blade reached like a hook around the shield's edge and bit at his left shoulder. His lion-embossed spaulder absorbed the damage, but Prentice felt himself deflected in the air, falling away to his right. Lashing out wildly with his sword, he missed the rider completely, just managing to catch the stag's flank. The beast's snorting and roaring was cut short by an agonized scream, and the creature fell away just as Prentice reached the ground, doing his best to absorb the punishing impact with a body roll.

Breath blasted from his chest and limbs aching, battle-focus alone allowed Prentice to get his feet back under himself and he turned to watch his enemy from a deep crouch, just as a hunting lion might after a foiled spring upon its prey. His head throbbed, and he suspected his helmet had been knocked askew by the fall. There was no time to risk adjusting it. Prentice's strike must have caught a sinew in the stag's rear leg, for as it struggled to rise, the trailing limb was refusing to support any weight. Its rider had tumbled clear of his mount's fall with all the art of a trained knight, and he came to his feet, sickle-like saber held in a ready guard. He shouted something in his own tongue that Prentice imagined must be a curse of sorts. The voice seemed strangely high-pitched for the body that produced it, but that meant nothing to the knight commander. He pointed his own sword once more.

"I am the Ashen Man," he shouted. "Know me as *they* know me, and you might outlive this night."

Inwardly he knew the words were ridiculous. Even if the fey champion could understand Kingdom speech, why would he not already know who Prentice was? And exactly what power did being the "Ashen Man" give him? It was all pagan rubbish as far as Knight Commander Baron Ash was concerned. But that was the point—the name Ash was his because his enemies had given it to him. If they feared it, then why not use that fear?

The fey leader charged at him and Prentice rose, shield ahead to block the cut. The fey was skilled, though, and almost as soon as the round steel blocked Prentice's eyeline to his attacking blade, the enemy reversed his cut and swung it around the opposite edge. The inward curve found the open path between Prentice's shield and sword. Razor sharp steel bit into the edge of the knight commander's helmet, and though Prentice tried to reverse the direction of his shield's movement to deflect the point with the circular rim, as well as making a desperate parry with his blade, he still felt the sting of a cut to his face just beside his eye. The pass was complete, and the two combatants faced each other again in the roaring, shadowed madness of the night. Prentice could see by his opponent's level expression that this was not the first such duel for either of them. His smile widened a moment as he wondered what Baron Ironworth would have thought of this opponent. Prentice was facing him with the deceased knight marshal's blade, after all.

At the edges of his vision, outside his focus on the bladesman in front of him, Prentice could see other deer riders circling the champions, cutting him off from the rest of his men but respecting their leader's honor combat.

Fools, he thought. *One of you should charge me from behind and have done with it.* Prentice looked earnestly over each shoulder, trying to keep the main of his attention on his opponent but watchful in case one of the other fey made the sensible decision. From what he could see, the circle was nearly two thirds closed. Soon enough he would be trapped. It occurred to him that he was experiencing a similar lack of common sense as that which he was despising in his foes. Practicality dictated that he should sprint for the remaining gap before it was too late.

I'd never make it. Prentice barked a mad laugh and kept his focus on the dismounted fey leader. His curved blade rose, ready for the next assault, when suddenly a Grand Kingdom accent shouted from the not-yet-closed gap in the circling enemy.

"Lions hunt in the pride!" called the familiar voice. "In the field they are never alone. Roar!"

CHAPTER 57

"Lyrach?" Prentice shouted, calling the name out almost like a curse. The ex-squire-turned-commander's-groom had been ordered to remain with Prentice's mounts, along with the ostlers, Master Solft, and the rest of the mule train. It had been a harsh decision, but Prentice had felt he had little choice. Even though Lyrach seemed to be maturing as a Lion, the knight commander's two main impressions of him were either that he was a traitor, waiting for the ideal moment to strike, or he was a tearaway youth, hungry for an opportunity to throw his life after glory. In either case, a battle like this was too great a temptation to put in his path. Yet as Prentice cast another swift glance over his shoulder, he could see Lyrach was here and dressed as a Roarsman line first, complete with lit matchlock, no less. Anything more the knight commander might have thought to say was swallowed by the retorts of five gunners firing.

"Second rank, fire," Lyrach ordered. When had he learned the Roar's drills? "First rank, reload."

More iron shot ripped across the battlefield at close range. Either by fluke or a cruel genius in Lyrach's directions, four of the first five shots were not even aimed at Prentice's fey opponent nor any of the others circling but at the wounded stag. With a heart-wrenching cry that was half deep cough, half scream, the sovereign of the forest collapsed where it stood, its heavy body crashing into the dust. Its mighty head tipped to the ground, and it breathed a loud final breath. The near supernatural tie that Prentice suspected existed between mount and rider seemed further confirmed as the fey champion's belligerent expression dissolved into instant grief. It was an emotion shared by his companion riders, and as one they began a moaning ululation, nearly identical to the mourning song shared by the fey of the Azures. Prentice wondered how long the pair had been bonded. Fey seemed inhumanly long-lived, and that beast could have been any age by his estimate. If God were to reveal from heaven that this stag was the very first of his kind, alive since the garden of Eden, Prentice did not think he would have been surprised by the revelation.

The Roar was not concerned with their enemy's grief, however, and they kept up their overlapping volleys. One deer and two riders fell, and that was enough to break their will. They fled, one bravely riding into the circle to collect his leader and take him away to safety. One last volley followed them before Prentice called them to cease fire. They did as commanded, and Lyrach immediately directed them towards the edge of the bluff, where the rest of the gunners had now driven off the slingers and were firing down into the massed Redlanders below. Their shots crackled like a bonfire in the night, and the flames of the fake camp were obscured by their smoke. The few remaining Fangs on their feet looked to protect their captured ground, watching in case the deer riders rallied and returned.

Still holding his shield and sword, Prentice awkwardly wrenched his helmet from his head, dropping it to the ground, and his temple throbbed as from a mighty hangover. Whilte appeared at his shoulder, his prophet's rod returned to a mere broken-bladed stick. He put his fingers to the cut on the side of Prentice's face.

"Is it bad?" Prentice asked. The injury did not feel bad, but he knew truly sharp blades could be treacherous in this regard. Their cuts could be so fine that they might feel like little more than a scratch but would penetrate so deep that they found an artery. He had seen several men bleed out from such wounds.

Whilte's matter-of-fact healer's tone of voice was comforting in its lack of comfort. "Likely won't even scar," said the chaplain dismissively, and even as he spoke, Prentice could feel the pain lessen under his touch, even the blood drying up.

"Poor beast," said one of the Fangs, looking at the slaughtered stag.

"Better it than us," said another, who was missing his sword and had his right hand clutched up under his shield. The limb was probably broken.

Prentice looked at the beast.

"'The creation is subjected to futility,'" he recited sadly, recalling words of holy scripture. They had never seemed so true to him as in this moment. Twice in a year he had survived battle at the cost of a glorious creature's life—the unicorn last summer in the Reach, and now this lord of the forest here at the furthest west known to Kingdom folk. He was not sentimental in general, and he knew that animals, just like mortals, lived and died, sometimes cruelly. Nevertheless, there was something truly sad in the ending of this magnificence.

"'Subjected to futility but in the hope of being freed from the bondage of corruption,'" Whilte said, adding more from the same excerpt.

"Is that your lesson, Chaplain?" Prentice asked, not meaning to sound as bitter as he did.

"It is," Whilte answered, undeterred. "You know as well as I do, Knight Commander, it was never the Almighty's intention for creatures like this to be used as weapons of war or as tools for tyranny. This beast's death was caused the day it was turned to battle. It has only taken this long to catch up to it."

Whilte had been present when Prentice was forced to slay the unicorn in order to free it from the Serpent Witch's gore-soaked control. Whether the chaplain felt the same sense of sadness or simply picked up on Prentice's emotions, it was clear he at least understood the knight commander's misgivings. Whilte stepped away to the wounded Fangs, following after his duties as healer. Prentice stared at the dead stag a moment longer, then shook his head. The battle was not yet done, and he had no time to be maudlin. Sheathing his sword, he took up his dropped salet and turned it over to see if it had been damaged in his fall. It looked serviceable and fitted back to his head readily. Knights and traditional men-at-arms wore hoods of cloth or mail, or else quilted arming caps, to help their helmets rest comfortably on their heads. The mass production needed to keep the Lions in armor meant that such comforts had been left to go by the board. He knew many of his militia wore scarves or wrapped rags around their heads, though in the heat of summer many simply chose to endure the steel, preferring hardness to warmth. Prentice himself had used a tree-sap glue to stick two wedges of folded leather into his helmet, a barely comfortable solution that hadn't mattered to him much because as commander, he often went bare-headed to see or be heard better on the field. It had been the irregularity of the little leather pads that had allowed his helmet to shift on his head when he landed on it.

"An arming cap," he told himself, deciding that it would have to be a priority when they returned from this campaign. If the archduchess had solved her coin problems by then, he would also press her to make such caps available to all the militia.

From below the ridgeline, the recognizable drumbeat of "hold ground" echoed upward, along with a haggard but throaty cheer of victory. Prentice reached the brink and looked down to see the Redlanders breaking and being driven away. Roar down at ground level joined their fire to their fellows' on the height to harry the painted spearmen deep into the night.

"Cease fire," came Guillam's bellowed command from along the ridgeline. As the senior Roarsman, he was the only officer Prentice had brought with him to the heights. "They're well out of range now. Enough wasting shot. This night's still got other business."

The gunners grounded their weapons and began the task of post-battle cleaning and servicing, while others headed back north to where Brother Whilte's mule had been tethered. Aside from carrying the chaplain, the pack animal's other duty for the night had been to bring heavy coils of rope. These would be tied to trees and fed down bluff to let men climb with more cables yet. The mule team and other animals would be fetched around by the north route, but the rest of the company would mount the cliff directly under the watchful protection of the Roar. The night would not be concluded until the entire company was united and camped on the heights. Pleased that everyone knew their duties and were attending to them, Prentice moved along to find Guillam. As he did, he also found Lyrach nearby. Saying nothing, he grabbed the ex-squire by his elbow and dragged him over in front of the corporal.

"Corporal Guillam," he shouted in his parade ground voice, and the man snapped to attention, clearly a little surprised despite his usual attitude. "I gave orders that my groom should remain with the animals. Can you explain to me what he is doing here, under your command and in the uniform of a line first?"

Guillam's eyes narrowed in suspicion, but it was a doubt backlit by mischief, and Prentice was reminded of Turley. The two men had a similarly insolent response to the world, but the corporal was not quite as carefree as Prentice's best friend.

"He asked," Guillam said simply. "And since one of them lead stones broke Halbot's neck a few nights back, we had the uniform going spare, so I give'd it him."

So akin to Turley did Guillam seem for a moment that it was almost all Prentice could do not to laugh. The uniform was not the point. Before he could say anything more, though, Lyrach stepped up and saluted him, then removed his helmet and tucked it into the crook of his arm the way a knight would.

"My Lord, Knight Commander Baron Ash, I must report that I have defied you," he said with a clear voice. Unlike

Guillam, Lyrach's expression was completely serious. "Also, I have deceived Corporal Guillam. After asking permission to see the dead Halbot's body, I took the man's uniform pieces and weapon and secreted myself amongst the Roar, all without the corporal's knowledge."

Prentice did not need to see the look of surprise on Guillam's face to know that was a lie. He looked back and forth between the two of them.

"Why?" he asked Lyrach.

"Seems he wanted to join the fight," Guillam said first, but Prentice held his hand up for quiet and kept his gaze fixed on Lyrach. This looked like the exact kind of adventurism that the knight commander had wanted to curb, but there was something about the way the younger militiaman was standing tall that gave Prentice hope of maybe more.

"You were ordered to watch over my horses," he told Lyrach. "To have left that behind is frank dereliction.

"It is, My Lord," Lyrach agreed, making no apology.

"And to wear another man's uniform? To take a rank that you have not earned? If a knight claimed rank he did not have, what would the punishment be, militiaman Lyrach? Do you know the typical sentence?"

"Execution by hanging, forfeit of all honors, rights, and rewards," Lyrach answered in a clear voice that quietly impressed Prentice. Lyrach was making no attempt to shade his actions or defend them. He was even working to take full responsibility, trying to shield Guillam from consequences, even though it was obvious the two of them had been acting together. It occurred to Prentice that in one sense, that alone was the most surprising and telling part of this whole unexpected affair. He gave Guillam a raised eyebrow, and the cocksure junior officer only shrugged.

"He *did* save your life," Guillam said, frowning thoughtfully, as if his only contribution to the conversation from now on was as an advisor. It was a point well made. Prentice looked down at the ground and sighed, making it look as if he was wrestling with the conundrum. In truth, he was testing Lyrach, letting the man have a chance to give in to his nerves or impatience, or else to show that he really had matured. The silence stretched on, Lyrach saying nothing, and Prentice finally found he had to nod, even though it pained his skull to do it. Looking up again, he flashed Guillam a wry grin.

"A *line first* of the Roar?" he asked, mostly rhetorically. Guillam answered anyway.

"Lad's a natural, if you can believe it, Commander," he said with a shrug. "Started to shoot with us only a little while ago, just as for merriment like, and now he's almost as good a shot as I am."

Lyrach coughed, his first gesture in the whole night to speak on his own behalf, and Guillam rolled his eyes.

"Alright, a hair's breadth better than me, if we're being all truth-telling," the corporal admitted. Prentice raised his eyebrows. That was as close to high praise as a man like Guillam would ever likely rise. The knight commander looked back to Lyrach, and his mind was almost made up. He just had one more question—the most important one, in fact.

"Why?" he asked Lyrach.

"I had to, My Lord," Lyrach answered readily. That was not going to be good enough for Prentice, but the ex-squire continued to explain. "They have been hounding us. Lions have died, others are injured. This was to be the telling battle, the ambush reversed. Everyone knew it, and you even said so yourself, My Lord."

Finally, Lyrach's disciplined reserve was being disrupted by a sense of emotion in his tone and manner. Even his posture reflected an earnest inner tension.

"I couldn't...I couldn't stand by and not fight," he said, real pain in his voice. "If we failed, if we were broken, then we would have had to turn and run. I couldn't leave another battlefield knowing I had left my friends...my brothers...to fight and die. Not without fighting myself, Knight Commander. I swear Boots and Dusty are well cared for. I made sure of that."

Now that he had begun to plead his case, Lyrach's words were pouring out. What impressed the knight commander was that in all of it, there was not even the shadow of a breath about glory, promotion, or even victory. Just loyalty. Prentice held up his hand for silence, and Lyrach managed to still his tongue, though it looked difficult for him.

"Alright, Lyrach, despite what privileges might accrue to that uniform, you will not be spared," he said, adopting a more formal tone useful for giving pronouncements. "Your latrine-digging duties are extended to the end of this campaign. You are going to be digging and burying filth for the whole company until we all set foot back in the Reach. Also, in the next few days you will find a suitable man for the task and begin teaching him the arts and skills of a groom. His performance will be your responsibility until he is ready to replace you."

"I am no longer to be your groom?" Lyrach asked, and finally a sense of regret appeared in him.

"Of course not," Prentice told him. "I am not going to waste a talented line first holding Boot's and Dusty's bridles. Now, go to."

Lyrach blinked, seeming frozen in disbelief.

"You heard the knight commander, Line First Lyrach!" Guillam bawled at him. "Find yourself a shovel and get us some slit trenches dug quick smart. I want that finished by sunup. And make sure you trim that long-match on your gun properly. A bad end doesn't always hold enough flame to light the powder right."

Lyrach saluted proudly and almost ran off to his punishment duty.

"He's a good lad, really, for someone who used to fancy himself becoming a knight," Guillam said readily.

"And you are an insubordinate bastard," Prentice told him quietly.

"Never denied it."

Guillam tipped his head and casually reached up to his beard, picking a bit of scorched powder from the bristles. Several of the hairs on his chin were well burned from repeated firings because the act of aiming his gun brought the trigger mechanism so close to his face. Impacted dots of powder, not to mention minor burns to chin and cheek, were a hazard of the Fangs' duty.

"Lions hunt in the pride?" Prentice repeated Lyrach's words from the battle. "Never alone in the field?"

Guillam nodded.

"That's how you explained it to us back in Fallenhill," Guillam said. "Made sense to me then and I shared it with him to explain the difference. Mates at your back, that's what you want. Knights, they're so used to climbing over each other for glory, they never fully watch out for their mates. Looks like once he got that clear in his head, it all just fell into its place for him. Was like that for me, too."

Prentice felt humbled to hear his own words repaid to him, not in anger or defiance but as received wisdom, precious for its proven effect. Guillam saluted and Prentice returned it. The corporal then moved away to supervise the men who were beginning the climb and hauling on the bluff.

The Gryphon Banner Company would be safe to rest a day by the time the sun came up.

CHAPTER 58

Amelia awoke in darkness to the sound of people's voices. Drowsily reaching up, she felt someone catch her wrist and hold it. Something rubbed against the back of her hand, like the bristles of a hairbrush, and Farringdon whispered something to her. It was hard to make out what he was saying.

"Some water...," she moaned, realizing that she felt very thirsty. Something was pressed to her lips, and she sipped at it. As she laid her head back, she realized that her eyes were still closed, and she smiled, falling back to sleep.

"He's young and hale, and by the looks the ribs have not pierced any of his innards," a woman with a croaky voice was saying. "You lot with your wars keep me on my toes. At least his coat of plates took the worst of it. You say he was hit by a flying board? Looks more like half a falling tree by the bruising. He's dashed lucky it didn't break his back."

The woman speaking sounded aged and very annoyed, and while Amelia realized she was speaking about Sedgemark and the piece of exploding bridge that has struck him in the back, she could not understand why the woman was so angry. Was she angry at Amelia?

Another woman spoke now, and Amelia tried to lift her head and open her eyes as she recognized Spindle's voice. A soft hand, different to the one that had caught her wrist, pressed down gently upon her forehead. Amelia tried to object but found the wetness against her lips again, and in her thirst, she sipped readily.

"This?" the old woman was saying. "Tincture of Lady's Flower. Aids in sleep to rest the mind."

Spindle said something indistinguishable.

"I already told you not to fret about that," said the old woman, sounding annoyed once more. "He took the brunt. The lady is bruised, fair enough, but no bones were broken, and there's no sign of bleeding within or ruptures. It's her mind that's fair troubled, not her flesh. She needs her rest."

Spindle objected earnestly and the woman made a surprised sound. The hand pressing on Amelia's forehead moved down to her abdomen, pushing in a number of places. Dully, as if somehow feeling her own flesh from a great distance, Amelia became aware that her back was sore. It did not worry her, though, and while she knew she did not like the pain, it was not too great.

"You're right," the old woman said, grunting with surprise. "You've a good eye. Maybe you missed your calling. Should've been a midwife."

Spindle said something else, but her voice grew suddenly distant, and Amelia realized she must be falling asleep yet again.

———◆———

There was the sound of water flowing and Amelia looked around to see she was standing on the banks of the Murr River, just west of the Aubrey bridge. The sky above was moonless, but the Rampart was a glittering white, and the whole land about her was lit with silver light, as on a night of a full moon.

Amelia knew this was a vision. It was not the first time she had had one, and while this was a kind she typically only had while dreaming—more ethereal and less natural to her mind—she did not feel sleepy. Indeed, she somehow recognized that for the first time in a long while, her mind was not clouded or dulled. Her toes felt cold, though, and she looked down to see that she was standing in the flattened reeds where Farringdon and the workmen had salvaged the broken piece of cannon. It looked like her feet were weighing the reeds down more heavily now and the water was seeping through from the bank beneath.

Nearby, Amelia began to hear the sounds of water being lapped up, as if by an animal, and she moved through the reeds and riverside fronds to find the mighty angel lion which she had seen in other dreams, head down, drinking from the flow. In the silvery light, the droplets of water that splashed from its tongue seemed to glisten especially brightly, as if being taken up by the angel. The water had acquired some part of the celestial being's glory, or else the angel was extracting something otherwise unseen from within the water itself. The creature lifted its head from the surface and shook its mane, the cloud of starlight-white hair billowing and scattering a fine spray of glistening droplets. Then, it turned to look at Amelia, and eyes that flashed golden and seemed deeper than the space between the stars stared into hers. Amelia did not feel afraid in its presence, not when it was like this. At other times in her dreams she had felt fearful, especially when the creature was enraged and doing battle with other mystical forces, but now she was quite relaxed in its presence. She was utterly certain that this being was a messenger from Almighty God, and the visions it brought to her, though sometimes terrifying, never proved false in the end. She had grown to value their guidance.

"Can you really, though?" she heard a voice whisper in her ear, and she turned to see a little dark-winged thrush perched upon her shoulder. It hopped about on one leg and sang a song that seemed too slow and mellow for a warbling bird. It's song formed words, and as it twittered, Amelia understood its questions and doubts. "You are in exile, lost again without the support you need. Silver have you none, loyal hounds are all fled from you, and your ladies are in happier marriages than yours. Should a proud archduchess be so poor in the things she deserves?"

Amelia found herself repeating the blue-feathered bird's words and wondering if they were not hers. After all, they were true, were they not? And what use were cryptic revelations now when her problems were not secret, but the only solutions were all beyond her? She was about to ask the angel lion, but as she turned from the bird, she saw that the awe-inspiring creature was already at her side. With a huff, it swatted at the little thrush, and it flittered away, just out of reach, although it did not seem like the lion was using its full power to strike. Its swat had seemed casual, almost perfunctory.

"Why chase it away?" Amelia asked, not sure she doubted its words. As she watched, the little bird flew up from the river, north, towards the hill where the cannons had been. In the manner of dreams, she did not lose sight of the creature, even as the distance grew, and she saw that it joined an odd flock of other birds, all mismatched, circling the crown that still smoked from the fire of the explosion. Amelia watched the flying birds, wondering if they were carrion eaters, feasting upon the slain gunners who were more dead men upon her conscience.

"Would you see?" the angel asked her, its voice rumbling like thunder heard at a distance. She nodded, not even looking away from the ruinous summit. The creature walked out over the river and Amelia followed. This was not the first time she had walked upon water in her dreams. The Murr was as dark as the Dwelt had been in other visions, but when she looked to her right, she could see the Aubrey bridge, its middle section seeming as if some monstrous river beast had risen up and taken a bite out of it. A long gap was missing, with only a few broken remnants of the stone footings poking through the river like the smashed teeth of a defeated pugilist. As she saw, she wondered if the Reach even possessed the masons and carpenters necessary to repair it. For its part, the angel lion seemed supremely indifferent to the wreckage, only leading the way across the water, through the reeds on the other side, and up the hill.

As she climbed, Amelia noticed two things at once, and both made her sick in her stomach. The first was the smell of burned iron and gunpowder smoke, the lingering stench of the furious explosion. She twisted her nose against the stink and felt her teeth clench in anger. The other thing she noticed was just how many different types of birds there were in the circling flight above. She saw ravens and gulls, thrushes and parrots, even peacocks and others she could not name. The angel led her around the hill, following the same path upward that existed in the waking world. As they passed the secondary ridge, she looked down to see the bulwark Farringdon had ordered on the day, and there were her battlewagons, abandoned, with militia bodies strewn upon them.

More guilt for her soul.

Beyond the bulwark, down on the field, she could see bodies of horses and riders, knowing them to be the dead of Farringdon's lancers. Amongst them a pack of hounds circled, licking at the blood of the slain, as well as their own wounds.

"Robant," she said and the hatred in her voice surprised her, not because she did not expect to have such an emotion but because of its intensity. It was like hearing sounds while under the water and then hearing them anew after breasting the surface. The hate was not fresh, but she was recognizing it afresh.

"More than half are mere pups," the lion said without stopping, and as she looked once more to the field, Amelia realized it was true. So many of the hounds she could see were not fully grown. "The leaders of the pack are so many slain, and the newborns are rising to the hunt too unready."

THE MANTIS AND THE MIRRORED SKY

Amelia wanted to ask what that cryptic pronouncement meant, but the angel had led her to the very summit of the hill, and she looked on it with horror. Even in the unearthly, silvery light, she could see the ground was blasted black, so that the very earth was stained by the event. Would any amount of rain and spring growth cleanse the awfulness of this place?

"Why did God punish me like this?" she asked the angel, feeling resentful that no vision was given earlier to turn her from this course. If the Almighty so loathed her engines of war, why had no prophet, no wise man or sacrist come with a single warning? Even a penny prophet shouting in her town's streets might have penetrated to her heart with a caution. Or the angel itself could have come. "Why did you let this happen to me?"

"Did it happen to *you*?" the lion asked mildly, though the rebuke in its words was unmistakable. It looked over the hilltop, and Amelia followed its gaze to see the slain. She could not pick Yentow Sent's body from the others, but the dead were there, burned by flame, torn and cut by shrapnel, and ripped apart by the pure force of the blast.

"I bear the guilt," she whispered, and the lion rumbled disapprovingly. From the flock above, a single raven swooped down, an oddly grey, sickly creature. It dropped to the ground in front of the archduchess and began to hop back and forth.

"Guilty. Guilty are you," it croaked tauntingly. "No love of God for you. No love. Guilty. Guilty."

Amelia felt tears streaking down her face, certain that because of her hubris, all this mockery was deserved.

"Hmmph, ravens," the angel muttered. "They who once fed the prophets at His command now eat the words of Truth and grow fat. The sweet words will turn bitter in their stomachs and their fatness will make them slow when the day of wrath comes. They will not be able to fly away from the judgement."

And what is that supposed to mean? Amelia thought bitterly. She was about to demand an explanation from the celestial messenger, wanting answers to her problems and guidance away from her pain. Before she could, though, the angel lifted its head and spoke to the flock above.

"Reveal yourselves," it commanded, and the power of its voice caused the birds to break in their circling flight as if buffeted by a storm wind. Amelia remembered the story Prentice told of how the angel had loaned him its voice during his confrontation with the Serpent Witch at the end of the drought. She had never quite understood what he meant, but if he had wielded this authority, even for one word, against the fallen Sir Haravind, then she could see how the Serpent Witch had been driven away. Amelia was only standing next to this creature, and its command had almost driven her to her knees. In front of her, the mocking raven fell flat, its wings splayed on the ground, and its song became a croak.

"Lies," its voice said weakly. "Heralds for liars, loaned to a sickly eagle. Starved and dying are both we and our eagle."

A "sickly eagle" is Daven Marcus, Amelia thought, recognizing *that* image at least.

From within the flock, a vulture-headed peacock rose from the others and announced itself with a proud screech before flying with impossible swiftness away to the west. Amelia watched it go until it was out of sight. She wondered at that, thinking that it surely represented nothing she could name. In previous visions, the peacock had stood for Bluebird, the minstrel and Inquisition agent, but he was no longer in the Western Reach so far as anyone knew, was he? Before she could ask about it, Amelia heard an echoing sound from the far west, a cry that was at once the roar of a lion and the hunting call of a hawk.

Prentice's gryphon? Amelia thought, and she was horrified as the peacock returned from the west, carrying an odd tuft of fur in its beak. Was that from Prentice? A trophy? Was her faithful knight commander dead in the far west? She had thought Prentice slain for a time last summer, and it had broken her household's hearts. Was this a warning to prepare to grieve in truth this time? The peacock swept in a wide circle around the hill, and as it did, the hounds at the foot of the hill all took to howling. Then, as the bird flew away to the northeast, the pack loped after her, the puppies and young dogs leading the way.

Another bird dropped from the flock, so plump and short-winged that Amelia wondered how it could have flown at all. It began to stalk about the hilltop, moving amongst the bodies.

"Falser am I than even the raven," it sang in the bluebird's voice, but after it had begun, the voice changed, seeming to have a different accent, and then another. The tone continued to shift, sounding as if it spoke from many heritages, as both man and woman, even sometimes as a child. If it was false, as its song proclaimed, then which of those voices was true, or were they all lies?

"Come see my work," it called with its many-toned song. Amelia looked to the angel for confirmation and the celestial nodded its head. She walked the short distance through the carnage to the strange, fat bird. As she approached, it flicked its tail, which was shaped almost like a harp, with some straight feathers and some curved, all projecting upward behind it and waving about proudly. The bird stood beside one body, and for a moment that body was alive and whole again. Horror and hope mixed equally in Amelia at the sight.

"I am slain," the body said, eyes staring straight into the sky. The odd bird bent down and pecked once at the living corpse's neck, and with a new flow of blood, the man died once more.

"Mine now," the bird said, and it spoke with the dead man's voice. It turned to Amelia. "Come and see what you do not know. See what I have done under your eyes, unseen while you watched."

It strutted away a short distance and found something else half buried in the scorched and battered earth, like an animal's body made of iron. The multi-voiced bird tapped its beak on the metal—not a harmonic ring, as of a bell or gong, but a dull, unmelodic tink. The metal rose up from the earth, revealing itself to be in the shape of a lion but fashioned entirely from black iron. It was no living thing, like her militia or lady bodyguards. In all her dreams, they had been white lions, like the angel but less fine. This was just a lifeless construct. The dirt dropped away from the metallic beast, and it stood, still as a statue, mouth open in a lifeless roar.

A lion of metal? My cannons? Amelia wondered. Was this strange bird the instrument of God's vengeance? Was this part of the vision a revelation about the pronouncement? How could that be if the strange bird was "false" as it claimed? God was not false.

As she watched, the bird strutted around the iron statue, studying it like a professional craftsman. It bent down, and in one swift motion, pecked out a section of the lion's throat, spitting that piece of metal away. Then it bowed to the ground and seized up one of the pieces of the shrapnel there. It placed the jagged scrap into the gap in the creature's throat where it sat, obviously out of place. The bird waved its wing over the site and the piece suddenly fitted perfectly. When she looked closely, Amelia could just make out the seams where the foreign part was, but otherwise, it was indistinguishable.

"Unseen, unseen, too clever," the bird sang, and Amelia suddenly noticed that others of its kind had joined it, all of them singing together in their multi-tonal voices. "Too clever for him. Clever stupid, not so clever now."

They looked at the recognisable corpse of Yentow Sent, now seen lying nearby, and Amelia felt a rising disgust at their behavior. The Masnian smith had been an arrogant and prickly man, but he did not deserve such scorn, especially not in death. It seemed the angel felt the same, for it intervened with a firm voice.

"Enough," it commanded, and the birds fell silent at once, like chastised children. "Go to, frauds. Others will find you out and pluck your wings."

Almost petulantly, the birds turned away and strutted from the hilltop. Amelia wondered where they were going and what further evil they might do before their wings were "plucked." The ironwork lion collapsed as they left, falling into shrapnel. Men appeared, coming up the hill wearing leather aprons and bare feet, to collect the fallen pieces. They were astonishing to Amelia, though not because of their appearance. In all respects they were like most other craftsmen found in any part of the world. It was because they were mere folk, not symbolic animals or celestial creatures. She almost never saw mortals in dreams like this. They carried away the fallen pieces, and as they did, one of them paused to tug his forelock to her like any loyal yeoman of the Reach would do. On his shoulder she could see that the part of the lion he carried included the false piece, still fitted neatly at the seams.

"When you wake, follow the workmen," the angel lion told her as the men hauled away the wreckage, leaving her alone on the hilltop with the celestial messenger. "They will give you the key that will unlock the cage of lies about you."

Amelia nodded and looked down at the dead around her. The angel began to move away, and she sensed the dream was ending. Still, she felt dissatisfied, resentful that these folk had had to die in her service.

"Why could I not receive this warning earlier?" she demanded, ignoring the cautionary fear she felt at her own impertinence. How did one challenge a being like this and not be afraid? If its wrath fell upon her, she would be dead in an instant. Still, she resolved to have her question answered.

"Why?" the lion asked her back.

"That their lives might be spared."

"Of all men that have lived, few, if any, will not taste death."

Amelia was surprised and annoyed by that answer. In one sense it was true, but in another it completely missed her point.

"Why did they have to taste it at my table?" she demanded, using the same metaphor.

"Is it your table?" the angel asked, and again Amelia was taken aback. "Just because you have been allowed to extend invitations to your own guests does not make you hostess of the feast."

That made a kind of sense as well, but still Amelia was troubled. Her annoyance though, gave way to a deeper pain.

"Deaths like this taste bitter. Iron is an ugly taste in my mouth, in my flesh. Why was it allowed?"

"Because nails in the flesh are no defeat when resurrection is the victory."

"I cannot resurrect anyone," Amelia protested, still not relinquishing her sense of responsibility for the dead around her.

"No," the angel agreed. "But the one who can, will. Until he does, all the dishes of the feast, sweet and bitter, must be served. And all must eat their share. Drink the wine and find the workmen. They will give you the key. Then all you must do is unlock the cage for yourself."

The lion was already walking away down the impossible south side of the hill. Frustrated and losing her temper, Amelia tried to follow it, but as she stepped over the edge, she lost her footing and tumbled downward to lie uncomfortably amongst reeds on the ground. Everything was dark and she tried to lift her head. It ached, though not as badly as she would have expected from such a fall. Then she felt someone holding her near the nape of her neck, taking the weight and relieving the pain.

"Drink this, lovey," the old woman's voice said, and Amelia felt a cup pressed to her lips. She sipped watered wine and opened her eyes, only to blink painfully against the light of a new morning, even through the canvass of a tent's sides. "This'll help you awake a little. Time to see if we can get you moving again."

"How long have I been asleep?" she asked.

CHAPTER 59

The Gryphon Banner Company rested that one morning just back from the ridge, then marched after noon as they had before. Prentice warned them that this would be the last half day of marching from then on. Victory over the ambush had cost the company twenty-three dead and forty with various wounds, most of whom could still walk once Brother Whilte had seen to them, and Prentice took the main of that last morning's rest considering what was best for those wounded. In any other campaign, they would be left back, either sent home or ordered to make camp and await the company's return. There was no possible way they would be safe enough to be left by themselves in this hostile land though, and detaching enough hale militiamen to defend them would fatally weaken the rest of his force. In the end he decided to divide the mule team's remaining supplies between the healthy, every man carrying a sack, a barrel, something. Then slings were rigged to poles tied to the mules, easily cut from the abundant deadwood, and the wounded who could not walk were carried in those.

"We could make rafts and float them along the river," Sergeant Gennet suggested.

If only we had the time, Prentice thought, shaking his head.

"We have to put distance between us and the river," he told them. "No more following the flow so closely where the will-o'-the-wisps can track our movements and the *imzuss* can send ambushers amongst us easily."

"Didn't seem like them bloody deers come from the river," Corporal Porth said. "Nor them slingstone flingers."

"No, perhaps not," Prentice agreed. "But the Redlanders did. We smashed most of their chariots, but even if they have more, these hills will not favor them." He turned his head to look west and upward at the towering slopes not too many leagues away. "We will find flat tops to camp upon each night and give them a hedge of pike and shot to come through if they want to harry us. I am afraid the nights of few sentinels are over. Everyone will be serving at least half the dark on watch duty."

"Won't take long for that to get tough on even the healthy," Gennet warned. "Especially marching in hills."

"Then pray we do not have to do it for too many days," Prentice told them, and that was the last he wanted to discuss it. In the back of his mind, he had always known the moment would have to come when his race westward would face the ascent into the mountains. Time and again he had thought to want for Jannomoch's boats, to have somehow brought them up onto the high plain and to travel the river at speed. If they had, it might have even been possible to ignore the rising slopes almost completely. After all, he had seen the fey lake and the Murr flowing out of it. It was broad and navigable right from the headwaters, and every sign was that the ancient upland fey culture had used boats to travel their entire land from that lake all the way down to the scarp over Radengon-Beyond-Dwelt. Even if they could have taken them up the escarpment quickly, though, boats on the river would have made perfect targets for the slingers. And as it turned out, there was the second ridge and falls, another barrier to terminally delay riverboats.

So, here they were faced with the most unjustifiably optimistic part of their campaign—a headlong drive into an upland territory against a foe who knew the lay of the land under an unknown time limit. By any reasonable measure, it was a recipe for disaster. If they had the Azure Mountain fey with them, as he had originally intended, Prentice was sure they would have had a much more even chance. Nonetheless, they had come too far to turn back now, and even if they did, they would be fleeing toward a Reach that was far distant and still in as much danger as when they left, or perhaps conquered already.

Remember when all you wanted was to catch Inxyphos? Prentice asked himself, smiling bitterly as the company began to climb into the foothills. *Or even just the Serpent Witch?*

Just how many enemies did they have waiting at the end of this march?

They camped on a hilltop as planned, and at dawn a few scouts went to fetch water while others ranged ahead, searching for parallel pathways west. An uncomfortable morning's walk on steepening slopes turned up something unexpected—the first tributary to the Murr they had found since coming to the drought-cursed land. No more than a thin stream, it trickled down a cliff face from one of the vanguard heights of the mountain range, across a hill slope, and into the river. Where it ran, no grass or tree grew, though. It was the first of a number like that.

Toward evening they came across another spring that would be deep enough to cover their feet if they stood in it. It flowed down such a minor height that Prentice set men to see if they could use it to refresh waterskins without having to go to the river that night. When some followed it to the summit, they discovered the remains of a fey settlement all but hidden around a rock pool just under the crest. It was exactly the kind of place where fey would be expected to make a hamlet, and the water in the pool was surprisingly deep and fresh, likely fed by a mountain spring. Prentice diverted the entire company in that direction to make the ancient village into their next night's camp. Even as the main of the force was climbing to the hamlet, two lines were sent into the little pod-like huts to ensure they were empty and not a hiding place for another lurking ambush. Like the ones Prentice had seen by the side of the dragonfly lake and up its cliffs, these huts clung to the rock faces around the pool, although not to any height. They looked to have been grown in place the same as the others, as if they were the husks of the seeds of some enormous climbing vine. The scouts found no danger within, but when he arrived, Solft immediately begged leave to investigate the dwellings, fascinated by any aspect of fey culture, whether native to the Azures or this far mountain range. Once he had permission, the scholar departed with a lit oil lantern and Prentice did not see him again for hours.

How much oil do we still have? was all the knight commander thought to wonder. Military matters were the whole of his mind's concerns for now. In fact, he was sure he would have less and less time for intellectual diversions until they had reached the lake and done what they came to do.

"And that is what, exactly?" he muttered as he chewed some gristly mule meat and washed it down with mountain water. He stared into the little flames of a tiny campfire set just for him a little apart from the others. When the archduchess had raised him to a baron, Prentice feared that his men would grow to resent him, seeing him as one of the tyrants who made a yeoman's life miserable. Now, as their long march was nearing its end, his men were indeed keeping their distance from him. Until now, he had hardly noticed, but in this much more enclosed space it was almost obvious. There were occasional, surreptitious glances and conversations kept quiet. Were they afraid he had led them to their end? The food situation was not yet dire, but it was possible they were already eating into their supplies for the return journey. When the time came to fight, they would have to win and capture supplies or else possibly risk going hungry on the return march.

"We've got sentries up on those rocks above us like you ordered, My Lord," Gennet said as he approached through the close camp. Brother Whilte was with him.

"Good man," Prentice told him. "Last thing we want is for the fey to sneak slingers up there and rain more leaden hail down on our heads."

Gennet agreed with a nod. Prentice bent down to pick up two cups from beside his fire, offering one each to sergeant and chaplain, then bent again for his own.

"Just the spring water," he apologized to them. Gennet raised his cup to the knight commander. Toasting with water was supposed to be ill luck, but Prentice raised his cup in return, nonetheless. Whilte joined them, giving Prentice a knowing glance. He was surely aware of the superstition as well.

"Everyone is nervous, I take it?" Prentice asked and the sergeant looked down into his cup, nodding grimly. Whilte was somber as well. "They did not swear on for this?"

Gennet stayed silent, and Prentice did not blame him. He was a loyal man, and pressing him like this was asking him if there was mutiny brewing. No faithful man-at-arms even liked to imagine such things.

"Things are not too dire," Whilte said noncommittally.

"We swore on to march and fight," Gennet said at last. "In return, you swore to feed us, pay us, and point us at your enemies' weaknesses, not into their jaws. I don't think any of us imagined we'd be marching this far, but you haven't pointed us wrong yet, My Lord Knight Commander. We all know that."

"You know I am not as sure of my target this time."

"Well, don't tell anyone else," Whilte said with a stern face but an amused gleam in his eyes. "We're following the glorious Baron Ash, Defender of the Reach. Where his road leads, that's the way we go."

"And what if it goes nowhere?"

"Then don't tell us," Gennet said, still not looking up from his cup. "All honor due, Knight Commander, we don't care. Where and why, that's your duty, and we need you to shoulder it. It's more than we want and more than we can bear. We've got our own burdens to carry."

"Have a care, Sergeant," Whilte said in a tone that urged caution, but Prentice was glad of Gennet's bluntness. The truth was, it *was* his burden to bear. His men did not need to know of his doubts or his certainties either. Making them carry his fears was as great a dereliction on Prentice's part as a sentry who fell asleep at his post.

"You are right, Sergeant Gennet. Thank you," Prentice told him sincerely. He let the matter drop then, and after a period of silence, Gennet drained his cup and returned it.

"I'll go to my evening's rest, with your permission," he said, saluting, and Prentice dismissed him with a salute in return.

"'Lonely is the head that wears a crown?'" Whilte intoned softly once Gennet was out of hearing.

"You keep reciting poetry like that, and I will have you tied to a tree," Prentice said. "See how lonely you feel when we leave you here."

"I am never alone," Whilte answered with prayer-like solemnity, even though his smile never wavered in his eyes. "The spirit of the one true God is ever with me."

"Lucky you," Prentice said, more bitterly than he meant. Whilte's expression gentled. He put a brotherly hand on the knight commander's shoulder.

"He is with you, too. You know that? As you are lord and commander over all these, so He is over you, if you let him."

Prentice nodded.

"You are not convinced?" the chaplain pressed.

"I marched us out here, mind focused on our duty alone. Cut the foe or break on his armor, like any mere blade. But I think I never fully understood how far we had to come and what a distance of this kind, accursed and ancient, could truly be like. Have I led us out here to merely fail and die far from home?"

"This *is* home, Prentice."

Prentice stared at Whilte as if the man had suddenly regrown his lost leg and started to jig and reel. The chaplain snorted, as if he had to choke back a guffaw.

"You should see yourself," he said, and Prentice found his good humor infectious. The commander smiled, though thinly. The chaplain went on to explain himself. "No, not here in these hills. This is not home. This is enemy country if ever a place could be called such. But the Gryphon, your company, *this* is home for more of us than you can imagine."

Even that explanation caused Prentice to shake his head in wonder again. Whilte was not finished.

"You doubt me? Think back, then, to what it was like when you were convicted. When they transported you across the mountains to die. You've told me little enough of that time, but I hazard I can guess some as well. You felt cast off, discarded by all righteous society, and alone amidst monsters. Hatred was all about you, from the highest to the lowest, and even the ones who were like you loathed you because they loathed themselves. You waited for death and only wished that it would come with the mercy of swiftness. Am I not right?"

Prentice nodded grimly. Whilte's insight was astute.

"How many of these around you felt the same, do you think?"

"More than a few, I would say," Prentice said, considering it.

"And you would be right. From what I've seen and heard, more than half of your Gryphon Banner Company is made up of ex-convicts. Not since the days of Fallenhill has a company of the White Lions had such a majority of the convicted."

Whilte stopped and looked Prentice in the eyes. Prentice could tell the chaplain was looking to see if his words were having the desired impact.

"I do not understand your point," Prentice told him, "unless it is to remind me how lowly we have all been."

"My point is, My Lord Knight Commander," Whilte said, frowning, "that you have made a place for such men, and they are not what they once were. I just want you to see..."

He paused and looked into the night sky, mostly crowded out by the protective rock face around the village cleft. Then he shook his head.

"When we marched with Prince Mercad and the then-duchess made you captain of the rogues, you made a speech on a barrel on a night like this."

"How do you know that?" Prentice asked. He had given that speech to convicts in the dark before dawn while the rest of the army had prepared for glorious battle.

"We used to watch you for the amusement of it," Whilte confessed guiltily. "Lord Ironworth had let it be known he wanted you left to whatever commands your lady liege had given you, but that didn't mean we couldn't have a squire or page spy upon you and tell us the tales so we could laugh at you around our warming fires while you slept in the open, in fetters and chains."

Prentice could well imagine the contempt the knights on that march had felt for the convict "captain" of the rogues 'foot. It might have infuriated him once, but it seemed so long ago now. He had risen far from that lowly day, and many of those who laughed at him were doubtless dead. Hating men already in their graves was pointless.

Whilte continued the story. "In that speech, you offered men a chance to do their morning's business or else do it on the march, like pack animals, walking in their own filth. We laughed over our own breakfasts that morning, but you were wiser than us all. You gave worthless, powerless men a sense that they yet had some strength to exert, even if just to pick where they did their leavings."

Prentice remembered explaining exactly that to Turley, years before, as he had reached for any little thing to extend his charges' odds of survival. It had done too few of them any good, to his mind. Whilte saw it differently, it seemed.

"You don't know all the stories that are told, Prentice, nor should you. Legends take care of themselves. Only vain popinjays like Baron Liam or Sir Whilte, the self-impor-tant-Church-knight-in-need-of-humbling care what others say about them behind their backs. But every one of those stories tells of one thing. You make men around you stronger. You take wretched scrap iron and sprinkle whatever you can into the forging, the secret dusts that only the master smiths know that turn iron into fine steel. Gennet, Guillam, Lyrach, and almost every other man here, Knight Commander. They all count themselves better men because of you. They don't march as rogues on the chain but because you are at their head. They'll walk to exhaustion and fight to the death just for the privilege to fall under your banner. Trust yourself to God as they have trusted themselves to you. The Lions are their home, and you have given that to them."

"My home is with Righteous and my child," Prentice said quietly, not arguing, but wanting to be honest.

"Rightly so," Whilte responded. "And there again, do you think Cutter the rape victim ever imagined she would be Lady Righteous, Baroness Fallenhill, mother of a beloved child?"

Prentice smiled at that. Whilte's encouragement was lifting his spirits in spite of himself. He whispered an inward prayer of thanks for the chaplain's knowledge of his own art.

"You are a gifted man, Brother Whilte," Prentice said.

The chaplain nodded, accepting the compliment.

"In the meantime, I must rest, Brother. All the faith in me in the world will not save us if I do not get at least some sleep.

"You might be surprised," Whilte said, clearly having returned to being contrary rather than actually sermonizing. "But since we are speaking of the meantime, I have one last request. Several of the men have come to me, asking for baptism. It seems they have never been taken properly to church, and they are wanting to fill the absence."

"Because they are not afraid at all of dying under my banner," Prentice mocked gently.

"Oh no, that's exactly what they're afraid of," Whilte returned. "Or more specifically, while they don't mind if it happens, they just don't want it to happen here in a fight with demonic forces without the guarantee that the Lord will keep their souls from the devil's grasp in the afterlife."

"Is that the purpose of baptism?"

"Not precisely," said the chaplain. "Nevertheless, I think they are sincere, and I will not deny them because their theology might not pass a sacrist's scrutiny. So, with your permission, I'll use the water here in the morning. We'll be done by the time you're ready for us to march, I promise."

"Then I will not deny them either, Chaplain," Prentice said.

Whilte tugged his forelock and withdrew, prophet's rod and wooden leg clomping away. Prentice smiled and sank to the uncannily parched ground, only paces away from a source of fresh water. He sat cross-legged, thinking to watch the fire for a time to let his mind relax. He suspected he would be unable to sleep much but at least hoped for some kind of rest. When he heard his name called later, he opened his eyes, surprised to find that the sky was lightening to dawn and he was lying flat on the ground, his cheek gritty with dust.

CHAPTER 60

"Lord Commander! Knight Commander Ash. Call for the commander."

Blinking, Prentice thrust himself upright as his injured shoulder flared in protest. He had fallen asleep in his brigandine, a foolish mistake, and now his exhausted flesh had the additional burden of having spent hours in awkward positions.

"Oh Lord," he groaned and tried to stretch his limbs. Before he could do himself much good however, a Claw militiaman ran up with a fearful expression and saluted.

"Please you, Lord Commander, you must come at once."

"Are we attacked? From which direction?" Prentice asked as he pointed for the messenger to lead him wherever he was needed. The man shook his head, and Prentice realized there was no sound of matchlock fire or the shouts of men being arranged into defensive positions.

"Not an attack," the messenger said, "but it's something...something mighty weirdly."

"Mighty weirdly"?

Prentice could only wonder what that might mean, and he was surprised that the runner led him no more than three dozen paces to the rock pool's edge. There was a crowd of militia gathered there, four of them stripped to their smallclothes, whom Prentice assumed were Whilte's baptismal supplicants. Everyone was looking at the water, and Prentice pushed his way through the crowd to see Whilte seated in the pool, the water only just reaching his waist. The chaplain must have been sitting upon a submerged rock so much of his body was above the surface. The religious man looked as if he were deep in thought, his one hand resting on his staff upright in the water while his eyes stared into the middle distance. As he looked closer, Prentice could see Whilte's eyelids were fluttering, like a man having a seizure, and his jaw was slack.

"What happened?" Prentice demanded of no one in particular, then looked about and noticed Corporal Porth amongst the unnerved gawkers. The older officer looked to his right and Prentice saw that Master Solft was amongst the crowd as well. The scholar's eyes were wide with horror, his expression a tortured mix of fear and guilt as he tugged his forelock.

"I only asked him to look for me," Solft said.

"Look at what?" Prentice demanded sternly, feeling a strong concern for the religious man he was growing to consider a close friend.

"The plinth, the stone beneath the water," Solft explained, pointing to where Whilte was sitting. "He was already in the water and the baptisms hadn't begun. You've no idea how little I've found to inform us, My Lord. I thought there might be writings in the huts—something—but nothing."

"Never mind the damned huts!" Prentice cursed. "What about this rock?"

Solft nodded apologetically.

"I thought I saw it under the water when the baptizers came with their lanterns," he said. "I just asked the chaplain if he could see what it was. He moved over and said it was a stone block, squared off, but with a rough top. I asked if it could be a plinth, like the one the other obelisk stood on back in the Radengon water. He said yes and I...I..."

Solft choked off with a guilty sob. The Lions around him regarded him with borderline contempt. One of the stripped men took up the story with a cold tone.

"He asked the chaplain if there was any writin's like, carvin', what-have-you. Brother Whilte said he couldn't see none and then this milksop asks if he can feel any. The chaplain leans on his rod, using his free hand under the water, and then he just stopped, like. Big breath out, as if he was goin' to make a dive underneath, but he just settled down to sit like this, his eyes gone all mad and his breathin' like he's been runnin' for leagues."

Prentice noticed that Whilte did seem to be breathing strangely. Not gasping exactly, but drawing in air in long sips, like a man trying to calm himself after a heavy exertion.

"And no one has tried to pull him out?" Prentice asked.

"I warned 'em not to, Lord Commander" Corporal Porth said. "Not 'til you were fetched. 'Cept for the scholar here, you're our most learned man, and since he's part reason for the whole problem, I kenned you'd want to have a say 'fore anything else was done. If it looked like the chaplain were gettin' worse ere you got here, I'd have ordered somethin' done."

Prentice nodded his approval at Porth and looked back to Whilte. Whatever was happening, it clearly had possession of the chaplain's mind. Given what little had been gleaned about the magick of the waters, he had no idea if this was because of the *imzuss,* the serpent women coven, mantis sorcery, the fey, or indeed some other power native to this spring and disturbed by their presence. He felt a momentary annoyance at Whilte for taking a risk like this but then realized what a hypocrite that made him. It was no worse than the risk he had taken when he salvaged the iron mantis mask. Indeed, Prentice's survival then would have been a reasonable cause for the chaplain to think this broken chunk of masonry was much less of a threat.

Someone must get him off that rock, Prentice thought, watching the chaplain's calm face and disturbed, trembling eyes. His first instinct was to go himself, as it had been at the obelisk under the scarp, but he remembered his conversation with Whilte the night before. These men marched under his banner, and it was his duty to lead them well and get them home. If both he and

Whilte were taken by whatever power this was, how was *that* leadership? Prentice turned to Porth and the runner who had called him originally.

"Go fetch some rope," he told the militiaman. To the corporal he said, "I survived last time, and odds are I will be alright this time as well. If this does go awry though, tell Sergeant Gennet that the company's only quest is to return safely to the Reach. The archduchess will send a greater force later, if needs be, but no one is to march a step further west without my command. Understand?"

Porth clearly had no idea exactly why Prentice was giving these orders, but he saluted, and the knight commander was content that they would be passed along without error. He began to unbuckle his brigandine and detach the other pieces of his armor, doing his best to suppress the groans his aching flesh wanted him to make. By the time he was down to his breeks, rope had arrived, and he tied it around his chest, under his arms.

"If I start to go...like that..." he said, pointing to Whilte, "Then pull me out straight away, understand?"

It seemed a ridiculous instruction from one perspective. The stone Whilte sat upon was barely five paces from the shore. Except that they might tip the insensible man face down into the water if they slipped or cut him with the edges, they could probably fish him out with the back spikes of their halberds. Barefoot on the dusty ground that should have been moist at the edge of a pool like this, Prentice touched his finger to the side of his nose, as if acknowledging a joke no one had told, and stepped into the water. It was deliciously cool. Sweat and dirt he had not even realized was caking his feet sluiced off readily.

Perfect water for a baptism, he thought and shook his head. It took three more steps and he was staring straight into Whilte's face, barely up to his knees in the refreshing pool. He bent down, listening to the chaplain's breathing and watching for any sign of recognition. There was none. Whilte's troubled eyes were barely open, and if they could see anything, it was another place far beyond his knight commander's presence. Prentice reached out one hand but slipped a little on the rocks under the water.

"Watch out, Baron," Solft called earnestly and several of the tension-filled men around him groaned in annoyance. Prentice did not find the scholar too distracting, but he understood the men's exasperation.

He reached out again, this time for Whilte's rod, Prentice's own old partisan, to use it as a balance before he tried to pull the chaplain's weight off the stone. As soon as his fingers circled the wood, Whilte's eyes snapped open, his pupils wide, like a man desperate for a single spark in deep darkness.

"Noon today," the chaplain declared earnestly. "Then noon of two more days. Then will be the midnight new moon and the sky once more can be opened. The fleet swarms at dawn the next morning."

After speaking these words, the chaplain fell forward, collapsing into Prentice's arms.

"Pull them out," Porth commanded, and the rope started to go taught.

"Never mind," Prentice shouted back, "I have him. I will bring him out."

With that, he drew up Whilte's full weight from sitting and half dragged him toward the shore. The chaplain was clearly groggy but not insensible, and by the time they left the water, Whilte was working to keep his feet under him. Then, he seemed to come more fully awake still and grabbed at Prentice.

"I saw it!" he all but shouted. "The truth. The truth of these waters."

"What is it?" Solft interjected before Prentice could ask, his concern almost immediately washed away by a hope for new discovery.

"These springs are from God," the chaplain answered readily. "All through these mountains. Folk fled here when the mountain was flung into the sea and the waters were turned to wormwood. God gave fresh springs so that not all would drink the poison water and die. That is why there is so much power in these waters and why the Redlander curse cannot banish it with drought, only suppress its life-giving. Even the obelisks are not as old or as potent as the waters themselves."

Prentice supposed that made a kind of sense, though he mostly had to wonder from where this new revelation had come. Had Whilte seen a true vision from God? When Prentice himself had been in the vision in the water and had spoken in defiance of the mantis and serpent coven, it had been as a prayer to the Almighty. Perhaps it had also somehow touched upon the power that dwelled in the waters themselves. He knew he had no magick or holiness of his own to use, so it could easily have been the power of the lake or springs like these, assuming Whilte was correct.

"There's more," the chaplain continued, showing no doubt in what his time under the broken stone's sway had revealed. "Even the fey don't remember how to enter the water as easily as you did in Radengon. They have to use the obelisks, the dragonfly perches, to move in the water or open the sky to other waters, and the Redlanders must shed blood over and above that. Large magicks, like moving many boats or many folk, can only happen at key times, such as after a binding of a new moon."

"Is that why you said the fleet swarms after a new moon?" Solft asked, but Whilte looked confused.

"What fleet? What swarm?" he asked.

"You spoke of a fleet and a new moon," Prentice explained. "As well as some other times."

"I don't remember any of that," Whilte said. Prentice accepted the chaplain's words for now and looked him up and down.

"How do you feel?" he asked.

"Fine, but there's something else I need to tell you, a secret unknown to the fey or the Redlanders."

A secret? Prentice wondered, and he reflexively held up his hand for Whilte to stop speaking. He looked to Porth.

"Everyone to their duties, Corporal," he said sternly. "We still have to march today." He looked at the undressed men who had hoped to be baptized. "Not this morning, goodmen. Perhaps another day."

If they were disappointed by the delay to their religious commitment, the men did not say anything. Prentice waited a long moment until all the others had moved off, although Solft remained without asking permission. The knight commander considered dismissing him as well but knew that would only be out of petulance. Whatever secret Whilte had to reveal, the scholar's opinion would likely be useful, if not necessary. Prentice turned to Whilte.

"Now, what is this secret?" he asked quietly.

CHAPTER 61

"A little bit more, Your Grace, and I think we'll have it fitted proper...sorry, proper*ly*."

Amelia stood with her arms out as Spindle sewed the last fitting-stitches into place on her new dress. The fine blue and silver lioness dress that had been the archduchess's pride and joy had become so filthy, not to mention damaged, that the seamstress had insisted upon replacing it. As Amelia recuperated, Spindle had created two underdresses from simple linen. However, since the cloths the lady-in-waiting had brought from the south were lost with the evacuated camp across the Murr, she had been forced to be truly creative with the overdress.

"Where did you say these colors came from?" Amelia asked as she looked at herself. The dress she was wearing was predominantly yellow and red, two colors she did not typically wear, but that was only the beginning. It seemed that wherever the cloths had been located, Spindle had been forced to make do with many mismatching pieces, so that one set of panels in the overdress were olive green, while another piece around the collar was classic Reacher cream. "I feel like I'm wrapped in the banners of a dozen noble houses. I look like an army on the march."

"I suppose you do some, Your Grace," Spindle agreed.

"Good lord, you didn't thieve some nobles' pennants, did you?" Amelia asked. Spindle looked up from under her liege's right arm and gave a conspiratorial smile. Amelia put a scandalized hand to her mouth, but Spindle only shook her masked visage.

"Of course not, Your Grace. If I get caught dippin' and takin', how would that reflect on you?" she said, returning to her sewing. "Most of this material I bought from the Veckander mercenary prisoners. The last of them were marched off these last few days and lots were well eager to sell some of their fancier clothes to line their purses for the journey."

"Well, that certainly makes sense of these sleeves," Amelia said, looking at her arms draped not in the classic winged sleeves of a Grand Kingdom lady of rank but in the ruffles favored by successful men-at-arms in the Vec. Amelia did not recognize the heavy cloth of which they were made, but it was soft and comfortable and of a beautiful lavender color sewn through with purple threads. As she studied herself, she realized that her lady-in-waiting had exerted a fresh genius with this garment, for while it was multicolored, every shade was deliberately placed, symmetrical down the axis of her body, so that even as she seemed as colorful as a minstrel's motley, there was nothing of a patched or haphazard appearance about her. Sewn from a dozen clashing and complementing colors, it still projected status.

"There, done," Spindle said as she stood back. "Fine enough for her grace to go about her camp without shame. Only sorry we cannot give you better jewelery and more than a caul. Don't want you mistaken for a fishwife."

"The pearls are fine," Amelia said, and she touched her hand to the little cap-like covering that was pinned on the back of her hair instead of the usual coif. As with everything Spindle produced, even something so simple projected fineness. "And the caul is perfect for a warm day in a military camp."

Spindle accepted her words with a curtsey and stepped back again, returning her needle and thread to their felt case and that in turn to the basket she kept for her sewing. Somehow, in the flight across the river when so much was abandoned in their other camp, Amelia's lady-in-waiting had not lost her sewing kit. It made the archduchess smile.

"If it suits you, Your Grace, shall we take a turn in the summer sun?"

Amelia cast a glance to the little old woman who was seated on the ground on the opposite side of the tent next to the sleeping Sedgemark. A dumpy creature with spindly arms and legs named Pollyusas, she was the healer who had attended to the archduchess and the sergeant throughout their convalescences, as well as calling occasionally on the still recovering Master Welburne. Now the woman picked at a few nuts in a bowl, tending to the sleeping militiaman with a cold compress upon his brow. Sedgemark was mostly recovered from his injuries, the healer had declared with confidence, but he had taken a little sickly while doing it and would need another day or two's rest.

Her opinion of Amelia was a different story.

"Go on, duchess-lady," the healer said impertinently, spitting bits of nut skin from her lips as she spoke. "You needed your rest, but you had that, so now you need some sun. Any more time hiding away in a bed and you'll turn indolent, and I won't have that on my conscience."

Amelia bestowed a graceful nod upon the little woman, and after gesturing for Spindle to lead the way out of the tent, stepped into the sunshine for the first time in five days.

Five days, she thought as she blinked at the brightness. Most of that time had been spent in sleep, and had been restful for that, although yesterday the enforced inactivity had started to grate. *I most definitely want this.*

"Where shall we go first?" Spindle asked, and as they turned along the narrow pathway between tents, the lady's hired guards dutifully fell in behind them. In every direction, the sound of the camp going about its business filled the air. Militia could be heard marching, as well as the noises of animals being moved, and from somewhere nearby came a smell of bread baking that made Amelia's mouth water. Just this little sense of normalcy buoyed her soul immensely, and she smiled as she considered her lady's question. Her reflexive answer was sadly the one she knew she could not follow.

"If I could, I would visit my husband first," she said. To Amelia's way of thinking, she and Farringdon had not yet reconciled, but she did know that he had sat by her side for the first two days she was unconscious after the bridge exploded. She had been only vaguely aware of him, but she thought she could remember him apologizing when he was forced to leave her. There had been rumors of further mercenary forces moving toward Aubrey and he had gone to reconnoiter the situation.

"Barring Farringdon's company, I think my next best choice should be to visit the garrison at the bridge," Amelia said. "I owe them my thanks for their loyal defense."

Yesterday she had learned that two Lions had died on the bridge when it was destroyed, and a few more were injured, mostly as she and Sedgemark had been by flying pieces. Since then, however, the destruction had mostly served them well, making the possibility of attack from Robant's forces almost negligible. However, Knight Captain Farringdon had still left orders to keep watch and patrol the banks in case they tried to cross by boat.

"Will you walk, or do you prefer to ride?" asked Spindle.

"It would be good to take a moment with Silvermane soon," Amelia said, "but I think a walk would suit me better this morning."

They headed off westward, seeking the road to the bridge, when a tink-tink sound caught Amelia's ear and she turned aside to seek it out, following an instinct from her dream. Coming around the back of a large tent with a single wooden wall on one side, she found an open-air smithy. The smell of coal smoke and hot iron filled the air as two heavy-set men, one older and the other younger, worked around a forge and anvil. Amelia knew them immediately as two of the men who had helped Farringdon with salvaging the piece of cannon from the riverbank.

The older man had a hot billet of indistinct shape on the anvil, and he was hammering it methodically, while the younger stood by the fire with a bellows in hand—likely the man's apprentice and possibly his son. The two were of a similar type—burly and full of belly. As Amelia, Spindle, and her guards watched the smith working with his hammer, the younger man's eyes went wide with surprise, and he tapped his senior on the shoulder.

"What?" the older man demanded, and the younger pointed at their aristocratic guests. The smith dropped his billet in surprise, the few tiny remaining fronds of grass on the muddy ground catching instantly alight at the ruddy metal's touch. The man himself sprang back with a nimbleness almost inconceivable in one his size. Torn between the unwelcome danger and the unexpected visitors, he managed to tug his forelock quickly, while positioning his feet better for safety.

"Your Grace," he said, and clasped the tongs and hammer in his hands across his belly. "How may I serve you?"

"I..." Amelia paused and thought about why she had come here. She looked to Spindle, who obviously had no idea but was ready to step in and perform her duties. Amelia shook her head and Spindle stepped back again. "I wanted...I wanted to ask you, good smith, about the cannon metal you salvaged with my husband some days ago."

"Whatever you wish," the smith said readily. "I have it over here, if you need to see it again?"

Amelia still didn't know exactly what she *did* wish but nodded for want of any better response. The smith bowed a little and then handed his hammer and tongs to his apprentice.

"Fetch that up," he said, pointing to the fallen billet, "and get it back in the fire and heating up. See how cold it's gone? Can't work it like that. Put it in the coals and watch it close, mind. Don't you take your silly eyes off it and let it burn. You ruin another piece of good steel on me, and I swear I'll tan your fat hide for a new work apron."

The apprentice nodded fearfully, but from the way his eyes kept shifting over the two fine ladies in his master's workshop, it seemed he was more intimidated by their noble presences than by his master's threats. The smith led the way into the shade of the tent, away from the fire in the open front.

"Sorry 'bout that, Your Grace, but I got to tell him," the smith said, apologizing. "He's a good lad in the main, but he can be a distractable lump if I don't keep him on a short leash."

Amelia accepted the apology with a nod, and the smith pointed her at the broken piece of cannon lying on the ground near one of the tent walls. Now that it was removed from the river and the mud and grass cleaned away, it almost looked like the half-rotted carcass of some strange creature. The central barrel was split open more at one end than the other, and around that end, the rings that had been supposed to help contain the force had been ripped apart so that they curved upward like a kind of forged-iron ribcage.

Ribcage? Amelia thought, and the word cage echoed through her memory from the dreamscape. *The key to the cage.*

"You are...going to...salvage the metal?" she asked, realizing the limits of her knowledge of forging. She could scarcely even understand the specifics of what she was looking at.

"Planned to, Your Grace," the smith said ruefully. "But ain't nothing I can do until we get back to a bigger workshop than this'un. I might do better to try taking it up to Fallenhill and sell it back to the smiths that made it."

"Why is that?"

"It's too big for any fire I can make and too solid forged for me to break apart with hammer and chisel. Me and the boy took turns for near on a day and next to nothing. You can see our fruitless marks there."

He pointed to a section that did indeed look badly scratched and dented with small marks, different than the more torn appearance the initial explosion must have created.

"Is it truly so strong?" Amelia asked, wondering how the cannon could have failed if it was so well made. Then again, if God had judged it, how could it not have failed?

"It's got to be to take the kick o' black powder when it goes off," the smith explained, looking down at the forged wreckage with the respect a farmer might have for a tree stump that refused to be pulled from the ground. "It's forged from lots o' bits, and to break those bits apart, I'd have to heat them back up. I just can't make a fire big enough, and even if I could, me and the boy wouldn't be strong enough on our own to pull it out o' the coals and put the chisels to it. Bitten off more'n I can chew with this one, I fear."

He nodded with a frown and then looked up with a sudden rush of fear.

"Not that I'm complainin' like, Your Grace. I'm well thankful for the salvage. It's just I got to..."

Amelia lifted her hand and waved away the man's apology. He fell silent immediately. She stared at the scrap, but in her mind she was seeing the lion made of metal in her dream. Even without really thinking about it, she was looking for the odd, out-of-place piece that the multi-voiced bird with the distinctive tail had put there. Nothing seemed the same shape as that at all on this blackened iron, but perhaps she was being too literal. She remembered how the piece in her dream had seemed to fit perfectly, but she had been able to clearly see the edges.

"Are there any...seams to split?" she asked, realizing that she did not really even have the vocabulary to describe what she was looking for. The making of things was her husband's area of interest. Her mind turned much better towards people and politics.

"Well, Your Grace, in a sense 'tis all seams," the smith explained, pointing a scarred finger as he described what there was to see. "The barrel there is made o' strips of iron, forge-welded one to the next up their sides until they curve all around to make the cylinder, like. It's dashed fine work, truth to tell."

"It is?"

"Oh yes! They said he was a wizard at the forge, that Masnian master, and lookin' at this, it shows. I could do a long forge weld like any two o' these pieces, that ain't nothin' but journeyman work. But to put them together and around like this, the whole thing gettin' heavier and heavier and sinkin' out the heat while you try to put the next weld on. Pfwhee!"

The man whistled and shook his head in appreciation.

"Then after all that, he's got to wrap these bands and weld them in place..."

The smith bent down, ostensibly to demonstrate something further of the late Master Sent's genius, but his voice trailed off. He rubbed his fingertips across one piece of the metal, then jumped them back to another piece and carefully traced that.

"Goodman smith, are you well?" Amelia asked, and the smith started, as if waking from a dream himself.

"Your pardon, Your Grace?" he said and tugged his forelock yet again. "I...it's just that you asked about seams and...well blow me down, these seams are rubbish."

"Rubbish?" Amelia repeated, and she looked at Spindle as if the word was in a foreign language.

"Rubbish, goodman?" Spindle asked, taking Amelia's glance as a lead. "The work of the wizard at the forge? Rubbish?"

The smith shook his head in complete disbelief.

"Ain't no master smith done *these* welds," he said with the certainty of scripture. He pointed to the part of the wreckage where the barrel was still mostly intact. "These ones. These are quality. But these other ones here, these ones that failed? I wouldn't accept this work from my twit out there, let alone a journeyman or master. Look here."

He pointed to one of the opened bands, to its ends.

"This jagged bit, that's where the welds failed. The powder's kicked it apart with all its force. But this part of the metal should be jagged all along that seam. Instead, it's smooth here on this part. That weld was never complete. It only held in two spots. And this one? This band was never even welded at the ends, just butted together like cheap mail links."

"So, it was not as strong as you first feared?" Amelia asked, trying to get a clear picture of the implications of this discovery. "Is that why it failed?"

As soon as she asked the question, Amelia felt a strange rush of emotion, remembering the way Farringdon had tried to persuade her that the explosion had been a mere mechanical failing, not the judgement of God, which the Church knight with Robant had pronounced. In her self-condemnation she had rejected his explanation, and now it seemed he might have been correct. She suddenly wished even more earnestly that he had returned from his scouting.

"It failed, I'm fair close to certain, Your Grace," the smith said, his tone growing more uncomfortable with every moment. "Because it was made to fail."

"Someone caused it to fail?"

"No, someone *built* it to fail."

The singular rush of emotion that had made her long for Farringdon suddenly whistled up in her soul until it was like a storm, thundering in her ears. She felt her face flush, and like a dark land lit by an instant stroke of lightning, Amelia saw many things at once.

Firstly, she had no doubt that the smith was speaking truth—certainly truth as he knew it. Secondly, she knew that if the cannon had been built to fail, it was not Yentow Sent who had done it. The master had loved his cannons, calling them his "daughters." Even if that had all been a fraud, Amelia could not believe he had built them to explode only to stand beside them in the battle, suicidally lighting the touch-hole himself. Knowing that, she was faced with an impossibility. Somehow, someone had managed to sabotage Yentow Sent's greatest love right under his nose. They had affected the welds and kept it secret. Surely the Masnian would have trusted no one but himself, and perhaps his closest journeymen, to work on the cannons, so since it would not be the master himself to do treachery, there could only be one possible conclusion. Whatever had been done, it had to have been done when the cannons were being constructed in the workshops in Fallenhill.

Amelia remembered the birds from her dream, particularly the bluebird that had sung doubt and confusion into her mind at the first. She had felt and seen the power of the real Bluebird's song during the drought. Then there had been the mocking raven, hating her and lying, according to the lion angel. Lastly, there was the bird of many voices, the one that had stolen a dead man's voice to speak with—a dead gunner on the hilltop. In the instant flash of revelation, knowing Bluebird's song was the first, Amelia knew this was the work of the Inquisition, and that somehow, whatever other fell craft that fallen brotherhood's agents could wield, one or more of them could fool everyone around them, pretending to be whoever they wanted. They could sing the songs of other birds, speak with other voices, and appear as someone or something they were not. Amelia felt sick to her stomach as the final truth struck her like a hammer blow.

There was a traitor moving unseen and undermining them at every turn—a traitor in Fallenhill.

CHAPTER 62

The hut had a wooden door, a rare thing in Fallenhill, since most of the barracks only had blankets covering their entries. The occupants of this building were more important than the average recruit, however. With habitual stealth, the young woman pushed the door and slipped swiftly inside out of the warm night's air. The walled camp was patrolled after dark, and while the girl had a perfectly legitimate excuse for being out and about, it was better not to be noticed at all on this evening's business. She closed the door behind her gently and stalked across the room to the bed and crib.

Both pieces of furniture contained important targets, and the crib was closer, with the bed being against the wall. Nevertheless, the girl's plan would be safer executed at the bed first. She paused to look at the crib only in passing, barely making out the two snug bundles in the slim moonlight coming in through the gap at the bottom of the curtained window.

"Who's that?" a woman's voice from the opposite corner of the room called. The girl froze, still looking down. The preferred target was not in the bed.

"'s just me, Flick," she said sweetly, careful to sound a little embarrassed. "I'm back."

"You been gone awhile, my girl."

"Sorry 'bout that Baroness Righteous," the girl Flick said, curtseying without turning, but reaching into a sleeve to draw forth a stiletto. "I just couldn't bear to be gone from these two bundles o' joy."

"That right?" Righteous asked from the shadowed corner. "You sure it wasn't just that your elopement partner didn't show for you? Left you twistin' in the wind, feelin' foolish, did he?"

"That too," Flick said, hitting the exact pitch that a disappointed and embarrassed young woman would use when forced to admit she had been played false by the local village heartbreaker.

"Well, we all make mistakes," the convict-baroness said knowingly, and Flick breathed a little easier. Gulls who were taken in by a sob story were easier targets to aim for. "And I do love my babes, too. Only, I can't see as even I would come back from the dead for 'em."

"Flick" froze in place, not even a third of the way into the turn that would have made "her" ready for the charge.

"I don't understand," she said.

"Flick would've said she didn't ken, but that's neither here nor there," the baroness said. For the first time, "Flick" heard the steel tension in the woman's voice and realized the night's business was not going to go as planned, not even close. "Was canny enough, put her body out on a grassy slope far from the village, let the wolves do for the hiding. Be years before the remains were found, most like in some old wolf den, and by then who'd remember some fool girl who'd run off long ago. Only it seems like the local packs got more taste for sheep than girls. We found her before the wolves did."

"Is that what you 'ken'?" the girl who was not Flick said, her girlish voice deepening naturally as her neck thickened and limbs changed shape. It was clear that stealth was no longer necessary. Better to move to a more combat-ready form.

"It was Franken who figured it, actually," Righteous said. "He was right livid to think someone in his charge was undermining his training, or mine, so he did some quiet digging.

Seems a recruit was seen sneaking about with one o' my maids, but none had gone missing, so he feared he had a rapist murderer in the camp. You might have heard some stories about why the Sergeant of Training would never put up with such a thing in Baron Ash's fiefdom."

"The locals tell all kinds of fey tales," the assassin who was not Flick said in a now distinctly manly voice. He had turned but still could not make out the Baroness Righteous's exact location. The woman had cunningly chosen the darkest part of the room from which to keep watch. No surprise there, and in fact the assassin was pleased to see his assessment had been accurate. He had watched Righteous since she had arrived in Fallenhill and had gauged her as a genuinely cunning opponent, with steel-edged instincts. Of course, being right about how dangerous she was seemed of little consolation now that he had to face her.

"So how does this hand play out?" he asked, trying to draw the conversation along so he could get a better sense of her location through sound, if not by sight.

"This hand's done," said Righteous. "You've played your cards and now you pay what you owe."

"I might still have one card to play," the assassin said and swept the stiletto into the shards of moon and 'part-light so it could be seen, then held it over the crib. "One stab, and *Baron* Ash is an infant short. Given how many steps away you are, maybe I can get both and maybe you and he will have to start again, if he ever gets back from the west."

The dagger held poised in the air, but not a single sound came from the darkened corner. Then the assassin cursed himself for a fool. He plunged the dagger into the crib only to feel the deadly point punch straight through a lifeless bundle of cloth. Of course, Baroness Righteous had not left her children in harm's way.

"Ready to tally up?" Righteous asked, and there came the sound of a blade being slid from a sheath. The assassin guessed it to be a dirk or other fighting knife.

She wants to do it herself, he thought and took that as a good sign. Canny, the convict-baroness might be, but she was still a streetfighter at heart. You could take the mutt off the cobbles, but the cobbles would always be in the mutt.

"Steel in the 'part-light, is it? Very well," he said, adjusting his accent to that of a Denay street urchin, issuing a challenge by mere tone—a challenge he was sure the street-fighting "peer" would recognize and find impossible to resist. Spending his entire life posed as folk that he was not—young and old, male and female, low-born and high—the assassin was an excellent student of people and cultures. He had been there when Righteous had gone into labor, having only just taken Flick's face the night before, and had seen the baroness resist all feminine instincts for the chance to get to grips with her rebellious students—a rebellion the assassin had expertly fostered. The baroness was desperate for a straight-up fight to vent her frustrations upon, and that was the bait the assassin dangled in front of her.

There came the noise of female feet shifting forward, and the assassin sprang backward onto the bed, aiming to draw Righteous into the light from the window while he retreated to the shadows, reversing her advantage. He landed adroitly, feet either side of the bundle of bedclothes, which was the fake sleeping body that made the bed look occupied. He watched the shadows, still listening for Righteous's footfalls and ready for a thrown dagger out of the darkness. Then his right thigh exploded in pain, once, twice, and again, though by the third time, he was already half-falling, half-jumping from the bed to escape.

"What the...?" he called, but his well-trained mind had already fixed on the answer. The scar-faced twit was hiding in the bed. The lad must have been still as a stone, holding his breathing. The ambush had been perfectly set, indeed, and the assassin had stumbled straight into it. The problem with living continuously fooling all others around you was that it became easy to forget how they might fool you in return.

Knowing the night's mission could not possibly be accomplished now, the assassin decided to aim only for escape. He would get outside and call for the guards, pretending to be one of the trainee maidens who had heard the commotion in the baroness's room. Moving swiftly in the night, he would call again with a sentry's voice, passing the alarm dutifully while rushing toward the women's hut to investigate. Three or more shifts of voice and body in the shadows, and by the time they knew for sure he was gone and were just starting to follow the trail of his blood, he would be in the workshops, tying off the injuries and posing as the Masnian journeyman smith who had been his base identity for the past three seasons—since before Bluebird had failed, in fact. The plans of Sanguine's Inquisition were ever wheels within wheels. The assassin would have to devise a plausible excuse for limping while his body healed. He had no idea how badly his leg was injured, but white laud painkiller, expert misdirection, and iron force of will would hopefully allow him to conceal the injury long enough to fake an accident at the forge.

Firstly though, he had to escape this room. His body struck the packed earth floor with a thump, and even though his badly slashed leg was agonizing, he managed to roll to a reasonable crouch. He threw his stiletto full force at the curtain on the window, striking it with a heavy enough whump to distract them, to make the two opponents in the room think he was aiming to escape that way while he dashed for the door. He felt, rather than saw, Baroness Righteous passing close by, close enough that he could have taken her, but that was too great a risk now. Then he was out the door and into the night.

The first dagger took him straight in the belly, even before his throat was half transformed from male to female. Eyes wide in disbelief, he collapsed, and two strikes aimed from either side of his head bit only air. They were the last two to miss, however, as female hands, despised for their low birth and weaker physical stature, combined their limited training and strength together to drag the assassin to the ground and plant their own blades in his flesh. His last word was an anguished, multi-tonal cry that made no sense to man or beast.

"Oh, holy God in heaven, what is it?" Daisy asked as she and the other maids looked down on the assassin's slain form. It was wearing Flick's dress, though several of the seams were torn, especially at the shoulders. The chin was stubbly, and the throat and right arm were clearly a man's. Still, Flick's brown eyes stared lifelessly from the mostly female face. The girls all looked horrified in the lamplight, and Righteous was sure several would have nightmares in coming days.

"*Brakkis effar*," Solomon said, his blooded blade still bared in his hand.

"What?" asked one of the girls.

"Skin changers," Sergeant Franken said solemnly, holding one of the two lanterns up to light the body. He was there in command of three full lines of White Lion recruits. Baroness Righteous had wanted the duty of ambush to fall to her Lace-Fangs-in-training, as was their right to avenge Flick's death, but she and Franken had been of the same mind that it was not worth risking failure over. If the hidden assassin had proved to possess mystical powers for combat as well as stealth, they wanted to be sure they had overwhelming force available to themselves. The assassin was *not* to escape.

"You mean you seen things like this afore?" Daisy asked. The girls' concerned expressions turned to amazement as both Solomon and Franken nodded.

"Seen, faced, and watched Baron Ash go one-to-one with," Franken said.

That made Righteous smile with pride. "Except," she said, "*Brakkis effar* are Redlander folk, and whatever else he was, he weren't no Redlander."

"So where did she...he...it come from?" Daisy asked, her look of horror not abating as the conversation went on.

"I don't know," Righteous told them, "but there are others seeking the answer to the question, don't you fear."

CHAPTER 63

Lady Dalflitch knew how she was regarded by the people of Dweltford Castle, not to mention the town at large. She expended significant effort crafting and maintaining her image—that of a vain, indulged, airy-nosed prancer, a gossipy wench with a head full of jewelry, dresses, and little else. In truth, while she always appeared to have the finest garments and baubles she could afford, both for herself and her husband, not to mention a fondness for very expensive wines imported from the northeastern islands of Aucks, she was utterly unafraid of poverty, filth, or desperation. Her life had proven to her that no matter the height in society to which one rose, it was only ever a more visible platform from which to fall. She had even once spent several nights sleeping on a makeshift stable floor, imprisoned with her future liege lady and clinging together with her for warmth.

Because of such experiences, Dalflitch was never fearful to acquaint herself with any lower hall, back corridor, or forgotten niche, cupboard, and closet wherever she was living. In fact, she made a point of doing so. In her youth, she might have imagined herself as a queen or princess, dwelling only in marbled halls on finest silks, but as far as the "fallen lady" was now concerned, nobles who kept to the comfortable rooms of their estates were only ever encouraging rats in unseen corners. The juiciest whispers, and the most dangerous, were always spoken in the shadows. For this reason, she found her husband's newly acquired position as Castellan of Castle Dweltford absolutely invaluable, since it put every key to every room in the castle in his hands, which was to say in her hands.

Even so, the castle dovecote was putting her assiduous curiosity to the ultimate test. A small brick outcrop on the intersection of two of the castle's western walls, the little building almost resembled a kind of beehive from a distance, even though it was actually the equal of a good-sized yeoman's hut. Up closer, it became easy to pick out dozens of arched openings in the dovecote's curved sides, through which the castle's messenger birds could easily fly. There was one doorway, half the usual height of a typical door, and after stooping to enter, the lady seneschal, wife of the castellan Sir Turley, always found herself assaulted by an atmosphere that must surely be inimical to mortal life.

While it was shadowy within the roost, the dovecote's position out in the open meant that in winter the cold winds blew through it, and in summer it baked like a poorly ventilated oven. Worse than these, though, was the acrid sting of the smell. Droppings streaked the walls and guano layered the dovecote's stone floor to a depth of a handspan at least. Dalflitch could confirm that fact for herself because there was a narrow path through the filth from the doorway to the middle, just wide enough for her to stand with her feet close together. It was as if someone had come to shovel the floor clean and then decided that only a simple strip, one pace long and half that wide, was all that was needed. It was like a channel through a miniature landscape of bird dung. The air was filled with dust from the droppings, along with a cloud of down that rivalled a morning fog for its density. Dalflitch's eyes burned, and she clutched a perfumed kerchief to her face as she tried to decide if she more wanted to cough or sneeze or cry.

All three at once, if I could manage it, she decided.

In niches between the openings on the walls all around her, a greatly diminished flock of messenger birds cooed and fluttered in the dimness that was not so cool, although cooler than outside. In previous years, the roost might have been full, but the drought had stopped many of the brooders from laying, and war always consumed birds with its dangers and depredations. So few were they now that in fear of losing the chance to rebuild the flock, neither Baron Prentice nor Marquis Farringdon had taken a single messenger bird with them, increasing the "stay-at-home" Dalfitch's sense of tense ignorance, not knowing what was happening abroad with either half of the province's armies. It was a disappointing and frustrating situation that the lady seneschal was already taking steps to correct, although the bankers' embargo was putting a crimp even on that simple task. Remembering her particular reason for braving this monument to bird leavings, Dalflitch searched the shadows near the walls until she picked out the birds' keeper, a leathery goblin of a man who wore a hessian hood as guano-streaked as the bricks around him.

"Over here," he called softly when he saw she was looking at him.

"Certainly not!" Dalflitch replied. Under no circumstances was she going to walk across his fiefdom of filth. She suspected she was going to burn her dress and shoes as soon as she took them off as it was. "You come here."

The keeper shrugged and shuffled toward her, kicking up a further cloud of filth as he approached. He had his hands clasped in front of him, and as he drew near, Dalflitch realized that he was gently holding a bird in them. The little head darted and bobbed in his grip, and when he stopped just in front of the lady-in-waiting, he brought the creature to his lips and kissed it tenderly. Dalflitch waited for the man to say something, but he seemed entranced by his affection for his charge.

"Well?" she asked at last, not wanting to play the imperious lady but eager to get as far away from the dovecote as was possible while remaining on castle grounds. She resolved that her afternoon's business would now consist primarily of a long, hot bath.

"Well, what?" the man responded, eyes still upon his bird.

"You called me here."

"You wanted me to," he insisted. Before Dalflitch could refute that notion, he went on. "You said that if Suzy Blue here flew in, I was to tell right quick. So, I come to tell you. The kitchen girls wouldn't let me down the steps inside, so they took to seek you out and sent me back here to wait."

"Suzy Blue?" Dalflitch repeated. As she did so, she realized it was his name for the bird in his loving grip, and as that insight resolved itself, she swiftly connected the rest of the reason why she had needed to come. There were very few of the castle's messenger birds deployed around the Reach, but this was the only one she had deemed sufficiently important that she was to be summoned immediately if it arrived.

"Give me the message," she instructed and held her hand out. Keeping one of his own hands on his precious pet, the keeper fished two little slips of paper out of his sleeve and passed them over. Dalflitch cocked an eyebrow.

"Two?" she demanded.

"Both come in this mornin'," the keeper said with a shrug as he returned his attention to his favorite in his hands. "Well, one in the predawn. He must 'ave roosted close overnight and then come afore the sun. Suzy here was just after 'im, as I broke me fast."

"Have you read them?" Dalflitch asked, scanning first one note and then the other.

"I can't read," the little man responded with amusement, as if the notion itself was a jest. Dalfitch nodded. Even asking the man was an act of wariness that bordered upon paranoia because she knew, before she had fully unrolled the papers, that they should be enciphered—written not in letters but in coded symbols prearranged before the birds had even been taken away in their cages.

"Good man," she said and pulled a guilder from the purse tied to her wrist while she tucked the messages safely away inside. She offered the keeper the coin, but he gave it a look of the same amused diffidence. Dalflitch pushed it on him, nonetheless.

"Buy Suzy Blue a juicy worm or something," she told him, then turned to leave. She was just straightening again from the dovecote's tiny entrance when he called after her.

"Saw that shadow again last night," he said.

"Where?" Dalflitch asked, her mind mostly directed to the matters on the papers in her purse.

"Same as before, over the old vegie patch," the keeper said, pointing to a spot along the battlements no more than twenty paces distant. It was a seemingly random location that looked west over the water, and even though it held no military significance, directly below it was the dead garden with its one important prisoner. The distance from the top of the wall to the ground was thirty feet if it was an inch, beyond the ability of an elderly woman to climb, but someone on the battlement might climb down.

Dalflitch looked into the courtyard of dead earth, then back to her purse and the slips of paper in within. She had not needed her codebooks to decipher either of them, and while one contained dire news, both would require immediate action. She noticed some down on her sleeve and brushed it off, shaking her head. Taking in one deep breath, she enjoyed a moment of fresh summer air and sunshine outside the dovecote. That would have to do to restore her spirits, she decided, since she would certainly have no time for a bath this afternoon.

****

The key to the castle.

It was an expression known to yeomanry up and down the Grand Kingdom. They used it to mean an unbeatable hand of cards, or a permission to some action which could not be denied, such as a magistrate's letter for the seizure of goods, a

winning play of some kind. It was a simple phrase, easily understood, and not in the least bit applicable to any true castle in
any demesne in the entire land. Some castles might have a single
key for their main gate, but they all had innumerable keys for
all the other doors, gates, and important locks. Some might be
in the hands of a doorkeeper or a captain of the house guards,
if there was one. A seneschal would have a key to every one of
the castle's strong rooms and lock boxes. In Castle Dweltford,
several of the stewards also had specific keys to individual rooms
that were their areas of responsibility.

It was for want of one *specific* key that the shadow stole
along the western battlements for a third night this summer—a
simple piece of iron to unlock an insignificant-seeming part of
the castle, and every attempt to acquire a copy had met with
failure. The new castellan, the half-crippled ox with the vain
wife, must have had at least one of the keys, but his shameless
spouse had scoured up every copy that was known to exist, and
as loathe as the shadow was to admit the fact, she had done an
excellent job of it.

Tying a purloined rope to the crenelation, the shadow lowered the other end into the empty courtyard. A thirty-foot
climb with rope was mere child's play to him, and even in the
dark, the shadow felt no fear of the drop. From the dovecote
across the way there came a sound of wings fluttering and a
muttering voice—the dotard bird keeper. The shadow was still
undecided as to whether the simple-minded twit needed to
die but thought he would have to have made up his mind by
the time he climbed back up. It was not that he was reluctant
to kill, especially not one of God's misbegotten creatures like
the keeper. It was merely a professional consideration. In any
household a death created disruptions, and disruptions led to
discovery. It was always best if any task could be accomplished
unnoticed. The shadow suspected the dovecote's one mortal
occupant had observed his presence already but was reasonably
confident that the keeper could not possibly identify him in full

light. Nevertheless, the shadow's masters did not accept "reasonably confident" as a standard. Less clean, but much safer, for the keeper to join the main target in the afterlife tonight. Break his neck and throw him from the wall, make it look as if he fell. It would not fool everyone, but it might delay making all the connections for an hour or two more, and the shadow could do a lot with two hours.

Down the wall by the rope as easily as walking, the shadow stole toward the old tool closet's door, the dimmest whisper of candlelight showing in the gap underneath. Pushing the door, the shadow stepped within.

"I've come for another visit, mother," the shadow said, using the lady seneschal's voice, or a fine enough mimicry. Stealing a voice whole could only be done with the dead, but a lyrebird's song could turn itself to almost any sound with enough exposure to learn by.

"Too late," whispered the Ragmother hoarsely.

"Must you complain every time?" the shadow said, making a quick guess at what the true lady seneschal would likely say in this situation—if not the exact words, then again, another fair enough approximation for so late in the night. "I come when I must."

"No," whispered the Ragmother and her voice suddenly became much stronger. "Too late because she's already dead. She died yesterday morning, if you can believe it. Your timing was just that bad. Oh well."

The shadow recognized the voice as the one it had just been mimicking. The woman on the cot was not the target Ragmother but the Lady Dalflitch herself. Several realizations flickered through the shadow's thoughts in rapid succession. Firstly, the plan to assassinate the Ragmother and take her place had to be abandoned outright. Secondly, the shadow's mission had been unmasked to an unknown degree, and so remaining in Dweltford Castle had become both dangerous and likely pointless. It would have to go to its bolthole in the town and wait to see how things played out. Lastly and most regrettably, the shadow knew it had to kill Dalflitch here and now, which would create massive disruptions. Disruptions were acceptable for key assassinations, but they also made watching too difficult and unreliable. Disruptions meant watchfulness and change; peace and somnolence were much easier to spy upon. Still, it could not be helped. No matter how well or how often the Inquisition did its divinely appointed work, the judge of all souls still set His own timetable for the life and death of most mere mortals, and by all accounts, the elderly river woman was long overdue for her day of reckoning.

All these considerations flashed through the shadow's mind in a near instant, and it launched itself at the new target on the cot that was needing to be silenced. Even before it began to move though, the heavy, spike-flanged head of a mace crashed into its right shoulder, lifting to fall again and again on its head, back, and lastly hip as it fell to the floor.

The slattern brought her ox, the shadow thought—his last thought, in fact—as darkness claimed him, and his soul departed the mortal realms to discover what the Almighty truly thought of those who killed mercilessly in His name.

****

"I wanted him alive," Dalflitch said, knowing that her annoyance was more because of her own mortal fear than because she disapproved of her husband's actions.

"And I wanted *you* safe, my beauty," Turley answered his wife, and she smiled at him despite herself.

Dalflitch looked down on the slain man, clad in simple homespun garments like any other kitchen hand or lower servant.

"That's two now," she said, sounding more satisfied than she felt. "How many more do you think there are in the Reach?"

"By the look of him, and the way he mocked your voice, half the castle could be," Turley said. Dalflitch nodded. It had been unnerving to hear her own voice coming out of the infiltrator's mouth. The possibility that there could be any number of such folk concealing themselves in the West, ready to do all manner of ill to their liege and her rule, was terrifying.

"Course, I wouldn't think being that level of tricksy was an easy thing," Turley went on. "Take the right sort, with the right flair, and then you'd have to train them, maybe for years like."

Dalflitch was inclined to agree.

"They might be a select talent, something only some are born with, you think?" she mused. "Like healers?"

"I was thinking more like Prentice," Turley said. "He and me, we're of a strength. I'd take odds I'm a touch more, with my good arm. But he's got art with weapons I never even knew there was to learn. And you could sit me in front o' books day and night for the rest o' my days, and I'd never be the sage he is."

Dalflitch looked up at her husband's face in the sparse candlelight. He was a brash and cocksure man, but in some senses, she knew it mostly for an act, just as her own shallow rumor-monger persona was more affected than real.

"However many there are, we now have other work to set to," she told her husband, kicking gently at the corpse between them. "Let's get this one somewhere better lit. I want to search him before we give him over to the gravedigger. Then we need to start readying for the new banner's march."

"I don't like the notion of setting off without Prentice here to take the lead," Turley said.

"Neither do I," Dalflitch agreed. "But I like the notion of her grace's rivers being blockaded even less. Especially if it's true that Aubrey bridge is gone as well."

CHAPTER 64

*T**he obelisk is cracked.*

That was the secret Whilte claimed to have seen revealed while he was entranced upon the stone. Springs rose throughout the mountains and fed the mystical lake and the upper Murr, bringing lifegiving water that was full of magickal power—water that was lifted from the deep earth by the ordinance of the Almighty himself, according to the chaplain. It reminded Prentice of the story of Noah and the first flood when it was said there was no rain upon the earth, only water rising from springs in the ground—a time when giants were said to roam the lands.

And now one of those springs is cracking the foundation of the obelisk that was built to contain and channel the water's power, Prentice thought.

That, or the brutal misuse the Redlanders were putting the power to had broken the stone, and the spring was rising into the cracks. Prentice could imagine either scenario. What he was unsure of was why this "secret" had been revealed to them and by whom? Whilte insisted that he had no memory of speaking about noons and dawns and new-moon midnights, so it seemed his accidental oracular moment had at least two parts to it, and that was something with which Prentice had no experience. His visions and dreams had always been singular, as had all the ones Archduchess Amelia had shared with him. They had sometimes seemed confusing, or even obtuse, but they were never multi-faceted, as if bringing separate messages.

What did it mean?

These thoughts turned Prentice's mind as the company made its slow way through the foothills, trying to keep the river as their guide. By midmorning they had had to backtrack a short distance once already when a scout party returned to warn them that the path they were on led only to the dead end of a gully wall. It was pure guess how long ago there had been enough rain in this region to wear a gully in the land. Another mule had almost been lost, along with his ostler, when part of the slope had given away, and Prentice had decided to walk rather than try to keep his saddle and risk a fall that would almost certainly be serious for Boots or Dusty.

"Looks like we're going to have to switch back toward the river, My Lord," Gennet said after consulting with the rest of the scout parties. "One of the lines say they made it almost five leagues north and could see another five from a spot they took as a lookout. There's nothing but cliff face and dead trees as far as they could see. Maybe there's a pass going west somewhere farther up, but not one we could follow and still keep any track of the Murr."

Prentice accepted his sergeant's report and let Gennet change the direction of the march. Soon, the company was descending a steep slope at the foot of a mighty cliff to a narrow, parched sward beside the Murr. The first grassy field they had seen since leaving Radengon, it was sparser the farther it emerged from the gorge out of which the Murr flowed, but seeing it from a height, Prentice thought the near meadow became more densely grassed as it went further back around the foot of the mountain. Perhaps this was the current boundary of the drought—as far as it had advanced west, finally yielding a little to allow the river to water some of the earth. It was an encouraging, if grim, sight.

"My Lord Commander! Call for the commander!" a Lion shouted from near the bottom of the slope, echoing off the mountain's rocky face. The call was passed up the hill, and

Prentice summoned a militiaman to take Boots's bridle while he moved to answer the request. Sliding and skidding down through the dust, Prentice wondered what his people must have discovered that needed his immediate attention. At one point during his descent, he looked upward, and seeing the sun, he realized it was almost noon.

If this is not one of our cryptic appointments, then it must be coming before long, he thought.

No sooner had Prentice reached the point where the slope bottomed out beside the flowing Murr than he saw why he had been summoned and knew that, almost certainly, this was his "noon" event. Sitting cross-legged on a broad, flat rock in the middle of the yellowed grass were two fey. Around the pair, a crowd of militiamen stood watchfully, weapons drawn, while others searched the nearby slopes and river for signs of an ambush. As he approached, Prentice gave the area a visual search of his own. The river was as dark as it had been for leagues, though it was narrower at this point. On the other side, the riverbank was little more than a strip of pebbles that immediately soared upward in a sheer cliff face for hundreds and hundreds of feet. Where the stony wall finally reached a ridge, a sparse few dead boughs could be seen overhanging. If any fey were hiding on that side, they were invisible, not to mention part spider or squirrel. Prentice could hardly imagine any other creature clinging to the sheer rockface.

This side of the river was little better, for while there was the grassed sward on the bank, it was overtopped by an even taller sheer cliff, as devoid of life or ledges as the southern side. The dry grass might have concealed some fey from others at the river's level, but as his men descended the slope to this waterside path, they would surely have been able to make out signs of any hiders. As he thought about it, Prentice realized that in years past the flat space where they were standing had probably been underwater itself. Without the drought, there would have been

no way to walk this path at all, for there would have been no
path.

Partly distracted by these observations, Prentice did not give
the pair of waiting fey his full attention until he was much
closer. When he did, he was surprised to realize he recognized
them both. The one on the left was the bereft, withered horse
archer from his meeting with Benjamin in the grasslands of the
Reach. It seemed almost a forgotten history to Prentice now,
though he did recall the fey man's name had been Dahyoor, or
something similar. He was dressed as he had been, in buckskins
and plain tunic, with no colored patterns or linen armor. When
Prentice had first met him, he had seemed half-starved, and that
had not improved. Beside him was a figure much less lowly,
and Prentice was astonished to realize it was the mighty warrior
who had ridden the sovereign stag in the ambush against the
Lions. He was more upright, stronger, and haler than Dahyoor,
and his spirit did not seem as broken. Nevertheless, there was
an equal air of despair about him, of loss and mourning. Like
the horse archer Dahyoor, he had no weapons and no distinct
aspects to his garb, no armor or markers of status. His leaf-like,
scaled byrnie was gone, along with his gauntlets and greaves. He
wore just a plain tunic, not dissimilar to his companion's.

You have both lost your life and kept drawing breath, Prentice
thought, recognizing the emotion in the warriors' expressions.
He imagined his own countenance had been the same in the first
days when he had been transported west of the Azure Mountains, bound to the chain, convicted of heresy. It was a sense
of raw brokenness, still too angry, too proud to have settled to
resignation.

Give it time.

The western fey man's skin was so like milk that he seemed
as bleached by the blazing sunlight as the land they had just
crossed. He did blink and shy away from the brightness of
the morning, but neither he nor Dahyoor tried to shield their
eyes—the horse archer's a deep brown and the other's an emer-

ald green. The stag rider stared at Prentice, sneering slightly, it seemed, and addressed him in the fey tongue. The knight commander had no way of knowing if it was accented or even a different dialect. It sounded similar enough to his ear, but Prentice knew that could just be self-deception, a trick of his own thoughts. After the pale fey finished his statement, he kept his attention on Prentice, as if he expected an immediate answer. After a moment, he looked askance at Dahyoor and slapped the more pitiful fey upon the shoulder. Dahyoor scowled back, but his companion only nodded aggressively and pointed at Prentice. With a sigh, Dahyoor looked to the Lions' commander, and Prentice wondered if companion was the right word. Overseer seemed more appropriate.

"Captain called Ashen Man," Dahyoor began in heavily accented Kingdom speech. "I am bid to speak to you for..."

Prentice held up his hand and commanded Dahyoor to silence. The fey rider seemed surprised but did as Prentice wanted, tilting his head quizzically. Prentice looked over his shoulder to the nearest line first.

"Send for Master Solft," he instructed, and the man went off at a run, heading back up the rough slope and calling for the scholar. Prentice turned back to Dahyoor. "We will wait for my translator, so that I may know for certain what words are being spoken in my presence."

Dahyoor shrugged, showing he was too indifferent to be insulted by Prentice's imputation. The pale fey looked from militia commander to archer and back, then slapped Dahyoor's shoulder once more. The two exchanged terse words, and the pale fey's unhappy expression deepened, but Dahyoor appeared to lose interest in explaining after a short space and the pair fell to grim silence, with Dahyoor as dejected as ever and the other dissatisfied but without options.

"Miserable pair, ain't they?" Corporal Guillam said, appearing at Prentice's right shoulder.

"If I come to need your opinion in this matter, you have my solemn promise I will ask you for it," Prentice said curtly, not taking his eye off the two fey, and Guillam stepped back with a salute.

"As you say, My Lord," he replied in a tone that told Prentice exactly what kind of smirk he had on his face without having to look. For his part, Prentice did not want to be distracted even for a moment. Whatever was happening here was too significant to risk putting a foot wrong. When he had heard Whilte's trance-like pronouncement this dawn, the knight commander had no idea what to expect. If he lived to be a hundred, he doubted he would have guessed it would be this.

The tense silence stretched on as fey and Lions watched one another with undisguised mistrust. The sun beat down and Prentice could feel the sweat trickling down his back, soaking his arming doublet under his brigandine. From up the slope came the sounds of pebbles and dust scattering as the messenger who had been sent for Master Solft returned with the scholar and his riding mule, aided by a number of other militia helping to keep man and beast from slipping to a dire injury. At last, Solft was standing at Prentice's side, his sunburned face even redder from the exertion of rushing.

"My Lord," he said breathlessly, tugging his forelock. "You called for me."

"Master, Dahyoor and his...companion...here have a message for us," Prentice told him. "I would have you assist interpreting from the fey language."

Solft nodded and looked to the two fey. For a long moment he only stared at them both, and Prentice assumed he was getting his breath back. Presently the scholar gave Dahyoor some kind of greeting, and with sour looks on both fey men's faces, the conversation began again.

"Ashen Man, so called, the Verdant fey set me now to speak for them," Dahyoor said.

"Verdant fey?" Prentice repeated, brows knotted. Dahyoor explained in swiftly spoken fey tongue and Solft nodded.

"Verdant is the name these far western fey have for themselves," the scholar explained. "It is an...ancient...name, apparently."

Prentice smirked a little at the irony of the native folk of this desiccated land calling themselves "verdant." Such was the passage of history that that which once had obvious meaning might become near nonsense in the light of passing ages.

"Speak then, this message from the *Verdant* fey," Prentice told Dahyoor, making his expression sober once more. Dahyoor looked to the Verdant fey and the rider of the fallen stag began to speak.

"The Verdant fey were told by the Untrue and by the Wind Rising kin that you were a force of death, Ashen Man," the Azure fey began.

"Wind Rising?" Prentice repeated, looking to Solft. When he realized the knight commander wanted him to answer, the scholar nodded apologetically.

"The name for our kind of fey, from the Azures. 'Wind Rising,' just as the ones from here in the west are called Verdant. The Untrue is the fey name for the Redlanders as a nation."

Prentice nodded. He already knew the term "Untrue" but was surprised to learn that the mountain fey had a name for themselves, one they had not bothered to share with him despite supposedly affording him the status of an honorary elder. For not the first time, he wondered if this "elder" status was not some kind of private joke amongst the horse-riding fey. He also noticed that as Solft was explaining, Dahyoor was looking back and forth between the Verdant man and the scholar. There was something about having to pass this message that offended him, even under the blanket of his own broken pride.

The disjointed conversation continued.

"The Verdant Fey did not fear your coming because they have watched the dust claim their land for a..." The last word was untranslated.

"I'm not sure, My Lord," Solft said with a pained expression. "I think it means a thousand years, but it also seems to mean a time too long to be remembered."

"Good enough, Master," Prentice told him and looked back to Dahyoor.

"They say they did not fear ash when the dust made by the thirsty sun cannot creep into their valley. Then you took the life of the one who walked the forests since the Earth Writhed, the Monarch of the Shadowed Green."

"I think he means the great stag," Solft explained, but Prentice stilled him with a hand to keep Dahyoor from being interrupted again.

"He says that he was only the last in a line of Monarch riders, going back uncounted generations," the horse archer said, and there was an even deeper tone of bitterness in his voice, thickening his accent even further. "A creature that knew the days when the sweet water first sprang from the mountains, that once roamed forests not only in the west, but all the way east until where the living water falls to the green. Once, over all the heights was his voice heard, now no more."

As the words were spoken, Prentice could almost see the ancient forests stretching across the western highlands that were now desert and the sovereign beast ranging through them proud and kingly, like the unicorn of the Azures and the Reach. He felt the sense of loss rise afresh in himself, the acute grief and regret that had touched him when he had seen the stag slain at the ridgetop ambush or the unicorn in the ruined village. Both deaths were tragic, and he could not deny that fact, but even as the mourning for a beauty destroyed settled upon him like a suffocating cloud, something from underneath, from the dark, cold bottom of his soul rose up against it. He remembered others slain, such as in the anonymous riverside village and in

Fallenhill; he remembered Baron Stopher, cooked alive in his own armor while his people burned before him; he remembered starved children hunting for rats in Aubrey's ruin and Sir Gant's salute before throwing himself into certain death, for what else was there when the Redlanders came upon a land? Worst of all, he remembered the undercroft at Halling Pass Castle where a serpent witch had sacrificed innocents to produce more misbegotten beast-men—a serpent witch that this proud warrior's people were now harboring with the rest of her *imzuss* from the judgement that she deserved—judgment that Prentice's liege had sent him to deliver.

"Tell him that if he did not want his precious animal to die, he should not have helped feed his people and mine to the blades of the Untrue," he told Dahyoor through gritted teeth. "He blames us because he lacks the courage to accept his own responsibility. We held the blades and guns, but he rode his beast upon them."

For the first time Dahyoor's face registered an emotion other than malaise or anger, and he was obviously afraid—not terrified, perhaps, but hesitant. He looked to the Verdant warrior but said nothing.

"Master Solft, can you translate?" Prentice asked.

"I think I can...but..."

"Then do so."

Hesitatingly, Solft turned Prentice's harsh words into fey speech, and even before he had finished, the Verdant stag rider's expression was a scowl of unreserved hatred. He half raised himself from his cross-legged position as he released a stream of invective in his own tongue, pointing denunciations at Prentice's chest. Around the stone where they sat, militiamen tensed, weapons ready.

"Master?" Prentice asked when Dahyoor did not translate the enraged diatribe.

"I...um...I..." Solft fumbled, and it was not clear if the scholar had not understood, or if he had understood and was too frightened to give the meaning.

"His wrath is directed at me, Master Scholar," Prentice said coldly, not looking away from the infuriated fey. "*My* wrath, should it be provoked, will not fall upon you."

Prentice saw Solft nodding in the corner of his vision and heard the jowly man swallow heavily.

"He calls...us...children, My Lord. Bratty children, I think his word meant. He says that we...'*etsk*'...it means damage...break..."

"Destroy," Dahyoor said sourly, giving Solft the more correct translation.

"We 'destroy' things we do not understand," the scholar continued. "Things we do not realize are difficult to replace. Impossible, perhaps."

Prentice nodded.

"*Etsk*," he repeated, forming the word as faithfully as he could. The Verdant fey man nodded ferociously and pointed at Prentice's belt. Looking down, the knight commander realized he was pointing at the champion sword in its sheath, with its unicorn-horn grip and the tassel from the dead creature's mane. Prentice pulled his swordbelt over his head and held the blade up in its cover. Then he drew it forth and held the blade out, showing it to the enraged fey who snarled at it like a cornered wolf at hunters closing in for the kill.

"Tell him this, exactly this," Prentice said, not caring if Solft or Dahyoor made the translation. "This blade is a tragedy, a calamity forged in steel and quenched in blood that should never have been shed. I carry it because it has fallen to me. I carry it because I have worn chains and survived. I have seen the bodies and the iron chains upon the stone, have seen the blood that binds the lake and the Verdant folk. I carry this abomination because I know that some slaveries can only end in blood and death. Enslaved things must be freed."

Prentice hated speaking those words, even though he believed them. The Verdant warrior listened with his proud stare, and as Dahyoor translated Prentice's declaration, the pale-skinned man recoiled, sitting back on the rock. He spat a terse reply at the Lions, scouring the armed cordon with a hateful glare.

"He says that sometimes the only alternative to death *is* slavery," Solft interpreted.

"And sometimes death is the better alternative," said Prentice.

When that statement was translated, the infuriated fey tossed his head with a snort of derision that required no interpreter. Prentice shook his head gently. He understood the fey man's rejection of the word, and he felt something of a hypocrite as he said it. After all, hadn't he endured long upon the chain, choosing slavery over death himself? Regardless, philosophical questions were not why these two had come. In fact, Prentice could not see why it was that Dahyoor was here at all. Why would Benjamin send this fallen member of his folk as a representative? The Verdant rider had said the Azure fey had told of Prentice's coming or confirmed the Redlanders' tales about him, which made it sound as if the two kin folks were on terms of some kind, but Dahyoor's presence did not fit with that picture. He was as lowly to Azure Mountains fey—Wind Rising, as they called themselves—as a convict was to Reacher society.

"Ask him why they are here." Prentice told Solft, and the scholar dutifully fumbled the fey words.

CHAPTER 65

After Solft's question another long silence stretched, and Prentice studied the Verdant fey's expression. The emotions there were not so alien as the man's appearance. Anger and shame were ubiquitous among the races that walked the earth, it seemed. Knowing that this was the one who had ridden the Monarch stag, the latest in a long line, made Prentice think that he must have been a champion of his people. He must have striven and trained in his youth, fought and competed, just for the privilege of that role, and now he would be remembered as the one who rode the sovereign beast to its death.

Like Sebastian, Prentice thought, remembering the earl driven by his pride to rebel against Archduchess Amelia in the drought. No, these fey were not so different, for all their ancient wisdom.

"He says that he is outside the camp," Solft said, and Prentice was broken from his contemplations, not realizing that the fey had started to answer the question.

"Outside the camp?" Prentice repeated, wondering what that meant precisely, but before he could ask for more, Dahyoor snorted derisively. "Did you get that wrong, Master?"

"I don't think so, My Lord," Solft said, scratching at his beard with a puzzled expression on his face. "He said it twice."

"Twice? He said it twice?" Prentice wondered at the expression spoken twice and then smiled. "He is between camps."

"Oh, of course," said Solft, and Dahyoor offered a smug nod.

"What camps?" Prentice asked. "The Verdant and the Wind Rising?"

Before Solft could translate, Dahyoor scoffed. The stag rider muttered a short question and the horse archer answered quietly. Then the Verdant fey scoffed as well and began to speak loudly, gesticulating grandly as he pointed in many directions, as well as up at the mountains and down at the river.

Prentice looked to his own translator, but Solft's limited knowledge of fey speech failed him as the pronouncements went on. He shook his head apologetically.

"Forgive me, My Lord," he said to Prentice. Behind him, Prentice heard Guillam tut with disgust at the softer man's failure, and he turned to look the corporal straight in the eye.

You think you could do better? he thought, certain Guillam would read his meaning in his expression. The corporal tilted his head and gave an unapologetic, one-shouldered shrug. Prentice looked back to the fey, who were quiet once more, and then at Dahyoor directly.

"Are you going to tell us his meaning, or do you want us to guess?"

Dahyoor's expression hardened to another scowl, and he bared his teeth a moment. These two were together, but they were not allies, of that Prentice was becoming certain. Initially he had suspected that the Verdant might have dominated Dahyoor because he still retained more honor despite his recent defeat. Now though, the hostility between them seemed deeper than mere social structure. Dahyoor had accepted his own people's disdain without any resistance. Benjamin might as well have put convict fetters on Dahyoor's ankles, and the broken rider never flinched. But he had resentment for this stag-riding war leader of his people's kin. What else was between them?

"They are a people in two places," Dahyoor described the Verdant fey, grinding the words through gritted teeth. "On the mountain lakeside and in the last ancient forest. They are split by their pact with the Untrue, *lasmour rahsiis.*"

Prentice looked to Solft, who worked to translate quickly since Dahyoor did not stop to allow time for interpretation.

"They deserve it...or should deserve it, I think. It is a complicated..."

Prentice stilled Solft with a hand.

Serves them right, he thought. *That's what Dahyoor means.*

"The *brakkis effar* take what they want from the cliff clingers, and the forest warriors are left free," Dahyoor continued to explain in a terse voice that was showing more contempt by the moment. "Except when the Untrue summon for battle. The Verdant keep their waters and their trees at the price of their people. Their riders are proud still, but their pride serves the Untrue, protects the Untrue when the serpents and vermin demand. The Witch came to bind us with the secrets her sisters learned to bind *them,* to bind the Verdant. Verdant secrets to bind the Verdant, shared from the oldest oaths."

Dahyoor's contempt for the Verdant fey was suddenly undisguised, and Prentice thought he could see why. His people—the horse archer fey, Wind Rising—had been bound to the Serpent Witch through blood sacrifice and the enslavement of the unicorn. By the sound of it, the Verdant fey had cooperated far more in their own bindings to the witches of the Blood Sects, perhaps even taught them how to do it.

"They betrayed you," he said to Dahyoor, and the bereft fey's eyes narrowed, moist with unshed tears. His jaw clenched and he nodded ever so slightly, as if even admitting the truth might have robbed him of all self-control. Prentice felt sure he understood what had happened between the two peoples now.

"You came straight to them with a message of liberation after the drought broke," he said, eyes on Dahyoor, as if he and the outcast horse fey were the only two people on the ravine floor, alone in the sunlight that would only strike this ground between mountains at midday like this. Shortly, the passage of the sun across the sky would overshadow this tiny river pass. As if that were some kind of pressure to his thoughts, Prentice outlined what he was thinking without pause.

"You were sent to tell them the Serpent Witch was overthrown, that all the serpent witches, all the mantis men, the *imzuss* and the *brakkis effar* of every kind could be overthrown. A new power had come to the lands, a power that frightened the cabals of the Untrue. You had seen it, and you brought the news of it to your kin, but they...would not listen?"

Dahyoor nodded and looked away, saying something in fey speech in a tone so hateful, it was as if the words themselves burned his tongue, and he could not get them out of his mouth fast enough. The Verdant warrior beside him shifted, and for the first time, his expression was tinged with some traces of shame.

"Hunted, like game," Solft interpreted, quietly. Prentice nodded and understood. He remembered his vision from the lake, with the huts on the cliffside and the forest in the distance, blocking the mouth of the secret valley. The villagers were like serfs to the Redlander occupying force and the deer riders were vassals, allowed limited freedom in the forest, but only if they paid fealty with service, protecting the cabals and keeping out all others, even their Wind Rising kin. And when the horse archers had come from the east with a message of hope to overthrow tyranny, the vassals had turned on them and hunted them down, either at the command of the Redlander cabal or from their own loyalty to the pact. This was the shameful secret that had broken Dahyoor and led Benjamin to ignore his obligations to the Western Reach. The two fey nations were kin, family, and like an argument between family members, not even friends or allies could be brought into a betrayal like this until it was settled between family. Except that they had forgotten one thing—by action and by adoption, Prentice Ash *was* family to the fey, supposedly.

"Between camps?" Prentice repeated, and suddenly he understood the Verdant warrior better as well. Dahyoor gave him a knowing look—no smile to it but encouraging nonetheless. The Monarch stag was slain, so the champion rider had no more place with the vassals in the forest. He was as outcast in his way as Dahyoor. Was he expected to return to the village and accept a place as a serf, a peasant belonging to the cabal now? Would they even let him return? Perhaps he would be the perfect candidate for a sacrifice, a formerly bolder and more independent fey, now broken and failed, like an uppity convict given an especially brutal flogging as a lesson to all the others. Perhaps they would make him wear a collar and keep him on a chain, as it seemed they did to the failed Serpent Witch who had lost the power of the unicorn. Was that why he was "between two camps" now? He could no longer ride with the deer riders, but had not returned, or *would* not return, to the villagers, broken and clinging to whatever pride he had left.

Prentice looked to Solft.

"Best you can, Master, say exactly these words to our Verdant friend," he told him. Looking straight at the Verdant fey, he carefully composed his words. "You watched us from the long water as we crossed the desert. You have seen me ride, surely? I have fallen from the saddle before and likely will again."

The Verdant fey snorted a contemptuous laugh and Dahyoor showed an involuntary smirk. Prentice allowed himself a smile at his own poor horsemanship.

"*Palpolon*," he said, nodding his agreement at their assessment of his skills. "But sometimes, when we fall, we can see the path between two camps that cannot be seen from the saddle. A path that no others have seen. Is that not true?"

Dahyoor gave his fellow messenger a knowing look and the Verdant warrior slowly nodded.

"Has he seen a path like that?" Prentice asked, and Dahyoor nodded as well. Prentice looked to the pale fey and waited, and it seemed as if everyone in the ravine paused to wait with him. Even the sound of the last few Lions still descending the slope behind them felt distant and muted. Only the river burbled, as it had continuously in their hearing since the day they had climbed the scarp and begun their march into the west. With grim deliberateness, as if it hurt him, the Verdant fey spoke, the hatefulness gone from his expression for the very first time.

It may well be causing him pain, Prentice thought as he listened, remembering the way in which the Serpent Witch's magick had killed a fey archer elder when he resisted it in the Reacher village last year. This time, as he spoke, Dahyoor did not hesitate to translate all his words.

"There is blood between us Ashen Man," said the stag rider. "You alone have put blade to the Monarch of the Deep Forest, and by your strike he was weakened to your fire-iron spitters. Now the riders strive to prove themselves, to take the place I have fallen from, but none of them rides the Monarch. They do not know if another can become as he was.

"The Untrue have commanded me to find you and take your blood. If I bring them your slayer's blade, with your own blood on the edge, they will make of me a new Horned Man. This is their promise for your blood."

Was that where the first Horned Man came from? Prentice wondered. *Was he one of your people?*

The Lions muttered and grumbled, taking the fey man's words as a threat to their leader, but Prentice stilled them by making a dramatic gesture of re-sheathing his sword and fitting the belt once more around his waist. The sign was obvious to all. If the Verdant and Redlanders wanted his sword, they could come and fight for it. The stag rider bowed his head and nodded wearily. Then he continued his story.

"They fear you, and they are right. Since the long, ancient ride westward, our people have feared the coming of your people. We pitied Wind Rising, who took the duty of watching the mountains for your hateful warriors. When the riders of horses came with their stories of you, of how you had killed the unicorn and broken the Serpent, we thought they had betrayed the ancient vows. They had made peace with the enemy that drove us across the mountains. The Untrue told us that the Wind Rising had ambushed and betrayed their envoy, the Serpent they had sent to seek alliance, so that all the betrayed might stand united once more against the merciless preachers of mercy."

Listening, Prentice doubted that the Verdant warrior had used the term "Untrue" for the Redlanders if his people saw them as allies. Perhaps Dahyoor did not want to translate the Verdant word for the Blood Sect peoples. He also wondered if the Inquisition were the merciless preachers of mercy to the Verdant folk. For that matter, what were Inxyphos and his men to them at all? If the Verdant thought the Wind Rising had the duty to prevent the Grand Kingdom coming west across the Azures, then what did they think of the Redlanders and the Inquisition working together? What pattern did those threads of the tapestry weave?

"I am older than any of your people or the Wind Rising," the stag rider was translated, and his voice was becoming cold again with sullen anger, as if he blamed Prentice or the White Lions for the sadness he was expressing. "When I was a child, our boats roamed all the waters of our land. This was all forest, deep so that even noon was evening under its branches. Only the farms of the farthest east were struggling, building well channels to bring the water with life. The Untrue promised us their aid. They first came to buy our boats, for nothing made in their land traveled as the ones we grew for them, not even on the brackish waters that remained from the Writhing. Our land died, went to salt and dust, and they promised aid, binding us to tighter and tighter pacts for vows they then broke. In our hearts we know that they *are* the drought, they *are* the curse, and that their pacts can no more heal our land than venom can make a corpse to live. But we cannot speak this truth that we all know. We are bound by blood upon ancient blood."

"Tell him the Wind Rising are no longer bound, despite the Serpent Witch's abuse of the unicorn," Prentice said to

Dahyoor, but the horseman shook his head wearily, as if the words were pointless.

"He knows already. He does not believe."

Prentice put his hand to his sword's hilt once more. "Is this not enough proof?"

"It was not enough for Benjamin."

That caught Prentice by surprise, and his eyes narrowed. He stared, about to insist that Dahyoor explain, when the Verdant warrior demanded attention once again.

CHAPTER 66

"You are the Ashen Man," Dahyoor translated. "You are a death thing and the blood on you stinks across the desert."

Several of the militiamen growled at yet another insult to their leader, but Prentice was unconcerned. He had already claimed nearly as much about himself when he had flashed his unicorn-horn-hilted sword in the sun.

"You have come to kill the Untrue, which we cannot do," the Verdant continued belligerently in the face of the militia's anger. "Do that and leave, and there will be nothing more between us."

"It's an odd way to offer peace," Guillam muttered, and Prentice agreed enough not to bother trying to quiet him.

"No, it isn't much of a deal," Sergeant Gennet concurred, and Prentice realized that virtually the whole of the company was now standing around, having arrived to listen to this bleak parley.

"It may not be, Sergeant," Prentice said quietly. "But it might still be one we have to accept."

He fixed Dahyoor with his gaze and lifted his head.

"What does he say about the Blood Sect members—the cultists, the ones amongst his own folk?" he asked.

Dahyoor translated Prentice's question and the Verdant champion's reply was short.

"He says, 'They pass unseen,'" Dahyoor returned.

Prentice shook his head. That was not good enough. "They do *not* pass unseen. I have seen them. They wear the tattoos, something no *kreff* yet has achieved. If they are not *imzuss* they are still more..."

Prentice heard Solft cough politely and stopped to see what he wanted.

"My Lord, the...uhm...the Verdant man did not exactly say they pass unseen," he explained, quite openly, and Prentice glanced at Dahyoor to see if the horse archer had any reaction to being caught in a lie. Solft continued. "I couldn't understand what he *did* say, but the way he said it, the tone and phrasing, was the way the Wind Rising say *their* phrase, '*We pass unseen* .'" I think Dahyoor was transposing for us."

Prentice turned fully back to the two fey, thinking. To "pass unseen" was the way of the Wind Rising. It was their article of faith. If this other fey was citing *his* people's credo, it had one likely meaning.

"Our Verdant friend is telling us it is none of our business, is he? That once we kill the Redlander cabal for him, what his people do is not our concern?"

Dahyoor nodded slowly.

Definitely not good enough, Prentice thought. There would be little point in slaying the *imzuss* and the other Redlanders if they left devout initiates of their cult behind amongst the fey. That would not make the Reach safe.

"The cultists will only bring the Redlanders back or else become an *imzuss* themselves. Tell him to let us help and we will cut out the corruption, root and branch."

Dahyoor translated and the Verdant gave his aphoristic response.

"He said the same...," Solft began but Prentice cut him off.

"I recognized it this time, thank you, Master." The knight commander drew in a hot breath and sighed. There was only one question left to which he needed an answer. "What will happen if we refuse his help?"

Words were translated and the response given. The Verdant rider seemed all but smug in the certainty with which he spoke.

"He says you will never pass through the forest valley alive. Amidst the deep green, the Verdant are lords." Dahyoor looked down to one side, his drawn face a mix of frustration and pain. "His words are not a boast."

So, we have a bad deal or no deal, Prentice thought. *An incomplete victory or certain defeat.* It was not a choice he would accept.

"Tell me," he asked, "was it this Verdant rider who sent the messages of times through the stone in the water?"

When Dahyoor translated the question, the Verdant fey nodded solemnly.

"These times you mentioned, they are important and specific?" Prentice asked. The fey nodded once more.

"Each noon can be a meeting, for they are distracted with their rituals," came the translation. It was obvious "they" were the priests of the cabal, rebinding the lake waters. "They call a few through the sky to make themselves safe against you once more. One boat each time."

Two more crew's worth of spearmen and beast-men, Prentice thought. Probably no chariots, though. That was not an insurmountable challenge for the Gryphon Banner, if they were past the Verdant riders and their "valley of death."

"Then, at the new moon midnight, they will bind the waters whole once more," the fey went on. "The dragonflies will be mantis claimed again completely, and they will bring all their boats through the sky in the dawn, one whole swarm, to fill the lake and to send them upon the flat between the eastern river and the eastern mountains."

The invasion goes into the Dwelt on that morning, Prentice thought. *A swarm of ships, full of spearmen and mantis warriors. This deal he is offering is clearly the only chance we have to stop them in time.*

Prentice knew it was possible that the fey man was lying about the time available. Despite Dahyoor's conviction about the power of the Verdant fey within their own land, the knight commander might be willing to try a brute-force approach if given no other choice in getting to the dragonfly lake. But ever since he had seen the vision while he was drowning, he had felt the pressure of time, the growing danger to his liege, his land, and his love.

And the child I have never seen, he thought hopefully, but he pressed it down into a quiet corner swiftly. Now was a time for courage and cunning, not hope.

"What is your pledge then?"

"Bring your death. Lay your hate blade upon the necks of the Untrue, spit your iron-fire into their flesh, but spare the Verdant people. Then we will take the dragonflies once more, and we will send you home in the reflection on the water," the fey champion promised. He turned to look sneeringly at Dahyoor. "Then the Verdant will be unseen and all will be *kreff* to us." It seemed clear he was including his people's Wind Rising kin in that pronouncement.

"If your people will still hear your words," Prentice told him, "tell them that we will spare those who stand aside. We will even leave the slingers alone if they stay clear of us on the field, but if they stand between us and the Untrue or the merciless, their blood will be upon their own heads."

After interpretation, it was clear such a thing was unacceptable to the Verdant rider.

"He insists you swear not to attack his people. Only the Redlanders and the other *kreff.*"

"He's a bold mongrel," Corporal Guillam muttered, and Prentice was surprised when he was hushed by Brother Whilte, who was standing between him and Sergeant Gennet. Prentice could not remember the last time he had not heard the chaplain's clomping, peglegged approach. It was an indicator of how intensely he was focused on this meeting with threadbare envoys of ancient peoples.

"Tell him exactly this, Dahyoor," Prentice said, formulating his oath carefully in his thoughts. "Tell him I will pledge in the name of the Lioness Mother and her throne that the *kreff* will spit no iron-fire and raise no steel against his folk, either from the forest or the lakeside, if he will bring us to the lake in time to stop the cabal, the *imzuss*, and let us leave the Verdant fey lands unmolested all the way back to the Reach itself."

Dahyoor passed the details, and the Verdant's response was unmistakable.

"He so swears," Solft translated.

"Tell him to swear on the blood of his people already shed, and to be shed, that binds them to the Redlander coven," Prentice said further. Solft quailed and Prentice heard one or two of the watching Lions draw in shocked breaths. Even Dahyoor looked discomforted by the suggestion. Prentice, however, was as unyielding as the stag rider.

"Tell him these oaths will bind us by the highest values of our people. If he wants his folk freed, he must entrust them to us as we entrust ourselves to him."

Solft's voice trembled as he fumbled the interpretation, and when his knowledge of fey tongue began to fail him again, Dahyoor grimly finished the message. The Verdant rider's visage contorted in rage and hatred, more unvarnished even than it had been throughout the entire meeting. For a moment, Prentice thought he might have pushed too hard, but the Verdant fey's attention suddenly shifted warily to the river. He looked up at the sky and the shadows falling from the ravine sides. Noon was passing.

Our moment of secrecy is waning, Prentice thought.

With eyes like flint and a scowl of pure venom, the stag rider nodded and spoke words like flung spears or leaden slingstones.

"He so swears, My Lord," Solft said with a tone of horror and remorse, as if he felt personally wounded by the dark oath Prentice had just extracted.

"Then so do I swear, in the name of Archduchess Amelia, Lioness of the Western Reach and by her throne, the Lions will raise no weapons against you nor fire upon you, even if you assault us," Prentice said. Inwardly he was shocked by how many times he had freely given his liege's word in oaths and promises. He might have called it a bad habit—her grace often did—but it seemed to yield useful results, in the main. He was sure once she learned of this oath in her name though, assuming he lived to tell her, she would not be pleased by it.

Just let her be pleased with the outcome.

"Dahyoor will stay as our guide," Solft conveyed as the former stag rider stood suddenly upon the stone. The armed men around him tensed, unsure what he would do next. "He will bring us to the place where the Wind Rising fey are so that they can fight beside us against the Untrue. This pledge will be the last time Verdant blood will be shed to bind another."

Until the cultists amongst you find a reason to use the rituals again, Prentice thought.

The rider jumped down off the stone and several Claws made to hedge him back with their halberds, but Prentice called them off. The enemy champion walked swiftly to the river's edge, and as his first step touched the water, he was simply gone, with nothing but empty air where he had been standing. Men gaped in astonishment, and some looked to heaven prayerfully.

"He certainly has power," said Whilte.

Prentice looked at the river.

"He rode the Monarch of the Deep Forest," the knight commander said grimly, using the Verdant fey's own title for the slain stag. "He has power to move through the water and to send you messages through it."

"That was *him?*" Whilte asked, surprised. Obviously, he had not been present for that part of the conversation. Prentice nodded.

"The words, at least. I would say he has, or had, something of the authority of an elder, if his artifice and power are any evidence."

"But does the pledge have power to bind him or his folk?"

"The blood of his people and the compacts made under it have cursed forest and farm to become desert for hundreds of leagues in all directions, even over land fed by *that* river." Prentice pointed at the Murr nearby. "I doubt anything bound to that blood could resist its power."

"So, seems you've sworn us, by desert-making blood-power, to stand and take as many stag charges and slingers' shots as they want to throw at us, eh, My Lord?" Guillam asked sourly, clearly letting his mood make him forget his promise to speak bluntly only amongst senior officers. "Why'd you do that?"

"Because we need to reach their lake before the Redlanders send their fleet to Dweltford, and it seems we have but few days left to do it," Prentice explained. "We have a bad chance or no chance."

"That's as may be, but how's our chances goin' to be gettin' to these Redlander witches if them snowy fey can get in the way? What are we goin' to do? Say 'boo' and try to shoo them off?"

"Watch your lip, Corporal," Gennet said sternly, obviously assuming that no matter what latitude the knight commander was allowing to Guillam, this was a liberty too far. Prentice smiled coldly at the Roar officer.

"We will not raise our weapons to the Verdant fey, Corporal, because we will not need to. The Azure fey will clear the path for us. My pledge binds the Lions and the throne of Dweltford," Prentice said. "It says nothing about Benjamin and his *keshiyaa.*"

Guillam whistled in appreciation of his commander's cunning, and others who overheard chuckled, but Master Solft was clearly discomforted with such calculated oath-making.

"If you play them that way, My Lord, they will never forgive us, or you," the scholar said in a dread tone. "You will be a monster to them forever."

"I am already a monster to them," Prentice responded, his lips a tight line and his eyes narrow. "The Ashen Man, a thing of death, remember?"

Solft looked to Dahyoor, who was now sliding off the rock, his sullen expression back in place, and Prentice understood the scholar's concerns, but he did not share them.

"You will pit kin against kin," Solft said.

"Kin are already pitted against kin," Prentice told him, waving to his officers that they should form up to follow Dahyoor, their new guide. "And I promise you, Benjamin will welcome this chance for revenge."

CHAPTER 67

The Aubrey bridge was not the smoking ruin Amelia had imagined, though as she thought about it, it had been almost a week since Robant's black-powder ploy. Now, as she approached it by the road, it looked to the archduchess that it was much as it had been when she last had seen it. It was not until the corporal commanding, a man whose name she did not know, led her along the bank a little way that she saw the damage for what it was. Strangely, in the bright afternoon sun, it looked much less terrible than it had in her dream.

"It's really just them two spans there," the corporal explained, pointing to the gap in the middle of the ancient river crossing. Across three sets of footings, the boards and side walls were simply missing. The pillar in the middle barely poked its way above the water, and the footings on either end of the gap showed cracked stones and other damage.

"For a while there, bits'd fall off and either sink or float away," the corporal explained, "but looks like it's mostly settled now, Your Graceship."

"Your Grace," Spindle corrected reflexively from her spot behind Amelia. The corporal looked at the masked woman like she was a ghost, then tugged his forelock obediently.

"Sorry, *Your Grace*."

"Has anyone checked the damage more closely?" Amelia asked. The corporal shook his head vehemently.

"The...uhmmm...," he paused and looked from Amelia to Spindle and back. "The *orders* are that unless and until that army across the water makes off, there's to be no one of ours risking 'emselves on the bridge. If the fellows over there make a go of it, we're free to let 'em try anything they like. Once it looks like they might actually make a proper go of a crossing, not just droppin' in the water like, then we give 'em a taste of Roar shot. That's the orders."

"Knight Captain Farringdon's orders?" Amelia asked, guessing the cause of the corporal's pause. The junior officer nodded, looking even more frightened than he had of Lady Spindle's correction. Amelia could hardly blame him. The last time she had been here, she had berated her husband for disloyalty and implicit cowardice. She imagined not one of the men garrisoning the bridge that day would be eager to mention their knight captain in her presence again.

"If those are his commands, then you do well to follow them," she told the corporal, keeping her face in her expression of courtly reserve but making sure her voice was warm. It would take time to correct the damage that the "whispering little birds" of the Inquisition had done to her marriage, as well as her reputation. She might as well begin the long task of restoring them sooner rather than later, and endorsing her husband's orders in public was not a poor start. The corporal tugged his forelock, and for a moment the memory of Amelia's dream chilled her. She had realized while talking to the smith that there was some kind of Inquisition agent, as secretive and likely as empowered with arcanum as Bluebird had been, who had been working to sabotage the cannons Master Sent had built. Standing now in the bright sunlight by the bridge, she realized she had no reason to suppose that agent, whoever they were, had not come south with the cannons as well. If they were so secretive as to be like mimics, then what was to stop them from hiding amongst any of these men, right here?

It could be this corporal, so obsequious. Amelia turned to speak to Spindle and drew in a horrified breath when she realized it could be Spindle herself. The archduchess almost recoiled, nearly seeing her lady-in-waiting's concerned expression as a true mask to conceal murderous intent, but when she thought of how it was she even knew these truths, she nearly laughed at herself instead. There had been no warning in her dream of ongoing danger to her person, only to the cannoneers and the master smith whose forging was usurped. Why would a trustworthy dream reveal only half a threat? She knew the dream was trustworthy because the smith's assessment of the wrecked cannon had confirmed it. Moreover, as she thought about it, Amelia realized that any scion of the Inquisition that wanted her dead had just had five days with her in one place with few attendants watching. They could have done the deed then. If they could have faked a true weld to the perfectionist Master Sent, they could surely have bypassed a few sentries or stewards. It would not even have had to be a stiletto in the night, a tiny manipulation of the healer's draughts, or an unction in her food when the cook wasn't watching. These would easily have done the job. There was no point in living in fear and mistrust. If she did that, Bluebird and his "flock" would have her caged forever.

"These others are reinforcing the banks in case Baron Rob...sorry, Duke Robant, tries for a boat crossing?" she asked the corporal, pointing to where men were digging at the riverside.

"Some, Your Grace," he confirmed, "Others is for Roar's ramparts for facin' south."

"South? Why south?"

"Knight captain's orders again, I fear. When he rode off, he said to make it so we can defend both riverside and landward side. Seems there was word of another Veckander army, or part of the last one, seen hereabouts."

"Another army?" Amelia remembered that some force under the Golden Heron's pay had been ranging in the south, but she had not thought of an entire *second* mercenary army. Even as she considered this news, the sound of hoofs beating on the road turned her eyes southward and two of Farringdon's lancers pelted up, their mounts' bits dripping foam. One of the two lancers was the company's sergeant, Nunel. He reigned in his mount and saluted without leaving the saddle.

"Your Grace, the knight captain bids me tell you that a Golden Heron force is but few hours' march away, coming on the road from Trachester. The camp is to be roused and arrayed as he left orders, with your permission."

"These are my husband's orders?" she asked. "Why does he send you?"

"I think, Your Grace, that the marquis thought you still indisposed," Nunel said with impressive politeness. "He would surely not have merely sent me with orders for the Lions without regard to your person otherwise."

Amelia sighed inwardly.

Everyone thinks they must step on eggshells around me now, she thought. She had so much to correct.

"The marquis is my husband and Knight Captain of the Western Reach," she said in her strongest voice. "While I march with the White Lion Banner, he may dispose of my person as he sees fit. And at other times as well, perhaps, but that is not the business of this afternoon."

"Your Grace?" Spindle said behind her with affected breathlessness. It pleased Amelia that for once it was she who shocked one of the Lace Fangs with her speech and not the other way around. For that experience alone she felt a debt of gratitude to Spindle's instructress, the Forever Countess.

"Nevertheless, Sergeant Nunel, the meaning of my question was to ask why my husband has not come himself?"

"The knight captain remains with the main of the lancers, hoping to harry and delay the enemy's approach, Your Grace."

Amelia looked around at her militiamen, caught in uncertainty in her presence. Bluebird had done his fell work well indeed, undermining her with the ones who should be able to trust her the most. Well, no longer.

"We have our orders, Lions of the Reach. Let us go to as the knight commander instructs and make every use of the time he wins for us."

She turned to the corporal whose name she still did not know.

"See that a full defense is prepared here and make ready for the rest of the Lion Banner to join you. Pick dry spaces for supplies, as much will be transferred here directly. And have eagle eyes on the north bank. The dog Robant might have a coordinated crossing planned. He doubtless has captured many rivermen's craft with his blockade. When he sees the Veckanders coming to assault us again, he might try to use them to put us back into the jaws of the wolf."

Amelia's confident and authoritative tone must have touched something in the corporal's mind, something deeply drilled, as he forgot to tug his forelock but instead saluted her as he would any other senior officer. Amused, the archduchess turned away, leaving the man to his duties. She looked up at Nunel once more.

"Sergeant, no doubt you have other instructions from my husband, but first I must call upon you to carry me in your saddle with haste to the camp."

"I have orders to see to your safety, Your Grace," Nunel reported dutifully.

"Excellent. Since my safety will be best achieved by uniting the whole of the company in a single, strong location, and I will be best able to assist in that back in camp rather than wringing my hands uselessly here, you will take me *there*."

Nunel looked at Amelia with a suspicious expression, as if he doubted her reasoning but could find no way to refute it. With a bow in the saddle, he shifted his weight and offered her his hand. She reached for it, but just before taking it, looked to Lady Spindle behind her.

"Your other man can carry my lady-in-waiting," she said. The second lancer saluted without hesitation and walked his horse forward to offer his hand to Spindle. Before she took his, she looked to her two hired guards.

"We'll run along behind," one of them said, not looking like he enjoyed the prospect.

"You will stay here and ready a place for your mistress and myself, to which we will send the rest of your guard contingent to assist you," Amelia commanded. The man's expression seemed to harden a little and he sniffed.

"We answer to Lady Spindle," he said flatly. Amelia's eyes went wide, but Spindle spoke first.

"You answer to me, and I answer to her grace." The lady gave the pair a firm look, but Amelia was not satisfied. She stepped away from Nunel's horse for a moment and stood directly in front of the hired bodyguard.

"Aubrey is now part of the Western Reach, of which I am sovereign in name, title, and power," she said, her voice almost pleasant, but her intent unyielding all the same. "In these lands you answer to me only after God Almighty. If this does not suit you, I will happily have you put in irons to await exile when my forces have time. Because of your loyal service to my lady-in-waiting, I have afforded you certain privileges. Do not forget by whose hand you enjoy them."

The guard blinked, as if surprised to see Amelia's comfortable and controlled sense of her own authority. He was doubtless used to the shrill and unruly woman that treachery and magick had created. He and his partner looked around themselves, as if only now realizing they were in the midst of a large body of armed men sworn to Amelia's service. The archduchess gave them a gentle but knowing smile. It was not their fault they had spent too long in the presence of a whining and sickly housecat, but it was time they realized the Lioness was back with her pride—time that everyone did.

The two lancers took Amelia and Spindle swiftly on their chargers back to the main camp where it looked as if some word of the approaching army had begun to circulate. There was a tense buzz of conversation and many Lions stood around, weapons in hand, or putting their armor pieces on.

"My orders are to rally the company and be ready to fight or march upon the enemy's appearance," Nunel said as he let Amelia down to the ground gently. "One of my men already went to seek Sergeant Sedgemark."

"He was still abed as of this morning," Amelia told the sergeant. "If he is unable to rise, you will have to pass the word to the corporals and line firsts of the foot yourself."

Nunel accepted that, but Amelia had further instructions.

"Our stores are currently in the charge of a handful of merchants with quartermaster duties. I will go to them now and explain what is happening. When the Claws and Fangs are in order, have them come by lines to the stores and each man will take a single piece of our victuals with him to the bridgehead. God willing, we will defeat this army as easily as the last, but if we do not, I will not allow them to take our supplies as we took my husband's uncle's."

"As you command, Your Grace," Nunel said, and he turned his mount around some of the tents, leaving Amelia and Spindle alone, but only for a moment as Markas appeared with two drummers and an escort of four halberd-wielding Claws. He marched straight to the two ladies and all seven in the little cadre saluted together.

"Your Grace, with your permission, you need an escort," he said bluntly. Amelia cocked an eyebrow at him. The last time she had seen him was at the bridge when he had stood up for Farringdon against her. She had thought him as impertinent as her husband then, but he had volunteered to go onto the bridge knowing that the gunpowder might already have been set beneath it. Courageous. As she remembered the day, Amelia also realized that far from crassly insolent, as she had perceived him under the influence of the Inquisition's whispered charm, he had actually been diligently polite.

"Should you not be with the banner?" she asked without malice.

"Sergeant Sedgemark holds post by the standard, Your Grace," Markas explained readily. "The healer says his back is not yet strong enough for him to move about too much, though I think he's about ready to tell her to take a swim in the Murr. But since he and me are of a rank, being as Captain Prentice made me Banner Sergent—equals as it were—we swapped duties. I'm seeing to the assembling of the lines, sending all to the banner as the rally point."

A drumbeat began to echo over the camp. Amelia looked up.

"Rally on the standard, Your Grace," Markas reported, knowing the signal reflexively.

Amelia nodded, accepting his explanation. She looked to the drummers standing behind him and he followed her eyes.

"You're the archduchess, Your Grace, peer of rank and liege," he explained. "Wherever you are, figures you're going to need messengers, especially since the stewards are set with breaking down the camp and hauling to the bridge. Goes double, I reckon, since Knight Captain Farringdon ain't with us at the moment neither."

Amelia smiled at the dutiful man with the white-linen noose around his neck.

"Excellent work, Banner Sergeant," she said earnestly. Looking over her little company of guards and attendants, with the sounds of the camp breaking around them, she formed a swift list in her mind of the important tasks she wanted completed before she returned to where they would make their riverside stand.

"Lady Spindle, go to your husband and see him northward with the rest of your guard contingent," she said. "Keep them with you both until you are returned to the river. Fetch from our supplies anything important you think to save. Be prudent,

My Lady. I do not want to hear of you being weighted down with a dozen bolts of cloth. What you cannot carry, I do not want. Take the time to fetch Silvermane and your own horse, but do not weigh them down with extra goods. Master Welburne, yourself, their saddles, and tack—these will be burdens enough."

Spindle curtseyed and turned to go, but as she did, Amelia added one last duty.

"Also, look in on the crone who did my healing," she said. "The gifted healers go where they will but offer her safety and succor if she is like to accompany to us to the bridgehead."

"As you command," said the Lace Fang, and then she was gone. Amelia turned to one of the two drummers, a fair-haired boy of no more than ten.

"Are you fast?" she asked him, remembering how proud Solomon had been, running messages all around the castle through the end of summer and into autumn and winter, despite the cruel injury to his face. This boy nodded with an eager smile that made Amelia wonder how many battlefields he had yet stood upon.

"I want you to run, swift as you can, to Sergeant Sedge-mark, and tell him that her grace says that our militia may have some unexpected folk amongst them heading to the river. Folk in rags, looking hungry and wan. They are to have our protection. Can you remember all that."

The boy nodded again. Amelia gave him a flick of her head to send him on his way, but he seemed to not understand the gesture. Markas gave him a gentle clip on the shoulder.

"Her grace has given you an order lad. Don't you tarry."

The boy rushed away into the growing chaos, forgetting to salute in his haste. Amelia turned to the other drummer, who seemed even younger than the one just gone.

"Is there a beat that summons Lions to aid the comman-der?" she asked him. He nodded, as awestruck to be speaking to the liege of the entire Western Reach as his departed partner had been. "And do you know that beat?"

He nodded again.

"Well, have it ready in your mind, for I have some tasks yet to perform before I can head to the river. If they take me too long, I might be caught out, and I will need your drum to call a greater escort. That will be your task. Your comrades are stout men, but four Claws cannot fend away an army all alone."

The drummer looked to the escort militiamen and clearly liked being called one of their comrades. Markas ruffled the boy's hair affectionately. Then the banner sergeant looked at Amelia.

"Where would you have us go, Your Grace?" he asked.

"When his army occupied Cattlefields, Prince Garrodmin trapped the survivors of Aubrey between his camp and the haunted ruin, there to starve or be abused for sport," Amelia said. "I have not subjected them to such a fate, nor will I abandon them to another Vec army that might repeat Garrodmin's sins."

Markas nodded, then stroked his dark beard thoughtfully.

"I know they don't seem like they got much to leave, Your Grace," he said. "But like as not, they won't be quick to make to follow us. They dug in there on the rump of their own town for almost two years now. If they were like to run, they would sure have done it already."

Amelia understood Markas's true meaning. The forlorn survivors under Aubrey's walls were not likely to accept any offer to move on, even in the face of a threatening army. Nevertheless, she had to give them the chance; they were her people. She would make sure that Markas and his men remained watchful for the coming enemy and listened out for any signaling drumbeats. It was some risk to go so far from the rest of Lion Banner, but as she led her little escort westward at a brisk march, Amelia felt her spirits lifting higher than they had been for weeks. She was out of the cage of fear that had been built by whispers in her thoughts.

The pride was yet in danger, but the Lioness was free once more.

CHAPTER 68

The morose Dahyoor led the Gryphon Banner Company westward through the high gorge along the grassy edge of the river, with massive cliffs overshadowing their passage. Prentice glanced at the sheer rock faces and marveled at the forces that must have cracked the mountains apart to allow the river to flow between them. He was also watchful for any secretive ambush waiting in unseen clefts. Mostly, though, his attention was focused upon their guide. The fey rider still seemed the same beaten-down outcast Prentice had first met back in the Reach grasslands—spindly of limb, walking slump shouldered, wearing the reproach of his people's harsh standards. The knight commander knew the posture well. Every convict transported over the Azures walked that way.

Prentice was concentrating on Dahyoor so fixedly that it was some time until he noticed that as the gorge continued westward, so the grass under their feet became fresher. They were almost completely through the gap, with the sky becoming open ahead of them, before he realized that at least half the fronds under their feet were green amidst the bleached stalks of straw. Their guide rounded a final corner, and while the mountains opened up, their view did not, for they were at the foot of a forested valley so rich with green growth that it was as if they had just stepped into another world. The grass continued for a mere handful of paces and then it was a wall of verdancy—Verdant fey, indeed.

Men gasped as they came out of the gorge, and many stopped in the midst of the column. Prentice could understand their awe. He felt it in himself. After so many weeks of only lifeless dust, the sudden riot of myriad greens and other living colors was almost an assault upon the vision. Trees as tall as church steeples marched in dense thickets almost right to the ravine entrance. Flowers bloomed at the side of the river, which rapidly disappeared under branches and hanging vines. The air itself seemed thicker, and breathing brought intoxicating scents of water and seeds on the wind, of rich earth and living things. Looking upward to either side of the opening in the cliffs, Prentice could see some trees climbing slopes and growing up the heights to overlook what was likely a bowl valley, probably larger around than Lake Dweltford, an impossible pocket of primeval life secreted behind bulwark peaks.

"I hadn't realized how much I had forgotten what such greenery might look like," Solft muttered as he stared at the vibrant tableau before them.

"No wonder they kill to keep all this safe," Sergeant Gennet added, moving past the scholar. Although he seemed as awed as the rest, the sergeant still obviously had his mind on his duty, and he moved ahead of the wonderstruck militiamen, eyes searching the shadows under the green for signs of danger.

No wonder they call themselves Verdant, Prentice thought, and he felt a momentary respect for the stag rider's sneering pride, as misplaced as he felt it was. This was something ancient, something mere mortals in places like the Western Reach and the Grand Kingdom had forgotten. If the fey had taken it upon themselves to preserve this, that must surely have been like unto a holy cause, at least at one time. Even so, blood sacrifice was the wrong food for this life and a loathsome chain to bind it with.

Hypocrite, he told himself as he remembered that he had just used the exact same blood to bind the stag rider to his oath. The memory of it soured his enjoyment of the moment like milk left in a drought-struck sun. He was about to give Gennet the order to wrangle the company back to the march when he became aware of Brother Whilte waiting at his shoulder once again, quietly regarding the same wonders but with a sense of weighty thought.

"Master Solft has asked you to speak with me, has he Chaplain?" Prentice asked, looking into the forest once again. "The scholar has hoped that we might win the Verdant fey to our cause as we did the riders in the Azures, and he is heartbroken that I have poisoned all that?"

He heard Whilte draw in a surprised breath.

"I sometimes forget just how shrewd you are, My Lord Knight Commander," the chaplain said. "What I do not forget is that you are not by nature a treacherous man, Baron Ash. You are not a natural liar."

That caught Prentice by surprise. It was a good opening gambit.

"Did you not say you knew about that speech I gave on a barrel, on the march to Fallenhill," he replied, not about to be softened by a mere compliment, no matter how well crafted. "If you know what I said that night, then you know that I lied then for a start, promising convicts freedom for the risk of their lives in the coming battle. I had no power to make that promise. I have done that to convicts and militia more than once since becoming her grace's *Captain* of the Rogues. I have lied many times in her name."

Prentice had not meant to put any emphasis on the word captain, but nonetheless it came out in a harshly derisive tone, as if he despised the lying man that Prentice had been as much as the knights of that time had.

"And has she ever refused to honor her word, given by you?" Whilte asked.

Prentice looked down but had to shake his head. She had often chastised him for his presumption but never refused his word on her behalf.

"She even gave you her signet at one point, did she not?"

Prentice raised his head again with a sigh.

"I assume you think this is significant, Brother," he said wearily.

"Of course, it is. The Archduchess Amelia trusts you with the future of her realm, from least mongrel to her own husband and children."

"She has no children."

"She will. And what is their future benefited by making sworn enemies for them."

"We are here to secure that future!" Prentice declared, his voice rising and disturbing birds nesting under the canopy. He whirled upon the chaplain and Whilte met his gaze. The religious man was calm, but there was pain in his eyes. He was conflicted, and Prentice could understand that, but he had no space for it in himself. Not now.

"I understand the master's concerns and yours, Brother, truly I do," he said earnestly but with a firm tone. He was not pleading, not now. They were too far from home to have a leader who doubted himself. This was the sharp end of the campaign, and even bad decisions were better now than vacillation and indecision.

"But what else would you have me do, Brother? That was one of their champions, one of their elders, if that word has the same meaning to the Verdant fey. What did you hear in his voice?"

"Regret; sadness."

"But no responsibility," Prentice said vehemently. "He is like Sebastian was, adhering to his old ways, hoping to reclaim his old honor and status while the land dies around him."

"Can you blame him, after all his people have heard and seen of us and what they have suffered by the hands of the Redlanders?"

"Some of them are Redlanders," Prentice said, and his eyes narrowed coldly to stare at Whilte. "Some of them are converts, worshipping at masks and magick water like the 'skip crews that we came out here to stop. I saw them by the lake."

"Frightened men will submit to the devil if they do not believe that God can save them."

"And they will be no less rebels against heaven for their fear," Prentice spat back. He remembered his own rage against God, the fury that his faith had been betrayed and the despair that came because he did not understand at that time that not everything done in the name of God was done in the service of God. Even so, this was not the same. There was a difference between a frightened man, grudgingly going through the motions of faith to save his own skin, and a believer who could pass the tests necessary to persuade dark priests of their devotion. Since no Reachermen had yet been found with the tattoos, it seemed no mere *kreff* had ever reached that level of devotion. Inwardly, Prentice shuddered as he imagined the kinds of acts that might be necessary to take that step.

"*Bleed or shed blood;* that is their credo," Prentice said, feeling fury rising within, the match of the forest king rider's anger but cold for all that. "I saw them on the lakeside. Not mere supplicants but converts, believers. *You* understand what kind of devotion Redlander witches demand of their initiates."

"You could look into their hearts?"

"I could see the tattoos on their skins! They bound themselves by blood and took the livery of their new masters into their very flesh. Even the unicorn, drenched in blood and draped with the skins of the dead, was not so ensnared as that."

Whilte fell to silence for a moment, either feeling chastised by Prentice's tone or else allowing the knight commander a breath to settle his own emotions.

"Perhaps he means to purge the blood faith from his folk alone," the chaplain said at last, referring once again to the fallen stag rider. "His intentions might be pure."

"Even if they are, I cannot afford to trust him," Prentice said ruefully. "He wants to go back to what was, in his people's distant past, but even then, when the Verdant fey ruled everything that was the desert we just crossed, they lacked the power, the cunning, or the will to stop the Redlanders from taking their own society from them, even while they watched their land poisoned unto dust. There is a fleet waiting on a coast, somewhere in the world, filled to the brim with *brakkis effar* and painted warriors, all primed to shed the blood of the Reach and likely the Grand Kingdom after them. We could sacrifice and die to slay the cabal that controls the dragonfly now and set the Verdant free, only for the cultists amongst them to hand the whole damned thing back to the Blood Sects at the next new moon. Twenty-eight days later and Dweltford could be swarmed regardless. I am charged to protect the Reach, and I have come out here into the wilds at the edge of the known world to break the mirror in the sky. In service of that goal, there is very little I will not stoop to. The hatred of a fey folk who already despised me for the crimes of my ancestors is little enough price to pay!"

Whilte nodded thoughtfully, clearly mulling over his leader's words. Prentice hoped that would be the end of it, but it was not.

"All that makes sense," the chaplain said at last, "but you are not by nature a treacherous man."

"You think I want to be?" Prentice retorted, thinking that he should restrain himself. Even as he stared at the persistent chaplain, though, he felt the rage within him retreat, quieting like waves settling as a wind dropped. It was not Whilte with whom he was truly angry.

"I think, My Lord," Whilte said solemnly, "and Master Solft agrees, that a millennium ago something happened to peoples no one remembers, but the scars of betrayal remain even to this day. Fey, Grand Kingdom, Redlanders, Broken Kings, or the Untrue—by whatever names those days are called—the hatreds from that time, the longings for revenge, have poisoned whole lands and have bound entire nations to slavery and slow deaths.

Whatever else we do here, it will be useless to our children's children if it repeats the past thousand years' mistakes."

"Somone gave you the vision of the crack in the obelisk, Brother," Prentice said quietly. "I do not believe it was the witches or the others of their cult. Not even the stag riders."

"No," Whilte conceded. "I think it was a higher vision, as well. But perhaps it was given to show that we need not fear. If the ancient springs are from God, then perhaps the Almighty is counseling us that He will see to their liberation from the Redlanders' control."

"And perhaps he is commanding us to break this defiance of the purpose of His gift," Prentice countered. "If the water is from Him, then blood sacrifice and the power to send boats of slaughterers amongst the lowly at will were surely not the purpose of the gift."

Finally, Whilte looked down, nodding as he acknowledged the breadth and complexity of the issues facing them.

"These are difficult matters, Knight Commander," he said at last, lifting his head and meeting Prentice's gaze. "I do not envy you this burden."

He turned to go.

"Thank you, Brother," Prentice said after him. Whilte stopped, and as he turned back on his wooden leg, he sank slightly into the soil.

"Why thank me?"

"Because you are right," Prentice answered, and he meant it. "These are difficult matters, and they should not be decided without consideration. Though you are not a *true* prophet, your wisdom is not *inconsiderable*."

Whilte looked up at his "rod" with its broken spearhead and smirked.

"And," Prentice added with a smile of his own, "because calling me 'not treacherous' is the closest I have come to a compliment from a devout churchman in many a long day."

"You pay me a similar compliment, calling me a 'devout' churchman," Whilte quipped back, and he wrenched his pegleg from the richer earth to hobble away on his staff. Prentice went in search of Dahyoor. The dishonored horse archer was sat in the grass, a mere skin-draped skeleton almost, waiting on his charges without impatience or pleasure, it seemed. His head hung low, as it always did.

"You are going to guide us through that?" Prentice asked him, looking at the mighty green darkness. Dahyoor looked up, and when he saw the direction of Prentice's gaze, snorted derisively.

"No," he said flatly and looked to his right at the curve of the mountainside. "There is a path there, hidden, to rise above the treetops and lead around to the valley where they have trapped Benjamin and his *keshiyaa*. It will be hard, but we should make it in two days, if you do not often stop to waste time like this."

"If time is tight, why not cut through the forest?" Prentice asked. He asked as a merely practical consideration. It was not a path he preferred by any means. Looking at the myriad insects buzzing over the water, he thought of his most wounded still carried in slings between mules or on the animals' backs. The journey would be a misery for them for a start.

"*They* would know you were there within a hundred paces," Dahyoor answered, speaking of the *imzuss* as he looked into the green with undisguised contempt. Prentice could not tell if his scorn was for the Gryphons or for the Verdant fey. "Your number would be halved before sundown, and the rest would not survive the next day. They would pick you off with stones from the underbrush, and you would never know where or how many they were."

"They pass unseen?"

"No, but you are *kreff*."

Wilfully blind, Prentice translated for himself. *Lord God, I hope not.*

CHAPTER 69

As Markas had predicted, the forlorn clutch of villagers still under Aubrey's walls were unenthusiastic about moving on from the home they had clung to through occupation and starvation. Even as Amelia explained that there was another Veckander army approaching and that she could not guarantee their safety if they stayed, she could tell by their expressions that they wanted to say no. Then a woman who hugged a bone-thin toddler to herself, her own frame almost as wan and fleshless, came forward with a wary expression. Amelia wondered what grief this mother felt she needed to express to Aubrey's supposed new liege, now driven away within weeks of arriving by yet another conquering force. Whatever the woman's accusations, the archduchess resolved to weather them with grace. If that was all she could give, then that was what she would give them.

"You the duchess lady from up north?" the woman asked with a distinctly Veckander accent. "The one what has all them men-at-arms and merchanters?"

"I am," Amelia said. She smiled at the toddler as the woman adjusted him on her hip. Amelia guessed his age as perhaps three, older than was typical to still be being carried, but she doubted the boy felt safe anywhere else in the whole world.

"I went to them merchanters, just like you told us, and they give me anythin' I asked for," she said. "First flour and milk us had in years. We had nowt since the animal boat folk come down the Murr. I made bread, t' first bread my Lowel here had ever tasted, and he...he..." She paused a moment as tears formed in her eyes and she adjusted young Lowel in her grip once more so that she could wipe them away. "He asked me, 'mam, is this cake?' Cake, he asked! Simple ruddy flat bread, not much more'n flour and water, and he thought t'was cake. Ain't right a free Vec child should grow up not e'en knowin' bread from cake. And weren't our own 'princes' what give him his first taste. It was you. Wherever you go duchess lady, I'll want to be there."

Amelia felt tears of her own welling in her eyes, but she forced herself to smile at the young mother, remembering the baby she hoped was still growing within her own womb, too small yet for her to show to the world.

"I do not know, goodmother, whether we will all be eating so well in coming days, but while I am safe, you and Lowel and all your fellows will also be safe; and while I eat bread, so will your little one."

"Then I'll come," the woman said.

"We will wait while you fetch your valuables but only what you can carry."

The young mother snorted, but not coldly.

"Got nowt that's valuable save Lowel and this blanket I'm wearin' for a shawl," she said. "I'll come right quick now."

Other villagers gathered around nodded, though some turned away, clearly not persuaded. One rushed off and returned with a three-pronged river-fisher's spear, and the rest showed that they were ready to flee with the clothes on their backs. Amelia wished she could take them all but was glad that some, at least, would trust her. In short order, a small crowd of filthy and downtrodden folk were following her escort company back to the captured camp that was now more than half empty. A thin column of foot militia was already marching up to the bridge, and even one or two of the tents had been broken down, Amelia assumed to transport as well. She was feeling encouraged by the signs of progress when she heard the blast of a horn to her right, the south, where the road led on to Trachester.

"Now for that beat, my lad," Amelia told the drummer, then looked over her shoulder at the following peasants. "Quickly now, and be ready to leave the road. I don't know how many riders they have ranging ahead, but if they engage us, we will do our best to draw them away from you. Hopefully they will not take you prisoners before they have faced us in battle."

The wearied peasants nodded their understanding, but one asked, "Do we go back to the village then?"

"No!" Amelia said vehemently. "I have given instruction to my Lions, and they are to afford you all protection if you go to them. See those lines going to the river? Follow them. They will let you hide behind them if it comes to clash of arms before you are safe."

The archduchess had to almost shout to be heard over the clamor of the young drummer beside her, beating out the call for assistance for all he was worth. The peasants began to jog uncertainly across the field, cutting the corner of the road, while Markas ordered Amelia's escort to double time march straight to the remains of the camp. Even before they reached the edge of the abandoned bivouac, a full cohort of Lions, one hundred Claws, Fangs and Roar, marched out in answer to their liege's summons. The corporal commanding saluted Markas, who explained the reason they were called, and Amelia rapidly found herself in the middle of two lines of fifty armed men, diligently protecting her person. Shortly after that, they reached the banner standard to find Sergeant Sedgemark and another half cohort holding the rear.

"With my back, old fellow, I didn't feel quite up to carrying the standard," Sedgemark explained merrily, as if they were meeting on a village market day and not a battlefield. "What say we swap duties back once more?"

"So I do all the hard work while you stand around?" Markas asked in mock annoyance, pulling the standard pole from the dirt.

"Well, we can duel for it, if you want," Sedgemark replied readily, signaling his group to merge with the escort and turn towards the river. "Winner gets to pick?"

"If your back's like you say, might be my only chance to beat you anyways."

"This is all very droll, good Reachermen," Amelia said, cutting across their banter as the horn sounded once more from the southern road, "but perhaps you might save it until after your reports to your liege?"

Both men suddenly looked at the archduchess with expressions so horrified that Amelia could barely keep from laughing. Both tugged their forelocks earnestly, obviously distraught that they had forgotten her place amongst them, but the truth was it made her happy to see. She took it as a sign that they were returning to their trust in her that they joked so in front of her, as if she were one of their natural senior comrades. Prentice often spoke of the humor the militiamen shared at times of stress, and in her private moments, Amelia confessed herself a little jealous that she could not be included. Of course, Righteous, Spindle, and Dalflitch made up for some of that, which probably explained why she so enjoyed it now. Spindle was wonderful company, but she missed her other ladies-in-waiting.

"Your Grace, the report, as it stands, is an army of something like two thousand footmen have been seen marching up the Trachester road," Sedgemark outlined as they marched, his tone now completely serious. "Seems they have no horse with them, but Sergeant Nunel said that they did have, just that Knight Captain Farringdon engaged them, so however many they are, they must be tied up there."

"What is their composition?" Amelia asked. "How many banners march together and what kind of arms do they field? Especially, what missile weapons? We will need to see our Roar deployed to see them off, if we can. Better a shooting duel at the start than letting them set up pavises to hide behind, especially while we have no horse to flank with."

If the two sergeants were surprised by Amelia's use of military terms and strategic principles, they showed no sign, only nodding and tugging their forelocks. A fearful thought concerning their ready agreement struck her.

"Unless, of course, my husband left other, wiser orders," she said quickly. Sedgemark shook his head.

"Nothing more specific than to hold at the bridge, Your Grace."

"And do my ideas seem right to you?" she asked. Now the two officers exchanged troubled looks. Amelia did her best to smile in a heartening fashion, despite the nerves she felt as she was nearly frog marched toward safety. "Oh, come on, you nellies, surely Knight Captain Farringdon has asked for your opinions of his plans at least once or twice. Knight Commander Prentice asked his senior men more than once, even in my presence."

"That's a truth," Markas said, with the White Lion banner waving above his head as he marched, the corners flicking in the breeze.

"Well, in that way, Your Grace, your idea about archers or gunners or what how seems sound," Sedgemark said. "And it sure suits my preference—get into the enemy early 'fore he gets a chance to set himself ready for me."

"That's 'cause you're always a better sword than the ones you face," said Markas.

"I've faced Lady Righteous," Sedgemark retorted, implying that he was not the superior to the Baroness Lace Fang at the very least.

"And I've been stupid enough to try bushwacking her husband," Markas came back. "First in or last don't make a lick o' difference with him."

"Good thing the Knight Commander's on our side then, aye gentlemen? At least we don't have to face *him*?" Amelia chimed in and both officers looked at her as if she had grown a second head. Calling men of their meanness of birth "gentlemen" was likely far outside their usual experience, not to mention a peer of the realm deigning to jest with them. There would be time for them to mull over the unexpected compliment and odd circumstance at another hour, or else it would not matter. She needed to know about the approaching force, likely hired by the Golden Heron. "So, what about *this* enemy?"

"I heard word of crossbows, or the like, from the early scouts, Your Grace," Markas said.

"Then Roar ahead makes sense."

"When we get there, I'll set some lines out ahead in the grass, skirmish order," Sedgemark offered.

"If the enemy comes in columns, they will not likely lead with their own crossbowmen," Amelia mused. She knew well from several sources that men armed with missile weapons were vulnerable to horsemen or fast infantry and so were typically held back in safety until an army might array completely. That was the White Lions' way as well, keeping the gunners within their ranks until the company could deploy its columns and squares in proper order.

"We could send 'em to skirmish along the column like," Markas ventured. "Tell the Roar to hide in the long grass until they see the archers, then spring up and 'whack 'em unexpected."

"Could that work?" Amelia asked.

Sedgemark was not optimistic. "Might, but too many ingredients to spoil the brew, as my uncle might say," the sergeant said, shaking his head. "These Veckanders might see our Roar too soon to spring the trap, or they might smell the smoke. Worst of all, we might get only one shot away, do sod all damage, and then be run down by horsemen anyway. If we try to send them down the columns, they'll wind up a long way from our main body."

"Goodly points," Amelia said with a nod. "We will follow your original plan and set skirmishers initially. If they do not draw the crossbows to a shooting duel at the first, we might try again once battle is joined."

"As you command, Your Grace," Sedgemark said.

At the head of their escort group, the leading corporal called out to the main bridgehead defense like a herald. "Her Grace! Her Grace! Make way."

Militiamen arrayed for battle shifted their ranks, and the archduchess was ushered into the relative security of the rough fortifications on the bridgehead. Just as the hundred or so were dispersing to their places in the larger formation, she caught one last exchange between the two sergeants who had seen her safely to this point.

"Your uncle worries 'bout ingredients in the brew, does he?" quipped Markas. "What is he, a goodwife or a witch, stirring his cauldron over the fire?"

"He's a brewer, of course," Sedgemark replied without offence. "He's always sworn that *true* beer is water, hops, barley, and yeast. Anything more only clouds the amber, so he says. And heaven help the fools that put fruits into their fermentation."

Sedgemark whistled, as if the horror of his uncle's wrath over "incorrectly" brewed ales would be a sight to behold. As the two men went to their own duties, Amelia sought out Lady Spindle and prayed that Sedgemark's uncle would be the most horrifying tale she heard this day. She doubted it would be a prayer that was answered.

Chapter 70

The path into the mountain heights was everything Prentice might have feared it would be, and he began to wonder if the green would not have been the better option. Single file almost continually, either steeply upward or steeply downward, the path wended across cliff faces and down into crevice-like ravines. It did possess the virtue of being almost continually out of sight of the Verdant's forest valley, but its narrowness and complexity meant the Gryphon Banner Company were strung out in a line over a league in length. If the pale fey of the far west were to ambush his people now, there would be no possibility of organizing a defense. The trail was so narrow at most points that it was all but impossible for one man to pass another without pitching his fellow down a cliff or into the branches of one of the vastly tall trees that grew up the slope. At one point Prentice stepped into a cleft to allow the column past so he could check on the wounded and the rearguard, then found himself stuck at the back end of the column for more than another hour's march before he could work his way back along the line.

By late afternoon, Dahyoor finally led them to a small gully with a burbling mountain spring coming down its back wall, just large enough for the whole body of men-at-arms to gather as one. Prentice was of two minds about letting his men use the spring to refresh their canteens and waterskins, since it seemed now that almost any water source might reveal their presence to the waiting Redlander cabal. Dahyoor was not so concerned and cupped water for himself to drink before scooping handfuls over his head to spill down his back.

"The witches cannot sense you in it?" Prentice asked him, but the broken horse archer only shrugged apathetically. Resisting the temptation to vent his anger, the knight commander looked over his parched command, hot and sweat-drenched from climbing the mountain slopes in armor and realized that ultimately it was a risk they would all have to take. Secret from the coven would be worthless if they all died of thirst. He gave the word, and cohort by cohort the Gryphons refreshed themselves or comrades as best they could, then the ostlers and the mules.

"How fare Boots and Dusty?" Prentice asked Lyrach after he had managed to get a drink for himself. The new line first of the Roar was proving diligent in his duties and had been training a replacement groom for Prentice's horses, a militiaman named Chortesman. The new fellow was not anywhere near the necessary level of skill to protect the two mounts from the dangers of this mountain trail, however, and so Lyrach had temporarily taken the duty up once more at Prentice's request.

Who would have thought Turley was one of the few horse thieves we would have in the Lions? Prentice mused as Chortesman watered Boots under Lyrach's direction while the line first himself checked the horses' shoes and legs for injuries and rubbed down their flanks to help the muscles rest.

"He's a stout heart for all he's a placid fellow, My Lord Commander," Lyrach said, looking Boots over affectionately. Dusty was a little way off, already attended to.

"Good thing they both are," said Prentice. "Can you imagine a spirited charger in this terrain?"

"A danger to themselves and their rider," Lyrach agreed. Chortesman nodded along with his superiors' conversation but made no move to involve himself in it.

Satisfied that the company would be able to replenish their water completely, Prentice made his way over the rough ground

to the head of the gully, a narrow opening high on a cliff, shielded from view by a stand of bushy-boughed evergreens. The little
stream simply ran out the opening and down the rock face.
In all, it made the gully an excellent hiding spot, completely
concealed from the broad valley below. Prentice found Dahyoor
crouched against one of the tree boles, holding on to a single
branch while he leaned out some from the cliff, eyes scanning
the deep forest.

"Thinking of jumping?" Prentice asked quietly as he approached. The wizened fey man turned back to him and
scowled a moment before his expression shifted morose once
more, and he shrugged. He went back to looking out over the
canopy.

"What is it like down there?" Prentice asked.

"The way it was supposed to be," Dahyoor answered readily,
but his tone soured even further. "At least that's what the elders
want us to believe. Full of life and impossible to conquer. Supposedly."

The drought is *conquering it,* Prentice thought, but kept it to
himself.

"Your elders, or the Verdants'?" he asked instead.

"Both, I think, but I don't know, *kreff enkreffra.* We never
saw the elders of the Verdant, never heard their words. They just
turned on us at the fire while our axes and bows were still on our
saddles. We had food in our hands, and they raised their curved
blades over us. It was unthinkable."

Prentice knew what treachery by folk who were thought of
as kin could feel like. He and Archduchess Amelia had been
there the night Daven Marcus slew his own father in front of
hundreds of witnesses and then tried to lay the blame at the
feet of the Western Reach and its liege. Prentice had even felt
a similar, personal sting when his father had disowned him for
heresy, preserving himself and his family at the cost of his son's
love and loyalty. These were not the strongest memories that
came into his mind, however. What Prentice most remembered

was a campsite in the Reach, almost a year past, where a pitiful band of refugees had settled down in the late afternoon for a sparse meal and been shot through with arrows—slain, every man, woman, and child—if not by Dahyoor himself, then by others he would call kin. Prentice had to work to keep himself from feeling some sense of satisfaction that some of the Azure Mountains fey now understood what that kind of horrifying surprise felt like.

Justice is not found in pretending some match of murder for murder, he thought. Prentice did not fear to see a criminal executed for their crimes, if that was what law demanded, but that was not what this was. One crime did not expunge another. Nevertheless, guilty or not, Dahyoor was suffering, and Prentice could see no point in berating the fey man for unrecognized evils now.

"*Kreff enkreffra,*" Prentice repeated quietly.

"It means..." Dahyoor began to explain, but Prentice cut him off.

"I know what it means. Tell me, Dahyoor, are you our guide because you are between two camps as well?"

Dahyoor nodded slowly. He tugged at a long stem of grass growing in the cracks near the roots of the tree he clung to, and when the stem snapped, he threw it over the edge to twist and fall gradually on the light breeze.

"And because I already knew the way out of the valley. The stag elder didn't want that secret shared with the *keshiyaa,*" he added after the grass frond fluttered from view.

"It is why I am permitted know your name, isn't it?" Prentice asked. Again, the fallen horse archer nodded slowly. Prentice kept on. "Benjamin will not let me know his true name, and you never told me the stag elder's either, not even a false name."

"He has never shared it with me or with Benjamin," Dahyoor explained. "He is as outside the camp as I am, but he clings to his pride, like his people betrayed us and kept *their* pride." He spat over the edge.

"You do not keep some of your own pride?"

Dahyoor sneered. "*He* has not run across the desert, hiding from the relentless kin, surviving on bitter grass and swift sips of water. Run, not ridden, because whatever the shame, your elders had to know the truth, had to hear of the betrayal renewed."

"Even though it cost you everything," Prentice said, understanding the personal sacrifice Dahyoor had embraced, choosing a shameful life over an honorable death for the sake of the Wind Rising fey folk. How many times must he have wanted to turn and face the Verdant fey hunters, to die in full, just as he had partially died when his horses were taken from him. "And for that, you are outside the camp."

"Benjamin wanted to avenge us, to give me vengeance. That was why he followed the Inquisition *kreff* into the dragonfly's lights, but we were made *kreff* by kin. We did not know that there was more than one water here. The serpents snatched the Inquisition to safety at the far lake and diverted the *keshiyaa* to a pool in a rock pit—a paddock for a prison. It is enough to hold our horses and the *keshiyaa* and no more. Already, when I left, there was too little grass for the herd. They are eating horsemeat so that not all our beasts will starve."

Benjamin's riders are killing some of their horses for food, just because they don't have enough grass to feed the whole herd, Prentice thought. He marveled at how effectively the Verdant struck at their kin, either individually, as in Dahyoor's case, or in groups. It would not be long and more Wind Rising fey would be dead without their kin having to fight even one battle with them. *Assuming the cabal does not use them for sacrifices first.*

"This is a family matter, and that is why Benjamin did not involve us," Prentice said, more stating a fact than asking. "Do you understand 'family matter'?"

"Your word family is too small," Dahyoor said in typical disregard for Kingdom manners. "But you mean what is true."

"I am named an elder of the Wind Rising, as well as *kreff enkreffra*," Prentice told him. "Does that not make me family, too, if only by adoption?"

Dahyoor cocked his head to the side, a curious expression on his face. It seemed this notion had not occurred to him.

Pity, Prentice thought, feeling a thin thread of bitterness in his heart for a moment. *If it had, we might not be in such a desperate position with only bad choices in front of us. Of course, we might not have raced across the desert to get here in time to stop the mantis in the mirrored sky either.*

"Benjamin does not fully believe the story of the death of the unicorn and the defeat of the Serpent Witch," Dahyoor admitted after a moment.

"He thinks this is a lie?" Prentice demanded, putting his hand to the unicorn-hilted blade on his belt.

"He says that if a proper warrior had faced the Serpent Witch in the village of blood, she would not have escaped and the unicorn would yet live."

"A proper warrior? He means a rider, not *palpolon*?"

Dahyoor shrugged again, but this time he wore a mocking smile as well.

"There were hundreds of 'proper warriors' in that village, and not one of them could raise a hand to the Witch," Prentice said, his voice harsh. For all the fey liked to imagine themselves different from the *kreff*, chosen to protect the ancient virtues of the forest and the mountains, they were just as vulnerable to foolish pride and arrogant self-importance, it seemed. For every Earl Sebastian or even Daven Marcus, there was a Benjamin or a Monarch stag elder.

"Not all the Wind Rising were bound under her blood," Dahyoor said quietly, as if reluctantly revealing a hidden truth. "The more blood she bound upon the unicorn, the more we heard her call echoing over the mountains and the harder she became to resist. Some managed to keep themselves from her by riding into the farthest valleys all the way north to near the hot forests. That was where Benjamin took *us*. He wanted to slay the Serpent Witch but could not resist the song over the mountains. Then we heard the roar in the night—the voice of one lion that thundered louder than her song in our hearts. And following that, the cry—the *dying* cry—of the purest of mane and horn."

Dahyoor paused and sighed, leaning himself over the edge, held back by the branch. Prentice wondered if the heartbroken man planned to let himself finally fall over the precipice. It must surely be in his thoughts.

"We came back swiftly. We know ways in the mountains."

Prentice nodded, having a good sense of what kinds of powers to travel the Azures and the grasslands of the Reach the fey archers possessed. He relaxed a little when Dahyoor swung back onto the ledge more securely.

"We came back, and the elders told us the tale of the *kreff* Lioness Mother, the true reflection of the false Serpent Witch. And of the *kreff enkreffra* who was her chosen man, the adopted elder who had set us free by committing a worse crime than even the ancient sages could name. They told us this impossible tale, and Benjamin nearly drew his axe against his own people. Even the Serpent Witch had not made us do this, he said. For his fury, the Wind Rising elders commanded that he would take a name the *kreff* could see and be the one to bring the Lioness Mother's words to us so the blood debt could be honored."

Prentice thought it would not be a bad way to force an unruly vassal to accept a new state of things, but as much a recipe for trouble as for peace, as the current state of affairs bore witness.

"The Serpent Witch did not need to ask any Wind Rising to slay Wind Rising for her," he observed. "By the time she needed what they did not want to give, they were already bound to her. She did all her own slaying when she wanted blood."

"And now you have killed two ancient forest elders and bound the Verdant by the blood of their own," Dahyoor said, implying that Prentice's actions might be on a par with the witch's.

"I do not want to send kin against kin," the knight commander answered, refusing to consider whether Dahyoor's comparison was just or not. "But Benjamin would not hesitate to order you against the Verdant in battle, would he?"

"He would not trust me to give me any orders, not anymore. I have been seen and my name is known."

"He will be willing to lead his *keshiyaa* to an attack?" Prentice rephrased, certain Dahyoor had understood his original meaning. Did the lone rider truly consider himself apart from his people, or only when it was convenient? "Not just against the Redlanders, *imzuss*, or Inquisition, but against the stag riders and the villager slingers?"

Dahyoor dropped beside the tree once again, sitting upon his haunches in the shade of the branches and staring out over the forest.

"Benjamin is very angry," he said quietly. "Angry at you and all *kreff*. Angry at the Untrue and their return to betray us once again. Angry at the Serpent Witch and at our kin for letting themselves be bound. Most of all, he is angry at himself for not being strong enough to make right all that he thinks is wrong."

"None of us is that strong," Prentice said. "That is why we need the savior." It was an oddly faith-filled comment, especially for a man despised by many churchfolk as a heretic, but as he said them, Prentice realized he understood and believed his own words. Dahyoor cocked his head again but did not argue.

"Benjamin does not want to be saved. He only wants to fight."

Fine by me, Prentice thought. *Let him turn his anger to some good.* It was what Prentice sought to do in himself and in the failed and criminal folk he led as militia.

"He does not want only to fight," Prentice corrected. "He wants to see his enemies die. That was why he let Inxyphos' men ride away, wasn't it, when we ambushed the cultists at the lake?

He wanted to watch *kreff* fight *kreff* and then turn upon the survivors." As he said it, Prentice also realized that Benjamin had not expected the Lions to overcome the Inquisition that night.

Because we had no horses.

"Yes, *kreff enkreffra*," Dahyoor agreed. "Benjamin will attack the Verdant for you, but he will hate you for asking."

"Sounds like he will hate us whether I ask or not," Prentice said.

"That echoes with truth," Dahyoor acknowledged. "What can quench that hate, do you think?"

Why are you asking me? Prentice wondered, and then he looked more closely at Dahyoor, seeing something in the fey man he had not understood was there before. The outcast rider was not just a starved man of a foreign people, stripped of his place amongst his own—outside the camp, as it was said—or between two camps, as the Verdant named it. He was dying bereft of all understanding of this new world around him. Nightmare legends from a thousand years ago had set fire to the world, and the ways of fey society had let the whole of the consequences fall upon Dahyoor's shoulders. Likely, Benjamin felt something similar, and the stag rider, too, and in a sense, Kingdom folk like Earl Sebastian as well—proud warriors and other members of communities who sacrificed almost all to protect their folk, and for their efforts they found themselves rejected, accursed, and expected to die.

Or made to ride against kin with new allies that should by any former measure be enemies. Benjamin must bridle to his very core at being told by his elders to let the kreff *see him and his riders. And against the Verdant, against other fey who should be like unto family.*

Prentice looked back at his own loyal company, grabbing their moment's respite in the shadowed cleft in the rocks. Whilte was back there somewhere. If there was any evidence in all the world of the possibility of turning hate to peace, even to genuinely brotherly love, then surely it was Prentice and the one-legged prophet-chaplain.

"I know your people say you are outside the camp," Prentice told Dahyoor without looking back. "But you are in *this* camp now. I give you a place by our fire and a share of our food, always."

Dahyoor snorted in derision, and Prentice was not surprised. For a millennium the Wind Rising had hidden from Kingdom folk as a prudent man hides from a prowling wolf pack, passing unseen. The history between them, as long forgotten as so much of it was, was a bloody one. What Prentice was offering probably seemed like pitiful consolation, like taking away a man's house and offering him a ragged blanket to shelter under instead.

"You know my scars," Prentice persisted with the broken horseman. "The merciless preachers of mercy did that to me. The ones who think that a loving God gave them the powers of devils over men. Then they transported me over the mountains, which was their way of putting me outside the camp, and they left me there to wait to die, just as you are waiting to die without Benjamin's *keshiyaa*."

Dahyoor looked up with a start, plainly surprised that Prentice understood even that much of his emotions.

"For the longest time I did wait to die," Prentice told him, looking into his dark, almond-shaped eyes. "I let them crush me flat, and what they did not crush, I held down with my own will. I sweated and bled, crawled in the dirt and ate dust for them, waiting for the last breath to flee my body. Even when the Redlanders came, I only cared—when I cared—because it was something different to do with my days. Then the Almighty sent the Lion, and also His son, as it happens, to tell me that I was not to die outside the camp. That I was to make a new camp and that he would send ones like me to sleep by its fires.

"He made a new and deadly thing of me, so that those who would serve *His* enemies would be made to fear—those like the

Untrue and too many of your Verdant kin, sad to say. Then he showed me how to make new things out of others as well. Your elders have seen that many new things are being made in the Western Reach, things that Benjamin and the stag riders are trying to reject. You could be one of those new things if you wish. No longer rejected."

"The elders do not know what this new thing will look like," Dahyoor said. "They sit on their saddles around the fires, telling the old stories and the new, trying to decide what the newest stories will be. They dither and speak of everything falling apart like a horse blanket with its stitches pulled. Everything might unravel, and it frightens Benjamin. It frightens me."

"Would you rather be afraid or dead?" Prentice asked. It was a question he had asked himself many times as a convict, or at least some variation of it. "Come be a new thing and show them that you are not unraveled amongst the *kreff*."

For the first time he could remember, Prentice saw a genuinely hopeful expression in Dahyoor's eyes.

"What would I do in this new camp of yours? Would you make a Lion of a fey?"

"I do not know," Prentice said, having not thought that far ahead. Then he realized what he really needed from Dahyoor. "I am sure I will find other things for you in time, but for now, I need you to lead us truly and swiftly to Benjamin's *keshiyaa* and to persuade him that whatever the new things will be, the Wind Rising, the White Lion, and the Gryphon need not be enemies and need not hate one another. How does that sound?"

Dahyoor nodded slowly, then picked up a loose pebble and threw it out into space.

"Alright, *kreff enkreffra*, you have seen me outside the camp and invited me to share your fire. We will see what new thing we can make and if we can bring Benjamin along to make it with us."

He stood and moved easily around Prentice, back into the gully, pausing just past the knight commander.

"You sit in the saddle like an old woman with rickets," he said directly. "Your horses do not trust you, and of the men you set to care for them for you, only one even comes close to knowing anything. The other is useless."

"Are you angling to claim my mounts?" Prentice asked, more amused than offended.

"Pah, they are too soft, like thistledown," Dahyoor said dismissively. "Old women's horses for a rider like an old woman. But I will teach them to trust you better. Perhaps you will no longer be *palpolon* before you die."

Prentice chuckled and gestured with an open hand for Dahyoor to lead the way back to the rest of the company. They were almost back when Prentice had a last thought.

"Best you not tell too many others all that we spoke of," he said. "Visions and hopes are one thing, but claiming I once spoke with the Son of God—that can get men's backs up. Discretion is better."

"Why would I tell *kreff* anything?" Dahyoor responded, and Prentice shook his head at his own foolishness.

Imagine counseling a fey to discretion. Twit.

CHAPTER 71

As it happened, the White Lions stood their posts through most of the afternoon as the army advancing from the south, diverted for a long space once they reached the remains of the vacated encampment. The few militiamen sent as scouts to determine what was happening returned to report that the newcomers seemed to have paused to ransack what was left, which drew more than a few comments of low wit from amongst the waiting ranks.

"Well, this is just rude," Sedgemark said once the sun looked to have reached midafternoon. He bent back and forth, apparently trying to stretch his healing back muscles.

"Should we have marched out to meet them?" Amelia asked, wondering if there was some military etiquette she had failed.

Markas's response instantly dissuaded her of that. "There's nothin' they'd like better, Your Grace," he said. "We're dug in strong here. We've got little diggin's all up and down our front to interrupt charges and firin' steps for the Roar, which are stronger than even the wagons, and we've got them here, too. Out there, we'd just be two brawlin' prize fighters, sluggin' each other on market day. In here, we're the next best thing to behind castle walls."

Amelia, her sergeant of the foot, and her banner sergeant were all standing on one of the remaining wagons at the rear of the entire company. The others that had managed to cross the bridge on the original day of battle had been badly damaged by the detonation. The wooden planks that had been salvaged from them had been incorporated into the two reed-and-mire ramparts that had been built on each flank of the road to the bridge. With thick, sunbaked mud walls, nearly five feet in height to stand behind, not to mention being able to rest their guns upon, the banner's two Roar contingents would be able to fire over their comrades' heads for the entire battle.

The road itself had been crisscrossed with shallow trenches, most no deeper than one or two handspans, but too wide for a horse to leap easily, especially a destrier in steel barding. No horseman would risk his mount charging over such a hazard, and so the White Lions were almost as secure from heavy cavalry charges as they had been when Earl Sebastian had tried to charge through the sudden mud of the refilling Lake Dweltford at the end of the drought. Markas's comment about brawling prize fighters made sense in that context, and as she thought about it, Amelia inwardly chastised herself for her naïve question. What did it matter about military etiquette?

For years now, Prentice has shown the cruel fruitlessness of such etiquette when it only serves the needs of the strong, she thought. Knight Commander Baron Ash would never have worried about such questions, she was sure. As she continued to appreciate the strength of the defenses around her, she realized Farringdon had not made that mistake either. He had ordered these preparations for the Lions for precisely these reasons.

Oh Lord, I owe him many apologies.

Some indistinct shouts floated over the river, and Amelia turned around to look at the north bank where many of Duke Robant's force were standing and watching, apparently alerted to the coming conflict by the sound of the approaching horns. It pleased Amelia to think they might be as frustrated with the long delay as she was.

"Are they making any moves to cross?" she asked, noticing that some of the knights there were on their horses but not many.

"Still looks more like a crowd of bored nobles than a company in array, Your Grace," Sedgemark said, turning to look with her. "We have men with the best eyes set to watch for any movement. We'll hear as soon as there's anything to see."

Amelia accepted his reassurance with a nod.

"At least they have no boats ready yet," she said. "If they do plan to cross once the battle is joined, they would still have to take the time to embark even before they began to row."

"Unless that's not all of them, Your Grace," said Markas grimly. "They could be out at the bank like this to make it look like they're all here but have a team of boats just around in the Dwelt, with men all aboard already. One call on a horn, and coming downriver with the flow they could get to us in half a candle, I reckon."

Amelia looked toward the confluence of the Dwelt and the Murr and shook her head in horror. She had never even imagined such a tactic.

"How do you keep it all straight in your heads?" she asked in wonder.

"Knight Commander Ash taught us well," Sedgemark said loyally.

"He schooled us not to try and keep it all in our heads at once," Markas added. "Me, Sedgemark, and Nunel split the duties between us today. I've been thinkin' of the water and what the dog Robant might be doin' to cross on us. And when."

At the mention of the lancer sergeant, Amelia looked over to the firing step on the right where Sergeant Nunel was taking temporary command of the Roar. Since none of the other lancers had yet returned but were still out wherever Farringdon was, the horse gunner sergeant had offered himself and his companion to join the regular Roar.

"How does *Prentice* keep it all in his head at once?" Amelia asked of no one in particular, as she looked back from the gunner positions.

—

"I do not know, Your Grace," said Sedgemark. "None of us do. Master Turley, your chief steward, says that we waste our time trying, for if we ever do develop the talent of thought that would let us think as the Knight Commander does, that would be the day of our last full night's sleep on God's earth."

"Prentice doesn't sleep well?" Amelia asked, realizing as soon as she had that it was so. She had never known him to take enough sleep, He was forever driven to do better and searching for the time in which to do it.

"So Master Turley says," Sedgemark confirmed and he shrugged.

Amelia looked to Spindle, standing dutiful and quiet beside her. The Lace Fang shrugged in response to her mistress's unspoken question.

"Other than the Baroness Righteous, I can't think of anyone who would know better," she said.

A sudden blast of a trumpet cut off the conversation, and the last two scouts who had been ranging ahead of the massed ranks sprinted back in and up to the wagon.

"They're comin'!" one announced as both saluted.

"Get to your posts, then," Sedgemark ordered.

Amelia looked over the heads of the ranked militia standing in front of her to where the Golden Heron army was now marching northward up the road. As their column drew closer, she could see they were only infantry, with no cavalry ranging about or prancing forward in parade-ordered companies. That was a good sign and should mean those troops were still somewhere else, engaged with her husband's force. There were, however, two officers, or leaders of some sort, at the head of the column, and they sat upon horses. Behind that pair marched a standard bearer, the equal in pride of Banner Sergeant Markas, but the black and gold standard this man carried was vast—nearly three paces square. The man who bore its weight seemed like something of a giant, in fact, perhaps six and a half feet tall, at least. It reminded Amelia of the defeated Vec

King Kolber's banner, cloth so long it had needed two heralds to carry and now fitted as a trophy under glass in the high table of her Great Hall. Veckander armies favored impressive heraldries, it seemed, perhaps as a compensation for the shortness of their histories and traditions. Kolber's united Vec army had lasted only a single summer, after all.

Watching the two mounted figures resolve, Amelia could see that one was clearly a mercenary commander, dressed in white steel armor like any Kingdom knight, while the man beside him wore robes of bright yellow and black. They drew closer at a mere walking pace in the unhurried manner of confident armies, and as they did, Amelia realized that she recognized the robed man; it was Jerrod Froster, the Golden Heron factor who had so disdained her in Dweltford and been ejected from the Counting House for his presumption. Seeing him at the head of an army-for-pay made her wonder whether there would be any motive of personal revenge for him in the coming battle. Had his masters chosen him for this task, or had he volunteered? Remembering his sneering self-confidence, she would not be surprised if he had. The memory of that contempt triggered another thought, and the archduchess involuntarily glanced over her shoulder at the north bank of the river and the Kingdom knights gathered there to watch.

"Sergeants, I have an important request of you," she said, addressing Markas and Sedgemark. They both listened intently, eyes on the approaching force as Amelia outlined what she wanted. Soon enough, though, they both regarded her with looks of horror, but she remained resolute. "I must insist you promise to do this for me."

"Your Grace...," Markas began, but immediately ran dry of words, shaking his head in disbelief.

"The knight commander would flog us raw if we did that," Sedgemark said. "Like as not, he'd swing the whip himself."

"He would understand, once I explained," Amelia told them, but the sergeant was not persuaded.

"Even if he did, your husband, the knight captain, would surely not be so permissive."

"You have already done something like it at his command," Amelia said. She looked to Spindle. "My Lady, the Lace Fang, will testify you are commanded, and she will even assist you if need comes."

Markas and Sedgemark turned to Spindle, plainly unconvinced that she would assist in the archduchess's orders. Spindle's expression under her mask seemed to indicate that she had similar doubts, but she bowed her head obediently all the same. Amelia had one other command to give as the mercenaries facing them began to array methodically from columns to a front of ranks wider from left to right than the lines of the Lions.

"I will pass *that* command to Nunel, Your Grace," Sedgemark said obediently, "then with your permission, I will take a place with the central cohorts. The foot commands will be best heard from there."

"Go to, Sergeant," Amelia said, and Sedgemark clambered down from the wagon, moving with less uncertainty for his back than before. Perhaps the prospect of combat had distracted him from his unhealed final twinges.

The mercenaries continued to array, and the jingle of their mail coats danced in the afternoon air. They were foot soldiers predominantly, with conical steel caps on their heads. They wielded spears and shields, reminding Amelia of the painted warriors of the Redlander crews, though she felt these men-at-arms seemed more naturally ordered, as well as wearing heavier protection.

Does that mean we will be trading heavier blows? she wondered. Would this battle be slower or swifter than one against the spearmen of the west?

A gap appeared in the enemy array, slightly to the right of center as the footmen shuffled sideways, creating the space into which marched a single company of crossbowmen. Standing in triple rank, Amelia counted across their front as they formed up, reaching twenty-five. Multiplied by three ranks, that made seventy-five men with steel, cross-barred missile weapons, carrying boxlike leather quarrels upon their hips. Akin to their spear-armed fellows, they were dressed in flashing steel mail, but most were without helmets. Many of the Roar did alike, since helmets could interfere with their weapons' aim and effect. Amelia assumed it must be the same for the crossbowmen. Their position in the line, arriving later as well, made it obvious how fruitless her prospective plan to engage the crossbows early with the Roar had been. The enemy clearly had no intention of letting such a conflict eventuate prematurely. Perhaps later in the battle.

After what seemed an interminable length of time, runners rushed from each unit of the Golden Heron army to the center, apparently to say that all were in their assigned places. Once they had given their reports and returned to their respective detachments, Jerrod Froster and his mercenary captain geed their horses forward, followed by their standard bearer and a handful of other footmen. It seemed to Amelia that they were also leading a third horse with them, but she could not make it out easily behind the enormous black and gold cloth. The unmounted creature, only half seen behind the fluttering banner, gave her an ominous feeling.

CHAPTER 72

"The Golden Heron would parley before being forced to conflict," shouted a man in a black surcoat with a yellow bird and circle symbol predominant upon his chest. "Will the laws of chivalry prevail? Will decency be honored by the invaders from the west?"

Cheeky devils, Amelia thought, *calling us the invaders from the west, as if we and the Redlanders are the same thing.* The notion galled her, and she was certain the slight was deliberate, especially couched in notions of decency. Decency would have been for men of the Vec, princes and bankers too, to help the wounded survivors of Aubrey's occupation. Instead, the few who had weathered occupation, torture, and starvation were now crouched a short distance behind her, hoping to stay safe in the coming battle. She gave Markas a single nod as company standard bearer.

"Tell your chivalrous heralds to step forth, and they'll get heard," the banner sergeant shouted back.

The man nodded and marched the short distance to where the Heron banner and its command troop stood waiting. After a moment, Froster and the captain came closer on their mounts, flanked by two spearmen. The banner remained a short distance back. They stopped no more than ten paces from the Lions' front rank. It impressed Amelia that they had the courage to get so close, having spent more time in the gap between armies herself than she ever wanted to again. Courage or contempt, she imagined, one or the other. They sat in their saddles staring at their enemy for a long moment, and then the mercenary captain lost his temper, it seemed.

"Well? Where's your commanders? Are they so craven they only cower unseen amongst you?" he challenged, and a grumble of offense rolled through the White Lions.

"Quiet in the ranks," bellowed an unseen corporal, followed by the short drumbeat for silence, and Amelia's disciplined men-at-arms were instantly still. It filled her with a sense of pride and respect. Taking a leather speaking trumpet from her lady's waiting hands, she put it to her lips.

"I am right here," she shouted, not fully trusting the trumpet to carry her words the distance. The mercenary threw up his arms in disgust, as if Amelia's answer had somehow confirmed some poor opinion of his, while the banker Froster held up his hand dismissively.

"Do you not trust our word, Duchess Amelia?" he called. "Are we to be judged by your own poor example? Will you not come forth to speak with us openly?"

"A snide banker who plays politics and has brought a gang of hired cutthroats to my lands?" Amelia shouted back, investing as much sarcasm as she could into her distorted voice. "What possible cause would I have to mistrust your word, Master Froster?"

"We are here to represent the Grey Hill Compact, Duchess," Froster replied. "And our men are at least paid. Can yours say the same? I hear that the pale slug Welburne had hopes of bringing you silver but, alas, has failed. Such a pity your witchcraft cannot whistle up some coins to pay your militia with."

Little snot, Amelia thought, but she also smiled. Apart from the nonsensical accusation of witchcraft, Froster must have heard that Caius Welburne had returned from Masnia without any moneys. Perhaps one of his guards had been captured during the flight across the western highlands. Froster likely believed that there would be no loan of any kind, which meant he would not be searching other avenues for her gold from the far south. That made her men's pay at least a little safer, she hoped.

She looked over her shoulder at Spindle, and though the Lace Fang was as formally correct as she ever was these days, Amelia knew her well enough to see the fury in her eyes at hearing her husband called a "pale slug." Jerrod Froster would do well to never find himself alone with the Lady Spindle any time in the future.

"Loyal men of the Western Reach do not fight for coin," she shouted back. "They are fed, clothed, and sheltered amongst brothers of the pride and are gifted a stipend for their loyalty to spend upon themselves and their families as it pleases them. They are in no rush to take a guilder, though. Not all men possess the souls of misers and bank clerks."

At the distance between them, Amelia could not easily make out Froster's expression, although the mercenary captain seemed to be scowling. The banker shook his head mournfully, as if feeling great pity for the woman he was speaking with.

"It saddens me we could not be more civil, Duchess," he began once more, and Amelia cut him off.

"Archduchess," she declared. "I am Amelia, first Archduchess of the Western Reach. You continually mistake me, Master Froster."

Again, the Heron's man shook his head.

"I am bid by the Grey Hill Compact members to inform you that your arrogated status as an *arch*duchess is denied by them," he shouted. "Meeting in council, they have disallowed your title and claims to Aubrey. They have named you a pretender and we are here, at their request, to begin your ejection from the Vec."

Heaven deliver me from men meeting in council to decide my life for me, Amelia thought, sighing and frowning.

"Is that all, Master?" she asked, wearily putting the trumpet to her lips once more. Must every battle her devoted Lions fought be prefaced with this kind of drivel?

"No, Amelia," Froster shouted back, and he reached behind him, where one of the men obscured by the Heron banner rushed forward to hand him something. "I have a message and a gift as well."

Amelia was still puzzling his sudden use of her given name, when she saw the banker begin to unroll a scroll with all the formality of a herald giving a pronouncement. A thrill of fear ran through her at the sight of it.

"Stop, master banker," she shouted into the trumpet, her voice becoming a little shrill. "DO NOT READ ONE WORD!"

Froster looked up, obviously taken aback some by her sudden rise in tension, but he only shrugged dramatically and turned back to the parchment in his hands.

"Take my warning seriously, Master," Amelia shouted at him. "I have given orders to my gunners that if you read so much as a single word out loud from any document, they are to fill you full of shot without hesitation. See, a line of them waits to your left. They will not hesitate."

Froster lowered the scroll once more and looked fearfully where Amelia was indicating. She could see by his expression that he could easily make out the eight Roar, loaded to bear, set at the front of the Lions' array. If she meant her words, and she did, then Froster would have little chance to survive their volley, and that must have been obvious to the clerk in yellow and black.

Amelia knew how irrational her fear of writing upon a piece of parchment would seem to those around her, but she had no choice. As unlikely as it was that this parley might lead to the Heron mercenaries quitting the field that they might be bought off or otherwise persuaded not to fight, she had to take the opportunity. She remembered, however, the spell-like power that the brother elder had exerted over her when he read the Church's scroll to her before the battle with Robant and before the sabotaged cannons detonated, seeming to confirm the false pronouncements.

In her dream, the brother elder had been represented by the mocking raven, and she was determined to never fall to such liar's powers again. Perhaps it took an initiated agent of the Inquisition to wield such magicks, or perhaps the art of it allowed it to work when read by any literate person. Amelia would not take the risk. She had even given Markas and Sedgemark orders that if she seemed to lose the sense of herself again, to become enraged and paranoid, that they were to take her away, bind her hands and gag her mouth until a sacrist could be sent for to exorcise the sorcery. That was the instruction that both men had almost refused for fear.

Whatever the meaning or background, until she could consult the Godly and learned, such as Sacrist Fostermae or Master Solft, she would not risk hearing any word read to her by a foe, and likely not by many friends either. With an exaggerated shrug, Froster lowered the document unread and returned it to the servant who had carried it.

"Will you at least allow me to offer you the Compact's gift?" he said with a theatrical wave of his hand.

Amelia made no effort to answer him, only lowering the trumpet and using her free hand to rest on the wagon's wooden side. She was becoming weary of all this posturing, even as she felt she had the better of it so far. As she watched, the horse she had seen partly hidden behind the banner was walked forward, led by a groom in mail but wearing different colors from the rest of the mercenary company. It was clearly a warhorse of some sort, with a military saddle and tack, and across its back was a heavy burden that Amelia's eyes swiftly resolved as a slain body, likely the mount's rider. The late afternoon sun was beginning to color everything differently in its golden light, but Amelia could just make out the blue leather of the figure's brigandine armor. The body was a White Lion, most likely one of Farringdon's lancers. It was a grim sight, but Amelia knew it would have been unlikely that none of her husband's riders would have died. Then her mind began to connect the pieces of this presentation and she scowled in fury at the callousness of it.

"Our riders have driven away the remains of your cavalry," the mercenary captain declared, apparently at a signal from Froster. "They have fled to Longshepherds, the few that have survived, that is. Their leader stood to defend their retreat, however, and he was taken prisoner. Enacting the existing prescription, sentence pronounced by the Grey Hill Compact in council, he was executed for the crime of surrendering to the Grand Kingdom."

The legal scholar in Amelia almost wanted to laugh. As much as the Grand Kingdom refused to make legal accommodations with the Vec princes, so it seemed the princes had precluded their own from doing the same in reverse. Her husband had been condemned by his former peers for surrendering his princedom and his ancestral seat to her. That part of her thoughts was small, however. Instead, there was the rushing terror of a second widowhood visited upon her youth once again. What did it matter whether the curses the Church spoke over her were true or not if the realities of her life made her accursed? With gritted teeth, she choked down her horrors and blinked away incipient tears. If her husband was lost, then such was life. Now was not the time to mourn.

A fully armored Fang stepped out of the lines to take the horse's reins from the groom holding them. From the red hair poking out under the helmet, Amelia knew it was loyal Sedgemark, taking the lamentable duty upon himself.

"The Compact demanded his head," the mercenary captain shouted. "An ancient prescription, apparently. His horse and body we return to you as his widow. We give you this night to grieve. Come the morning, we will demand your surrender or else drive you into the river."

The lines parted to allow Sedgemark to lead horse and slain rider into the formation, and like a funeral procession's escort, they formed an aisle for the fallen to be brought directly to Amelia's presence. There was a gloomy silence across the whole company as the animal's hoofs thudded like a slow, mournful drumbeat on the packed earth of the road. Cattlefields road had seen too much bitter life and death in recent years.

They want to break my heart and sap our will to fight, Amelia thought. *That is why they've done this, and why they wasted the time to array for battle, even when they had no intention of fighting us today. They wanted us to see how strong they were. They want us intimidated and grieving.*

From across the river Amelia heard jeers and insults start to be shouted, mostly unintelligible, but recognizable by their tone. Right on cue, Robant's force were taking their part in this funereal play. The archduchess looked down on the ruined, headless corpse, realizing that whatever had killed this man, it was not the beheading. She had seen men so slain before and knew the kind of gore that that dreadful wound brought with it. There were some crimson smears upon the animal's grey flank, but it was simply not enough blood. This man's heart had stopped beating before his head was severed, she was sure of that. Even as she looked, other details presented themselves, and Amelia began to smile.

"Banner Sergeant, what color is Marquis Farringdon's horse?" she asked loudly, though not into her trumpet, so that while some of her nearby militiamen would surely have heard her, there was little chance Froster or his mercenaries could.

"Well, it's grey, your Gr...," Markas began, looking at the horse in front of him before stopping and realizing the present animal was at odds with his memory. "No. Chestnut, Your Grace. The knight captain rides a chestnut, not a grey."

"Quite so," Amelia said, seeing her smile infect the banner sergeant's expression as well. "And as loyal a Reacherman as my husband is, he still wears the white steel breastplate his father bought for him when he won his spurs. Any White Lion knows that."

She looked down at the brigandine-clad body with widening grin, which she then schooled for a moment to a more somber expression. Whoever this was, it was still one of her loyal men-at-arms, and his death was a cause for grief. Nonetheless, the failure of the enemy's ploy delighted her more than she could contain. That, mixed with the relief within her of not being widowed again, combined to form an irresistible alchemy of joy.

My child yet has a father, she thought, and her happiness broke into a dawning smile. *If God is kind, then I will yet see my husband in the land of the living. I will ask his forgiveness for all my unkindness and kiss him for my love.*

She smiled at Spindle and said simply, "It's not Farringdon."

The lady-in-waiting returned the smile with a nod. "No, Your Grace, it isn't."

Word of her conversation was spreading through the ranks, and the militiamen who had thought themselves bereft of their young commander were muttering as they learned the truth of the enemy's ploy. Amelia was so delighted that she could hardly contain it, and though she did not want to seem disrespectful of the slain man, she let herself release the emotion. She burst out laughing, the feminine peal of it ringing over the late afternoon field.

"Good God!" Jerrod Froster shouted, sounding truly aghast. "She really is a witch!"

That only made Amelia want to laugh even more, and around her, the Lions began to join in. It was a little forced, and obviously mocking, but it followed the Heron's command troop as they rode away to their own lines, likely to spread the story of the cackling witch duchess and the madness with which she infected her followers. Shortly enough they would decide that she had seen through their ham-fisted ploy, but in the immediate term, they would rather see her as a madwoman, heretic, and slattern. Let them. Amelia did not answer to any of them.

Having delivered their message and attempted intimidations, the mercenary company withdrew a short distance and began to set camp on the field just in front of the Lions' bridgehead. Raising no tents, they kept their ranks in a broad semicircle, attempting to cordon the Reachermen off against the riverbank.

"Sergeant Sedgemark, take that faithful man's body off his horse and let us see if someone can determine his name. His family must be informed and their needs looked to," Amelia commanded loudly. "If he cannot be named, we will bury him here by the roadside and a marker stone will be set to record his sacrifice in days to come. Then let the company be fed and rested by cohorts. It will be a cold camp tonight, but a pleasant summer evening for such, I think. The kind of night Reachermen love for an open-air meal, wouldn't you say?"

"I would indeed, Your Grace," Sedgemark called back, and then he moved to enact her orders, a drummer somewhere in the company rattling out the appropriate beats.

Amelia turned to Lady Spindle.

"My Lady, I am sure you would like to see to your husband's needs for supper," she said. "But before you do, I would call upon your company. I mean for us to visit now with each cohort and speak with each loyal corporal personally. Thank them for all their diligence this summer. Twenty or so visits should only delay you about an hour from your wifely duties. Would you do me this service?"

"It would be my privilege, Your Grace," Spindle said, her courtly voice sounding almost natural now. Amelia dismounted the wagon, and with Spindle at her shoulder, moved along the lines to speak with each junior officer, thanking and encouraging them. It was fully dark and reed torches were being lit and passed around by the time she was finished. Out in Cattlefields, the Heron's force sat by their own campfires and sang unknown songs in the night.

CHAPTER 73

Dahyoor found the Gryphon Banner Company a thin stretch of mountainside pasture to camp the night in, and the fatigued troop dropped to the rare patch of grass thankfully. Prentice stood on the relatively flat ground and was himself grateful for the simple relief for his aching legs. He gazed up at the jagged peaks that crowded out so much of the night sky, cutting like serrated blades across the growing light of the Rampart.

We are not even a third of the way up most of these, he thought.

Some of the peaks had snow upon them, even in the mid-summer heat, and he wondered how hard it would be for his company if the path they were following had to climb any farther. He had heard that the air was thinner in the lungs at great height. Mountain folk were known to speak of difficulties in gaining breath when climbing to snowcapped peaks. This altitude was tough enough on his armored body and on his men's as well, he thought. Too many days marching like this and they would have no hope of fighting a battle at the end.

Thankfully, we only have one more day, one more night and one more dawn, or else it will not matter what condition we arrive in.

Prentice shook his head, smiling ironically at the notion that this was something for which to be thankful. He took a swig from the waterskin tied onto Boots's saddle horn.

"He's doing alright, *kreff enkreffra*," Dahyoor said from the horse's bridle. "He doesn't like the heights, but his legs are sound."

"That is good," Prentice said, then added, "And in this camp, Dahyoor, I am Knight Commander or My Lord. Not *kreff enkreffra*."

"Oh yes?" Dahyoor said with his typical tone of bored indifference.

"Indeed, yes," Prentice replied, injecting a sliver of steel into his tone.

"Alright, My *Lord*," said the fey man, and he put two fingers to the shaved part of the side of his head. It was an odd gesture that puzzled Prentice for a moment until he realized the horse archer was mocking the Grand Kingdom gesture of tugging the forelock.

"Close enough," the knight commander said with a chuckle and turned away to check on the rest of the company. Lyrach intercepted him soon after.

"Chortesman is not much pleased at being replaced, My Lord Knight Commander," the line first reported.

"Does he think he was doing a better job than a fey horseman would?" Prentice asked, and Lyrach only shook his head.

"*I* couldn't do as good a job as the fey man. Only half a day and already that's obvious. I would just say that Chortesman is concerned you have some cause against him for his dismissal."

Prentice was pleased with the ready way Lyrach admitted Dahyoor's superiority as a groom. A mature man could admit when he was outmatched without it stinging his self-esteem. The knight commander kept a stern expression, though. He did not want to encourage grousing, no matter how natural or understandable it might be.

"Let Chortesman know that it, of course, has nothing to do with his service, which was loyal and worthy," Prentice told Lyrach. "But under no circumstances tell him you raised this with me."

"Why not?"

"Because your command will never trust you if they think you cannot handle such a small matter as this without 'running to daddy,'" Prentice explained. "They must know you understand my decisions and can enforce them by your own strength. One coherent command from militiaman to line firsts to corporals and then sergeants, all the way up to the knight commander. No one has to jump the line because the word is the same from first to last."

Nearby, some of the militia had set a pit fire, a narrow shaft in the earth, with two angled side shafts to draw in fresh air and feed fuel through. It was a form of campfire that allowed for reasonable heat without letting light be seen far distances. By its limited glow, Corporal Guillam flashed his commander his characteristic grin.

"What about the knight commander?" he mocked, showing that he had overheard some of Prentice and Lyrach's conversation. "Who does he answer to?"

"To the archduchess, of course," Prentice said readily. "And before you ask, she answers to God Almighty. So, you see, it goes from God to the archduchess to *me*! Remember that as you sit there and chew, corporal."

"Lost the last o' me chew," Guillam said, hawking and spitting on the ground beside the firepit.

"See, God is showing you who is in charge already," Prentice said sardonically.

"Best not to let the chaplain hear talk like that," Lyrach said, surprising Prentice by appearing to take Guillam's side. "It might go from God to the archduchess to you, My Lord, but the Almighty still sends his own stewards down the line when he sees the need. Seems the top of the line doesn't have to follow the chain of command so strictly."

Guillam and other men gathered around the fire chuckled at Lyrach's joke, and Prentice found himself approving inwardly. Sycophants and thralls made for poor militiamen.

"If Brother Whilte sees fit to rebuke me, Line First Lyrach, I will of course attend to his words, as he is a holy man of God," Prentice said. "But whether it happens or not, it will never fall to you to know about it. Surely one of you low-born louts must have a gong farmer friend, and they would tell you that filth runs always downhill. If the Almighty must skip the archduchess and send the chaplain to rebuke me, be assured, you will not want to be underneath to be splashed with the runoff."

The men around the fire chuckled again, and Lyrach crouched down with them to warm his hands by the limited flame. Summer or not, at this height the night was cooling swiftly.

"Walked into that one, son," Prentice heard Guillam tease as he left the men by the firepit to inspect the rest of the camp.

"I'd say we both did, with respect, Corporal," Lyrach returned, and the next chuckle was the last thing Prentice could hear of that conversation.

Picking his way through the grass in the darkness, Prentice was surprised to come upon the chaplain immediately next, bent over the softly groaning figure of Master Solft, who was lying on the ground in pain. Other wounded were laid out nearby, resting as comfortably as possible. Their journey in the heights was surely the hardest of all.

"Problems, Brother?" Prentice asked when Whilte took a pause in his ministrations.

"Our good scholar has developed some ulcerated sores upon his feet," the chaplain explained. "I have treated them and prayed for healing. Now I think it best if he stays off his feet for the rest of the night."

"I've been riding my mule almost the whole way here, My Lord," Solft's plaintive voice explained from the shadowed ground. "My boots are not made for these kinds of uphill struggles. I'll come good again once we're out of these mountains."

"You realize, Master, that our goal is yet within these mountains?" Prentice said.

"I do," Solft said and hissed, presumably at his own discomfort. "I'll persevere and not hold you up, Baron Ash. I swear it."

Whilte stood and moved a little closer to Prentice.

"For a man more accustomed to a writing desk than a forced march, he is doing commendably," the chaplain observed quietly.

It was true, Prentice could see that for himself. The soft, round, and pale man who had barely escaped High Sacrist Quellion's rabble rousers a year ago was all but gone now. His skin was still perpetually red, but with his coat removed for the heat, the undershirt he wore in the day hung upon him like a tunic. He had taken to using a length of rope as a belt since his leather one had no notches he could utilize. His limbs were slender, too, and his frame seemed half its size. Given what this campaign west had cost him physically, there could be no doubt as to his devotion to the goal.

"Stay with us, Master," Prentice said, only half joking, given how thoroughly Solft appeared to be wasting away. Too much longer and he might rival the scarecrow-like Dahyoor. Hardship stiffened a man, but excess could kill him just as well. "I have a notion your learned insight will be needed again before the end of our journey."

"The descriptions of your vision of the lake to which we journey have me entranced, My Lord," Solft said in a cheerfully suffering tone. "I will not falter before then, God in Heaven willing. I must sketch and record it; I simply must."

"Devoted man," Whilte observed with an approving whisper.

"And you, Chaplain?" Prentice asked, equally quietly. "How are you enduring our mountain march?"

"My knee aches, both of them do, in fact, but I imagine that is part of the Almighty's purpose for me."

"You do not think the Lord would show you some mercy, alleviate your pain as He did Master Soflt's through your hands?"

"This is not merciless, Knight Commander," Whilte said with confidence, and in the darkness, Prentice could imagine the man's grimly determined smile. "It is pain, not suffering. A thorn in my flesh, no more than that, and a perfect reminder to humility in all."

"May the Almighty honor you as you seek to honor him," Prentice said earnestly. As great as the ancient grudges had been between himself and the chaplain, this humble, penitent Whilte was a man whose faith impressed him. "How are our wounded traveling?"

"Some recover, but Greg of Ramatswash died in the sun this morning. We buried him under rocks."

Prentice nodded grimly. He knew the man's name but did not remember his face.

"And what of you, Knight Commander?" Whilte asked. "Have you decided what the end of our march will be like?"

"You know the decision is not mine alone. Our allies and the enemy will have some say in it, at least," he said, more sharply than he intended. His men were dying, and immediately the discussion had turned to what mercy he planned to show the enemy? He suspected that Whilte was talking on Solft's behalf as well, speaking to the scholar's desire to preserve the Verdant fey as a possible source of the lost knowledge he craved almost more than life. These were burdens Prentice did not want to shoulder.

"I will pray the Lord reveals his will to you," the chaplain said. "A path of honor, without need for treachery or abuse of allies."

"Better a path that leads to safety for the Reach," Prentice retorted and turned on his heel to walk into the night. He had gone only a few paces when he stopped.

"Thank you, Brother," he said, without looking back at the chaplain, doing his best to mean it.

Whilte's prayer was not unworthy, for all that it touched upon matters Prentice counted as secondary in importance.

CHAPTER 74

Two mornings had dawned fresh and clean upon the mountains, and despite their aches, the Gryphon Banner Company rose on each one and formed up. On the second morning in the heights, most were hoping for a swift journey down from the slopes, finally. Below them, the impenetrable green bowl of the forest had grown to seem less a deadly mystery and more a hidden relief worth almost any risk. Flat ground to march upon was the grumble that sounded amongst the campfires and packing bedrolls. The sun was just blazing over the shoulder of a distant peak, like the open door of a glowing forge in heaven, when Prentice consulted Dahyoor as the new groom gave the horses a drink of water from a skin bag.

"Noon today, that was the message," he said.

The fey nodded.

"What will we find then?"

"Then we will reach the paddock in a pit where Benjamin's *keshiyaa* is held."

Prentice did not understand the reference to a pit, but Dahyoor's use of the word paddock was significant to his ears. Paddock was a *kreff* word—a field with a fence around it. No Wind Rising fey would think to do such a thing to the grassland, to try to imprison it. The knight commander sought to envisage what kind of space was containing the horse archers, and what his men might have to do to free them from it.

"The stag rider will meet us there, will he not?" Prentice
went on.

"I have told you once and once again already," Dahyoor said
impatiently. "Can you not hear, or do you not listen?"

It was true that the fey man had already given the knight
commander this information. In their two nights and days on
the mountain slopes, Prentice had repeatedly quizzed Dahyoor
about the planned rendezvous with Benjamin's force. He did
not like that he was obligated to lead his men to someone else's
schedule, one he had no part in planning. It felt like a restraint, a
shackle, like having the convict chain on his feet again. And like
every convict with new fetters, Prentice found himself worrying
at the iron, trying to find some space, some gap, some way to
minimize the discomfort. So, he returned yet again to ask about
the details.

"I listen each time," he said directly. "And still, I will ask
again, as many times as I feel the need. One glance, even a hundred studied glances, is sometimes not enough. Would you have
me lead as *kreff* lead?"

Dahyoor shrugged, as if to imply Prentice might have no
other choice, but he nodded and gave the details again.

"The rider will be there, for he will be needed to open the
way in the rock. The pit is wide and deep, and no gate enters it.
Only through stone or water can it be reached."

From previous discussions, Prentice understood that this
"pit" was a gorge of some kind, with a spring water pond in
it. They would have to enter it "through stone," but whether
that meant some kind of mystical transition into solid rock
or following a hidden tunnel, Dahyoor was never quite clear.
Prentice was starting to think all fey took a perverse pleasure in
being obscure in their speech. Perhaps it was revenge for being
forced to let themselves be seen.

Talk of where the *keshiyaa* was held led him to the last pieces
of his conversation with his guide, not concerning pathways or
moments in time but the difficult and inevitable conversation

that was coming between Prentice and Benjamin—the ostensible ally who would much rather be an enemy. Prentice had an approach in mind for that, and he tested his theory again with his one expert, but Dahyoor was even less unequivocal on this subject. At least on this question Prentice was sure the exiled fey man was not being deliberately difficult. Reestablishing a working relationship with Benjamin would be challenging no matter what happened. It also would not help that he would be arriving in the company of the stag rider, the leader of kin who had betrayed Benjamin's horsemen and kept them imprisoned for weeks.

"And you are sure that if the stag rider does not assist us, we will never free Benjamin and his followers?" Prentice asked. "We cannot find the way through the rock for ourselves?"

"Can you swim through stone or walk through sky?" Dahyoor responded dismissively.

I have enough trouble riding my horses, Prentice thought wryly, already mostly resigned to accepting Dahyoor's words and the stag rider's plan. He found Sergeant Gennet and quietly gave the order to begin the day's march.

Along ledges and narrow paths, the string of men and their remaining animals slowly descended toward the valley's level. Around midmorning they arrived at a shallow ridge line, on the other side of which was a smaller tributary valley, long but barely two hundred paces across. Carpeted with forest, it was still much less dense and primeval than the main craterous bowl which they had been skirting. A stream flowed from rocks at the head of the valley. As near as they could see, nothing moved amidst the stripe of trees between the two stony spurs, certainly no fey riders on the backs of broad-antlered deer.

"We should refill our skins as we pass through," Prentice said to Gennet when they paused behind the lip of the ridge.

"No," Dahyoor insisted. "We must cross here. It is the only path, but once we are under the trees, we come into the Verdant's sight. They will be able to see us. When we cross, it must be swift. Since *you* cannot hide, we will not stop."

"His lordship has spoken," the sergeant muttered, rolling his eyes.

"He is our guide. Not much point having one if we do not listen to him," Prentice responded, but he smiled and lifted his eyebrows. Before the order to cross the ridge was given, he moved down the line to find the corporals.

"Make sure no one takes any wild swings at the woods while we are down there," he explained to the initially perplexed Porth and Guillam. "They have all kinds of forest arts, these Verdant folk, perhaps even the kinds of thing we might dismiss as fey tales. Well, now we live in a new age of ancient fey, and God Almighty alone knows what they are capable of. It could be that the Verdant will sense a blade against a beloved tree or something similar. Stealth is paramount."

"Fat rector in our village used to tell a tale in the drinking house," Porth said, "'bout how a dryad spirit could live in nixie trees, and if she felt a woodsman's axe on her favorites, she might come and cut off his head in the night with his own axe. Rector told us we should never take to the deep forest to cut wood without he gave us a prayer first to keep us safe from dryad magicks. 'Course he always charged a fresh tankard for a prayer, so not everyone took him serious like."

"Lots of villages have a sacrist or rector like that," Guillam said, sneering.

"And for all their venal ways, perhaps they remember some truths," Prentice warned. "Mayhap it was all child's fables, but I do not want us finding out the hard way that some was based on fact."

"I'll pass the word to the boys, My Lord," said Porth seriously, and after saluting, he moved off. Prentice caught Guillam's shoulder before the corporal could go to his own charges.

"The Roar are all carrying full loads of powder, I assume?"

"Always, Knight Commander," Guillam answered, seeming surprised that Prentice should feel the need to ask.

"That is good for now, and for up until today's noon," Prentice told him. "This meeting with Benjamin's horsemen might be on the up, or it might be a trap of some sort, so I want them ready for a fight."

"I thought you kenned the fey horsers as still on our side."

"I do, for the most part, but the Verdant are a cold-edged mystery. They could be thinking it fine sport to have us all together in one place—horse, fey, and Lions—and then cull us all at once."

"We'll make it cost 'em if they do," Guillam asserted.

"We will," Prentice agreed. "But after we are linked up, if all goes as planned, I want you to collect all the spare powder you can from every Roarsman. Leave each man no more than one decad of shots premade. I want the rest in sacks and barrels."

"Ten shots only is a short fight," Guillam objected, giving his commander an uncertain look. "If we get into a proper battle, we'll burn through that in a trice."

"I know," Prentice said, and he frowned, acknowledging the corporal's concern. "But I have another use for the powder."

"Can I ask what?"

"There's a crack in the base of the magick stone column at the end of the lake, the one that lets the mantis men and serpent cabal send their ships through the sky. Before that mongrel fleet I saw gets its chance to fly through to Dweltford Lake, I mean to detonate that stone and cut off any chance it could ever happen."

Guillam whistled quietly. "Mighty bold, My Lord Knight Commander. Sure'n you ain't no gelding."

"And my wife is well glad of it," Prentice joked back. "Now go to and pass my word to your men."

Guillam saluted. As Prentice moved away, he added one last question.

"Is this what Brother Whilte and the scholar man's been ridin' your back about?"

"I told you the other night, Corporal," Prentice said sternly, but with mischief in his eyes. "Commands, not grousing, are like dung; one flows downhill, the other never flows back up."

"From the *scholar* to the chaplain to you?" Guillam opined, showing what he thought of the situation. "I thought you answered to the archduchess and she to God. Where's the Master Solft come into it?"

"He knows things you do not, Corporal," Prentice said, recognizing that Guillam had a point but knowing he had nothing to gain from indulging it. "Things *I* do not. According to scripture, God once made a donkey speak to give a rebuke to a prophet."

"Oh, righto! A donkey made to speak," Guillam said and saluted with a smirk. "That makes much better sense to my kenning."

CHAPTER 75

The sound of hooves mingled with the dawn beat echoing over Cattlefields as the two facing armies awoke to find little had changed in the night except that the Golden Heron's hired horsemen had returned from their distraction with Farringdon's lancers. As the rest of the mercenary force returned to the places they had occupied the previous afternoon, the horsemen formed up on the left flank.

"It was dark when they rode in, Your Grace," Sergeant Sedgemark reported as he offered Amelia his hand to help her up to the battle wagon command post once more. In front of her, the disciplined Lions were similarly arraying themselves in their cohorts again—sword, pike, and halberd edges bright in the dawn light. Wisps of long match smoke tickled her nostrils as the Roarsmen lit their slow fuses to ready their weapons. Amelia strained to look southward, feeling a little stiff in her muscles but not as terrible as she might. Her freshly made peasant bed was far from the softest thing she had ever slept on but was not uncomfortable for all that.

"So you didn't see if they brought any prisoners?" she asked Sedgemark, following the line of thought from his statement. The sergeant shook his head.

"Sorry, but no. Our scouts say that mayhaps they have returned with some extra horses, captured from somewhere, but they cannot give a true count. It might be the knight captain's lancers, but we need not give up all hope yet. He could be out there still with some, or even most, of his lancers yet in the saddle."

"No one knows this land better than the marquis consort, Your Grace," Markas added, obviously trying to be encouraging. "He could go to ground so they'll never find him and then make back and come at their rear. You watch."

"Thank you," Amelia told the banner sergeant. "So now we wait and see what the morning brings us?"

"We could have a sing-a-long, if it is that you're bored, Your Grace," Sedgemark offered.

"No thank you."

Just be glad my lady, Spindle, is not here, good Sergeant, Amelia thought. *You would surely be receiving another of her newly developed and finely attuned disapproving stares for a comment like that.*

Amelia had given the Lace Fang instructions to watch over the civilians in the rear during the early phase of the day since they had no one else to take charge of them and keep them out of trouble. It also gave Spindle an excuse to be near her husband, who despite his protests, still seemed slow in recovering from his flight through the hills. The Welburnes's hired guards would be more than sufficient to keep order amongst the refugees also, freeing up the whole of the Lions to face the Heron's force.

The archduchess studied the enemy, comparing what she was seeing to what she had read in her years of research. After standing upon many battlefields in one capacity or another, she was beginning to realize just how difficult strategy and tactics truly were to explain. The treatises of war, historical ones from previous ages of the Grand Kingdom, as well as modern ones from the Vec and other lands farther afield, rarely had diagrams for battle, but when they did, they were always drawn from the eye of a bird, as if flying high above. That made it easy to see the arraying of lines and formations, the right moment to give an order, or the wrong tactic to adopt. Even when she had not understood everything she read, Amelia had known it at least made some kind of sense. As she stood now on the ground, or near enough to it on the battle wagon, she was astonished at how hard it was to even translate what she had read to what was happening in front of her.

Start simple, she counseled herself, hearing the admonition in both Prentice's voice and Farringdon's. She smiled. *What can we see?*

The massive heron banner was placed in the center of the line this morning, a space created for it between the two largest bodies of spearmen. To her left, the enemies' right, they had more spears and shields. To the right, their left, they had the crossbowmen halfway to the end of the line and then the newly arrived cavalry at the very end. From what she could see, the horsemen were heavily armored but not as heavily as King-dom knights. They seemed more like her husband's lancers in weapons and armor. She wondered if that meant they would also have the short guns the lancers favored.

"To the left they are only one type," she mused out loud. "Only spear and shield. To the right, they have all their diversity of weapons, both the crossbows and the cavalry as well. Why is that?" .

Despite her recent efforts to acclimate the sergeants to her involvement in battle, both Sedgemark and Markas only looked at her in bewilderment. She nodded to each one in turn, in-dicating that she was asking a serious question and expected them to answer. The two looked at each other, blinking, and then faced toward the enemy, studying the lines that were slowly starting to march forward.

"I really couldn't say, Your Grace," Markas answered first.

Sedgemark was stroking his ginger beard, though, clearly trying to give the question more thought.

"I ask because we are more evenly arrayed," Amelia said, looking to left and right. "Have we made a mistake? I do not see how we could know ahead of time where the best place to put ourselves was, other than as we have."

"That is because we are on the defensive, Your Grace," Sedgemark said. "We are tied to this spot by our defenses and the river. There's no way to use the land to force them to come at us where we want, so we make our defense as evenly as we can."

"And is *that* a mistake?" she asked. How did a leader on the field make a decision when there were so many possibilities?

"No, Your Grace. We're not spread too thin, and we've got even numbers with the enemy force, so this is strong enough."

Amelia recalled something from one of her strategy books.

"I read once that as a battle goes on, lines shift sideways as each man flinches away from the enemies' weapons just a tiny bit," she said. "Not as a coward, but just sensibly trying to keep the main of himself behind as much shelter as he can, such as his own or his comrade's shield. Even the most well trained and stoutest of heart do it a little. But across a line of dozens, or even hundreds, those little bits add up to a big shift, like single grains of wheat filling a town granary store until it builds up to a mass that could crush a body."

Sedgemark nodded, apparently to show that he was listening, but he offered no reflections on her thoughts.

"I also read that commanders take steps to stop the drift," she continued, "including anchoring one side with a heavier troop less inclined to flinch because its protection is greater or its power overwhelms the enemy there. Is that this, would you say?"

The young sergeant shrugged, shaking his head.

"Could be, Your Grace. It's not something the knight commander or the captain's ever talked about, near as I remember."

"I reckon they've got themselves a plot with their crossbows," Markas said suddenly, and Amelia turned to see his eyes narrowed in shrewd appraisal.

"How's that, Banner Sergeant?" she asked. With no one able to confirm or deny her own theory, she was not about to dismiss any others without consideration.

"Well, they've only got their one lot of them crossbows," Markas continued. "It ain't like the Roar, in amongst us all. They can only use theirs in one spot. So, I'd reckon they plan to hammer that spot hard as they can, make right pincushions out of us there."

He pointed and Amelia looked to the Lions who were exactly opposite the mercenary crossbowmen, then to the methodically advancing foe. They were a bare few hundred paces away now, and already the cavalry seemed to be slowing, dropping back somewhat. Why? She looked again to Markas and saw beyond him that Sedgemark had likewise developed a canny expression.

"So they will focus their attack there?" she asked, nodding to the point in the Lions' formation.

"Maybe," Markas said, and Sedgemark developed a knowing smile.

"They will, Your Grace, but like as not, there'll be few spearmen in that attack," he said.

"How can you know?"

"Because of their horses," he said. When she shook her head at him, he happily explained. "They can't charge us easily because of all the trenches we've dug, and if they've heard anything of how the White Lions fight, they'll know better than to charge us head-on anyway. We love knights foolish enough to throw themselves on the Claws for us."

He and Markas both shared a snorting laugh, and Amelia smiled, buoyed by their confidence.

"So what are they doing?" she asked, still wanting the enemy's plan deciphered for her, if it could be. "What have the crossbows to do with the horses?"

"They will hammer those cohorts there, in front of them," Sedgemark continued. "Their crossbows'll probably not come too close for a long while, and they'll likely stop just outside the range of the Roar, since we've put *them* at the back of us here. They'll look to make right spiny anteaters out of our boys in the

Claws and Fangs, so much so that we'll have to respond. We'll have to break one or more of our cohorts out of their nice safe wall and march them straight at those filthy quarrel shooters. Then, what will happen?"

"Then they'll be out in the open," Markas said, clearly picking up Sedgemark's thought before Amelia could. "Out in the open and with a whole mess of horsemen on their right flank. We like knights to ride straight on, but from the side it's not such a fun dance to go to."

As the two officers explained their thinking, the stratagem revealed itself to Amelia as readily as the dawn that had just cleared the horizon. It was surely the most likely thing Froster and his hired captain planned, and it thrilled her to think her company would outwit them.

"So all we need do is to keep to our formation where our defense is strongest?" she said happily.

"Except that will mean a lot of wounded and dead men in those cohorts," Sedgemark countered, his smile becoming a more somber expression.

"Anteaters, pincushions," Markas agreed.

Amelia cursed inwardly.

Winning hands are rarely built on the play of a single card, she thought, imagining it as something Dalflitch or Righteous might say. *What other cards do we have in our hand to play that would save those loyal militiamen from becoming corpses?*

CHAPTER 76

There were no trails through the strip of forest at the bottom of the narrow valley, so the Gryphon Banner Company was forced to move as a crowd, clustered in small groups. Thankful that the journey was a short one, Prentice was still uncomfortable at his men-at-arms' forced disorder. He felt his skin crawling, imagining eyes watching from every shadow, under every bush and branch. His head swiveled about, trying to watch every direction at once. It did not help that even in a dell that was truly no more than two hundred paces across in the space between what amounted to two rocky walls, the green canopy was still so dense that not even a quarter of the way in they could no longer see any mountains overhead. The air under the trees was also not as cool as he had expected; it was muggy and thick to breathe.

As focused in purpose as the directions he gave them, Dahyoor stayed ahead and led Boots and Dusty at a surprisingly spry pace through the underbrush. Prentice worked at remaining in the rough center of the company, seeking to keep both their leading guide and their trailing rear in sight at the same time. It was a fruitless effort, and he frequently found himself giving soft-spoken encouragements for his footsore men not to slow down. The last of the company passed him as he stopped by the narrow stream to watch them go when down the valley he saw a strange movement in the gloom. At first, he thought it a trick of the sunlight through the leaves, but as he watched, he realized he could see it better when there were shadows than when the sun shone through in patches. Then he could tell it was moving over the water as well, and he knew what it was—another will-o'-the-wisp.

Stepping swiftly out of the space the stream created through the green, Prentice hid behind a bush and watched the flitting insect-like light. It was moving back and forth, and after a moment more, he felt he had reason to hope it had not seen him.

Or the ones who look through it have not, he thought, realizing he still had no true notion of whether the wisps were living things unto themselves or merely projections of fey magick. He ducked as swiftly as he dared behind the nearest tree and caught up with the rearguard, feeling perversely like a nervous mother hen as he urged them to cautiously and quietly press onward across the narrow valley. He could feel the sweat trickling down his face and back from a combination of the moist warmth and nervous tension as he did his best to keep watch through the thick foliage for the deceptively unthreatening blue-green glow. The men ahead of him also quietly passed word up the line that the tiny spy had been sighted. Most of the company already had some sense of caution about the wisps from experiences by the river in the desert, but apparently Dahyoor had been passing some extra warnings since joining the company more fully.

Not far, Prentice thought, realizing he could just make out their goal ridge drawing closer despite the enclosing canopy. Then he heard a familiar scratching sound, as of a flint against steel, followed by the fizz of a long match. A Roarsman was lighting his matchlock's fuse. Risking making a more revealing noise pushing through the scree, Prentice rushed towards the sound. Not far ahead, though, with numerous fallen branches and tough, low-growing bushes between him and them, Prentice could see two Roar, pointing southward. It took him only a moment to realize that they had also seen the will-o'-the-wisp, and like a fool, one had loaded his firearm, preparing to shoot at the floating light.

Unwilling to gamble a countermanding shout, Prentice looked for the shortest distance between himself and the two gunners. He risked plunging through some kind of low-growing fern and was glad it did nothing to entangle his legs. Even so, his progress was too slow, and while the loaded roarsman's partner turned as he heard Prentice coming, the one intent on making the reckless shot had his weapon to his shoulder, with the support rod propping his barrel's weight. The knight commander watched in helpless horror as the gunner crouched down slightly to aim the propped firearm upward more easily and depressed the trigger. Prentice crashed into the fool's partner just as he saw an anonymous, leather-gauntleted hand snatch the weapon away from its owner right at the pan, so that instead of lighting the powder, the dogshead snapped down on the back of that glove, scorching the leather like a burning taper being stubbed out.

With a hissed curse, Lyrach heaved the heavy matchlock around to rest butt-down upon the ground and rubbed the back of his left hand against his side. His glove had a distinct burn mark where the trigger he had just intercepted had struck.

"Are you addle-headed or just the son of a mad goat?" the line first demanded of the gunner in a furious whisper. "We've been ordered to go with stealth, and you want to take a snapshot? Your mother must weep to have a worthless block of wood for a son!"

Prentice drew in a relieved breath, louder than he meant, and the two Roarsmen and their junior officer turned to look at him.

"Everything alright, Line First Lyrach?" he asked, trying to sound noncommittal and not at all enraged.

"All is well, My Lord Knight Commander," Lyrach responded quietly. "I was simply making sure these two men understood how to fulfill their orders, including the latrine trenches they will be helping me to dig and fill from now until the day we return to the Reach."

"Carry on then," Prentice told him, noting the concerned but chastened looks on the faces of the other two. He pointed at Lyrach's glove. "You have a burn there, did you know?"

"Yes," Lyrach said, handing the gunner back his matchlock and tapping at the damaged leather. "Must learn not to get too close to a burning long match."

"Quite so," Prentice whispered his agreement. He pointed them to move on, and as the three started off, he nodded at the loaded firearm. "And make certain that match is fully doused. We have no need for it here, and a good scout will smell the smoke a half league away."

The reprimanded Roarsman saluted and spat on his own glove tips to wet them before pinching off the fizzing spark.

Prentice watched them go, pleased at the way Lyrach had chosen to handle the situation, not abandoning his charges to the wrath of the knight commander, but when he looked back to find the tiny light that had caused the stir in the first place, it was easily located. It was no longer dancing in the air but hovering in place no more than fifteen paces away. Looking at it felt like being stared at by a predator.

We have not passed unseen, he thought, and shaking his head, knowing there was nothing else that could be done now, he rushed after the rearguard. Stealth was no longer an option.

CHAPTER 77

"W are the sky!" came the cry again as another flight of crossbow launched, iron-headed quarrels arcing through the air toward the Lions' positions. Beside Amelia, Markas lifted up a Fang's shield to provide her and himself cover from incoming bolts. In amongst the Claws holding their position in cohorts, Fangs were doing the same, their "umbrellas" making a surprisingly good job of protecting from the dangerous "rain." Few of the bolts flew far enough to threaten Amelia on her wagon, but some had struck the sides, and she had learned to snatch her hands back under the shield's protection after one bit into the wooden edge of the wagon no more than a span from her fingers.

Sedgemark had already left to take his place in the main body of the footmen, so Amelia was alone with the banner and the banner sergeant on her raised platform. Although things were going well, it seemed, it was unnerving to stand while volleys of bolts, seventy-five at a time, fell so close. More than a few men had taken injuries already.

"How many shots can they make before they run out of bolts?" she asked as she watched the crossbowmen put their weapons to the earth once more, one foot in the stirrup as they turned windlasses to ratchet back their weapons' tensile strings. It was a powerful war crossbow that needed a windlass.

"I doubt they'll be out anytime soon, Your Grace," Markas said loyally, lowering the shield once again to rest his arm between shots. In front of the wagon, two militiamen carried a comrade between them from out of the formation, brown-fletched shaft protruding from the gap between the edge of the man's helmet and the bloodied collar of his buff coat. From the look of it, the quarrel was at least halfway into his chest, and as she watched, Amelia saw the man cough an excruciated gout of blood from his mouth and then fall limp in his comrade's hands. He was dead. The two militiamen recognized his passing, and after grimly looking at each other, they simply lowered his body to the ground. One went straight back to the formation while the other looked up at the wagon, meeting his liege's eyes soberly. Amelia felt the sudden sting within, the temptation to guilt and self-recrimination that had come upon her at the hilltop when the cannons exploded, and the inner reproach that robbed her of all confidence or hope. This time, however, it was not coupled with the power of whispered sorcery—simple-seeming words covering curses and eldritch machinations. Looking into her loyal man-at-arms eyes, the archduchess saw no recriminations, no reproach. Instead, his expression was resolute and, to her amazement, proud. The militiaman saluted and then turned after his friend to return to the battle proper.

If he can be proud to stand the field with his liege, Amelia thought, *then his liege will be proud to stand the field with him.*

A cacophony of steel crashing on steel echoed from the left side of the field where the mercenaries were pressing hard, working to keep the Lions on that side occupied. The spear their basic footmen carried was much shorter than the White Lions' pikes, so the front ranks of the mercenaries' formation was forced to do nothing but protect themselves with their steel-rimmed wooden shields while they tried to get closer to thrust back. If they did close well enough to use their own weapons, however, they came into range of the halberds of the Claws—the Lions' rear claws, as Prentice called them. A spear wielded one-handed was a deadly weapon, but the spiked axe-head of a halberd was wielded two-handed. Its user could bring his full strength to bear in every stroke and thrust, and the blade was heavy enough to hack at a shield until it was no more than a tangle of firewood hanging uselessly on a man's arm. Spear and shield in mail versus pike and halberd in buffcoat and brigandines was the kind of warfare the White Lions were trained for—that and unhorsing Kingdom knights too foolish to see that their reign on the battlefield was coming to an end.

The call to shoot came again from the left flank gunner bastion, and the matchlocks spat fire and iron into the enemy. To keep their own comrades safe, the Roar were firing into the mercenary ranks far back from the line of the melee. Amelia feared it might do no good, but searching to see where the iron shot had landed, she was pleased to see spearmen flinching or even falling, leaving gaps in their formation and reducing the support the rear ranks could bring to the front. In fact, it seemed the chaos that Roar shot brought to their formation was spreading, and the attack was faltering. It was the second time already this morning. Soon, the Heron spearmen would have to withdraw and reform or else break completely. Amelia was watching for that moment when she was distracted by a man loudly cursing nearby. She looked down to see a Claw militia-man pushing his way out of formation, carrying what looked like half a pike shaft, one end ragged like a broken branch.

"What ho, militiaman?" she called, and when he heard her, the man immediately stopped and tugged his forelock before holding up the broken piece of wood.

"Cursed unlucky roarshot hit my pike," he shouted. "Split the wood, and the point just fell off, useless.

"I'm sure it was no more than a fluke," Amelia said, and she was surprised by the response he gave her.

"No doubt, m'lady. I'm only raw 'cause that's a shot that didn't kill one of those buggers comin' at us." He tugged his forelock once more. "Beggin' your pardon, but I got to get me a replacement and get back to the fightin' afore the fun's all over."

The man dashed away to seek a spare pike, but it seemed he would be too late for this assault. The mercenaries on the left were falling back already. Jeers followed them as they turned to flee, a final volley of gunshot giving them impetus. Lions called for their own lines to come back into order, and they held position as wounded allies were brought back for help and enemies were policed. Dead mercenaries were left where they fell for now, but the wounded or surrendered were dragged aside by pairs of Fangs—watchful, with their own shields and swords ready for desperate treachery.

Markas's shield rose over Amelia's head once more, and she looked to the right and into the sky to see how the duel with the crossbowmen was progressing. Another shower of quarrels fell and, again, most were harmless but too many were not. In her heart she could feel her own tension rise with every volley, and *she* was only fearful of the rare, overlong shots. She could only imagine the nerves of the men standing in their formation. It made her wonder if they could be made to hold themselves back for the whole of the battle. If their nerve broke, they might charge into the fray out of sheer desperation, and then it would not matter that she, Sedgemark, and Markas had seen the Heron's trap with their cavalry. Her militia would have fallen to it regardless.

"What can we do to help them?" she wondered aloud.

Beside her, Markas followed her eyeline and divined her meaning.

"'Tis only a pity we don't have the marquis' cannons, Your Grace," he said in a matter-of-fact tone. "They'd've made skittles of the crossy-bow folk, no mistake."

Amelia looked at him aghast, knowing that she was staring as if he had just suggested a child sacrifice to the Redlanders' demons, but she couldn't help it.

"You would want those monsters on the field again after what happened?" she demanded, doing her best not to give in to her old feelings for the iron beasts.

"It's all monsters on a battlefield in a way, Your Grace. Even us ordinary men like. When the Denay king hurled big stones on us, I swear it made a man want to run. I reckon them cross-bows'd make a run for it, too, if we could hurl some big iron fists at 'em." He stopped and shrugged before looking back toward the crossbowmen working their windlasses for their next shots. "'Course the Denay bronze monsters didn't blow up on their own crews neither, so better some o' *them* than the ones what did the hilltop in."

Amelia nearly laughed at Markas's simple reflections.

It's all monsters on the battlefield, she repeated in her thoughts. Then, she shook her head. Perhaps every army needed the possibility of the horror that monsters knew—the ability to release rage upon the enemy who would not yield. That horror did not have to come only from monsters, however. That was why Prentice had brought her a pride of lions, superior in their way to king's dragons or Redlander beast-men. Lions could unleash the fury and yet remain regal in the pride, like the angel lion from her dreams and Prentice's dreams as well.

"If the knight captain was back with us, his lancers would pack them off right quick, too, I'd say," Markas said. "If they did it at a full charge, timed from the side just right, they might even do it in a swing around and not get pinned by their spearmen or even them horsemen. Course, that's if he was here."

The banner sergeant stopped and gave Amelia an apologetic tilt of the head. She nodded with a gentle smile. In the midst of a battlefield like this it would be perverse to think only of her own fears and sufferings, but it was sweet to have someone acknowledge, even for just a moment, her worry for her missing husband.

Well, my darling, she thought of Farringdon, *if we have neither you nor your cannons nor your lancers to help us, what can we do to keep us alive, and for how long? If you have an answer, come back to us with it soon.*

CHAPTER 78

Dahyoor led the Gryphon Banner through a series of dry gorges and defiles with no signs of water and little growth of any kind. Only that they were clearly on much higher ground and could not see west in the least, it seemed almost like they had returned to the desert again. Worse, this time they were without the lifegiving water of the Murr close to hand. Prentice was sure the men around him must be noticing just how vulnerable their position had become, and he wondered that he was not perceiving more signs of incipient mutiny. He watched for whispered conversations under mistrustful expressions, for odd groups clustered together out of the order of the march, and for any of the signs of rebels about to declare that they would go no farther—not that Prentice would blame them if they did. He could feel the tension souring his stomach as their mission led them farther and farther away from anything familiar.

Only let us stop their swarming fleet, he told himself, *and then let the Verdant keep their rider's pledge, and we can march home.* He snorted with derision at this reckless trust to hope. He had led these sworn men-at-arms to the edge of their world, and still they were following him. They deserved better than just hope.

Leading his command to their doom was only half of his fear, though. The other half was that they would all die and still not stop the Redlanders. Whatever else he had to do, that could not be permitted.

"And so, back to hope," he muttered.

"Did you say something, Knight Commander?" Whilte asked from nearby. The chaplain pulled off the straw hat he had scared up from somewhere to protect his sunburned tonsure and waved it at his face, no doubt doing nothing but washing hot air across himself. The mountains were truly testing even his patient endurance, and it seemed he needed to lean ever more heavily upon his broken-spear rod. Prentice guessed that he was trying to take some of the weight off his amputated stump. Nevertheless, the chaplain forced a ready smile, however much it seemed like a demanding effort to do so.

"Nothing that bears repeating, Brother," Prentice answered, stopping as some of the militia marched past. Dahyoor was leading them along a low ridge on the north side of a cliff that might well have stretched upward all the way to one of the mountain peaks. Other than picking east from west by the sun, there was no other way for the Reachermen to know where they were.

"Noon is almost upon us," Whilte observed. At the head of the column, Dahyoor stopped, holding Boots's bridle, with Dusty trailing, and keeping the animals' heads turned away from the downslope of the ridge. Prentice pushed past the men between them who had stopped as their guide had.

"Time is close, Dahyoor," he said. "Can we afford to stop?"

"We are here," Dahyoor answered.

"Here?" Prentice repeated and looked around. All he could see was the cliff face and narrow trail, the steep downward slope, and the other mountains in the distance. "Where?"

"Here."

Lord deliver me from having to take a fey man at his word, Prentice thought grimly. Having no cause not to believe Dahyoor's statement but wanting something to do, he ordered one line to continue along the ridge up to the next curve of the mountain while others took shelter from the sun in the sparse shade offered by the cliff. He gave orders that men should rest if they wished.

"Your scouts will find nothing," Dahyoor said with an unimpressed frown. "This is the place."

"How can you be so certain?" As far as Prentice could tell, they were stopped in front of a random piece of rock wall. "What marks this point from any other?"

"*Kreff*," Dahyoor said with a shrug and a condescending smile that made Prentice want to punch him despite their differences in size and weight. Before he could say anything more, he heard the stag-rider champion's voice not ten paces from where he was standing. Behind the Verdant fey, a section of rock that had only a moment before been a solid surface now revealed a narrow defile, just wide enough for two or three men to walk side-by-side.

"Where the hell did he come from?" an astonished militiaman exclaimed as he and others who had been sitting literally beside the sudden gap in the rock now scattered in alarm, reaching for weapons.

"He says you were seen," Dahyoor interpreted. "The *imzuss* knows where you are. He wants to know why you were not more cautious instead of blundering about like stags with mating sickness."

"Mating sickness? What is that?" Whilte asked, and Prentice thought it was hardly the most salient question.

"When a hind goes into heat, the stags can smell," the Wind Rising fey explained. "If a stag cannot track, cannot reach the hind, he becomes more desperate, charging into trees and brush, even hurting himself to get to her. Seeming sick—mating sickness."

"Tell him the way was long and we did not want to be late," Prentice said, not interested in a lesson in forest husbandry.

Dahyoor did as instructed. "He says, 'Instead, you are early, and you were seen.' Now he will show you the way, but your battle will be harder when you reach the lake."

The stag rider turned and entered the newly opened gorge, not even looking over his shoulder to see if anyone was following him. Prentice looked to Whilte, and the chaplain shrugged. Dahyoor led Boots and Dusty into the gap and waved for them to follow him.

"In you go, Gryphons," Prentice said and pointed the way.

"What happens if the walls close behind us?" one of them asked quietly as they entered in.

"Then I guess we get trapped in the rock. What d'you want to fear more—crushed, stabbed, or dead o' thirst?" his mate answered. Prentice imagined most of the company had had a similar conversation or two over the preceding days. How much more demanding could their campaign become?

Prentice waited until the last of the company had passed, including the wounded on their remaining mules and the ostlers who handled them. If the Gryphons returned safely to Dweltford, Prentice resolved that he would petition the archduchess for stipends for each of these men for the rest of their lives, or for their families if they did not survive. They had earned that much, at least.

As Corporal Porth brought up the rear of the company, Prentice joined him in marching into the narrow confines of the gorge, and while it was claustrophobic, the high walls at least shaded them from the direct sun. Only ten or so paces inside, they found Solft, standing by himself as if left behind. He was rummaging in his satchel, drawing out a piece of fine parchment and a stick of charcoal.

"What on earth are you doing?" Prentice asked.

"I'm taking a rubbing, My Lord," Solft said as if his explanation was self-evident, and he pointed at a spot on the rock face in front of him. As Prentice looked, he saw that inset into the rock was a metal plaque, somewhat corroded, although nowhere near as pockmarked as the iron mask at the falls had been. Prentice wondered if Solft was still carrying the heavy artifact with him somewhere in his belongings, realizing he had not laid eyes upon it since the day he had almost drowned to recover it. The plaque in the rock here was also iron, or more likely, as Prentice studied it, a form of steel. It was embossed with some kind of writing and images.

Steel is not usually used for such, Prentice thought. Bronze or brass, even copper or gold were preferred in the Grand Kingdom for a purpose like this. It was easier to work an inscription into such metals. As he was watching, he had a sense that something had changed, and Prentice looked about to see that Porth had noticed as well. The two exchanged a wary glance as they tried to determine what had happened. It was the salt- and pepper-haired corporal who first noticed that the opening at the end of the defile had closed again. From this side, the narrow channel in the rock ended in an apparent cul-de-sac. Prentice imagined the outside looked like a cliff wall once more.

"It was the change in the air around us," he told Porth who was regarding the sudden wall with deep distrust, as if the stone might continue to close and crush them at any moment. "The outside wind, light though it was, was suddenly cut off."

"Should we, I'm thinking, not tarry then, My Lord?" Porth asked, his expression making it clear that he had only one answer he hoped to hear. Prentice gave him an easy nod and looked to Solft.

"Come, Master, we have no time for sagely inquiries."

"But Baron Ash, look at this." Solft held up the charcoal rubbing he had taken of the inscription.

"I am sure it is fascinating..." Prentice began, hardly looking at the ancient and foreign combination of letters and inscrutable line diagrams, but Solft's enthusiasm cut him off.

"Here, do you see it?" said the scholar, pointing to one part of the rough copy and then to the corresponding part of the plaque.

"Master, we do not have the time."

Solft was still holding up the rubbing, but his head was down now, and he was hardly listening as he rummaged again through his bag, which was hanging awkwardly from his shoulder. Prentice was about to seize him by the arm and manhandle him away when the scholar suddenly bounced upward, the Borrosod codex in hand and held open to a page.

"Look there," he said eagerly. "At the edge of the page. Can you see it?"

Prentice tried to look between the two documents being held in his face, the book in one of Solft's hands and the rubbing in the other. Nonetheless, as he did so, his eyes involuntarily followed the scholar's instructions, and he compared the respective points upon the pages and stopped a moment. In the illuminated border of Borrosod's page, the line drawings on this plaque had been reproduced as a pattern. Once seen, it was quite unmistakable, although Prentice doubted he would have noticed it if Solft had not pointed it out, certainly not in such a transient exposure as simply walking past down this ravine. Master Solft was something of an expert on notions hidden in the illuminations of historic documents, and this only proved it. Even so, there was the immediate possibility that if they took too much more time here to ponder this discovery, it would be the last question they ever considered.

"Master, we must go, now," he insisted, waving the pages away and taking hold of Solft's upper arm to turn him about. As he was being maneuvered the scholar noticed the change in the end of the defile, and his eyes grew wide.

"Good Lord, the rock is simply there," he said breathlessly as he was being bundled away. "How astonishing."

"Yes, and if circumstances allowed, I would certainly encourage you to stay and study that as well," Prentice said.

"Perhaps we could return some day."

"Lord deliver us, I'd rather go drinking in the Weeps," Porth said, and he and Prentice kept the distracted Solft walking at the best pace he could manage while packing his papers back into his satchel-like bag.

CHAPTER 79

For the better part of an hour the disgraced stag rider led the company through the winding ravine. Sometimes the gap narrowed to less than enough for two men, but it never grew wider than space for three. The walls echoed with the tramp of their footsteps and the jingle of the armor and weapons, but those sounds seemed strange as they were reflected from the stone. After a time, Prentice decided the strangeness must be because of the lack of other sounds, such as birdsong or the sighing of any breeze. The ravine floor was as still as a tomb and quite unnerving when he stopped to think about it.

"It seems to be only one continuous passage," Solft said at one point. "Fascinating."

It was a true observation. In all their travel "through stone" they did not pass a single intersecting pathway or separate ravine. There were no gullies or other cracks in the stone, only the singular defile.

Of course, if intersections are hidden like the opening was, indistinguishable except by fey augury, he thought, *we might have passed hundreds of intersections and never known it. This mountain could be more of a rabbit warren than the back alleys of Dweltford, if that is the case.*

A little while after that thought, Prentice encountered the first piece of evidence that made him think he might be correct as he and Solft noticed another steel plaque seemingly at a random point in the stone. Prentice nodded at Solft's unspoken question and stopped with him as he drew out his equipment to make another charcoal rubbing. When he was done, the two made quick time to catch up with the rest of the Gryphon Banner, though Prentice noticed that Solft was wincing as he walked. His feet were still quite sore, it seemed.

At last, the company emerged onto a narrow ledge that curved from a height around the smooth-seeming side of a bowl valley in the rock of the mountains. The stone was baking in the afternoon sun so that the air shimmered with the heat. Militiamen cursed when the force of it struck them after the relative cool of the ravine shade. The valley had few trees, and one half of its floor was taken up with a depression filled with a pool of dark water. Around the edge of that water was a dusty strand that might have had grass growing upon it if not for the herd of more than a hundred fey ponies, which had doubtless cropped every shred of greenery down to the dirt during their weeks of imprisonment.

When he stepped onto the ledge and felt the blast of heat, Prentice realized he could see all the way to the front of the line around the bowl of the valley, and he saw that the vanguard were now only ten or fifteen paces from the nearest cluster of Azure Mountains fey, standing together and watching the arriving Lions the way guests at a revel might regard late arrivals—curious and suspicious but not overtly hostile. As he looked, Prentice saw the Verdant rider move out in front of the Lions, while Sergeant Gennet, near to the head of the column, was immediately working to reestablish military order, forming the militia into their cohorts. Sweating, red-faced, weary men showed admirable discipline in allowing themselves to be so directed. From somewhere closer to the horses, Prentice saw a group of fey men move toward the spot where the Lions were forming up, and he recognized the one leading them as Benjamin. Abhorring the risk he was forced to take, Prentice began to push through the column ahead of him, taking the chance of knocking someone over the edge but desperate not to allow the two fey leaders to confront each other without him present. The next few moments would be crucial, Prentice was sure, and he did not want the pair's shared bitterness to run his plans aground before he even got to open his own mouth.

"Hold!" he shouted almost without thinking, still dozens of paces from the valley floor, and his voice echoed around the rock walls.

Most of the riders from Benjamin's *keshiyaa* looked up, seeking out the source of the command, Benjamin included, but the stag rider only continued walking into the open space as more and more Wind Rising gathered around him. Prentice marveled at the pale fey man's self-assurance, unarmed in the midst of folk he had helped to imprison, and realized he had seen this kind of arrogance before in overseers who strutted amongst their convict charges, secure in the knowledge of their rights over life and death. Secure, that was, until they pushed a step too far and one or more resentful imprisoned decided it was worth dying to take the bastard with them.

Looking down and judging the slope of the remaining distance between where he was on the ledge and the valley floor, Prentice stepped off and skidded the ten or so feet downward, managing to keep his feet but only just. Not waiting to fully regain his balance, he sprinted awkwardly across the rocky ground toward the stag rider. Gennet clearly had no idea what his commander was doing, but he dispatched a line of Claws in Prentice's direction nonetheless, and they trotted forward, sweat dripping down their faces, to act as an escort for their leader. By the time they reached him, Prentice himself was beside the Verdant fey man and Benjamin was no more than ten paces away.

"Stay there," Prentice told the stag rider, holding out his hand in front of the fey, who looked at it with exactly the same level of indignation and contempt that an overseer would have felt for a convict in the same situation.

"What are you doing here, *kreff enkreffra?*" Benjamin asked as he approached. Whatever surprise he felt at the Gryphon Banner Company's appearance was hidden beneath his contempt for the Verdant fey Prentice was keeping in front of. "Are you here with our traitor kin?"

Prentice shook his head impatiently, feeling momentarily breathless in the hot air after his swift dash from the ledge. He was in no mood to deal with Benjamin's paranoia. Keeping one hand raised to the stag rider, he lifted his other to the *keshiyaa's* master.

"Both of you, just wait," he commanded, trusting that the Verdant fey would be able to divine his meaning from his tone, at least. Not pausing to see if they would cooperate, he looked about for Dahyoor or Solft to translate for him. The scholar was still at the back of the descending militia, but the fey exile was nearby, and Prentice waved him over. He left the horses behind him as he approached, and one of the fey at Benjamin's shoulder muttered something in their own tongue. Another laughed sneeringly, but Prentice snapped his head around to glare at them. The chuckling fey's eyes narrowed as he recognized the challenge in Prentice's expression, and his amusement hardened. Dahyoor reached Prentice's side, and the knight commander nodded in his direction while keeping his eyes on Benjamin.

"My man, Dahyoor, here, is going to translate for me so that everyone knows what is being said," Prentice told him. "I do not want family squabbles getting in the way of the rest of today's matters."

"What matters do *you* have here?" Benjamin demanded of Prentice, though his eyes immediately slipped past the knight commander to the Verdant fey. It was clear that "family squabbles" were the matters the Wind Rising leader most wanted to address.

"I have a few concerns, Benjamin, including with you, but the most important is that we are going to destroy the Redlander cabal here in the mountains of the Verdant fey, breaking their control over the dragonfly lake for good."

"You have seen much that *kreff* should never have seen!" Benjamin said hatefully. One of the two fey behind their leader sneered once more at Dahyoor and muttered something to his fellows again in their own language. Prentice had no way of knowing exactly what had been said, but he felt Dahyoor stiffen beside him and could guess the insults in their words. He put his hand to his sword hilt.

"Benjamin, tell your man to still his tongue or he will have to prove to me that he is worthy to keep it," he ordered, eyes on the offending fey man. "The days of the White Lions enduring the insults of the Wind Rising to our faces have passed away."

Benjamin's companions looked ready to accept the challenge, and the *keshiyaa* leader himself was clearly indignant to be spoken to so directly. Before he could say anything, however, Prentice turned his back on them and walked to his horse. Over his shoulder he gave Dahyoor a nod, and then as the fey guide came over to Boots's saddle, Prentice handed him a small bundle of kindling, along with flint and steel. Dahyoor took them and walked to a spot between their horse and the fey. There, he knelt on the ground, cleared the dirt and began to set a fire. With the heat, the kindling was bone dry, and setting a small campfire took mere moments. In the meantime, Prentice began to unbuckle Boots's saddle. Over the last few days' march, he had asked Dahyoor if this was not a squire's task or a groom's, but the fey man had been adamant that amongst the Wind Rising, an elder handled their own saddle. As he hefted the heavy leather bags and seat from Boots's back, Prentice's eyes met the Verdant fey's. In this moment, the stag rider was the wild card that could tip the game the wrong way, but Prentice was glad to see the pale man simply watching calmly, even seemingly a little curious. That was all Prentice needed for now.

Hefting the saddle to the fire, Prentice laid it down on the ground. The Grand Kingdom saddles were not designed to be sat on without a horse, so he and Dahyoor had devised a system to prop the leather up by stuffing the saddlebags and bedroll through the middle to mimic a horse's back. Once the saddle was reinforced, Prentice sat on it like a chieftain presiding over some barbaric ritual, something his proud instructors at Ashfield would likely have been appalled to see—the indignity of a Grand Kingdom man, a baron of the peerage at that, behaving like a tribal "mutt" from a far land, like Aucks or north of Quenland.

You already put me out as a heretic, Prentice thought, as if those instructors were present. *Once you stick chains on a man's ankles and soul, it is surely no surprise what he becomes capable of.*

After sitting on the saddle, he nodded to Dahyoor, who returned the gesture, indicating that everything was set. The exiled fey moved swiftly across the ground from where he was kneeling to sit cross-legged at Prentice's left side. Again, Dahyoor had answered Prentice's questions with this insistence: in this context, the left hand was correct. He did not explain if that might change in other contexts. With everything set, Prentice looked to Benjamin in the hot afternoon sun, blinking from the bright rock and sweating like a farmer at the plough.

"Welcome, Benjamin *keshkirae,*" he said with an open hand, giving Benjamin the full respect of his title as a *keshiyaa* leader. "Take a place by the fire."

Benjamin and his closest exchanged looks that equally combined disbelief with indignance. They were clearly astonished to see a *kreff* follow Wind Rising tradition so accurately, but they were also offended that their ways might be so known by *kreff,* as well. This was the moment of highest risk, the turn of the gambit card, as it were. If Benjamin played fully to his anger, Prentice and his banner company would be fighting a battle right here in this tiny "paddock" in the rocks.

And then we will all likely die, he thought. *Either at each other's hands or the Redlanders'. Either way, the Western Reach would belong to the serpents and mantis before the end of summer.*

Looking around the valley, Prentice could see the other groups of trapped fey moving closer, obviously fascinated by the sight of a *kreff* acting as an elder of their clans and doubtless curious as to what their leader would do.

Benjamin looked from the fire to Prentice and back again for a long moment. It was clear he had no idea how to respond. The rules of his society, upon which he had relied all of his life, fixed him in place, giving him no clear move in any direction. One of his offended companions said something dismissive, and Prentice assumed he was counseling his leader to reject this whole ceremony as false. To his credit, Benjamin rebuked his man, recognizing that disdaining Prentice at this moment might also mean disdaining the tradition of their people that Prentice was enacting.

Behold, Benjamin, God is doing a new thing with all our peoples, Prentice thought, eyes fixed on the *keshkirae's* face. *I am one of the tools to make that new thing. We all are, or else we are the old thing that is being overturned. Reject that if you wish, but know that the Verdant, the Redlanders, and the Grand Kingdom's nobility all know in their hearts that it is true. Even the merciless Inquisition knows. And they all fear its coming.*

Benjamin walked forward until he was standing by the fire, but he set his face in a hard expression. His eyes fell upon Dahyoor.

"He has no place by our fires," he said, and even in the brutal heat of that afternoon, the coldness of his words was unmistakable.

Prentice could not help but smile. Heat was tough to endure, but he had tasted the rage of the Lion—the rage of God himself at the sins that poisoned His creation—and no heat could compare to the fires that were stoked from that righteous truth. And as for cold?

My heart is colder than yours, my friend, and you should be thankful it is.

CHAPTER 80

Prentice met Benjamin's hard stare calmly.

"Dahyoor has a place by the Lioness Mother's fires, by *my* fire," he said calmly and then gestured to the little flame roiling in the scorched air. The Wind Rising riders were watching, fascinated, some still clearly aghast but many more simply unable to make full sense of what they were witnessing.

"He has surely fallen low enough to sit by the *palpolon* elder, would you not say? Beside the elder who walks with a horseless *keshiyaa*?"

Prentice smiled as he spoke and was pleased to see several of the watching fey smirk at his joke. Some sneered, as well, but he was less concerned with them. They would sneer no matter what he said. What mattered was that he could show a place, a connection, a path between the old ways that were faltering but might still be profitable and the new thing he was building on his liege's behalf. Benjamin stared for a long moment at Prentice. The fey leader was not carrying a visible weapon; horse archer fey always kept their weapons on their saddles. Nevertheless, there was a chance he would attack. Dahyoor had been insistent on this. The *keshkirae* took one more step forward and then slowly sank to sit, cross legged on the ground.

Audible sighs and gasps sounded from fey riders, and behind him, Prentice was fairly certain he could hear similar noises from the militiamen standing guard. He had discussed some of the possibility of this moment with Whilte and Solft, as well as

Dahyoor, but he had no idea how much they had explained to others. Everyone present, though, seemed to have some notion of the historic potential of this meeting.

So let us get it right, Prentice thought.

"Tell me of these new things you think to make, *palpolon* elder," Benjamin said, and while he looked like he was trying to be openly sincere, he was obviously struggling not to simply give way to anger and contempt. Prentice had to give the fey man credit. He was waging war on his own instincts for the sakes of his followers and his people.

"I will speak of new things, but first..." Prentice told him and paused look over his shoulder at the Verdant fey still watching closely. He was pleased to see Master Solft was beside the stag rider and appeared to be giving an interpretation, since the meeting was being conducted in Kingdom speech.

"First," Prentice repeated, turning back to Benjamin, "you have a cause of blood against kin. Speak your cause, as much as you must tell."

This was another important moment, one Prentice and Dahyoor had planned with great care. Since Prentice was the elder at this fire, when he spoke on a matter, that matter was concluded. His word was as close to law as could be, just as if he were speaking as a nobleman in his own court.

Which you actually are now, Baron *Ash,* he told himself, ignoring the feeling of ridiculous irony that caused him.

But since his words would be final, it was significant that he gave Benjamin full space to speak his grievances first. It was a gesture of respect, and from his eyes, Prentice could see that Benjamin understood it and perhaps even appreciated it.

"The Verdant broke covenant with kin," Benjamin said, and there was no disguising the hate in his voice. "Around their fire they drew blades without cause and slew us. We had their food in our mouths and our weapons upon our saddles. They killed our horses and our riders. Worst, all this they did in service to the

Untrue, whom all fey kin have sworn to allow no fires between until all earths are no more."

Benjamin fell silent, glaring at the Verdant fey over Prentice's shoulder.

"The words Benjamin *keshkirae* speaks are true," Prentice said. "Blood is between the Verdant and the Wind Rising. The White Lions and the Lioness witness this blood and stand beside Benjamin and his *keshiyaa* as far as he must ride to wash the stain away."

Of course, all this would have been so much easier if you had just told us this from the beginning, you stiff-necked mongrel, Prentice thought, keeping his face as neutral as he could.

"Nevertheless, the Lioness has made a pact with the Verdant," Prentice went on. Every word he said now had been worked out already with Dahyoor, and Prentice watched assiduously to see what impact his speech was having on the proud, betrayed, and imprisoned fey. "We have sworn together to end the Redlander cabal, the serpents, and the mantis. Until that is done, we have sworn to raise no blade, no gunners' shot against the Verdant, rider and slinger both. Can you bear this, or does the blood between you have no patience?"

This was yet another key moment. Prentice was openly giving Benjamin the freedom to scuttle the entire plan with the Verdant fey. He meant it, too, because he knew he must. The fey of the Azures, the ones like Benjamin who had not seen his combat with the Serpent Witch and the unicorn, had come to a cliff, a ravine that they had baulked at trying to leap. If Prentice wanted them to trust him, he had to show them that the ground on the opposite side was stable and that not every tradition was going to be abolished. This was the thing Earl Sebastian had never seen—the possibility that the new future would keep the worthy parts of the relinquished past. Of course, Sebastian had had other voices whispering fears to him in secret, which had not helped.

"What if we cannot leave our cause of blood with the herd?" Benjamin asked in fey fashion. "What if it must be carried with our saddles?"

"Then it must be carried with your saddles," Prentice answered, accepting the word. "The Lions cannot break their oath for this, but neither will we block your path. Your *keshiyaa* must ride its own path, and we will be allies at the end. We must find a way to end the Redlander cabal, and soon, but the Lioness does not ask you to give up what you must carry with your saddles."

Benjamin nodded thoughtfully and then looked up at the Verdant fey once more, his expression less hateful and more contemplative, as if weighing his options.

"What does *he* say?" the *keshkirae* asked.

"He does not sit by this fire until Benjamin has said what is true," Prentice said, and Benjamin nodded even more meaningfully. Prentice had just told Benjamin that whatever he chose, he would retain place with Prentice, regardless of what it cost with the Verdant fey. It looked as if Benjamin fully appreciated the endorsement.

"We can leave the cause of blood with the herd until the Serpent Witch, her sisters, and the crickets who walk as men are thrown down. We will not leave the cause of blood behind us on the trail, though. Do not doubt that."

"You are *keshkirae*," Prentice told him. Benjamin's riders followed him, and it was his right to lead them wherever he chose. That was the way of things amongst the Wind Rising fey. Prentice touched Dahyoor's shoulder, and taking the signal, the exiled fey stood and went to fetch the Verdant man the short distance to bring him into the circle of their fire.

"Go, fetch your saddle," Prentice told Benjamin. "You should not sit at the same height by my fire as your blood foe."

Benjamin's eyes went wide with surprise, and he stood. Before he left to fetch his saddle, he looked to Prentice with a last question.

"What of between us?" Benjamin asked quietly, and Prentice took that to mean what would be done about his rebellion, leading the *keshiyaa* into the dragonfly mist, as well as earlier thinking to let the Inquisition and Lions kill each other in the swamp near Dweltford.

"We have never sat at a fire together before—yours, mine, or another's," Prentice said to him. "What true matters can be between us if no elders have bound us, nor have we to each other?"

Benjamin nodded, and for the first time there was no acrimony in his expression as he looked at Prentice.

"*Kreff enkreffra,*" he said, then smirked. "*Palpolon* elder."

Prentice smiled back at him and inwardly sighed with relief as Benjamin went to fetch his saddle. That was half the afternoon's mission completed. He looked to see the stag rider approaching cautiously, waiting in bewilderment to be invited by the "elder" of this campfire.

Now comes the difficult part.

CHAPTER 81

The day was almost over, and the Lions had weathered the fighting well, as near as Amelia could see. Sometime in the midafternoon the crossbowmen had stopped shooting, though the why of that was not clear. The archduchess wondered if they had finally run out of ammunition, but Markas thought it more likely they had decided to conserve what they had left.

"Odds is they've figured their plan ain't goin' to work today and they want to save what they got for some other ploy."

That made sense to Amelia, and she let it stand at that. From the look of things, their spearmen were as frustrated with their fruitless strategy as their crossbowmen.

Let them be exasperated, Amelia thought. *They have hurt enough of our men in the process.*

The militia's discipline and will still seemed sound to her as she looked at the orderly troop that had stood almost a full day in rank, only sparing themselves time to take cups of water brought by runners. Apparently, several of the refugees from Aubrey had volunteered for that task, and the threadbare scarecrows rushed back and forth up the lines carrying small barrels they filled from the river.

"North, across the river," came a call from behind her. "The knights are moving."

Amelia looked over her shoulder to see Robant's force—the whole of it, it seemed—taking to their horses and riding westward toward the Dwelt and the Reach proper. She looked up at the sun and guessed there was still an hour or two of daylight left, being that it was high summer, and the sun would be up until well into the evening. Even so, if Robant was leading them to the cleverly hidden boats Markas had imagined, he seemed to have left it late in the day to make his move. If she had to judge between the Vec forces and her own, she thought it was the enemy who were more dispirited by the battle's progress. Trying to catch her militia in the jaws of the wolf now looked likely to break the bottom jaw before it saw the Lions badly bitten.

Nevertheless, the archduchess stood tense on her wagon vantage point as they waited for the sun to go down. When the Golden Heron army began to withdraw to their camp, her relief was so strong that she felt her knees almost go out from under her. She sagged against the wagon's edge and took long breaths.

"Drink of water, m'lady?" a voice offered, and Amelia looked up to see one of the refugees on the ground beneath her offering up a wooden cup of water. "Nice and cool, not long out o' the river."

"You say, 'Your Grace,'" Markas counseled the man. "Her Grace is not a m'lady. She's a 'Your Grace.'"

"Sorry, Your Grace," the man said earnestly, tugging his forelock. Amelia smiled and reached down to take the offered cup.

The things that matter to us, she thought as she drained the water that was indeed still cool and fresh.

"Thank you for your service, good yeoman," she said as she handed the empty cup back.

"Sorry, Your Grace, I'm no yeoman. I'm a serf, bound to Aubrey farmlands by my grandpap's debt-pledge. That's why I'm still here. Ain't no member of my family gone wayward. We got a name for that, hard earned."

"Not anymore, good yeoman," Amelia said, marveling at the thin wire of pride in the core of this half-starved man. Life had worn him to the bone, and his commitment to this one truth made him stay on his master's lands, even though it might have killed him. "As liege of Aubrey, I declare your grandfather's pledge paid in full by your service this day. You and your children after you are freed to make your way in the world. If you have no place to call home, you are given now the right to claim unowned land anywhere within the Reach and build there what you will. What is your name?"

"Adam, Your Grace," the man said in an awestruck tone, as if he were experiencing a religious vision.

"Then, Adam, to the throne of Dweltford you are Adam Waterman, who served rightly on a day of battle. Tell your children the tale and give them the name after you."

"I will," the newly named Adam Waterman said, forgetting to offer any sign of respect as he wandered off, a beatific smile on his face. Amelia watched him walk away and then looked up to see Markas staring at her with a similar expression on his own. When he saw that she had noticed, he bowed his head.

"What is it?" she asked. Markas bit his lip thoughtfully for a moment and then said simply.

"We love you, Your Grace."

Amelia felt tears well in her eyes, and she looked away, dabbing at them with the corner of her winged sleeve.

"Oh shush, Banner Sergeant," she said. "You'll have me weeping on the battlefield. I'm supposed to be the Lioness."

"Sorry, Your Grace," Markas said earnestly, and Amelia had to choke back a guffaw at the foolish feelings the situation raised in her.

Once the sun started to set, the command was given for the company to break ranks, and militiamen traversed the short distance to where they would sleep the night under the soft sounds of the river flowing past. It could have been a pleasant evening's camping if not for the danger they had faced and would face again come the new day.

"We cannot remain here like this indefinitely," Amelia said as she ate her evening meal. "How many days will they keep us pinned here, trying to wear us away like this?"

"Hard to say, Your Grace," Sedgemark answered through mouthfuls of a fried river fish, likely catfish, or its cousin, cobbler. "They tried hard to make it hurt today, but other than getting one nasty cut for every hundred or so crossbow bolts they shot, we got the best of the fighting by far. I think they weren't really ready for fighting Lions, though you can see they'd thought about it."

That seemed true, and while her faith in her militia was, if anything, increased by the day's performance, Amelia knew it was not a strategy they could keep up indefinitely. Even if everything else remained equal, they only had enough shot for another full day of battle like this.

"Knight Captain Farringdon was firm in his command that we should hold out as long as we can," Sergeant Nunel said. Whenever the archduchess consulted him, he always defaulted firstly to her husband's orders. His devotion to his leader was impressive.

"But how long can we do that?" she asked.

"As long as we must," the lancer sergeant said faithfully, and while Amelia appreciated his sincerity, she also knew there came a point when any strategy might begin to fail, even if it had won every engagement up to that point. Faith tempered with wisdom, as Prentice might say.

And mixed with a good smidgeon of canniness, Amelia heard Turley add in her mind, and she smiled. She yawned then and was about to retire to her reed bed when the sound of shouting came from the direction of the river. Her command staff around her all looked up from their rough meals and listened to see what could be made of the fracas. Was it Duke Robant's knights arriving at last? She nodded to Sedgemark and he dropped his plate of fish to quickly rally a cohort of foot.

"Beat general call, Your Grace?" Markas asked.

"The men need their rest," she said, knowing how much she herself was enjoying the chance to sit and eat. "They can have it until we know what is happening for sure, but fetch a drummer and let him have his sticks in hand."

Markas saluted and left his own meal by the fire as well. With only Nunel and Spindle as escorts, Amelia headed for the riverside to see what new trouble was disturbing their night. By the time she arrived, multiple patrols of sentries were waving torches and lanterns back and forth on the bank, trying to pierce the darkness over the water. There were shouts and splashes, and someone thrashed their way out of the river not far from where she was standing.

"Name yourself," a sentry with a halberd demanded, holding the swimmer in the shallows at weapon point.

"Reacherman," the fellow spluttered, spitting out mud and river grass. "Loyal Reacherman!"

"We've been pilotin' on the river blockade since soon after the duke from the east sent his knights to hunt us down," the dripping riverfolker said as he sat under guard just up beneath the Aubrey bridge footings. He paused as Sergeant Nunel handed him a hot cup of passionflower tea, which he took thankfully in both hands.

"You were manning the blockade?" Amelia asked, shocked at the revelation. The riverman was immediately defensive.

"Not for ourselves or nuthin'," he insisted. "We was hidin' at first. But they snatched up our boats and strung these long chains through 'em. The river flow's not simple as some road you can just string a rope across and call it a fence. After two days they'd already had two times where a chain snapped and a craft swung free some, tangled up one or more others and sent the lot to the bottom. After the drought, we was only just startin' to come back to life like. If we let them knights just keep chainin' up our boats and runnin' 'em to the bottom, there wouldn't be no riverfolk life south of Griffith come the end of summer. Some of us figured we'd offer to steer the boats so they at least didn't go under."

"So you thought to help her grace's enemies in choking off the river trade?" Lady Spindle demanded. In the torchlight, her half-masked face plainly intimidated the riverboatman.

"It ain't so simple as all that," he protested fearfully, eyes go-ing from the mysterious woman to the more open-faced-seeming liege lady of the Reach. He shrugged as he explained his actions. "Loads of us have 'skip crew family, or friends like. It's the river, ain't it? We figured we'd handle this "blockade" for 'em, make a big show of turnin' boats back in the daylight and then let the 'skips through in the dog watches. And we'd make sure word got to you and up to Dweltford 'bout what was goin' on. 'Cept someone got hungry fingers and took a purse of guilders to sell us out. We figure it was one 'em mask-worship folk. Bloody fools. Who fancies there's gods in a mask made of wood or copper? If that's the case, why in a mask and not in a boat or an oar? Could use an oar with a magicky 'god' in it." He shook his head. "Anyhow, word got back to the knights and suddenly there were a couple of executions and men-at-arms put on some of the boats come each sundown. Weren't no skippin' from then on, with things like that."

Amelia nodded, both pleased to learn that the riverfolk might have thought to act as loyal Reachermen and unsurprised that Robant had been so ruthless in handling the smugglers and their plots. She wasn't sure how she felt about mention of mantis cultists still being about on the river, but the riverman's rejection of their teachings was a comforting revelation.

"Tell us then why you are here tonight," she pressed. "Did you manage to set your boat free from the blockade? And what was the fight on the river about?"

"That was loyal against traitor, that was," the riverman said with a mischievous smile. "There ain't been no way for us to do anythin' 'cept whatever the dog and his men told us for weeks. We tried all things, but either we had to stay nights in the chained boats or else we were chained up ourselves, stuck in the work crews, diggin' the walls and trench, and a big pond for their daft little forts on the side of the Dwelt. They got themselves well hid behind walls, figurin' to stay a good long while, from their talk. 'Enforcements, that's the word they kept sayin' to 'emselves night and day. Stick it out 'til rare 'enforcements come to help 'em."

"Reinforcements?" Amelia corrected, and the riverman nodded after taking another sip of warming tea.

"That's the word."

"What do you mean they were having you dig a pond?" Nunel pressed before the man could return to his story.

"A pond, a big hole in the ground they wanted filled with water," the riverman retorted, as if being asked a fool's question. "What do you think I meant?"

Nunel looked to Amelia, ready to cuff the man for his insolence, it seemed, but she was more concerned with getting the story concerning the blockade. A pond or whatever other oddities Robant's knights were insisting upon was of less interest to her. She gestured for the riverman to continue his tale.

"They figure to have friends, these 'enforcements, comin' from the west and the east. We figured on the ones from the east bein' sent from the kingslayer, but we never heard nothin' 'bout someone's from the west. There was a tale told 'bout a Reacher lion army out in Radengon at the start of summer, but sure'n they would be your men, wouldn't they, Your Grace? They wouldn't be comin' for to help the dog's boys."

That rumor must have been about Prentice's Gryphon Banner Company, Amelia assumed. The other force, the one for which the knights were waiting, must have been the Inquisition knights that Prentice had gone to hunt. But surely they must be dead or in chains by now. Even with the Inquisition's magicks, they could not hide from the fey riders in the west for the whole of summer, could they?

Does that mean that Prentice is not yet even returned from his campaign? Or worse, defeated?

That notion troubled Amelia deeply. She had assumed that Prentice had returned to Dweltford by now and would be rallying the full new company from training in Fallenhill to march to her relief.

"Has there been no word from Dweltford yet?" she asked, holding her hands hidden in her sleeves so that no one would see them clenched in tense fists. The riverman shook his head with a cocksure smile.

"No word, 'cepting another bloody army marched straight down from the lake, not even stoppin' at Griffith. Got the jump on the dog's knights and all. Should've seen 'em wetting 'emselves and sendin' riders off for help."

"Oh, thank God," Amelia said, putting her hands to her mouth a moment. "Prentice must have returned after all."

"The Dweltford convict with the magick sword?" the riverman asked at mention of Prentice's name. He shook his head. "Didn't see no tell of him. This army had two womenfolk at the head. The pretty one they say used to be a princess or somethin', though no one's supposed to say cause her ears hear everythin', and the other deadly one in the mask, the one what done for that prat, Fulford. They were the ones in charge, not to mention a gaggle of skips' girls floating about, learning to be proper ladies, so it's said. They marched down on the little forts this morning and lined 'emselves up to fight. Some knights come early on to back up the crew in the forts, but that only made a hundred or so, and the lady's army, it was like to thousands, so someone who can count that high said."

Dalflitch has led the company south with Righteous? Amelia wondered, casting a troubled glance at Spindle. *Where was Prentice then? Had he died on the campaign? Did they bring his company down without him because he was lost?*

The thought made Amelia's heart break for Righteous, a new mother widowed, and then she felt a further worry as she realized that her lady should not really be marching so soon after giving birth either. The needs of the Reach were demanding indeed on its new peers, it seemed.

"When it got all befuddled, some of us lads figured time was comin' to break the blockade up, give the dog's boys more to think 'bout. Then they come to do it 'emselves. We figured we were to be let off the hook, but no, they just wanted to set a boat off with a message for down the Murr. The 'enforcements they told of, they had word of them comin' by boats from Bridgetown, or somewhere roundabouts there. They wanted to send a messenger to say, 'make best speed.' Come and save us, more like."

The sodden man paused to give a contemptuous snort, then carried on.

"A riverman they trusted got the message cargo to carry and we were told to take 'is boat off the chains for 'em. I told my mates this was a shot to get the traitor and end the blockade for 'em, and we made best use of the moment. Got dicey for a space. Couple of rivermen and one or two men-at-arms went into the river. Worse for them than us. We can swim. Coats o' plates ain't so good for that."

He smirked readily once more and swirled the dregs of his tea around in the cup before downing it in a last swig.

"Would've been better with some gin in it," he said.

"Be thankful you got that, cheeky otter," Nunel told him sternly. Amelia held up her hand for peace. She had more important concerns than the riverman's gratitude.

"What of that messenger?" she asked. "The one sent for reinforcements."

The riverman hung his head and frowned remorsefully.

"Sorry, Your Grace," he said. "I poled my skiff like a mad devil, I swear I did, and I ran him down alright, but I missed my count. He had an extra pair of hands aboard. While I was fightin' to knock one in the drink, the other scab got a gaff hook under my feet. Had me over the side 'fore I knew it. They got away, I'd say."

Amelia nodded her head and stepped off, leaving the rescued boatman to her guards. Nunel and Spindle followed her.

"It is good to hear that a relief army has come in force from Dweltford, but news of support coming for Robant by boat is unwelcome," the lancer sergeant offered. "Still, unless those knights prove more brilliant in defense than we have yet seen, or those reinforcements run themselves up the river in a single swift day, I think we can take hope that we are no longer to be pressed upon two sides. We will be able to return you to the Reach soon, Your Grace."

"Aubrey is the Reach," Amelia said reflexively, her mind still more occupied with the details of what she had learned.

"Forgive me, Your Grace," Nunel apologized. "I meant the Reach proper."

Amelia was tempted to correct his correction, but she was too distracted to care. She had enough spare thought to bid the line first who led the nearby sentries to see the boatman be fed and released to wherever he would go, and then she began to move away, back into the camp.

"Relief will be welcome, Your Grace," Spindle said quietly at her shoulder. "And it sounds like some of those blockade boats will be swiftly available to use once Lady Dalflitch's force captures those forts. Even if the fight goes on some more, we should not starve."

"Lady Dalflitch's force?" Amelia repeated, shaking her head. What was happening to the world that ladies-in-waiting were bodyguards and captains of armed companies? Where were the worthy men, the men to take up the burdens of war?

They are my enemies or else dead in my service, Amelia thought and immediately rejected it as an unworthy notion. Nunel, Markas, and Sedgemark were all plainly worthy, and while she would not rush to promote any of them, if it came to it, they should be able to take the reins, at least for a time.

That is assuming my two most favored men are lost to me. Hard enough upon myself, but poor Righteous, too? If we must be widowed, Lord, let us at least look upon our husband's bodies.

Her first husband had been murdered by poison in her absence, and never seeing his body before it was interred was something that had hurt more than she had imagined it would. It had been as if she had had no chance to bid him farewell on his journey into the world to come.

Better they both still live, she thought. *But if not, please, Lord, let us see their bodies.*

CHAPTER 83

T he Verdant elder sat in the place Dahyoor led him to, halfway around the fire between Prentice and Benjamin's spot. The *keshiyaa* leader took a short while to return with his saddle, which he placed on the ground in his previous space and then settled himself upon it with the proud dignity of any peer of the Realm.

"A Wind Rising fire set by a *kreff* in Verdant fey land," Prentice said once Dahyoor was back at his spot beside the knight commander. "If our elders or sages ever imagined a day like this one, they never shared the story with *my* ancestors."

Dahyoor interpreted for the Verdant rider, while Benjamin simply nodded silently. When the translation was finished, the stag rider said something terse, clearly aimed at Benjamin. The *keshkirae* started, almost rising from his saddle, as if ready to avenge an insult with violence. Then he sat back and sneered at the Verdant man, turning his head away and nodding to Prentice once more. It was a perfect moment for Prentice. The Verdant had tried to split the meeting apart, to sow chaos, but Benjamin had returned to his tradition, the peace of a welcomed campfire, the peace the Verdant had defiled. If the stag rider had tempted him to violence now, the dishonor would have been shared. Instead, Benjamin had held his honor, and in the process honored Prentice. The Verdant rider's sneer soured further, and all mockery left his eyes, replaced with the kind of sullenness that once had characterized Dahyoor's expressions. For the first time since the White Lions had arrived in the mountains, it was the Verdant elder who was the outsider. Prentice doubted he had ever imagined this could happen. Playing Wind Rising off against *kreff* had likely always been his prime strategy.

"What is your plan?" Prentice asked the pale man.

The Verdant elder did not respond, only scowled as he looked back and forth between the others seated around the fire. Tiny though it was, it seemed to be heating the already oven-like air further, and Prentice dreaded the thought that his sweaty face might look weak to the equanimous fey. He had noticed that both kinds of fey folk endured the weather with much greater peace in their bodies, and he wondered at how the Almighty had fashioned similar mortals so differently.

Musings for another time. Be mindful, he chastened himself and wondered how to push the Verdant man to speak. All this ritual might be necessary, but according to his calendar of noons and midnights and dawns, it left them little time to do the most important things.

"Is this expected?" Prentice asked Dahyoor quietly. The fey shook his head.

"His pride is choking him," Dahyoor whispered back. "He is made small in our sight, and he doesn't want to speak as the least one by this fire."

Another Liam, Prentice thought furiously. He did not have time to coddle the wounded pride of a fallen champion. The Reach's need was too great. Thinking to prompt conversation by drawing a map on the ground to plan their move against the Redlanders, Prentice took his sword in hand and began to rise. Immediately Benjamin shifted his weight forward, as if to stand as well.

Damn, I am the governing elder of this fire, Prentice thought. *When I stand, the meet is over.* He paused for a moment, sitting back on his saddle fully. Benjamin did the same. Then the knight commander reached to his belt and unhooked his dagger in its sheath, the one his wife had given him, the one Solomon had once tried to "borrow." Memories of his wife and the lad he counted as an adopted son almost slapped Prentice in the face, and he had to force them down savagely. This was a moment that required steel focus. *Keep your head in the fight.*

He handed the dagger to Dahyoor.

"Use this to draw in the sand there," he said, indicating where he meant. "I will tell you what I want, starting with a shape like the dark of a snake's eye, curved at the sides, pointed top and bottom."

Dahyoor looked at Prentice with a confused expression, some wonder and something even resembling happiness. He accepted the dagger, and using the weapon in its sheath, he drew what Prentice commanded in the dust beside the fire. On his hands and knees, Dahyoor had to scrabble past the Verdant fey, and the elder pulled back slightly, speaking an angry question.

"He wants to know what is happening," Benjamin translated, and Prentice was truly encouraged.

"This is the map of the lake where we will fight," Prentice explained, and Benjamin interpreted the words while Dahyoor continued to trace the shapes at Prentice's instruction.

"Draw a dragonfly at that end and put these pebbles on this side, at the other end. They are the settlement on the cliffside. Draw a river coming away at that end."

Each piece was drawn in the dust or placed, and both Benjamin and the Verdant fey started to pay closer attention. Prentice noticed a few desiccated leaves lying on the ground nearby, and he pointed Dahyoor to those.

"Put them in the lake. They are the Redlander boats. Ask him which part of the lake they moor in."

Benjamin asked the question, and the Verdant shrugged, muttering something that was obviously going to be unhelpful.

"In the water, he says," was the translation.

Prentice rolled his eyes.

"Where? By the settlement? Up against the sacrificial plinth? Under the shadow of the dragonfly?"

Given the size of the lake, anywhere was likely reachable by Redlander oarsmen and magickal sails within a half hour, but even that short a time might be significant and something they could exploit. As it was, the Verdant fey was far from helpful. The best they could gain from him was that the boats tended to move about the lake, though Prentice doubted they did not follow a recognizable pattern.

And if we had time to watch, we might find it out, he thought. *No matter.*

"Ask him where he plans to lead us," he told Dahyoor.

When the question was repeated, the proud elder sneered again.

"He says to the lake."

"Remind him that he wants us to kill the Redlanders and not harm his folk," Prentice said in exasperation. "We need to know where they are and where he will lead us out of the mountains. How far into the forest will we come out of these secret paths, for example?"

His words were translated and the Verdant fey scoffed, giving a reply more in keeping with his usual contempt.

"He says that if he released you into the forests, you would fall before you saw the lake water," Dahyoor translated. "He says we should have explained what it would be like, since we have been through it already."

Bloody fool, Prentice thought, recognizing the vain taunt in the Verdant's words. *You want to be free from the Redlanders but not so much you will give up your resentment and pride toward your own kin?*

Dahyoor showed almost no offense at the Verdant's words, but Benjamin's jaw appeared locked in fury, his teeth likely grinding like millstones on grain.

"Ask him where he will bring us out, then?" Prentice said, glad for the *keshkirae's* restraint.

The Verdant fey sat forward and poked a finger into the sand near the dragonfly end on the settlement side of the lake. From the memory of his vision, Prentice recalled this was all rock and cliff face, with a bare pebbled strand perhaps wide enough for a double column to walk but nowhere to fight a battle. He was about to ask for clarification when the Verdant elder began to trace a long line up around the dragonfly and then down the other bank of the lake until he stopped it about halfway on that side.

"He says the paths through the stone will follow that line but will only exit there."

Prentice did not believe for a moment that the only exit to the mystical paths was on the far side of the lake from the fey folks' settlement, but most probably the stag rider had no intention of bringing them any closer to his people than necessary.

"He says we will fight them here, on the grass beside the water," Dahyoor finished. The Verdant sat back with the air of having issued a great pronouncement.

"Far from everything important to him," Prentice observed, and Benjamin snorted, apparently recognizing the self-serving nature of the Verdant's plan. "How does he propose that we get the serpent cabal to come across the water at us? He wants us to kill them without ever going near them?"

The question was passed, and the answer was so improbable that Prentice had to keep himself from openly scoffing.

"He says he will go to them with a plan to capture your head," Dahyoor explained. "He will say that he has led you to a trap but needs their help for your capture. Then he will bring them across and we will use iron and fire to break them. Then he will call on some riders he trusts to finish it."

"What about the merciless?" Prentice asked.

"He says that *kreff* are *kreff's* problem," Dahyoor said, passing the translated question and answer.

"Point out to him that our oath does not bind Inxyphos' people," Prentice said, looking the Verdant man in the eye. "They will be free to attack and slay the Verdant fey."

The interpretation was given, and the Verdant elder answered with a disdainful shrug.

"He says the same—*kreff* are *kreff's* problem."

Surely he does not imagine we will fall for this? Prentice thought. *Is he truly planning to play all sides against the middle? Was even Benjamin this foolishly proud? If we look able to overthrow the Redlanders, he will come to his people as their savior. If we fail, he will look for his moment to seek my head in the battle and accept the Blood Sect "blessing" to become a Horned Man. He has been an unchallenged leader for too long. He does not know how to recognize when he is outmatched.*

Prentice found himself meeting Benjamin's eyes, and there was a sense of shared understanding there he had never had with the *keshiyaa* leader before.

"He thinks he is cannier than we," Prentice said, and Benjamin nodded once, slowly. Dahyoor did not translate these words, likely sensing that Prentice did not mean them for the Verdant.

"The forest is impenetrable, and only a trick of the wind on an arrow could take the Monarch from under him. He thinks all *kreff* are blind still, even when they can see him," said Benjamin.

A trick of the wind on an arrow? Prentice repeated in his mind. *We might say fickle fate. The Verdant is giving no credit to us. The loss of the sovereign stag is just a fluke that he need not fear repeating. Benjamin is right. Our "friend" here still thinks we are too stupid to understand what is happening. Even if we were, the Redlanders would not fall for this. They will likely devour him once they see what he is trying to do.*

"If this is the wisdom of the Verdant fey, what can save them?" Prentice asked, still looking at Benjamin.

"Their error is now seen," the *keshkirae* responded. "It cannot be unseen again."

So, what then is our plan? Prentice thought.

"Ask him how long it will take to get from here to where he will let us out of the stone pathways."

CHAPTER 84

T he Golden Heron mercenary force took the field once again, and the Lions formed up as well. Neither side was in the hurry they had been in on previous mornings, and the sun was many hours over the horizon by the time the Heron's trumpets sounded and they began their advance once again.

"Now let us see if we are as clever as we hope we are," Amelia said to Lady Spindle, who had asked to attend her liege this morning. Her husband was no longer abed and had taken to organizing the refugees as a way to keep his mind active. He had also insisted that she cease from "mothering him" as well, apparently.

"Will they do the same thing that failed yesterday?" Spindle asked.

"Not if they're canny," Markas ventured. "But they might figure their last try just hasn't had a chance to work yet."

"They will be disappointed if they do," Amelia said with more self-possession than she felt. In the predawn hours she had taken some time to devise a new strategy with her sergeants for dealing with the crossbows. It had seemed a goodly plan come sunrise, but now she was feeling the lost sleep and found her confidence waning. Nevertheless, she set her face to her courtly reserve and projected the dignity of the Lioness. If nothing else, these days of command were erasing the memory of the shrill madwoman the Inquisition's whispers of grief had tried to turn her into—at a dreadful cost, though.

The crossbowmen on the right were almost to their shooting point, while the mailed spearmen on the left were likewise advancing, slowly it seemed. She could imagine they were reluctant for *another* slugging match they were sure to get the worst of. Both wings might soon be surprised. It was the horsemen, though, that Amelia watched most closely. It could be that they would swing the battle yet, but if they did not form up as they had the previous day, her plan would only be half as effective, if that.

"'Ware the sky," came the shout as the first volley of crossbows fell upon the waiting Lions. "Umbrellas" were raised as before, and the iron-tipped shafts clattered off protective steel or else thudded to the earth. Only one or two bit flesh, eliciting groans of pain and calls for men to be carried out for healing. As soon as the volley was done though, Sergeant Nunel gave a bellow and a new drumbeat rang out, one that had not yet sounded on this battle.

"Roar forward!"

The White Lion Banner Company fielded around four hundred Roar gunners. For the first days, they had kept to the mud ramparts on either wing of Amelia's defenses, fifty at a time, running up the rear ramp to fire and then withdrawing to reload while the next fifty came to take their shots. Like waves of shot upon a beach made of bodies, it had proved a very effective firing tactic, as long as the enemy kept coming on. The advancing spearmen on the left had learned to fear it. On the right, the crossbowmen had stayed at the longest range and been relatively safe. No longer.

While the crossbows were down, windlasses turning to draw back the strings, two hundred Roarsmen in four lines of fifty emerged in ranks and fired four successive volleys into the opposing missile troops. Nunel and Sedgemark had assured Amelia that the most likely thing the crossbowmen had been told to expect was an advance by Lions in formation to charge them down. If that happened, the crossbows would be expected to run back while the smaller company of spearmen on their right moved to intercept the charging militia. Once they had done that and the Lions were bogged down, the cavalry would have swung around and charged in from the right, mauling the pike and halberd from the side where their weapons were unready. That was what they expected the Heron wanted, but Amelia was determined not to give it to them.

Cries of pain and terror rang across the battlefield as smoke began to interfere with Amelia's sight of the enemy lines. The one thing the Heron crossbows had not expected, it seemed, was return shooting from the Roar. She peered through the mildly obscured air, watching men in mail who had thought themselves safe recoil from shot they could not see coming. Amelia had never been on the receiving end of matchlock fire, but Nunel assured her it sounded like angry hornets, buzzing through the air.

"Will they rally?" she asked herself, watching closely. The rest of her plan with her sergeants depended upon how the Heron force responded to this change in her side's tactics.

"Only four things they can do, as I see it, Your Grace," Sedgemark had summarised. "One, they can pull back. Safe, simple, and I'd say their canniest move. Two, they can try to make a duel of it, their crossbows against our gunners. That might work, except the matchlock's a faster and easier reload than a crossbow, and as near as they've shown us, they haven't been trained to do it in the quick rolling volleys that'll let them keep up pressure on us like we can on them. We should win a duel comfortably.

"The third possibility is that they get their spears afoot to march into the gap between us, act as living pavises as it were. Then they can try keeping up the same shooting, arcing over their fellows' heads."

"Will they accept that kind of duty?" Amelia had asked as they sat around the early morning fire.

Nunel and Markas had shaken their heads readily, and Sedgemark seemed to agree.

"I wouldn't like to try to order the Claws and Fangs to that," he'd said. "Not without some plan more than to just keep throwing shots back and forth at each other."

"Then what is the fourth possibility?"

The three sergeants had all looked to each other then. This was what they agreed was most likely.

"The horses on the flanks are readied for a charge. If they see the Roar out front of our protective pikes, chances are good they'll call that a juicy target and try to sweep them away. Horsemen live for the charge, even our knight captain's new lancers, and these fellows spent all yesterday waiting for an opportunity that never came."

"And so you think they will come on if they see the Roar sitting out front ahead of the Claws?"

Amelia remembered asking that question as she peered through the haze at the enemy's wing where their horsemen were formed up awaiting their hammer-blow chance. In front of the Lions, the Roar had begun to reload, and while some of the crossbowmen seemed to think to make a race of it, at least half the enemy missile shooters had begun to crouch down or pull back some, delaying their own attacks in hopes of protecting themselves even a little. Their place on the battlefield had just become so much more dangerous than they ever expected. The firing continued in its slow waves, and in small but significant numbers, the enemy company was being whittled down.

"There goes a runner to the spearmen," Markas called, pointing to that part of the Heron's line where a man was seen dashing across.

"And another to the horses, I think," Spindle added, peering in the other direction, though it was harder to see there as the smoke was denser. The morning breeze was already pushing powder fumes more to one side of the field. The three on the command wagon watched closely, and then it became clear what response the enemy had chosen.

"The horsemen are coming to the charge," Markas declared. Amelia looked to the Roar, vulnerable at the front of the formation, and had to resist the urge to shout a warning to Sedgemark and Nunel. There was no chance the two men could have heard her above the crackle of matchlock fire and the clamor of battle on the left where the spearmen were advancing with a little more confidence, since they had not yet been fired upon by the other two hundred Roarsmen. Steel was beginning to clash on that wing, and her sergeants knew their business in the next phase. They needed no word from her.

The horsemen moved cautiously in a wide sweep, apparently waiting to see if the mere threat of their presence was enough to drive the gunners back to the safety of the pikes and halberds. Her Roar continued their fire so that the crossbows were now definitely falling back, seeking safety out of their enemy's range. She could not see clearly with a quick glance, but it looked as if several were wounded or even lying dead on the open ground. Then Amelia's attention was on the horsemen. They had crept forward until they were only a couple of hundred paces distant. Good cavalry could turn that distance into a charge in moments, yet still the Roar kept firing, intent only on breaking the crossbowmen. A trumpet sounded and trained coursers leaped forward as a mass. The mercenary horses were charging.

In a matter of heartbeats, hooves were shaking the earth, hammering their riders over the ground, lances held upright but soon to be leveled at their victims. If the Roar's shot was a series of persistent crackling ripples on a far shore, this was the thundering of a tidal wave, and the riders had no cause to fear, for if they did not crush the gunners under their steel and muscle, they would simply roll past and sweep back around. No gunners would risk coming out to shoot again without bringing their pike and halberd allies with them, and then the horse would have their favored flanking targets.

Amelia looked from charging enemy to exposed Roar. Timing now was paramount. It should be safe, even if their strategy failed, but one error could turn a clever trick into a bloodbath. Less than a hundred paces between the two forces now, just barely enough time for the Roar to run back to sanctuary. Then, a drumbeat sounded—one that had never been heard before, not on any field by any Lion, and one that had been decided in the predawn planning to be unmistakable. The two hundred exposed Roarsmen who had been waiting for the signal turned on their heels, and hefting their heavy weapons and support poles, rushed back into the formation behind them.

At the same time, in response to the same signal beat, the other two hundred Roar, who had not fired a shot yet this day, stood up from their hiding places amongst the long river grasses further out from the White Lions' right flank. In two long, offset lines, a hundred each, they rose with their matchlocks already loaded to fire. Suddenly, the cavalry's flanking charge was itself flanked, and as one, two hundred gunners fired into them. Just close enough that some of their iron shot would even punch through steel plate, their one massed volley wreaked havoc upon the charge. Horses and riders on the flanked side fell, and as they did so, many tumbled into their comrades. Skilled riders swerved instinctively, but being attacked from an unexpected direction, they spoiled others in the mass who didn't understand what was happening and did not expect to have to maneuver so suddenly.

As many as a third of the cavalry were injured, either horse or rider by shot or impact, and the charge center dissolved into chaos. Fearful that the riders might recover swiftly nonetheless, the revealed ambushers now sprinted back toward the center of the White Lions' line and the safety of the Claws once again. By the time they reached that security, the original two hundred who had acted as bait had also withdrawn, and far from charging at exposed gunners, the cavalry was faced with the choice of abandoning the charge completely or else throwing themselves onto the defensive hedge of pike they had been so committed to avoiding up to this point. Very few chose the second option, but it mattered little from the Lions' point of view.

The right side of the charging cavalry, the side that had been farthest distant from the enemy and thus was shielded from the ambush shot by their comrades' bodies, began to curve their charge away, giving the entire action up as a bad loss, knowing that they would have to make the turn tight to avoid overrunning the shallow trenches in the center front of the Lions' position. What they did not know was that in the last dark hour before the dawn, working feverishly despite their fatigue, Archduchess Amelia's militia, aided by the barely alive villagers, had dug a myriad of fresh trenches in front of their right wing and covered these with reeds and rushes cut from the riverside. Up close, they would fool no one, but at a distance, the horsemen had never seen them. Now that they tried to ride across them, the cavalry had no chance to safely maintain their pace. A handful more fell, unhorsed as their mounts stumbled in the haphazard shallow digging, while most were forced to rein in their pace, picking their way slowly and carefully over the deceptively uneven ground. Following riders were forced to pull up or else crash into their leaders. The orderly charge was hemmed in on both sides and with no hope of maintaining their built-up speed, reduced to a walking pace.

Now the Roar emerged once more to fire in single lines at a time, never too far from their protecting allies. Twenty and thirty gunners per rank stepped forth, placed their guns upon their stands, and fired into the mass. Then they withdrew to reload and the next came after them. There was no aiming, just a continuous swarm of fiery iron hornets lethally stinging the desperate cavalry. No riders in the Vec had ever experienced this. Rare were the Grand Kingdom knights who had felt the bite of waves of matchlock fire and survived. When the ceasefire command came, the Golden Heron's mercenary cavalry was reduced to less than a quarter of its strength. The survivors who were able limped away, while wounded animals and riders floundered, horses whimpering, some even screaming, and men-at-arms groaning in pain.

"Fangs out," was shouted, and the drumbeat carried the command. Sword- and shield-armed Fangs, who yesterday had weathered the near continuous hail of crossbow shots falling from the sky, now rushed from the lines with clear commands. Any who yielded were to be taken prisoner. Those who would not were to be dispatched. Some few horses were simply riderless and to be retrieved. The injured animals were to be put down humanely and left where they were. The Lions did not even have the space in their defensive strongpoint to butcher the carcasses for meat.

Amelia watched as her Fangs leaped amongst the charnel morass, capturing many more than they slew. She felt the grim satisfaction that this action had reduced the enemy's power significantly. In fact, it would likely be the turning point of the entire battle. Nevertheless, she could take no pleasure in it. The cries of the wounded and dying would never be sweet to her ears, whether they were her own loyal men-at-arms' or her enemy's.

"We might as well be in a damned tunnel!" Corporal Guillam cursed in a whisper as the Gryphons marched along the narrow passage the Verdant elder had opened for them in the rock. Prentice's campfire meeting had resolved by late afternoon, and Benjamin had gone to explain to his closest warriors what would be happening. There had been some tension to that discussion as well, it seemed, although Prentice had ordered all militia and other Kingdom men to keep well clear. The whole thing was between the *keshkirae* and his *keshiyaa*. The militia cohorts were ordered to refresh themselves by the water, to grab whatever food they could, "cold camp"—an inappropriate term in the given location—and be ready to march as soon as the fey horse archers were.

The Verdant fey leader stood aside while the rest of the afternoon's affairs were settled, but Prentice had Gennet set a number of men to watch him closely, including one of the company drummers.

"He might have a plot in mind or just think to give this away as a bad loss," the knight commander told his sergeant. "I want him kept away from any of the walls. If he does open a pathway through the stone without us, I want the drums summoning every nearby Lion onto him before he can slip through and close it behind him."

If the Verdant fey understood what Prentice's men were doing, he never said, but by the time the fey had their horses saddled and ready to journey, the fallen stag rider was clearly in as foul a mood as he had been since the day he and Dahyoor had waited for Prentice by the Murr.

"He could be having second thoughts," Whilte agreed when Prentice asked the chaplain for his opinion. "But even if he is, we are no more at risk from treachery now than we have been before. He could easily have walked us into an ambush or tricked Dahyoor into doing it for him, many times."

That was Prentice's assessment as well. When the pale fey had at last opened what was to be the final pathway through the rock, there was no more to do but pass the word for the Gryphon Banner Company and the *keshiyaa* of Benjamin of the Wind Rising fey to follow. Now, after many hours, the sun had set, and the darkness in the tight defile was, as Guillam observed, as deep as if they were underground. A few torches had been lit, but whenever someone suggested more, the Verdant leader made it clear that each extra light was a greater risk.

"He'd rather we bruised ourselves silly smacking into the rock," one militiaman had muttered after Prentice sent a line first to have him douse the rushlight the militiaman was carrying.

"Like shadows in the night, eh, My Lord?" Solft asked as he managed to squeeze up next to Prentice in a broader section. "Ghostly riders once more, perhaps."

Prentice sniffed with a half-smile. When the fey horsemen had first started to come down out of the mountains to attack the Reach on the Serpent Witch's orders, they had been referred to as ghostly riders, barely seen before their deadly attacks struck. Now, as the few flickering lights available cast looming shadows upon the walls and the fey horses moved with their usual near-mystical quiet, the title seemed fitting once again. Ghostly riders indeed.

"Just pray the Lord blesses us to come upon the Redlanders like ghosts, Master," Prentice joked with the scholar. "And keep you close to Sergeant Gennet the whole day coming. I have given him instructions to see you safely back to the Reach with the rest of the wounded should something happen to me."

"Is something likely to happen to you and not to him?" Solft asked with typically insensitive, scholarly curiosity.

"Ask me again if you see me at the end of tomorrow," Prentice said, and then ushered the scholar ahead so that they did not form a blockage in the narrow path.

At what Prentice guessed was an hour or so after midnight, the Verdant fey sent word through Dahyoor for the knight commander to order the dousing of all lights.

"His lordship's orders again," Gennet joked, but in short order the entire secret company was plunged into near total darkness. Only by looking straight up at the night sky, with its sparse starlight and reflected moon glow, could they tell any difference from the pitch of their surroundings. The fey had much less difficulty with the darkness than mere men, but even they were not able to see well, and every man groped his way forward with a hand upon a fellow's shoulder or a piece of saddle tack, or similar equipment.

"Shoulda played out some rope for us all to hold," someone muttered at one point, but he was quickly shushed up and down the line.

For half an hour or so, they made their slow way forward, almost silent until a dusty, biting clang of steel striking rock echoed along the passage and every man froze.

"What the hell was that?" Gennet hissed, his fury clear even in a whisper. Word passed quietly up and down until the answer returned.

"One of the Fangs had his shield over his head, didn't know there was a spur in the rock above. He hit it."

"What's he doing with his bloody shield over his head?" the sergeant demanded. Whoever was reporting had anticipated this question, however.

"He said he was covering it. He kenned if the slinger fey were going to ambush us, likely it would be like this, in the dark where there was nowhere to run and nothing to see. He was worried about slingstones on his head."

"Not the most foolish thing to be worried about," came Brother Whilte's opinion from the inky shadows.

"No, but he still made a bloody racket for his worry," Gennet declared. Prentice saw no point in getting involved, and now that someone had made a potentially dangerous mistake, he trusted the rest of the company would be on the watch for similar errors. Some short while later, their sightless trek came to a sudden stop. Whispers summoned the knight commander, and Prentice pushed his awkward way forward to find Dahyoor waiting with the Verdant fey.

"It is here."

"What is on the other side?" Prentice asked.

"The lake."

Prentice rolled his eyes in the darkness—ask a fey a simple question. The same sudden shift in the air occurred, and it was as if a dim lantern had had its covers removed, so that, while it was still dark as he looked out of the newly formed opening, he could make out the lake valley before him but barely.

"I would have liked a better chance to prepare," he whispered, but neither Dahyoor nor their Verdant guide answered. At least he could pick out their silhouettes in the night now. The stag rider gave what sounded like instructions and then was gone through the gap. Dahyoor followed him, and Prentice stepped out far enough to let men pass so he could see what kind of terrain waited for them. The ground underfoot was rough, like broken stones, and gently sloped downward. Prentice's hands felt the soft touch of long grass fronds, and he felt sure they were in exactly the location the Verdant fey had promised. He moved toward the more open space of sky above, and the stone wall of the valley fell away completely.

To his right, perhaps a league away, a tiny glitter of yellow lights climbed upwards, like a column of fireflies rising from a cluster upon the ground. That was the fey settlement, the vine-like knots of huts that rose up the cliffside, with others at the foot near the lakeshore. Recognizing that, Prentice looked to his left, the opposite direction, and there he saw the source of all this place's threat and power—the dragonfly atop its enchained plinth. In the darkness, the metal body and crystalline wings seemed to glow dimly, far less brightly than the lantern lights from the settlement. It was like moonlight reflected on poorly polished metal, but it had the coruscating colors of the insect wings' refractions. Even as Prentice watched, the glow grew and the sound of the wings pulsed over the valley, causing the very air to thrum like a bowstring. The men exiting the passage gasped, and some stopped to watch the valley and sky lit in the rainbow glow. Then the light faded, and in its absence, the lake seemed so much more distinct, as if the surface of the water were being polished.

"He says he told you, you were late," Dahyoor reported as Prentice found him dutifully staying close to the fallen Verdant elder who likely plotted to betray either them or his people, despite the oaths he had sworn, it seemed.

"Let him say what he likes," Prentice told his man. The main of his attention was on the lake itself, searching for signs of the Redlander boats already waiting on the water. Redlanders slept in their crews frequently, so except for the cabal in the Verdant fey settlement, he expected the main of their beast-men and other warriors would be with those craft, waiting to attack, if this had been a plot all along. Even if not, this was one of the riskiest parts of his plan. If the Redlander forces were ready for him, waiting in ambush again, the Lions would be easy prey, half inside the stone passage and half out. As far as Prentice was concerned, the Verdant fey could make all the snide comments he liked, as long as he did not betray them to the Redlanders at this point.

For what seemed like an hour, the Gryphon Banner and Benjamin's *keshiyaa* snuck out onto the grassed slope in single file. It was surely nothing like that amount of time, but to

Prentice's nerve, it might as well have been. Finally, Benjamin's mount walked past with the characteristic stealth of a Wind Rising horse, and its rider leaned down from his saddle.

"I am the last," he said.

With so little time since their reconciliation and no good opportunity to speak privately, Prentice had had to trust in Benjamin's instincts for this next part of the plan, trust that the *keshkirae* would understand what was necessary. He was thankful when the fey archers moved to gather themselves into a single force and waited while the militia were assembled into their own cohort ranks. It was far from a silent activity, and difficult in the darkness, but with the pulsing dragonfly lights and the hum in the air, it seemed increasingly likely they had arrived unseen.

For now.

Prentice passed the word to Gennet that every man with a blade was to keep it sheathed. Halberds and pikes were to have their edges covered with whatever thick cloth men could find. Helmets were to be removed, and once in position, they were to sit or lie in the grass until the time came to march or fight. All their safety for being unseen would be banished if some foe saw the dragonfly glow glint off a piece of polished steel.

When that was done, Prentice gave Guillam a nod and found Brother Whilte seated on a rock, rubbing the area of his knee just above his wooden leg.

"I require your assistance with a matter, Brother," he said quietly as Guillam moved ahead to be ready for his task. "It is urgent, and I need you not to question me until the end."

"I will give what service I can," Whilte said, and by his tone it seemed likely that he did not like the requirement to not question.

"It may be that nothing will be asked of you, chaplain, but if something is needed, it is a something only you can provide."

"Alright, Knight Commander."

Whilte wearily pulled himself up by his staff and hobbled along as Prentice crossed to where he had left Dahyoor and the stag rider waiting.

"Where are your people at this moment?" he asked the Verdant.

"The ones not for the ritual will be in their huts or the forest," Dahyoor translated.

"How many will be involved in the ritual?"

"Those of the cult."

Prentice managed to keep his temper at that response. By this stage he no longer hoped for helpful answers from uncooperative fey. Nor from cooperative, truth be told.

"What specifically do you want from us?" he asked. The Verdant elder was silent for a long moment in the dark, making Prentice think that even at this late stage the fallen stag rider was unsure where his best advantage lay.

You picked the battlefield for us and have decided which enemies we are allowed to fight, Prentice thought coldly. *And still you are afraid you have not given yourself enough advantages?*

Prentice was sure the Verdant fey wanted exactly what Benjamin had wanted in the swamp near Dweltford—for all the *kreff* to destroy each other and leave his people alone. Too bad for him. His people were too deeply in marriage with the Redlander Blood Sect. They could not escape this day without some hurts. Nevertheless, Prentice was determined that he would honor his pledge to the letter, all of his pledges—to the Verdant fey; to the archduchess; to the Reach; to his men, Gryphons and Lions; and most of all, to his wife.

The coruscating light hummed down the valley once more, revealing at last, for just an instant, the Redlander boats afloat in roughly the middle of the lake, perhaps a half league from where his troops were sitting in the grass. At that distance, an eagle-eyed Redlander would not need the telltale of a steely glint. It was a precarious position, and Prentice's only comfort was that Redlanders seemed singularly poor at imagining themselves under threat. He had never known them to be diligent in posting sentries.

Looking back to the Verdant fey, Prentice managed to see his expression by the fading glow. He seemed so condescending and hateful that the knight commander was surprised the man was holding himself back. With his alien features, he looked for a moment more like a figure of nightmare than a mortal in the multicolored light. If Prentice had never looked into the eyes of a *brakkis effar,* he might have imagined this fey man was a devil sent from hell. As it was, he was only a strange and hateful mortal to the knight commander's eyes.

"You can see the boats," Dahyoor said, translating the Verdant's words, leaving out the contemptuous tone. "Attack them. Slay them if you can."

Goading me? Bit late for that, Prentice thought, and in the darkness, he did not bother to conceal his own condescending smirk.

"What will you do?"

"Go to the *imzuss*, tell them you are here, and the boats require their help. Your fire iron spitters are many and you have freed the Wind Rising traitors."

Dahyoor growled a little at the word "traitors," and Prentice could imagine the will he needed to keep from striking the provocative stag rider.

"And they will believe you?" Prentice asked. Dahyoor translated the question twice, and still the man did not answer. Dahyoor asked a third time, looking like he might strike the Verdant fey in his anger, but that only elicited a sniff of derision in the dark.

"Perhaps they will call the warriors of the forest to guard them, but that might take time," he answered at last, and even through the translation there was an obviously calculated wariness in his response. Prentice was sure he was weighing up how much he could reveal. It was so flagrant, so inept as a form of deception, that it made the knight commander want to laugh with disdain. He had known Grand Kingdom nobles like this fey man from the farthest west, individuals who lived every day with such an overwhelming sense of their own superiority that they never considered how obvious their thoughts might be to those they imagined their inferiors. Daven Marcus the Usurper was the worst Prentice had ever known, but there were many others.

"What if they call more boats through the sky? They must be able to do that soon, even if they are waiting for dawn to bring the whole fleet."

The light pulsed again, and by it the Verdant fey looked truly surprised—either that Prentice had guessed this possibility for himself or because it had not occurred to the elder before this.

This fool led them for decades? Prentice wondered.

The fey composed an answer, and Dahyoor turned it into Kingdom speech.

"Fight hard. Threaten their boats, and if more come, move down toward the river mouth so that none can escape without suffering your spitters' fire. Then they will be forced to fight you, even the *imzuss*."

That might be a plan, if we had three times our number and a dozen of Marquis Farringdon's cannons, Prentice thought dismissively.

"And if the fey riders come out of the forest for them? Or the slingers from the village? What then?"

"Fight harder or suffer your vow."

That was what Prentice thought. The Verdant elder was confident now, thinking he had turned Prentice's oath back against him. He hoped the Gryphon Company would win the day based on his hard-learned fear of the power of the Roar and their matchlocks, but if they did not, the Verdant elder was trusting that his stag riders would join fearlessly in the battle because any militiaman who resisted them would die under the curse of the vow that bound Lions and Verdant. Prentice imagined the elder had already tried to pass some word of this to the guardians of the forest by whatever means a dishonored stag rider might be able to make himself heard.

"You think that's the trump card in your hand, don't you?" Prentice muttered and touched Dahyoor's arm to keep him from translating. "Sorry to say, I married a very sharp player, and my best friend has never not had a spare trump up his sleeve. Between them, they have taught me never to trust to just one card, no matter how high suited."

CHAPTER 86

H e gave a single cough, the signal for which Guillam was waiting, standing a sparse handful of steps behind the Verdant fey, and before the treacherous fallen elder knew what was happening, he had one arm twisted behind his back and Guillam's hand clamped across his mouth. The stag rider was a warrior, a former champion, and likely had been since before Prentice or any of the Reacher men-at-arms had even been born. It was expected he would try to wrestle free, but Prentice drew his sword immediately, holding the edge close to the Verdant fey's throat. To his left, Dahyoor drew the dagger Prentice had let him keep and put it to the elder's side as well. Three on one, with two blades drawn and poised, the fey man ceased his struggles. In the next pulsing glow, the man's terrified eyes lanced at the knight commander, incensed that he was betrayed before he could betray.

"Brother Whilte, if you sense even the slightest bit of fey magick or Redlander sorcery, you must do what you can to suppress it. Use your gifts for us now."

Prentice did not look back at the chaplain but kept his eyes on his target, trusting that his next words would allay Whilte's misgivings about what was happening.

"You think we are mad," Prentice told the elder, and Dahyoor repeated his words in hissed fey speech more acid even than a serpent woman's curses. "You think I am going to bring your people's blood curse upon us before we even face the Redlanders. I tell you, only if you force us at this moment. We do not plan to kill you, and if you do not resist, you will see the dawn. But I am a 'death thing' as you have said, and I do not trust you. So, we will face the Redlanders our way. We will hunt the Inquisition out of your settlement our way as well. Until we are victorious or dead, you will be our prisoner. I do not know if your powers are by word or gesture, or by sight or hearing, so the next few hours will not be comfortable for you. Console yourself with knowing that I will honor every word of my pledge to you. You have had your plans, but if my plan succeeds, your people will end the day sending us away for good. Keep hope."

The Verdant fey's eyes darted around his captors, with the hate-filled wariness of a trapped animal. Prentice and Dahyoor kept their blades in place as Guillam removed his hand from the fey's mouth and plucked a roughly made wood and leather bit-gag from his belt. He reached around and forced the stick piece into the fey's mouth and then gathered both of the leather strips tied to the end with one hand behind the fey elder's neck. Once he had both, he risked releasing his wrestling grip, and swiftly grabbing the two strips with one hand each, he planted his knee into the elder's spine so that the former champion was held cruelly in place, painfully poised on the point of falling backward while the corporal tied the leather strips tightly. When he was done, Guillam released the elder and the fey man fell forward on his hands and knees, snorting angry, desperate breaths in through his nose, sounding like an enraged animal. Guillam dropped upon him, having pulled a length of rope out from his belt, and began to bind the elder hand and foot.

"You've done this before, I'd say Corporal," Whilte said, somewhat aghast, but thankfully not objecting to this harsh solution to the problem of the traitorous elder. Guillam spared a moment to grin at the chaplain.

"I didn't get these scars on me face by accident, Chaplain," he said happily. He wrapped rope carefully about the man's wrists and then pulled another length for the ankles. When he pulled out a third piece of rope, Prentice started to wonder how far he planned to go.

"He seems secure, Corporal Guillam," he said with a cocked eyebrow.

"I seen a hedge wizard once, you know, them ones that do market day magick shows that village sacrists all say ain't real magick but tricks o' the hand, quicker than the eye and all that. This hedge wizard did things I swear I couldn't ken, and when he did, he always waved his fingers all tricksy like. I been kennin', what if these feys does tricksy finger things? Best be sure, don't you think, My Lord?"

As he explained, the corporal bound the Verdant elder's individual fingers with coils of the rope. It looked distinctly uncomfortable. Prentice glanced at Whilte, who seemed amused while showing at least some empathy for the imprisoned enemy. If anyone could have confirmed Guillam's suspicion, it was Dahyoor, but Prentice suspected his translator would have no interest in alleviating this pain and so did not bother to even ask. Instead, he sent the former Wind Rising fey to fetch the other officers he needed. The time had come for final battle plans.

Once the trussed-up elder was removed to a quiet distance, Prentice briefed Whilte, Gennet, Porth, and Guillam in the intermittent light, along with Benjamin and one of his trusted riders who remained unnamed, Dahyoor, and Lyrach, since the line first would have a specific part in the coming day's battle. Solft was there as well, without invitation, but quietly standing nearby, charcoal and what must surely be his last piece of parchment in hand.

"This is what we have come looking for," he told them. "And you can see it is as ancient, mysterious, and outright bloody terrifying as all our worst nightmares told us it could be. Between us we have fought monsters and men, and seen angels strike with the fury of God's own wrath. We have faced legends, sorcery, and odds that every wise man would call unwinnable."

Prentice paused to sigh. He was tired, tired in his heart. Not bitter, but weary, and deeper still, angry—angry at the fate that had brought them here to die at the edge of the world. He looked to Whilte and heard the chaplain's voice admonish him in his own thoughts.

Are you angry? Yours is only a single lifetime's worth of wrath to bear. Imagine how God feels, seeing the abuses of his creation and his peoples. He bears long with us, but his wrath must eventually be poured out.

So it is, Brother, Prentice thought. He looked over the darkling water, like polished black glass—night mirrored in the midst of night. As that water had been brought from the earth when the other waters were poisoned, so now it was a spring that was about to see the unleashing of a divine wrath, he hoped. *Only let the coming storm swamp the Redlanders, their cabal, and their boat, and let us somehow ride out the maelstrom.*

In simple terms he outlined his full plan, giving each part of his too-small-seeming force their deployments.

"When do you want us to set the drums a going?" Gennet asked when Prentice was done.

"Leave it until the pre-dawn or as long as you can," Prentice told him. "But when you do start the beat, make sure you have your back to the rock wall, and keep someone watching—the ostlers will be best for that—and be ready. If the fey send a force through the rock somehow, you might find yourselves pinned between two foes. If you are pressed back to the wall, you should be able to keep them from forming up too easily before you notice."

"Not enough space," Gennet concurred. "Could be hard to keep the wounded safe if it comes to that."

Prentice nodded solemnly. There was nothing else he could think of for them.

"And we're supposed to get by with a decad each?" Guillam asked, grousing more than needing confirmation.

"You can come with me, if you like," Prentice offered, looking at Lyrach. "Perhaps you can swap places with the line first here."

"Not bloody likely," was the corporal's response, and his lips worked absently, as if longing for a piece of his missing chew.

"Just keep your few shots back for the beast men. Roarshot is still our best weapon against them. And you will have the chaplain with you. His wisdom will help against *brakkis effar* as well."

"In that regard, My Lord Knight Commander, I would be better use if I went with you," Whilte said earnestly.

"You will not be able to keep up," Prentice replied flatly, hating that he had to be so direct with the loyal chaplain. He would much rather have Whilte with him and had no doubt that the brother would walk straight into the gates of hell on his one good leg if even only one of the White Lions needed rescuing there upon the threshold, but for this night's work it would not be enough. "Endurance you have, deeper than the waters of this lake, Brother, but your days of swiftness are passed. You know that."

Whilte accepted Prentice's words with no more objection.

Satisfied that each of his militia officers knew their places for the coming battle, Prentice gave them one last, dire set of instructions.

"The aim is for that fleet to never come through the sky," he told them. "No swarm upon the Reach. If we do not stop them, do not doubt we here and our homeland far to our east will be overwhelmed. If we fail, if we do not stop them, do not dig in to the last around a tattered blue and silver rag. We are not crusaders or ancient knights to make a noble and pointless final stand. Go to any fey archer who will help you and make for home. They have arts of the land. Some of us might make the distance. Dahyoor here has already done it once."

"Will you make it home, do you think, My Lord?" Lyrach asked quietly.

"If we fail, Lyrach, then I will already be dead," Prentice replied honestly.

"Then that is how I think it will be with all of us," the former knight errant answered, and the other Lions all nodded, even Guillam. Prentice was glad it was too dark for them to see the tears in the corners of his eyes. He saluted them and they returned it.

The officers went to their assigned places, Lyrach staying close to Prentice. He stepped away a handful of paces to his last duty, speaking quietly with Benjamin. There were no complex gestures between fey in moments like this, not even the basics like tugging the forelock or saluting, so Prentice simply gave his last instructions.

"From here to where the lake becomes a river in front of the forest, that is your *keshiyaa's* bounds," he said, pointing from where they stood eastward along the lake's southern bank. "In that space, pick your own enemies and fight as you see fit. My oath to the Verdant does not bind you. Shoot your arrows as you see. The Lions will hammer the Untrue. Your aid will be valued, but the stags may yet come for you out of the forest."

"We left our blood debt with the herd," Benjamin told him, reiterating his loyalty.

"The traitor kin may see you and bring the debt to you afresh," Prentice responded. "You are *keshkirae*, so sees the *palpolon* elder."

"We pass unseen, *kreff enkreffra*" Benjamin said, nodding. It was a simple moment with no extra emphasis, but somehow to Prentice it felt like a bending of the knee.

"The elders saw well when they saw Benjamin *keshkirae*," Prentice told him.

"Not yet, but dawn is coming."

There were no more instructions to give, but Prentice had one more question, a frivolous one, but he might be dead soon, so there was no reason not to indulge himself this one little piece.

"If you can tell, why are you 'Benjamin'?" he asked. "Of all the *kreff* names, why choose that one?"

Benjamin smirked. "The *kreff* sage, the no-longer-fat one, he told a *kreff* legend of a tribe of chosen, beloved of the All Maker. He said they became lost to all others and were never seen by the world again. Benjamin, they were called. He said the *kreff* would recognize it as a name, so I took it. *Kreff* did not take it as the chiding I thought they would."

Prentice smiled and almost laughed. Forced by his elders to adopt a *kreff* name for his own peoples' sake, Benjamin had chosen the one that sounded most to fey ears like their ways. A lost tribe, all but forgotten to history, sounded like passing unseen. He had thought by calling himself Benjamin he was telling Kingdom folk and Reachermen that they should have no right to see him. What an irony, then, that he only adopted a perfectly mundane name that told *kreff* nothing and yet made him fully, acceptably named in their sight.

"An elder should know the names of the riders who ride beside him," Benjamin went on, and Prentice was astonished by what his words implied. The knight commander had certainly not planned to ask what it seemed the fey archer leader was offering. "If you see, whom will you show?"

"I..." Prentice had to pause, taking a moment to make sure he picked the best words for what was coming. "I am sworn to the Lioness Mother, and she may command me that she may see. But to all others, you are Wind Rising, and you pass unseen."

"*We* pass unseen," Benjamin corrected, and he held Prentice's eyes for a long moment. "I am Dahyonraa from birth to the saddle and still there this dawn."

Prentice nodded, hoping he showed well how much he appreciated Benjamin's gesture, and then he realized how familiar the *keshkirae's* fey name sounded. He looked to Dahyoor, standing a short distance away and then turned back to Benjamin, eyes wide in shock.

"Your brother?"

"Cousin," Benjamin corrected gently, "but close like brothers. We took to our saddles together the same dawn."

No wonder you were so angry, Prentice thought, and he bowed his head again. When he lifted it, Benjamin was looking at the sky.

"You have a hard march and not much night, *palpolon* elder," he said and then turned away to where his horse was waiting obediently nearby.

Prentice shook his head in wonder and went toward his own small force, waiting to begin their particular gambit in this mad battle against ancient curses and present evils.

"Whatever happened to the halcyon days when it was just a handful of us, half naked and starving, against a company of knights ahorse in full harness?" he joked as he walked.

"I'm sorry, My Lord, did you say something?" Lyrach asked, but Prentice waved him away. For the next few hours, they would have no breath to spare for conversation.

CHAPTER 87

A melia watched for sundown, unable to keep her eyes from flicking to the Murr over her shoulder, hopeful to see relieving boats sent by Dalflitch's force after defeating Duke Robant's occupying knights. So far, the river remained clear. In front of her, the battle was at a quiet pass and had been since an hour or so past noon. The Golden Heron had been well and truly mauled by her forces. Their cavalry would never form up again in this battle—all the sergeants agreed on that—and the last footmen's advance might have been generously described as reluctant. The crossbowmen, however many of them had survived, had not reappeared on the field either.

"We're pretty much at the point where we could drive them off," Sedgemark had offered not too long ago. "Even without the Roar."

For all its success, the concentrated use of her gunners to ambush the horsemen had consumed almost all their remaining black powder, rendering the weapons virtually useless. The lack of ammunition Amelia had hoped would befall the crossbowmen had now come to her own missile troops.

Amelia did not think Sedgemark's confidence was misplaced. After all, the sergeant had used the same judgement to break Prince Garrodmin's forces at the beginning of this campaign, and the youthful officer seemed to know foot tactics as well as anyone. Nevertheless, Amelia remembered that her husband had insisted that they remain in this defensive position, and she could not order them to break from it without feeling like she was betraying him.

"Lord God, let that be wisdom and not just fear of a second widowhood masquerading as loyalty," she prayed quietly and looked to Spindle behind her. There was a single trickle of dried blood on Spindle's left sleeve from where an errant crossbow quarrel had grazed her in the last moments before the ambush had begun. Amelia had been concerned for her lady's safety, but Spindle seemed more annoyed with the damage to her sleeve than injury to her arm beneath.

"'Ware the south!" a voice shouted, and Amelia looked to see what the lookout must have noticed. Over the heads of the dejected Golden Heron force, a dark cloud could be seen rising. For at least half an hour, the archduchess watched it grow, thinking at first that it might be smoke and wondering if the mercenaries had set her captured camp ablaze in a fit of frustration at being so thoroughly rebuffed. Then she realized it was not smoke but columns of dust, such as heralded the march of many men-at-arms.

"An ominous banner, I think," she said. Beside her, she heard Markas sigh heavily. Still, with one hand on the company standard, now with two fresh holes in it from truly long-flighted crossbow shots, he also had his shield dutifully on his arm. Putting the protective "umbrella" down for a moment, he removed his helmet and rubbed at his sweaty scalp with the leather palm of his gauntlet.

"That looks like it could be a lot of new fellows comin' to join us," he said, and his voice sounded heavy in Amelia's ears. He was tired. They all were. "'Course if we're lucky, these boys'll tell the newcomers how foolish it is to attack us, and they'll lose their nerve."

Amelia gave him a disbelieving glance and he shrugged.

"Worth hoping, wouldn't you say, Your Grace?" he added.

It was her turn to sigh wearily. She looked to the sky once more.

"How long yet until sundown?" she asked.

"It would seem at least another hour, Your Grace," Spindle said, also looking to the sky.

"Surely they will not go straight from the march into battle so late in the day?" Amelia said hopefully, but neither Markas nor Spindle seemed confident to agree with her sentiment. After another quarter hour of the candle, by her estimation, it seemed the archduchess's hopes were indeed fruitless. The arriving forces marched directly up on the left of the Heron's lines. The beleaguered mercenary army seemed to collapse in on itself as the diminished line merged into a single right wing and the reinforcements formed themselves into a new left wing.

From Amelia's vantage, they had arrived with another significant body of men-at-arms afoot, though these only in buffcoats and steel caps but still with spears and shields. They also brought two large cadres of horsemen, each equal in numbers to the cavalry force the Lions had destroyed in ambush. Worst of all, they appeared to have three separate units of crossbows. Each was only about fifty in number, but taken together, they were many more overall. As they appeared and took up position in the front of the lines, the original Heron crossbows returned to the field as well, apparently encouraged. Once the force was positioned, the arriving command troop, looking to be made up of at least ten knights ahorse, bearing three impressive banner pennants, rode across the front of the lines to join up with Froster and his enormous black and gold standard. As they crossed the front, the newly arrived forces cheered their leaders, and the sense of high morale spread until the entire combined force was cheering.

"Markas, send runners for Nunel and Sedgemark," Amelia said, and the banner sergeant immediately moved to fulfil her command. When he was gone, she stared at the renewed enemy, feeling as she did when she had looked out her window at the drought-afflicted lake. "How high can you count, My Lady?"

"Not that high, Your Grace," Spindle said. "My Caius can do it, no doubt. I can fetch him if you need."

"No, thank you," Amelia told her. The question had been rhetorical, but even if not, she would not summon Caius here. There would be little point. Soon enough her sergeants had returned from their places in the line, both tugging their forelocks but not bothering to mount up onto her wagon. She did not begrudge them; they might have to rush back to their place in the ranks soon enough.

"What do we say, good Reachermen?" she asked.

"At least four thousand now, likely closer to six," Nunel said, giving Amelia the rough count of the enemy. "More than we had when we arrived, and that was when we had full barrels of powder and a lancer company."

Amelia felt her face sour and knew she was too exhausted to control it. It wasn't Nunel's fault their situation was now so dire, and he hadn't reminded her of her lost husband deliberately. Even so, she frowned and shook her head.

"How long can we last against...all that?" Amelia waved her hands at the enemy.

"Noon tomorrow, Your Grace, if they don't attack until morning and don't realize for a while that the Roar are empty," Sedgemark said, and by his eyes it was clear he hated giving such an assessment. Nevertheless, he was too loyal a man to lie. "If they know now about our powder and are feeling like making a swift matter of the whole affair, they could come at us straight away and have us in the river not long after the sun goes down. That'd be messier for them, even full speed, since dark fighting is no one's idea of a harvest fest revel, but it'd still end the same way."

Amelia looked over her shoulder at the river again, vainly hoping to see relief boats coming, Dalflitch or Righteous in the prow, but there was nothing but the open water, starting to glow fiery in colors of the setting sun.

"Could we send a swimmer to see how close our relief force is?" she asked.

"We could, Your Grace," Markas said, "but that wouldn't mean much before tomorrow morning at the earliest, sorry to say."

From the south, the enemy trumpets sounded, and Amelia looked up to see half the newly combined command troop riding forth, their banners flying under a flag of truce. She turned to Spindle.

"Let's get down nearer the front," she said, moving toward the wagon's steps.

"You do not wish to use the speaking trumpet?" her lady asked, and Amelia nodded.

"Bring it, if you will, My Lady. I will use it, but this late in the day my mouth is too dry to shout too loudly, and even with the trumpet, I would have to shout from here."

Spindle bobbed and moved away to fetch the leather cone. Amelia held her hand out for Markas to escort her down the stairs.

"Leave the banner here, good Sergeant," she said. "It will only have to come back, anyway. Come, Reachermen, let us see what fresh insults we must endure from men with too much coin to care how many they kill."

CHAPTER 88

The pebbled strand on the north side of the lake was an agony to march along, doubly so as they did their best to make good time and remain stealthy. The stones were not small underfoot, being more typically the size of a man's fist. As such, they slipped uncomfortably with every step so that the two- or three-league walk took over an hour and made their feet and legs burn with the exertion.

"Not long until dawn," Lyrach muttered quietly, but Prentice did not even nod. He had been watching the sky since they had reached the tight gap behind the dragonfly, carrying the main of the company's powder supplies in barrels and sacks. Every time the dragonfly pulsed its refractive light, Prentice cast an involuntary glance upward, fearful that the serpent coven had finished their ritual early and the mirror was about to disgorge its deadly swarm.

The powder was left behind now, wedged as best they had been able into the foreseen crack at the bottom of the obelisk, under the darkness and pulsing glow of the insect on its perch. The stench of rot at the foot of the defiled artifact reminded Prentice of the depths of the Ditch Prison in Aubrey, where he had gone to rescue Farringdon, and found the extent of Redlander depravity. And of the cell under Ashfield where he had been tortured and judged a heretic. In a way, it made sense the Inquisition found themselves allies of convenience with the Blood Sects—both institutions were masters of cruelty. The corpses hanging slain from the chains around the stone had looked like ghosts or other ghoulish monsters in the unnatural light, and more than once Prentice's men had stopped in their duty to simply stare in horror at the atrocity. It had taken much of Prentice's own will to keep himself and them focused upon the task.

"Not long until the fuses'll be lit," one of the militiamen muttered from down their single line of march.

"Long enough," another whispered, but Lyrach shushed them. It was little needed, as imminent danger made grousing seem pointless.

Three of their number had been left behind with the duty of lighting the fuses, fashioned from lengths of Roar long-match, but differently treated to burn more swiftly. That trio had orders to light when they could see from their hiding spot to the edge of the water clearly without the glow from the dragonfly's wings. They were not to wait for full daylight, just the ability to make out the water's edge. Then they were to light and make for the rest of the company, still waiting on the grass where they had come into the valley.

Prentice had left them there and marched the rest of his little force—ten of the best Fangs and five Roar, plus Lyrach—as stealthily as possible down the north shore strand toward the fey settlement. Their purpose was to raid directly into the odd town, sneaking up to the stone causeway where the cabal conducted their rituals and slay as many as they could before anyone knew they were there. He made it very clear to his tiny assault force that they should stick to the water's edge because under no circumstances were they to shoot or cut at a single Verdant fey. That would be an act to damn them all.

"Can we punch 'em?" one of the Fangs had asked, "or smack 'em with a shield?"

Prentice nearly laughed when he realized he had no idea if such an act would violate his pledge, but in the dark he had only said, "No." Anything else might have been taken as tacit approval and brought down the curse.

So now, the many parts of his precarious plan balanced on which thing happened earliest. If they reached the cliffside village first, his force would not hesitate to throw themselves at the cabal, seeking to kill all or enough of the witches to stop the ritual in its tracks before the fey and any other Redlanders or *brakkis effar* stopped them. Although it would be a suicidal assault, it was in some ways the outcome Prentice preferred. He had called for volunteers to this duty, but even so, he could not send a single man to this kind of risk and remain behind with honor. Besides, he had to be sure the Serpent Witch died. This would be his one chance for that. Also, somewhere in the valley was Inxyphos, most likely near the cabal, and he was another priority for Prentice.

If the dawn came first, or some enemy sentry noticed the Gryphon Banner Company on the south bank, then Gennet and his men were to stand up and to begin belting on the drums, drawing as much attention as they could, especially from the boats in the water. It might even be that the Verdant elder's proposal would work in this, causing some of the *imzuss* to cross the water to that fight on the opposite bank. That would ideally make Prentice's assault the easier.

Of course, if dawn came with no discovery, it was possible that the gunpowder would detonate before their enemies knew anything, and in that eventuality, the ritual should be made impossible, and every fight would become a battle to flee the valley. Then Gennet and the Gryphons would march straight east toward the forest to press their escape.

In every branching possibility, Benjamin's *kehsiyaa* were to offer support, attacking wherever they thought best, but especially acting as a shield against the Verdant riders if the stags were summoned from the forest to protect the Redlanders.

The last, and least desirable possibility was that the ritual would be completed, and the mantis ships would come through. Then it would become a battle to the death, with every man and fey archer killing as many enemies as they could before they fell. While asking men to fight to their doom was a despairing notion, if it came to this outcome, there would be little point thinking anything else. They would only be the first corpses of the mountain of dead the mantis swarm would make of the Western Reach.

And so, Prentice all but flinched, glancing upward at every pulse, and fearing the mirror above. The light in the air from the most recent pulse faded and Prentice realized that the sky's purple color was no longer a result of sorcery. The predawn hour was on them. Sunlight would soon be touching the peaks, and everything would be visible. He noticed that the boats in the water were no longer beyond his sight, and the water itself was no longer night black. He and his men would be spotted soon, no matter what they did.

"We make for the fey town, best speed," he told his men, and began an ungainly rush over the stones. They were no more than fifty paces from the first huts and their feet scraped loudly, but stealth was too late. The light was nearly enough to see the whole length of the valley. The fuses were surely already ignited and the lighters now running back to join the company. The platform and causeway in the water were clearly visible as well, and Prentice was struck by how much they were exactly as he remembered them, as if he were looking from the surface of the water in his vision again.

On the dais stones, the serpent coven writhed and invoked their demon gods by torchlight, seemingly soaked with gore. Their scaled skins were wet and crimson, while in their hands they waved metal-edged bone knives. Prentice remembered the brutality of sacrifice that the original Serpent Witch had used to bind the unicorn and how unspeakable that had seemed. In comparison, this was beyond the mind's ability to comprehend. As in his vision, there was a single representative mantis man present, also sprayed with blood but with random-seeming gouts, as if he remained aloof from the ritual and was only splashed because of his proximity.

Knives plunged ceremonially, and a whimper was barely heard over the witches' hissing song and the pulsing air. Then the mantis moved, hefted up a dead fey body, and tossed it over the edge where it fell amongst many others in the lake water. For a moment, Prentice froze as the insectoid *brakkis effar* appeared to look straight at them, but it did not react. Perhaps enraptured by the ritual or lost in bloodlust, the mantis man only turned back to watch as another victim was drawn up onto the platform.

Arms bound and gagged, the sacrifice was a pale fey, and it seemed he was being led by another Verdant fey man, this one marked with Redlander tattoos. If known practices were holding, Prentice expected the two were actually relatives—such was the level of sacrifice the Blood Sects' viciousness demanded of their devotees. After the sacrifice of a Wind Rising fey and then a Verdant had been insufficient for the coven to drive Prentice's vision presence out of the lake water before, he imagined the *imzuss* was now using all the power it could muster, including the direst of sacrifices.

"We will come around the waterside edge straight for that platform," Prentice told his men, most of whom were staring utterly aghast at the ritual. In his deeper thoughts, their commander feared for their souls, doubtless to be scarred by what they were witnessing. It disgusted Prentice to his core, but then he knew what the Inquisition did to its prisoners in deep holes in the ground. This was not far beyond that. What concerned Prentice more, though, was how clearly he could see his men's faces. Dawn was all but here. He cast a horrified glance at the dragonfly and obelisk, as if by looking he could will the powder to detonate.

Still, there was nothing.

"When I say go, full pelt, no holding back," he whispered to his team. He specifically turned to the five Roarsmen. "As soon as they see us, pepper those witches 'til you have no powder left. Only stop if a Verdant man or woman runs up on the platform. Do not shoot them. If some of the slingers come out for you, or even a fey child with a blunt stick, you throw off your guns and dive into the water. Swim for the south bank. The Azure Mountain fey will give you cover."

Prentice had chosen the five Roarsmen who claimed they were the most confident swimmers for exactly this purpose. Their initial impact was to shock and disrupt, but without the protection of the Claws and Fangs, they could not stand in a melee and were commanded to swim for safety. As for the Fangs that Prentice had with him, he had assured them that their task was to get him to the platform, and then they could stay or swim as they desired.

"The archduchess will not even charge you for the loss of your shields or swords if you have to cast them away," Prentice had joked. "I promise you, I will be in the water right behind you once I have given the Serpent Witch her final taste of steel."

The five Roar loaded up and sighted on the crimson-dripping platform, ready to support the assault. The Fangs slipped along the stones until they were crouched behind a hut, halfway into the village. Every Verdant fey must have been caught up in the ritual, or else hiding from it, for they saw almost no locals other than a line of pairs—bound sacrifices and their one escort each—awaiting their turn with the bone knives. On the far side of the jetty altar was another crowd of other tattooed fey, standing as if bewitched, eyes focused on the slaughter. Doubtless these were the ones who had made their sacrifices already. Prentice wondered how he would have responded to them if he had not already sworn not to raise his sword against them. Was half the settlement being put to death for this one ritual? Could they hope to survive as a people?

From the other end of the valley a rumble sounded, like thunder heard at a distance. The powder had detonated. The mantis man looked that way, perhaps puzzled by the unexpected noise, and Prentice turned as well. He watched the obelisk and thought he saw what looked like a cloud of smoke billowing around the base, but so much less than he hoped for. It rose perhaps to the height of fifteen or so feet, no more than a quarter of the way up the obelisk. It swirled around and then slowly began to settle. The rumbling echo died away.

"It did nothing. Not a dashed thing," Lyrach muttered, horrified. Prentice felt the grip of dying hope enclose his heart and sighed.

I once expected to die in a cellar under Ashfield, he thought, *and many other days in many other places, including by the whip under Liam's gaze. This is not much worse than those things. Not even more lonely, not really. Lord, let my blade strike true and cut through the Reach's foes. Let me be as Samson, tearing this place down upon my head so my wife and child live free.*

The witch coven seemed not to have even noticed the failed powder explosion, simply continuing in their ritual carnage. Another fey sacrifice fell, and the body was cast into the lake where it dripped its life fluids over a mound of corpses easily half the height of the stone platform. If every pulse of the wing-light through the night had been timed with a sacrifice, Prentice was not surprised to see half a graveyard's worth of dead mounted up out of the water. Strangely, for all the gore upon the stones, the water around the corpses seemed almost clear, as if the power drained from the blood also turned the crimson to water. Now the wings of the dragonfly statue at the other end of the valley moved as they had all night, but their drone ceased to be a pulse and became a continuous sound, a vibration that shook the air up and down the valley. It echoed off the cliffs and set the surface of the water dancing. In an instant, Prentice's muscles were tense and his jaw ached, as it had every time he had been this close to the power. His salet helm obscured much of the sound, covering his ears as it did, but nonetheless, the shaking still entered into his very bones. A quick glance at his men made him think they suffered similarly.

Above, the sky had turned to lensing glass, and the Redlanders' far coast was coming into view, a bay full of more boats than Dweltford had huts, or so it seemed. The mantises were about to swarm through the mirrored sky.

"Now is our moment," Prentice said, thinking they might still be able to disrupt the magick while the cabal were distracted. The ritual had been cut short at this point during his vision, and perhaps it could be again. Eyes on the platform and ready to launch himself to the attack, he drew his sword quietly and raised his hands to signal the gunners to start firing. The motions made him shift his weight slightly and his foot slipped. For the first time since the Gryphon Banner Company and Wind Rising fey had arrived in the valley, someone not a Redlander or Verdant fey touched the water of the lake. The witch's hissing song cut off abruptly, and the mantis man turned to look straight at them.

"Fire!" Prentice commanded and threw himself forward, splashing through the mystical shallows, eyes fixed only on the bloodied dais and its accursed priesthood.

CHAPTER 89

J errod Froster sat his horse in the midst of the extended command troop while behind them the various banners and pennants fluttered and snapped in the rising evening breeze, unusual for this part of summer. Amelia hoped it was not a bad omen. Beside the Golden Heron banker, his original mercenary captain sat scowling in the fading daylight. He looked nothing like the insouciant sellsword he had seemed during their first parley. Likely, he resented having seen his expensive and powerful cavalry reduced to ruin. He may well have lost close comrades as well. On Froster's other side was a broad-shouldered and powerfully built man with a manicured beard and closely cropped dark hair. His features were handsome, and he had a strong jaw. From the fur trim of his cloak and the complex embossing upon his plate armor, it was clear he was another Vec prince. On his opposite side sat three more men-at-arms, almost as richly panoplied as their leader.

"Do you still fear to look us in the eye, witch?" Froster shouted across the few paces between himself and the first row of steel points leveled at him. "See, I have brought no prayer books or Bibles to frighten you with. I will read no holy writ in your hearing. Let us meet under a last flag of truce."

Archduchess Amelia watched the enemy leaders from a space created for her midway inside the lead cohort. She could not really make out their faces in the gathering gloom, but since she still did not trust that Froster and his armored companions would not try something rash, hoping their steel plates would protect them long enough to snatch her away, she would go no closer than this.

"I see you have new friends," she spoke loudly into the leather cone, ignoring Froster's jibe about reading the Bible. Either he knew about the Inquisition's attempt to ensorcel her with written words, or he was simply playing into the image of a witch that they wanted painted upon her. Either way, there was nothing to gain by debating the truth of it here. "Do you think to be courteous, or shall they remain impolitely anonymous?"

"I am Tarningcrest the Fourth, Prince of Rosedale," the regal knight declared before Froster could introduce him. "These here with me are my sworn bannermen, and I would not sully their names by speaking them to you, northern slattern. We are here to throw your rabble back across the Murr and to drag you in chains to Grey Hill, there to cut off your head for your impudence in seeking to conquer a sovereign princedom of the free Vec."

"A pleasure to meet you too, Prince Tarningcrest," Amelia replied and several of the nearby Lions chuckled. The prince had the dignity not to be too visibly offended, but he scowled with clear indignation. Amelia found herself too tired to be much pleased with her own wit. "Have we come together once more to exchange invective, or did you have some business to transact?"

"Business? Are we mere merchants to haggle with?" Tarningcrest demanded.

"Her father was, they say," the doleful mercenary captain shouted. "Just a jump-up who bought a cheap frontier province from a decrepit, and after killing him in his sleep, she has taken to calling it her queendom or some such."

"I may be the daughter of a merchant," Amelia shouted back, feeling her temper slip a little, "but I am not the one here in the pay of a bunch of cowardly, fat bankers. I do my own bidding, not the Heron's, nor that of any other men of commerce.

Ask Master Froster what merchants get for impudence like this in the Western Reach."

Chew on that, she thought, knowing it was petty, but more fed up with being talked down to than she had expected to be.

"She is every bit the shameless reprobate we were told to expect," one of the prince's anonymous men declared, as if he was discovering the shocking depravity of a brothel masquerading as a church.

"Her grace is lawfully married before God to one who was the prince of this realm until he surrendered it to her in troth," Spindle called from Amelia's side. The Lace Fang looked furious, speaking in her liege lady's defense and ready to champion her honor further. Amelia put a hand to Spindle's arm and the lady-in-waiting fell silent.

"If you have words of parley to speak, gentles, then may we be about it?" she called into her trumpet. "My good militiamen have been waiting all day for their dinners, and I would not delay them longer than necessary."

"Let them wait..." the mercenary captain began to retort, but this time it was Froster's chance to still an underling speaking out of turn.

"Your force has had a successful few days, Amelia of Dweltford," the banker said. "But you surely can see how the ledger is now balanced? Now it is you who are on the deficit side."

Amelia wondered if Froster was using a mercantile metaphor to mock her or because he thought it apt. Either way, his basic point was correct. Her force was significantly outweighed now that Prince Tarningcrest and his army had arrived.

"Sad enough that your husband is lost to you and with him any legal case you might have made to claim Aubrey," Froster went on. "Now I fear you will be unable to make any military attempt either, since you are hedged in and the moneys you have been hoping to smuggle through the Eastern Trade Road will not be coming to you either."

"Eastern Trade Road, that's what the Veckander's call the road that runs through Bridgetown, Your Grace," Spindle whispered. "They've caught Caius' caravan."

Amelia shook her head, keeping her attention on Froster.

"Your weary men, hungry for their dinners, cannot hope to defeat us. And even if by some hellish false miracle they managed it, you have no coin with which to pay them. They will die for nothing or win nothing in victory."

"We ain't graspin' sellswords, Veckander," an anonymous voice cried out from the Lions' ranks. "We fight for honor and blood!"

"We fight for the Lioness," another shouted, and suddenly the ground was shaking as hundreds of polearms hammered upon the dirt while Fangs stamped their feet and banged the pommels of their swords upon their shields. The banker and prince both recoiled at the spontaneous demonstration of loyalty, as did their companions. Their horses shifted nervously under them, and by what little light they had to see, it looked like several of the Vec command troop thought they were about to be attacked.

"Bring them to heel," Amelia told Markas, shouting in his ear to be heard. The banner sergeant began to bellow for quiet, and while it took a while for the command to be heard, calm slowly spread over the militiamen once more.

"Is that your answer, witch duchess?" Froster asked as he struggled to keep his unnerved mount still beneath him. The creature was almost wheeling, snorting fretfully as it stepped back and forth.

"My answer to what, banker?" she spat back. "I have heard no terms yet, only insults."

"Yield to our authority, little jumped-up bitch," Tarningcrest said. "You're a brat out of place and we'll insult you however we like. I'm not young Farringdon to be awed or affrighted by a clutch of rogues afoot."

"And if I yield, you take me to your Grey Hill and cut my head off? That is the whole of your offer?" Amelia said quickly, fearing her men would take umbrage at another round of affronts. She wanted this conversation ended as soon as possible. She was tired, and while it might salve her pride to resist these arrogant men to their faces, nonetheless, the fact of their power was unmistakable. She had only one priority left at this point.

"You will be taken to trial before the Compact in Council," Froster explained. "If they find you guilty, your head will certainly be forfeit. Of course, if your cause is just, as you claim, you will be judged fairly and be let to live."

The Heron banker's face was a mass of shadows now, the sun finally fled beneath the horizon. In moments, Amelia would be unable to see any of them. Even so, Froster's voice seemed full of mockery. It was clear he believed the only outcome of any fair trial would still be her death.

"You have said nothing of my militia, of my retainers," she said, and a different sound of affront and discontent began to creep through the White Lions. "What is to happen to them upon my surrender?"

"Your Grace, you can't think..." her banner sergeant began, but Amelia cut him off.

"Shut up, Markas," she said, far more coldly than she intended. He went quiet immediately, and Amelia looked to him, frowning apologetically, but in the failing light she could not be sure he could read her expression at all. In the meantime, Froster had deferred the question to the prince, since it would be his authority that dispensed with any prisoners.

"They are invaders, but loyal, and it seems they have committed little pillage," Tarningcrest said grandly. "There is no reason they could not serve some typical labor and then return to their homes. We do not convict criminals to the same extreme as you Kingdom folk. Aubrey is a haunted ruin, so they say. I could have them tear it down and use the stones to begin a fresh, unsullied, town—perhaps here, closer to the bridge to commemorate my victory."

You haven't won yet, Amelia thought, but it felt like a bloodless retort in her mind. She had stood fast for herself and for Aubrey and its people. She had obeyed her husband's last command to the best of her ability, and her men-at-arms had shown admirable strength in the fight. By any measure, they were the superior warriors on this battlefield. Now, she had no horsemen and likely no husband. Wherever Farringdon was, he was surely wounded or slain. The bridge that linked her land with this new province had been destroyed, and even if it was whole, her army could not use it to withdraw because the other side was occupied by another force that it seemed was stubbornly refusing to break, even though she had a second company fighting for her on the banks of the Dwelt. A day ago, she had felt triumphant; now, she was tired, staring the extermination of too many good Reachermen in the face in the night. Fresh wolves were at the door and the latch was breaking. She and Prentice had made the Reach strong, but no one land could be strong enough to resist the entire world—Redlanders, Inquisition, Veckanders, and Grand Kingdom usurpers. Her forces were trapped in the jaws of not one wolf but an entire pack. She gave her men a glance, and though none were looking at her, she could feel their loyal resolve. They would die for her, she was certain. She could not pay them, and they knew it, but it did not matter. She could not lead them to victory, and still they wanted to fight. They could not retreat. The river that guarded their back also hemmed them in, and there was nothing she could do about that, not in the time she had. There was only one thing she could do for them. She could save them from death, but even as she tried to form the words, the gall in her mouth stilled her tongue.

The Lions of the pride deserved better than surrender.

"Will you give me this night to consider your terms?" she asked, and something like a groan sounded around her.

"What difference will one night make?" Tarningcrest mocked, but Amelia ignored him.

"Will you grant it?" she pressed.

There was a moment of silence. The battlefield was fully dark, and few torches had been lit in the windblown inkiness. If the Heron force proposed to attack now, it would take an hour at least just for them to ready enough light and arrange for the fight. Surely one more night was nothing to ask.

"Have your last night, petty duchess," Froster said. "Come the morning your rebellion against God and propriety ends, one way or another."

"Assuming you live that long," another of the Veckander company sniped, though Amelia could not see who in the darkness and did not recognize the voice. She wondered if they were threatening her with assassination, or if they were teasing her with the prospect of a mutiny. Shaking her head, Amelia turned away. If there was one thing she was certain of, it was that these loyal men-at-arms around her would not rebel. Not this night.

"Tell them I'm finished," she said to Markas.

"Her grace has concluded this parley," he shouted as Amelia walked away toward the river and her bed of reeds and rushes. She doubted she would get much sleep this night.

"Go now while the flag of truce protects you. She will give her word in the morning."

Markas sounded truly indignant, as if he would rather tell the Veckanders to stick their parley in their own backsides. The command troop rode away, their horses' hooves thumping in the dark. Shortly after, the dismissal beat sounded, and the Lions went to possibly their last dinner as loyal Reacher men-at-arms.

CHAPTER 90

Prentice was thrashing through the shallows as the mantis warrior sprang into the air towards him. At the same time, the five Roar fired, and while the bullets missed the hominid insect, one of the serpent witches fell dead, her head split by iron shot. Prentice had faced mantis warriors before and he knew many of their capabilities, so the enormous leap was no surprise. He was already dashing sideways out of the path of the springing attack, with his sword up ready to deflect the *brakkis effar's* path. Today, he did not have a shield with him, only the long sword wielded two-handed. His purpose was not safety or survival but a carnage to end the carnage on that damnable stone platform.

The mantis descended, both serrated, sword-like forearms leading. Prentice was slightly out of his line, but the insect warrior twisted in the air so that he might slash the knight commander on the way past. One chitinous claw "blade" was aimed to tear out Prentice's throat between his helmet and his brigandine where he had long since forsaken wearing a gorget because of the desert heat. The second claw would surely sever Prentice's leg through the knee, if not through the thighbone itself.

The first time he had fought a mantis warrior, Prentice had worn no armor and wielded only a cudgel and dagger, neither of which had been very effective against the hard, chitinous skin of the insect warriors. But Baron Ironworth's champion sword was nothing like those simpler tools of war. It was a masterpiece that had been twice fashioned to be perfect, much as Prentice himself had been—once as a knight and again as a convict. While Prentice would never love the blade, he knew its capabilities. Like him, it was a "death thing."

Even before the mantis warrior struck the water, Prentice took a second step aside, and from the high guard that Iron-worth himself had used the day he had nearly defeated Prentice, the champion sword chopped a brutal downward sweep, severing both serrated forearms and coming back up into its guard again, like the spoke of a wheel. The blow knocked the mantis sideways, water spraying up as the beast-man landed awkwardly. With inhuman speed he twisted to get his legs under himself properly, but Prentice was not finished. He had seen mantis swiftness too many times to give it any space. Before the *brakkis effar* could even fully realize the brutal loss of his weapon hands, Prentice followed, slashing so that his blade fell wherever it desired. These cuts were nowhere near as forceful as his first, and most deflected from the armored hide, but it did not matter. The pressure was relentless, and soon enough one bulbous eye was sliced open, and then a rising cut took the mantis under one of his legs as he tried to lift it for a kick, and his body was toppled over once more. Prentice leapt upon him, pressing him down to the rocks under the water, and aiming carefully, thrust the point of his blade through the creature's uninjured eye. The carapace of its skull cracked like the shell of a nut and the warrior lay still in the water.

The Roar fired a second volley, something Prentice had worried they would not even get a chance to attempt, and another two serpent women took wounds, though neither fell. On the dais, it seemed indecision reigned. Some of the witches were clearly intent on maintaining their ritual, while others were calling for assistance to deal with the attackers. In the midst of the rising chaos, Prentice thought he heard the clank of an iron chain and assumed that was the Serpent Witch he had come to find. In one sense, one individual witch in the midst of the cabal was a pointless target, but he had given his word to his mistress, and if he had to die, he would do his duty in the process. He was no mere convict anymore.

Although Lyrach had come along as a Roar line first, the young man-at-arms was carrying a Fangs' sword and shield, and he was leading the rest of the hand-to-hand fighters swiftly between the village huts, aiming for the raised flagstone causeway from the shore to the platform, the only place where there were steps upward to get to the serpent witches. With almost no hope of survival, Prentice had little fear of his men violating his pledge to the stag rider elder now, but he was pleased to see the Verdant fey seemed too confused by what they were seeing, too torn between the ecstasies of the ritual and the agonies of sacrifice to make any kind of resistance. The Fangs bullied their way through the fey with their shields, meeting virtually no opposition.

"For now," Prentice thought, and he ducked involuntarily as a third volley of Roar shot passed overhead, the hornet buzzing of their passage almost swallowed by the throbbing of the dragonfly. With the serpents driven back from this side of the dais by Roarshot, Prentice decided not to waste time going for the stairs. He was already standing knee deep in water too icy for the dry heat that cursed the land outside these two valleys. That cold was awakening the cold within his own soul, and he almost smiled with the insanity of his next thought. Thrashing the water to foam, he charged at the funereal mound of the unholy butchered and mounted upon the slain like a sepulchral staircase out of hell itself. Bodies slid underfoot and his balance threatened to fail, but he had eyes only for the rise, and when he reached the top and started to tumble forward, he sprang for the side of the platform. His foot touched the stones and pushed him upward farther, so that his hands could reach out for the lip of the dais. With his sword in his right, that hand's fingertips slipped almost immediately, but his left held, and he swung wild for a moment before making a second, wrenching attempt. His weapon slammed on the stone surface with a clash, and he had enough grip to scramble up onto the top.

Having attained his goal, he knew he had just got in the way of his gunners, but he heard a volley fire again. There were splashes in the water in the corner of his vision and he looked to see that the five Roar were now shooting at a Redlander boat. He had no time to watch closely, but from a swift glance it seemed to be a new one, not one of the ones that had already been in the lake. The swarm had started to come through the sky. It would all be over soon, but as he scoured the dais with his gaze, Prentice saw that the still living witches were only six in number now, plus the one he most wanted, kneeling still like a pet, yanking at her chain that was anchored in the stones. She seemed completely lost to panic.

Be ready for the venom, he told himself, smiling now with the cold fury of battle. Everything had shrunk once again, shrunk down to the single purpose of defeating his enemy before they handed him over to death's harsh mercies. As he moved immediately sideways to create a difficult target for the serpents to spit upon, Prentice was almost pleased to discover that the Redlanders were not the only ones on the stone platform. Previously out of sight on the far side of the dais, apparently an observer once again, was Brother Elder Inxyphos, wearing his silvered mail and his Inquisition tabard stained with fine sprays of blood. It seemed a right metaphor to Prentice's thoughts.

"Heaven damn you to eternal torment, Ashen Man," the Inquisition knight exclaimed. He quickly hefted the helmet under his left arm up onto his head, leaving the strap hanging loose.

"I have already survived the merciless blessings of the Inquisition, thank you," Prentice retorted, and he smiled. Inxyphos did not return it.

"As nothing compared to what awaits you," he said, and he drew his sword.

Prentice heard one of the serpents hawk from their throat, preparing to spit, and gambling on the likely tactic, he dodged back the way he had come. As he hoped, the venom had been aimed at where he had been going, and the change of direction made the miss very wide. It did, however, bring him close to Inxyphos, who stepped in with a slash of his blade. Prentice caught the stroke and pushed off with the engaged edge. By fluke, it shoved the pair of them apart just as another gout of venom flew their way, sizzling in the throbbing, multi-colored air between them.

"Careful, Brother," Prentice mocked, smiling even more broadly. "Seems your allies do not care who they hurt in their hunt for my head."

"I'll take your damned fool head," Inxyphos declared, and he came on with a whirling series of strikes, aiming for Prentice's face. The champion sword intercepted and checked them all, though the force of one was such that Inxyphos's point managed to flick around and clip the side of Prentice's steel helm. He hardly noticed. His defensive techniques had brought him close to the edge of the platform, which was a risk that Inxyphos could clearly see, but it had also brought him around so that the Inquisition knight was between him and the serpent witches. If they tried to spit at him now, they would get Inxyphos first.

Suits me, Prentice thought, and he felt his icy grin again. If one was to die, then surely this was the exciting way to do it.

From the shoreline behind him, he heard the sounds of battle becoming even more chaotic. He thought he caught words being exchanged in Kingdom speech, insults and battle cries, and not from one side only. Inxyphos's Church millitants had entered the fray, it seemed, and his Fangs were now going toe to toe with them. Prentice hoped they lived long enough to taste some personal victories over the elite men-at-arms of the Church's fallen institution. Redlander battle cries were sounding over the water and the distinctive rhythm of Lion drums seemed to be perceptible under the drone of the dragonfly. In every direction was an insanity worthy of a vision of the end of time, and Prentice was resolved he would deliver his liege's justice to the liar knight in front of him and the chained snake a few steps farther on. Then let God come to judge his soul; he had done what he could.

There was a crack, like the retort of a chain snapping but louder than was imaginable. It echoed over the entire valley so that it seemed to come from everywhere at once. Then there was a tearing noise, as of a long cloth being sheared by a blunt blade. It began and then stuttered and then began again, followed by two more cracks, not as loud but still echoing. Inxyphos looked up and the few serpent witches still speaking their hissing enchantment ceased as well, their heads looking to and fro in a growing panic. Behind Prentice, the sound of the melee on the shore trailed off, and as it did, the knight commander realized the drone of the dragonfly magick had become intermittent as well. The coruscating light that made a mirror of the sky began to swirl, the blanketing madness becoming more like a mist and less a ubiquitous glow. One of the serpent witches screamed, and her sisters joined her as they looked where she pointed to the other end of the valley. A massive crack had appeared in the stone of the obelisk, and as Prentice risked a glance, he saw a chunk, surely tons in weight, break away and splash into the water. As it fell, the rest seemed to shift, and the wings of the dragonfly faltered, the light and the drone fading for a moment. The remaining weight of stone seemed to try to fall, then held, likely barely contained in place by the myriad chains of sacrifices wrapped around the artifact.

For how long? Prentice wondered exultantly. In the water much closer, there was a heavy splash and splintering explosion as another Redlander boat, apparently failing in its transition, had fallen from the impossible above-below height and been smashed apart by the impact. It was a guess if any of the crew might have survived. Likely, if the hit had not killed them, it would have stunned them enough that they would soon drown.

"Looks like no one is leaving this valley now," Prentice told Inxyphos. "And no more will be coming through."

The brother elder glared at him with the fury Prentice imagined the agent Bluebird had felt when Spindle put her poniard through his knee.

CHAPTER 91

A melia picked at her plate of fish stew, dipping her silver spoon into the mix and drawing up a sauce-filled portion, only to let it drop back into the plate uneaten. It was not that the stew was unappetizing. Indeed, it smelled exceptional for such a simple dish, but she had no desire to eat or do anything, if her heart was any guide.

She could see militiamen and servants moving in the corner of her vision as she sat alone, staring into a campfire. They watched her, knowing what she knew, facing what she was facing, and willing her to the course of action she could not abide. More than once she noticed Markas or Nunel carefully intercept an approaching figure—some earnest Reacherman intent of violating protocol for the chance to reassure her of their loyal willingness to die in her name. For years now she had wrestled with the folk of the Reach, from the peerage down to the lowliest convict, trying to wring from them the obedience she needed to let her guide the land through this war. Bringing nobles like Duggan and Sebastian to heel had seemed overwhelming, but by comparison, this unstinting loyalty was torture.

"I would never have credited it," she whispered to herself, setting her plate aside. Shortly Spindle arrived quietly at her elbow to collect the uneaten meal.

"Someone has some hard tack, Your Grace," she said, "If the stew is too rich for you, dipped in fresh water, it would be not too bad for the stomach."

Amelia smiled and shook her head.

"I think I will try to rest awhile," she said. "I'll eat in the morning."

"Very good, Your Grace. Would you like me to brush your hair?"

Amelia stood with a smile, shaking her head.

"I won't sleep in my coif but there's little point unpinning the whole thing, My Lady."

"If you say so, Your Grace."

Amelia could tell by her tone what Spindle thought of that, and for a moment she was reminded of her long serving and long-suffering chaperone matron, Bettina. At least *she* was safe in Dweltford.

Amelia turned toward her reed bed, head down, to keep from meeting anyone's eyes. Even that much contact would be too painful, she was sure. Her Lions deserved victory, and she was going to take their sliver-like hope of it away from them to save their lives.

"Have you made up your mind, Your Grace?" Spindle asked, unable, it seemed, to keep her own nerves from this one presumption.

"In the main, Spindle," Amelia answered. She would not lie to her friend. "You know I really don't have much choice."

"They mean to kill you. You cannot let them take you."

"They do not know I'm pregnant yet," Amelia said. "Once I am in their hands, I will tell them. No sentence, however unjust, can execute a mother with child. I may not know as much Vec law as I do Grand Kingdom, but I know that much."

Spindle put her hand to her mouth, eyes wide in horror. "Oh, good Lord, Your Grace, I had forgotten. In all the madness of these days and Caius' needs, I had forgotten your condition."

"Better for us all that you did, Spindle. Can you imagine what these Reachermen would do if they learned the heir to Dweltford was growing in my womb? They would throw themselves into the river and make a bridge of their own bodies in the hopes I might cross and escape. No, better by far that this has been a secret. I have barely begun to show, but it is at least enough that Froster and Tarningcrest will know it is no ploy to dodge their wrath. I will have a trial eventually, but summary execution will not fall upon me."

"Always assuming they don't just claim it weren't Farringdon's and that you carry some bastard," Spindle said, again too affected by emotions to keep from presumption.

"Always assuming," Amelia agreed, and finally she waved her lady-in-waiting away so that she could go to her bed in the little area of privacy created for her by a series of cloths tied to posts, like a tiny tent with no roof. Pulling away her coif and shirking her brightly colored overdress, she lay in her shift, hair still pinned, and wished for sleep to come. She doubted that it would, and lay staring at the Rampart across the sky and the half-moon shining its light on the world.

So peaceful, she thought. *Watching stars is not a sad way to spend one's last free hours.*

She and her first husband, Duke Marne, had watched stars together from a balcony on their wedding night. It had been a pleasant time, and the memory comforted her more than she imagined it could because it must have been some hours later when a sentry's call awakened her.

"...the river," was all she caught as she sat up, blinking her eyes.

The river? she thought hopefully, imagining Dalflitch's breakthrough force. She stood up just as Spindle poked her head into the tiny, private space.

"Boats on the river, lots of them," she said, and Amelia smiled at her.

"Our relief?"

Spindle shook her head, sombrely.

"From the east, Your Grace."

The east? Duke Robant's reinforcements. Amelia remembered the mockery of the anonymous Veckander knight. "Assuming you live that long."

This was what he must have meant. The Grand Kingdom's reinforcements had arrived. Would they sail past to relieve Robant's main force, or would they turn aside now and assault her camp. She knew which tactic she would favor in their place.

"Let's get me dressed, Spindle. Morning did not wait for my decision, it seems."

Taking no more time than she needed to get her overdress back in place and her coif pinned once more, Amelia led the way to the riverbank where the rump of the bridge met the now useless road. There she found a cohort armed and readied, facing eastward into the darkness, Markas and Nunel with them. There were torchlights visible, bobbing on the water not too far away.

"Sedgemark's rallyin' the rest, Your Grace," the banner sergeant informed her.

"How many boats are there?" she asked.

"Too many, Your Grace, and bigguns too, so the scouts reported when they spotted 'em coming upriver. There's word of men in steel in some of the prows, so we know they're not fishers."

"What are they doing?" she asked, noticing that the lights were not approaching as swiftly as they might.

"My guess is that they have decided to offload on that side of the bridge," said Nunel. "They won't want to risk crossing the fallen gap in the bridge at night. Too many snags there under the water. The rest of the arches, they might try, but they'd have to slow for them, too. Might as well just offload that side as try some clever poling in the darkness."

"Well, as long as they aren't inconvenienced," Amelia muttered. She turned to Markas.

"Fetch the standard, Sergeant, and several torches or lanterns. The banner must be well lit. I do not want them to miss it when we furl our colors."

The sergeant looked at her, his crestfallen expression obvious even in the poor light. He moved away slowly, and Amelia felt a cruel temptation to hurry him, seeing so many of the waterborne torches drawing closer.

"Name yourselves!" challenged a sentry who had obviously decided the boats had drawn close enough to surrender their anonymity. Amelia cringed as she waited to hear the name of the Grand Kingdom noble who would end her rule. She wondered if she would know them.

"Boatmen of Bridgetown," came the reply, "late of Earl John's service."

"Who do you serve now then?" the sentry called back, and a voice Amelia had thought perhaps to never hear again answered out of the closing distance.

"They now give loyal service to the newly risen Baroness Penelope," called the voice, "Service she has graciously offered to the Western Reach and its knight captain."

"Farringdon?" Amelia cried, and she rushed into the darkness ahead of the single cohort readied to defend her. They would no longer be necessary. She nearly slipped as she reached the very edge of where the watergrasses met the land, and moved back and forth watching the lead boat and where it would come ashore. There in the prow, unmistakable in his steel breastplate even if he hadn't removed his helmet, was her husband. His boat stopped and a gangway was run out. No sooner had it splashed into the shallows than Farringdon was dashing down it, his armor-weighted form causing the boards to flex. Then he was at her side, sweeping her into his arms, and Amelia felt tears rush like a storm.

"My darling, my love," he murmured in her ear as he held her close. "I'm so sorry. So sorry I was away so long. I feared for certain we would be too late."

He was sorry?

Amelia could barely believe her ears. She had all but named him craven and sent him to a death trap from which he had escaped only by pure wit and cunning. She had indeed cursed him for a fool to his face more than once under the influence of the Inquisition's fell arts. And in all that he had served her and the Reach and fought with utter devotion.

And *he* was sorry?

Amelia had so many things she wanted to say, so many apologies to make, so many questions to ask. But as she leaned back in his arms to look into his dear face—not well formed enough to be handsome but more delightful than any other would ever be—she had one thing she had to say first.

"We are with child," she told him and smiled as fully as she had since summer began. "Three or four months now."

Farringdon peered at her as if he suspected she might be lying or seeking to fool him somehow. Then he burst out laughing—a joyous sound she wished would never cease.

CHAPTER 92

Prentice watched as Inxyphos's eyes narrowed in cold calculation. Behind the Inquisition man-at-arms, the serpent coven was wailing, worse than when being wounded by Roarshot. If they had any power left to exert, they had not gathered their wits enough yet to use it. The brother elder, though, looked much more focused, and Prentice readied himself to receive the Church knight's next assault.

He was astonished when instead, Inxyphos turned around, and with a sweeping stroke, clove one of the witch's heads from her shoulders. Then he kicked another aside and dove to the stones, half tumbling, half scrambling, with arms reaching out, hands grasping like a miser trying to keep from spilling coins out of a damaged money bag. The knight even dropped his sword, to Prentice's complete disbelief. When he came up to his feet for a fraction of a moment, the knight commander saw that Inxyphos had snatched up two of the witches' ceremonial daggers.

"Another time, heretic," he said with a sneer and then jumped from the dais into the water. Prentice dashed to the edge, one eye still to spare for the remaining serpent women, who were now shocked from their despair by Inxyphos's treacherous retreat. Their hate-filled gazes were fully fixed on the one White Lion on the stones beside them.

"Ashen Man! Ashen Man!" hissed the Serpent Witch, still bound by chain and collar, pointing a claw-like hand. Trying to watch everything at once, Prentice twisted his head back and forth, seeing Inxyphos limping awkwardly through the shallows, apparently injured from his jump. A crash in the water signaled the fall of yet another Redlander boat failing its transition, growling screams of terror accompanying the drop as some crew members were tossed clear. His tiny Roar contingent was still loading and firing into the water, hunting the few fallen enemy who might look like they could swim. The clash of steel interspersed with monstrous bawls from further up the lake told of Gennet and the main of the company in the thick of a desperate melee.

A body bumped into Prentice from behind just as one of the witches spat a gout of venom, spoiling his attempt to dodge aside. The jet of poison never struck him, however, as the bumping body revealed itself to be Lyrach, who reached across in front of his commander to interpose his shield between spittle and target. The vile ichor splashed over the metal, blistering the surface and spraying fine droplets into the air. Lyrach and Prentice both recoiled, though the young militiaman kept his shield high as he blinked and coughed.

"They all said the stuff burns the eyes, but by God, I never imagined this!"

"Do not let the chaplain hear you taking oaths by the Almighty like that, Line First," Prentice said happily, using the confusion of Lyrach's intervention to get himself safely back from the edge.

With two swordsmen facing three witches yet standing, Prentice felt no hesitation. He let Lyrach pick his own target, and the two comrades charged at the scale-skinned women, breastless like all cold-blooded creatures and barely human anymore. Talons raked at them and one more tried her venom, but expecting it, Prentice was already back-swinging with his blade as she hawked, so that the unicorn horn hilt with its silver lion head pommel crashed into the witch's jaw, smashing it like a clay pot. The woman fell insensible, but her spittle still seared across part of Prentice's arm. It fizzed on the metal, and as he brought his blade around again, he heard a snap. The caustic poison had rotted through the leather straps on his spaulder. The embossed lion's head now hung loose and useless for protection.

Ignoring the inconvenience, Prentice hacked at the leg of one of the two women who were concentrating on Lyrach, trying to get around his shield. There was a cut on the line first's neck, it seemed, and his right sleeve was torn where it looked like a clawed hand had turned the cloth to ribbons. Once the knight commander halved the pressure he was under, the militiaman turned full upon his remaining opponent and slammed his weight into her in a shield charge. It was likely he meant to knock her to the stones, but misjudged the woman's lesser resistance, and he nearly followed her over the edge as she cartwheeled away with a scream. The last fighting witch, the one Prentice had hamstrung, fell backward to the stones, and he ended her hissing rage with a straight thrust that split her sternum.

"Take a bad shot there, My Lord Knight Commander?" Lyrach asked, nodding at Prentice's damaged armor while he recovered his own balance. Prentice looked to his shoulder, thinking to either settle the misaligned armor piece or remove it for later repair. The dribbling remnants of the venom on the steel and leather of his harness threw fumes into his face as he looked closely and he snapped his head backward, coughing and spitting. Face turned away, he tucked his sword under his arm, and using one hand, wrenched at the spaulder several times until it finally tore free.

"Do not let me forget that, Line First," he commanded as he dropped the marred armor piece to the stones. Then he looked to the sky. Like the blurry eyes of a hungover morning, the image of the Redlander fleet in its far bay was shifting in and out of focus. Boats and their crews seemed trapped in the translation, sometimes on the water of the lake, then suddenly back in the bay above. It was an insanity that Prentice doubted even

Redlander minds could endure. Each time the image resolved and became confused once more, screams could be heard, as if wafting closer and farther away on an intermittent breeze.

A stream of hissed Redlander speech drew Prentice's eyes back to the dais and the Serpent Witch—the failure who would have been queen of the Reach, now a pet for her sisters. She was cursing him, he had no doubt, and the fury of her loathing was unmistakable. Prentice almost wanted to laugh, except he feared that if he did, the madness all around would overtake him. Instead, he set his focus upon his duty. The cold of his battle rage had receded, but the anger that underlay it was not abated. He stalked toward the crouching beast-woman who shied from him exactly like a fearful animal.

Live as a beast, die as one, he thought, but then he shook his head. He had not come merely to put down a rabid animal. He had a judgement to deliver. The Serpent Witch tried to draw up a spit of venom, desperation unmistakable even in her yellow eyes, but it seemed nothing would come. Prentice wondered if her sister's imprisonment had somehow restricted the power within her. Perhaps the iron collar somehow choked off whatever inhuman organ it was within her flesh that produced the venom. For whatever reason, the last and least witch of the coven was unable to stop him as he kicked her, driving her sideways to the blood-slicked flagstones. As she fell, Prentice placed his foot in her back, keeping her flat down in the crimson.

From the other end of the lake came an odd sound, like the metallic pings of hot metal cooling. Looking up, with Lyrach beside him seeking out the sound as well, Prentice realized it was the last few heavy iron chains on the obelisk failing. The ancient stone finally toppled, and the dragonfly's wings ceased, the carved insect crashing into the water and the crystal shattering from the force. Where the obelisk had stood, a geyser of fresh water spouted, possibly the original spring that had been capped now fully unleashed. It burst upward while the stone mass that had tamed it now sprayed a wave ahead of itself, like a ripple from a child's rock thrown into a pond but far too large for so benign an image.

"The mountain cast into the sea," Lyrach muttered as they watched the swell roll down the valley, washing up on the strand and reflecting off the north-side cliffs.

"God preserve the Lions," Prentice prayed, and as his eyes searched out the Gryphon Banner where they fought on the flat southern bank, he feared for their lives. The wave was rumbling down the lake, easily the height of a man and with the power to sweep away any mere force of infantry. Then he smiled with utter relief as he saw the light, the holy light of Whilte's prophet's rod, shining over his loyal militiamen. By faith, he knew they would be safe. Beneath his foot, the Serpent Witch uttered a whimper, and Prentice looked down to see her head up, staring to the shattered other end of the valley and the approaching deluge.

"A baptism comes," he said, kneeling on her back and grabbing her chain, wrapping it around his gauntleted left hand close to her head so he could control her, forcing her to watch the onrushing wrath. Putting his head close to hers, he whispered where her ears should have been. "A baptism to cleanse this place, but not for you."

She tried to turn her head toward him, but Prentice yanked on the chain and kept her facing forwards at the water rushing down upon them. As it drew closer, it looked to him as if it surely would be high enough to crest the dais.

"Lyrach, tell the others to get behind the stone walls," he shouted. "They have moments."

If the line first heard him, Prentice did not look to see. He had his last task to perform. He slid the blade of the champion sword under her throat.

"*Brakkis effar,* creature of blood," he pronounced, doubting she could understand his words but determined to do what was right, what was necessary. "In the name of Amelia, first Archduchess of the Western Reach, and the Wind Rising fey of the Azure Mountains, I deliver now judgement upon you. For kin slain, thefts and banditry, occultism, heresy, blasphemy, suborned rape and pillage, and enslavement, you are sentenced to die. For the ancient beauty you perverted, feebly commemorated in this blade, you will die by its edge. Go now to whatever awaits you in eternity."

Prentice wrenched his sword upward, draw cutting as he did so, and the singular edge severed the cultist's inhuman head from its shoulders. Her brownish, discolored blood sprayed upon the stones, mingling with the life flow of all the others lost for her people's depravity, and then the deluge struck the podium and Prentice felt bathed in the icy wash of a thousand years of judgement unleashed.

CHAPTER 93

"They kept pushing us eastward," Farringdon explained to Amelia as the White Lions began to embark on the large, flat-bottomed lighters sent in flotilla from Bridgetown. "I thought it was a good thing, drawing the Golden Heron's horsemen further away, giving Sedgemark time to bloody the rest of their force. I knew we could trust Knight Commander Prentice to drive Robant's contingent away, and that meant that you only had to hold the bridgehead until the north bank was clear."

"There is no word from the knight commander, I fear," she told him, and he scowled, clearly disturbed by the unwelcome news.

"We captured a riverman on our way here who said that a full Lions company had marched from Dweltford and was besieging Robant's blockade forts as we speak. He had been sent to fetch reinforcements for the duke, and we made sure that missive will never reach its goal. But how is it the second banner marched without Baron Ash?"

Amelia looked up at her husband. Since he had stepped off the boat, she had been loath to be more than a handful of paces from him. It was taking all her will not to hold his arm and cling to him like a lovesick maid with her first suitor.

"Dalflitch and Righteous are bringing the second banner company. That is the word we have," she told him.

Another cohort marched past, carrying as much of their kit as they could salvage up the wooden gangplank of the next transport boat to take its place by the bank. The previous craft, now fully loaded, was being poled into the dark center flow of the Murr to float away eastward. As overladen men tromped with heavy boots onto the planks, archduchess and marquis were treated to the bizarre performance of a corporal whispering an infuriated call for quiet. Embarking the entire camp, spartan though it was, would take hours, and if they were to escape safely, it had to be done in secret. Even so, thousands of armed militia, servants, and all their remaining provisions could not be transported in utter silence. Reachermen were not fey.

"Well, whomever is commanding, Robant will find himself with no relief coming, not now that we have their boats," Farringdon said with a self-satisfied smirk. Amelia's eyes went wide. In a night full of surprises, that was a surprise further still.

"How?" she asked.

"Bridgetown has changed loyalty in the civil war, my love," Farringdon explained. "The earl had been sworn to Daven Marcus, apparently, but he was old and sick, so the Usurper had a trusted cadre in the town to enforce his will. They were like their master, it seems, and built a great deal of resentment against themselves. They were gathering these boats to ship the rest of Robant's force, all the reinforcements Daven Marcus planned to send. Then the old earl died in the night. Even before the bells were rung, the new baroness, Penelope, gathered some of her own loyal knights and seized Daven Marcus' sworn swords. They put them in chains and hanged a few after swift trials before dawn."

"Swift trials, indeed," Amelia agreed in a shocked voice.

"As I say, my love, they had built up quite the hoard of resentment. At any rate, when Daven Marcus' force arrived at Bridgetown's gates, they found them closed and were told that Baroness Penelope now considered her earldom a free land, akin to the Reach, until such time as the peers of the Grand Kingdom resolved the violations of proper succession to the throne in Denay."

Amelia smiled and nearly laughed, only keeping her propriety for the sake of the sober duty that lay unfinished about them.

"Thus, the boats were ready and waiting for Baroness Penelope to hand them to us for our needs in exchange for certain promises I trust you will not mind my having provided."

"I doubt I will," Amelia agreed in principle, but Farringdon was still dancing around the part of the story she most wanted. "None of this tells me how you came to be in Bridgetown to even ask."

Farringdon stood back a moment as a blinkered horse with hessian sacks on its feet was led past and up a gangway. Then he stepped closer again.

"As I said, we were trying to keep the Heron's horsemen drawn away, but we were forced to go to ground for a time in a small woods near Aubrey's border with Longshepherds, right at the south. We hid not more than six hours to avoid a reasonably clever ambush, but by the time we emerged, the enemy cavalry had simply withdrawn. I thought about trying to reengage them, but that would mean risking riding back into other ambushes. I still would have, but by chance we happened upon some men from the court of Longshepherds' earl, a man named Arnock."

Amelia had not realized that the Vec had earls, always assuming that every peer independent enough to have his own seat in the Vec automatically declared himself a prince.

"It was Arnock's men who told us about the situation in Bridgetown and that the baroness had sent emissaries to the earl's court to ask for contact through to our forces here in Aubrey. Arnock had never been close to the old earl of Bridgetown—understandable since each swore allegiance to a different nation—but they had been civil neighbors, and the baroness was quick to offer favorable terms for any traders or free men who wanted to bring their goods through her domain—releases from tariffs and taxes for a decade or more."

"But why? What love has Bridgetown for us?" Amelia asked. She had never heard of this new baroness, Lady Penelope, and knew of no existing relationship between Dweltford and Bridgetown. As far as she was concerned, they were as strangers to each other.

"Bridgetown is in almost a worse way than even the Reach, to hear tell of it, Your Grace," Farringdon said, and Amelia noticed that he had switched back to her title. He was about to unfold something of political significance to her, she realized. "They are sieged by Daven Marcus' denied force on their north, but on the south bank, the situation is even more dire. The Heron's man Froster might boast of taking you in chains to the Grey Hill, but the compact has all but broken. Every prince is up in arms, taking to solving their every dispute at sword point. At least two different armies, some with hired men-at-arms from Masnia, are marching on Bridgetown's southern gates. They don't have enough troops to hold against both jaws of the wolf, and the baroness wants to borrow the Lions for that task."

Amelia shook her head. As she understood it, Bridgetown's name was well deserved, for it was literally a single large town settled upon a series of islands in the lower Murr and linked by bridges. In any other context, it would be no more than a knight's fief or a baronet's, at most. But because it controlled all the trade between the Vec and the Grand Kingdom—at least whatever did not come by boat from the Reach—it was a vastly wealthy and militarily crucial strongpoint. The earldom had been a valued prize for royal favorites for centuries, and the current baroness's family had only possessed it for a little under a hundred years. It was no surprise to Amelia, after all she had been through to keep control of her own lands, that Lady Penelope was contemplating radical options to help her keep her family's seat.

"So, Your Grace, with your permission and begging your forgiveness if I have erred, I have pledged the Lion Banner in your name until the coming of the next spring," Farringdon explained. "I have also offered Baron Ash's services to train Bridgetown a militia of their own after the Lion's model. Of course, if Prentice is lost to us, perhaps others could fulfil that role."

"Let us not despair of the knight commander just yet, Knight Captain," Amelia said. Prentice had defied her anticipations too often to write him off at this stage. Considering Farringdon's news, Amelia recognized that he had presumed much in negotiating this alliance in her name, even only temporarily. Nonetheless, it would save her militia's lives, which was her highest priority this day.

Not to mention my own life and our unborn child's, she thought and smiled at Farringdon once again. She would be very old indeed before she felt she had fully recompensed this loyal spouse for the devotion he had shown her in the face of the Inquisition's whispered curses.

"Your Grace, if I may intrude?" Spindle said quietly, appearing out of the night.

"What is it, My Lady?" she asked as Spindle smiled and curtseyed at the marquis knight captain, newly returned from the dead.

"Some of the refugees are begging to speak with you, Your Grace," Spindle said. "I would have dismissed them as a nuisance at an hour like this, but I know you have taken a personal interest more than once. And they are a desperate folk."

"They are, Spindle," Amelia said with a nod. "I will go to them. Knight Captain, I know I can trust you here with this duty."

"My purpose and my pleasure, Your Grace," Farringdon replied with a courtly bow, perfect even clad in his steel plates.

CHAPTER 94

"We love you, Your Grace," said Lowell's mother, still hugging her toddler to her waist. The sleepy boy seemed barely aware of the quiet chaos around him in the night, but his mam and her fellow refugees all had worried faces. "We all do. Coz of you, ain't one of us had an empty belly since we come to your camp. But we are all serfs, indentured to Aubrey."

Amelia looked over their earnest expressions and her heart broke for them. They were afraid they would be left behind when her army retreated on its boats. Whatever else Froster's mercenaries might do, the archduchess knew they would likely vent their frustration at being bested on this small pack of villagers once they learned the "witch from the west" had escaped them.

"Adam, who used to be a ditch digger, he tells us you released him and give him the name Waterman," the scarecrow-thin mother continued. "He's off now, loading barrels on them boats for your men-at-arms. He says his indenture's done and he can settle wherever he pleases in your lands. Is that the truth?"

"It is," Amelia said.

"Then please, Your Grace, release us, too, or take us with you. There ain't no Aubrey Conclave no more. All the guild masters is dead. There's no one to speak our case to or pay any indenture no more. We know stories of Tarningcrest. Beggin' your pardon, but he ain't known to be kind. Not cruel especial, just not kind. He'll see us as chattel, and we'll be packed off to live another generation or even ten as serfs on his land. Some of us were to have free children, our indenture finished with us, but with no conclave records, he won't believe us."

Several others nodded their heads, grimly affirming the fate they were convinced awaited them.

I fear for the petty vengeance of frustrated mercenaries, but that would only be one in an unending series of miseries for these folk, Amelia thought. *And it sounds as if, far from protecting them as his newly acquired subjects, Prince Tarningcrest will only add to their wretchedness.*

Amelia looked at sleepy Lowell and made a decision.

"Lady Spindle, send to Knight Captain Farringdon that a space is to be made on these boats for every one of Aubrey's remaining population, highest to lowest, who wishes to come with us. And explain to him that word is to be passed that each last one of these folk is under my protection. Whoever abuses them will answer to my justice."

"As you say, Your Grace," Spindle said, and she moved away quickly to pass her liege's commands. Amelia looked back to the poor community of desperate survivors and felt a pang of guilt that it had taken her so long to come to their rescue.

If it cannot yield at least some good, then let politics be damned, she thought as they all looked to her as if she were some kind of angel from heaven. A mischievous smile lit her lips for a moment in the fluttering torchlight. If they thought she had done well by them, they had yet to hear true blessings.

"Every one of you must go to the boats in a moment, but before you do, hear me," she said, raising her voice a little so that they would all hear her. They all had to know. "We will not be going back to the Reach just yet. I don't know if you have heard, but these boats will be bearing us to Bridgetown. Once we get there, there will be some while before my Lions are billeted and everyone knows what is happening. While that is the case, you must stay close to the Lions' fires. There you will find proper treatment and meals for yourselves and your children."

THE MANTIS AND THE MIRRORED SKY

The Aubrey folk nodded thankfully, but their arch-duchess was still not finished.

"Once I am in position and able to access my funds, you will be summoned to my factor. He will record your names for the conclave in Dweltford. Be ready when you come to tell the factor, for he will ask your family names as well."

"We is serfs. We don't have family names," one of the refugees said.

"Then you must choose them for yourselves," Amelia told him. "I picked one for Adam Waterman, but you cannot expect me to do that work for all of you. Once you have your name and it is recorded, you will each be given ten guilders in coin and released to whatever future seems right to you, but if ever you wish to seek service with the Reach, my household will take you in. Tell your name and a free place—openly sworn, not indentured—will be found for you. Just tell your names and you will be accepted."

Many of the threadbare folk were openly crying, their cheeks glittering in the night, and one or two rocked on their feet as if they wanted to embrace her or kiss her hand but were too afraid yet to risk the impropriety.

"Thank you, Your Grace," one said almost breathlessly, and the others all joined in. Amelia held up her hands and shook her head.

"All this awaits our escape first. Grab whatever matters to you and head to the flotilla. We are not safe or free just yet, not even I."

They tugged their forelocks and Amelia stepped away, finding Spindle returning swiftly in the rising breeze.

"The Lord sends a breeze to snatch us away from the wolf's jaws," she told her lady.

Spindle smiled at the metaphor. "I hope that's how it seems to them lot," she said, casting a nod southward toward the enemy. "It'd be a real chuckle to see their reaction when they find us gone come sunup. Not that I want to linger around for it."

"No, nor I," Amelia agreed.

In the end, the archduchess boarded the final riverboat as the predawn was turning the black sky to purple and the stars and Rampart were fading. Despite their fears, they had embarked every last man, woman, and child. Even Silvermane and the other horses were safely away. Prince Tarningcrest and the Golden Heron would awake to find nothing of the White Lions but some lonely torches burning out and a scattering of discarded rags or broken tools—that and a bridge no one would be able to cross for many a day.

Amelia looked westward from the stern of her boat to where the night still reigned on the horizon. The Dwelt was back there, and on its banks, an enemy besieged by her other men-at-arms. How long would that conflict last, she wondered. Would the Grand Kingdom force currently shut out of Bridgetown's northern gates be sent west by land to reinforce the dog Robant's incursion into the Reach, despite having their boats "purloined"? Would the Lion Banner Company end up committed in Bridgetown while her land was invaded around the southern tip of the Azures? One of the main purposes of bringing Aubrey into the Reach fully had been to secure that border of her lands, controlling both the north and south banks of the Murr in a single unified defense against Kingdom armies. Instead, it remained a half-open door that could be kicked in at any moment. And somewhere, far beyond the river that was the Reach's deepest artery, Prentice was missing with his chosen men, some fey allies, and an enemy plotting to attack the Reach again from the mysterious west. It was a relief to be rescued, and her husband's return was a joy inexpressible to Amelia's mind, but her future seemed the way it always seemed—utterly uncertain.

Perhaps it would always be so.

From behind her, Farringdon approached quietly. He had shed his armor and was wearing only breeks and a surcoat of soft cotton. He wrapped his arms around her waist and pulled her to him so that they were both looking into the lightening west.

"Pregnant mothers need their rest, so I'm told," he whispered.

"I've heard that as well," she replied, pressing back into him and taking a moment just to enjoy his presence.

"Even the ones who are archduchesses," he persisted.

"Even them?" she asked.

"Even them."

Amelia turned in his arms and kissed him. Then she traced her finger down the line of his crooked nose, tapping his chin at the end.

"Alright, good husband, since we are in private, I will accept your unspoken urging and seek some rest."

He smiled at her and released his hug, taking her by one hand. "A bed of sorts has been prepared. It is mostly old sacks, but I managed to find a bit of soft cloth to cover them with. It should be reasonably comfortable if you can bear the smell."

"I'm sure it will be quite acceptable, husband," she said and followed where he led to a quiet spot between some of the boat's open-deck cargo. She lay down while he promised to keep watch for her so she was not disturbed.

"I think you overestimate your ability to shield me from disturbance or my ability to rest regardless, one of the two," Amelia told him. Nevertheless, she fell rapidly to sleep before the day had even fully dawned. Farringdon strung another sack between two boxes so it sat above her head, shielding her from the sun, and she rested so deeply that when in the late morning a desperate portion of Robant's force thundered past on the north bank, whipping their mounts to foam in full retreat, the archduchess barely stirred. Later, when she was told of the incident, Amelia felt a little disappointed at having missed it, even though she enjoyed the sleep immensely.

"Tell the boatmen to put us up against the north bank a moment," she commanded in the late afternoon. "And find a volunteer. We must send a scout back to see how the other company fares."

CHAPTER 95

As the deluge receded, bodies of all kinds were washed upon the shore, some of them sacrifices, torn apart and long dead, but others twisted and broken by the force of being swept against rocks by the singular floodwater. Many were spearmen, tattooed crewmen fallen from their failed boats. Others had the shape of men but the fur of beasts or skins of insects or serpents. The *brakkis effar* had not survived the failure of the *imzuss* magicks any better than their lesser initiates. The grown huts of the Verdant fey had proved more resilient than Prentice could possibly have imagined, with more than half still in place, but of those that remained, almost all were cracked or broken from their foundations, such that few looked immediately useable for living.

When the wavefront had crashed into the dais, Prentice had expected to be washed away or drowned, ready to accept his own death as the price for the Serpent Witch's end and the breaking of all power to send the mantis into the Reach. As it was, the water washed him from his feet and he was bruised and battered but managed to hold on by the Witch's chain. The serpent's already decapitated body and separated head were washed away. When the tumbling maelstrom had passed, Prentice found himself close to the edge once more, with his arm twisted in the iron links. By the time he had managed to untangle himself, Lyrach appeared from the churned shallows at the foot of the dais, having followed his commander's instruction to the letter.

"Worst bath I ever had," the militiaman sputtered and stood up. Then he slipped and half fell against the stone wall of the platform, crying out in pain. "My foot!? Oh, for sure, it's broken. Hurts like the devil!"

He gingerly leaned back and lifted his right leg out of the water, grimacing.

"Well, looks like it is still on straight at least, Line First," Prentice said with the heartless humor convicts and men-at-arms all shared in moments like this. "Surely it cannot be hurt too bad."

"Bad enough, thank you, Knight Commander," Lyrach retorted, but he laughed, and Prentice joined him. They were alive. Why be bitter about injuries they would survive?

Lyrach took his time making his awkward way out of the shallows, and as he did, Prentice left the platform and walked to the shore by the causeway, collecting three more Fangs who had also managed to shelter behind the lower wall the jetty offered. They were sodden and a little bruised but happy to have survived. Of the Roar who had done so well in keeping up their oversight fire during the assault, nothing could be seen. They had been completely swept away. At least two lost Fangs were washed against the broken huts, but one of them had an obvious wound that must have been caused by a weapon.

"The Inquisition knights," one of the surviving Fangs reported. "They come at us from behind the sleepy fey once the shooting started. You said not to fight the white ones, and that weren't hard, but it seemed a fine thing for us to go after Churchey traitors."

"You did well if you took them on by yourselves," Prentice told the man sincerely. Inxyphos had had nearly fifty men-at-arms by the last count. Elite Church knights, they should have found no trouble dealing with ten Fangs, even with the element of surprise on the Gryphon Company's side.

"Sure, it weren't all of them, Knight Commander," the survivor Fang continued. "Looked like most of them were off keeping their horses ready. They planned an escape of some sort for certain, even before they knew we were here. I'd lay money on that."

"So did they get away? Surely, they did not make the forest before the water caught them," Prentice mused and looked east to see if any horses or men in mail and Church tabards were washed up somewhere in sight. Another of the Fangs answered that question for him in a horrific fashion.

"They fled the same way they escaped us in the grass-lands, My Lord Knight Commander," he said, rolling his shoulder and trying to find a comfortable position for his dented and deformed shield.

"Through the mists?" Prentice looked up the valley to the fallen dragonfly. Its power must not have fully failed before Inxyphos could invoke it for himself. "They have learned the secret."

"They sure *looked* like they knew it, their brother leader man at least," the Fang explained. "I saw him grab one of his fellows from close by like, wrap his arm around him like they were old friends, brothers in arms. Then he thrust one of them serpent bitch daggers straight up under his man's throat. Tore it out like stripping leaves off a switch and waved the blood off the bone edge like he was pointing a scepter at the air. And the mist rose up all around them, rainbow fog, just like before, and his whole lot were disap-peared again, same as."

Prentice nodded, watching his man's face as he absorbed this bitter news. Inxyphos was alive, gone, and knew at least something of the Redlander blood magick—enough to transport his forces away in the midst of this disaster. What other Blood Sect secrets had he learned in his time with the cabal? What was he going to add to the Inquisition's existing store of eldritch knowledge?

"We saw a whole mess of horrors here, Knight Commander," the witness to Inxyphos's actions went on. "Things I expect never to forget, but I'll tell you this for nothing...I haven't ever seen a horror like the way those men in mail just stood there, po faced, and let their bossman kill another one of them just to get them home safe. What kind of a fellow does that? One of the Gryphons, one of my cohort brothers, could kill my wife and child right in front of me, and while I swear I'd do him in for the crimes, I'd still have to force myself to it. I couldn't just slash his throat like that, even for such a betrayal. I just couldn't. And I couldn't just stand and watch someone else of the banner do it. It wasn't like the fey folk, all dreamy like too much drink or healer's laud juice. They just calmly let it happen. I don't know what kind of man can do that, but I couldn't."

"Neither could I, militiaman," Prentice said. He had never heard the term "cohort brother" before, and it pleased him to discover it amongst the militia, but the Fang's grim declaration was as bitter for the knight commander as it should be for every White Lion. No militiaman should be able to treat another like a resource, a useful tool, or piece of livestock.

Whatever the Inquisition are, Prentice thought, *I think none of us knows them as they truly are. Not even I.*

That notion surprised him, and it lurked in the back of his thoughts the rest of the day. With the few survivors of the assault team, he set about finding something Lyrach could use as a crutch while they together all kept watch for any Verdant fey who might have been lurking and feeling vengeful. The main of the destroyed bodies left scattered up against the valley walls were all pale, but it surely could not have been the whole of the settlement's people, Prentice was sure of that much. All but the lowest of the huts clustered on the cliffside had been above the level of the water, for a start.

The survivors helped their hobbling comrade along the rocky north shore to the point where the lake had formerly drained away into the beginning of the Murr River. The old definitions had been transformed by the force of the flood, a new channel washed into the weir-like stones of the lake's east end, and crossing to the south seemed a dicey proposition for the wounded Lyrach with the stronger flow. Or perhaps it had always flowed so strongly, and it was only drawing this close that revealed the danger. While they looked for options, some dazed survivors followed them out from the ruined village.

"Look out," one of the Fangs called, turning to face the approaching fey, sword and shield at the ready. The other two Fangs, who were supporting Lyrach between them while he tried to make a broken piece of pole work as a walking staff, looked over their shoulders. Prentice put his hand to his sword hilt as well, but two arrows flew suddenly over their heads and skittered across the pebbles where they struck in the gap between the militiamen and the sullen crowd of surviving Verdant.

"*Kreff enkreffra,*" a voice called, and from the other side of the water, three Wind Rising stood in their stirrups. Sixty or seventy paces distant, neither Prentice's group nor the rider's pale kin had any doubts how deadly fey archers could be from that range. With the Verdant watching, some of the riders waded their ponies slowly into the flow a short distance, testing the water. They appeared to decide it was too difficult even for their tenacious beasts to risk, and they paused to discuss some other plan, bows still in hand. Two reached into their saddles and began passing something back and forth, while the third kept close watch on the north bank. Then something unintelligible was shouted and an arrow was launched on a high, arcing course over the water. There was a length of twine trailing behind it. The riders were sending them a rope. As he realized what it was, Prentice watched it fall, the arrow smacking into the strand not far from where he stood. As soon as the twine began to collapse behind it, the water began to drag it away, and the knight commander dove painfully to his knees to snag the end before it was lost. Once he had it in his hands, he realized that the twine was surely too thin to take all their weight and drag them through the water. Even one man would likely be too heavy and their armor surely too much of a burden.

Looking up to his would-be rescuers, Prentice heard them call something more in fey speech, and then one of them began to make winding gestures with his free hand. Smiling, Prentice hauled on the twine, and as it started to coil in his dripping gloves, he saw the riders feeding a much heavier cable attached to the other end of the twine. With slow, continuous motion, cautious in case rough handling caused the lesser twine to unravel from the heavier, Prentice drew the cable to himself. Once the rope was in his hands, he lifted it up to show the fey on the other side.

"We have help to cross, Reachermen," he declared over his shoulder, and the two helping Lyrach stumbled closer on the uncomfortable bank. The one keeping guard backed away, managing to look menacing despite his awkward steps.

"One at a time, d'you reckon, Knight Commander?" one of the two helpers asked.

"We might do well to cast off our brigandines to reduce the load," Lyrach suggested.

Looking across the water, Prentice saw the fey riders share the other end of the rope between two of them and loop that around the horns of their saddles. He smiled.

"I suspect they will be happy to take us all as a single lot," he said, "Armor and all."

It took some arranging to fit all five survivors onto the end of the cable, each man holding on with enough space not to spoil the others. It would surely have been safer to go only one at a time, or even by twos, and discarding their armor would have made the matter easier on the horses, no doubt. But Prentice did not trust the Verdant fey not to give way to vindictive despair, making some kind of suicidal rush to take one of these unfamiliar men-at-arms into the dejected afterlife with them, absorbing arrows to overwhelm the last man or two left on this side. And once they had crossed to the other side, there was no telling whether further combat awaited, so yielding their armor was not desirable either. The best option of another bad selection of possibilities was for them all to cross at once.

I am forced to make a lot of these sorts of decisions, Prentice told himself, smirking wearily for a moment.

The five Lions waded into the fast flow as far as they dared, and Prentice gave a signal. The fey took the slack, and all five men were suddenly yanked off their feet as the ponies began to back away from the other bank. Lyrach shouted in pain again, his foot likely striking the bottom for a moment, but otherwise the crossing was methodical and much swifter than they expected. Each one supported his fellows as best he could, and while they all swallowed more water than they wanted, none came near to drowning. On the other side they fished their soaked bodies out of the shallows and helped Lyrach onto his one good foot as well. His "crutch" was lost in the crossing, no doubt washed away into the forest. Perhaps one day it would float all the way to the meeting with the Dwelt. Prentice wondered if his Banner Company would even beat it there. The Gryphons were safe enough right now, but they were yet far from home.

From the other bank, the crowd of Verdant fey survivors began to keen, a seemingly wordless sound that reminded Prentice of the Wind Rising fey's song of mourning. The pale faces turned away, as if turning their back on an escaped enemy, and their rhythmic wail began to echo off the cliff wall. Looking to the fey riders who were coiling their rope and twine, Prentice nodded his thanks. The fey of the Azure Mountains returned his nod in their fashion and then looked across the water at their grieving kin. Their expressions were not hate-filled—not exactly—but they were pitiless.

CHAPTER 96

Prentice sat on a boulder, listening to the marching beat of the company's drums as they advanced across the grass toward the head of the valley. He watched them coming on, the silver and blue Gryphon Banner at their head. Beside the colors, the vanguard was carrying something else above their heads, something that Prentice struggled to identify. As they drew closer, however, he realized it was a person, and soon enough he could see the tonsured head of Brother Whilte, bobbing above the marching militia.

"Quite the triumphant progress," he said as Sergeant Gennet approached and saluted. Prentice stood to return the respect.

"The men insisted, and I saw no reason to deny them," the sergeant explained, apparently uncertain as to whether his commander would take affront at the breach of usual discipline. Prentice only shook his head, watching the lead cohort carefully handling the chaplain down to the grass and stones.

"It was the damnedest thing, My Lord," Gennet continued. "One moment I figured we'd done our duty, and it was time to beat retreat; the next, that wave is bearing down on us and we're sure to die. Then Whilte rushes to the left flank—he'd been in the midst of us the whole battle up to then—shouting "no" at beast-men and holding them in place with his words so Fangs could smack them about. Then he's there, prophet stick held

high and praying like the voice of God, and the water, it just
went around us."

Gennet gave Prentice a doubtful glance, as if he expected
the knight commander to scoff or something similar, but then
he shook his head and continued his story.

"It didn't take long, but for that one space, I swear the water
was over the height of my head. It just flowed past me, sweeping
the Redlanders away like sticks in a stream. From hard-pressed
to saved in the blink of an eye. It was like that story sacrists tell
when God split the sea for folks—walls of water. I've already
heard men calling the chaplain Moses Whilte, you know."

The company's new Moses clumped happily over, smiling
with some embarrassment at the praise and back-slapping he
was receiving at every turn.

"They insisted I shouldn't have to walk the whole distance,
My Lord Knight Commander," he said, tugging his forelock.
Then he looked Prentice up and down and seemed to notice
his waterlogged state. "You had a tougher time of it, I see. Sorry
I wasn't there to help."

"You helped all I needed, mighty prophet," Prentice said.
"Men will tell of your deeds for ages to come."

The chaplain winced as if in pain, but Prentice only chuckled.

"Fear not, chaplain, I promise my awe will not let me forget
that you are but a man."

"How many of you were wounded?" Whilte asked.

"More died than survived," Prentice told him grimly. "But
Lyrach needs your attention most urgently. Were you the only
one carried down with us, or is our erstwhile guide still here?"

"Still trussed like a roast, Knight Commander, and brought
along," Gennet confirmed. "You want I should have him
freed?"

Prentice nodded.

"Have him brought along once he has the feeling back in his
legs. We have another confrontation yet. And start fetching the

wounded and others as well, if you have not already given the order."

With no word from the stag rider elder, and with the swiftness of their assault, no other deer-riding fey had emerged from the forest before the flood. Since then, a growing band had been coming forth from the dense green, many of them wet and some clearly injured. They were ranging about in the narrow sward on the south side between the end of the valley and the first trees. Whatever they thought to do in response to a battle they had not known was happening, they were contained for the moment by Benjamin's *keshiyaa*, who were continuing in their assigned duty, horses riding back and forth, bows in hand and ready. With their place being farthest of all from the obelisk, the Wind Rising had been the best able to respond to its collapse. By the time the rush of water reached them, most had been able to retreat up to a relative high point, and the valley opening out just before that had dissipated much of the force. As a consequence, only a handful of the Azure Mountain archers had been lost. Their herd of spare mounts had not fared so well, however, since riders who barely had time for themselves could not rush back to save the animals left farther off, cropping grass. Most of the *keshiyaa* had lost one or more changeover rides. The injury to personal wealth was further coloring their already poor attitude towards their kin, as far as Prentice could see. He walked to a point close behind their rough line that blocked entry to the valley and waited until Benjamin noticed him and rode up.

"Dahyoor should bring you a horse, *kreff enkreffra*," said the *keshkirae*. "Elders do not approach *keshiyaa* at war on foot."

"*Palpolon* elder, remember?" Prentice answered. Benjamin shrugged. "Dahyoor will be fetching them up, along with our friend from the traitor kin. How fares the *keshiyaa*?"

"They watch for a hunter's moment, but the Verdant are canny and stay beyond hunting bowshot."

Prentice assumed hunting bowshot was more accurate shooting, rather than the raining volley shots of massed Wind Rising riders. While he would not begrudge the horse archers taking potshots at the Verdant, he was glad it wasn't happening. After the destruction of the last hours, there was no telling what the grief-stricken deer riders might do. Every now and then another wail of mourning echoed across the water.

Benjamin rode a short distance to join some of the others of the *keshiyaa* as Dahyoor and the Verdant elder arrived, the pale fey now released but his limbs still stiff and weakened. He staggered with every second step it seemed. His expression was enraged, and he approached Prentice with a fixated glare, as if he intended to avenge himself barehanded. Behind him a short distance came Corporal Guillam, with the removed bonds slung over his shoulder and a skinner's knife in a plain leather scabbard in hand. He had had to cut some of the tight knots away, apparently.

The fallen fey leader stalked up to Prentice with ungainly steps and unleashed a tirade in his own tongue. His arms waved with his anger, as they had so often before, but it was clearly too painful to stretch them fully, so every gesture seemed misshapen and somehow crippled. The knight commander felt the image fitted well to the man's spirit and character.

"He accuses you of lying and betraying your pledge," Dahyoor translated, his calm voice contrasting distinctly with the elder's tone. "He says he hopes the Lioness devours you for breaking your pledge in her name. He says…and he says…other things."

Prentice wondered what kind of threats or insults Dahyoor found too extreme to translate.

"Tell him it is done," Prentice said. "As my word requires, not one of ours struck down one of his."

Dahyoor did as instructed, and the elder exploded, his voice becoming shrill and his gestures beating the air like a mad prize fighter. He pointed to the collapsed obelisk and the broken dragonfly, resting now half out of the water. He gestured to the cliffside huts and then at the forest.

No, not the forest, Prentice thought. *He's gesturing at his erstwhile followers whom he had planned to take under his leadership again. Little chance of that now.*

Prentice felt no sympathy for the vaguely pathetic figure, now broken on the wreckage of his own failed cunning. Dahyoor started to translate the raging fool's words once more, but Prentice cut him off.

"Just tell him that the blood that bound me binds him and them." He pointed to the forest riders watching from their safe vantage. "Tell him that he must tell *them*, or when we march from here, they will suffer for his oath."

Dahyoor passed the message, and the elder finally stopped shouting, staring at Prentice in sheer disbelief. He ground out fresh words with quieter menace.

"He says you killed many of his folk," Dahyoor explained. "You broke the stone. You brought down the gold and glass creature of rainbows. The oath is broken."

"If I have violated the oath, why do I still breathe?" Prentice responded, cold eyes fixed on the incensed fey. "No blood claims my life. The *imzuss* are gone and your folk are free. Pay your debt and be glad. Go tell your people what they must do."

By the time Dahyoor had translated the entire word, the elder's shoulders had slumped, and he blinked a few times before turning toward the forest and slouching off to his former allies, the ones who had exiled him for his previous failure.

"Miserable bugger ought to be thankful," Guillam said, coming closer now that the conversation between leaders was over. "He was with the wounded and the mules. Whilte's miracle saved him as well, even though he didn't deserve it."

"Did you deserve it, Corporal?" Prentice asked absently as he watched the milk-skinned fey taking his message to the forest riders.

"Lord no, Knight Commander!" Guillam said happily. "I kenned that wave had come to wash me away to the judgement, like the sacrists all said would happen. Well not exactly, like. They all said a baptism was supposed to wash my soul, but I didn't feel like that one was going to make me too clean."

Prentice chuckled and looked down at his sore feet for a moment.

"Did you want me to go to the sergeant?" Guillam asked in a much more serious tone than was typical. "This looks like it might go awry. You might want some Gryphons rallied at your back."

"Not just yet, thank you, Corporal," Prentice said sincerely. "This is a fey matter for now. We will let Benjamin have the honor of dealing with it first. But be ready; I might change my mind quickly."

Guillam saluted and then stood silent next to Prentice. There was the crunch of footsteps on some rock somewhere behind them and Solft's voice called out.

"Do you have a moment, Baron Ash?"

"Not now, Master," Prentice replied without turning.

"I promise it is important," Solft pressed, uncharacteristically insistent.

"As is this, Master," Prentice retorted. The elder had reached his people and a conversation had begun.

"It really is very…"

"Be quiet, Master Solft, or I will have Corporal Guillam here drag you off."

Prentice did not expect Solft was being frivolous and likewise doubted he would actually have to carry through with his threat. Nonetheless, the conversation he was watching at a distance carried the entire weight of his company's future. How or even whether they ever returned to the Reach might be decided in the next few moments. The elder was looking up at another Verdant warrior mounted on a stag, though one far less impressively antlered than the Monarch of the Forest had been.

They were arguing as savagely as the elder had berated Prentice. The elder held out his hand, demanding something, and the rider shook his head. The elder persisted, hand still out. The rider looked to some fellows nearby, some of whom looked to be fey women, although there appeared no distinction between men and women as to who rode a stag and who a hind.

At last, something was handed to the rider, and he passed it over to the elder, still on foot. It was the fallen rider's sword, the inwardly curved blade flashing in the midday sun as he drew it from some kind of animal-skin cover. Holding the weapon in one hand, the elder turned on his heel and began marching directly back toward the Wind Rising fey and Prentice.

"What's he think he's doin'?" Guillam asked. "Is he goin' to attack us all by himself?"

"He is going to prove that the oath is true," Prentice said, sure in his heart that his guess was correct.

"He can have no honor. They will not let it to him," Dahyoor said, adding a fey's insight. "All he can do is save them from his error."

"Yes," agreed Benjamin, who had walked his horse closer again.

"What's going to happen then?" Guillam asked, seeming nervous. The elder had crossed nearly half the distance now and had raised his sword high, as if he thought to charge the rest of the space for one mighty strike.

"He is about to die," Prentice said, convinced it was true, only wondering how and whether he should allow the broken fey to make an attack first to see if the power of their oath would slay him outright. Would the other Verdant fey believe if a *keshiyaa* arrow or Guillam's sword took him? As it happened, the decision was not Prentice's.

From the forest edge, there was a whipping sound, and a swift-moving sling stone arced at the elder's legs, smashing one out from under him. He collapsed to the grass and half raised himself to look back in the deer riders' direction. Another stone whipped from the treeline, and another, until a hail battered the elder's body permanently to the ground. It was possible the fey man was not dead, but Prentice did not think he would live long from his wounds.

A lone fey voice called from the forest, the words barely audible in the distance.

"His oath dies with him," Dahyoor translated. "The forest remains death for *kreff* and the traitors who make peace with them."

Prentice hung his head wearily.

"What does that mean?" Guillam asked.

"It means the path home is going to be as hard as the way here," Prentice said, looking up as he rubbed at the back of his head. He was tired. It had been a long night. "We have to go give Sergeant Gennet the good news and start a full assessment of what supplies we have. I doubt the good folk across the water will want to sell us anything, so we will have to be rationing right from the get go, I suppose."

Or raiding from them, he thought but did not add. The White Lions were never supposed to steal from common folk, not even in enemy territory. Prentice and Archduchess Amelia both had always had it in mind that pillage and plunder would be forbidden to the Western Reach's militia. The problem was, when the Lions had been conceived, the notion of being this far from home with a hard march ahead never occurred to either of them. He sighed and turned, almost crashing bodily into Master Solft, the waiting scholar having crept forward impatiently, seeking the knight commander's attention.

"Really, Baron, this is quite urgent," the shorter man pressed, and Prentice felt his temper slip more than a little.

"You are a distractable little fellow, Master Solft," he said harshly, his voice rising. "Your capacity for fixation on your own interests is well attested, but even you must see the dire state we find ourselves in. The Lions are far from home with only bitter paths ahead of us. Whatever you have to discuss must wait!"

"No, it cannot!" Solft responded, if anything even more firmly than Prentice. "Brother Whilte requires your attention immediately!"

"Brother Whilte?" Prentice wondered, and was pleased he managed not to think, *what now?*

CHAPTER 97

"How long has he been like this?"
Prentice was staring at Whilte, who was standing, insensible, with his one good foot in the edge of the lake water, facing east.

"Only a short while," Solft assured the knight commander.

"He wasn't tryin' to baptize folks again, was he?" Guillam asked, having accompanied Prentice rather than fulfilling the order to round up Gennet and the other senior officers of the company. "After this morning's flood I would've kenned the boys have had enough of water and dunkings."

"Did I not give you orders, Corporal?" Prentice remarked as he studied Whilte. The chaplain's eyes were moving under their lids like they had in the spring in the deserted village.

"I passed them along to a line first, Commander," Guillam said casually. "See, the sergeant's already on his way with Porth. Might as well just stay here with you and watch."

Prentice scowled but was too distracted to make more of the issue.

"What is he holding in his other hand?" he asked as he moved around the statue-like figure of his chaplain and friend. Whilte's right hand was on his staff, as always, holding much of his weight. His left hand hung by his side on the water side of his body, obscured by the folds of his tunic.

"This," said Solft, and he lifted a piece of the mask that Prentice had torn from the smaller obelisk in the falls in Radengon Beyond Dwelt. It surprised Prentice to see it was broken.

"When did you pull it apart?" he asked. He would not have credited Solft with smashing an ancient artifact. The scholar's life was a fight to preserve the forgotten things. Splitting the mask seemed so uncharacteristic.

"I didn't, My Lord," Solft said earnestly, holding up the half piece in his hands. "That's what I have been trying to say. The mask was in my luggage on Helperman, my mule. After the wave passed, the poor beast was beside itself. I went to calm him, and he reared. He's a mule—stubborn, of course—but he's never done that before. As he did, one of the pieces fell to the ground out of my bags. This one, in fact, just like this."

Prentice turned to look at the scholar, cocking an eyebrow at the overly detailed story before squatting down as near as he dared come to Whilte, trying to see the other piece, the one in the chaplain's hand.

"Baron Ash, I put the thing away for travel," Solft said. "I've not looked at it since before the ambush on the heights. With the upland's haunted aspect and the odd powers coming from the Murr, I didn't feel safe to bring it out."

"Wise decision, I am sure."

Prentice was barely listening to the story's details. He was more concerned with Whilte's condition. The last vision had been triggered by a message from the Verdant elder, though it had brought additional, divine information with it. That elder was dead now, or dying, so from where was this trance coming?

"You don't understand me, My Lord," Solft persisted. "The mask was in one piece, wrapped in parchment and that wrapped in a leather bundle tied tightly with twine. I had stopped the eye holes with mud, remember? Tell me, do you see mud now?"

He held up his half of the mask, and while he looked cautiously, Prentice could see daylight through the honeycomb holes in the carved insect eye.

"Someone has been interfering with it?" he asked. "Perhaps using it for themselves?"

"I don't see how. I tend to wander about, but Helperman is so often with me."

Prentice looked around himself involuntarily, reflexive suspicion making him feel as if a spy or traitor might be lurking close by. Knowing the sensation for foolish paranoia, he forced himself to ignore it, pushing it away by force of will. As he glanced about, though, he noticed many of the Verdant fey, gathered on the opposite side of the lake, still watching him and the rest of the Reach forces. Every now and then the mourning "song" could be heard softly upon the breeze. They were several hundred paces distant on the north bank, far enough that Prentice did not really fear any sling attack, but the calm way they were staring was unnerving, nonetheless. Likely they were fearful themselves and keeping watch to see what these destructive invaders might do next. He stood and looked at his friend's face. It was serious but not showing any pain or fear.

Well, we cannot leave you like this, Brother, Prentice thought, and he remembered the last time. He was about to reach out and touch the enthralled clergyman when he also remembered that the last vision had been prompted by a small spring and a broken plinth. This one was happening in the much more powerful lake and the shadow of the fallen dragonfly. It might be somewhat more dangerous.

"Corporal Guillam," Prentice called and turned to see Gennet and his other summoned officers approaching, not to mention yet another growing crowd of onlooking militia, likely drawn more by the fey across the lake than the chaplain's odd condition. "How would you like the free chance to body tackle your commander and drag him away from this water with no consequences? Maybe even a thank you?"

"Would I what!" Guillam said like an eager apprentice being let out to visit his sweetheart. "I'd give the last of me chew for a shot like that."

"You said you were all out of chew."

"Alright, the last of me next batch."

"Well, if I go vision-headed like the chaplain here, you pull me away," Prentice told him.

Guillam thumped his brigandine in salute and started to peer closely at the knight commander's face. Despite his jesting, his expression looked serious and not the least bit eager. Prentice touched his fingers to Whilte's staff hand, and the chaplain's eyes opened.

"A light, a path through the forest and all the way to home," the brother declared eagerly. "A road of light, growing dim, but not yet dark. We must be swift or lose it forever."

Prentice looked directly in Whilte's now opened eyes but was not entirely convinced he was being seen. He gently reached for the other piece of broken mask in the chaplain's hand, careful not to set his foot in the lake water, even a little.

"Best give me this to me," he said mildly, glad he was still wearing his fighting gauntlets and would not have to touch the mystic object with bare skin.

"No," Whilte declared and snatched his hand back, holding the iron fragment up in the daylight over the lake. "Trust me, I can see it. There is a way home. The Lord can light our way, but we must go swiftly and with faith. It is too dark for us under the forest any other way."

"Brother, whatever we must do, you can explain it to us once we step back from the lake and you give me that little bit of iron."

Whilte shook his head. Prentice watched him closely, fearful that whatever the vision was, it had left him possessed. Having spent time "in" the waters himself, and knowing how many slain *brakkis effar* there were about, not to mention other Blood Sect cultists and sacrificed fey, Prentice had little trust that a vision born of this moment was not treacherous. And one telling him to rush was doubly untrustworthy to his mind.

"We have not much time," Whilte insisted, and Prentice could see his eyes looked clear, that he was in his right mind, but still the knight commander would not be pressed. He had led his men to the end of the Murr on this quest. He was done gambling their lives on hope and duty. His only duty now *was* to their lives.

"Trust," Whilte said.

"I do trust you...," Prentice began, but Whilte cut him off.

"Not me. Trust the one who showed you the light under the willow when lion and serpent first clashed in the Reach. Trust the one who loosed your chains."

Prentice blinked. In all his life he had told only a few people of that vision, the first of all the ones he had seen since the Redlanders came upon the Western Reach. Two were women—his liege, Amelia, and his love, Righteous. The only other two were his closest friends. One was in Dweltford and the other waited for him in the afterlife. Prentice trusted each of them utterly. None would have revealed the details of this vision to anyone, not even Whilte.

"'His word is a light to my feet,'" Prentice recited from the scripture, unsure where he had first learned the adage.

"It will be," Whilte said with a beatific smile.

Prentice released his touch and stepped back, pausing for just a moment to see if breaking contact would somehow return the brother to his trance or otherwise stop what was happening. When nothing changed, he turned to his men.

"Sergeant, corporals, gather the Gryphons, every last one," he shouted, feeling himself smile a little drunkenly. Was he really doing this? "We are going home. Fetch all our animals and the wounded. Anyone who cannot walk gets carried. I'll put a man on my own shoulders if need be."

"What's going on, Knight Commander?" Gennet asked, his loyalty clearly being stretched by the possibility that his leader had gone mad.

"Brother 'Moses' there is about to part the sea for us once more, and like the Israelites, we must be ready to hurry across before the waters close again."

Gennet, Porth, and Guillam shook their heads, eyes wide in wonder, and they looked past Prentice to Whilte who was now lifting his prophet's rod into the air. A glow was beginning to form around it, like the reflection of the sunlight upon the water, but softer, not so sharp upon the eyes.

"Quickly, Reachermen," Prentice shouted. "I will take the word to Benjamin's *keshiyaa*. When I return, I expect us to be ready to leave this valley, and I mean never to come back."

CHAPTER 98

The little fort on the eastern bank of the Dwelt was no more than wreckage now, as the second White Lion Company policed the area, stacking up the slain and accounting for their own wounded. After boasting that they would hold the earth and log-walled encampment until doomsday, Duke Robant's fort had broken within a sparse hour and a half once the militia marched to the attack. Whatever further reinforcements they had expected after the Grand Kingdom duke moved in his whole company of knights never eventuated. The newly minted company of Lions—the militia that was supposed to have been commanded by Knight Commander Baron Ash—had lined up by cohorts at dawn, following Sergeant Franken's command under Lady Dalflitch's leadership. Baroness Righteous would have had the right to command, given her status, and in truth a large part of her wanted to, but her first loyalty was to her two babies. It was sacrifice enough, as she saw it, that she had brought them south with a wetnurse. Much as she might long to order Lions to avenge her husband on Robant's force, she chose the path of mother first.

"Look close, girls," Righteous said to her charges, the trainee Lace Fangs, as she led them around the small fort while it was being put into order post battle.

The assault had been expected to be difficult but not uncertain. Then, shortly after dawn, just as the order to begin the attack was about to be given, a glow of rainbow-like light had been seen over the tops of the log walls. Fearing magick, Franken had given the word for them to hold back and watch. The glow faded, and for a short while everything was as it had been. Then the gates were flung wide, and a small column of riders had emerged, galloping hard. Expecting attack, Franken and the Lions had waited, but almost immediately the column had turned south toward the Murr and the Azure Mountain foothills. Later, they would be seen riding east along the riverside back into the Grand Kingdom.

Not one to miss a golden opportunity, Franken had ordered an immediate foot charge, something the Lions rarely practiced but were capable of all the same. The pike and halberd had reached the open gate before all the remaining knights in the fort even knew that a battle was on. The rest had been swift, brutal, and utterly one-sided. Of the two hundred or so men-at-arms within, about fifty were slain, another thirty or forty wounded, and the rest surrendered.

"You want us to look at this?" asked Daisy, turning her nose up at the dead who were laid out in a row, receiving rites from a sacrist chaplain whose name Righteous did not know.

"Indeed, I do, my fillies," Righteous said, though the term was far more an affectionate one now than it had been at the start of summer. "The day will come—not *might* come, *will*—when her grace will need you to defend her, and it will look like this. It will be grim and filled with death. It'll smell like a cesspit had a child with a butcher's shop, and it'll look just as bad. You need to be ready for that, 'cause while you're turning your nose up like a proper lady, the last assassin—the one hiding behind the curtain and waiting for you to drop your guard—is about to spring."

The trainees all nodded, earnestly absorbing every word. Righteous watched them make the effort to remain dignified and not turn away, but it was clearly not easy. Why should it be? This was the part of war no song ever told about and no monument ever commemorated. This was as ugly as it got.

"Here, Prancer," an anonymous militiaman with a crop of dirty blonde hair called, whistling at the young women out of place in their simple but elegant blue overdresses. "If it's too much for your delicate stomachs, I'm sure me and my mate can distract you. Be much sweeter, I promise."

"You'll be bloody lucky," one of the women retorted but was cut off by a short, discrete cough. She turned to see Lady Dalflitch, standing as poised as if at her own wedding. Righteous smirked as the beautiful seneschal's imperious gaze swept over the militiamen, silencing them, before reaching the student maids.

"Baroness Righteous has instilled in you the steely spirit that is the core of a Lace Fang," Dalflitch said, teaching as naturally as any governess. "That *is* the 'fang,' as it were. Now we must garb that fang in lace, which is the reserve and dignity of a lady. Archduchess Amelia has faced princes while dressed only in rags and the muck from the floor of a stable, yet her poise, her dignity, her courtly manner shamed every lady in Rhales. So it must be with you, too. Let louts catcall as they will. They are no more to you than a mutt in its kennel. You need never hear or see them except in the service of your mistress."

The girls all curtseyed in nearly perfect manner. It was one of the first skills Dalflitch had taught them, and many of them were already better than Righteous at the simple-seeming motion. Dalflitch acknowledged them with a nod of her head and moved on, inspecting, with Franken slightly behind her and Solomon at his elbow. 'Duelist' had become the company's chief messenger on the march south, not quite ready to take up a place in the Claws or Fangs but far past being consigned to the position of mere drummer. Lady Dalflitch had even begun to teach him how to ride a horse.

"What the hell's that?" an alarmed voice called, and everyone looked to the sodden depression that took up the whole south side of the captured compound. Like a pond full of nothing more than mud puddles, no one had understood it when they saw it, though they noted that many of the prisoners either feared or loathed it. There was a single post set up in the middle, with a bug mask on it like the one Prentice had found in the swamp near Dweltford. On seeing it and being reminded of her still missing husband, Righteous had furiously commanded it be taken down and smashed. A militiaman had made two steps down into the mud to fetch it and slipped on a body half buried in the muck. As he clambered out, he found others. All the mud covered them, it seemed. Likely, they were rivermen who had been enslaved to dig the odd water feature in the first place. Franken had called the man back and asked that they be let to wait until a sacrist skilled in dealing with such things could be fetched. Words like black magicks and Redlanders were whispered.

Now, the mask on its post seemed to be glowing. Righteous watched, wary of a multihued glow like the one that had heralded Robant's escape. It was possible the whole bastion was some kind of magickal trap designed to kill Reachermen. This light, though, was not like the earlier rainbow light. This was sunlight like the healthy glow of a spring day. The mask atop its post seemed to be heating up, becoming first dull red, then bright, then glowing golden such that it looked ready to melt. Militiamen scrambled backwards from the pond, fearfully watching what was happening. The glow was almost too bright to look upon, and then the mask *did* begin to melt, dripping apart like fiery oil.

Where the droplets struck the mud, a steaming fog arose, no more than the height of a man's knees, and from within that fog came a sound like the burbling of a stream. The sound soon grew to a rushing noise, like a river over rocks, and water burst forth from the foot of the post, flowing into the pond and turning the half-hearted mud pool barely covering the corpses into a full body of water, suffused in every part by the softening mist that glowed with sunlight. Through that cloud, from post to the very edge of the water, a deeper glow formed together, like a pathway of fireflies or golden will-o'-the-wisps. Walking that path, staff above his head like a holy man in a cathedral's stained glass came Brother Whilte, his filthy clothes wreathed in light. He walked on the surface of the new water until he stood on the pond's edge, then turned back to face the post now missing its mask.

Following the same glowing path across the water came two, then four, then a whole first cohort of Lions, marching in column. Their armor was as filthy as Whilte's clothes, and many had faces that looked drawn and pinched with hunger and thirst. Their skin was darkened from days in the sun, and there was a hard, unyielding look in their eyes. Righteous knew that look, and she did her best to still her hopeful heart as she watched a miracle occur. She wanted to hope, but could not bear to be disappointed, if that was what was coming. Better to be patient and suffer a small fall from bad news than to rise to the heights of hope and then be thrown down.

I have been prayin' though, she thought, and fearfully wondered if it had been enough. The sacrist that had blessed her babies had told her that "enough" was not a wise word to use with God's love and mercy, but that only sounded like so much sermon talk to Righteous.

Horses began to emerge on the sunlight pathway, with fey archer riders, and their hooves struck splashes as they galloped for dry land. After what must have been at least fifty horsemen, interspersed with more marching Lions and other animals, one of the fey archers turned his mount aside and pulled up in front of Franken and Solomon.

"Do you command?" he asked, and the sergeant looked to the Lady Dalflitch, standing as awestruck as all the rest but as reserved as she no doubt felt able to be. The fey rider turned to her.

"You are not the Lioness mother," he said, noting her hair, it seemed. Dalflitch's sable mane would never let her be mistaken for the fairer-haired archduchess.

"She is some way away," Dalflitch said politely. "I am her lady."

If that was of interest to the fey rider, he gave no indication. He looked upward to the east where the few peaks of the southern Azures could be seen.

"The mountains sing, the Wind Rising," he said and smiled broadly. With no further explanation, he rode out of the fort, and Righteous wondered if he would ever be seen again.

After a short while, no more fey riders emerged, and the men afoot, including some ostlers handling a number of half-dead-seeming mules, trickled away as well. Righteous watched them emerge and struggle to get their animals over the path, using their hands to shield the cantankerous creature's eyes. A single fey man who looked almost mummified, so tightly was his skin stretched over his bones, emerged leading Prentice's first horse, the buckskin with the dark mane, and Righteous bit the inside of her cheek. She sniffed once. Her man's horse wasn't coming home led by another because he was safe, she was certain.

I won't never forgive him, she thought, unable to express her fear any better way, just before the last Lion, the man who had also been the first, came riding out on the road over the water. As dirty as his men, skin darker than she imagined it could ever be, and missing one of the spaulders on his armor, came Knight Commander Baron Prentice Ash, riding his newer horse, the red bay with the white socks. He stopped in front of Brother Whilte and dismounted wearily, clapping his hand on the chaplain's shoulder. Something heavily liquid, like dirty wax, dripped from the fingers of Whilte's left hand. Then Prentice lifted his other hand and wrapped it around Whilte's right upon the staff. Prentice gently brought the rod down to the ground, and Whilte seemed almost to collapse into the knight commander's arms. The light vanished, but the water in the pond remained, glinting in the suddenly less bright sun.

"Thank you, Brother," Prentice said, his voice audible for those watching close by. Whilte nodded and let himself be handed off to one of the militiamen who had just marched out of a sunlit fog as if they had been crossing a log bridge over a country stream. Righteous watched her husband look up at the amazed faces watching him from every vantage of the now overflowing bastion. He scanned them and smiled with obvious relief. Then his eyes found Righteous, and it was as if his sight alone lifted her off the ground. She took two steps involuntarily, ready to run straight to him.

Fool skirts, she thought, hating that they would slow her down, and she remembered her students standing around her. Without even knowing she was doing it, she cast a glance at Dalflitch, meeting her eye. Although the lady-in-waiting was clearly as enraptured with the event as Righteous felt, still her back was straight, her hands hidden in her wing sleeves, and her dignity undiminished. Righteous straightened her own posture and put her shoulders back.

You are a baroness, now, she told herself. With the barest of hand gestures to ensure that her lace half-mask was in place, she walked delicately to where her husband was watching. Pausing the proper distance in front of him, she curtseyed, and when she reached the bottom of her dip, he bowed to her. Then they both stood straight once more.

"You are dirty and late, my husband," Righteous said formally, as if speaking at an afternoon picnic.

"I am, my wife," Prentice replied to her. He reached up and stroked the neck of his horse. "You've not met my friend here. Allow me to introduce you. This is Boots."

She could see his eyes glittering with his adoration as he spoke, and it made her shiver in the warm sun. These were the best moments in all her life. How had this mighty man noticed Cutter the street knife? She didn't care. He had, and now he was hers, just as she was his.

"I'm sure your horse is very nice, but your children have been growing quite impatient with their father's absence. How long did you expect them to wait to be given their names?"

"Children?" he asked her, and she felt herself smirk with mischievous delight.

"Twins, a boy and a girl," she explained with a nod. "Quite the handfuls. No doubt they take after their father."

She looked at him as his expression seemed to fill with a stream of thoughts. Then he simply beamed, and destroying all her carefully crafted decorum, seized her up and swung her around in his arms. Boots whickered quietly and turned his head away from the sudden whirl of her skirts. Then Prentice kissed her—not with the wild, passionate kisses that would come later, in private, but sincere, tired, and truthful.

"You are a miracle of God, Baroness Righteous Ash," he said, and then kissed her again. Righteous closed her eyes and let it happen, but from over her shoulder she heard Dalflitch giving yet another lesson in decorum.

"There are times, rare though they are," she was saying, "when even the courtliest reserve must give way to some emotion. You will have to learn your own judgement for each case."

EPILOGUE

"And must the martyr expire? Or is partial blood sufficient?"

"A question I never thought to ask. My apologies, Sanguine."

The soft-seeming, dumpy, true head of the Inquisition turned to the knight in his silvered mail and fresh surcoat. The brother elder had been much disheveled and far from dignified when he and his escort had ridden into the rectory stables in Otney three days previously. Now he was restored to his former self, it seemed, clean shaven again, mail polished and gleaming in the lamplight. Even his limp was gone, no doubt having received some healing.

You are making a number of apologies since your return, Inxyphos, Sanguine thought as he returned his attention to the fresh cadaver upon the stone-topped wooden table. Tied in place, with his mouth gagged, the anonymous man was truly not long dead, and his passing had been excruciating. Sanguine's attentions were far more focused upon the man's injuries than his sufferings. He studied the precise cuts for placement and execution. In a moment he would summon back his scribe, who would create exacting diagrams of the martyr's condition for posterity.

On a second table not too far away, another body, fully alive but no less blood soaked, was making a series of agonized groans, interspersed with guttural screams. Unlike the first, this one had not been gagged but had a brass funnel forced between his teeth through which sacrificial ichor had been poured. Under its influence, empowered by blood sorcery, the man who had once been human was now a monstrosity with a toothed beak, tendril-like fingers, and legs like the hind legs of a dog sprouting from a hairy torso. Yellowed eyes glared madly at the ribs of the ceiling vault above.

"Is it always like this?" Sanguine asked.

"So their priestesses insisted," Inxyphos confirmed. "I saw the process done many times and participated twice."

Sanguine nodded and held out his hand for the vicious blade which Inxyphos had just used to ritually draw power from the one man and provide it for the transformation of the second. More tool than weapon, the heavy bone dagger was serrated on its edge, which was further enhanced with a sharpened copper strip that became a wire to wrap around the handle. A crude thing, apparently carved from a thigh bone, perhaps of a horse or similar. Looking closely, Sanguine could see the ancient writing his institution knew as the Lifeblood Prayer embossed in tiny sigils. Even those seemed unrefined when compared to the millennium-old records of the originals contained in the Vault's library. While the Broken Kings' descendants remembered some things the Inquisition had forgotten, they had lost much more to the depredations of time.

Good.

Sanguine thrust the blade's point into the mad, failed beast-man's belly, allowing him to die, though not speedily. Both martyrs had served their purpose, but Sanguine was not being deliberately cruel; it was simply a longstanding point of pride that no death in the Vault Above the Pit was ever swift. The Inquisition's leader cleaned the blade and his hands on the apron he was wearing and then placed tool and cloth on a third, smaller table.

"And the form? Is it always made like this without their charms?"

"That is what they believe," Inxyphos agreed, turning to follow the master of their order. Sanguine noted how well the Church knight had managed to keep most of the blood from spraying on his new white tabard. He was undecided if it spoke to an admirable precision or a fastidious vanity.

It could well be both, he thought.

"What do you believe, Brother Elder?" he pressed as he led the way toward the door.

"From the rituals I witnessed, the one to be transformed names their chosen totem and that becomes their form," Inxyphos explained. "Some falter on the threshold, as it were, and the priestesses all shout mongrel at him, which transforms him into one of their hounds, the ones that so often have beaks as well. If their devotee is lacking in false faith, he dies or becomes such a beast. The ones that hold fast through the whole ritual gain the form of their totem. It seems entirely dependent upon the will and focus of the subject, though of course, the snakes talked of acceptance by blood spirits and other heresy."

Sanguine nodded. Inxyphos's interpretation certainly made some sense.

"We shall have to test your thoughts further," he said non-committally.

"Naturally," agreed the knight. "We have the complete process now, and we can make as many attempts as we desire."

"Yes. A pity the rest of your mission was not the same level of success."

Inxyphos paused, and for the first time since entering this chamber, he showed a measure of discomfort. Sanguine was almost surprised. Did the man truly think to escape without chastisement?

"We all did as we could," Inxyphos said with a dismissive wave of his hand, affecting a feigned confidence Sanguine found painfully transparent. He despised falsehood and felt it should be reserved only for the fools his institution had been formed to shepherd through the world to the judgement.

"The Western Reach was to fall to the Broken Kings," Sanguine said with the same even tone. "Was that not your instruction?"

"My instructions, as you well know Sanguine, were to facilitate the invasion for the priestesses in exchange for their secrets. I returned with all that could be learned and offered the damnable frontier up to them on a plate. I did everything short of cut their meat for them and feed it to them a nibble at a time, like babies just off the teat."

"You could have killed this ex-convict for them," Sanguine mused.

"I was instructed to give them what they wanted, and they demanded him for themselves. I fulfilled the orders I was given. If they choked on their meal, it is hardly my fault they didn't know how to chew."

Sanguine paused at the door. At one level, it was impressive that Inxyphos thought to be belligerent in his own defense in this fashion. There were not many in the service of the Inquisition who would think to argue with its master. Nonetheless, failure of this level was unacceptable.

"One last question, Brother Elder," Sanguine asked. "Is it true that the sacrifice must always be some relative? It seems their pagan religion must need to encourage their women folk to breed continually if that is the case, just to furnish them with sufficient bodies for the altars."

"Familial relations are stronger," Inxyphos explained. "But any strong connection adds to the power, even institutional, such as the Aubrey prince's blood and the sky control that stopped the Murr."

"Perhaps the Murr will be stopped for good now that their dragonfly is toppled."

"I saw an impressive spring burst from the fractured rock," said the brother elder, almost dismissively, "just before we escaped. I would not fear for the river's flow just yet."

Sanguine nodded and offered Inxyphos a wan smile that felt every bit as false as the emotions the brother elder was expressing. He shook his head sadly.

"And you are sure the dragonfly is gone, its power destroyed?"

"It toppled, and its colored mist barely took us back to the boy king's henchmen before it faded. I lost four retainers in the transition. Even worse for the Blood Sects, their boats were dropping from the sky like rotten fruit at the end of the season. The fools gathered their invasion in one swarm and suffered for their hubris."

"Hubris, yes," Sanguine repeated and pushed the door. "I would say you have shown a deal of that, Brother Elder Inxyphos. You might do well to be careful."

With the door open, two of Inxyphos's banner knights were revealed, standing guard under lanterns hung in sconces on the wall.

"It could easily have ended up being you on one of those tables."

Inxyphos seemed to swallow, and any sense of confidence appeared to drain out of him, as if his blood had indeed been let from an opened vein. He cast a glance at his two loyal men and seemed to take courage. He nodded and, to his credit, offered no false smile or bravado.

"It could indeed," he agreed, "save that it is I who knows the ritual best, and I lack any close attachments to exploit. I am sworn to Mother Church and the Vault Above the Pit. All other obligations are foresworn."

"Rightly so," Sanguine agreed, nodding a dismissal. In the fashion of their institution, Inxyphos made no sign of respect, only stepping through the door and gesturing for his men to follow him. They fell in behind, and after two steps, one hefted a leather bag over his head while the other tackled their former commander to the flagstones, wrestling to control him while the breath was choked from his body.

"They will only bring you to unconsciousness, Brother El-der," Sanguine said calmly. "Your service to the Inquisition is not yet completed. While your point about close attachments is well taken, you will understand, I hope, that we will not take your word for it. After all, surely your institutional connection to Mother Church and the Vault Above the Pit is sincere and strong. As to your being the only one who can perform the ritual properly, I have seen it and will pass on what you have taught me. At first, we will likely struggle to get it right, but I am sure we will muddle through."

At last, the lip of the bag around Inxyphos's head had choked him to stillness, and the two knights hefted up his body to take it back into the chamber he and Sanguine had just exited. From down the underground corridor, one of the master's chosen scribes approached carrying a scribing board, as well as pens, charcoal, and a bag full of paints, brushes, and parchment. Record of the night's next tasks would be thorough and accurate in every important respect.

"Shall I await you inside? Will he need to be gagged?"

"Yes, gag and chain him, then begin your notes on the two martyrs," Sanguine said. "I will return soon, but I do not think I will turn my attention to Inxyphos for some days yet. In the meantime, I will be at the Master's Bench. I have a letter to write to Cerulean. I think we may have found an excellent new tool for his next task. He will be most pleased to put it to use."

"Will you need it enciphered?" the scribe asked.

"Yes," Sanguine confirmed. "But I will make sure I have my wording precise before I give it to you."

The scribe nodded and went into the cell while Sanguine walked away toward the Vault Above the Pit—the true chamber with that name—known to so few individuals that Sanguine knew each by face, even the ones who had myriad faces.

Several less of those now, he thought and felt an actual tinge of bitterness. The bitch in the west was proving to be a singu-larly annoying thorn in his flesh—she and her convict mongrel.

Inconceivable as it was to him that the Inquisition might have a mistaken policy, not for the first time in recent years he regretted the decision to allow Chrostmer to declare a crusade against the fool Kolber's invasion of the Reach. If they had not, the "Ashen Man" would now be a long-forgotten corpse buried under the cellars of Ashfield and the Western Reach in the hands it should be—theirs. Sanguine was not superstitious, certainly not so much as to believe in something as random as luck, but he did sometimes wonder what Heaven thought it was doing when it let dangerous wild animals like this Prentice loose upon the world.

Never mind. Wild animals were easy enough to hunt down, as evidenced by the heretic's own damnable successes. And there were hunters yet, eager for the chase, not to mention new ones to be made.

To that end, it was time to write to Cerulean.

GLOSSARY

The Grand Kingdom's social structure is broken into three basic levels which are then subdivided into separate ranks: the nobility, the free folk, and the low born.

The Nobility

King/Queen – There is one King, and one Queen, his wife. The king is always the head of the royal family and rules from the Denay Court, in the capital city of Denay.

Prince/Princess – Any direct children of the king and queen.

Prince of Rhales – This title signifies the prince who is next in line of succession. This prince maintains a separate, secondary court of lesser nobles in the western capital or Rhales.

Duke/Duchess – Hereditary nobles with close ties by blood or marriage to the royal family, either Denay or Rhales.

Earl; Count/Countess; Viscount; Baron/Baroness – These are the other hereditary ranks of the two courts, in order of rank. One is born into this rank, as son or daughter of an existing noble of the same rank, or else created a noble by the king.

Baronet – This is the lowest of the hereditary ranks and does not require a landed domain to be attached.

Knight/Lady – The lowest rank of the nobility and almost always attached to military service to the Grand Kingdom as a man-at-arms. Ladies obtain their title through marriage.

Knights are signified by their right to carry the longsword, as a signature weapon.

Squire – This is, for all intents and purposes, an apprentice knight. He must be the son of another knight (or higher noble) who is currently training, or a student of the academy.

The Free Folk

Patrician – A man or woman who has a family name and owns property inside a major town or city. Patricians always fill the ranks of any administration of the town in which they live, such as aldermen, guild conclave members, militia captains etc.

Guildsmen/townsfolk – Those who dwell in large towns as free craftsmen and women tend to be members of guilds who act to protect their members' livelihoods and also to run much of the city, day to day.

Yeoman – The yeomanry are free farmers that possess their own farms.

The Low Born

Peasants – These are serfs who owe feudal duty to their liege lord. They do not own the land they farm and must obtain permission to move home or leave their land.

Convicts – Criminals who are found guilty of crimes not deserving of the death penalty.

Military Order

Knight Captain, Knight Commander & Knight Marshall – Every peer (King, Prince or Duke) has a right to raise an army and command his lesser nobles to provide men-at-arms. They then appoint a second-in-command, often the most experienced or skilled soldier under them. A duke his Knight Captain; a prince his Knight Commander; and the King his Knight Marshal.

Knights – These are the professional soldiers of the Grand Kingdom. All nobles are expected to join these ranks when their lands are at war, and they universally fight from horseback.

Men-at-Arms –A catch all term for any man with professional training who has some right or reason to be in this group, including squires and second and third sons of nobles.

Bannermen – This is a special form of man-at-arms. These are soldiers who are sworn directly to a ranking noble.

Free Militia – The free towns of the Grand Kingdom have an obligation to raise free militias in defence of the realm.

Rogues Foot – A rogue is a low born or criminal man and so when convicts are pressed into military service, they are the rogues afoot (or "on foot") which is shortened to rogues foot.

Other Titles and Terms

Apothecary – A trader and manufacturer of herbs, medical treatments and potions of various sorts.

Chirurgeon – A medical practitioner, akin to a doctor or surgeon, especially related to injuries (as opposed to sickness, which is handled by an apothecary).

Ecclesiarchs – ruling members of the Church. Their ranks correspond (very roughly) to noble ranks. The ecclesiarchy refers to the power of the Church where it rules with its own power, like a nation within the nation. Monasteries, churches, cathedrals and the Academy in Ashfield are all part of the Church lands, where religious law overrides King's Law.

Estate – A person's estate can be their actual lands, but can also include their social position, their current condition (physical, social or financial), or any combination of these things.

Fiefed – A noble who is fiefed possesses a parcel of land over which they have total legal authority, the right to levy taxes and draft rogues or militia.

Frater – brother (from the Latin word)

Hoi Polio – the common folk

King's Law – This is the overarching, national law, set for the Grand Kingdom by the king, but does not always apply in the Western Reach.

Magistrate – Civil legal matters of the Free Folk and Peasantry are typically handled by magistrates, who render judgements according to the local laws.

Marshals/Wardens – Appointed men who manage the movement of large groups, especially of nobles and noble courts when in motion. They appoint the order of the march and resolve disputes.

Physick – A term for a person trained in the treatment of medical conditions, but without strict definition.

Proselytize – Attempt to convert someone from one religion, belief, or opinion to another.

Pugilist - A professional boxer.

Provost – (short for provost marshal) junior officers assigned to sentries or patrol for the purpose of military discipline. In the case of the White Lions militia, the typical rank of a provost is a Line First. Roughly equivalent to military police duty.

Republicanists – Rare political radicals, outlawed in the Grand Kingdom and the Vec who seek to create elected forms of government, curtailing or overturning monarchical rule.

Seneschal – The administrative head of any large household or organisation, especially a noble house of a baron or higher.

Surcoat – The outer garment worn by a man-at-arms over their armor. Typically dyed in the knight's colours (or their liege lord's colours in the case of a bannerman) and embroidered with their heraldry.

Te tree – A tree, known for its medicinal properties.

The Rampart – A celestial phenomenon that glows in the night across the sky from east to west in the northern half of the sky.

ABOUT MATT

Matt Barron grew up loving to read and to watch movies. He always knew he enjoyed science fiction and fantasy, but in 1979 his uncle took him to see a new movie called *Star Wars* and he was hooked for life. Then *Dungeons and Dragons* came along and there was no looking back. He went to university hoping to find a girlfriend. Instead, the Lord found him, and he spent most of his time from then on in the coffee shop, witnessing and serving his God. Along the way, he managed to acquire a Doctorate in History and met the love of his life, Rachel. Now married to Rachel for more than twenty years, Matt has two adult children and a burning desire to combine the genre he loves with the faith that saved him.

Learn more at:

mattbarronauthor.com

Also By Matt Barron

Rage of Lions

Prentice Ash

Rats of Dweltford

Lions of the Reach

Eagles of the Grand Kingdom

Serpents of Summer

The Mantis and the Mirrored Sky

The Bears of Bridgetown

Be sure to check out our other great science fiction and fantasy stories at:

bladeoftruthpublishing.com/books

Made in the USA
Coppell, TX
31 March 2024

30757258R00444